ember glen

BRYNN FORD

More from the Author
www.brynnford.com
brynn@brynnford.com

series note

The **Ember Glen** trilogy follows the forbidden romance of Mercy and Arlo
All three books are included in this omnibus.

reading order

EMBER GLEN TRILOGY
Spark of Madness
Blaze of Misery
Embers of Mercy

content warning

This dark romance series involves many triggering elements which may be upsetting for some readers. A complete list of tropes and triggers can be found on the author's website.

www.brynnford.com/triggers

spark of madness

EMBER GLEN | BOOK ONE

BRYNN FORD

playlist

Stream on Spotify
bit.ly/spotify-brynnford

Arsonist's Lullaby by Hozier
Devil's At Your Door by SWARM & TINYKVT
Savages by MARINA
Devil on My Shoulder by Faith Marie
Never Alone by Krigarè
Soldiers by FJØRA & Neoni
Witch Hunt by VISTA
Almost Touch Me by Maisy Kay
Pyrokinesis by 7Chariot
Heaven by Julia Michaels
Dangerous by The Tech Thieves & Besomorph
Devil Inside Me by Halocene
Repeat After Me by KONGOS
Do You Love by machineheart
Rise by Katy Perry

For all the women who were told what to believe…
Seek truth through the madness,
and when it's necessary, dissent.

chapter one

Mercy

CHAOS LOOMS, THEN sharply descends like the quick stab of a blade through supple flesh. My anxiety over tonight's service has reached its peak, pounding through my heart and pulsing adrenaline through my veins.

Tonight, we serve the Impulse beneath the full moon.

We serve, though lately I've come to think of it as something else— something I don't have a word to describe, and I wouldn't dare speak it even if I did.

Hyatt Price circles the flickering orange flames of the bonfire, his golden eyes glowing like a predator's in the night…and they're fixed on me. I knew he would seek my service tonight. He's been whispering his intentions to me every day for the last week. The anticipation of it has given me adrenaline fatigue.

I step backward in my short black lace-up boots, a twig cracking beneath my feet as they carry me toward the surrounding forest's tree line. He sees me retreating and his pace quickens toward me.

Why me?

Debauchery falls like the black embers cast from the licking flames, sparking ash spewed out from the fire. It rains down to set our world on fire with the release of the Impulse in a monthly ritual where our men purge.

Servants have already been claimed. One woman is being ravaged in front of the fire, while another is beaten senselessly in the shadows. All around, the air is ripe with the scent of smoke, sex, and sin.

And Hyatt approaches to use me.

He marches right past three unclaimed servants dressed in their black corsets and lace. One of them is Ivy Jane, who I know for a fact takes great pleasure in serving the urge for violence. Yet after a quick appreciative glance at her curves on display, Hyatt continues, heading straight for me.

I take another step back, though I know there will be hell to pay if anyone sees me retreating. I should be marching toward him. I should be waiting on my knees for him, knowing he's coming to use me. But no matter how hard I try, I can't plant my feet. I can't bend. I can't sink to my knees and welcome his purge.

I'm a sinner…a rebel.

I'm weak.

I watch as Hyatt's expression hardens, his pace quickening toward me, violent rage gleaming in his deceptive glowing gaze.

And then a hand closes around my wrist.

Jerking me toward him, Theo Hughes pulls me into his hard chest and bends to kiss me, claiming me before Hyatt can even reach me. I allow a sigh of relief against his bruising lips. Theo's urges are nothing to balk at, but they're manageable. I can survive Theo—I have time and again—but I don't know if I'd survive Hyatt.

As Theo drags his soft lips from mine, he turns his head, looking over at Hyatt, who's standing at our side. "Better luck next time," he says, clapping him on the shoulder. "Mercy's mine."

"You'll be done with her eventually," Hyatt says, his lips twisted devilishly at the corner of his mouth. "And then I'll take my turn with her."

"I wouldn't wait around," Theo replies, reaching around me and curving his palm around my ass cheek.

I swallow hard as Hyatt narrows his eyes, holding my stare. Heat burns through his gaze, scorching me with the promise of untold violence and pain. He holds me there, forcing me to take the fire before he blinks and turns his eyes to Theo. "Fine. Plenty of other servants." He reaches out to pluck a strand of my long blonde hair, twisting it sharply around his finger. "Just know I have my eye on you, Mercy Madness."

He turns on his heel, returning to the bonfire where Ivy Jane stands with a proud smile upon her cheeks as he approaches her. Hyatt glances over his shoulder at me before fully giving his attention to her.

"You're lucky I'm looking out for you," Theo murmurs.

I look up at him as a moment's relief tugs away the incessant throb of adrenaline, allowing me a brief reprieve. "Thank you."

He lowers his voice. "I saw you retreating from him. Someone else could've seen. You need to get yourself together, Mercy. You're a *servant,* and you need to accept it."

"I accept it," I tell him, though it may be a lie.

My lack of acceptance is rebellious, but I don't aim to rebel. I want to survive here, though sometimes I find it difficult to justify that desire.

Theo's hand latches around my throat and he squeezes, restricting my air flow as he pushes me back against the tree trunk. His other hand slips beneath the torn black lace of my skirt, shoving it aside and quickly seeking my sex, finding me bare without the barrier of undergarments—which we aren't allowed to wear during service. He unceremoniously shoves two fingers inside me, his rough skin scraping along my dry inner walls.

"Why aren't you ready for me?" he growls as he leans against me, his lips beside my ear. "What do you think Hyatt would've done to you if he'd found you dry and unprepared like this?"

I turn my head to the side, looking out at the campfire and the licking orange flames as depravity claims our village. Theo pumps his fingers harshly, grunting as he grinds his body against mine. He's trying to draw slickness and desire out of me, though it's for his benefit, not mine.

I sigh, watching as Hyatt playfully threatens to push Ivy into the flames. She screams and he laughs, a pulse of collective pleasure at the sound of her horror ripping through the crowd.

Men thrive on our horror, our pain, our misery. It's their burden to carry as they live their lives suppressing their natural and overwhelming urges— that instinctual, primal need for violence and sex, and the mixture of them together.

It's why we serve the Impulse tonight. It's why we allow them a regular outlet to purge. It's why we live to serve.

Purging is the only way they can control it.

Except I don't believe that.

Theo's hand leaves my throat, but only to allow him space to sink his teeth into the side of my neck, eliciting a yelp from me.

"I want to hear you scream like that," he whispers.

I gulp, assured that he will make me scream like that if it's what he wants.

"For fuck's sake," his voice is tinged with agitation, "get wet for me already."

"I⸺," I whisper. "I'm trying."

"⸺matter," he snarls, pulling his fingers out. He grips my shoulders ⸺fore throwing me down on the dirt. I land sideways on my hip, ⸺ing my skirt. "Hands and knees."

⸺gh everything within me begs to resist.

⸺rt me and use me, but it won't be as bad as it would've been with Hyatt. I should be grateful to serve Theo's needs.

I'm not grateful to serve any man.

The boning of my black corset digs into my pelvis as I maneuver into position for him. I arch my back as he flips up my skirt, exposing my bare bottom to the world—but I'm still more covered than most of the women around us.

Grunting, groaning, screaming sex fills the air.

I'm supposed to let it take hold of me, to let it fill my heart with passion for service so it can sink me in pleasure—pleasure derived from serving any violent or sexual desire that's demanded by the men of Ember Glen.

But it never works for me, and as far as I can tell, I'm the only one. I'm the only woman who seems to think this way, or maybe the others just don't let on. I'm having a harder time hiding my truth as time goes on. I'm a bad seed, and I deserve to feel the pain of service.

Except...I don't deserve it at all.

Theo slams inside me, thrusting into my dry pussy with painful force as he grips my hips.

"It only hurts because you weren't ready for me." Always trying to shift the blame. "What's wrong with you?" he asks as he fucks me from behind.

Nothing's wrong with me.

Everything around me is wrong, but it makes *me* wrong to think it. To speak it would get me killed, so I pinch my eyes shut against the burning pain between my legs as Theo thrusts, and I let the single teardrop stray from the corner of my eye in aching silence.

I keep my mouth shut and let Theo sink into his cravings. Eventually my body succumbs to his movement, slickening with fake arousal to ease the sharpness of his intrusion.

We live to serve; we serve to live.

I repeat our mantra in my mind, pretending that I actually believe it until some part of my mind that aches to please demands control. I let that part of me take control, happy to let it, knowing that it will give all the other parts of me some sense of peace. Maybe not peace, exactly, but a reprieve, nevertheless.

With his brute strength, Theo flips me over, my back landing harshly on dirt and stones and twigs. He hooks his fingers into the top of my corset and yanks, forcing my breasts to peek out of the top.

I blink up at him, reminding myself that sometimes he's kind, that he stepped in to spare me from Hyatt's raging, that he's someone I might consider a friend if we ever interacted outside of service. But as he ber over me, planting his fists in the dirt on either side of my head, all I c is a faceless foe.

Maybe something *is* wrong with me.

I wish I could be like the others. I wish I could let myself enjoy this. I wish I could feel my purpose in this as I'm meant to.

He lifts his hand and tucks my hair behind my ear, almost sweetly, deceptively so. Then he sinks inside me again, thrusting with slow, deep strokes, coaxing something out of me, too kindly tricking me into pleasure. I feel it for a moment, a tug deep in my core, and a single shockwave of pleasure I know I should let myself sink into.

But it's lost when he slaps me across the cheek so harshly that my head snaps to the side. His palm presses to my cheek and the pressure of it soothes the ache for a moment—until the pressure becomes too great. He presses down against my face with bruising force as he picks up his pace, fucking me harder, faster.

Gradually his hand slips down, fingers wrapping around my throat, squeezing. I reach for his wrist, grabbing hold of it with both hands after a minute of painful pressure takes my breath away.

He's unrelenting.

He's supposed to be.

"That's fucking beautiful," he groans as my eyes widen, silently begging for air. He loosens his grip just long enough for me to suck in a greedy breath before his hand tightens again.

I panic as he skirts the edge of release, as his thrusting turns to manic fucking. His eyes darken as he pants, teasing me with his breaths that I'm not afforded the same privilege of having. My body bucks beneath him as he comes, as he shouts his pleasure into the night, and it mingles with the sound of so many others.

Moaning, panting, shouts of pleasure…screams of pain.

After Theo spills inside me, he hoists me up by his grip around my throat, pulling me into a sitting position with my legs still spread for him, my knees bent at his hips while he kneels between them.

His hand slips up to pinch my chin, forcing it up as he bends down over my face. "It's no wonder Hyatt wants you to serve him; once you're warmed up, your cunt is divine."

He spits in my face, and I flinch, turning away as his hand slips back into my hair. He holds my head steady as the other hand strikes my cheek again.

"Happy to serve," I mutter half-heartedly, speaking my script as he rubs his saliva across my cheek.

His fingertips drag to my mouth, wiggling against my sealed lips until I let them part. He shoves two fingers inside, stroking them along my tongue, toward the back of my throat until I gag. Only then does he drag them back out.

"Damnit, Mercy," frustration touches his tone, "give me something. Fucking *anything.*"

I have a nasty habit of disengagement during service.

I've been told by others that using me is like fucking a corpse—but I have to disappear to avoid speaking my mind, to keep myself quiet, to stop myself from fighting.

I should be more enthusiastic to serve my purpose, but I'm simply not. I wish I could be like all the others.

I close my eyes, trying to find the actress within, though she's buried so deep. "How can I serve you better?"

He bends, my back arching as he looms over me, pressing an almost sweet kiss to my cheek. "Give me something. Literally any emotion would serve me. Passion, lust, anger, hatred…fight me if that's what you feel. Just wake the fuck up and *engage.*" His lips slip back along my face, coming to stop at my ear where he whispers, "Everyone's watching you, Mercy."

My eyes snap open to take in the scene where sex and violence surround me. I glance around at the clusters of people, taking in the sight of women offering themselves with passion and purpose—because it *is* our purpose in Ember Glen. They fall to their knees, part their lips, spread their legs…They take a hit and rise for another; have their head slammed to the ground, only to lift it again for more.

But no one is watching me that I can see.

I turn my head to look at Theo. "What?"

"People talk about you," he says, catching my gaze with his dark eyes. I see honesty there—there's no room for anything but raw, painful truth when giving in to the Impulse. "They call you a sinner."

"I'm not a—"

He clamps his hand over my mouth. "It's what you look like when you give me nothing. You're supposed to serve happily, so do your God-given duty."

"Just tell me what you—"

He drops me, and I land hard on my back as his eyebrows knit together. "Get on your knees and offer your service with enthusiasm." His eyebrows lift expectantly. "Now."

I steel myself as I scramble to get on my knees, blinking up at him. "I offer myself to honor the Impulse." I speak the scripted words like a prayer at the altar of his feet. "How can I serve you?"

His hard chest rises and falls, his palm landing on the side of my head, stroking down my white-blonde waves. "That's better," he murmurs. "You know I'm only looking out for you."

I know he is…I do.

I know he cares about me.

Yet the more I serve, the more everything around me feels so wrong. I'm not doing a good enough job of hiding that, and I really need to. I need to bury my internal dissension so deep that no one can dig it up.

But how?

I nod, forcing a small smile. "I know. How can I serve?"

"No!" a sharp cry pierces the night, collectively jerking our attention toward the sound.

I twist to keep my eyes on her as a girl with wild eyes shoves a man near the campfire and runs toward us, racing for the forest just beyond. The entire village hesitates from their collective madness at the brilliant sound of a word no servant should ever speak, especially not while serving the Impulse.

I recognize the girl with the wild mane of long ashen hair—Delle Carter. She just turned sixteen last week, and this is the first time she's serving. My heart races as I see the fear on her face—I recognize it as the same fear I had when I had turned sixteen over four years ago.

Her eyes catch hold of mine as she approaches, her skirt floating behind her and shadowing the firelight at her back as she runs. The world around me slows, as if I'm trapped in a nightmare with her, trying to outrun a threat that's moving faster. But reality snaps back into focus as she blurs past us, chased by three men in quick stride.

"Who is that?" Theo asks, and when I turn my eyes to look up at him, I find his are fixed on the girl beyond my back being chased into the forest.

I clear my throat. "Delle. Tonight is her first—"

He holds up a hand to silence me, his gaze fixed far beyond me—and I already know he's going after her.

It's fine.

He can have whoever he wants.

But it's not fine—I need him to claim me to keep me safe from the others.

"I'm going after her," he confirms, but I hardly hear the words because he's already running.

I look over my shoulder to see him dart off into the darkness of the forest, his strides quickly carrying him to match the speed of the other men chasing the poor girl before they all disappear into the night.

I hold my breath as they vanish in silence, waiting for the inevitable sound of it…and it comes, her scream piercing through the night once she's caught.

I turn forward and bow my head as I release my breath with an unsteady huff, my fingers curling into the lace covering my thighs. I should stand. I should go and find one to serve. But I can hear my pulse thrumming, pumping behind my ears, adrenaline running like rivers through my veins.

Run.

I want to run, too.

I want to disappear into the darkness.

I push to my feet and straighten my skirt, then press my modest breasts back into the corset and adjust it.

I raise my foot to take a step forward, intending to walk back to the campfire and present myself for another's use. And that's when another piercing scream, more horror-striking than Delle's, rips across the night.

My wide eyes snap to the burning fire, and I see it shift.

Feral flames streak away from the containment of the bonfire, rushing across the camp, but it's not a blaze set along the forest floor or burning through the trees. It's a servant, her skirt bathed in fire that threatens to consume her whole. She runs, flames chasing her, burning up the fabric, racing to greet her skin and burn her flesh.

Hyatt Price stands behind her, holding a torch of his own making, his twisted smile bright with delight for what he's done to her. It's not until her beautiful, raven-black tresses catch flame that I realize it's Ivy Jane screaming and running, begging for help.

But she'll get none.

She'll go down in literal flames to serve the Impulse.

And she'll be honored for her sacrifice.

I lurch as bile rises in my throat, bending sharply with a dry heave and catching myself with my hands on my thighs. I swallow it down, panting heavily through my sudden nausea. When I lift my head, I see Hyatt move in my direction. He sees that I'm unclaimed, that Theo has left me, and now I'm on my own.

I rise and take a step back as he picks up his pace.

Another step, then another, committing the sin of retreat with each pad of my foot against earth.

A sin with my right foot, a sin with my left...

And when I realize I no longer care if anyone sees me retreating, knowing my fate is sealed no matter what I choose, I turn on my heels, and run into the forest.

I stood as a servant, and now, I run as a sinner.

chapter two
ARLO

THE IMPULSE DRIVES my hunger, the same as it does for everyone else. But it's the anticipation of our nights of purging that's the most thrilling for me—sometimes even more thrilling than the nights themselves.

The Impulse is painful for some—the suppression of a man's natural, God-given urges for sex and violence. I suppose I've always been a little twisted finding pleasure in that pain. The denial is intoxicating for me. Skirting the edge of release for as long as I can amplifies the relief once I finally let go. And there is no better way to skirt the edge than with a little voyeurism.

I take a sip of ale from my mug, then tilt my head back to rest against the tree trunk at my back. I feel one with my primitive nature, sunk down low against the earth, sitting on soil with one knee lifted to rest my arm against. If I were to press my palm to the ground, I imagine I might feel the vibration of pleasure from Mother Earth as we submit to our primordial needs—as our women fulfill their purpose by serving our masculine urges.

I have every intention to participate in tonight's festivities, but not until I'm ready. As a member of the Control, I'm used to standing back and watching. It's actually a rather fitting role for me to be one of the authority of Ember Glen. I have a level of patience unrivaled in our village. That patience is what allows me the ultimate release after extensive time spent in persistent, delicious anticipation.

There's always a mad rush at the beginning of a night of purging, such as now. The hounds have been released, so to speak, and the men of Ember Glen chase their prey like rabid dogs, quickly seeking and selecting a servant to unleash upon.

Watching this is my favorite part.

Taking another long sip from my mug, I cast my glance around the glowing firelight at the center of the camp…watching, waiting. I reach down with one hand to undo the two buttons of my waistcoat which I wear over a gray button-up. The leather gloves I often wear are placed on top of the coiled rope resting on the ground beside me. My sleeves are rolled up to my elbows, and the gradually cooling air breezes across my forearms.

I watch the flames dance against the dark shadows of the campsite and the black trunks of trees looming beyond. It's rustic, a good setting for primal release, though I enjoy my clean, elegant living at the Homestead with the other members of the Control. Yet being out here in this part of our village, with the servants and men of our community, it makes the impulse to purge that much stronger.

This night is feral.

A scream near the campfire draws my attention, and when I glance over, I see Hyatt Price playfully threaten to push Ivy Jane into the fire before pulling her away. Her fright sends out a pulse through the village, an electric shock which triggers desire to use and abuse.

I slowly inhale, dragging in an aching breath of anticipation as I let my desire simmer deep inside. Several servants are unclaimed; I could take any one of them now and satisfy the throbbing ache of my thickening cock, but still, I bide my time.

I scan the circle from where I'm seated, my gaze settling to watch one pair and then the next, observing the men of Ember Glen as they use their creativity to purge with servants. I spot Ellary Hill stark naked, on her hands and knees in the dirt, getting fucked from behind. My gaze travels her naked form appreciatively—I think I'd enjoy sinking inside her, but I don't think she'll be the one I take to satisfy me first tonight.

Nearby, I see Cambria Miller, still fully clothed, hugging a tree. Her wrists are bound with a rope on the opposite side of the trunk. She screams with pure delight as Killian Cole—a fellow member of the Control—spreads her legs and drags the tip of a blade down the back of her thigh, a thin stream of blood slowly tracking down her bare leg.

My pulse quickens as I watch the blood flow, the subtle violence of the act and the slow drip of blood along her medium brown skin builds anticipation that rushes through my veins with an insistent *whoosh*. I adjust my cock with one hand as I shift against the ground, then take a long drink of ale as I continue to watch.

"No!" The shout of protest immediately catches my attention, my head snapping toward the sound.

Servants don't say no—on this night or any other—and it won't be tolerated. I see Delle Carter dart from the campfire, running toward the forest, her hair whipping wildly behind her as she sprints away. I scramble to my feet, prepared to run after her, but another villager and two members of the Control are already chasing her—two more than necessary to bring a servant under control.

And then I see one more, Theo Hughes, take off at a sprint to chase the group into the dark forest.

That's interesting.

He's a member of the Control, too, and surely, he sees enough men are after her already. In his wake, he leaves a girl on her knees…the same girl he chooses nearly every time we purge.

Mercy Madness.

I'm perplexed by her.

She's attractive, though her appeal has declined over the last year or so—at least that's what I hear from my brothers. By all rights, she should be in high demand. Supple flesh, round curves, skin like porcelain begging to be reddened with a smack of a hand or the flow of blood. Pink lips that dip to a perfect, permanent pout, sinful, sultry bedroom eyes, and soft waves of long, white-blonde hair.

She is service in the flesh, a feast for the eyes, though her passion is severely lacking. It's the reason my brothers find her less appealing than she should be. It's also the reason the Control has been watching her. Her history is riddled with small rebellions which, kept unchecked, could lead her to revolt.

I gaze upon her curiously as she tucks her breasts back inside her corset. She hesitates, gathering herself, as if she isn't enthusiastic to find another to serve.

What is she doing?

A shriek breaks through the night like a lightning strike, so thunderous and bright it can't be ignored. The chaos is drawn to the fire, and soon I see why—Hyatt Price holding a torch and Ivy Jane awash in flames.

I'm mesmerized by the walking fire for a moment, the movement of the orange and yellow glow as it burns her skirt to ashes, licking at the ends of her long, black hair. There's a stagnant pause as silence surrounds us, allowing the sounds of her horrified screams to echo through the trees as she chokes on her own voice.

I say a brief prayer in honor of this sacrificial servant, "*Malo mori quam foedari.*"

Death before dishonor.

It's quite a glorious end for a servant so willing as Ivy Jane. I can't imagine she'll survive this.

I could put her out.

It's an odd voice inside me that thinks such a thing, and I don't understand it. Though I suppose I didn't always understand my natural impulses, either. I had to be taught to sink inside every dark thought in my mind and push myself to indulge each of them without prejudice in these nights of purging.

I was taught to indulge any impulse that begged from deep within me… so perhaps I should indulge this strange impulse to put her out all the same.

I set my mug on the ground and retrieve my black overcoat. Then my feet carry me in Ivy's direction, intent on covering her to smother the flames. As I walk toward her, I see Hyatt move around her, staring at the spot where I saw Mercy standing. I turn to look and see if she's there, though I'm not sure why I bother.

She *is* there…but she takes a step back.

Oh, don't you dare.

Don't you fucking dare, Mercy Madness.

Don't retreat.

She turns, and she *runs*.

Hyatt sprints, zipping with his torch alight, the heat of the flames brushing over my skin as he streaks past me.

Two servants have now retreated—Delle and Mercy. They've run from their purpose and have fled into the forest.

This won't be tolerated.

They'll face punishment for this.

I drop my coat and chase after them.

chapter three
Mercy

MY CONSCIENCE NAGS as my lungs burn, fear running blazing heat through my veins. I glance back as I run—*I'm not supposed to run*—and the only thing that's visible is the orange glow from Hyatt's torchlight. He'll burn down the whole damn forest just to light me on fire.

I don't know exactly where I am in the darkness, but I'm comfortable among the trees. I'm familiar with the feel of twigs cracking beneath my boots, and the meager piling of leaves just beginning to fall, crunching with each step. I often travel through the forest to get to the open fields of wildflowers beneath the mountains that surround Ember Glen. So while I can't see my hand in front of my face, I don't fear the dark; I don't fear colliding with the trees blocking my path.

"I'm going to bathe you in flames, Mercy Madness!" Hyatt shouts, his voice is faraway, but echoes through the trees.

My heart slams against my ribcage, pulse thrumming with the insistent need to get away.

Get away, get away, get away.

Tears burn behind my eyes as I pump my legs harder, faster. There's going to be hell to pay for doing this, for running away, but I think—I *hope*—the punishment can be no worse than being set on fire.

I'm fast, but I'm not fast enough to outrun the pace of his determination. His voice is too near when he calls my name again.

Climb.

I skid to a stop, reaching out into the darkness and grappling to find the nearest tree. My knuckles scratch across the bark when I find one, and I press my palms against the trunk, reaching in front of me and high above my head in hopes of finding a low hanging branch I can climb. I circle the tree with quick side-steps, feeling all around.

Good fortune finds me. The side of my hand bumps up against the stubbed remains of a branch that must have fallen away. Feeling around, I find another branch above it, just within reach. I think I can pull myself up onto the remains of the broken branch and climb higher.

It's that or continue trying to outrun Hyatt, and my lungs are already screaming.

Climb.

Grabbing hold of the higher branch, I plant my foot on the tree trunk and hoist myself up. I grunt with the effort as I climb, managing to place my foot on the stub. I use it as leverage to climb onto the higher branch. I steady myself, ensuring it will hold my weight as I find my balance before reaching, searching for another branch to climb.

The orange glow of Hyatt's torch approaches, burning enough light around me that I can see the shadow of a limb at chest-height in front of me. Without hesitation, I scramble, jumping from the branch I'm standing on to wrap my body around the one in front of me.

The lace of my skirt catches and tugs behind me, as if it wants to pull me back. But I pull against it, lifting my leg over the limb, pulling enough that the lace snags and rips, a piece of it tearing off as I wrap my body sideways around the branch, hugging it, and holding on tight.

I settle just in time to see firelight move into the space beneath me and the dark shadow of Hyatt's form attached to it.

He's not running.

He's slowed to a walk.

He must know I'm nearby.

Turning my head, I place my cheek against the rough bark, and I can see the torn strip of dark lace caught on the stub I climbed from. I squeeze my eyes shut, ridiculously wishing that *he* can't see it if *I* can't see it.

"Mercy," he sings my name tauntingly as he creeps between the trees twenty feet below me.

All he has to do is look up, and he'll see me.

Quick footsteps from behind him pad across the dirt, plodding to an abrupt stop. "Where is she?" I hear a second male voice, along with the sonorous pounding of my heart.

I open my eyes to look down, wondering who it is, uselessly hoping it could be Theo, that he might be willing to rescue me. I know it isn't him, though. I saw the look in his eyes when he ran after poor Delle—he was lost to the Impulse.

"She's near," Hyatt replies as I see the top of another head approach. "I'm claiming her. She's mine."

"I'll help you find her."

No!

"Help me find her if you wish, but I'm telling you now, she's *mine*. I've been waiting for my turn with her," Hyatt says.

"And you should've had your turn by now. She retreated, and that won't go unpunished."

"She won't need punishment from the Control by the time I'm through with her. My impulse to defile her is strong."

"Then find her and purge." I see the other man snatch the torch from Hyatt. "But don't burn the forest like a damn fool just to spite her running from you."

"I need the light." Hyatt lurches forward, reaching for the torch, but the other man draws his arm back, holding it away from him.

"You're lost to the Impulse. I won't allow you to set fire to the trees just to serve it."

Hmm.

A rational thought from a man during a purge?

Hyatt postures, stepping closer to him, moving unnervingly close into his space. But this other man doesn't step back; in fact, not a single muscle twitches as he stands his ground.

"I have an impulse to fight," Hyatt hisses in a way that would be intimidating to me…

But it isn't intimidating to the man in front of him. He takes a step forward, forcing Hyatt to move back. "Then go find your servant and fight."

Hyatt places his hands on the man's chest and shoves. "Maybe I'll fight you."

He takes a step back to catch himself but pushes forward again, shoving into Hyatt's space, coming in chest to chest. "Back off, Price. I'm warning you."

Hyatt throws his fist, but the other man catches it in his palm as it *smacks*. I stifle a gasp as he twists Hyatt's arm, spinning him to face away before kicking the back of his knee, causing him to buckle. When Hyatt drops to kneel, he wraps his arm around Hyatt's neck, squeezing him into a chokehold.

The man is strong, holding him with one arm, the torch still held out in the other while Hyatt claws at his forearm, trying to pull his grip away. Hyatt struggles against his hold, but the man's hold remains tight, keeps him still, squeezing and squeezing until suddenly, Hyatt collapses. His arms drop away and his body slumps, and when the other man lets him go, Hyatt falls sideways to the ground, unconscious.

He choked Hyatt until he passed out.

I watch with wide eyes, afraid yet curious for what will happen next. The man holds the torch over Hyatt's still form, watching him for a few beats, as though he's making sure he's really down.

Then, with a snap, he turns his head in my direction, chin tilted, eyes landing on mine as if he's always known how to find them in the dark.

He takes a step closer, gaze locked on mine as the fire crackles, and a curious expression spreads across his cheeks. "I believe it's now your move, Mercy Madness."

Arlo Rainn.

My heart drops to my stomach as I realize who stands before me. He's one of the Control. He's witnessed the extent of my failures as a servant.

Retreating.

Running.

Hiding.

I'm a sinner…and he's going to send me straight to hell.

chapter four

ARLO

THERE ARE SEVERAL words that could describe how I'm feeling about this situation—interested, fascinated, and curious all come to mind. Yet none of them quite capture the pleasure that comes from the anticipation of her next move.

I didn't have a plan when I ran after Hyatt chasing Mercy into the forest, and I don't have one now. I could walk away if I wanted, let her do what she will, knowing that she'll face punishment for her insolence once the sun rises. I could pull her down from the tree and use her to serve my needs—finally satiate the sexual desire rushing through my veins from the thrill of the chase.

Instead, I take a step closer, then I stop and wait.

I watch as she slowly pushes herself up to a sitting position on the branch, the shadow of her form gradually moving where she straddles the limb. Her hands remain in front of her, pressed to the branch between her legs, gripping it with fear.

She should be frightened.

"It appears you have two choices." I casually take another step toward the tree. Her bright blonde hair gleams behind the firelight as I move the torch in front of me to cast her in the light. "You can stay where you are, and hope that I have no interest in you. You can pray that I'll walk away so you can remain here in hiding for the rest of the night—regardless of the fact that you've already crossed the line so severely that you'll never recover from the punishment you'll receive. That is a choice you could make…though, you should also consider that perhaps I'm just as lust-blind as Hyatt." I creep closer, inch by inch. "Perhaps I'll set the tree on fire. Perhaps I'll rip you from it and burn your flesh just to hear you scream."

Her shoulders straighten and her face hardens. "You won't."

My eyebrows lift in surprise. I'm surprised she spoke, because for some reason, I expected her to be meek and fearful. After all, she ran from her duty when she should've been kneeling, grateful to serve, regardless of the pain inflicted.

"Your other choice is to run," I finish. "Come down from your perch, little sparrow. I'll even let you have a head start." I take a step back, sweeping my arm out to the side as if welcoming her down to the forest floor.

I let silence settle between us, though I can sense it's unsettling for her. A grin twists at one corner of my lips as I wait, savoring the festering quiet which precedes her response.

I'm not sure what I expect her to do.

I'm not sure what I hope she'll do.

With a sharp movement, she lifts one leg, bringing it over the branch before turning sideways to sit. She hesitates, her hands pressed to the bark on either side of her hips. She looks down at the ground, then her eyes flicker sideways to glance at me surreptitiously. She kicks out her foot and lets it swing, as if she were going to jump, but thought better of it.

"What will it be?" I prod.

She looks over at me. "What will my punishment be? How will I be punished for running from my duty?"

"I don't know," I tell her honestly. "Your cowardice will be brought before the authority of the Control for a vote."

"So it's cowardice, then?" she scoffs. "Not wanting to be set on fire?"

She asks as though she doesn't know, and my eyes narrow at her, wondering why she's so combative about who she is meant to be, how she is meant to serve her community. "Coward, weak, spineless…*selfish*. Choose whichever word draws the most meaning for you."

Her lovely lips part in surprise as her eyes narrow, taking personal insult from the words. They aren't untrue; she knows her role, her purpose, her duty—not only did she fail to fulfill it, but she *ran* from it, and hid from it.

Remarkably, it's this sentiment that gives her a nudge, and she makes the leap, pushing her bottom off the branch and falling to the ground. She lands hard, her knees buckling from the momentum of leaping from such height, but she manages to keep herself upright as she bends.

She rises slowly, and my breath catches in my lungs as I watch her shadowed form lift from the ground. Perhaps it's the sweep of her long, platinum waves over her shoulder which brush over the swell of her breast. Maybe it's the gradual manner with which she lifts her chin, her eyes rising to meet mine. It could be the intoxicating manner in which she fills the black corset…or maybe it's the glow of her pearly smooth skin stretched taut around her fleshy thigh where it peaks through the split in her skirt, begging to be marked.

Sweet sin.

"I'm not selfish," she says defiantly.

I smile at her, amused by her boldness. I suppose she knows just how much trouble she's already in and assumes she can't make it any worse—though, I'm certain she can make it much, much worse.

With one arm, I shrug off my waist coat, then move to a brush-free clearing a few steps away where nothing but soil covers the ground. With a suddenness that makes her audibly gasp behind me, I drop the torch, the flame flaring as it catches air on the way down. As soon as it hits the dirt, I open my waistcoat, position it above the flame, and drop it. The light goes out with a puff of smoke as I effectively smother the fire.

I hear her step back, her boots crunching over twigs and leaves—one small step, then another.

I whip around to face her, but remain in place. "Are you going to run?" I'm met with silence…sense-heightening silence. "Think twice, Mercy. Because a chase sounds like fun for me."

I hear the breath she forces out with a frustrated *oomph*, and her annoyance calls to me. I've never interacted with a woman in quite this way before—where she's combative, hostile, resistant. I think I'm enjoying the resistance, though I know I shouldn't. It's should put me off entirely because her actions are disgusting. She's defiant of the ritual sacrifice she was born to give each month beneath the full moon; the sacrifice of self to satiate the hunger of men.

I listen for the crinkle and crunch of leaves and twigs beneath her boots, though she tries to muffle the sound with each slow step.

Why hasn't she run yet?

Hyatt groans, stirring from his unconsciousness nearby, and that seems to be the trigger she needs to act. I hear her turn, hear her padding with quick steps along the forest floor, and I give chase.

I run, following the sound of her footsteps until I can see her outline in front of me. I open my arms and wrap them around her waist as I barrel into her, grabbing hold as I plant my feet to stop. I lean back, lifting her from the ground as I step backward to steady myself.

"Hyatt…" she whispers with urgency, her quiet plea in protest of my capture.

My back hits a tree behind me. I set her down and spin her in my arms to face me, turning and shoving her spine against the tree.

"Please don't—"

I slap my palm over her mouth when I hear Hyatt move, creeping to his feet in the darkness.

"Quiet, or he'll hear you," I warn.

She stills, though her anxiety rises. I feel the warm puffs of breath from her nostrils as they rush down the back of my bare hand. I feel her soft lips against my palm, and I want to feel her softness against every inch of me. I move closer, molding my body to hers, pinning her to the tree.

Sweet sin.

The way she feels is divine. Her soft curves are a perfect contradiction to her sharpened tongue. The lust she inspires is maddening—something that wraps around me and takes hold with a swiftness I couldn't have predicted.

My cock thickens, straining behind my slacks, and my hips jut forward to seek relief. I shift my hand across her lips, along her cheek as I move in close, whispering against her ear, "Quiet. Don't make a sound. Remain silent and I'll do the same." I comb my fingers through her hair, threading through the silky strands. I feel the wisp of her breath against my cheek. "Stay quiet and I'll keep you safe, right here, until he loses interest and goes away."

She doesn't stir.

She doesn't speak.

Her chest is the only part of her that moves, the gentle rise and fall as she breathes rocks me into a state of blissful longing.

I wonder how soft she is between her legs…Are those lips the same precious pink as the pout on her face?

I let my free hand move as footsteps crunch in the distance, and I hiss, "shh," against her ear as I sweep aside her skirt. I brush my knuckles along the inside of her thigh, nearly groaning at the silky smoothness of her skin and how her muscles tense against my touch.

Slowly, I drag a finger up her leg until I reach the apex of her thighs. She flinches, stifling a gasp as I pull my finger along her slit, dipping in to the knuckle. She rises on her toes, her body slipping upward as though she's trying to lift away; yet, when I push a little deeper and press against her inner wall, she drops in my hold.

Her hands, which she'd pinned to her sides before, snap up to clutch my biceps, the burrow of her fingertips pressing buttons inside me I didn't know existed. My lips press to the side of her neck as I stroke inside her, adding another finger.

"I—"

"Not a word."

Sinking deeper, I curl my fingers, stroking and gently pumping, savoring the wetness that so easily coats my fingers. I wonder if it's all from her or whether Theo's release is still dripping from within her.

Her grip on my arms tightens while I stroke her, tightens further when I grind my cock against her body. I'm finding it difficult to contain myself, and a groan beckons from deep in my chest, threatening to roll up my body and escape with a roar. I smile against her neck as I swallow the sound, feeling the muscles in her throat contract as she swallows, too.

I bring down my thumb to circle her clit, and with a jolt, her back arches from the tree. Her face falls forward to land on my shoulder. Somehow I find my free hand swooping around her, stroking down her soft hair, caressing with a gentleness that doesn't make sense.

It's when her hips roll forward to seek more pressure from my hand that I feel overwhelmed with the need to make her come. I bring my hand from her hair to her hip, fingers curling around her ass and dragging her into me. With the squeeze of my hand, I encourage her to move—I need to feel her fuck my fingers with gratitude for the unearned concealment I've offered her from Hyatt.

She feels incredible, inconceivably warm. Her cunt is unlike anything I've ever felt before, though I can't place exactly why. It isn't just her cunt, though—it's every inch of her.

Our breaths mingle with heat as she rocks on my hand. "Come for me," I demand, "but don't you dare make a sound."

chapter five

Mercy

I'M WARM AND wet, pleasure circling my center in a way I've never felt before.

I feel weak.

I feel strong.

I feel shame for the release that threatens to unravel me…yet I crave it all the same.

I dig my fingers into his arms as my core tightens, clenching around his pulsing digits. My breaths quicken as I rock against his hand, intoxicated by the way he holds me, the warmth of his body aligned with mine…the way his hardness presses to my stomach.

I feel held by him, and somehow, it's centering yet disorienting all at once.

I bury my face in the crook of his neck as my climax awakens, pulsing through my swollen clit while his fingers work with mastery.

Come, but don't make a sound.

A command I can follow.

I'm not unfamiliar with my body or the feeling of self-pleasure. All of us—the servants of Ember Glen—would spend a week at Sanctuary following a night of service. We'd gather to rest and reflect in reverence of fulfilling our duty; we'd heal and mend those injured in violence.

For many nights, we would share our experiences with one another in a safe space. No one is allowed in Sanctuary except for servants and the Control who watch over us. And even they can only enter with the permission of us all. It's the only time we have any power in this place.

Some weeks in Sanctuary were living hell—if someone had served an excess of violence, we lived their pain with them as they healed. But occasionally, there were nights of service more manageable than others, when no one was injured, and we'd spend our nights recounting our experiences in sexual service.

Inevitably, there would be some girls who would become lustful in their remembrance. Self-pleasure isn't allowed unless a man demands it of a servant during a night of service beneath the full moon—which they rarely did because men don't care about a woman's pleasure. I suppose that tiny rebellion was part of the appeal. It was an unspoken secret we kept for each other, the silent seeking of release by one's own hand beneath the sheets when the lights went out.

I was never left particularly wanting after serving; though, like so many of the others, I was left unsatisfied all the same. Service is about the men, but those nights are for us. And I would sometimes indulge while in our safe space. Though I did it out of spite and contempt—not as a lust-fueled rebellion that I'd seek forgiveness for by dutifully serving.

And that was how I had always come before, silently, secretly, because I never once came from service.

Arlo turns his head, running his nose along the sensitive skin behind my ear, letting out a soft hum as he exhales, and that tips me over the edge. My body spasms, my grip tightens, and I arch against him as every muscle in my body tenses. Then comes the release as a strangled moan fights its way up my throat.

His hand moves to cradle the back of my head, pushing my face down into the curve of his neck. "Bite down and keep quiet," he whispers, and *oh*, how that makes me clench around his hand, spurring my release to its peak.

I clamp down on the soft fabric covering his shoulder and let it muffle the moans that wish to escape. I've never climaxed from the touch of another, and it makes my head spin.

How did he do that?

How did he make me come like that?

He strokes my hair as I twitch, as my body suddenly goes limp against him. His lips press to my cheek as he holds me through this oddly comforting let down.

"See?" he whispers. "You can be obedient when you want to be. I think Hyatt's gone away now. I don't suspect he heard a single moan," he thrusts forward against my middle, "or whimper."

I feel breathless and shaky. "H-how can I serve you?"

He lets out a groan that vibrates across my cheek. "That's what I wanted to hear."

With a suddenness I don't expect, he releases me and steps back. My knees are so weak that I slump as they buckle beneath me, the fingers of one hand grazing the dirt as I brace myself with the other palm against the trunk of the tree. I steady myself, then push back up to standing, watching him retreat into the darkness.

He's silent, taking a step back, then another.

I can't stand the silence.

"Do you want me to—"

"I want nothing from a sinner like you, Mercy Madness. Enjoy the remainder of your night in the forest. The Control will decide your punishment soon enough."

I hear leaves crunch as he turns and runs away. He runs away, leaving me there, panting, overwhelmed, stunned…and alone.

I SAT WITH my back to the tree for a while, basking in my confusion over what had happened and my fear of what will happen to me next. Somewhere in the midst of deciding whether I should return to camp and try to fulfill my duty as a servant, or give in to the fact that I'm already in deep trouble, I fell asleep.

Awakening now, the sun is rising, fog overcasting the streaks of orange glow that draw lines between the trees. The purging is over now that the sun is rising, and I know I'm safe. No man will touch me—not until next month's service under the full moon.

I push myself up from where I'd slumped over sideways across the ground, yawning as I draw up my knees to brush dirt from my bare legs, which are covered in goosebumps from the chill of night.

I inhale the fresh morning air as I let my head fall back against the tree, looking up at the branches overhead. Flashes of last night rush through my mind's eye—running, climbing, leaping from the limb, and trying to get away…Flashing to Arlo grabbing me and shoving me against the tree at my back.

A trembling breath shakes through my lungs as I recall the way he touched me. How his touch felt good, welcomed. And then he'd left me alone, and I couldn't understand it. I couldn't understand how he was so hard, how he had me at his mercy, but had somehow dragged himself away during a night of purging. He hadn't asked me to serve his needs, and I'm entirely baffled by it.

Why didn't he use me?

I should return and check in with my friends. They may worry about me now that the purge is over and I'm nowhere to be found at camp. I shouldn't be out here in the forest.

I drop my head forward, glancing around to gauge my location so I can find my way back to camp. The hazy orange sunshine tries to tear its way through the fog, peeking between the ash-colored tree trunks and casting a glow over the teardrop-shaped marigold leaves which are scattered across the forest floor. They're starting to fall rather early this year.

I stand, brushing dry dirt from my hips and smoothing down the torn remnants of my lacy black skirt. My shoulders sag as I walk, the brightly colored leaves beneath my feet sparking images of walking fire and the memory of Ivy Jane awash in flames. I wonder if she survived the night. If she's dead, we'll know it soon enough. Either we'll see her at Sanctuary or we won't.

Maybe I won't be seen at Sanctuary.

Maybe I'll be dead by then.

A shiver creeps up my spine as I recall just how badly I've behaved and how much I've sinned in failing to fulfill my purpose. Arlo Rainn had promised that punishment would be coming, but what that punishment will be or when it will fall is anyone's guess.

Perhaps I'm in so much trouble that it will be days before retribution finds me. I imagine my transgressions will be brought to the full attention of the Control, and a collective decision will be made. Slow-burning fear already crawls through my veins at the thought of what penance I'll be made to pay.

I come upon a fallen tree laying sideways across the ground in front of me. I lift my leg to step over it, and as my boot comes down to land on dirt on the opposite side, I gasp because my eyes land on the other servant who ran last night.

Delle Carter.

Her small frame is curled around her center and tucked against the fallen tree. Her corset is gone—I spot it discarded a few feet away. Her skirt remains, but it's torn and tattered around her bruised legs. Her bare back is covered with a bloody crisscross pattern of welts, made by a whip.

Is she dead?

I shake myself from my hesitation and run to her, crouching beside her, and placing my hand on her arm. "Delle…"

She jolts, swinging her arm back with the force of her entire body turning toward me, hands coming up defensively, prepared to fight me off. I fall back, landing hard on my ass, but quickly shift onto my knees and scramble toward her again.

"It's okay," I soothe, gently grabbing hold of her swinging arm. "It's okay…it's over. You're okay."

Her pretty hazel eyes widen, her expression awash with fear. But as she blinks, her gaze moves across my face, flickering down my form and taking me in for what I am—a fellow servant and not a threat.

She takes in a stuttering breath. "I-I'm…"

Nothing follows.

I push matted hair from where it sticks to her forehead, where I imagine sweat slicked her skin as she was used last night. "It's okay. The night is over. You don't have to be afraid anymore."

You always have to be afraid.

I let a small smile touch my lips to offer her comfort, but the comfort only allows her space to grieve. I watch as she swallows so hard that her throat bobs, as tears gloss over her eyes, as her breaths quicken into a hiccup which turns into a sob. She clutches me as she begins to cry, and I grab hold of her, easing her closer as she turns onto my lap. She lets her tears spill onto my bare thigh at the spot where my skirt splits.

I stroke her hair as I sniff back my own tears.

I feel relief that this girl I hardly know has survived.

I feel pain for what she must have gone through.

I feel hopeless that serving will never become easier.

"Let it all out now," I tell her softly. "Release everything you're feeling right now because you can't take it back with you, love. We're meant to be strong through this; we're meant to be proud to serve."

She sits up with a sharp snap and looks at me pointedly. "I'm not proud!"

Her arms cross over her chest as she realizes her top is bare. She blinks and her face contorts, twisting from anger to embarrassment as her eyes meet the ground.

What do I say to that?

I'm not proud either, but I'm meant to be. We all are. And before this very moment, I've never heard another servant say as much aloud. I'm frightened of our shared sentiment because it means she'll suffer the way I have suffered for years—lacking the ability to take pride in our God-granted duty like the others.

I swallow the unease climbing up my throat. "It's a lot to take in. The first night isn't easy for anyone—"

"The *first* night? Is *any* night easy? How could it be? How could this ever become easier?"

"Delle, I—"

"I can't do this! I won't do this again!" she shouts.

I grip her cheeks, squeezing enough that she can't shake from my hold as I turn her face to meet mine. "Don't ever let me hear you say that again." I narrow my eyes on her. "If they hear you say that, the consequences will be dire."

She opens her mouth to argue, but I silence her with the force of my words.

"*No.* Listen to me." I lean in close, our noses nearly touching as I hold her stare with significance. "I understand you. I do. But no one else in Ember Glen ever will, and if you speak the thoughts in your mind, you will pay dearly for them. You may already be in trouble for running from service. I can only hope the Control will offer leniency as it was your first night." I loosen my hold, allowing one of my hands to stroke the side of her head with a sisterly kind of comfort. "You don't share these thoughts inside your mind. You hold your head high. You show your pride for service. You do what you must to survive. And when the emotional burden of your sinner's thoughts becomes too great, you speak of it to me and *only* to me. Do you understand?"

She blinks slowly, a lonely tear slipping from the corner of her eye, trickling down her rosy cheek. "I'm not a sinner."

I close my eyes and let my forehead fall to hers. "I know." Her hands wrap around my wrists where I hold her steady, though she isn't trying to pull them away—she's holding on. "I know you're not." I let go and pull her close, wrapping my arms around her, trying to give her the comfort I wish someone had given me after my first night of service.

I let her hold on to me for as long as she needs. Eventually, she loosens and pulls away. I stand, retrieve her discarded corset, and bring it back to her.

"Just hold it in front of you," I tell her as she positions the garment to cover her breasts. "We can tend to your back at Sanctuary."

Delle gives me a small nod, and a softly uttered, "Thank you," before we begin our walk back to the campsite, which is on the way to the village and Sanctuary.

I see the smoke of the extinguished bonfire rising in the distance, the gray tufts of ash slowly lifting between the trees. It brings me a contradictory sensation of panic and relief all at once.

The service is over.

The purge has ended.

The Impulse of men has been satiated...for now.

Yet, I still hold the fear from witnessing what had happened to Ivy Jane—from Hyatt chasing me with a torch and what he meant to have done to me.

Arlo Rainn saved me from that...and brought me pleasure in its wake. I place my hand over my pounding heart as we emerge from the trees.

"Mercy!" I hear Ellary call and turn my head to see her rushing toward me.

A smile touches my cheeks when I see her. Her straight brown hair flows behind her as she runs to me. She collides with me, pulling me into a hug that I welcome. Then, with my hands on her shoulders, I nudge her back to arm's length, quickly looking her over from head to toe—a habitual check for injuries. There's a bruise on her collarbone, but otherwise, she looks well.

"Where have you been? Were you dragged into the forest?"

"You could say that..." I hope she doesn't ask for more. "Are you okay? Are you injured?"

"No, I'm fine," she tells me, and by the look on her face, I can see she's being truthful. "The Higgins brothers claimed me and took turns with me the entire night."

I exhale with some relief. The Higgins have strong sexual urges, but they've never been particularly violent.

"Where's Cambria?" I ask, concerned that she hasn't approached yet.

Ellary's expression twists. "I need your help to take her back to Sanctuary...she's injured."

Urgency tenses my shoulders. "Where?"

She leads and I follow. We rush around the smoky remnants of the bonfire, to the opposite side of the circular clearing surrounded by trees. I hear Cambria's hissing and labored breathing before she comes into view. Her onyx hair forms a tangled frame around her beautiful face, though it's contorted in agony where she lays. She's on the ground, curled on her side, rope still twisted around her wrists where she must have been bound, though I can see the other end has already been cut free.

"Cambria." I slam to my knees at her side, and Ellary mirrors me. "Where are you hurt?" I ask, scanning her form.

"Everywhere," she hisses.

Her legs are streaked with dark, dried blood. Her skirt—which covered down to her ankles last night, despite the slit that cut all the way up her thigh—had been torn to shreds. It hangs in tattered pieces where a knife must have slipped through the fabric to cut her skin beneath.

"Oh..." Delle breathes out on a whisper of horror from where she stands somewhere behind me.

As I carefully inspect her skin, I see the knife has touched Cambria nearly everywhere except for her face. Bloody streaks have dried down her arms and across her chest—her skin must be burning from the sear of it.

"We'll help you back to Sanctuary," I tell her. "Can you stand?"

"My toes..." she whimpers.

"What?"

I look to Ellary as she explains, "I think they might be broken."

"Her *toes*?" Delle gasps.

Ellary nods. "Her right foot. The other seems to be okay."

I feel too much.

I feel her pain as if it were my own, and I feel my face grimace with her agony.

"Oh, Cambria…" Ellary's voice is laced with empathy and pride as she brushes her knuckles comfortingly along Cambria's cheek. "*Malo mori quam foedari.* You served so bravely last night."

My eyes snap to Ellary, my jaw tensing against her words.

Malo mori quam foedari—an ending to our prayers so often spoken in Ember Glen. It's said to mean that we should seek death before dishonoring our roles of service. Everyone in Ember Glen says it, but the prayer is really only meant as a reminder to servants.

I know Ellary means well. She only says what she's meant to say; she only thinks what she's meant to think. She's a victim of our indoctrination as much as anyone else. And just like everyone else, she's entirely unaware of it. She means to honor Cambria and her strength—of which, they both have mountains worth—but my sins have overcome me in such a way that my mind sees it all differently now.

They still serve with pride in the name of our god.

Why can't I believe the way they do?

A glance down at Cambria shows the small smile that touches the corners of her lips while tears glass over her dark eyes. I see the gratitude she has for her agony.

Regardless of what I believe and what I don't, this is our reality. This pain is real, and I wish I could bear it for her so she didn't have to. But this pain can't be held by any one of us alone—it must be held by all of us.

It's our burden.

Our duty.

Our curse.

With great care and taking our time, we help Cambria from the ground, working together to carry her through the trees and back to the village of Ember Glen, seeking out our Sanctuary from the madness.

We come out through the trees like warriors returning from the battlefield—injured and tormented from the horrors of war.

Only this isn't a war.

It's our life.

chapter six

ARLO

THE CONTROL STAND watch over the foggy morning as those who serve begin to emerge from the forest. The seven of us stand side by side, forming a line across the large open space of the village square. It's a matter of showing honor for our women who have served the Impulse as they cross to return to Sanctuary—a space where they can rest, heal their injuries, and reflect in reverence of the good work they've done.

I bend to brush away dirt that hides the shine of my black derby shoe beneath the tapered leg of my fine-cut black slacks. I huff as the dirt only attaches itself to my black leather gloves and rise while I brush my palms together. I adjust my waistcoat over my gray button-up before shoving my hands into my pockets.

"Be still, brother." Theo's head is turned toward the trees, away from me, and he watches carefully. "You've been fidgeting all morning."

I blow out a heavy breath. "I'm unsettled."

Theo briefly glances at me with furrowed brows before turning his attention back to the forest. "Perhaps if you'd purged as you were meant to, you wouldn't feel that way."

"I had my release."

I hadn't.

I was desperate to come when I'd left Mercy.

I'd meant to grab another woman to serve me, but the mere idea of it felt…unsatisfactory. I should've fucked Mercy. I'd even gone back into the forest to find her once I realized she hadn't returned to the campsite to serve her duty. And I had found her, at that very same tree where she came on my fingers.

The clouds were clearing from the sky and the full moon shone brightly above her, as if it were placed there just to bathe her in moonlight for my eyes' pleasure. Her bright blonde hair glowed like starlight shining down from above.

Yet, when I saw her there, pacing, fighting an internal battle I couldn't see with my eyes, I'd been too fascinated with watching her to approach.

Fascination had quickly turned to obsession, and I couldn't tear my eyes away from her. Not as she paced, not as she sat, not as she reached between her legs and rested her fingers there with confusion in her expression—she was confused about me and what I'd done to her.

I'd wondered if it was the first time she felt pleasure.

I'd wondered a lot of things about her…so many things that minutes creeped into hours. I watched until she fell asleep, and before I knew it, the night was coming to a close. I had to leave her to return to the Homestead before daylight—and without a single release of my own.

I'd squandered my only opportunity to satisfy my impulses for the next month. I missed out on the physical pleasure I was meant to take, all because I'd lost myself to the curiosity in watching *her*.

"Here she comes," Theo mutters, running a hand through his mess of sandy blond hair, and I don't know exactly who he means.

I look across the vast, gravel-covered square toward the trees, and I see her.

Mercy.

Her platinum hair shines in stark contrast against her black clothing. And she's not alone. She's helping Ellary carry Cambria—and I'm not surprised. From what I've gathered, the three girls are close.

However, I am surprised to see young Delle close behind, clutching the remains of her corset to cover herself. Frankly, I'm surprised to see her walking on her own. Last I'd seen, she was taking a harsh whipping.

We watch as the group of girls make their way across the open square, small pebbles crunching and kicking up around their feet. It's thirty paces or so from the trees to the end of our line, and we stand in waiting as they pass the first of us.

"Thank you for your service," Owen says from the end as they pass.

Another two paces ahead, they cross Ryker. "Thank you for your service, ladies."

Each of us thank them in turn, standing still as they huff and struggle to carry Cambria across the vast square. They pass Theo, who offers his thanks with a cursory glance at Delle. And as they approach where I stand—second to the last in our line—Mercy's eyes meet mine, though she quickly looks away.

A grin curls my lips. "Thank you for your service, *sinner*."

I'm not entirely sure why I feel compelled to remind her that she's sinned, but I do. And the way her gray-blue eyes narrow on me as she sets her jaw makes something inside me stir—whatever it is slithers up my spine, coiling around my nerves and squeezing.

She doesn't say a word as they pass. She arcs an eyebrow as she gives me an appraising look, and then her eyes leave me, stealing my breath as they do.

The way she turns from me feels as though I'm a flame being snuffed out by the breeze of her disapproval.

My fingers twitch in my pockets with the desire to put pen to paper—she's walking poetry and my hand aches to write her. I don't know how she's managed to evade my senses for so long or how she's suddenly triggered such an awareness within me.

It's no matter. Her demeanor is insolent. She's sinned and punishment awaits her.

BY MID-MORNING, THE girls are all accounted for and safely tucked away at Sanctuary, save for one. Ivy Jane's remains are being prepared for grievance and honor at a servants' ceremony that will take place later in the week. It's probably good she didn't survive being lit on fire; I imagine the recovery from such an event would have been excruciating.

The seven of us cross the village square. The town is at our backs, and the Homestead manor is in front of us. Gravel crunches beneath our feet as we walk the empty space to the sprawling mansion estate where we reside. The people of Ember Glen live in their humble homes in the village, but we—the seven men of the Control—live here at the Homestead. Our space is superior and separate from the residents.

Our manor is made for kings, which we are in our own right. Perhaps not kings exactly, but keepers of our realm.

Decision makers.

Overseers.

High priests ensuring the godliness of our domain.

Our stone manor spans the square, from the forest line on the eastside, to the Sanctuary on the west. Rising high behind the Homestead are the peaks of the Ember Glen mountains. Beautiful and shielding, the mountain range surrounding our valley village serves the purpose of keeping us separate from the outside world, protected from its evils.

I glance over my shoulder at the Sanctuary—the old cathedral on the westside of the square—before looking over at Theo. "You left Mercy Madness alone last night."

"I did."

"Hmm."

"Did you have a thought about that, or are you just verifying facts?"

"I'm curious about it...You frequently claim her on nights of service."

Theo sighs. "For a long time, I found her fascinating. She thinks differently, and it was fun to entertain it for a while. However, as of late, her thinking has turned in the direction of defiance and apathy."

"Are you aware that she ran last night?"

I feel the collective attention of the Control turn their eyes to me, Theo's head swiveling to look at me squarely as we move toward the wide stone steps leading up to the manor.

"No, I wasn't aware," Theo says, a twinge of concern detected in his voice.

"Who ran?" Killian asks from down the line.

"Mercy Madness," I say. "She ran and hid from service in the forest."

My foot comes down on the first step, and I stop on the second step when I realize everyone else has halted. I half turn to face the group.

"Unprovoked?" Owen asks with his pensive blue-eyed stare.

"Not exactly." I turn completely to face them, moving down to the first step. "It was after Hyatt Price set Ivy Jane on fire. I saw him run after Mercy with his torch."

I see unease strain Theo's features—dark eyebrows drawing a line over his brown eyes as his shoulders tense. His reaction—that he has any reaction at all, really—to my story about Mercy causes something like jealousy to bubble up in my chest, and I'm not fond of the feeling.

"I left her unclaimed when I chased after Delle Carter," he says.

"And Hyatt noticed. He came after her, and instead of welcoming her fate to serve his violent urge, she fled in cowardice." I swallow around the word. I'd said it to her last night, too; and while it's the appropriate word, it just somehow doesn't taste quite right.

"Delle ran, too," Ryker points out.

"She's sixteen," Theo counters. "It was her first service."

"This needs to be addressed immediately. We should take it to the Elders," Killian suggests.

I nod. "I agree. It's a transgression worthy of severe punishment."

"It may be worthy of death considering how rebellious Mercy's been as of late. She's developed a history of bad behavior. How long do we allow it before losing all control over our community?" Killian's stare narrows in consideration. "That girl thinks too much for her own good."

He's right, though I admit to myself that Mercy's unpredictable thinking is what drew my attention to her last night. There was a strong anticipatory thrill in not knowing exactly what she would say or do, whether I could find a way to break her, shape her, to discover her buttons and exactly how to push them to get her to do what I wanted her to do.

She's a challenge…not easily controlled.

And though the mere idea of overcoming her is exciting, I understand why it can't be tolerated. Allow one woman to think for herself, and all control is lost. She becomes a danger to herself with her foolish ideas and poses a risk to the very values our community was founded on one hundred and fifty-two years ago.

Intrigue on my part isn't enough for me to argue for her life.

Was I thinking about arguing in favor of her life?

Theo sighs before making his way up the steps. "I've warned her about that."

We follow behind, all of us climbing the thirteen stone steps to the concrete landing.

Killian scoffs, showing me his profile and his tuft of brown hair tied back in a knot. "And yet she still had the audacity to run and hide during service? She makes a fool of you in extending that kindness to her. At her age, she should be a model servant."

Theo reaches the main entrance first, two large wooden doors, intricately carved with images of wildflowers that seem to leap out from the wood itself—dozens of three-dimensional flowers that resemble the grassy fields leading out to the mountains. He pushes his sleeve back to reveal the black band permanently fixed around his wrist—just as all the men of the Control have. He waves the device adorning his wrist over the concealed scanner above the door handle, and the locking mechanism beeps once before we hear it release.

"I've been more than kind to her," Theo agrees as he pushes the door open, and we all filter inside. "I claimed her last night, as I did the first time Hyatt went after her. I'm aware of how brutal his impulses are, and some part of me wanted to spare her. I know I shouldn't have…I should have let him have her. She offers me nothing in service—no passion, no pride, no gratitude."

We cross the ornate floor where the burgundy and gold tiles are laid to form a sunburst pattern—a massive design that expands all the way across the large, circular foyer. The sun's center lies directly beneath a golden chandelier that's more decorative than it is functional. The space is dimly lit, save for the natural light filtering through the large windows on the west side—our home can seem a little grim, I suppose.

"She's been given too much leniency," Killian says.

Naturally, we gather in a circle surrounding the sunburst—not intentionally nor ritualistically. This is simply how we've always come to stand together and discuss important matters.

Wesley rubs his dark palms together. "It's not like we can manage every ill-formed thought that flits through the servants' minds."

At that, I find myself wondering what ill-formed thought is flitting through Mercy's mind right now. I wonder whether she'll think of the way I made her come on my fingers when she lays her head to rest at Sanctuary tonight. The idea of it makes my cock twitch.

Sweet sin.

I should've fucked her last night while I had the chance.

"Something has to be done about Mercy Madness. The new servants are impressionable," Killian says, "and this sets a poor example for them."

"Then something should also be done about Delle Carter because she ran, too," Ryker adds.

"I think Delle could be afforded some leniency," Theo says, crossing his arms. "It was her first night."

"It's no excuse, whether it's the first or the fiftieth. How many first-timers have behaved that way?" Killian asks.

"None come to my mind in recent memory," I reply.

"Exactly." Killian points to me. "They know their place before their first service."

"I don't think Delle presents a concern," Park offers, tossing his head as a strand of black hair falls across his tawny skin. "I'm sure she's learned her place after last night." He looks to Theo. "You went after her. What happened once she was caught?"

"She was effectively put in her place," Theo confirms. "I don't think she'll be an issue again."

"It's Mercy who poses the threat," Killian says. "The pattern of defiance she's developed; the fact that she ran and hid last night…How long has she been in service? How old is she now, twenty? Four years of monthly service. Her actions last night were blasphemous. She's a sinner, and we have to make an example of her."

The men nod in agreement, as do I.

She *is* a sinner.

And yet…there's an odd prickling at the back of my mind that makes me feel uneasy. I can't place the feeling or why it's there. Perhaps it's my weakened state since I didn't effectively purge last night.

Yes, that must be it.

My impulses are clouding my mind, and I need to be careful about my thoughts and decisions until I can satisfy my impulses at the next service. My brothers in God are right; Mercy is a sinner, a bad example for the younger servants, and she must be made an example of.

She must be punished.

I let out a heavy sigh, forcing my breath to blow away that useless feeling of unease. "Then it's decided. Mercy Madness must be punished. I'll alert the Elders that we need to meet."

chapter seven

ARLO

I ROLL MY pen along the dark wood table as we discuss the fate of a sinner whose name stirs lyrical thoughts inside my mind—thoughts which beg to be put to paper.

This is a manner of torture for me, having jumbled words inside my mind without the time or space to scratch them out with my pen. It has me struggling through this collective discussion between the three ruling Elders and the seven members of the Control.

I clear my throat and push back to straighten in my seat, intent on engaging with reason and sound judgment, as it is my duty.

The Control are seated at the black semi-circular table in the courtroom here at the Homestead. The room is a large, barren square, starkly different from the rest of the manor, where everything is elegant and opulent.

This room has black walls and furniture, and a cold, slate-tiled floor. The two light sources are strategically placed—one above the center of our semi-circular black table, and the other directly above a spot on the opposite side where it can serve as a spotlight over the accused who would stand before us.

This room is where we cast judgment over the sinners and lawbreakers in Ember Glen. Fortunately for us, this room is hardly used, thanks to the grace of our God. Because God commands that we indulge during each full moon, the Impulse of men is satisfied, such that the rest of our days are free from violence, debauchery, and sin.

The three Elders appear on the projected screen on the black wall opposite where we sit. Due to their advancing age, they remain physically excluded from the general population. It's crucial their health be maintained so they can provide guidance to Ember Glen, to ensure we follow the guiding principles set forth by their forefathers, who founded our community set away from the world after a new civil war split the nation.

We were all lucky to have been born here.

No one knows what horror still exists in the world around us, what vile demons and sinners lurk on the other side of the mountains that surround us.

"I have a suggestion," Clyde says, snapping me from my thoughts. The flickering triangle of light points from the projector across to the far wall, showing his face in its own square on the screen aside the other two Elders.

"Please," Killian says, "we'd be grateful for your guidance."

"It hasn't been done for a while," Clyde continues, "but I think it's necessary to reassert your authority. You must send a message to the other servants that their sins won't be tolerated. I think Mercy should be made to participate in the Trials of Dissension."

I lean away from the table, my head tilting in curiosity as my arms fall to the armrests of my chair. "The Trials haven't been executed in what, forty years? Fifty? Certainly not in my lifetime."

"Yes, forty, maybe forty-five," Clyde confirms with a nod. "It certainly has been a long time. I was a child then, maybe seven or eight years old."

"If I heard correctly," Theo says, "they tried to do away with the Trials altogether after that last round. Why is that?"

Ryker leans back in his chair, lacing his fingers together over his wavy, dark blond hair, and stretches back. "They stopped because they lost five servants."

"Five? That many chose to participate?" Owen asks.

"There was an unusually high number of participants that year," Edgar—another of the Elders—confirms. "The sinner was required to participate, of course, but then four other servants volunteered."

"And none of them passed? None survived?" I ask.

"They all survived the first round, much to be expected," Clyde says. "I think three survived the second round, and the final round took the rest."

"I think it's fair," Killian says. "Mercy Madness should be made an example of."

"I don't think anyone here disagrees with that," Owen says, "but perhaps we should take some time to discuss the past trials. I'd like to be fully aware of the punishment we're proposing."

Park leans forward, placing his forearms on the table and clasping his hands. "I'd like to do that review, as well. I suppose I don't have a good understanding of the trials, as I can't imagine why a servant would *volunteer* to participate."

"For a chance at freedom," Lawrence—the third Elder—explains. "A sinner is forced because they've already dissented from our ways. But if a servant thought that they somehow deserved a different life than the one God chose for them, then they could volunteer to participate with the promise of a new role in our society should they pass the trials—the promise of a domestic life."

"But no one ever passes," Park says.

"Right," Lawrence confirms with a sharp nod. "Because the trials weren't meant to be passed."

"And yet there were volunteers?"

"Who could possibly understand the mind of a woman?" Clyde chuckles. "Their judgment is poor, and the decisions they make are untenable. Some are as boldly brave as they are stupid, thinking that somehow they will be *the one* to pass."

I realize I'm tapping my pen on the table and abruptly still my hand. "Then the trials are torture. A means of punishment for a sinner, and a device by which to draw out any other servant with divisive thinking."

"Precisely," Edgar says. "Use the trials to draw the approval of the villagers—it will be seen as a fair ruling and prove to be healthy entertainment for them. You give the promise of absolution for the sinner's soul through their participation in the trials. And any servants who might find your sinner to be...*inspirational* will be put in their place. Either they'll volunteer to participate, or they'll see what the sinner faces in the trials and remember why it's best for them to keep their mouths shut, their silly ideas to themselves, and serve with pride and dignity."

"So, what about Delle Carter?" Theo asks, and I'm starting to see the pattern of his concern for her fate. "Admittedly, I feel a pang for how far Mercy's fallen. I've tried to be a friend to her, to keep her in the light, but clearly, I've failed. I understand that an example needs to be made of her," his leg twitches beneath the table as he speaks, "but Delle...she's young. She has years of service ahead of her. She can be managed, reformed in the eyes of God."

"But fleeing from her purpose? It's shameful, regardless of her age and experience," Killian counters.

"Transgressions can be forgiven with atonement," Theo reminds him.

"The three trials *are* atonement—reparations for the sake of the soul before death. The sinner will prove herself through the ultimate acts of service: Service of the Flesh, Service by Sacrifice, and Service from Bloodshed," Clyde recites the three trials.

"But I think Delle's soul can still be saved in *this* life," Theo asserts. "She'll witness Mercy's trials, and she'll learn. If she's a true sinner, we'll know, won't we? If we allow other servants to volunteer, she'll come forward, we'll know, and then the trials will take care of her."

"Fair point." Killian nods.

"I think we're all neglecting to ask a question with a very important answer here," I say. "What happens if a servant survives the trials?"

The Elders laugh, then Lawrence says, "That won't happen. If they survive the second trial, it's the third that will seal their fate…and you make sure of it."

We make sure of it.

So, that's it, then. The Trials of Dissension are a certified death sentence.

"Let's put it to a vote. All in favor of Mercy's participation in the trials…" Killian says.

Hands rise in favor from Killian, Wesley, and Ryker. Theo seems reluctant, but then slowly lifts his arm.

Breathing you in is sweet sin,
transgression worthy of fire and brimstone.

Words suddenly spring free in my mind, words that need to be chased and explored.

Mercy needs to be chased and explored.

With the thought, I immediately raise my hand in agreement. She draws too much interest and is clouding my every thought. She needs to go, or else I may lose myself in the overwhelming intrigue of her strange personality.

Park and Owen raise their hands as well—a unanimous agreement, of course.

"It's settled then," Killian declares. "Mercy Madness will participate in the Trials of Dissension."

"You'll need to elect a warden," Lawrence says. "Someone who will be responsible for looking after the trial participants. They'll be moved to reside in the Homestead manor during the time between trials."

"Why?"

"For several reasons," Clyde says. "First, to ensure they are immediately separated from the other servants. The last thing we need is a sinner sullying the minds of our most precious commodity. They'll also need to be protected from the villagers. There's record from one of the earliest runs of the trials where the villagers took it upon themselves to round up the participants, tie them to stakes in the center of the village square, and burn them alive."

Ryker chuckles. "Well, that certainly seems more expedient."

"It offers no absolution for the soul," Theo explains. "Isn't that the ultimate goal at the end of the trials?"

"Yes," Lawrence confirms. "And allowing them to seek that absolution absolves us of any responsibility in judgment. The trials decide their fate."

Absolves us of responsibility?

My mind must truly be muddled, as that sounds like hypocrisy to me. How can we say that the trials decide their fate if the trials are fixed? If we're meant to ensure their fate by the third trial, then how do *we* find absolution?

I shake my head and run my leather-gloved hand across my short beard. I didn't purge last night. I must be out of my mind.

"How do we select a warden, then?" Owen asks.

My hand lifts and I speak beyond conscious thought. "I'll do it. I'll volunteer to be the warden."

What the hell am I doing?

I need to stay away from this girl, this sinner who makes a mess of my thoughts.

"That was easy enough. Anyone opposed to Arlo serving as warden?" Ryker asks the group.

To my detriment, no one disagrees. I've just volunteered to keep myself close to Mercy Madness as we bide time until her death. Though that worries me for my clarity of thought, it excites me for the anticipatory denial that being in her presence will bring. I won't be able to have her, and that will only heighten my anticipation for the next full moon when I can purge my impulses with another servant.

Yes. This will be good practice in self-control.

"Congratulations, Warden Rainn. You get to babysit the sinner," Killian says, drawing a low chuckle from the Control.

"It will be my pleasure," I say…and I think it actually will be.

I CLIMB THE marble steps to the second floor and turn right at the landing. My steps are quick as I pad over the runner covering the hardwood floors in the hallway—a traditional rug design of crimson and gold. My room is at the far end of the hall, and when I reach the door on my left, I use the band around my wrist to unlock it.

I slam it shut behind me and ensure its locked before crossing the ivory carpet to my desk. I pull out the chair and sit, huffing out a heavy breath as I stare at the beige wall. My desk is pushed up against it, sitting between two windows that look out to the rolling mountains.

I open the drawer on my right-hand side and pull out my leather-bound journal and fountain pen, placing them on the neatly organized desktop before me. I peel off my leather gloves and drop them onto the desktop.

I stretch and flex my fingers, observing the uneven texture and pinkened color of the scars from my old burns. The roughly textured surface of scarring on my left hand extends from my wrist, twisting along the back of my hand, and stretching to the bends of my pointer and middle finger. A circular patch covers the back of my right hand, thankfully stopping before reaching my fingers, allowing me full movement without pain—if I couldn't write, I don't know what I'd do.

I keep my hands covered most of the time, but not because I'm hiding them. I keep them hidden because these scars are for *me*. My scars are a reminder of how little self-control I had in my youth.

I unwrap the leather cord from around my journal and flip to the next empty page, smoothing my hand down the center to press it open. I uncap my pen and quickly scribble the two lines that had come to me earlier:

Breathing you in is sweet sin,
transgression worthy of fire and brimstone.

I move my pen to the next line, letting a dot of ink bleed out from the tip—hoping the words will bleed out from me, too. And soon, they do.

You are heat.
You are flame.
You are smoking ash which floods my lungs with each delicious breath I take.

My breaths quicken as I draw my pen across the page. Memories of Mercy in my hold as I brought her to pleasure dance across my mind. I remember each drag of my fingers inside her—each twist, each stroke, each thrust—and the sound of her secret, warm breaths puffing delicately against my skin.

I'd never felt anything like her before.

Burn, sweet sinner, and I'll bathe in flames with you.

Heat washes over me as the image of her sets fire in my mind's eye. She is the same as the flames where I burned my hands in my youth—a flickering light that calls to me, heats me, begs me to be burned.

I will disintegrate to ash at your feet.
And my remnants will beg for your grace, your sin…your mercy.

"Mercy," I breathe her name aloud. "Sweet, *sweet* Mercy." I scribble on the page.

Send me to hell, you demon of delight.
Burn with me.

I drop my pen, suddenly heavy with the weight of words I didn't know I was holding inside my mind. I lace my fingers behind my head as I stretch, leaning back in my chair. My cock is hard, and it's all because of this girl—this *servant*—I had hardly noticed before.

What is it that changed?

What removed her cloak of invisibility?

It was her running that made me stand and take notice, but I don't know if that's where she drew my sudden obsession.

No.

It was the grip of her fingers on my biceps and the rocking of her hips as I made her come. It was the way she bit my neck to muffle the sound of her orgasm.

It was her pleasure…the way she fought against it but took it all the same.

"Fuck." My palms drag down over my face.

I slap the journal shut, coil the leather cord around it, drop it in the drawer, and slam it closed. I hadn't felt a need to lock that drawer before, but I feel the need now. The poem must be kept secret, a shameful thing I need to hide.

I use the band on my wrist to engage the magnetic lock on the drawer before shoving to my feet so forcefully that my chair topples over backward. I ignore it and march toward the bathroom, stripping my clothes off as I go.

I walk straight across the white-tiled floor to the far corner of the bathroom. The shower has no doors, just a rainfall showerhead from the ceiling and a drain at my feet that I can walk straight beneath.

Naked, I step beneath the showerhead before turning it on, letting the cold water spill down my body. I don't turn the tap to warm—I need the shock of cold to wake me from this shameful longing.

There's nothing to be gained from wanting Mercy Madness. She's been sentenced to death, and I've volunteered in a way to be her reaper.

I rub cold water over my face as I wonder what the fuck I was thinking volunteering to be the warden of the trial participants. I find myself hoping other servants will volunteer, because then there will be others to focus my time and attention on.

Yet, I also find myself hoping Mercy will be the only one, hoping I might have moments with her alone.

What sins would I commit with her alone?

A shudder rips through my spine.

I'm going to need a bathtub full of ice cubes to shake this blasphemous desire.

Breathing you in is sweet sin,
transgression worthy of fire and brimstone.

You are heat.
You are flame.
You are smoking ash which floods my lungs with each delicious breath I take.

Burn, sweet sinner, and I'll bathe in flames with you.
I will disintegrate to ash at your feet.
And my remnants will beg for your grace, your sin…your mercy.

Mercy.
Sweet, sweet Mercy.

Send me to hell, you demon of delight.
Burn with me.

chapter eight

Mercy

I SLEPT ABOUT as much as Cambria did last night, which is to say not much at all. She was in pain, and though she was stubbornly, bravely calm about it all, her silent screaming called to me.

I stayed by her side, waking every time she did. We splinted her toes as best we could, but I'm afraid they won't heal well. I worry she'll be in pain, that she'll walk with a limp. The cuts all over her body were mostly superficial, though painful nonetheless, I'm sure. Only a few of them were deep enough to need stitches, and Ellary took care of those with her nimble fingers.

I'd laid in the bed beside Cambria's in the chapel where we all sleep, our beds forming a large circle in the open square room. Pews once filled this space instead of beds—I once saw an old, faded photograph showing when they were still in place, but it must have been long before Ember Glen was founded. This space has been for servants to gather and rest as far back as I can remember.

Though I'd laid down to rest last night, I didn't really sleep. Between Cambria's pain and my concern for Delle, I couldn't find peace. The wounds on Delle's back were tended to, but her soul was broken. My ears strained all night, listening for the sound of her crying as I knew the tears would come eventually. And when they did, I was there to comfort her in an instant, staying by her side until she fell back to sleep.

Then, when I went back to rest again, Cambria's whimpers of pain called me to her, though she'd urged me to go back to bed. There wasn't much I could do except be there for her.

I hate it.

I hate watching someone I care about be in pain. I wish I could take the pain for myself, so she didn't have to.

The sun shines through the stained-glass windows, signaling the girls to awaken, though I've been awake for hours.

"Mercy," Cambria calls in a tired voice.

I move from my position on the floor at her side, rising onto my knees and taking her hand. "How are you feeling?"

"I'll be all right," she says quietly. "Did you sleep at all, or have you been up worrying all night?"

She knows me well.

I give her a small smile. "You know the answer to that question. Are you in pain?"

Her features wince as she shifts, and she presses her eyes shut. "You know the answer to that question," she parrots.

I sigh. "I can get you something for the pain."

"No. It's not that bad. And you know I want to feel it."

She always wants to feel the pain. She revels in it, as do many of the others. They take pride in their injuries and feeling them deeply, knowing it means they've served well.

It saddens me in a way I can't explain, in a way I *wouldn't* explain to anyone in Ember Glen. No one would understand me.

I take hold of her hand and squeeze gently. "I know you do, but I wish you didn't. I hate seeing you ache."

She rolls her head on her pillow, turning her face to look at me. Her black hair is matted around her sweaty cheeks, and she gives me a smile. "Be happy for me, Mercy. I served well."

My chest tightens. "You always do."

"Did you rest at all last night?" Ellary's cheerful voice comes from behind me.

I glance over my shoulder and smile at her approach, glad she's not injured as well. "Not at all."

"Well, I'm up now," Ellary says, her striking green eyes showing a calmness I've never felt. "I'll watch over Cambria. You should get some rest."

"I'm too alert to sleep. My mind is already flooded with thoughts."

"Your mind is *always* flooded with thoughts." She grins, shaking her head as she lowers to sit on the bed at Cambria's feet. "What have you been up thinking about all night?"

Pain.

Torment.

Fear for the future.

"Nothing interesting."

"Are you going to tell us how your night of service went?" Ellary asks. "What happened to you in the forest?"

She leans forward with interest, and I feel Cambria's eyes on me as well. Both wait with something akin to excitement to hear what happened to me.

What do I tell them?

That I'm a sinner awaiting punishment?
Do I tell them that I ran? That I hid?
That Arlo Rainn made me come against a tree?

A wave of pleasure from the memory ripples out from my center, rushing an odd feeling through my core that instantly makes me feel shame. I blink and shake my head to rid me of the memory. "I was…taken into the forest. There's nothing else to tell."

"Something interesting happened to you, *finally*," Cambria says softly, "and you won't tell us. I'm insulted." She giggles and Ellary chuckles with her.

I force a smile to touch my cheeks, but humor and happiness evade me. The memory of Arlo Rainn floods my veins with contradictions—heat and pleasure through my belly at the recollection of the way he touched me, fear and fury for the threatening promise he made for punishment.

"I want nothing from a sinner like you, Mercy Madness."

I swallow a lump in my throat at the recollection of his words and the unearned shame I somehow feel about them.

I know I'm a sinner in his eyes—in everyone's eyes, soon enough.

But I don't feel like I am.

I only feel like a woman trying to survive madness.

My heartbeat quickens, and I suddenly feel overwhelmed. I quickly climb to my feet. "Don't feel insulted." I pat Cambria's hand. "I promise, there's nothing interesting to tell you." I look at Ellary. "I think I'll go get some fresh air. Promise you'll look after her?"

"I always do," Ellary promises.

I grin, blowing them both a kiss before I turn away. When I do, the smile quickly drops as I let my face fall to accurately reflect my melancholy. I don't expect anyone to see, but I glance sideways and catch Delle's gaze fixed on me from where she sits on the side of her bed. She sees my expression, the emotional ache of my soul radiating through my frown. Instinct tells me to cover it with a smile, but before my lips twist, I see it—the same soul ache within her.

She's a mirror, reflecting me exactly as I was at her age four years ago, when disdain dripped from my pores.

But I know better now.

I know I have to hide it.

I let it slip and she saw it, and I don't want her learning bad habits from me that might get her into trouble.

I have to get away from here.

I smile at her before marching toward the two wooden doors that lead out to the village square. Grabbing hold of the long metal handle, I pull the heavy door open, letting the morning sun shine in and cast its rays across the dark wood floors.

I grip the layers of my black mid-length skirt. Though servants must always wear black, we're allowed to make more modest clothing choices outside of nights of service. I've put on a long-sleeve, form-fitting black top that covers my shoulders and has a sweetheart neckline. My high-waisted skirt is made of layers of lace that float around me in asymmetric tiers, and I always wear the same lace-up ankle boots. Lifting my skirt up to my knees, I prepare to run.

I plod down the stone steps and sprint over the gravel, sprinting across the open village square. My eyes are set on the tree line of the forest ahead, the small stones crunching beneath my feet.

I spare a single glance at the Homestead as I run parallel to the massive structure, sneering at its pretension before turning my focus ahead to the trees.

Are they in there right now deciding my punishment?
Has it already been decided?

I push harder, running faster, sprinting to the trees as my lungs burn.

But I don't stop.

I don't stop as gravel turns to dirt. I don't stop as open space becomes cluttered with tall trees that surround me as I cross into the forest. I don't stop for fallen branches, leaping over them as my feet crunch over twigs and leaves on the forest floor. I don't stop until I reach it—the tree where I keep it hidden.

I slow to a walk as I approach the tree and circle around to the other side. Stopping, I step in close, raising onto the balls of my feet and reaching my arm high. Slipping my hand into the open knot of the trunk, I feel around as I stretch, my cheek pressed against the bark. My fingers touch leather and I grapple for a grip on it. When I have a firm hold, I pull out the leather-bound journal and lower to my flat feet.

Looking down at it, I brush the dirt away—my mother Mira's journal. I'd found it three months ago while cleaning out my father's home in the village after he died. It was in the table beside his bed, which was odd because I'd never seen it there before. It was almost as if I were meant to find it— almost as if it were meant to find *me*.

I tuck it beneath my arm, and head deeper into the forest, heading for the one place where peace always finds me.

chapter nine
Mercy

AS I COME through the trees, my mother's journal held in my grip, I'm overcome by the radiant sunshine that dares to exist after such a dark night of service. Tufts of white clouds dot the brilliant blue sky, and the sun is warm where it touches my skin. I can't help but let it bring a smile to my face.

Ahead of me is the open meadow. It's laid out beneath the rolling hills, which lead out toward the mountains—my own personal sanctuary.

Wildflowers in shades of amethyst and ruby dance in the breeze with the tall grass—gems of color that shine brightly through a bleak world. It's a sea of bright life that calls to my soul. I breathe deeply, savoring the floral scent that mingles with the fresh mountain air as I walk among the wildflowers, my skirt dusting the grass as I move through it.

I hear a child giggling and look off into the distance to see a domestic woman and her little girl playfully chasing one another through the field. The grins and laughter between them bring a joyful expression to my face, yet it also brings a twinge of heartache.

Moving to my perfect spot in the center of the field, I tuck my skirt beneath me before lowering to sit, my head still turned to watch them play a few moments longer. The longer I watch the little girl—who's maybe seven or eight—the more my sadness grows.

That child is destined to serve—she's already been marked for it. I can see the lines of black ink on her forearm from here; and though the image isn't clear from so far away, I know exactly what it looks like all the same. All who've been selected to serve bear the emblem.

I set my mother's journal beside me and push back my sleeve, revealing the same design tattooed on my arm. Two black lines wrap all the way around my forearm, splitting apart an image of the same wildflowers I sit amongst, only the design on my arm is colorless.

I think the founders of Ember Glen must have imagined us as wild—colors too bright and bold invading their grassy meadow that they needed to subdue. In a way, it's quite a sad image. Black lines draw the floral landscape on my arm, but the image is devoid of color, lacking the joy that the real flowers bring.

I sigh, knowing the little girl would've been marked for service when she was five—that's when all the girls in Ember Glen have their fates chosen for them. The Control decides who will be marked to serve and who will be left for "domestic bliss"—their words, not mine. Though if you ask the Control, they'll say God speaks through them to select the future servants, and that they don't make the decisions all their own.

It's a lie if you ask me.

In truth, we all serve, but domestics will never have to serve the Impulse. Domestics are given the grace of a home, a husband, and children. Sometimes the children are their own, born of artificial implantation, and sometimes they're born of servants and assigned a family unit. In any case, the child playing happily in the meadow bears the mark of a servant, and it gives me the urge to charge after her, pick her up, and run with her up the mountains.

It's just a fleeting thought, though. It's not as though I could ever leave Ember Glen. Even if I could survive the trek to see what's on the other side of the mountains surrounding us, I don't know what horrors await.

There was a civil war born of politics and greed before Ember Glen was settled, and it destroyed a country they once called the greatest in the world—at least, that's what we're told. It's always said that we're lucky to have been born here.

I turn away and lay back, letting myself disappear among the green, purple, and red. I lift my mother's journal to rest against my belly, feeling the stitch of a small ache that never really goes away. It's not an ache of the physical nature…it's spiritual.

When I was younger, I naïvely hoped for children of my own one day, but that was before I understood my role as a servant. Once I began to serve, God saw fit to bring life to my womb on five separate occasions, yet he took it away every single time.

Each loss brought me such pain, tearing holes in the fabric of my soul that will never be repaired. But with the pain of lost life came gratitude for a tormented future that was spared. I couldn't bear the thought of bringing a daughter into this world, and so I knew the miscarriages were for the best, even though they pain me still.

Lifting the journal, I open it to the leather strap down the center of the page I had left off on. I find the next entry, dated July 8, 2171, when I was just a few weeks shy of my sixth birthday.

Sometimes I look at Mercy and wonder if I made a

mistake allowing her to be born. I wonder if I should have found a way to end the pregnancy as soon as the successful implantation was confirmed. But that thought never lingers long because the thought of how beautiful and perfect she is quickly replaces it.

Her smile is sunshine, bright and wide and warming everything she shines upon. She's full of lightness and life, naturally caring and concerned for the well-being of others. She notices when I'm sad—when melancholy over her future in service breaks through and shows on my face.

She comes to me in those moments and climbs onto my lap. She touches my cheek with her soft, tiny hand and smiles with those naturally pink lips and her unique silvery-blue eyes glowing up at me.

"It's okay, Mama," she'll say. "I'm here with you." Then she snuggles in close, hugging her arms around me tight.

And when she does, the whole world feels perfect... until she lets me go.

Then, all I can think about is her future of service. All I can think about is how she'll be hurt, how she'll be used by men.

They want me to take pride in that. They want me to be proud that I have such a beautiful daughter—a daughter who will serve so many in nights of purging.

But I'm beginning to think everything is wrong. I'm beginning to think God doesn't exist. Because if He does exist, how could He possibly allow this to be done to our daughters? How could He allow them to live through such horror?

Am I the only woman who sees this?
Am I the only one?
Am I wrong?
Am I a sinner with a demon's thoughts in my mind?
Should I take pride in knowing how Mercy will serve?
I don't know how I ever could.

My pulse pounds as I read my mother's words. She was afraid for me.

She questioned the beliefs of our community, just as I do. She wondered if everything we're told to believe is wrong. Her mind was that of a sinner's, her thinking so similar to mine.

Did she condition me for divisive thinking?

Are my thoughts rebellious because hers were?

Did she indoctrinate me against having pride in service?

Was she a sinner who made me question my beliefs?

No…No!

I refuse to believe any of that.

I'm not a sinner, and neither was my mother.

But if we aren't sinners, then that means everyone else is wrong. Air rushes from my lungs on a sigh. Nausea rolls through my gut with the dissonance of it all. Either she and I are right and everyone else is wrong, or she and I are wrong…and we both deserve to burn in hell for our sins.

Where is the truth in this madness?

I flip the page to read the next entry, dated a week later, on July 15, 2171.

I'm a sinner.

I have sinned.

I don't think there will be absolution for me.

Elijah found me with her.

I don't dare write her name, though it wouldn't matter if I did. They already know; they all know. The Elders, the Control, Elijah…

Oh, how I've hurt Elijah.

He found me tangled with her in our bed. I honestly hadn't expected him to return home so soon, and I was stupid. We were stupid.

We're sinners.

It's the only explanation.

I must have been wrong, so wrong to think against our beliefs, to question the existence of our God, to wonder whether the ways of our community are right or wrong. They're right…of course they're right, and I have sinned beyond forgiveness.

There must be a demon inside my mind, giving me the same sexual impulses as those of men. It tricks me, deceives me, convinces me to carry out sexual acts with a woman, and I'm weak. Women are weak...too weak to handle the Impulse. It's why God only burdens our men with it. They have the willpower to wait for the full moon to purge, while I had none.

I wanted her.

I needed her.

I thought perhaps I loved her.

But it's only the demon in my soul.

I'm a woman possessed.

I'm a sinner.

Elijah had to report my transgression to the Control, and my fate awaits their decision of punishment. I know I deserve whatever punishment they bring. I just hope that when I'm gone, another domestic can help Elijah raise Mercy to be stronger than me, holier than me.

All hope for me is lost.

But perhaps Mercy will grow to become the proud, willing servant I know she can be.

I flip to the next entry, dated July 21, 2171—my sixth birthday.

I've said goodbye to Mercy, and nothing in my life has been harder than that. My daughter, my love, the light of my life...She turns six years old today, but it's the last birthday I'll ever see.

My life will end tonight.

I know my fate is death; I've accepted it. But I don't accept the condemnation of my soul for all eternity. I asked to find absolution for my soul, but no grace was given by the Control. They find me too abhorrent. Perhaps God will grant me grace at the stake when I'm doused in flames.

Unless...there is no God.

Unless there is nothing after death.

If that's the truth, then dare I say, I'm glad I loved that incredible woman while I could. My hand shakes as I write this—the words are blasphemous, I know. But what does it matter now that I'm sentenced to death and my soul is already damned?

There's a simple spark of hope in my chest that maybe this is it. Maybe death is the end. Maybe eternal suffering won't find me, and life will simply be over when I die. That hope is all I have to cling to in these final hours of my life.

But oh, how I fear for my Mercy. How I hate myself for doing this to her, for sinning so catastrophically and leaving her behind. The tears running down her pink cheeks as I told her I was leaving forever were enough to shred what was left of my tattered soul.

She was fearful and sad and looked at me as though I'd broken her world. I have broken her world because I sinned.

But tonight I'll stand humbly at the stake, and I won't scream when they set me on fire; I won't protest. I'll receive my punishment, and though I know it's too late for my soul to be saved, I'll pray for God's mercy all the same. Likewise, I'll hope that God doesn't exist at all, and that this will be the end of my suffering forever.

All I ever wanted was to love and to be loved. It was never there with Elijah, though he never treated me poorly. It was only with her that I felt it, and I regret nothing.

No.

I regret everything.

I regret our stolen fates.

I regret our carelessness.

I regret that we didn't spend more of our numbered days together, sinning in secret.

I regret that I won't be here to protect Mercy.

Tears well, and one breaks away from the corner of my eye, slipping down the side of my face. My heart is broken. My mother had loved and been loved in return, and because it wasn't with the man she'd been assigned to be with, she was persecuted. She'd found love with another woman, and they murdered her because of it.

Love is a rare and precious thing in Ember Glen—something scarcely seen and only found by sheer luck. Domestic women are assigned their male counterpart, and the likelihood of them loving one another is improbable. Though I can't deny the hurt I feel for my late father over her adultery, the anger I feel for my mother's demise overshadows it.

How can murder be justified for one person loving another?

A shadow quickly obscures the sunlight from overhead, startling me. My heart sinks heavily into my stomach, but it splashes in the acid, scattering droplets that burn my insides as I look up and see why the sunlight disappeared.

A man stands above me, feet straddling either side of my hips.

"Good morning, Mercy."

I blink against the tears clouding my vision.

The sunlight glows like a halo around Arlo Rainn's head.

"Good morning," I return politely, curious about his appearance.

I swallow anxiously that he's caught me with my mother's journal—and on the page with an admission of her sins, no less.

I don't want anyone to see what's within these pages—it's my mother's personal thoughts. But more than that, it tells of her indiscretions. It tells of all her secrets, and my thoughts are scribbled in the margins. So, as he watches me, I move slowly, careful not to draw attention to it, careful not to move so quickly as to make it seem like I want to hide it.

I fold the journal closed and gently slip it down to rest on the ground beside me, releasing it, though I have the urge to hang on for safe-keeping. I know if he sees me willing to let go of it, then perhaps he'll assume there's nothing of great importance in there.

I press up onto my elbows, wishing I could sit up at least, unnerved by laying beneath him. The way he stands above me, feet straddling my hips, prevents me from moving.

"Is there something I can do for you?" I squint against the sunshine halo around his face, tilting my head and bringing one hand up sideways against my forehead as a shield.

"I could think of several," he returns, "but the night of your service has passed."

I swallow the lump rising in my throat. "There's always the next one," I say, my voice dripping with sarcasm.

I shouldn't have said those words, at least not in that sardonic manner. It's as though I can't help but try to get myself into trouble.

Careful, Mercy.

A soft smile tugs at one corner of his thick lips, twisting into his tawny beard and highlighting the long line of his dimple. He's handsome, there's no denying it. The glow of sunlight all around him really amplifies the hint of orange in his brown hair and beard—it reminds me of fire.

Orange and yellow flames flicker through my mind, rushing me back to the other night. Images of Hyatt and his torch flash to pictures of Ivy Jane moving as flames engulf her, which distorts into the flash fire I felt rushing through my veins when Arlo had me against the tree and made me come—

"There likely won't be a next one for you, I'm afraid."

I sinned.

I ran, and I hid.

I rebelled from my soul's purpose, and I was promised punishment.

He's come to punish me.

As soon as the realization hits me, I scramble, kicking against the earth to push myself backward and crawl out from beneath him. He ignores me as I awkwardly rush to my feet and back away; instead, he bends to pick up my mother's journal.

No!

I lunge for it, but he jerks his hand away, holding the journal beside his head.

"Give that back."

"No," he says plainly.

He slowly lowers it in front of him, thumbing open the pages.

I lunge again to snatch it, but he only steps back, narrowing his eyes at me with his head tilted toward the pages. "Stop. Your property is my property now."

"What?"

What is he saying?

I'm entitled to have my own things.

Except, the Control has license to take authority over the personal property of sinners.

And I'm a sinner now.

I feel frozen as I watch him flip through the pages, reading a sentence here and there. A shiver runs up my spine despite the warmth of the sun, and I hug myself, running my hands up and down my arms. Movement in the distance catches my eye; standing at the tree line, at the edge of the meadow, are the other six members of the Control.

Watching.

Waiting.

The notion of my death claws through my mind, scratching away all other thoughts.

Have they come to kill me?

Will I die today?

How will they do it? Burned at the stake like my mother?

"What is this?" Arlo asks, closing the journal and holding it up. "Is this your mother's?"

I hear him, but I struggle to respond. The very essence of my being is trapped behind a thick wall of ice inside my mind, frozen and paralyzed to thoughts of punishment and death.

"Forget it," he says with exasperation. "Come with me."

He holds out his palm, covered with a black leather glove, and I stare at it as if it's the strangest thing I've ever seen, as if it's the most terrifying thing I've ever seen…because it is.

If I take his hand, he'll lead me away, only I don't know where to and I don't know what will happen then. I don't know if I'll be hurt or tortured, or if I'll be killed immediately.

I lift my gaze from his hand to meet his stare. "Are you going to kill me?"

His eyes are blue—bright blue, like the clear sky above. They sparkle as he watches me, waiting for me to take his outstretched hand.

I think it's the first time I've ever really looked at him. I've only known him by name and in passing before the other night in the forest. I knew *of* him; I'd seen him and could identify him easily. But looking at him now, I know I've never truly *seen* him before.

"Not personally, and certainly not today," he offers. "Come along now. We have things to discuss."

"What things?"

He takes a step closer, and instinctively, I step back.

"Mercy."

"What's going to happen to me? Please. Can't you just tell me now?"

"I'm not going to ask you again." His offered palm twitches with threat. "We will drag you away if you insist on resisting."

Part of me wants to resist. If my fate has already been decided—and I suspect it has—then resistance won't change the outcome. Resisting might make me feel like I did something, that I at least tried. That part of me makes my knees bend with the urge to run.

Likewise, though, there's no point in that fight if it changes nothing. Something tells me I should save my strength for a battle yet to come, though I don't know what it is.

I take a step closer to Arlo, and slowly, I reach out to him, watching our hands come together in contrast beneath the bright shine of sunlight. The black leather looks menacing, held out above the colorful wildflowers and grass that sways in the gentle breeze. As I lay my pale hand atop his palm, his hand closes tightly around mine, caging it in his suffocating grasp.

My lips part with an abrupt inhale as he pulls me sharply, easily tugging me into his hold as his other arm—still grasping the journal—whips around my waist. I raise my head to look up at him, and he catches me again in his stare. The intensity of his blue gaze grabs hold of me and flashes through my memories, making my stomach flutter.

I remember the warmth of his bare hand as his fingers pressed inside me. Part of me wants to feel that warmth against my palm now held in his grip—but the leather grips me instead. His thick eyebrows furrow, drawing a line above his blue eyes. His expression is forever changing—it shifts and twists so quickly that my darting eyes can't keep up as they flicker about his face. I see the curve of his throat bob as he swallows, his arm shifting along my back.

Why is his arm still around me?

Why does he still hold me this way?

He blinks and his eyes shadow, like a shade slipping down and hiding the brightness. Still holding my palm in his, he releases his arm from my waist and turns before shifting into a fast walk, dragging me along beside him. "I'm taking you to the Homestead. You'll be under my charge for an undefined period of time."

"What does that mean?"

"Do you know how to be quiet?"

"I just want to know what's going to happen to me."

"You'll learn soon enough. Patience is a virtue, Mercy. You should practice it."

I huff out in stressful frustration as he pulls me toward the trees. The Control turns their attention to me as we charge toward the center of their gathering at the edge of the woods.

"Mercy Madness," Killian Cole says. "About time you were brought to justice."

"It's your reckoning day," someone else calls, but I don't see who as Arlo drags me past them, marching me through the forest.

"Bring the sinner to her judgment," another says, their voices following close, taunting me as they take me away for God knows what.

The taunting continues through the forest, twigs breaking beneath my feet, the crunching echoes bouncing off the trees all around me. The men's voices seem to drift into a swirling chorus that loops around tree trunks, swirls through the empty spaces between them, and bathes me in taunting noise.

As we break through the trees, the noise crescendos with the sound of voices ahead in the village square.

Adrenaline pulses through my veins as I stumble behind Arlo's quickening pace. My eyes take notice of who the rising voices belong to. The entire population of Ember Glen is standing in wait in the village square, just in front of the steps leading up to the Homestead.

Waiting.

Waiting for me.

chapter ten

Mercy

FEAR GRIPS ME, bringing my feet to an abrupt stop. Arlo jerks, but I plant my boots on the gravel, anger contorting my expression. His grip slips from my hand to my wrist. I try to pull my arm away, bringing my free hand to push down against his grip.

"Let go of me!" I shout, and my cry is met with the sudden deafening silence of the world around me.

Arlo stares at me, his anger bringing a sneer that pulls his lips across his cheeks. In a surprise move, he releases me and takes a step back. I turn to run, but I crash straight into Theo's broad chest.

I look up at him. "Theo…"

His expression is somber, sad, regretful—and that scares me more than anything. "I'm sorry, Mercy."

I take a step back as the Control circles me, making it clear there is no escaping my fate.

"You sinned when you were meant to serve," Theo says, as if the logic is sound and should be enough to make me accept this. "But it was the culmination of your dissenting thoughts, and it can no longer be ignored." He lowers his voice. "I warned you…"

He did warn me.

He told me I was being watched before he ran after Delle that night.

Heat envelops me, like a fire burning at my back as Arlo steps in close behind me. My pounding heart skips a beat. His fingers are too light, too gentle as they capture strands of my white-blonde hair and lift them back over my shoulder. His breath breezes across my ear as he leans in.

"Come with me, sinner. Walk with dignity to your reckoning, and I'll stand beside you."

I turn my head sharply, meeting his eyes as he slowly circles to stand at my side.

"I'll stand beside you."

I don't know what to make of such a contradictory statement.

I'll cast judgment upon you while standing at your side?

Righteous indignation catches fire in my chest as he once again holds out his gloved palm for me to take. I feel the snarl tug a sour grin from my lips.

Everything in Ember Glen is a contradiction—our faith, our beliefs, our values…Everything is just one sickening contradiction after the next.

So let them call me the sinner.

Bring forth my judgment and reckoning.

I won't pretend I believe their lies any longer. I won't go with willing acceptance to my death like my mother did.

I swing my arm to smack Arlo's hand away. "I don't need anyone to stand beside me, least of all men like you." For good measure, I spit on the ground beside his feet, out of my mind with fury.

My action stirs chaos, and the men descend. My eyes are caught on Arlo's, but he can't even get to me before another has their arms around my waist, lifting and dragging me away. I stare as Arlo remains fixed to the spot, as my body is carried away with the Control surrounding me, all except for him.

In his own rage, the sight of him draws me in, keeps my furious attention locked on him while I'm dragged away. His chest rises and falls as anger flares his nostrils; but strangely, there's a fluttering inside my stomach at the way his piercing eyes narrow on me.

He looks at me with passion.

He looks at me with fierce determination, with intent, with a plan. That shouldn't trigger my curiosity, yet it does.

It keeps me drawn in, zeroed in on him as he stomps after me. Arlo's rapt attention fuels me with anger, and I thrash against the arms that hold me, letting rage build as I'm spun away and dropped heavily to the ground again.

I land on my boots, but the forward thrust pitches my weight, causing me to stumble ahead. I'm determined not to fall. I find my balance and start walking before they can push me, moving toward the villagers gathered in the square.

The day is too bright for these dark events.

The villagers watch, confusion and anticipation mixed in their expressions. They probably don't know *why* they're gathered; they're probably just excited *to be* gathered. They must know by now that I've done something wrong. My sin is their entertainment—whatever my punishment will be is a spectacle for them.

Murmurs and whispers carry to my ears as I'm marched up the concrete steps toward the Homestead. Three of the Control climb to the landing ahead of me. They stop and turn to face me so abruptly that I nearly lose my balance trying to stop myself from falling.

A hand latches around my wrist, another pressing to the small of my back. The touch of fingertips grazing my spine with delicate control is shocking, causing a shudder to ripple through every nerve ending.

My head turns, and I'm not surprised when I lock eyes with Arlo. It's his leather-clad hand on my wrist, his palm on my back. With a quick jerk, he spins me around, and I suck in a gasping breath.

Clustered together in the center of the large gravel-covered square is everyone I've ever known. They're staring at me, judging me, waiting on bated breath to know why I've been brought to stand before them.

This is perhaps the first moment I've ever been glad that both my parents are dead—at least I don't have to see them gathered, staring with fear and embarrassment in their eyes.

A mass of servants, all dressed in black, emerge from the Sanctuary, realizing that there's a gathering that they hadn't been called to. It's only because it's the week after service—they're meant to be left alone in reverence, and this is a disturbance.

I'm a disturbance—a ripple in the perfectly flowing current of life in Ember Glen.

My heart pounds as the girls from Sanctuary quicken their pace, my stomach clenching in shame as Ellary recognizes me standing on the steps and rushes, pushing through the cluster of servants to meet the gathering of villagers.

I can't look at her.

I turn my head, gazing off toward the line of trees, quietly wishing I were back in the meadow among the wildflowers.

Too soon, Killian's bellowing voice drags my attention back to the unfolding nightmare. "Mercy Madness has sinned."

The dramatic hisses and sighs of disapproval that roll through the throng is nearly laughable—as if they hadn't already figured it out.

"On the night of our purge, Mercy turned and fled from a man as he approached her. She ran into the forest and hid in a tree. She knowingly, and willfully, refused to serve the Impulse, and her transgression cannot go unrecognized by our authority. Mercy has actively engaged in rebellion, not only by fleeing during service, but in her withdrawal from her duties to serve this community. She chose her own well-being over the well-being of every other man, woman, and child in this village. She has chosen not to fulfill her purpose as a servant of the Impulse, and in doing so, has put you all in danger."

I scoff, too angry to hide it any longer.

They aren't in danger because I chose to flee rather than be lit on fire, but it's what we've been made to believe our entire lives. As I learned today, even my mother was made to believe it—though she'd questioned it just like me. They've made us believe that our community is safe because men are allowed to purge on nights of service, and servants are honored for their sacrifices.

But we were never given the choice to sacrifice, so it's not sacrifice at all…it's slaughter.

In my obvious disdain, Arlo jerks my wrist, tilting my body harshly to the side. I grimace as he twists, bending my arm at the elbow and pinning it behind me. Pressing forward, my back arches away from the pressure, and I groan.

"Quiet, sinner," he whispers.

I lift my foot and slam it back down again, stomping on his toe. His leather shoe is hard, and I'm sure he doesn't feel a thing. Still, he presses harder, making my back arch deeper. His other hand wraps around my hair and tugs, forcing my chin skyward.

His mouth is against my ear, and he speaks so quietly that I don't think the Control surrounding us can even hear. "I will bind you so tightly that your veins bulge and your limbs go numb. Don't test me." The rasp of truth in his tone is jarring, and I still myself in his hold.

Gradually, he loosens his grip, his fingers slipping down through the length of my hair until it falls away entirely. He doesn't let go of my arm, keeping it pinned against my back, but he lets up enough that it no longer aches.

"Our eyes have been on Mercy Madness for several months," Killian continues. "She has become disengaged from our community; she's indignant and self-righteous. And this last purge was the culmination of her dissension. We've known peace in Ember Glen for many years, and we owe that peace to our nights of release. Praise God for the insight he's granted us over how to be a worthy community—a community of godly men and women who know their roles and fulfill them with grace. We cannot allow one ungodly servant to threaten the peace we've worked so hard to maintain.

"Yet, we must humble ourselves in God's good graces. We must seek absolution for the sake of this sinner's soul." Killian paces dramatically along the step beneath me as he speaks. "Though her dishonorable choices must be punished, we must offer her a chance."

A chance?

A chance at what?

I'm motionless, waiting on bated breath.

"The Elders have offered us their guidance and we are all in agreement of what must be done." Killian stops, turns his head over his shoulder to glance at me with a smug grin before turning to face the villagers again. "Mercy Madness is set to participate in the Trials of Dissension."

My ears roar, not with the murmurs and cheers that swell from the villagers, but with the quickening thrum of my pulse.

The Trials of Dissension?

I shake my head. "No," I whisper, but no one hears me. "No! This is a death sentence!"

"Pass the trials, and it's not," Arlo says.

I turn toward him as rage takes hold of me, his grip loosening and letting me go. "No one has ever survived the trials. No one."

He leans forward, coming into my space, making me crane my neck to look up at him as he bends over me. I can smell his minty breath. "Then perhaps you'll be the first." An arrogant grin spreads through his cheeks.

We both know that won't be the case. No one ever survived because the trials were designed to push one past their boundaries in the ultimate acts of service. Every last participant has met their death at the end of these torturous trials.

I'm disgusted by Arlo, sickened by all the men surrounding me—smug, righteous, arrogant, power-hungry men.

Does no one see it but me?

My mother did, but she was so misled that she still mistrusted her instincts.

"Get out of my face," I hiss.

Arlo's grin remains, though his blue eyes roam my expression.

What is he thinking when he looks at me that way?

And why do I care?

"You'll hold your tongue with me and show respect, Mercy, or I will make your numbered days a living hell."

I swallow the weight of his threat, feeling my eyes widen as the smug expression melts with the honesty of his words.

Abruptly, he turns to face the villagers. "I've been appointed warden of our trial participant," Arlo says. "Mercy Madness will be my charge and my responsibility from now until the trials have concluded." He turns toward the servants, all grouped together beside the other villagers. "Servants, as is tradition with the Trials of Dissension, you are all granted the choice of participating. Those of you who are proud servants—graceful in your acceptance of your role within our community, honorable in the eyes of God—you should find it an easy choice not to participate.

"But should any of you feel a blasphemous urge to participate in these trials along with Mercy, we are granting you the right to make the choice. If you pass the trials and prove yourself through the ultimate acts of service, then you will be granted reprieve from your role as a servant and assigned a domestic life.

"But make no mistake, the trials are brutal, and none have survived before. I suggest you think again should the unholy urge to participate arise. God does not show favor in this life to those who wish to deflect their duties." He looks over at me and catches my gaze with an unexplainable heat in his eyes. "Mercy has lost her way. She travels a trail of sin." He looks back to the servants and I blink away the invisible hold he has on me. "If you're a woman of God, you'll ensure you do not follow the path she has made with demons."

Arlo Rainn—my warden, my jailor, my *captor*.

I'll be his until the day I die.

chapter eleven

Mercy

I JERK MY arm from Arlo's grip and plant my feet in the center of the foyer as the men come to a stop in front of me. The door slams shut behind me as the Control circles around, making me feel caged in.

Because I *am* caged in.

I've never been inside the Homestead before…none of the villagers or servants have. It belongs to the members of the Control and to no one else.

I spin to see all of them surrounding me. Seven towering men in their fine clothes and pretentious expressions bringing me to judgment of my so-called sins. As I turn, the tiled floor beneath my feet catches my gaze. I'm standing on the center of a golden sun with seven swooping arms reaching out to form its halo—seven arms, and one man standing at the point where each ends. A lump rises in my throat and I swallow, feeling tension pull through my shoulders.

I open my mouth to speak, but to say what, I don't know. But their madness descends without warning, and any words I might've spoken are shoved aside by the forceful protest of my scream. All at once, they close in, my cage collapsing. Hands fall on me, grabbing my wrists, sweeping my legs out from under me, bringing me down to the ground. I thrash and fight at their team effort to push me down, but there are seven of them and the fight is no use. Quickly, they have me on my back, and it's a flurry of men above me, beside me, all around me.

"Turn her over," Killian commands, and there isn't an inch of my body that isn't being touched by someone.

I scream, thrashing and twisting violently as they work to flip me. I don't know what they intend to do to me, but it isn't hard to imagine what horrible things they might do while I'm pinned face-down on the floor with seven men controlling me.

"Mercy, stop," I hear Theo say, and the sound of his voice startles me.

I glance over at him as his hand slips behind my head and grabs hold of the back of my neck. I don't know why it hurts me that he's part of this, because he's always been part of this. He's always been one of the Control.

I just sometimes thought that he was my friend, too. Maybe that stopped when he chose to leave me and chase after Delle into the forest.

The overwhelming fear and heartache over what's happening to me brings tears to my eyes, and the trail down my cheeks triggers a resigned sob. My body relents in its fight and allows them to turn me, pressing me down into the hard floor, my black skirt spread across the sunburst tile like a dark spot on the sun.

I feel someone climb over my back, their knees straddling my waist. Then I feel the touch of leather kiss my skin, and I instantly know it's Arlo brushing his gloved fingers across the side of my neck. I go still, my breath held at his touch.

"Hold still," Arlo says as he pulls my hair back, brushing it aside and exposing the back of my neck. "We need to mark you for the trials. If you just hold still, it will only hurt briefly."

I'm a strong woman, but I have no strength in this moment. I'm subdued entirely, overpowered and overwhelmed. I don't even flinch at the news of pain and being marked. I just want them to get this over with—whatever this is.

I hold still, breathing heavily through several beats, doing my best to quell the waves of tears that threaten behind a sob. I feel Arlo's leather-covered fingertip trace a spot at the base of my neck.

"Here?" he questions.

"Yes, right there at the back of her neck," I hear Killian respond.

The leather leaves and it's replaced by a metal tip, and then a sharp slice sears pain across my skin. I yelp at the unexpected burn of it—a knife slicing a quick straight line at the base of my neck.

"Don't move," Arlo commands, and I'm obliged to listen as sadness overwhelms me.

He stands, the weight of him leaving my body, but it's quickly replaced by someone else. I feel the knife tip dig into my skin a second time, then slice sharply, drawing a short line of fire beside the first cut.

I cry as I feel the warmth of my blood pooling and dripping from the cuts. I let the tears fall freely as the second body leaves me, and another replaces him, as another slice sears my skin...then another, and another. The seven take their turn drawing bloody lines at the base of my neck, and once the seventh is etched on my skin, it's over.

They let go of me, and nearly all at once move back to their points around the starburst, leaving me in the center of the burning sun. Gasping and breathless, my body curls protectively around its center, though my palms stay pressed flat to the tile.

"There's no need to fear us, Mercy," I hear Killian say. "You won't be harmed in this house now that you're marked. As a trial participant, you're granted the privilege of living as one of us until your time is…over."

Until I'm dead.

I hear Ryker chuckle. "Last rites for a sinner."

"Your warden will make sure you have what you need during your time here, however long that may be."

I push through my palms and slowly lift myself. "How long?" I ask, my voice coming out unexpectedly hoarse, low, shaken.

"The first trial will take place in a little less than a month."

One month.

Goosebumps prickle along my forearms as I bring myself to a sitting position, my gaze fixed on the floor.

"Come with me, sinner." Arlo's smooth voice touches my ears and I feel the sound vibrate through my spine. "I'll show you to your room so you can dress in something more appropriate for your new status."

I scoff at his words as I bravely, but slowly push to my feet. I turn to face Arlo and see his outstretched hand once again—still covered by the black gloves I'm coming to despise.

Arlo's pointed gaze holds my attention, his straight expression steady and severe. "Take my hand," he implores, "and come with me."

I feel my hand lift and reach toward his. I'm aware of the movement, but I feel powerless over it. As my palm lands on his, something sparks and crackles between us—a strange emotion that feels inevitable, yet entirely unexplainable.

Arlo's hand closes around mine and he tugs, just as he did in the meadow. Air escapes my lungs as he pulls me against him, and our bodies collide.

I bring up my hands to push off his chest, but they're pinned between us as he dips his head to my ear. "I expect nothing less than your best behavior," he whispers, then draws his head back to look down at me, speaking loud enough for the others to hear. "It's understood that I'm your warden, and your needs will be met through me. If there's something you need, you come to me first. No one else needs to be bothered by your requests. Do you understand, sinner?"

"You can continue to call me that but saying it doesn't make it true."

I draw a chuckle from the men behind me, but my eyes are fixed on Arlo's serious features, my gaze drawn to the frustratingly plump lips that twist into a devilishly smug grin.

I hate his lips.

I hate his grin.

I hate the long dimples that cut down his cheeks.

I hate that, despite all the ugliness inside, he's objectively handsome. But when I raise my eyes to meet his, I feel an unwanted recognition.

I can't breathe when he looks at me.

"Up the steps, sinner," Arlo says, tilting his head toward the grand staircase in front of us.

He shifts to move beside me with our hands meeting in the space between us, my palm resting face down on his as he leads me elegantly up the steps. He behaves as if this were a delicate and regal moment, helping a fragile woman make her way up such a grand staircase.

He acts as though he's honorable for leading me so gently.

It enrages me.

We step onto the landing, and we turn right before he leads me down a long hallway.

"You'll stay in the room next to mine," he says. "That way I can keep a close eye on you and ensure your needs are met."

Part of me wants to remain silent in protest, but there's a much stronger urge to speak up, to lash out, to show anger. "What needs do you expect me to have that you're capable of meeting? I don't recall a single time in my life that all of my needs have been met."

He stops abruptly, turning to face me, my hand still in his. "Then consider yourself lucky to live what's left of your life here. In the Homestead, everyone's needs are met, save for—"

"Sex and violence?" I finish the statement for him. "Don't all the men of Ember Glen have that need?" I scoff.

He arches an eyebrow. "We do, of course."

"So, not all your needs are met here."

He tenses his jaw to fight the curling of his lips at one corner. "Obviously, you already knew that. Are we playing a game of semantics?" He drops his hand and mine falls, as well. He cocks his head to the side as he considers me. "It's funny that you mention it, seeing that the very reason you're here right now is due to your choice not to fulfill man's need for sex and violence under the last full moon. Here you are now, having your own needs fulfilled until the day you take your last breath." He takes a step toward me, and instinctively, I step back. "And aren't you ashamed of yourself? It was your duty to service the impulsive needs of men, and you refused."

"I served those needs," I argue, stepping forward and closing the distance between us. "I served dutifully for four years!"

"Do you have short-term memory loss, or are you just stupid? You *ran,*

Mercy. You fled and hid from service."

I flinch at his insulting choice of words but allow it to fuel my frustration. "My memory serves me well, and I'm much smarter than any man gives me credit for. I'm smart enough to know better than to let myself be lit on fire just for the sake of calling myself righteous. A god worth serving wouldn't—"

He presses closer and our bodies touch as he looks down at me with fury and passion. "Don't you dare speak another word, Mercy Madness."

I huff out a heavy breath as my eyebrows draw together in anger, my chest sinking rapidly. I want to speak, to retaliate, to agitate him. I want to rile him up further and invoke a verbal sparring match, but I don't know exactly why I want that. He's stubborn and self-righteous; a man who has the authority to uphold the doctrine I question and quarrel over in my mind on a minute-to-minute basis.

Then I realize why I want to speak against him so badly. It's because he's let me speak longer than any other man ever has. Truthfully, I've spoken more freely with him than I ever have, even with another servant. The realization is striking, and somehow, it fills me with a sense of gratitude—a sentiment he certainly hasn't earned. Yet it pulls through me, drags my shoulders back, forces me to soften my features, and concede to showing him that the sentiment is there all the same.

Sensing the change in me, he pulls back, rolling his shoulders and letting go of some tension he held there.

He lowers his voice to a heated whisper. "You'll watch your words here, lest one of my brothers with less patience than I have should overhear you and decide it would be best to drag you out and burn you at the stake…to spare the spectacle of the trials and the time granted to you in between." He turns and starts walking again. "This way."

"What do you mean?" I ask before following him down the hallway.

We approach a door—second to the last at the end of the hall—and he turns to face it. He pushes back his sleeve and uses the black band, which is forever fixed around his wrist, to release the lock. My gaze falls to the patch of skin visible between his sleeve and glove, and I notice a portion of his skin is bumpy, uneven—it looks scarred or something.

Is he hiding scars beneath the leather gloves?

He turns the handle and pushes the door open, waving his hand to encourage me inside. Reluctantly, I cross the threshold and enter the room. I take a couple of slow steps inside before I hear the door click shut behind me, and it makes me jump. I whirl around to find him in the room with me, door closed at his back.

"You're here as both a prisoner and for your protection," he tells me.

"We've granted you a courtesy by making you a trial participant; we've given you a chance—"

"It's hardly a chance."

He closes the distance between us with a single, long stride. "It's a *chance*, nonetheless. A chance at absolution for your soul, if not for life itself. But make no mistake that if you fall out of line, a swift execution can be arranged. Everyone in Ember Glen is aware that you're a sinner, and though I'm sure they'll all be thrilled to watch you face the trials, some would be so inclined as to take matters into their own hands and end your life more expediently."

His finger captures a strand of my hair and I narrow my gaze on him. "You should really consider our kindness in bringing you into our home. You should be grateful that you get to live this life of luxury while you can. Because you certainly haven't proven that you deserve it. I can only protect you if you tame your maniacal thinking and keep your pretty pink lips shut." His eyes drop to my mouth and my heart skips a beat.

I swallow. "Why bother to protect me at all?"

"Because I'm your warden, and you're my ward. Because it's the duty I've been given, and unlike you, sinner, I uphold the word of God."

He moves closer as I move back, and I realize only now that we've been doing this dance the entire time. My back hits one of the four posts of a bed behind me that I haven't set my gaze on yet. I gasp, twisting my head around to see the dark stained wood post as my body crushes into it.

He bends over me, and as I draw in a shaking breath, I can smell him— mint, pine, and open mountain air.

He smells like the meadow.

He smells like my happy place, and the realization of that twists in my gut, almost pleasantly so, but it quickly turns sour, spinning into nausea.

"You'll have no privacy from me, do you understand?"

I don't understand it.

I don't accept it.

But somehow, I find my head nodding as I stare up into his disarmingly bright blue eyes.

"Good." He tilts his head, his stare lifting to look beyond me, past my shoulder. "Go run a bath."

"A bath?"

His leather-covered finger plucks a strand of my hair again, running it slowly down to the end. "Are you asking me what a bath is?"

"Do you really think I'm stupid?"

"I think you're a servant and a sinner. I don't expect you to know much of anything."

My nostrils flare as I take in a furious breath, my voice deepening to match his condescending timbre. "I know how to care for myself. I know so much more than you'll ever give me credit for."

"That remains to be seen…though I don't expect to see much before the end."

The end.

My death.

I swallow hard. "How long do I have?"

"For what?" His body sways toward mine, and I let my back press against the wood post, hard and aching as my spine aligns to it.

"Until the final trial."

"Hmm," he hums. "I don't know. But as soon as I'm aware of your final day, I'll be sure to let you know."

His flippancy about my demise sets a fire in my chest. Without thought or care, I put my hands to his chest and shove. My sudden action takes him off guard and he stumbles back, slowly lifting his head and looking up at me from beneath dark lashes.

I've incited violence, and now he'll have a fair reason to retaliate. The Control are anointed by God to meet violence with violence in the name of keeping the peace—one of so many contradictions of our religious law.

His soft, full lips stretch wide across his cheeks to form a straight, hard line, indignant at my action against him.

Two swift steps bring him against me, his hand locking around my throat, then slipping around to the side of my neck, and spinning me to face away from him. Gripping the back of my neck, his touch sends a searing burn through my spine, reminding me of the knife marks still dripping blood down my back.

He marches me along the side of the bed, moving us past it and shoving me toward an open door at the back of the room. My shoulders tense and tighten, lifting against his grip as he shoves me forward. My boot steps from plush carpet to land on cold, hard tile—the transition mimics the contrast of Arlo, and it makes my head spin.

Just as fear weaves between my ribs and ropes around my heart, he stops…and lets me go. I feel the weight of his force drift away, and I whirl around to face him. My hands come up, ready to defend myself, but he takes a step back.

"Take a bath, sinner." He stands in the doorway, leaning his shoulder against the frame, standing so casually that I don't know what to make of it because I thought he was going to hurt me. "I want you clean before your skin touches the fine clothes we have for you."

I blink at him, confused. "Are you…are you going to stay there?"

He crosses his arms as he leans. "Does my presence bother you?"

"Yes."

"That's too bad." There's no violence in his expression. Instead, he smiles, his wide, thick lips turning upward and showing the long lines of his dimples.

He's disarmingly beautiful, and I know that's dangerous.

"Go on now," he says, tilting his head forward to indicate behind me.

I look over my shoulder and glance at the white clawfoot tub in the center of the bathroom. The space is starkly white. The walls are painted a soft, gray-tinted shade of white, and square, white tiles cover the floor. The vanity even has a white marbled countertop.

White, white, white.

No hint of color.

A space for cleansing.

"You seem nervous," he says, drawing my attention back to him.

Of course, I'm nervous.

Everything in my life has just changed for the worst.

I cross my arms over my chest, caging in my pounding heart. "I can't undress with you watching me like that."

"Like what?" he taunts.

He's baiting me into this little back and forth, and it leaves a sour taste in my mouth. I choose not to respond. Instead, I turn away from him and move to the center of the room, reaching over the edge of the tub to turn on the faucet. Water pours—clear, clean, and heavy—into the oversized tub. If my circumstances were different, I would find joy in the prospect of climbing into the warmth and resting.

But that's not my circumstance.

My shoulders jump and I startle as Arlo's fingers suddenly run across my shoulder blades. I feel his hand wrap around my hair, strands catching on the leather of his glove.

"Your hair…it's the color of the stars in the night sky," he says softly.

I wonder if I imagined him saying that at first. It's said in such a gentle way, in a way of wonder. It's jarring in comparison to the way he calls me a sinner.

It makes my heart beat faster.

I feel his hand turn, fingers combing through, leather catching on a tangle as he drags his hand down the length. I wonder why he doesn't remove his gloves to touch my hair, which he seems to be so enamored with. I wonder if it's stained and matted with drying blood from the knife wounds inflicted on my neck.

His fingers reach the end, and I feel the weight of my long hair drop against the center of my back, nearly reaching my waistline. I take a breath, and I think it's the first I've taken since he reached out to touch me.

Without preamble, he touches the zipper at the back of my high-waisted skirt and tugs with a sharp jerk. He pushes the fabric down over my hips and it quickly falls to my feet. I shudder at the sudden exposure of my bare legs.

Leather brushes my skin as his fingers wiggle beneath the hem of my top and tug it up. My arms lift naturally, too easily allowing him to pull it off over my head and toss it aside. I cross my arms at the sudden chill in the room…the sudden bareness and vulnerability in the way he's exposed me.

I'm left standing in my boots, bra, and underwear. I feel rooted to the spot as I watch the tub fill with water. The sound of it splashing against the porcelain tub echoes through the bathroom, and he's just standing there behind me, too close for comfort, quiet and still. I have to arm myself against him because I feel the strength of his gravitational pull, the way it tugs at my soul in a way I've never felt before.

I feel him so strongly.

It's terrifying, and even though the pull is warming, it makes me shiver from head to toe.

"Take off the rest," he whispers.

I steel myself and harden my voice. "Where is the line for you?"

"What are you asking?"

"The line, Warden Rainn." I call him that to dehumanize him—maybe if I can remind myself that he's my captor, my keeper, then maybe I'll forget about the way his presence melts my insides. "Where is the line between asserting your authority and being inappropriate with a woman?"

"That's a bold question."

"The question is bold, but you know the line is thin."

He chuckles, the sound low and rumbling. "Do I?"

"Don't you?"

He moves around me, circling to the other side of the tub, and my eyes never leave him. "The line may be thin, sinner, but I know where it's drawn." He bends, wrapping his gloved hands around the rounded edge of the tub and leaning forward on it.

I turn my gaze away from him, unable to look directly into his blue eyes, and I watch the water pour from the faucet instead. "I don't think you do."

"Are you going to enlighten me, then?"

I shake my head.

"No? Then perhaps you should admit that you don't know as much as you think you do."

I dare to lift my eyes and look directly into his bright blue stare. "I know far more than you give me credit for."

"You know *nothing*."

"Is this how the end of my life is going to be?" My head tilts as I appraise him with narrowed eyes, my palms rubbing over my arms. "Constantly being reminded of how stupid I am?"

"If you make it necessary."

"I suppose I should just keep my mouth shut, then? Keep my stupid thoughts to myself?"

A half smile tugs at the side of his mouth. "If you wish."

Indignation burns in my chest. With a snap, I bend, untying my shoelaces and kicking my boots off in a fury. I harshly pull off my underwear, stepping out and kicking it aside. I reach behind my back and unhook my bra, ripping it from my body and tossing it to the floor. I huff as I stare at him, refusing to speak, watching him watch me.

We stand and stare, eyes locked on each other as the sound of a waterfall rushes around us, echoing through the stark space. We stare until the tub fills, and as soon as it's full enough, I lift my leg over the edge and step in. The water is too warm, but I ignore the burn as I turn and lower. Arlo's hands lift from the edge, and he backs away as I sink.

Frustrated, frightened, and completely overwhelmed by Arlo's mere presence, I slip completely beneath the waterline. The hot water sears my skin, shocking me as it touches my cheeks, but I let it burn. It takes me from the moment and makes me feel free from this nightmare.

I'd happily stay beneath the water, holding my breath and basking in the all-encompassing warmth. But too soon, I'm torn from the heat.

Arlo's hand latches around the back of my neck, and I feel his fingers and thumb dig in painfully before he lifts me from the water. I gasp in a breath of surprise as he jerks my head above the waterline with jarring speed. My arms jerk out as an instinctive reaction, and my palms grip the edges of the tub as I rise.

Sitting upright, I whip my head to see him on his knees beside the tub. Our eyes catch and lock; his are narrowed, staring with such intensity that I don't think I could look away if I tried.

"What are you doing? Trying to drown yourself?" he huffs, anger tinging his features. "Suicide is a sin."

From the corner of my eye, I catch the red swirl of blood from my neck mingled in the water as it swirls lightly in the ripples and flow.

"What difference would it make since I'm already a sinner? And I wasn't trying to drown myself; I just wanted a moment of peace." I jerk my shoulders, forcing him to loosen his grip until he releases the back of my neck. My skin burns where he held me too tightly over the fresh cuts.

He tilts his head. "Do you think you deserve peace?"

"I deserve nothing," I sneer.

"Finally, we agree on something." The crease in his forehead ripples as his eyes flicker in bewilderment.

My lips snarl as I lean my face toward his. "We agree on *nothing*. I meant that I deserve nothing that's happened to me in this life. I didn't deserve to be chosen for service. I didn't deserve to be used and abused. I didn't deserve to be called a sinner, and I most certainly don't deserve *this*."

His expression surprises me, softening instead of hardening. "You don't believe you've sinned, do you?"

"I haven't. Not in the way I view sin."

"Sin isn't open for interpretation," his hand strokes down the back of my head, and that's when I realize he's still wearing the damned gloves.

Why didn't he take them off before reaching into the water?

Why does he wear them at all?

"It is when it requires me to put my life on the line," I tell him.

"God's requirements are clearly defined, and your role in this life is clearly defined. You defied your duties, Mercy. Argue it all you want, but you're wrong." He pushes to his feet and moves away, circling the tub. I follow him with my gaze. "You crossed a thick, dark, well-defined line in your role as a servant. The sooner you accept that, the more likely it will be that forgiveness will find you."

"What makes you think I care about forgiveness?"

"It doesn't matter if *you* care about the fate of your soul."

I pause. "Who does it matter to?"

He sighs, several beats passing before he speaks again. His eyes skim the length of my body, and I watch his Adam's apple bob as he swallows harshly. "You were right about that thin line; perhaps it's fainter than I thought. I'll wait in your room until you're done."

I watch as he leaves through the bathroom door, and I'm frozen, my fingers curled around the edge of the tub, my head permanently turned toward the door.

Why is he talking about the fate of my soul?

Why did he bring up the thin line?

Why did he lift me from the tub if he truly thought I would try to drown myself?

I know why. I won't pretend it's because he cares about my life, because I know he doesn't. It's because it would deny him the opportunity to punish me, to drag me through the pomp and circumstance of the Trials of Dissension.

I can't let him disarm me the way he threatens to. I can't let my guard down, because I can already sense all the ways in which he could ruin me. He could ruin my mind, my heart, my soul. He could find his way through my armor. He could find his way into the depths of my being.

And I can't live my last days with that kind of hope.

chapter twelve

ARLO

I SHOULD NEVER have offered to be the warden.

I shouldn't have put myself in this position with a fiery woman who inspires poetry…an attractive woman who inspires an inappropriate stirring within me.

Inappropriate.

That was the word she used to describe the thin line between authority and an abuse of my power. And indeed, that line was thin—thin, faded, and broken in places. The sight of her bare is what snapped the line for me, and it's my own damn fault because I neglected to purge. If I had, I wouldn't be seduced by her strong will, her starlight hair, or her sultry curves.

I need to pray.

I needed to purge at the last full moon.

That's the true issue at hand. It has nothing to do with her and everything to do with my failure to purge. Yet, it was her who held me so rapt with attention that night that I neglected my impulses.

I cross her room and sit in the ivory armchair facing the foot of her four-post bed. Her accommodations are fit for saints, and far too good for a sinner like her. She should consider herself lucky to spend what's left of her life here.

My eyes are fixed to her bed, to the cream-colored comforter threaded with gold stitches that create a floral pattern throughout. I hear water rolling and lapping as she moves in the tub, and I press my eyes shut, trying to focus on something else, anything else. My fingers curl around the armrests, my leather gloves soaked and uncomfortable against my skin as I dig them into the fabric of the chair.

I should just take them off, but I'm feeling vulnerable in the moment, and they serve as a shield. It's not as though I have an issue with her seeing my scars, but I'm not in the mood for her curiosity about them right now. I'm not inclined to share personal details from my life with her. I refuse to let her in, especially now when I'm reeling with urges I should've satisfied with her when I was allowed to under the full moon. If I had, I'd be thinking clearly now.

Eventually, I hear the whoosh of water as she exits the tub. I open my eyes and watch the open doorway, my pulse thrumming with the anticipation of her arrival.

My eyes want to take her in, to see her standing there, bare.

God help me.

I let out a breath when she finally appears, relieved to see her wrapped in a white towel. Her hair is dripping, and I watch droplets fall to her feet, landing on the tile and echoing in their splashing sadness for no longer mingling with her starlight tresses.

She looks at me expectantly, and I cast a glance toward the bed. "You can get dressed."

She looks at the dress I've laid out for her on the bed. Before, she only wore black—as all the servants wear—but as a trial participant, she'll now wear red, the color of blood and sacrifice. She'll have to sacrifice pieces of herself in the ultimate acts of service.

She takes a few slow steps toward the bed and reaches down, running her finger beneath the fabric. "It's beautiful."

Sweet sin.

The way the word flows from between her rosy lips makes something twist inside my chest.

Beautiful.

She looks up at me. "I'm supposed to wear this?"

I press my elbow into the armrest as I lift my hand, leaning to rest my chin against it. "Yes. You have a wardrobe full of gowns to wear."

"Why?"

"Would you rather parade around naked?" My fingers curl into a fist at the thought, and I lift my head before slapping my palm on the armrest. "Just get dressed, Mercy."

"I can't get dressed with you sitting there staring at me."

"Try."

She glares at me for a beat. "So the line is completely broken, then."

The line.

The thin fucking line between authority and abuse.

"Get dressed."

The same defiant look she had when she leapt into the tub and buried herself beneath the water touches her features. Without warning, she drops her towel, her bewitching eyes locked on mine. I force myself to hold her gaze, though my eyes beg to drop. She stares for what feels like the longest time—as if she's testing whether that fucking line still exists between us—

before finally letting go. With a sneer and a frustrated huff, she shakes her head before turning toward the bed and reaching for her clothes.

I cover my mouth to conceal the heavy, heated exhale that rushes from my lungs, swiping my fingers over my short beard.

"I'd rather be put to a swift death…" I hear her mutter, and I don't know whether she intended for me to hear it.

"Speak up if you mean to be heard."

Her head snaps and her eyes meet mine again so sharply that I feel knocked back in my seat. I clutch the armrests. "I said that I'd rather be put to a swift death than be tortured by you this way through the end of my days."

I'm surprised she said something; I'm surprised she met my gaze. Naturally, I'd assumed she'd humble herself when I called out her muttering. But instead, she met me with heat, raised her voice, and spoke her truth.

She's a sinner, I remind myself.

She's a sinner, she's a sinner, she's a sinner.

I know she's a sinner, yet her unearned self-pride pulls a smile through my lips. "Mercy Madness, you've yet to know torture."

I shove to my feet and stride across the room to meet her. My body moves me into her space against my will, against my better judgment. I watch myself step closer and closer to that line.

I turn toward the bed and she turns with me, and when I press closer still, she tries to step back…only the bed is behind her. She drops to sit, her chin tilting skyward to look up at me, her strange, beautiful eyes staying with me.

"I will make you a promise, though," I tell her.

"A promise?"

I bend, dipping so low that my forehead practically touches hers as I slip two fingers beneath her chin. Her sweet lips part, probably to protest my nearness, but I speak before she can. "A promise for you and the twisted morals that seem to rule your life. You will know what torture is before you meet your end."

Her eyes narrow on me. "My twisted morals?"

"Those are the words you choose to question?"

I've made a promise that she'll meet torture in her numbered days, yet she questions my assessment of her morals—it's baffling.

"Those are the only words in your statement that I don't understand."

"What don't you understand about them, sinner? Your morality presents with as much madness as your namesake."

"If you think it's mad to run from a man who chases after you with the intent of setting you on fire, then yes, call me mad."

My gaze drops from her eyes to her lips. "Are you referring to me or to Hyatt Price? I assure you, my intent was also to set you on fire when you ran from me in the forest."

I shouldn't have said that.

I shouldn't have thought it.

I'm mad myself—mad with impulses I needed to have served.

"And you did," she whispers.

My ribcage opens up, letting my heart drop heavily and sink in my gut.

She blinks and turns her head, quickly breaking the connection between us—a connection that shouldn't exist.

I step back, straightening to my full height. "Get dressed."

This time, she obeys, rising to her feet and turning her back on me. I stand and watch as she dresses quickly, and when she pulls the gown up her body, I reach for the zipper on the back of her dress. I don't waste time, though I'm tempted to graze her spine with my fingers. I zip it up quickly, then turn on my heel and storm toward the door.

"Go where you like within the Homestead, but if you try to leave the manor alone, you will be stopped. I'll come later and retrieve you for dinner."

Without sparing her another glance, I pull open the door, step out into the hallway, and slam it shut behind me. I stride down the hallway with no direction, simply moving away from the temptation of her as quickly as I can.

chapter thirteen

Mercy

I HEAR THREE knocks against the bedroom door; three dull thuds that somehow sound exactly the way I'd expect Arlo to knock.

"Come in."

It feels strange to extend an invitation. I'm certain if I'd said, "Don't come in," or "Go away," he would have rejected the protest and come in all the same.

The knob turns and the door swings open wide, revealing Arlo centered in the entryway. I'm perched on the very edge of the armchair across from my bed, my head turned toward him, and there's a beat where everything within me feels so light and weak at the sight of him that I worry I might topple forward onto the floor with so much as a gentle breeze.

He's dressed all in black, his clothes pressed in sharp lines and severe edges. His button-down shirt is open at the collar, hinting at curls hidden beneath. The waistcoat he wears has a silver chain draping from the second button to the small pocket stitched across its side. His sleeves are rolled up to his elbows, exposing the lines and sinews of his forearms, which draw my eyes down to his closed fists.

He stands with potency, his feet planted in a wide stance and his arms at his sides. It's the tan length of rope looped through his gloved and fisted fingers that makes my words catch in my throat.

"What…Why do you have that?"

"Come here," he commands.

I'm on my feet and moving across the room before a single thought of protest has a chance to fly through my mind. I think it must be fear that compels me to obey him without a thought. I don't feel fearful, though…not truly. Not in the way I've felt real fear through so many nights of service—shaking through my soul and quaking in my bones.

I come to a stop in front of him, my head bowed slightly as I fixate on the rope in his left hand.

His right hand floats toward me, and his knuckles lift to tap beneath my chin. "I don't need to bind you, do I, Mercy? I know you're a sinner, but I also know you're capable of compliance when it benefits you."

Compliance is such an ugly word.

Compliant is what I've been for far too long.

It wasn't until recently that I realized how blind compliance to a doctrine—one that didn't even make sense to me anymore—was dangerous. But he's not wrong; I am capable of compliance since that's what keeps servants alive. It was my rebellion that put me here, after all.

I shake my head, causing him to drop his hand. "No. You don't need to bind me."

His eyebrows twitch, casting an odd shadow over his bright eyes that brings a look of disappointment. I step back when he steps toward me, but then he stops.

"You only need to give me one reason to wrap this around your neck and lead you like a dog." His voice is calm and cool, as if his threat is nothing more than polite conversation. "One reason, one step out of line. Do you understand?"

I huff, not in anger, but in exhaustion. I'm so damn tired. I'm tired and hungry and too drained to fight. I nod, understanding what he's telling me, though that understanding doesn't lessen my confusion over what's happened to my life.

Nothing makes sense anymore.

I don't understand what we believe.

I don't understand the god we worship.

I don't understand why running from service is a sin.

I don't understand any of it, nothing at all.

Arlo's shoulders loosen and relax as he watches me, and something in his features soften. Then he turns, moving to stand beside me, holding out his left arm for me to take.

"I'm glad we understand each other."

The rope remains tight in his grip, dangling between us. I watch it sway for a moment before slipping my arm through his. With our arms linked, he pulls me closer to his side, and I feel the end of the rope brush my leg through the thin silk fabric of my crimson gown.

I flinch at the touch of it, but not in a fearful way. It's almost like being touched by him, like the rope is an extension of his hand, and he's just grazed my thigh. I push out a slow breath through my nose, trying to steady myself as he leads us into the hallway.

"Where are we going?"

"To dinner. I told you I would collect you."

"I wasn't sure you would..." I trail off, realizing I have no interest in making it known how much I doubt his words—how much I doubt every word…how much I doubt everything around me.

"If I tell you I'm going to do something, you can rest assured, I'm going to do it."

I don't respond.

We reach the staircase, and he leads me down. He's careful, as if he assumes I'm wearing the ridiculous high-heeled shoes I found in the wardrobe, but I'm not. I'm wearing my black boots beneath the elegant gown.

I smile to myself, thinking of it as a small, though insignificant rebellion. Trivial, yes, but it has meaning all the same. It returns some sense of pride to my heart, pride I need to get through dinner with the Control.

The voices of men carry from the foyer as we descend, and I spot a few of them standing on the starburst pattern beneath the golden chandelier. Killian and Ryker glance in our direction, and I feel the weight of their appreciative glances—glances that would indicate their interest in using me in service. I know they won't touch me outside of a full moon, but I don't feel any safer. I don't feel any less devalued and objectified.

We reach the bottom of the steps, and I see Theo enter the foyer, moving toward us from a dark hallway across the sunburst. His hands are tightly fisted at his sides and a furious, fearful look darkens his features. He spots me and stops abruptly, catching my eyes and holding for a beat. I see the movement of shadow from behind him—two forms shifting into view before emerging from the dark hall at his back.

Park steps into the meager light from the chandelier, the dim glow bronzing the shade of his tawny skin and making his black hair look even darker.

And then I see the ripple of black fabric as a servant steps forward, moving into the dim light beside Theo, who casts her a sideways glance.

"Mercy," Park says with a smile and a tilted head, "it appears you'll have a companion during the trials."

Delle Carter stands beside Theo, her face awash with equal parts determination and outright fear. It takes me a few moments of deep confusion, fueled by my unwillingness to accept what's standing right in front of me, to work out the scene.

Delle is here, and it can only mean one thing…

She's volunteered to participate in the trials.

I open my mouth to speak, to protest, to scream at her, and beg to know why. Arlo's arm unhooks from mine and lassos around my back instead, sensing my rising agitation. He opens his hand around my side to grip me, smashing the rope between my stomach and his palm in silent warning.

He bends and puts his lips to my ear. "Give me one reason, Mercy."

A warning.

My heart is torn between fear for myself and fear for Delle.

What was she thinking?

What has she done?

She's too young and naïve to make a decision like this, and I don't understand how they can allow it. She's sixteen years old. She spent *one* night in service. They can't really be thinking of allowing this.

I ignore Arlo's warning, shake myself from his grip, and charge across the space to Delle. "What are you doing?" I ask her, then look at Theo standing at her side. "You can't let her do this."

Theo's eyebrows stitch together over his brown eyes. "She has the right to make this choice."

"She doesn't understand the choice!" I shout.

I reach for Delle, placing my hands on her cheeks as she blinks at me through tearful eyes. "What were you thinking? What are you doing? Why? Delle, *why?*"

"I didn't...I couldn't..." she stammers. "After that service, I couldn't bear the thought of doing it again. Never again."

"This isn't the answer; this isn't a solution. Do you understand that no one has ever survived the trials?"

"I know." She nods, her delicate hands landing on my wrists. "I know, but there's a chance, right? There's a chance I'll pass, a chance I'll survive, a chance for something better than service. I have to try, Mercy."

A sob breaks free from her chest and she drops her hands, moving against me and wrapping her arms around my waist. I hug her tightly, wishing I could hug her tightly enough to take all the pain of this life away.

"You don't have to do this," I whisper. "You can survive a life of service. Some...some find joy from it, peace in doing God's work." I swallow hard because my words don't feel right.

They've never felt right.

"It's already done." Delle releases me and takes a small step back, turning to face away from me. She tugs her hair to the side, revealing the back of her neck. Seven fresh cuts still spill droplets of blood at the base of her neck.

They've already marked her for the trials.

"No..." The syllable falls from my lips in defeat.

It's already done.

chapter fourteen

THE CLANG OF knives and forks touching ceramic dishes echoes through the silent dining room. I wouldn't say it's unusually quiet, but the silent energy is certainly different.

There are two women present for our nightly meal—two servants, no less. It's not that their presence is bothersome, just that it's different. I think we all feel a sense of duty to curb our usual nightly chatter in favor of presenting ourselves properly with the weaker sex present. It's no matter that they are sinners, servants, trial participants...we must always hold ourselves to a higher standard than they hold themselves.

The round, wooden table we sit at is dark—nearly black—and Mercy sits rigidly in the seat to my right. A gold and crystal chandelier serves as the only light source in the room, and it casts a spotlighted glow on the center of the table beneath it. The central illumination casts shadows all around us, darkness shrouding the space behind our backs. I can see my brothers in God where they're seated, but it's black as night behind them.

Delle sits to my left—a new ward I'll be required to take care of for the trials. I feel uneasy about her presence. Truthfully, her decision to participate doesn't sit right with me. By all accounts, she's a sinner as much as Mercy is for running during service, but it was her first night and she is so young. We had elected to give her another chance, and in doing so, she had a choice.

She chose poorly.

She chose sin over learning and growing from her mistake, and now she'll be put through the Trials of Dissension.

Mercy clears her throat, and it draws my attention. I look over as she shifts in her seat, straightening her spine, and reaches forward for her glass of wine. I watch as she draws the goblet toward her mouth. The glass touches her soft, pink lips and my gaze is stuck there, trapped at the way they part, allowing the liquid to slip past them as she takes a sip.

I have a sudden vision of her bewitching me with her sinner ways, draining the blood from my body, and sipping it from a glass just like that. I wait for the repulsion of such a vision to take hold of me, to steal my appetite, but instead, I feel the weight of it sink inside me. My thighs tense as I feel a heaviness between my legs, my cock thickening inexplicably.

Sweet sin.

I don't know how I'll make it another month managing the impulses I should have purged. I need to be careful in how I handle Mercy Madness.

"We should discuss the first trial," Killian says, his voice cutting through the silence so unexpectedly that it nearly startles me. I turn my head away from Mercy to look at him across the table. "The Elders sent over their documents of the last three trials, and it seems there's some room for creativity."

I feel the shift in energy at my left and right, both Mercy and Delle raising invisible shields.

"Creativity?" Ryker asks. "How so?"

"The purpose that each trial serves is set," Killian explains, "but the means by which they are carried out leaves some room for us to decide. It ensures that no two sets of trials are the same."

"The first trial is Service of the Flesh," Theo says from where he sits on the opposite side of Delle. His jaw is tense as he speaks. "What purpose is that meant to serve?"

"As it's written in the Impulse Edict," Killian explains, mentioning the written religious law that governs Ember Glen, "servants must openly and eagerly offer the use of their bodies to the men of Ember Glen during nights of service. Under the full moon, their physical forms must be given entirely to performing acts of service that allow the men of Ember Glen to satiate their perverse sexual desires effectively, such that the domestic women of our community may continue to live their days in peace without fear of unwanted sexual acts being committed against them." He recites the edict from memory, as all members of the Control would be able to do.

Mercy sets her wineglass down on the table too hard, and some of the crimson liquid—which matches her gown—sloshes out, spilling onto the table. "Damnit," she mutters.

She lifts her white cloth napkin from her lap and works to wipe up the spilled liquid, though I notice her hands tremble. The rest of the room is silent as we all watch her dab at the red wine. The ways she trembles does something to me—twisting in my gut, making me feel uneasy. I don't enjoy watching her fumble and twitch through her nerves.

"Stop that," I tell her, reaching over and grabbing the cloth napkin and pushing her hands away. Dabbing with her napkin, I finish mopping up the spilled wine. I glance up when I feel the eyes of the room upon me. "Don't mind me." I nod. "Go on."

Killian blinks at me with a curious expression, but then continues, "Service of the Flesh is meant to be the ultimate act of sexual service."

I'm so utterly aware of Mercy's every breath, every twitch of every muscle, every slight movement in anxiety. It unnerves me for some reason, and I need to get control of it immediately. As soon as I finish cleaning the spilled wine, I remove the length of coiled rope where I looped it over the back of my chair. I push back my seat and swivel my body to face her squarely.

"What are you—"

"Shh," I hush her quickly as the conversation continues around us.

I grab hold of her wrists with one hand and tug them toward me. Before she can protest, I wrap them, circling coarse twine around both her wrists, looping and tugging it between. Around and through, and over again. Surprisingly, she doesn't squirm, she doesn't fight. I think she's in shock and it's frozen her in place. Once her hands are bound in front of her, I drop them in her lap.

"And how has this trial been delivered in the past?" Owen asks.

My eyes catch Mercy as she gapes at me, her wide, wild, silver-blue eyes blinking at me. She opens her mouth to speak, but I quickly lift her wineglass to her lips and tilt it. She can choke on it…or she can accept my kindness in taking control of her nervous actions.

A fierceness washes over her features as her eyebrows straighten to frame her narrowed and intentional stare. Closing her parted lips around the rim, she lets me tip another sip into her mouth.

My heartbeat doubles its pace as I watch her swallow, her throat working as she takes down gulp after gulp, nearly draining the glass.

"Once, there were three participants," I hear Killian explain, though his voice seems fainter than before, "and they were made to serve the entire village for a night." I strain to listen, but everything is fading around me as Mercy manages to draw my full attention. "Another time, there was only one servant, and she was made to…" His voice fades entirely to the background.

I watch Mercy drink, and when she's nearly drained the glass, I pull it away and set it on the table. I take my clean napkin from my lap and use it to dab at the corners of her lips. For good measure, I swipe my finger—covered by the cloth—across her bottom lip, intent on catching the wine that slipped out when I pulled the glass away.

But then I swipe again, even though I don't need to, noting the way the center of her lip has an extra tuft of plumpness that dips in the center to create that beautiful, sweeping curve.

"Arlo," Owen says, snapping me back to life.

"Yes?" I twist turn from her, placing the napkin on my lap.

"You're the warden for the trial participants," Owen says. "Do you wish to have a final say over the manner in which the trials are carried out?"

Yes.

No.

On one hand, I want that level of control over Mercy's fate—though I know that would be dangerous to my own suffering self-control. Furthermore, whatever is imposed on Mercy is imposed on Delle, and there's something about her participation that feels...bothersome.

"No," I decide. "I think we should decide collectively, as a group."

"I have a proposal," Ryker leans back in his chair, nursing a devious grin as he locks his fingers together behind his head and stretches back.

"Go on," Killian encourages.

"Perhaps the seven of us can come together to trial their ability to serve." His gaze shifts between Mercy and Delle. "Seven men for seven hours."

"Do you mean one per hour?" Park asks.

"Perhaps. Or perhaps not," Ryker leans forward. "If we're meant to push the boundaries of service, wouldn't more than one man at a time achieve that end? Given that a normal night of service allows for only one man per servant at a time."

"Seven men in seven hours." Park's expression indicates consideration. "I suppose that does have a nice ring to it. It feels like poetic justice."

I glance at Mercy without turning my head, curious to see her reaction to all this discussion happening right in front of her. Though she has no right to speak on any of this, I still find myself hoping this will provoke her, and I don't know why I hold that hope.

Perhaps because the thought excites me.

Perhaps that's precisely why I'm a danger to myself and everyone around me because I didn't purge.

In any case, she's seething at my side, her bound fists balled in her lap, and the corners of my lips twitch to smile.

"Seven in seven," Killian says. "I like the sound of it. But Ryker is right, one at a time certainly doesn't push the boundaries of service. It's a trial, after all, so we'd need to think on that."

My hand snaps to the side and I wrap my fingers around the rope coiled between Mercy's wrists. Lifting them above the tabletop, I drop them down without warning, and her fists collide with a *thud* that draws everyone's attention, as I meant it to. She huffs at me, but I ignore her.

"What if I string her up?" I offer. "Put her on display for a day inside the Homestead? Her body can be used by any one of us as we see fit. One at a time or multiple—she'll be helpless for seven hours."

"*Them*," Killian corrects me with narrowed eyes. "You said *her*, but of course, you mean *them*. You speak of one participant, but don't forget there are two."

My fixation on Mercy is evident, and I can't allow that. I need to get control of myself, lest I be judged for lack of self-control.

I clear my throat and ensure I'm turned squarely toward the table. "Yes, forgive me."

"I've seen the way Arlo binds women when he purges," Wesley says. "I think that could be an effective trial, to be left and used for so many hours."

"Let's put it to a vote," Ryker says. "All for seven in seven, say aye."

"Aye," the sound of the single word rings out in chorus.

"All opposed, say nay."

Silence.

"Give me fourteen hours," Mercy mutters.

I look over to find her head dipped slightly, her fierce eyes looking up through her eyelashes to stare across the table with a slow burning kind of fury.

Ryker grins with amusement. "Excuse me?"

"Give me fourteen hours and leave Delle alone. Let her skip this trial. Let me take the burden for her."

Sordid chuckles carry through the space, but the sound doesn't include my own. My stare is locked on her, humor evading me as I see the honest determination in her expression. She's serious. She would actually endure double the necessary time to spare Delle.

Ridiculous….intriguing.

My heart thumps an odd extra beat as I feel something I can't explain. It couldn't possibly be admiration or respect because I have no capacity for those feelings when it comes to sinners like her. And yet, those are the only words that come to mind describing the feeling.

There's a strangeness that vibrates through me, like dissonant chords being played simultaneously.

The laughter fades and dies.

"No," Killian says plainly.

"That's not how this works," Ryker follows.

Mercy lifts her chin and tilts her head, looking across the table and speaking with unearned authority. "And why not? It seems as though you're making up the rules as you go. You said it yourself…there is room for *creativity.*"

Sweet fucking sin.

This woman knows no boundaries. It fills me with fury, but oddly, it's only for the way she creates risk for herself. She has no concern for self-preservation. She understands no one has survived the trials and the likelihood of her own survival is equally low. Maybe knowing that her days are limited makes her bolder and more daring than she ought to be.

"No." Killian doubles down, harshly emphasizing the word. "And just for that ridiculous request, I think we ought to let Delle complete her trial first."

Mercy shoves to her feet, the legs of her chair screeching as they scrape across the floor and tumbles over backward. "Over my dead body," she spits.

"That can be arranged," Killian says, and the others chuckle.

I quickly slip on my gloves before standing, reaching out to grab the short dangling ends of the rope attached to her wrists. I tug on them, forcing her to spin away from the table to look at me. Our eyes catch for a heated beat, and I see rage swirling there, like a gray storm whirling around her irises.

It's rather beautiful.

I speak without looking away from Mercy. "If you'll excuse me, brothers, I need a moment to handle my ward."

"Please do," Ryker huffs.

"I'll be back for Delle," I add as an afterthought, nearly forgetting she's also my responsibility now.

"I'll see her to her room," Theo offers, and I nod without looking.

With a tug of the rope, I walk away, pulling Mercy along behind me.

chapter fifteen

Mercy

ARLO DRAGS ME behind him like a pet, and I don't think I've ever been so furious. But the way he charges forward down the hall and into the foyer makes me think he feels the same way, though I can't for the life of me figure out why.

I plant my feet when we reach the center of the foyer and stop on the starburst beneath the chandelier. I jerk back on my arms to stop him, and he halts and spins to face me. I'm ready to speak, to tell him what I really feel, but he beats me to the punch.

"What is it going to take to get you to understand your place in this life?"

Stepping forward, he invades my space in such a way that I'm forced to take a step back, but once I do, I refuse to take another, and I hold my stance.

"What life?" An honest question.

"Are you not concerned about the fate of your soul?"

I blink, my head tilted to the side. "There was a time when I was, but I'm no longer convinced I want salvation for my soul when the means to achieve it are so vile."

His eyebrows shift and lower as he narrows his eyes, not in judgment, but in grave concern. "You're lost. So lost, sweet Mercy."

I swallow the weight of his words.

They're true.

I am lost…I have been lost for so long, but it doesn't matter anymore. I'm a sinner; I'm beyond redemption.

I shake my head lightly. "And what does it matter now? I'm damned in this life. What difference does it make if I'm damned in the next?"

He steps impossibly closer and I lean away, my back arching. His hand snakes around me, his palm splaying across the small of my back to hold me in place. "You don't have to be damned in the next. Your soul can be redeemed. Yes, your fate in this life is sealed, but God will forgive you in the next life through your ultimate acts of service in the trials."

My breaths quicken at the touch of his fingers on my back, at the way he holds my stare with intensity and sincerity. "Why do you even care?"

His forehead wrinkles and he huffs a heavy exhale through his nose. "Because I'm your warden. It's my role to meet your needs, and that includes spiritual."

I scoff, "None of my needs are being met."

"You're clean, you're dressed, you're fed. Please tell me which of your extravagant needs aren't being met."

"Peace, comfort, friendship, compassion..."

"Those are wants, not needs." His finger twitches against my back, sending a jolt of electricity through my spine.

"I need them; Delle needs them. They can't be met here, not in this manor, not in Ember Glen, not with our vicious doctrine—"

He tugs me tighter against him as his free hand slaps over my mouth, silencing me with leather. He turns his head, glancing around us. "Watch what you say."

It doesn't matter what I say.

Not anymore.

I'm already doomed.

He spins me in his hold, turns us toward the staircase, and urges me forward. He releases me and I move immediately, climbing the staircase with stomping feet and swift steps. Jogging up the stairs, he quickly catches up with me, then lassos his arm around my side as he slows to match my pace.

He leans into me sideways and whispers, "I don't care what your fate is, Mercy Madness, but you will not be blasphemous to our faith. I won't allow it."

His words freshen my fury. I twist and jerk myself from his hold, then charge quicker up the staircase. When I reach the landing, I stop, whipping around to face him. "I won't be silenced any longer. If I'm meant to meet a torturous end, then so be it, but I will ensure the women of Ember Glen know the truth."

He laughs as he steps onto the landing. Creeping toward me, he holds my gaze, even while his hand drifts forward to wrap around the dangling ends of the rope attached to my wrists. He continues to walk right past me, tugging on the ropes until my arms are tautly drawn in front of me, and I'm forced to walk to avoid stumbling.

He drags me behind him as he moves down the hall. "Truth is our way of life. Truth is the Impulse, the urge, the need of men to purge the worst of their humanity—"

"Upon women who don't deserve it, who never asked for it."

"On women who were chosen by God to serve those needs." He stops in front of the room he says is mine, and he turns to face me. "You rejected God's favor when you turned and ran into the forest, when you hid in that tree, when you ran from *me*."

He unlocks the door and shoves it open, then his hand wraps around my elbow before he forcefully drags me across the threshold. Flinging me forward into the room, he releases me unexpectedly. My weight pitches forward and I stumble. I catch my balance and turn to face him as he closes the door and locks it.

Then he charges toward me, his intense stare scaring me enough to make me step back as he moves into my space. The force of him shoves me until my back hits the far wall across the room. He slams his palms against it on either side of my head to cage me in between his arms.

I can smell the mint on his breath as he glowers down at me, breathing out fire like a demon—like a man who needs to purge. Fear rises in my chest as my eyes widen at the way he watches me. While fear rises, sin descends, an unwanted clench of a forbidden feeling tugging desire low into my core.

My body remembers the warmth of his pressed against me, the touch of his fingers as they moved inside me, the overwhelming sinful sensation of coming at the touch of another's hand.

All the air escapes my lungs as he dips his head, bending closer. "Do you still want to run from me, sinner?"

"Yes," I breathe, and though I intended to speak honestly, it feels like a lie.

His plump lips part with a sigh as his forehead touches mine. "And if you did run from me again...would you want me to catch you like I did in the forest?"

"Yes." And that's the truest I've ever spoken.

It feels like the most blasphemous thing I've ever wanted, ever thought, ever said out loud. It's blasphemous to want my warden, my controller, my eventual executioner to touch me the way he did during a night of service.

I want it now.

I want it badly.

I want him to sin with me...and I don't understand the feeling at all.

It's perhaps the most shameful thing a servant could do—to admit such things to a man outside of the full moon and tempt him in that way when he's not allowed to act upon it. Yet I can't control the arch of my back as my body is called to his, as his warmth beckons me.

"You're a sinner," he whispers, his head rolling against mine. "You're a sinner and you want to take me down to the depths of hell with you."

"I want no such thing." My hands rise between us, curious fingers reaching out for him, though I don't know where to touch. "Not for me, not for you, not for anyone."

He solves the confusion over where my hands want to be as he sways forward, moving into me, crushing them between us.

"Liar." He drags in a deep breath and forces it out again, his chest rising and falling against me.

"What are you doing?"

"Be quiet."

"I need you to hear—"

"*Silence*, Mercy. I didn't purge and you're tempting my urges..."

"You didn't purge?" I ask in disbelief.

"Your sins stole my attention under the last full moon."

Indignation wrinkles my forehead at the way I'm blamed. "I did nothing but run from flames that threatened to consume me."

I feel his breaths, quick and shallow, nearly panting. "You made your presence known to me, and that was enough."

I don't know how to respond, so I say nothing. I wiggle my fingers and they graze the button on his waistcoat. Absently, I grab hold of it, my hands fidgeting as a result of my anxiety in this heated moment.

"Your hair smells like wildflowers..."

My heartbeat quickens as he shifts forward, his body kissing mine.

He's on the brink of immorality—closer than he should be to that edge—and dangerously near sin.

My first instinct is to push him back, to remind him of his faith, to encourage him to stay right and true, and to wait until the full moon to seek service for his needs. But something stronger than that takes hold of me, something warm and wild, like sparks threatening to ignite.

It feels wrong.

It feels dirty.

It feels good and necessary.

A true sinner's thoughts.

I try to swallow my desire, but there's something stronger within me, something evil that wants to unleash and take his soul, blend it with what's left of mine.

I dare to speak the words that should only ever be spoken in service. "How can I serve you?"

He pulls back with a snap, his head jerking to look at me as his arms drop from the wall and fall heavily to his sides. "What did you just say to me?"

"I asked how I can serve you?" Shame wells in my gut for offering service here, now, with *him.*

"It's not a full moon, and you're no longer a servant. You're a *sinner.*"

"Then perhaps it's not a sin to purge with me."

What am I saying?

I'm out of my mind with this begging sensation that lies heavily between my legs. "If I'm not a servant, and I'm not a domestic, then I'm really not anything, am I?"

He flinches, and I hang my head, feeling overcome with guilt, shame, disgust for losing myself within a moment's lust when I should be fighting, demanding forgiveness for myself...for Delle. I should be focused on the reason why he dragged me from the dining room in the first place. I should be focused on fighting to save Delle if my fate is already sealed.

I let my eyes flutter shut to block out my senses, to try to recenter myself. Yet as soon as I see darkness, I'm swept up, arms wrapped around my back, body dragged away from the wall, and lips landing heavily on mine.

Lips.

Soft, but bruising lips…

My eyes snap open.

Arlo Rainn is kissing me?

I lift my bound hands, press my fists to his chest, and shove. He stutters backward, catching himself on the arm of the chair behind him as he quickly lowers to sit. His hand comes up to swipe across his short beard as he watches me with disbelief.

Before I can think, before I can process, my feet move, stepping toward him. As I move, so does he. We crash somewhere in the middle of the space between us, and our lips collide with furious, sparking passion. His tongue presses to the seam of my lips, begging me to open for him, and in service, I do.

He needs my service, and I want to give it to him.

I never wanted to give my service—I always gave it with reluctance and out of necessity for my own survival.

So why do I want to give it now? To Arlo?

What is happening to me?

My tongue is timid where his is eager, swiping across mine, tasting me fully as his arms close around me again. It's like he forces desire into my mouth with the swipe of his tongue, and I swallow it down, letting it sink heavily, making my stomach clench and my back arch as my body sways against him.

He shoves me back against the wall, breaking our kiss for but a moment to grab my bound wrists, to lift them high above my head and slam them to the wall before descending again.

I gasp into his mouth at the shock of his force—shock that he's kissing me, touching me at all. This is beyond inappropriate—especially for a man in his position—and the rumbling voice of the servant that's still buried somewhere deep within me tells me how wrong this is, that he's misusing his position of power, that he's doing something he should be condemned for.

But my rebellious spirit is strong, engaged, eager for this connection with a man I only know in passing...eager for so much more.

It's wrong.

I'm wrong, he's wrong, wanting this is *wrong.*

Yet I part my lips and taste him as much as he tastes me.

If this is the flavor of sin, then let me be gluttonous for it. Let me burn in hell for the taste of it. Lust has me in its grips like a demon, sinking its claws into my skin and burrowing deeply.

His lips move, catching the corner of my mouth, my cheek, along my jaw beside my ear. "Your madness is spreading," he whispers. "I can feel the way you spark sin within me."

His hips shift and I feel his hard length press against me. I nuzzle desperately into his cheek as he kisses beside my ear. "It's not the spark of madness you feel, Warden Rainn..." I feel him tremble as his body moves, rocking into me. "It's—"

Sanity. Clarity. Divine.

Those are the words I mean to say, but he interjects with his own interpretation.

"It's the Impulse. It's because I didn't satisfy those urges when I was meant to." His mouth moves down the side of my neck, catching me off-guard with a wave of pleasure that causes me to whimper.

I find myself disappointed at his interpretation, but I know I shouldn't be surprised by it. It's what he believes; I used to believe it, too.

"Then satisfy it now," I pant.

He pulls his head back and regards me with a desperate expression. I see the self-control flicker across his bright blue eyes, but that control is lost completely when my hips roll forward unintentionally, desperately seeking the same relief he does.

"Sweet sin," he mutters.

He releases my hands and his drop to his pants, working with haste to unbuckle his belt. My eyes fall to watch as his long fingers work—the same long fingers he buried inside me and brought me to pleasure with. I sink without his body against mine, my back slipping down the wall as I bring my hands down between us.

This is wrong for both of us.

Yet the sound of his aching breaths, the sight of his trembling hands reaching to free his cock, the heat in his blue stare, and the pained expression of lost self-control as his lips part swirl around me.

He fills every sense, intoxicating me with his suffering.

It calls to me.

No matter how much I rebel, no matter how much I want to be free, no matter how much I question our doctrine and defy my unwanted role, there's still a desire within me to please, to serve.

As much as I hate it, I want to serve him. I want to serve Arlo Rainn for the way he overwhelms me, the way his presence consumes my rational thoughts and steals them, making me a desperate servant willing to drop to her knees and *serve*.

Why him?

How does he do this to me?

Guilt and shame threaten to grip me, to take hold of my mind, but I force them away. I can't bear it. I don't *want* to bear it at this moment. I want a moment's freedom from heartache, from the melancholy and fear and pain. Sharing this sin with my warden is the only way to find that freedom.

My bound hands reach out for his cock, but he slaps them away.

"Let me serve you," I say, my nipples hardening beneath my dress, breasts swollen and aching for touch as my chest heaves with each longing breath.

"Don't touch me," he growls.

He reaches for my hips, his hands latching on with a firm grip that nearly aches. He spins me around and slams me forward to the wall. I try to bring my hands up to catch myself, but they only get caught between my chest and the wall as he pins me in place with his body. I feel how hard he is as his bare cock presses forcefully against my ass.

"Warden Rainn…"

"Quiet, sinner."

His fingers are gentle as he runs them beneath my long hair, tugging it back over my shoulder and laying it softly down my back. His hands fall to my arms as his cheek slips along mine. He turns his head to press soft kisses on my cheek, working them back to my ear. The quick switch to gentleness has me stunned, immobile, and it has wetness dripping between my legs.

For a moment, I feel wanted.

No one has ever kissed me sweetly, softly.

No one has ever given me an erotic moment of gentleness and peace.

Then his tongue paints a wet, hard line across my skin, dragging up the spot behind my ear all the way to my hair line. I shiver.

"Do you want me?" he whispers.

My head nods, though it's turned, my cheek pressed to the wall in front of me. "Yes."

"Why?"

"I-I don't know..."

"I don't know why I want you, either."

His hands glide down my arms, dropping to my hips. He grapples with the fabric of my dress, his long fingers working to inch it up my thighs. His hips press, and he slowly grinds against my bottom, hissing his relief as he tries to let go of his waning control. "I should be repulsed by you, sinner... but you bewitch me."

His cock moves from behind me, and suddenly, I feel it sliding along the side of my hip, slipping across the silky fabric of my gown. My eyes dart down and my breath hitches to see his excessive thickness rubbing along my hip, watching as he works to wrap my dress around it.

He leans heavily, pinning me to the wall, crushing my hands between my breasts, and nuzzling his face into the crook of my neck. He works his hips, slowly thrusting, stroking his cock along my hip wrapped in the fabric of my dress.

I want this so much it aches. It aches between my legs, but it also aches in my heart, in my conscience. I shouldn't want this with the man who controls my fate, the person set to put me through the trials that will more than likely end my life.

But I think I need it right now.

I need to be touched, too.

"May I—"

I only manage to squeak out those two words before his hand wraps around my body, grips one of my wrists, and forcefully shoves my hands down. He moves them until they're between my legs.

"Do it, sinner. Show me your depravity and come with me."

His words lasso around me and tug everything to my center. My body sinks with the ache in my belly, the sick desire that makes me curl around it. My face scrunches with the pain of need, and I stretch my fingers, their tips grazing over my underwear. I whimper.

I need more.

My fingers stretch and bend, trying to reach the pulsing throb in my clit, but I can't with the way I'm pinned.

"Please..."

Arlo groans, hips thrusting, his cock slipping along my side. His thrusts push me harder to the wall, but if I shift my hips just right, the pulses make my clit slam against my fingers. Each thrust sends a wave of pleasure ripping through my body, and each beat between makes me more desperate.

His lips are on my neck, rubbing over my skin, parted and slick, and his breaths pant heat in their wake. The heat spreads and lowers, sparking something terrible, vicious, and truly depraved within me—it sparks a madness I can't control.

"More," I beg. "Harder. Faster."

Teeth nip at my skin as he groans, as his body curls, and his thrusts along my side hasten and grow in strength. "Sweet fucking sin…Sweet *sin*, Mercy."

He pounds against me from behind, one hand curled around the silk wrapping his cock, the other gripping my hip. His fingers dig into me painfully. He steps closer until the entire front of my body aches from being pressed so hard to the wall.

The ache is exquisite.

With the angle of our hips and the way he pins me to the spot, my fingers can finally reach and circle that throbbing nub. Puffs of breath escape me as we work fast and hard, chasing release together.

His nose nuzzles my neck, drifting back, and I feel it brush against my hair. He inhales deeply, and a moan escapes me as he whispers, "Wildflowers and starlight." His hand leaves my hip, and suddenly, it's wrapped around my hair at the base of my neck. He jerks back on it, and I whimper as my neck cranes, chin lifting skyward at a beautifully painful angle. "This is mine." He rubs his face in my hair.

Hair he called the color of starlight.

Hair he said smelled like wildflowers.

I don't think any part of me has ever been compared to such beautiful things.

In service, I've been called names—cunt, whore, slut—and parts of me have been referred to as fuckholes, and were used as such. I've been told my hair was good for pulling; I've been told I smelled like a good little bitch.

To have a part of me compared to wildflowers and starlight in the midst of such sinful lust…it's a sentiment more incredible than I can even begin to describe. Emotion swells in bryn chest, a deep, longing ache for more of that feeling overwhelming my heart as his body touching every part of mine overwhelms my senses.

"Come," I breathe. "Come for me, please. I want you to." I really do want him to—something I've never wanted for a man before. I want him to feel pleasure for the joy he's just sparked inside me. "You can use me. Any part of me. I won't tell a soul."

His grip on my hair tightens as his thrusts sharpen. I feel it swell as if he were inside me because every pulse of him along my hip pulses through my clit just the same. I'm so close, so quickly—quicker than ever before—and more powerfully than ever before.

He thrusts. He pants. He groans.

And as my climax looms, my clit swelling and aching, he shoves me over the edge with a whisper, "Come for me, starlight."

A sob escapes me as I come—as he comes with me—and he swallows it with a deep kiss over my shoulder. The pleasure peaks and my body trembles, quaking in waves that ripple out and back, out and back.

He groans into my mouth as his hips falter in their rhythm, turning him frantic. He bites my bottom lip as a strangled moan chokes him—and it chokes me, too. I feel like I can't breathe.

His hips surge forward at the peak of his release, and then he stills, his chest rising and falling heavily against my back as we pant together, as we come down from the high together.

Stay.

Stay in this moment with me.

Stay with me.

Arlo can't hear my silent pleading for him to remain in this bliss for just a little longer. He releases his grip on me slowly, gradually loosening. I feel him pull away, and I allow my gaze to fall to my side, watching as he drags his cock away, letting it slip through the silk, and wipe the remnants of his release all over it.

My body slumps as he steps back fully, and though he's still panting from exertion, I hear him already working the buckle of his belt, already leaving me alone in my bliss, and preparing to steal me from it entirely.

Slowly, I turn, pressing my back to the wall, slipping down until I sit on the floor, legs stretched out before me. Glancing down, I see my dress is ruined beyond repair. I lift my chin to look at Arlo, terrified of what I'll find in his expression. He's already put himself together again so quickly, tucked and fastened, looking as sharp as always…except for the red flush around his gorgeous lips from kissing me and the way his thick hair is tousled from our movement.

His head inclines and he watches me for a beat as he catches his breath. Then he steps over me, straddles my legs with his feet on either side of my knees. He crouches to his haunches so abruptly that it makes me gasp.

He pulls the leather glove off his right hand. I hadn't realized he'd still been wearing them while he fucked my silky dress. His blue eyes flicker across my face, and I stare into them deeply, watching as he processes something in his mind.

What is he thinking?

With his gloved hand, he reaches out to lightly lift my chin. With the other—and without looking away from my eyes—he reaches down to the smeared, stained fabric and swipes his thumb down, collecting some of the white residue.

He lifts that hand, his eyes darting to my lips as his tongue sneaks out to swipe across his own. Then he touches his thumb to my bottom lip, pressing in, slowly swiping his cum from one corner to the other.

A puff of breath escapes my parted lips at the feel of it and the way he claims me. At least it feels like he's claiming me, though I know that could never be the truth.

"Don't tell a soul, sinner. Promise me this will be our dirty little secret, and perhaps we can sin again."

His words are abhorrent. He knows what we did was wrong; he knows consequences would find him for this. I should tell...I should shout it down the hall and let them end him for this.

But, as sick as it is, I don't want that.

I *want* him to sin with me again. They could punish him for this, but it won't change my fate. If they insist on putting me through the trials— insist on ending my life and sending me to hell—then at least I can take his corrupted soul along with mine.

I nod slowly, feeling degradation and sin settle inside me for wanting anything from him so much that I would lie for his sins—when he isn't man enough to lie for mine.

He leans forward and presses a kiss to my cum-covered lips, then pulls back and licks them clean. Heat flashes through his eyes, sparking a fire within me that burns so bright and hot that it forces my shame to creep from the darkness and flee from the inferno.

I'm a sinner...I am.

And now, I'm a lying whore, too.

chapter sixteen
ARLO

WHAT HAVE I done?

I leave Mercy's room and go to mine, slamming the door behind me and locking myself in.

I used a woman; I purged my impulse with her. I wiped my cum across her lips.

Sweet fucking sin.

All the worse I asked her to keep the secret.

All the worse, she agreed.

My chest feels tight with the sinful pride of it.

Where is my self-control? My discipline? How did I lose it so easily?

I could blame her for my transgressions—Mercy fucking Madness. She is the sinner, and I could say she corrupted me, influenced me with her wicked ways. I could say she brought me into sin with her. But even I know that would be a lie because I *wanted* it. I wanted her, more desperately than I've ever wanted anyone or anything in my life. I wanted to sink inside her and feel her warmth wrapping around my cock.

I don't know what to do from here. I don't know how to control myself, but I must get myself under control.

I cross to my desk and sit, unlocking the drawer and pulling out my leather journal. I remove my gloves—which I'd left on while I fucked the fabric of her dress—and thumb open my journal to the next blank page before picking up my pen. I press it to the paper and within a minute, my hand moves, quickly working to scribe my mind's racing thoughts.

Light of the universe,
starlight in human form.

Celestial beauty and the scent of earth,
like the meadow and sweet mountain air.

Wildflowers and starlight.

She shines like the heavens,
and I am deceived.

She's born from hell.
Stars burn, and so does she.
Her light born from hellfire, lit from the spark of madness.

Wildflowers and starlight.

She ignites me, a falling star colliding with my soul, setting it ablaze,
spreading like wildfire.
She incinerates me with passion.

Intoxication from her heat burns my blood,
rushing it low with the swell of desire.
I'm overcome with the impulse to ravage, relief promised in her
warmth.

Wildflowers and starlight.
Starlight and hellfire.
Hellfire and lust and sin.

I lose myself in the sin of her, yet in that sin...
I'm found.

I sit back in my chair, reading the words on the page—blasphemous words of lust that shouldn't be on record. I tear the page from my journal and crumple it into a ball as I stand and cross my room to the fireplace. I draw my hand back, prepared to toss it into the fire, but the flame catches my attention and stills my hand. The dancing orange flickers with shimmers of white light that remind me of the stars—of starlight, of *her*.

Her starlight hair will be the death of me.

My grip on the crumpled page loosens, but I can't seem to let it go. I can't bring myself to burn the words that ring so true.

I unfold the page and read the words again.

I lose myself in the sin of her, yet in that sin...
I'm found.

I've never written with such ease; I've never written with such cadence. She's a muse as much as she is anything else.

She's also a sinner, a demon of lust who wants to possess me. And she did possess me for moments as we came undone, and I have no doubt she could do it again. She *will* do it again if I'm not careful.

I need discipline.

I need self-control.

I need to punish myself for this transgression.

I drop the crumpled paper on the carpet. I take the candelabra from the mantle and tip it toward the flames, dipping the wick of the candle into the fireplace until it catches. I pull it out and carry it to my desk, setting down the silver candle holder before lowering into my chair. I lift the long ivory candle from the holder and reach toward the flame, the tip of my finger hovering beside the dancing glow.

I revel in the anticipation of pain, the preemptive, knowing ache of my skin as I await the searing burn. I inch my finger closer, tempting the heat, yearning for the pain that reminds me why I need to control myself... Because if I don't, I will burn in hell, and this is the pain of the flames I'll feel for an eternity.

I push my finger toward the flame, but it twitches before it touches, and it gives me pause. The pause makes me feel weak, and I can't be weak—not with myself and especially, not with Mercy.

I drag in a deep breath and move my hand above the flame, hovering above the flickering tip. I force fear from my mind, and I lower my hand quickly, dropping it so the center of my palm falls into the fire.

I hiss as it burns my skin, groan as the ache deepens, as I let it heat my flesh and hope that it adds another scar. I remove my hand while the pain is still intense, knowing I will have burned too deep and deadened the nerve endings when the pain ceases. My hand is shaking as I turn it over and witness the red blistering flesh in the center of my palm.

I'll remember this mark whenever I think of Mercy as anything more than a sinner and a trial participant...whenever I think of her whimpers, her flesh, her starlight strands of hair.

This mark is for her.

This mark is *because* of her.

It's a reminder of the pain that awaits me in death if I let her drag me into sin with her.

But somehow, I already know it's a pain I'd welcome.

chapter seventeen

Mercy

IVY JANE'S CHARRED remains are on display in the center of the village square. It's bleak and gray today, a soft breeze cutting through the air. Arlo leads Delle and I to the black mass of servants kneeling in their dark clothes facing Ivy in rows. The villagers are gathered behind them, hands clasped and heads bowed in reverence. Arlo directs Delle with gentle gestures to the end of the front row of servants, indicating she should kneel beside the last servant there.

He doesn't show me the same gentleness.

His gloved hand lands on my shoulder and firmly grips me, twisting my body before shoving me down. I drop to my knees beside Delle and land hard on gravel, tiny rocks pushing against the fabric of my burgundy gown and pressing into my kneecaps.

I try to ignore the way Arlo broods at me as he backs away. He hasn't said a word to me since we...since we sinned together days ago.

I glance over my shoulder and spot Ellary and Cambria in the row behind me. I press a small smile through my lips, but it's not returned. They quickly avert their eyes, Cambria bowing her head and Ellary looking forward. Pieces of my soul crumble and fall with how they turn from me.

Though, I understand why they turn away. I understand what they think of me now. I'm no longer their friend; they can only see me as a sinner. They think I'm wrong, that I'm bad, that I'm going to hell. They think I betrayed their trust and sullied our friendship with my actions against service. I can accept why they would believe that, and I don't fault them for it, yet the evidence of their swift detachment still cuts through my chest like a blade, piercing my heart.

I could cry right now for the way it hurts me, but I don't. I don't want to give everyone the satisfaction of a sinner's tears. I take a deep breath that hitches with a begging sob, but I swallow it down and force my gaze to Ivy's dead body, reminding myself that if I hadn't run—if I hadn't *sinned*—I might've been lying beside her right now.

Worse, I might've been alive, suffering excruciating pain for the burns

Hyatt Price had threatened to inflict upon me.

Ivy's once smooth skin is red and blistered, and she's been embalmed to preserve the sight of horror—yet surrounding the horror is beauty. Her body is laid flat on a raised platform that's covered with a pure, white cloth draping down the sides and delicately dusting the ground. Wildflowers in shades of violet and garnet have been plucked from the meadow and laid around her body, encircling her form on the platform. Her beautiful ebony hair has been brushed and pulled out around her head, creating a halo. She looks angelic in her white gown, aside from the tragic burns and blisters that mar her skin.

The gloomy day surrounds her with appropriate melancholy, and though I wasn't close with her personally, sadness for the loss of her swells within me all the same. She was a servant—a sister—and she died the way I was meant to.

Wesley steps away from the rest of the Control, who stand in a line behind the platform where Ivy's laid to rest. A breeze whips around us, kicking up the black skirts of servants in a dark, ominous way.

Somberly, Wesley begins, "We've gathered in remembrance today. Ivy Jane gave her life in an act of service, and she deserves our honor, our praise, and our gratitude. She served the Impulse with dignity and grace. She served willingly and with pride for her God-given duty. She was honorable in this life, and though we will find peace in knowing she's found paradise in the afterlife, she will be missed. She'll be missed by her fellow servants. Remembered by the villagers as they go about their peaceful days—peaceful because of Ivy's sacrifice in serving the Impulse. She'll be held in reverence by the authority of Ember Glen. Her life will not be lost in vain. Let us take a moment of silence in her honor."

Silence settles quickly and uncomfortably, amplifying the sound of the wind as it rustles through the trees at the outer edge of the village square. I look beyond the Homestead in front of me to the mountains behind—I wonder if heaven is found at the peak.

My hair tickles my cheek as the wind catches it, blowing it sideways across my face with an unusual chill that makes goosebumps prickle up my arms. I turn my gaze and find Arlo's brooding expression—he's staring right at me. His gloved hands are clasped in front of him. I hold his stare as my eyes narrow, confused by the attention when his head should be bowed and he should be thinking of Ivy.

Perhaps he is thinking of her as he looks at me. Perhaps he's thinking how lovely she is for her sacrifice...how wonderful and honorable it was for her to step into the fire and ask to be burned. Perhaps he's thinking of how much I disgust him for running from the same flame, for refusing to serve when service meant pain beyond comprehension and almost certain death.

I sneer as I stare back at him, wondering why I haven't told anyone about our indiscretion yet.

Because I'm a sinner, and no one would believe me.

Because I don't want to tell anyone.

Because I want it to be our secret.

A heavy sigh escapes me, and I tear my gaze from him. Bowing my head, I turn my eyes to the ground.

"*Malo mori quam foedari,*" Wesley says, ending the moment of silence.

"*Malo mori quam foedari,*" everyone repeats in a chant…except for me.

I only mouth the words we use to end our prayers. They roughly mean death before dishonor, and Ivy Jane took them to heart. There's a pinch of shame in my stomach because she died to evade dishonor, and I was unwilling to do the same.

Wesley steps back into line, and Killian steps forward. He holds his arms behind his back and paces in front of Ivy. "Ivy Jane's remembrance comes at a time that forces further reflection on our lives here in Ember Glen, on our doctrine, the Impulse Edict, on God."

I lift my head as he speaks, feeling indignation rise at the tone of his voice. There's something about the way he keeps his hair long, pulled back into a knot at the back of his head, that makes him look pompous and arrogant. Perhaps it's just because he *is* pompous and arrogant that I think he looks that way, too.

"As Ivy stepped forward and offered her body to the service of a man's impulse, another servant fled from the very same fate. As we revere Ivy Jane's strength and pride in her role, we must reflect on the dishonor and shame Mercy Madness has brought to our community. As we mourn the loss of an honorable servant in Ivy Jane, we must equally mourn the choice of Delle Carter to dissent from the will of God." He points an outstretched finger at us. "These two have brought dark days upon Ember Glen. They've brought anger, sorrow, and reminders that demons lurk within the shadows, able to overcome anyone of us. But we will not let that destroy us. We will win this fight against sin and the sinners who commit them."

Against my will, my gaze lifts, seeking Arlo, though his gaze is already upon me.

"The Trials of Dissension will purge them of their demons, grant them absolution from their sins if they prove themselves worthy, and will rid Ember Glen of the darkness they've brought upon us."

I force a breath out through my nostrils, my chest sinking heavily, anger making it rise again sharply. Arlo's tongue slips out to wet his bottom lip before his brow furrows, narrowing his stare on me.

I want to look away from him.

I don't want to look away from him…I can't.

I don't hear the rest of Killian's righteous tirade. I'm locked in, my attention held, trapped in the way Arlo watches me. My pulse quickens as moments pass, as Killian's voice fades to a muted rumble, and the wind sounds like a roar as it flicks my hair across my face.

Wildflowers and starlight.

I can hear his voice in my mind, and the sweet words drop through me like a lead ball in my gut. My fingers curl over my knees, nails digging into my flesh as I watch the flicker of bright blue in his eyes, as something in him calls to me, compelling me to stay locked in.

It isn't until the service has ended and Delle stands beside me that I'm pulled from the trance. I gasp, feeling like I haven't taken a breath in minutes. Sound returns and voices mutter around me.

I glance over my shoulder as Delle says, "Mercy?" I see everyone is standing except for me, the villagers returning to the village, the servants hugging and chatting quietly.

I stand and pat Delle on the arm reassuringly. I turn quickly before Arlo can catch me and make my way over to Ellary and Cambria, who are locked in a sorrowful embrace.

"Ellary." I tap the brown tresses that hang over her shoulder.

They release each other and Ellary turns to face me, expressions of discomfort and judgment greeting me.

"You shouldn't be speaking with us," Ellary rushes. "Go back to your warden."

"I just wanted to say hello…" I peek around her to Cambria, "to see if you were healing okay."

Cambria crosses her arms and her brow furrows. "You can't speak to us anymore. It's not right."

"It's not— What do you mean, I can't speak to you? You're my friends. I need you."

Cambria leans forward. "For heaven's sake, Mercy, you're a sinner. We can't be seen talking to you." She glances around warily, looking at the other servants before she lowers her voice. "People will talk. They'll think we're sinners like you."

"I'm not a…" I know there's no use in arguing my virtue. It's what everyone believes, and I can't change their mind. "I just want to know you're okay."

"We're fine," Ellary clips, her features soft though her voice is sharp.

"We take care of each other. But we don't wish to speak with you anymore. We're so disappointed in you. You—" Her voice breaks and I feel it in my chest. "You broke our hearts."

I press my palm over my heart, rubbing over the aching, pounding muscle. "What?"

"You always had a different way of thinking, a different view of things, but I never would have thought you would sin this way," Cambria says quietly. "I never would've thought our best friend would condemn herself for eternity." Cambria breaks into a sob, and I feel my heart stop beneath my palm. Ellary slides her arm around Cambria's shoulders, pulling her into a side hug.

"You've brought this upon yourself," Ellary tells me. "We fear for you… we do. We pray for you every night. We pray you'll find absolution for your soul through the trials. But darkness and demons plague you, Mercy, and we won't risk corruption. We can't speak to you anymore." Tears well in her eyes, as they do in mine. "It hurts too much."

"It hurts to speak to me?" My voice cracks against my will as teardrops slip from the corners and run down my cheeks.

Ellary nods sadly as Cambria begins to cry.

"I'm sorry." Though I don't know what I'm apologizing for, I mean it.

I *am* sorry.

I'm sorry we were born in Ember Glen.

I'm sorry we were chosen for service.

I'm sorry my self-preservation hurt them.

I'm sorry we don't see our world the same way.

I step backward, not because I want to, but because I feel the weight of their disappointment drop between us, shoving me back.

"We'll keep praying for you," Ellary mutters. Her arm tightens around Cambria, and they turn away.

I take another step backward as I watch them walk away from me, and my tears fall like a river down my cheek. I close my eyes and let them fall, clutching my dress over my heart. My world has become so sad and silent.

The touch of leather against my cheek startles me. My eyes snap open as Arlo traces the trail of tears with the tip of his gloved finger.

"You're pretty when you cry, sinner," he whispers from behind me.

Sadness turns to anger, and I let go of the fabric at my chest to swat his hand away. "Don't touch me."

He snatches me by the wrist before I can bring my arm down, and whips me around to face him, bringing us chest to chest. "Are you finally seeing the full impact of your sins? Friends turning away from you?"

"They don't know what they're saying."

"I think they know exactly what they're saying. Your actions have consequences for everyone you care about."

I look at him squarely. "And what consequences will those you care about face when your sins come to light?" My threat of exposing our dirty secret is idle for now but reminding him that I could expose him is the only power I have in my life right now.

His jaw tenses and his eyes turn sideways, looking to see if anyone else is near enough to hear. "You haven't told anyone." It's a statement more than it is a question.

My shoulders sag. "No. I haven't."

"Good choice."

"No one would believe me."

"Probably right."

"And they wouldn't care if they did."

"You're very insightful for a sinner."

"Is that all I am? From now until the day I die? I'm no longer a person, only a sinner?"

He clicks his tongue. "There's that golden insight of yours."

I look at our hands between our chests, realizing only then that his gloved palm has slipped from my wrist to curl around my fingers. He holds my hand so tightly that I can't pull away—and I'm not entirely certain I want to. I look up at him and he sucks in a breath as our eyes meet, then he blinks and releases my hand.

"Come along now," he says. "Delle's already gone back to the Homestead, and I'd like to check on her."

I rise on my toes to look over his shoulder, spotting Delle climbing the steps behind Theo and Park. Suddenly, my attention is drawn to her and the need to protect is overwhelming. I don't wait for Arlo's lead; I move around him and stalk across the square at a quick pace. It's only a few steps before I feel his hand on the small of my back.

"I don't need you to lead me. I know where I'm going."

I twitch my hip, arching sideways and trying to shrug him away. His hand only slides around the side of my waist and grips me.

"Don't be ridiculous, Mercy. If I wanted to lead you, I'd place a collar around your neck and attach it to a leash."

I stop abruptly and look over at him. "I may be the sinner, but there's something *deeply* wrong with you, Warden Rainn."

He stares at me, blinking his bright blue eyes. "Just as there is with you, Mercy Madness."

He doesn't elaborate, nor does he wait for a response. He drags his hand across the small of my back, fingertips grazing in a way that's almost sensual as he drags his hand away. He gives me a quick smile that sets off a flurry of feeling in my stomach.

And much like a leash, his aura tugs me, dragging me up the stairs behind him.

chapter eighteen

Mercy

BACK INSIDE THE manor, I catch up with Delle at the top of the staircase. "Delle."

She stops on the second-floor landing and turns, waiting for me to climb the last few steps to meet her.

"Are you okay?" I ask her.

"I suppose." She absently runs her hand down her straight, ash-brown hair. "Are you?"

I sigh as I reach her and drag her into a hug, mostly because I need one, though I know she needs one, too. "Of course not."

I pull back and smile before releasing her, comforted briefly when she returns my smile with a weak one of her own. We walk down the hallway side-by-side toward our bedrooms—hers is the room next to the one I've been given.

"I saw you talking to your friends," she says. "What did they say to you?"

I sigh. "They're unhappy with me."

"I'm sorry." Her regret for me sounds genuine, and her head dips. "I was too afraid to speak with my friends."

I nod in understanding. Her friends probably feel the same as mine, or maybe they feel worse. Delle wasn't forced to participate in the trials; instead, she *chose* it. She chose to dissent for a practically non-existent chance at a life outside of service. As awful as it is, they probably hate her for it, and it makes my heart hurt for her.

"Well, I suppose we'll just have each other." We stop in front of her door and I give her a quick smile.

She grins, but there's no joy in it—only fear and misery. She glances over her shoulder, then lets her face fall slowly. She exhales fully as her head bows, and she lowers her voice. "I'm worried I've made the wrong decision."

Oh, Delle.

"Come with me." I take hold of her arm and drag her into her bedroom. I push the door open and pull her through behind me. I motion to the armchairs in the corner which face the foot of her bed, and she moves to take a seat, gradually and with heaviness in her steps.

I move to the bed, lowering to perch at the foot of it, pressing my palms on either side of my hips. "Talk to me."

"I don't know what to say. I…I don't really think I've made the wrong decision because I know I can't live as a servant. I *won't*. I refuse to. But I don't understand why…why we have to live this way."

I hear the heartache in her breaking voice, the sorrow of her soul. I know this deep soul ache that she's feeling. I felt it for months during my first year of service. Not to say that it ever really went away, but eventually, service felt normal—at least, as normal as it could be.

"I don't understand it, either. Refusing to understand and believe is why I'm here facing the trials and an almost certain death. It's why my life is over, Delle. I never would have wanted you to make this choice."

"I didn't want to make it either, but what was I supposed to do?" She begins to cry, and it claws at my soul.

I cross the room, quickly dropping to my knees in front of her as she drops her head into her hands and cries. Her pain swirls around me, encapsulates me in heartache so strong that it threatens to tear me in two.

I know how hard the transition to service is when you're sixteen. Though our training over the years gave us an idea of what our role would be, there is no understanding the depth of it until you're thrown into your first night of service. And Delle is like me, which makes it all the worse.

She thinks.

She questions.

She wonders.

And all those lead to rebellion.

We're warned about it, of course. We're preached to, repeatedly, about the pain that awaits us in the afterlife for rebelling against our servant role. The mere desire for something different is seen as a secret sin—one that will bring you to hell after death, though no one would know about it if you didn't speak it. We're taught that the only way to live a godly life is to find joy and pride in our role. It's perplexing how all the others seem to find a way to do it.

Unless…

Unless they're all living that secret sin and simply unwilling to speak it. The hand we've been dealt is a losing one, and there is no exchanging cards.

The only thing I know is that I would do anything to take this poor child's pain from her, to spare her the trials, to fight against the impossible and grant her the domestic life free of service that she deserves.

I think my aptitude for self-preservation is entirely lost as ideas for saving Delle run rampant through my mind. I'm meant to die in these trials; I'm the reason they're holding the trials at all. My fate is sealed.

But if there was a way to spare Delle the same fate...

I gently tug on her wrists to pull them away from her face. I wait until she lifts her head to look at me, trails of tears streaking down her pinkened cheeks. I reach up to brush my thumb across and swipe the drops away.

"Delle, is a domestic life what you really want? Is that the reason you volunteered to participate?"

Her voice is quiet. "I don't want to die, Mercy. I want to live, but I...Not like *that*...I can't live the life of a servant. How have you survived that life this long? How have you done it?"

"Truthfully, I don't know. I've just done what I have to do to survive."

She swallows hard and pulls her shoulders back, bringing her hands to her thighs. She sniffles before forcing a determined expression. "I don't want to do it. I don't want to serve, not ever again. If it means I die in the trials, I have to at least take that chance. I have to—" Her voice breaks as fear cuts through the determination and widens her hazel eyes.

I watch as the realization hits her, as the reality of her decision takes hold, as the thought of death and what that truly means strikes her. Her breaths quicken and sharpen, and her fingers move restlessly against her thighs.

She's not prepared to die—of course, she isn't.

"Mercy, I can't—" She takes in a rasping breath as she falls into a panic.

"Okay." I reach for her calmly, grabbing hold of her wrist and tugging her gently forward. "It's okay, come here."

I guide her down to the floor in front of me and wrap my arms around her, hugging her fiercely as she breaks apart. My breath catches in my lungs and tears spring to my eyes, but I force my emotions away, swallow them deep into my soul.

I stroke her soft ashen hair as she sobs, as we both drop from our knees to sit on the floor, and I cradle her against my chest. I let her release. I wait until her tears have all been spilled, until her breathing slows and steadies, until she starts to come back through the panic.

I don't know how long we sit like this. I only know it feels like an eternity that I have to force my own fears and pain and heartache away so she can release hers in the safety of my presence.

"I want to ask you a question," I say calmly, stroking her hair.

She nods against my chest, and I feel her tug away. I let go of my hold so she can pull back and sit up to look at me.

I give her a small, comforting smile. "If there were a way..." I hesitate in my words, not sure how to frame them, not yet sure whether they're worth anything. I tuck her hair behind her ear in my pause. "If there were a way for someone to take on this burden for you…if someone could take this pain away from you and allow you the chance at a domestic life without going through the horror of the trials…If someone wanted to do that for you and offered it, would you let them?"

Her forehead wrinkles in confusion, and I know I'm not being clear, that I'm not making any sense.

"What do you mean?"

"If someone else could go through the trials for you and give you the chance at a domestic life, would you allow them to do it for you?"

"Mercy, I don't understand what you're asking me."

"I just need to know, Delle. If there were some way I could bear it all for you, would you allow me to do that? Would you promise me you'd go on and live your happy domestic life after it's all over, after I'm gone, without shame or guilt?"

"How could I ever answer a question like that?" I see tears fill her eyes again, but the way they flicker with the possibility of living without this fear tells me exactly what I need to know.

I shake my head. "Never mind." I don't want to force an answer from her. I won't make her say it when I already know what it is. "It's an impossible question."

But maybe the answer isn't impossible.

I was sentenced to this, and she chose it. She was braver than I ever could have been, and that should be enough for her. It should be enough for her to be given the domestic life she deserves to have. I was given no choice, and I don't think I would've been as brave as Delle to choose this if presented with the opportunity. But I can find my bravery in her honor now; I'll meet her courage with my own and fight for the impossible.

I LEAVE DELLE tucked in her bed—she was so exhausted that I insisted she climb into it and get some rest for a few hours before dinner. Closing the door behind me, I run my knuckles beneath my eyes, catching and dragging what's left of my tears. I let out a heavy, shuddering breath before finding the strength to move.

I enter my bedroom one door down, and head directly to the bathroom. Looking into the mirror above the sink, I note that my eyes are a little red and the skin beneath them is puffy from crying. I can't go to Arlo looking this way. I need to convince him to help me, and to do that, I need to appeal to him.

I need to tempt him.

If I can tempt him to sin with me again, then perhaps I can hold it over his head, blackmail him into helping me convince the Control to let me save Delle. Even with his help, it's unlikely they'll let me do the trials twice to spare her the burden of going through it. Even if they allowed it, I'd probably die before I'm able to complete them and save her.

The odds are stacked against me, as close to zero as they can be. I don't even know if blackmailing Arlo would work. I truthfully don't know that any of his brothers in God would care if I told them he used my body outside of service—or if they would even believe a sinner like me. But I don't know what else to do, and I have to try something. I couldn't live with myself if I didn't try something, anything, to spare her.

This is the only thing I can think to do. It's the only plan that I have.

Tempt him.

Make him sin.

Keep the secret in exchange for his help.

My life already has an expiration date, and my soul is already damned. I may as well take my warden to hell with me.

chapter nineteen

ARLO

I FLING OPEN the door to my bedroom to stop the insistent knocking. "What?"

I'm taken aback at the sight of Mercy standing before me, her fist raised mid-knock, encased in her overwhelming aura of wildflowers and starlight. I expected it was one of my brothers with the persistent rapping at the door. If I'd had any inkling she would be calling on me unexpectedly, I wouldn't have answered the door with such indecency. My shirt is unbuttoned, hanging open at my sides, exposing my chest and torso.

She drops her hand as her eyes land on me, skimming down my front. My head inclines with curiosity to watch her scan me so boldly. She blinks a little too long before raising her chin a little higher, forcing herself to meet my eyes.

Her jaw is set, expression taut. "I'd like to speak with you."

"Then speak."

"May I come in?"

My pulse thrums at the request, both with anxiety and anticipation. It's a dangerous game she and I have been playing, yet I want to play it. I return her appraising gaze to drink her in, instant frustration tightening a knot in my stomach at her maddening beauty.

Her white-blonde hair cascades in perfect, tumbling waves over her slender shoulders, and even though her crimson dress is plain and hangs somewhat loose on her frame, she looks like an angel—a fallen angel, but an angel, nonetheless. She's a thing of beauty, once from heaven, though she's fallen from grace to rule in the kingdom of demons.

Against my better judgment, I step back, sweeping my arm to welcome her into my room. I watch as she breezes past me, her fingers twisting nervously in front of her as she moves across the room. I shut the door as she turns to face me, then leans back on the sideboard against the far wall. She curls her fingers around the edge at either side of her hips.

If only her fingers curled around me the same.

I move forward a couple of steps, then stop and cross my arms over my chest. I tilt my head, looking at her expectantly, and wait for her to speak.

"I've come to an unfortunate realization," she says, her eyes are downcast, staring at a spot on the carpet.

"Oh?"

"I can't win." She looks up at me, and the silvery blue of her eyes sparkles. "I refused to accept it before, but I accept it now. My life is going to end in these trials, and I can't go on pretending there's a chance I'll survive."

My arms fall to my sides as an odd pang strikes my chest. "What made you come to this conclusion?"

She regards me with a piercing stare. "I'm capable of reflection. In any case, I'd like your help, if you're willing to give it."

"I'm your warden; it's my role to help. But what exactly is it you want my help with?"

She swallows. "Finding absolution for my soul."

My breath catches.

I want absolution for her soul, too.

The thought of her burning for an eternity causes an ache I can hardly bear.

"I want that for you, too, Mercy."

"And I want it for Delle."

"She'll find it in the trials."

Mercy shakes her head, starlight brushing over her shoulders. "No, she won't." She pushes off the sideboard and takes a slow step in my direction. "She doesn't understand the choice she's made. If she could take it back, she would."

"What's done is done. She made the choice, and she has to live with the consequences."

"It's not right, Warden Rainn."

The way she recognizes my authority stitches a thread of desire through my gut.

"She's a child," Mercy goes on. "She made her decision out of fear. Her first night of service was rough…it was rough on all of us servants. Ivy Jane lost her life. Can you imagine one of the servants losing their life on your first night of service? It would make any first-timer fearful."

"You're not meant to be fearful. You're meant to have pride in your work."

"Pride takes time." She nudges closer. "It takes time to understand the benefit of our work to the community."

I slip my ungloved hands into my pockets and huff out a breath. "Now you're singing an entirely different song, Mercy Madness. I thought you had no pride in your role; in fact, you outright rejected it in sin. Your words are contradictory to your thoughts and actions."

She nods and grants me a tight smile before looking down. "I know." She looks up at me from beneath her eyelashes and the flash in her bewitching eyes tugs on that thread of desire, pulling it tighter. "But you and I are singing the same contradictory song, aren't we? You and I have sinned together, Warden Rainn."

I breathe out slowly, letting my chest sink as her eyes hold mine. "What do you want from me?"

Her head rises and our gaze locks squarely. "I only want your help to save a lost child from a life of misery and eternal damnation."

I chuckle, but it's humorless. "Oh? Is that all?"

"What do you want from *me*?" She dares to reach out her hand and press it to the center of my bare chest.

My reaction should be disgust at her obvious attempt at seduction, at her sinful promiscuity. Yet my reaction is one of sin—a clenching low in my stomach, a spreading warmth from my center, the twitch of my blasphemous cock.

I force myself to take a step back. "I want to save your soul, Mercy."

She takes a step forward. "And I think there's a way for me to save Delle's soul, too."

"Her soul will be saved through the trials—"

"No. It's not right, and you know it. If there were another way to repent, wouldn't you want that for her?"

"I want to follow the Edict…God's word."

Mercy shakes her head. "No, you don't."

She steps closer and I pull my hands from my pockets, reaching up to grip her shoulders and push her away…only I don't push. I grab and hold on as the front of her body kisses my chest and torso.

"I know you don't want to follow the Edict. If you'd wanted to, you would've purged that night in the forest. You wouldn't have fucked the fabric of my dress the other night in my room. You wouldn't allow me to be alone with you in your room." Her hands press to my chest, spreading warmth across my skin. "You're *indecent*, Warden Rainn."

Indecent.

The word drips from her lips.

It makes me hard.

It makes me desire indecency with her.

Squeezing her shoulders, I push her back, walking her quickly until her back slams to the wall behind us. I release her shoulders and slap my palms to the wall on either side of her, caging her in. I lick my lips as my eyes drop to watch the rise and fall of her chest.

My lips creep up into a cheeky smirk. "And you desire my indecency, don't you, sinner?"

Her expression is odd—a mixture of determination and temptation. The look of sinful wanting in her eyes is clear, but it's as though she fights against it.

Why fight it when it's so clear what she's trying to do here?

"You want to drag me into sin with you," I tell her, because it's obvious.

But I don't expect her response. "Yes, I do."

She reaches up to touch the sleeves of her dress and nudges them down her shoulders. The ill-fitting gown slips too easily from her body, revealing the tempting silk chemise she wears beneath. I stifle a gasp at the sinful look of her nipples peeking through the thin fabric, at the truly indecent way one of the thin straps slips down her shoulder.

I should step away.

I should demand that she leave.

I should call upon my brothers to save me from this temptation, but instead, I inch closer.

"Tell me why. Is it because you think you'll get what you want from me if I become a sinner like you?"

Her lips part as her eyes move around my face, searching for a place to land, the determination in her expression waning. "It's because it feels so good to sin with you." Her eyes finally land, fixing on my lips.

There's no hint of deception or dishonesty in her words, nor in her expression. In fact, the honesty rings so true that it punches through my heart, delivering a lightning strike to the good and righteous part of me, forcing it into a shock that renders it temporarily useless. That moment of shock is all it takes for her demon claws to reach into my chest and sink into my heart, delivering a poison of lust straight from hell.

I clutch her face and I dip to kiss her, but then she speaks, halting me. "I want to endure Delle's trials as her proxy."

What?

I'm already gone, lost in sin, so I ignore her, pressing my lips to hers and forcing a kiss that she eventually succumbs to. A pleasure-fueled whimper vibrates through her as I push my tongue between her lips and taste her— taste every drop of sin from her soul.

We devour each other for moments before the need to taste her flesh consumes me, and I leave a trail of kisses across her cheek, along her jawline, to her neck.

"I mean it," she whispers, her voice breathy and desperate as her body arches into mine. "She regrets the choice. I'll endure my trials and hers if the Control will allow me."

My hand trails down her body, moving from her shoulder over her chest, down the mound of her breast. Her hands touch my cheeks, and she lifts me away from her neck, pulling me into another shattering kiss. My palm squeezes her breast as her tongue dances with mine.

This is wrong.

This is sinful.

Yet it feels more divine than prayer, more righteous than atonement.

I let myself sink into the depravity. The weight of my desire for her is so heavy that there's no sense in fighting it. Fighting it will only make me sink faster.

I comb my fingers through her starlight tresses. When they catch on a tangle, I wrap my fist around the length and jerk sharply to the side. She whimpers but lets me pull, exposing the bare expanse of her ivory neck. I lick from nape to ear, tasting her fully and filling up on her sin.

"Will you help me, Arlo?" she pleads softly as her hands brush down my neck, my chest, fingers grazing the lines of my stomach until they hit my belt.

My hips rock forward against her touch. "Help you?" I pant against her neck. "How?"

"Convince them to let me do each trial twice. Once for myself, and once for Delle."

I stiffen at her words, confusion overtaking me. I lift my head to look at her. "What are you saying?"

"I want to win her a domestic life." She tugs at my belt. "I'm damned, we both know that. I want to sacrifice for her. If I complete all my trials, and hers, would the Control consider giving her a domestic life for my sacrifice?"

I release her all at once and take a step back. "You aren't making any sense."

Her chest heaves with heavy panting, and I can hardly breathe, watching the swell of her breasts lifting and lowering.

"One of the ultimate acts of service is sacrifice, isn't it?"

"It is…" I run a hand over my scruffy beard as my brow furrows, still trying to understand her through the pounding of my heart.

She pushes off the wall and steps toward me. "The Trials of Dissension are meant for the participant to perform grand acts of service. Sacrifice is a pinnacle act of service. I want to make a sacrifice to prove myself, and in honor of my sacrifice, I want the Control to spare Delle the fate she chose impulsively."

Her fingers toy with my belt buckle, and I drop my chin to watch her hands as they work.

"She made a mistake one time," Mercy continues. "She's not like me, and I think you all know that." She looks up at me and I meet her eyes. She unbuckles my belt as she speaks, holding my gaze. "I'm a rebel…always have been. My thoughts are blasphemous, and my actions are sinful. I understand why I have to participate in the trials, but Delle is different." She unbuttons my pants. "She's just a child who made a mistake…a misguided child who can find her way back to God." She tugs down the zipper and slips her hand inside before I can protest, wrapping her small hand around my cock and making me gasp. "I've always been a sinner, Arlo. Let me suffer twice and spare her. Let me suffer twice and give her a peaceful life."

She squeezes, and it feels like burning in hell—only the fire feels good searing my flesh. I wrap my hand around her wrist, squeezing tight to still her stroking palm.

"Do you deserve to suffer, Mercy?"

I feel the quickening beat of her pulse through her wrist as she nods, her gaze holding mine steadily, hardly blinking.

I bend and press my forehead to hers. "Then you will suffer greatly."

"I…I'll accept that."

I jerk her hand from my pants and bring it up to her chest, pinning her arm between us as I press in closer. "Yes, you will. You have no choice but to accept just how much you'll suffer in the first trial."

"I know."

"Oh, you have no idea."

"Tell me."

I let a grin touch my cheeks, then I tilt my chin and draw her into a consuming kiss. Grabbing her shoulders, I shove her down until her knees buckle beneath her, and she drops. She looks up at me, a sinner on her knees, prepared to sacrifice herself.

I grip her chin and brush my thumb along her bottom lip, so viciously tempted to press my cock against it. Instead, I drop to my knees before her, wrap my arms around her, and take her down to the floor. I force her onto her back as I stretch out above her.

"My brothers will want your pleasure in the first trial." I press a kiss to her cheek. "But you're not going to give it to them."

"I don't understand." Her fingers curl around the open sides of my shirt, pulling me down against her.

"If you want me to try to convince them to let you do this, then you're going to do something for me in return."

"What?"

I bend to whisper against her ear. "Denial, starlight."

She shudders and I feel it vibrate through me.

"Denial of what?"

"I know I'm the only man who's given you pleasure before, aren't I?" I kiss her neck. "That night in the forest when you came on my fingers…it was the first time by another's hand, wasn't it?"

"Yes."

"And I'll be the only man who gives you that until the day you die."

The haughty sound of her chuckle awakens something playful within me. I tear her hands from my shirt, lock her fingers between mine, and stretch them out above her head, pinning them to the carpet.

"Do you think there's any way I would ever find pleasure in being forcibly fucked by seven men?"

"Of course you would, sinner. Because I'll be there to make sure you don't forget the way you feel stretched out beneath me."

I roll my hips forward, and her legs part naturally, trying to make more room for me between them. The movement inches the short chemise up her hips, and that's when I realize she's bare beneath. I squeeze her hands in mine, let my weight fall a little heavier on top of her, aligning every inch of me with every inch of her.

Sweet fucking sin.

She sighs as her lips part, beckoning me to taste.

I dip my head, bring my lips to hers, and let them brush as I speak. "Promise me your pleasure belongs to me, and to no one else." My hips shift, grinding her down to the floor. "Promise me your sins belong to me, your flesh, your moans, your desire. Let it be for me, and I'll try to help you."

She tilts her chin, trying to steal a kiss, but I don't allow it. I drag my head back and let go of one of her hands, bringing mine down the side of her neck. I brush my thumb over the hollow of her throat, relishing the way her muscles work as she swallows against my touch. I slip my palm higher, stopping at her jawline to rub my thumb across her bottom lip. She puffs out a whimper that threatens to undo my self-control entirely.

"I promise," she whispers, and there's nothing but sweet, sinful sincerity in her gray-blue eyes.

"Promise me you won't tell a soul about this, about us…and I'll grant you that pleasure now."

Fuck, I'm losing control.

I'm not losing it…I'm letting her take it.

Am I going to hell for this?

"I promise, Arlo." Her voice begs sweetly, and her hips lift from the floor—and I believe her. "Please."

I groan at the word, at the way it slithers inside and coils around my desire, wringing out every last drop of lust to pool deep in the pit of my stomach. My head falls as my body drops its full weight onto hers, pinning her entirely. I bury my face in the crook of her neck, kissing and nipping with my teeth.

"Say it again, starlight."

"Please, Arlo. *Please.*" Her voice trembles, as does her body beneath mine.

Fuck absolution.

Let me burn in hell with her.

I slink down her body, my lips and tongue tasting her everywhere, down her throat, along her chest, over the swell of her breast spilling out above the silk.

She tenses and squirms beneath me as my mouth works its way down her body. I kiss the satin fabric over her stomach, turning my cheek to run my nose down her belly, sniffing my way down to the apex of her thighs.

My palms grip her hips, my fingertips wrapping around to splay across her bare cheeks, and I squeeze. She whimpers as she raises her hips, bucking against nothing to seek relief.

"Please…please," she continues to beg and all the goodness within me dies.

Her voice is angelic as she begs—contrite and needy. There's nothing even remotely sinful about the way she needs me. The way she needs me is spiritual, holy, *divine.*

In this moment, I am God, and she prays for me to grant her pleasure in mercy.

Sweet Mercy.

I grab the hem of her skirt, working quickly to shove it higher above her belly button. I press onto my knees to look down at her and see her bare, exposed, slick, and ready for me. I sit back on my heels, pressing my palms to my thighs so I can admire the perfection between her legs as she draws them back, bending her knees and spreading wide for me.

She's wet, glistening, so ready for my touch.

I didn't expect that, and the sight of it sends a pulse of dark desire through my veins that I can no longer deny.

Mercy rises onto her elbows, her pink lips parted, eyes hooded with desire. She doesn't speak a word, she just watches me with a silent plea in her

eyes—a needy plea that calls to me.
    I want to give this woman pleasure until it breaks her.
    And I want to break her slowly.

chapter twenty

Mercy

THIS DESIRE IS maddening.

I feel out of my mind, yet perfectly settled in my soul.

Arlo runs a hand across his lips as he gazes at my aching center. I'm exposed and open to him in the most intimate way—it's what I wanted, what I planned for. My intent was to lure him into wanting me, to seduce him into sin, and convince him to help me. I got what I wanted already, but now I want more.

I need more.

I ache for more.

"Touch me. Please," I beg him, watching as his broad chest rises and falls.

He licks his lips like he wants to taste me, and I want him to. My skin burns for it. Rising onto his knees, he shoves his pants and the elastic of his underwear down over his hips, and I watch with wide, wanting eyes as his thick cock springs free.

He leans forward with a snap, and I sigh, sensing relief coming. He wraps his arms around my waist and hoists me up, pulls me against him where he kneels. He shifts to sit as he settles my weight across his lap, positioning me to straddle him. He holds me close, palms splaying across my lower back, making me arc my chest forward.

His lips are aligned with my breasts, and his eyes flicker with anticipation as he scans the swell of them above the fabric. He presses a soft kiss between them, which hits me with a swirl of relief and stronger need all at once. My head drops back as he kisses his way across my chest.

I wrap my arms around his neck, but I don't need to hold myself up. His hold on me is strong and sure, heating me from the inside out.

One of his hands slips up my back, slowly working up the center, between my shoulder blades, then over my shoulder. One finger plays under the strap of the silk chemise, nudging carefully until it slips and drops down my arm.

My fingers creep up the back of his neck, sinking into his wavy hair.

It's thick and soft, and the feel of it in my grip is empowering…like I have a hold on him.

I exhale in a heavy rush as he toys with the silk over my breasts, easing it down, steadily exposing my flesh until he's freed them. The cool air breezes across my nipples, but his gaze upon them is warming.

"How can a sinner look so divine?" Arlo whispers, almost as if he's speaking to himself. He presses a soft kiss to the hardening peak. "So heavenly, so angelic?"

Another soft, almost sweet kiss, and then he runs the flat of his tongue over my nipple, sending a cascading swirl of pleasure down my center.

My lips part as I pant out a moan, and I struggle to speak through breaths of ecstasy. "Maybe…maybe divinity isn't what you think it is."

He kisses the hollow of my throat, trailing a line down my breast with a smug grin. "And I suppose you'd like me to entertain your sinner thoughts?"

"You're already entertaining them." I draw my hips back and rock them forward, my slickness spreading along his cock.

What am I doing?

What am I?

I feel wanton and flesh-hungry, as if perhaps I am the sinner he claims me to be.

He groans, his hands splaying across my back as he hugs me closer, burying his face in my chest. He takes in a shuddering breath, and I feel the way he fights against himself. I feel the tension as he tries to hold himself still, gripping me like his sanity depends on it.

Slowly, he lifts his head, gazing up at me with an odd softness in his blue eyes—an ethereal glow that looks like a cloudless sky, clear and vibrant, open to the heavens.

His gaze is heavenly.

His hold on me is spiritual.

The raw touch of our intimate parts is sacred.

To have him inside me would be divine.

I untangle my hands from his hair, slipping them back so I can cradle his face in my palms. I drop my forehead to meet his, holding his eyes with mine, breathing with him through this unexpected moment of connection I know I'll treasure for all my days.

I've never felt connected this way—engaged, wanted, needed. His eyes tell me a million different ways that he needs me, though he doesn't want it to be true.

He doesn't want to want a sinner.

I let the tiny ball of shame sink in my gut, let it roll through the coiling desire and mix with lust into a kind of need that feels filthy and wrong.

It's wrong, but I like it.

It's wrong, but I want it.

"I won't tell a soul," I promise him, and I think I mean it.

I shouldn't mean it. I shouldn't want to keep this filthy secret for one of the men set to ruin my life, but I know I will keep it for a moment like this.

"Please," I beg him for the millionth time, and a fire ignites behind his eyes.

Shifting, he reaches between us with one hand, fisting his cock. We both look down between us, watching as I lift my hips, as he angles the tip and brushes it through my folds. We pant through the tease, our breaths growing heavier and more desperate as we slip and shift into position.

And when he sinks inside me, the gates of heaven spread wide open and welcome us in glorious light. Our embrace tightens as we revel in stillness and the bright white light of pure and holy pleasure.

As a moment's relief gives way to greater need, my stomach tightens in dark knots of lust, and our bodies start to move. He encourages it when his hands fall to my hips and squeeze. I rock with him inside me, holding him close.

He groans with all the filth of a demon, and suddenly, we're cast out of heaven, forced back through the pearly gates before they're slammed shut to lock us out.

I don't mourn the loss of heavenly light as we're dropped down into darkness. My pace quickens as need builds. As his chest heaves and his lips part against my skin—as pleasure sinks us into the darkened depths of depravity—hellfire rises to greet us, and we welcome it with pure carnality.

Thought is lost.

Reason has fled.

Caution and fear have caught fire and burn to smoldering ash all around us.

"Oh…" My head falls back, and I moan, a sound I've never heard myself make before.

I've never found pleasure with a man—not until Arlo first touched me in the woods. And even that pales in comparison to the pulsing and tingling between my legs now.

His lips and tongue are on my breast, licking over the mound, swirling around the hard pink bud, and sucking it into his mouth. My body sinks, twitching around my center as warmth spreads and ecstasy builds through this ethereal sin.

"Yes," I encourage, the first time I've ever used that word in sex and meant it.

I want more, harder, faster.

I want every dark plea of my senses to be filled by him, fueled by him.

He tenses around me, his grip tightening, his lips falling away from my nipple as he takes in a rasping breath. "Come for me," he groans. "Punish me with your pleasure, starlight."

His fingers find my hair, curling and fisting a lock in his grip. He tugs my head back sharply, and I whimper as my chin shoots toward the ceiling. His thick lips brush lightly across my throat, the soft touch contrasting the rough way he keeps my head angled with the ferocity of his grip.

"Come, Mercy…" He trembles against me. "Now. Come now."

This would be the moment I'd fake it in service—not that it's common for men to want the pleasure of the women who service them, though sometimes they like it. But the way Arlo commands it—*no*, the way he *begs* for it—lassoes around me and tugs deep through my core. Leaning back, rocking my hips in this steady rhythm, forces him against a perfect spot inside me that pulses and swells, making me feel like boiling lava slowly rising inside the mountain.

His thumb sweeps softly over my nipple before pinching it in his fingers. He rolls it as he flattens his tongue, running it heavily over my skin from the hollow of my throat to the tip of my chin.

It sets off the explosion within me, and I erupt from my center, waves of heat pulsing through me as pure bliss ripples between my legs. My lips part to gasp through the wave of ecstasy. I barely notice the pain of him tugging on my hair harder, craning my neck deeper.

I can feel him swell inside me, and the thought of him coming with me touches my cheeks through a smile as my pleasure breaks. "Come with me," I whisper toward the ceiling as my twitching body stills.

He releases my hair so fast that my head wobbles, but he steadies it quickly with his hand, cradling the back of my head in his palm as the other grips my hip. He lowers me to my back in a rush, and I turn my gaze to him, trying to meet his eyes, suddenly excited, hopeful, somehow even wistful at the thought of him taking me this way…at the thought of him taking control to spur his release.

But his eyes don't meet mine, and his cock slips out. The sudden absence feels as overwhelming as if he'd torn a piece of my flesh from my body just to watch me bleed.

He drags himself away, scrambling unsteadily to his feet, cock still hard and proud, with a bead of liquid settled at the tip in anticipation of release.

He doesn't come back to fuck me.

He doesn't do anything to relieve himself.

Instead, he forcefully shoves his rigid length back into his pants, zipping and buckling with the most pained expression I've ever seen on a man.

"Arlo?" I don't understand what he's doing.

"Quiet. Don't speak another word to me, sinner."

Sinner.

The moment has passed.

The play and the pleasure are gone.

A deep ache settles in my chest as an unexpected longing to return to passion with him washes over me. I'd felt some peace in his arms, in the way he consumed every sense. And now the peace is gone, replaced by misery, heartache, and the dreaded fear of how limited my days truly are.

My climax was a lie.

The peace was deceptive.

He's one of the righteous collective, and I'm only a sinner to be used.

I press my legs together as he crosses to a dresser and pulls open a drawer. I shove my skirt down to cover myself and slowly sit up, then I climb to my feet. I collect my dress from the floor and hold it against my chest.

"I'll go," I mutter, moving toward the door as I pull up the straps of the chemise to cover myself.

"Stop," he hisses.

I turn to face him, but he's not looking at me; he's too busy sifting through the contents of his drawer.

"Go sit in that chair at my desk."

Shame rains down on me like a storm, and as I move to obey his command, I fear I may drown in it. I do as he asks, smoothing out my dress before lowering to sit on the wooden chair. I have a good view of the walls and the windows that frame the two sides of the desk—I almost wish I could see the view beyond them, but the curtains are drawn.

I hear him move around me, behind my back. My heartbeat quickens as he walks past me, going into the bathroom. Moments later, he returns, coming over to where I sit, stopping at my back. I can't seem to steady my breathing, my chest heaving out of control.

I hear him sigh as he lets out a heavy breath, and it's like an ancient monster breathing fire over me. When I feel his bare fingers gather the strands of my hair, the heat dissipates as a frigid breeze of warning combs through them.

His breaths are heated and heavy, blowing out a mixture of residual longing, prolonged aching, and rising anger. "You've gotten inside my head, sinner. You've made me lose control of myself, and it's time I take it back."

chapter twenty-one
ARLO

EVERY INCH OF me is screaming in pain, and I welcome it.

After losing myself to this dark demon of lust disguised as bright white light, I need the ache of denial. But fuck, how I want the release. I want to bend her over the bed and destroy what's left of her, then put her back together with mind-numbing pleasure.

Sweet sin, the way she came undone.

It did something to me—something that must be undone immediately.

She's a sinner, and she's meant to die.

I slowly comb my fingers through her white-blonde hair, taking my time to loosen the tangles my fisted grip created. I'm so intently aware of each shuddering breath she takes as she sits as still as a statue in the very chair where I sit to write my poetry—where I sit to write poems about *her.*

I begin to plait her long, luxurious hair. She turns her head in confusion to ask me what I'm doing, but I stop her.

"Face forward."

She stills, forcing out an anxious breath.

"There's something dangerous about you, Mercy. Something bright and dark all at once."

"I don't understand—"

"You've brought me into sin with you. I can accept my failings. I'll suffer the pain of denial and beg God for forgiveness for my loathsome indulgences outside of service. And I'll be forgiven because you tempted me, because you're a servant and you drove me to this. In the eyes of God and my community, this is all *your* fault."

"You're a hypocrite," she mutters. "All of you are."

I give a sharp tug on the end of her braid, eliciting a yelp. "So says the sinner. You've always been rebellious."

"Why will your sins be forgiven and mine won't?"

I tie off the end of her braid with a short length of twine that I pulled from my dresser drawer. The view of the coarse rungs wrapped around her starlight hair sends a shudder through my spine that makes my cock painfully throb. I stifle a groan as I work to loosen the braid at the base of her neck, flattening out the strands.

"Because your sins were your choice, and your temptation brought me to mine."

"You're unbelievable!" she snaps, trying to rise to her feet, but I shove her back down in the seat with a firm hand on her shoulder. "You *chose* this as much as I did. You let me fuck you, commanded me to come."

I tug on her hair again, forcing her chin up, craning her neck back far enough that she can look at me when I bend over her. "Because you *knew* I didn't purge and came here with the intent to tempt me anyway. Don't lie to yourself and pretend you didn't know exactly what you were doing. You used your body to get what you wanted, to spare Delle."

Her cheeks flush pink with fury as she fumes at me, nostrils flaring. But I've successfully managed to shut her up. I release her, and she whips her head forward with a huff.

"This...these starlight strands of hair...you must have been colored by demons, painted bright white to mimic the heavens as a lure for men. This temptation is too great."

Her chest heaves with fury, but her voice is lowered to a harsh whisper. "And now you blame my hair for your failure."

I pull the scissors I had collected from the bathroom from my back pocket. An unexpected tremor shakes through me as I grip them and open them, prepared to cut. She's not even aware that I'm holding them. Not even aware that I'm going to cut her fucking hair because it calls to me like a siren's song.

I bring the scissors to the base of her neck where I've loosened and flattened her braid. I spread the scissors open wide and hover them over the strands. I take in a steadying breath and shut my eyes for a beat as indecision washes over me.

Yet, I know I have to do it.

To save my tempted soul, I have to do it.

Snip.

I cut a chunk at the base of her neck.

She gasps, startles, tries to turn as her hands fly up to her skull. "What're you—"

I place my other palm on the top of her head to keep her still, and with forced determination, I *snip, snip, snip* my way across the line of her shoulders. Each snip echoes, slicing through the quiet room, a horrifying sound I feel rip through my chest, cutting me with regret.

Yet, I continue.

"Stop!" She wiggles, fighting against my grip which presses down on her head.

I cut all the way across, from shoulder to shoulder, and her braid drops free, tumbling to the floor in a heap.

"No!" she cries as I let go.

I bend to grab the fallen braid as she leaps from the seat, whirling around to face me as her hands reach behind her for the hair I now hold as a severed braid in my hand.

"Why did you *do* that?" Her expression is a mix of sadness, shock, and horror—you'd think I'd cut off a limb by the look of her face.

And it kind of feels like I did.

"If temptation is brought to man outside of service, the temptation must be removed," I quote the Impulse Edict, the documentation of the doctrine we follow in Ember Glen.

"My hair…" she gapes at me, "you cut my hair."

"I removed a temptation."

"You haven't removed *anything*!" She stomps forward, pressing into my space. "You're *horrible*," she spits. Her hands slam to my chest and she shoves me back. "You're *disgusting*. I hate you!"

I'm struck by her words. They physically pang as they hit my heart, forcing me to take another step backward. I swallow an odd lump that rises sharply in my throat.

She turns from me and stomps toward the door, and though I could let her leave—*perhaps I should let her leave*—I know I can't. I won't. I refuse to let her walk out that door right now, lest she do something phenomenally stupid. She might be hurt enough in this moment to break her promise and share our secret sin.

I slam the scissors and her braid down on my desktop and charge after her. I reach her just as she reaches the door. I circle her wrist with my hand, then tug and twist her around before slamming her back against the door. I pin her with my body, my cock aching, my heart hurting.

Looking down at her, I see tears in her eyes and note that the beauty of her hasn't relinquished at all with the length of her hair gone. I cut it just above her shoulders, but the choppy line of what's left still shines like starlight, still begs for me to touch its silky smoothness.

She holds my gaze with anger for a moment, but then a sob overtakes her, and her chin drops.

I don't know what to do.

Before I can decide, my arms move to encircle her, pull her away from the door, hugging her close. She pulls back, fighting against my arms, but I tighten my grip. I hold her until her fighting relents and she lets go, shedding her tears, burying her face against my chest. Her tears coat my bare skin, and I swear it feels like they're boiling, burning my skin…

It feels like the punishment I deserve.

No.

She's the temptation. She's the sinner.

I grip her shoulders and turn, pushing her backward as I rush forward with her to the dresser. I open the top drawer and remove a length of rope I normally only use on servants during nights of purging.

"No," she cries as I turn to her, gripping it in one hand and wrapping it around my palm. She takes a step back as I rush her, but she's not quick enough. "Don't!"

I shove her back toward the bed and force her to sit on the edge. I grip her wrist and lasso the rope around it, quickly tying a solid knot to secure it firmly. She swings her free arm at me with a closed fist, punching cleanly into the side of my stomach. Her fist pounds painfully into my flesh and I flinch, my body jerking away.

She stands, trying to make a run for it. Though the hit took me off guard, and my hand slips down the length of rope, I quickly recover, clamping my hand around the coarse twine and tugging. Her tied arm jerks back, dragging her entire body with it, and she tumbles into me. I grab hold of her and toss her onto the bed. I reach for her hips, twisting her body until she's laying back on the pillow.

I keep one foot planted on the floor as I lift the other knee over her body. She thrashes beneath me, bucking against my still hard cock, sending painful shockwaves throughout my entire body. I grit my teeth against the desire I still hold for her, my jaw tensing as I fight my lust.

God help me.

Tugging the rope, I tie the free end around the bed post. I manage to secure it entirely while she fights me. Once it's secured, I shift my weight back and huff out a breath of exhaustion from the struggle. The moment I take that pause, she reaches up with her untied hand, and slaps me across the cheek.

My head turns against the impact, hair falling across my brow. I snatch her wrist and slam it to the pillow above her head, then do the same with the other, thankful I left enough slack to be able to do so. Her now short hair fans out behind her head, the platinum strands looking more like a halo than the remnants of my temptation.

Yet the temptation still exists.

It's when she spits at me that the demon within her reveals itself. I feel it taking hold of me as my cock thickens dangerously. I can nearly envision her seductive tresses re-growing before my eyes in the way the tattered strands fan out around her. I can almost see them lifting ethereally from the bed and wrapping around me, taking hold of me, forcing me to devolve in depravity.

But the vision is only in my mind. Beneath me is just a sinner—a broken woman possessed by some demon of the mind, who twists her thinking and forces her to take everyone around her to the depths of hell in her seduction.

Not everyone around her...*just me.*

She's crafted from sin, born of the deviances and temptations I've struggled with since I was old enough to purge, since the age of sixteen.

She's my own personal demon...and I think I deserve her torment.

BY THE TIME I've taken the coldest shower of my life and willed my throbbing cock to deflate, Mercy has calmed herself to stillness, though she still huffs with seething breaths. I forcibly tugged the covers from beneath her and tucked her into my bed before climbing in beside her, leaving ample space between us.

I need a good night's rest, and so does she. Rest will give us both some clarity over what occurred here tonight. I need the clarity because I have no idea what has transpired between us or why it's happened.

Moments of frustrated silence pass in the dark as we both lie on our backs, staring up at the ceiling.

"I'll try," I tell her quietly.

I hear her head move against the pillow as she turns it in my direction. "What?"

"You wanted to take on Delle's burden, and I'm telling you that I'll try. I'll bring it to my brothers and let you make your case. But it's not the nature of the Trials of Dissension to allow one to take on another's burden, especially when she chose to participate. It defeats the purpose entirely. Don't get your hopes up."

She's quiet for a minute before she asks, "Why would you do that for me?"

"Perhaps there's a part of me that thinks Delle should be forgiven for choosing so impulsively. That maybe she should be given guidance and redirection, rather than endure this torture for a chance at a life that's really no chance at all."

"Is there any part of you that thinks I should be forgiven for my impulsive decision to run?"

Maybe.

I harden my voice, though my instinct is to speak softly. "After what transpired here tonight? No. You're the worst kind of sinner, Mercy. You're the kind of rebel who inspires rebellion in others."

"Are you saying I inspired you to rebel?"

"I'm saying you inspire sin."

"Call it rebellion or call it sin, but either way you say it, it's admission that you and I were the same for a moment tonight."

I bring my hands up, linking fingers behind my head, elbows jutted out and resting on the pillow. She's not wrong. It's bothersome that she's right, because it makes me like her—even if it was just for weakened moments, even if it was her fault for inspiring my desire with her sinful intent.

"A moment of weakness isn't a pattern worthy of punishment," I tell her.

She scoffs, tugging against the rope around her wrists—I'd had to secure both to the bedpost—and the wooden headboard creaks. "A man's moment of weakness should be as equally punishable, and it's disgusting that it's not."

I can't help but chuckle. "What the devil *are* you, Mercy Madness?"

I hear her sigh, and she speaks calmly. "I don't know what I am; I don't know who I am. But I know I don't belong here in Ember Glen."

"There's nowhere else for you to be. Ember Glen is the only safe place in the world."

"Then perhaps I should be glad I'll be dead soon."

The resignation in her voice is alarming, and it creeps over my skin with the vibration of warning bells. Truly, I don't know how else I would expect her to view her impending doom—it's just the clarity in her acceptance that stabs between my ribs, slicing right through my aching heart.

There's nothing else to say. There is no logic or reason I can counter her statement with. Perhaps she should be glad she'll be dead soon because it's so clear she doesn't belong here—and there's truly nowhere else in the world for her to go.

But what's most bothersome is the fact that I'm not glad for it. I'm not glad that this sinner will meet the fate she deserves. And that's a fact I can't reconcile in my mind.

chapter twenty-two

Mercy

"DELLE DESERVES ANOTHER chance," I plead my case before the members of the Control and the Elders on screen in the dark courtroom. "As the authority of this community, you should be guiding our youth, especially those who serve. Her decision to participate in the Trials of Dissension was impulsive, made after a particularly brutal first night of service. Her decision was a mistake. Not one of you here is above making mistakes. You may think I'm different because I'm a sinner, but at the end of the day, we're all human."

I don't know whether my words hold meaning to them, whether they'll understand my thoughts and their intentions, whether their minds are capable of the same level of rationality and compassion that I pride myself in having. I know they all think my thoughts are irrational, but they're wrong.

I know they are—they must be.

The heat of the spotlight shining down on me makes sweat break across my brow. The Control sits in a semi-circle in front of me, hardly visible as they're shadowed in darkness behind their black table. The courtroom is bleak, black, dark to inspire fear.

And it works.

Owen speaks first through the shadows. "No one forced Delle to volunteer to participate in the trials. In fact, we discussed her fate and whether she should be *forced* to participate at the same time we decided your fate, and we chose to spare her. We've already granted her leeway, and I find the tone of your argument to be presumptuous against our compassion for the people of Ember Glen."

"Agreed." Killian leans forward and folds his hands on the dark table. "I find it presumptuous and offensive. Our concern at all times is the well-being of the members of this community. It's the reason why sinners like you must be put on trial."

Wesley crosses his arms over his chest, leaning back deeper into the shadows that further darken his already dark skin. "This is a waste of our time." He turns his head, looking at Arlo at the end of the table. "You've got your hands full with these mouthy wards."

Arlo glances at Wesley, giving a small smirk from the corner of his mouth, though it falls away quickly. He says nothing, then turns his attention back to me, watching quietly.

"I've said this from the beginning," Theo speaks up, "Delle deserves another chance. But even I can't deny the fact that she *volunteered* to participate. No one forced her hand, Mercy. It was her choice, regardless of whether it was the right one."

"It was the wrong choice," I speak boldly. "It was her moment of weakness. That night of service where she ran was brutal. A servant died. Any new servant would be terrified of serving again."

"It was brutal," Owen says, "I'll give you that. But every full moon brings the potential for that level of brutality in service. It's the entire point. We purge our impulses when the moon is brightest and we're all at our celestial worst. Delle knew that before she served. She was trained."

"But you can't train the humanity from a person." My voice rises in agitation, and I take a deep breath to calm myself. "No sixteen-year-old girl can be truly mentally prepared for that. And she's certainly not mentally prepared for the trials. She doesn't understand what she's volunteered for. She doesn't *want* to participate. She was scared, she saw a way out, and she took it." We all know it was never really a way out, but who could've expected Delle to understand that? "I want to take the burden for her. Let me right her wrongs. Double my burden, and let my efforts absolve her of her sins."

"Mercy," Clyde speaks from the projection on the wall behind me, and I whirl around to face the three Elders, anxious for turning my back on the collective Control. "I'm sure you realize how absurd it is that you're standing here before us, asking for a favor. You're not in God's good graces, and we don't hold you in ours."

"Absurd, indeed," Edgar agrees on screen. "We could've burned you at the stake like your mother, but we've granted you this chance at absolution from the compassion within our hearts. And here you are, standing before us, asking us to change the rules because you think you understand something about humanity that we don't?"

"We hold the secrets of God as the Elders of this community," Clyde says. "We are the keepers of the Impulse Edict. We know what God wants for Ember Glen, and you know *nothing*."

Chair legs scrape against the floor behind me, and I turn to see Killian slowly stand, buttoning his black blazer. "I think we've all heard enough from you, Mercy. You had your time, now kindly leave us so we can pretend to discuss your ridiculous request."

I have to try one more time. "I just want to—"

"*Enough,*" Killian snaps and it startles me. He stretches his arm toward the door, pointing his finger. "Out."

I glance at Arlo, our eyes catching for a moment. Then he leans back in the chair, shrouding himself in shadow, hiding from me. Defeated, I nod slowly, then make my way to the door.

I WAIT IN the foyer, pacing across the starburst-patterned tile for another fifteen minutes before they've finished their meeting in the courtroom. I know it didn't go over well, and I don't expect they'll return a result in my favor, but I still have hope. I had to try.

I stop my pacing abruptly, landing perfectly on the center of the sun, as I hear the courtroom door click open from down the nearby hallway. The sound of male voices filters out and moves closer.

Killian is the first one out, and he pauses for a moment as his eyes land on me, the corner of his mouth quirking up with a sneer that makes me feel terribly uncomfortable. His eyes scan me from top to bottom before he moves again, crossing from the hallway into the foyer and heading in my direction.

Wesley and Owen follow close behind him as they all move toward me. They hardly veer as they approach, and my shoulders tense as I pull my arms close to my sides, shrinking myself to take up less space. But they still come in far too close as they brush past, heading for the staircase at my back.

"See you soon, sinner," Killian mutters, his shoulder bumping mine as he passes.

"Looking forward to that first trial," Wesley says at the same time.

Park and Ryker aren't far behind, sharing their whispers of warning, which make anxiety wash over me. All their words whirl around me like a tornado of dark promises for the upcoming trial, and suddenly, I worry that standing before them today has prompted them to hate me all the more. Their hatred will, in turn, prompt more brutality when it comes to the trials.

Have I just worsened my fate while trying to spare Delle's?

Five of them are on the staircase and climbing when Theo appears from the hallway. He comes close and stops just beside me, moving in so the front of his shoulder touches the front of mine.

The softness in his brown eyes catches me by surprise before he leans in to whisper, "Thank you for trying. I mean it." He looks sad—sadder than I've ever seen. Yet the gratitude he has for me is humbling…heartwarming.

He and I haven't interacted much outside of service, but we've spent enough time during those purges that we grew something akin to friendship—

however shallow it was, it existed, nonetheless. And he was always happy, always joyful and enthusiastic. I sense none of that now as our gaze meets, and it aches in my chest for him.

He gives me a tight smile before walking away, heading up the stairs behind his brothers. I sigh as he passes, but when I raise my eyes again, I see Arlo coming toward me.

My pulse quickens, and though I want to believe it's from the anxiety over waiting to hear what they've decided, I know it's not. I know it because I feel that swirl of wanting through my belly as my eyes drop to take him in.

The black sleeves of his button-down are rolled up to the elbows, revealing the lines of sinew in his forearms that draw my gaze to his large, gloved hands. His fingers clench and unclench, mirroring the anxiety I feel. I almost feel like the sinner they claim me to be when my eyes sweep lower to see the outline of his length beneath his perfectly ironed black slacks. When we meet in the center of the sun, my heartbeat stops altogether.

I blink up at him expectantly, tucking both sides of my newly shortened hair behind my ears. "What did they say?"

"The answer is no," he says flatly, his blue eyes scanning my face, "which was to be expected."

My chest sinks as I let out a drawn-out breath, feeling deflated, defeated. My head drops, knowing that I tried, but I failed. I failed to save Delle.

Arlo's fingertips tap beneath my chin, lifting my head and forcing me to look up at him. When I do, he moves his fingers to tug the hair from behind my ears. It's a clear assertion of his authority over me, a reminder that he cut my hair, that he controls me.

"I think there's something to be said about the fact that you tried," he says quietly, almost a whisper. "Perhaps absolution will find you yet."

He says the words with such earnest that they breeze right through me, blowing gentle embers of the fire from within him to brush against my soul, threatening to spark a fire I can't control. I hate the way it feels because of how much I love it, how much I crave it, how much I need it.

My head tilts against his fingers lingering beside my ear, and for a moment—just a brief, perfect moment—he opens his palm to cradle my cheek. And for that moment, I feel comforted.

But the moment is gone just as quickly. He blinks, eyes flickering and drawing him back to reality. I see the remembrance of who we are and where we're standing rush back in to the flush of his cheeks as he jerks his hand away and steps back.

"Come," he says, brushing past me toward the stairs.

Though I know he only means for me to follow, the alternative meaning of the word in the context of our heated moments of sin rushes shameful wetness to my core.

I follow behind him, lifting my long, red skirt so I don't trip. "What now?"

"I need to gather some things from my room, and then we're going to take a walk."

"Where?"

"You'll know when we arrive."

"Arlo, please…tell me what's going on."

He stops suddenly on the landing, and the abruptness makes me stop just a few steps beneath. I quickly grab hold of the railing to steady myself as the sudden stop unbalances me.

His eyes narrow on me. "Warden Rainn."

I can see the distress he holds within that single look, and it seems overwhelming. He wants formalities in front of the others…maybe he wants formalities all the time.

"Warden Rainn," I start again, "what's going on?"

He turns away and starts moving down the hallway. I hasten, jogging up the last few steps and chase after him. I want to grab his arm and stop him physically, but Ryker and Park stand only a few feet past, chatting casually, and Theo is near the end of the hall, knocking on Delle's door. So, I continue to meet his pace without reaching out to touch him.

I long to touch him.

"We've wasted too much time already," he says, still walking away from me. "It's my job to prepare you—both of you—and we don't have any more time to hesitate."

"I don't understand. Will you please tell me what's going on?"

"We're going to be away for several hours," he says. "Take five minutes to attend to your personal needs, and I'll come to collect you."

Before I can say another word, he rushes to unlock his bedroom door and hurries inside. It closes behind him, and the lock engages, effectively shutting me out. The sound of another door opening draws my attention, and I turn back to see Delle's door swing open, Theo pushing past her to enter her room.

What is he doing?

He shouldn't be alone with her. He's twenty-seven years old—the same as all of the members of the Control—and she's only sixteen.

Turning on my heel, I charge after Theo. I reach Delle's door just before it shuts, slapping my palms to the wood and shoving it wide. I nearly tumble through the entry in my haste.

"Mercy?" Delle says as I move toward them.

"What are you doing in here?" I ask Theo as he turns his head to look at me.

"Not that it's any of your business, but your warden asked me to retrieve her." He then turns his head again to look at Delle. "You have five minutes to take care of your personal needs. Then we're heading out and we'll be gone for a while."

Delle looks back and forth between us. "Where are we going?"

"You'll know when we arrive," Theo replies.

"That's what Arlo said," I confirm.

"Well, that's what he told me to tell you," Theo says to Delle, then looks at me. "Does she know what you did for her? What you tried to do for her?"

Tried.

Tried and failed.

Delle looks at me. "What?"

I shake my head pointedly. "No, she doesn't. I wasn't going to say anything, Theo."

He gives me an appraising look and it nearly feels like acceptance. He nods slowly, and though it looks like he's going to say something, he just reaches out to pat my shoulder with a tight smile.

"Okay," he says. "Five minutes, both of you."

Theo turns to leave, but not before casting a sideways glance at Delle, giving her a much more genuine grin before leaving us alone. The door clicks shut behind him.

"How often does he come to you?" I ask her. "You don't have to let him in, Delle. He has no right to be alone with you."

"Not often," she replies, her eyes fixed to the door behind my back. She blinks and looks at me. "He's been kind, and I—"

"Delle, you can't trust any of them. Do you understand me? Not even when they're kind to you…*especially* not when they're kind to you."

"I know." She nods and casts her gaze to the floor. "I know that."

"They're not allowed to touch you outside of service. Don't let them."

"No one's touching me, Mercy." Irritation shades her tone as she lifts her head to look up at me, crossing her arms. "That's why I'm here. It's why I volunteered to participate. I don't want *anyone* touching me ever again. I'll take death before I allow it."

All of them will touch her for the first trial—whether she allows it or not. My blood runs cold at the thought, and a shiver tremors up my spine. Yet I understand what she's saying—she's chosen this fate rather than be forced to serve.

"Okay," I say softly. "I just want to make sure you're okay."

She nods a little, though I still see the frustration in her expression—teenage defiance that was once a hallmark for me before months and months of service dulled my affect. I almost want to smile at it, recognizing my former self within her. Perhaps that's why I care about her so much. Caring for her almost feels like caring for my younger self.

Fighting for her feels like fighting for me.

A few moments pass as she relinquishes slowly, bringing her arms down to her sides. "What was Theo talking about? What you tried to do for me?"

I wave my hand dismissively. "Never mind. It doesn't matter. It didn't work, anyway."

"Mercy, did you...The other day you were asking me about whether I'd let someone take the burden of the trials from me...whether I'd choose differently if I could go back. Did you try to—"

"Don't worry about it, Delle. Unfortunately for the both of us, nothing has changed." The reality of my failure strikes me hard in the chest as I speak the words out loud. It threatens to knock me down, and I step back to avoid stumbling over my emotions. "Five minutes," I remind her. "Whatever it is Warden Rainn has planned for us, it sounds like we'll be together. It will be okay."

I smile at her before turning away, and my face drops immediately, our situation sitting heavily on my shoulders.

I tried to save her, and I failed.

I tried to save myself, and I failed.

I fear the outcome of the trials will be no different.

chapter twenty-three
ARLO

I KNOCK ONCE on Mercy's door as a courtesy before letting myself in. She stands at her window, gazing out at the mountains. The first hint of sunlight I've seen all day peeks out from behind the cloud cover, shining through the window and striking her as if she had called upon it herself.

She turns her head over her shoulder to look at me, her shortened hair whipping around her face like sparkling strands of shooting stars. Cutting her hair didn't lessen the draw of her starlight tresses, it only gave them more freedom to move and draw my attention.

Yet I quickly lose sight of her hair as it falls away, the strands framing her porcelain face, blushed cheeks, and pink lips—but more than that, my gaze is drawn to her gray-blue eyes which are glassy with the sheen of tears, glistening in the sunlight which sweeps across her face.

I should remain in place, let her feel whatever it is she's feeling without interference. But the messenger bag I packed drops heavily from my shoulder to the floor, and I stride across the room before I can stop myself. She turns her head as she brings her knuckles up to swipe beneath her eyes. I stop at her back, my arms aching to reach out for her, but I clench my fists to keep them at my sides.

"You tried," I quietly tell her. "It's more than most would do in your position. There's something to be said for that."

Her hair shakes with her head. "It's not that. I mean, it *is* that, but not *only* that." She turns and starts to brush past me. "Never mind. I'm fine."

I reach out and wrap my palm around her bicep, pulling her in front of me. "You're not fine."

She sniffles and blinks and a strained tear slips out from the corner of her eye. "You said five minutes. I'm ready to go—"

"Pretend I said ten minutes. Talk to me."

Her expression flickers, eyebrows dipping toward her delicate nose. "Why?"

"Because it's clear that you're going through something, and you need to talk about it."

Her head jerks back and irritation creeps through her features. "Going through something? Obviously, I'm going through something. I'm going through *everything*. My life is over. It's coming to a close and all for what? Because I've questioned? Because I've wondered? Because I ran to avoid a painful death? It's all wrong...everything is wrong, and I've never felt so afraid—" her voice breaks. "I've never felt so alone. I've never felt so lonely."

Her tears break free, and she brings her hand up to cover her mouth as she tries to hold them back, but the way it strains through her body to resist the purging of her emotions is something I can feel throbbing in my chest, in sync with the beating of my heart.

Before I know what I'm doing, my arms encircle her and tug her against me. Her hands land on my chest and push, but I tighten my embrace, holding her against me until her sob breaks free and her body goes limp in my arms. And then she cries, dropping her face against my chest, her hands fisting my shirt.

My heart pounds, pulse races, breaths quicken with the swirl of emotions that sweep into a tornado within me. Holding her while she cries makes me feel equally vulnerable and safe—like I'm home and free to exist in my feelings without the mask of authority I'm always expected to maintain.

A sinner shouldn't make me feel that way.

I sigh, allowing myself a moment to relinquish control and feel her. I know immediately it's a mistake...because she feels like something I'll struggle to let go of.

And I know I'll have to let go of her.

I count to twenty in my mind, granting us both that much time to exist in this state. And then I let go, steeling myself, hardening my shell, separating myself from her emotions.

Why do her emotions feel like my own?

I clear my throat, release her, and turn away. I walk toward the door and bend to pick up my messenger bag. "Dry your eyes, sinner. Let's go."

"Where are we going?"

"Somewhere I can prepare you for the first trial."

I COLLECT DELLE and Theo and lead them all back to the courtroom downstairs. Inside the dark room, there's a concealed doorway, hidden behind the table where the Control sits for judgment.

I lead Mercy, Delle, and Theo through the door—one that all the Control knows about—and down the hidden staircase. The first set of steps are wooden, and they creak as we descend. At the bottom, our feet touch stone, and on our right is another set of steps. These are carved from stone, created from the natural bedrock that lies beneath the Homestead. This is where wooden, man-made structures disappear, and natural rock supersedes.

I light a torch at the stone landing before leading us down the next set of steps—a long staircase that takes us down, down, down into the depths beneath the Homestead. At the bottom is a long, narrow pathway, and I lead us through the twisting corridor. The ceiling is low and rock walls surround us with dark, damp grayness as we make our way deeper into the darkness.

"Is this safe?" I hear Delle ask from somewhere behind me. "Where are we going?"

"Somewhere that we won't be interrupted or watched."

"Or listened to," Theo adds from the rear of our line. "Somewhere with privacy."

"Privacy," Mercy echoes him with a sarcastic tone. "I haven't known privacy since I was brought here."

The torchlight casts an orange glow around us, leading us with flickering light and heat.

"We're granted privacy for the purpose of trial preparation," I tell them. "It's in the Impulse Edict."

"A serious question for you, Warden Rainn," Mercy says. "How would one know it's in the Edict?"

"The Elders tell us." They're the guardians and interpreters of the Impulse Edict, and we rely on them to guide our community based on the written word of God. What we know of the Edict is what has been told to us by each generation of Elders. The only fully documented version of the Edict is in their care.

"And you just presume that the Elders always tell the truth?" Mercy asks.

"You're quite bold for a servant trapped in a cave," I tell her.

She chuckles. "I'm not a servant; I'm a *sinner*."

A smile spreads across my cheeks at her banter, as she throws my own words from previous conversations back at me.

"Is that where we are?" Delle asks. "In a cave?"

"Nearly," Theo says. "These underground tunnels lead to a cave system that runs through the mountains."

"We're going to the mountain?" Delle asks with a hint of childlike wonder in her tone.

I remember the first time I was brought through these tunnels and shown the caverns. It was shortly after I moved into the Homestead my first year as a member of the Control two years ago. I was filled with wonder, too, and my mind overflowed with poetry depicting the beauty of the Earth. I was filled with awe over God's creation, and the fact that I was chosen to be one of the few to bear witness to it.

Perhaps I should feel bad that a sinner is allowed to see it now, except I don't. It somehow feels okay that she sees it, it feels right. Perhaps a part of me hopes that seeing it will trigger her sense of awe and return her lost reverence for God and his creation.

A ten-minute walk through winding tunnels brings us to a wide open cavern. Towering high above our heads, stalactites hang from the ceiling as pointed cones of natural rock pointing down at us. The solid rock beneath our feet creates a flat, winding path through the same coned rocks that jut up from the ground surrounding us in rows and clusters of stalagmites.

Between the points of hanging stalactites and rising stalagmites is vast, open space, and it's filled with nothing but echoing darkness. It's eerie and ethereal all at once, and it never ceases to take my breath away.

"Oh…" Mercy breathes out the sound of wonder on a sigh, and I somehow feel relief in knowing she sees the same beauty I see here.

"This is incredible," Delle's small voice echoes with excitement.

"It is," I agree.

I lead us along a flat, narrow path of bedrock that years of men traversing have flattened out neatly between stalagmites. The flat path leads us across the open cavern to another tunnel, and a sharp turn to our right stops us in front of a large boulder.

Only the boulder isn't real.

I hand the torch to Theo, grip the false rock with both hands, and easily slide it sideways. Behind it is an opening to a space I've often retreated to be alone with my thoughts.

"Follow me," I tell them, taking the torch back from Theo and ducking my head to creep into the short tunnel.

A few steps take me into the grotto, a carved-out space as large as my bedroom and as dark as night. My torchlight sets a glow that allows me to circle the space, finding the three torches I'd fixed to the rock walls a long time ago, lighting each in turn. Two at the sides, one at the back, and a fourth spot at the front wall where I place the torch I carried in with me.

The space is dimly lit from the firelight with a shadowed, flickering glow. As Mercy makes her way inside, turning to reach behind her to help Delle through the small opening, her short tresses still shine as brightly as the stars.

What demon is within her that calls to me so loudly?

I drop my messenger bag and crouch to my haunches to open it, pulling out several lengths of coarse rope and drop them heavily onto the rock floor.

"What's that for?" Mercy asks behind me.

I stand and turn to face her. "Preparation. It's the reason I've brought you here." I look at Theo. "The reason *we've* brought you here."

Mercy's head inclines as she looks at me pensively. "Preparation for the trials?"

"The first trial," I confirm with a nod.

Staring down at the rope, she fidgets with her hair, dragging her fingers through the ends as if she could still stroke the phantom length I cut. Then she hugs herself, her eyes telling me that she's trying to retreat. Delle sucks in a quick, shaky breath just behind her, and it snaps Mercy from her retreat. She lets go of herself and reaches her arm back, turning her head over her shoulder to find Delle's hand and grabs hold of it.

It's bewildering the way the demon in her mind relents and allows her compassion for Delle. Perhaps Mercy's compassion is simply so strong that no devil or demon could overpower it. The thought stirs a flurry of extra beats through my heart.

I clear my throat and pull back my shoulders to stand a little taller. "I've been tasked with binding you for the trial. I think it's fair that we have some practice with what that's like beforehand."

Mercy takes a step back, pushing Delle behind her as she moves. "We're not meant to endure a trial twice. I won't allow you to bind us here."

"You will allow it if you want to be prepared." I try to appeal to her protectiveness of Delle. "You'll allow it so Delle will know what to expect and won't panic in the moments before her trial begins."

Mercy watches me discerningly, her eyes scouring my form from top to bottom, as if she can assess all my intentions—good and bad—with a single glance. Perhaps she can, but she'll find no bad intentions here.

"Tell me your plan then," she says carefully. "What do you mean to do to us here?"

"I mean to bind you with rope, to show you how you'll be bound for use in the trial, and give you a chance to prepare your mind for endurance through limited movement and the inability to escape of your own free will. I mean to help you prepare, as I said."

"And why is Theo here for this?" she asks me. "You're our warden."

"That's something we need to discuss."

"So discuss it, then. I assure you that you have our attention."

"To avoid exhausting my brothers, you'll be participating in the first trial simultaneously."

Her nostrils flare with a touch of anger. "We most certainly wouldn't want to exhaust your brothers while they defile us.”

Something like a whimper escapes from Delle, and the small sound makes something resembling shame tick through my heart for a beat. It passes quickly with the next beat, though, because I know my God—I enforce His Edict, and I will do His will in these trials.

“Collectively, it’s been decided that you’ll be placed in two separate rooms to ensure the validity of your experiences.”

Mercy stares. “You’re going to have to explain that one to me.”

“The trials are an individual endeavor, and this one is meant to try your ability to endure the passionate needs of men with your flesh. On your own, and without support or encouragement. You should consider this to be a good thing, Mercy. You won’t have to witness Delle’s trial.”

“And I won’t be able to support her, now, will I?”

“Tell me when you’ve ever supported another servant on a night beneath the full moon. Service relies on the individual—”

“And the collective,” she interrupts me. “Without my sisters in service, there wouldn’t be enough to fulfill the needs of all the men in Ember Glen.”

“True, but this trial doesn’t require you to serve the needs of *all* men. It requires you to serve the needs of *seven*.” Slowly, I step toward her. “In a way, you’ve won your case with my brothers.”

Creases form on her brow in confusion. “What do you mean?”

“They’re angry with you, Mercy. They were already angry with you for your sins and your pattern of rebellious thinking over your years of service. Perhaps it’s my fault for letting you speak your case in Delle’s favor today, but they feel insulted by the speech you gave asking to take on her burden. And the way they speak about taking out their aggressions on you in the trial, the way they speak about giving you what you deserve, means that their time and attention will mostly be focused on you.”

I watch her face fall as I speak, fear creeping through her features, though she tries to force a determined expression to hide it.

“With your trials taking place simultaneously,” I continue, “they’ll give you their worst, and Delle will be an afterthought. The anger you inspired in them today may very well have spared Delle the worst of them in this first trial.”

Even in the dark, I can see her throat bob as she swallows, quickly steeling herself as her shoulders pull back. “Good. Fine. That’s what I wanted.”

“Is it?”

She hardens her expression. “Yes. I wanted to take Delle’s burden, and I’ll take as much of it as they’ll give. Let them be angry with me if it should spare her their depravity.”

I nod, crossing my arms. "Good. Because they'll give you a mountain of depravity in your seven-hour trial, which will take place a few days before the next full moon."

"And you think you can prepare us for that?"

I drop my arms to the sides. "I can't do anything to prepare you to fulfill the lustful desires of my brothers, as sexual acts are forbidden outside of service." I cast a wayward glance at Theo, a natural movement of my eyes as I feel caught in a lie—no one can know of the things I've done with Mercy. "But I can mentally prepare you to endure the entrapment of being bound for hours and hours." I take a step forward. "Now, will you let me help you?"

Mercy blinks, holding my gaze, and though the light is dim and constantly flickering, I can see the thoughts swirling behind her eyes.

It's Delle who speaks, looking over at Theo. "Why are you here? What do you have to do with this?"

"The Control have decided that Arlo has his hands full with Mercy. They're concerned about her continued rebellion and what she might inspire in others during the trials. They don't want Arlo's attention divided, and they asked for another volunteer to be your warden," Theo says. "I volunteered."

Delle's eyebrows lift. "You're my warden now?"

Theo nods, shoving his hands into his pockets. "Yes. It means I'll be responsible for you during your trial—binding you, suspending you, adjusting the ropes to ensure your safety. I need to learn from Arlo. I don't want to hurt you, Delle. That's why we need to practice this. It's why I'm here, to learn."

"Okay," Mercy says, "then prepare us." She looks squarely at Theo. "But please remember that Delle is a *child*. I don't care what the Edict says about her age and her ability to serve, you will mind her with care in this preparation. Do you understand me?"

"I understand that you're a sinner, Mercy, and your words hold no meaning here. What you need to understand is that I have no intention of harming Delle. I don't have to be here; I don't have to learn how to bind her safely. I don't have to do any of this. So, if you think for a second that my intentions with her are malicious, then you're *wrong*. I volunteered to help her."

"I don't trust anyone's intentions, Theo," Mercy replies quietly, "not even yours."

"You don't have to trust me," he replies, "but maybe you should trust her to speak for herself."

Mercy looks at Delle over her shoulder, who meets her eyes and gives her a small smile and a grateful nod. "It's okay, Mercy. I chose this, remember? And I want to try. I know you think it's hopeless, but I want to try to pass these trials. I need you to let me do that."

I can feel the conflict within Mercy pulsing from her soul. She wants to protect Delle, but I think even she knows that she can't—not really. She bobs her head in understanding and side-steps away, letting Delle step forward beside her.

"All right then," Mercy says. "Let's prepare."

chapter twenty-four

Mercy

IN AN UNEXPECTED act of kindness, Arlo lays a soft blanket on the floor for each of us. I watch as he spreads them out and backs away, curious for all the unknown thoughts in his confusing mind.

Every time I think I have him figured out, he changes my mind. Sometimes—most of the time—I hate him. He's my warden, the man who judges me as a sinner, the same as the rest of Ember Glen. He's the man who cut my treasured hair as punishment for stirring lust within him. He's a man who will never understand me.

But other times I look at him and my heart skips a beat, my stomach clenches in shameful attraction, and my fingers twitch with the ache to sink into his hair. He confuses me, and though it's frightening, it's also exciting.

"Kneel," he says, turning away to grab rope from the rock floor, untangling a stretch of it and handing it to Theo.

Delle complies, moving to the center of the square blanket laid out in front of her and lowers to her knees. Her compliance is a learned behavior. Regardless of the fact that she ran from her duty on her first night in service, the same as me, her entire life leading up to that moment had taught her to obey—submission is what we were trained for.

A memory sweeps through me, capturing me in a trauma I'd rather tuck back into the dark corner in my mind. Interacting with Delle has brought me so many recollections of my teenage years. Here in the darkness of this cave, the recollections come so vividly, taking me back to one of my worst memories when I was only fourteen years old.

The Control entered our classroom unexpectedly that day and stood before our rows of desks at the front of the room in a menacing line. I remember them standing with such authority, dressed in tailored clothes that matched the sharp, pressed lines of their expressions perfectly.

Back then, the seven men who made up the Control were older. Arlo and his cohorts only came into authority two years ago, when they were twenty-five. When I was fourteen, the men comprising the Control were forty-six, nearing the end of their reign. Their age and experience only served to make them more intimidating.

When the Control stood before our class, one of our three teachers announced that they had come to assess our progress. I was surly as I leaned back, slouching in my chair, arms folded across my chest with an angry stare.

I didn't want to be assessed. We'd been learning about the male anatomy and the tenants of oral pleasure over the last several days, and I was disgusted by it, indignant that I should ever have to put my mouth on that part of a man. I couldn't comprehend why they would want such a thing if they could use my cunt just as easily.

One of the Control, whose name I can't remember, stepped forward. He was a forty-six-year-old man with silver strands streaking his thick black hair. He asked who would be willing to demonstrate their learning by serving him.

I'd scoffed, but every girl in the room shot their hands up high and fast into the air. They were eager to serve, eager to please, eager to serve God in their duty before their time in service even began.

Slowly, I'd lifted my palm and held it just in front of me. I didn't want to raise my hand at all, but I knew if I didn't, my teachers would scold me and beat me. My bottom was still red, welted, and sore from the last beating I'd taken for my attitude.

I'd turned my gaze away from the Control, disturbed by their wandering eyes and darkened gazes as they looked at my sisters. My stomach had turned in sick knots, and I'd prayed I wouldn't be called upon that day.

Relief came when another name was called.

Relief fled when I realized who it was.

They'd called Cambria.

I dropped my arms and straightened in my chair while nerves prickled anxiety through my veins. I hadn't been surprised she was chosen because Cambria was the most eager. She'd practically been bouncing in her seat with her hunger to serve as her arm stretched high in the air, her fingers wiggling in excitement. She was so excited about her role in life and that she would be an honored servant of Ember Glen.

She'd found pride that she was chosen to become a servant and was eager to please God in her service.

I remember her walking to the front of the room and the way the man watched her with thirst in his dark eyes. He'd commanded her to kneel, and her excitement had been palpable as she lowered to her knees. It was the same level of excitement that had rippled through the classroom and the girls who watched with wonder and whispers and innocent giggles.

They were all eager to see their sister perform well in service, to see the flesh of a real-life man rather than just the mannequins built for our practice—all because they'd been taught this was good, that it was wonderful, that it was Godly to kneel and serve the men of our community.

I'd searched the room, hoping my eyes would land on a single girl showing any attitude other than enthusiasm. I'd found no one—only me.

I'd wondered what was wrong with me, whether I was possessed or born from hell. I'd wondered how I could become better and whether I would ever be able to find joy in service. I'd tortured myself, wondering why I couldn't just be like everyone else.

The man at the front of the room revealed himself, sending a ripple of nervous whispers through the classroom. It had sent a ripple of nausea, stress, and fear through me. Then anger flushed out the anxiety, and it took hold of me. It possessed me, and I shoved to my feet.

"How can you be doing this now?" I'd demanded as the room fell into abrupt silence. "There is no full moon. You're only meant to purge on a full moon."

I recall the way the man stared me down with heat and fury, and the way it made me want to shrink away. But it had been the look Cambria gave me that filled me with guilt. Her look was one of annoyance, a pointed reminder that I should be quiet—and I'd known the look well. Truthfully, I wondered almost daily back then why Cambria and Ellary had remained friends with me given all the times I'd gotten myself into trouble.

"Come here," the man demanded of me, and the silent room held stagnant.

I hadn't dared a glance at my teachers. I didn't need further direction—a member of the Control had given me a command, and I had to obey above anyone else. I'd stepped out from behind my desk and slowly walked to the front of the room.

"Kneel." His hand was around his jutting erection, holding it out in front of Cambria, and I'd felt terrified at the sight of it. "Put your hand at the back of her head," he said to me, "and hold her in place. She'll want to pull away when I gag her, but she must learn to stay in place, all in the name of pleasure for the man." He looked down at Cambria. "You want to learn to do it properly, don't you?"

Cambria nodded eagerly. "Yes, of course."

"Good." He looked to me once again. "You. Do what you're told or face consequences by my authority in Ember Glen."

Rebellion had leaked through the odd mixture of fear and anger flowing through my veins. If he'd cut me open just then, I would've bled with dissent-tainted blood. I wasn't going to lay a hand on Cambria to help this man touch her with that monstrous appendage.

"No," I told him boldly.

And in an instant, I was overcome.

The Control encircled us, lifted me from the floor, and carried me outside. While Cambria was left kneeling in the classroom to demonstrate her knowledge of oral pleasure, five men stood shoulder to shoulder and surrounded me as the sixth took my virginity outside. He fucked me against the outside wall of the school building until I bled.

That was the day I learned to keep my mouth shut.

That was the day I learned it was best to kneel.

That event, and too many others that followed, helped tame the rebellious spirit within me before I officially began service at sixteen. But over the years since then, that rebellious spirit has grown bigger without me realizing it. She grew so big that she burst at the sight of Hyatt Price and his torch chasing after her beneath the full moon, and her return made me run, made me sin.

It's not a sin.

I'm not a sinner.

Regardless, I want this preparation. I don't want to go into these trials blindly. I want to know what to expect. I want to know what it's going to feel like to be bound by Arlo Rainn.

My pulse quickens as he turns toward me, and I step forward, gripping my skirt at my knees and lifting it so I can bend. I kneel at the center of the blanket, and though the fleece fabric is soft against my skin, the hard rock beneath is instantly painful. Arlo steps in front of me, and I cast a sideways glance to observe Delle watching Theo step toward her all the same. Her eyes are downcast, palms pressed to her thighs as she takes in shallow breaths.

"It's okay, Delle," I murmur. "I'm right here with you."

She glances at me, nodding with a weak smile before taking in a steadying breath. I return my attention to Arlo and the aching rhythm of my heart. Stepping closer, he drops the rope beside my knees, then works to roll up his shirt sleeves.

"We'll start simple," Arlo says as he exposes his forearms, taut tendons drawing lines to his hands. "You'll be suspended for the trial, but we'll work our way up to that."

I lift my chin to look up at him. "You took off your gloves."

His head is still dipped as he works on his sleeve, but his eyes raise for a moment, meeting mine from beneath his lashes. The fleeting moment of connection is intense, swarming my insides with a flurry of butterflies' wings.

He doesn't offer an explanation for why he took off his gloves, though I can guess it's because they restrict his dexterity in tying rope. I wish he would speak because the way he holds my gaze without a word as he rolls his sleeve is overwhelming.

I swallow anxiously and blink, dragging my eyes from his stare before taking a deep, steeling breath. I rub my palms over my thighs, looking down at my hands as though they're interesting enough to steal my attention.

Nothing is interesting enough to steal my attention from Arlo.

"There's a stark difference between what will happen here in our preparation and what will happen to you both in the trial, and I want to be very clear about that." He pauses, his arms falling to his sides. "Here, you're in control. If you want us to stop what we're doing or untie you, we will. But for preparation's sake, I'll encourage you to push yourself past what you think is your breaking point. Because you'll have no control in the trial; none of my brothers will stop if you ask them to. No one will untie you if you demand it. The more you can push yourself to withstand excessive time in bondage, the better prepared you'll be."

Quiet settles for a moment with the weight of his words. This trial will be much like a night of service, except for the fact that we'll be bound and suspended. My choice, my will, my self-control will all be lost in a much more significant way than it ever has been in the forest. I lift my palm, absently smoothing it down the side of my shortened hair—another symbol of my lost control.

Arlo steps forward and my downcast gaze lifts slowly, grazing up the length of him so close to me, until my head is lifted high to look at him staring down at me. "You may keep your clothes on if you wish, but you'll be naked in the trial. At some point you'll want to take the opportunity to know what the rope will feel like digging into your bare flesh."

Bare flesh.

There's something sultry in the way he says the words, as if he's saying them to me, and only me...speaking them like poetry.

Inexplicably, I wish we were alone.

My lips part as he reaches out and touches my cheek with his bare hand. Skin to skin, flesh to flesh, his touch is striking against the embers of desire that linger from our last encounter.

"What will it be?" he asks.

"I won't remove my clothes, not tonight," Delle says.

The sound of her voice seems muffled, far away, too quiet to compete with the roar of my soul as Arlo's fingers slip down the side of my neck.

"Brother," Theo snaps, and his voice is loud enough to break us. "Mind your hand."

I blink from the enchantment of Arlo's touch and look over at Theo. His eyes are narrowed where Arlo's palm touches my skin before he tugs his hand away sharply.

"I know you didn't purge," Theo says to him with righteous anger in his tone, "but there is no full moon tonight. You know better than to touch a woman like that outside of service...even a sinner."

Arlo clears his throat and takes a step back. "You're right. Forgive me."

I look up at him again, but the moment is lost. He bends to grab the rope, and he doesn't meet my eyes again.

Theo's warning reminds me that Arlo has already stepped across the thin line to abuse his power with me. I should have turned him in before...I should turn him in now, though we both know the Control would deny me and believe I was lying if I did. They would side with Arlo, and not just because he's one of them—it would be because they hate me, too.

It doesn't matter because I know I wouldn't tell them, anyway. It wouldn't change my fate. And if I wasn't aware of it consciously before, I am now—the sins of the flesh we committed together gave me the only moments of true peace and pleasure I've ever known.

And I want more of it.

Wrong as it is, if I'm sentenced to die, I'll keep his secret if it means I can share a forbidden passion with him until the very end, because I want more of this overwhelming need.

I'll take this secret to my grave just so I can revel in these sinful cravings a little longer.

chapter twenty-five
Mercy

A LITTLE MORE than two weeks of preparation in bondage have passed. I've spent every third night with Arlo, Theo, and Delle in the caves, and they have been nights of abject misery with Arlo's grazing touches and secret glances.

Otherwise, he's stayed away from me, avoiding me as much as he could. I've felt the distance he puts between us. He avoids me in the hallways, and he certainly doesn't come to my room. When I go to his, he speaks from the doorway and sends me away discourteously. He ignores me at meals, his words cold and curt.

But then we go to the caves where he binds me, and I *feel* him. His essence is braided into the ropes he coils around my body. I've come to feel freer when I'm bound by him than I've ever felt running through the forest or walking among the wildflowers in the meadow.

The anticipation of it is thrilling.

Of course, the thrill is always subdued, limited by the presence of Delle and Theo.

Tonight is different. I don't know where Delle and Theo are, and Arlo leads me through the secret door in the courtroom. The two of us descend the stone steps alone and traverse the winding tunnels through the caves.

He leads me along a different path than we usually follow, taking us through corridors that require us to dip our heads from low-hanging rock, and side-step through narrow openings. Some paths we travel are frightening in the dark, but I keep my eyes on the flame of his glowing torchlight, letting the flickering orange guide me through dark shadows that threaten to close in all around me.

We duck beneath a naturally formed stone archway, then step forward. He stops, and when I try to take another step to move beside him, he sharply throws out his arm, effectively stopping me from taking another step forward.

"Careful," he says, holding his torch out ahead of us with an outstretched arm. "It's a long way down."

I lean forward, gazing out in the direction of his light. Looking down,

I see the rock beneath our feet drop off into a vast darkness just a few steps ahead. When I realize how close we are to falling off the edge, it startles me, and I scurry backward toward the arched stone opening we came through.

I look over at him with confusion, and a sudden fear punches through my chest, shocking my lungs, quickening my breaths into anxious panting.

Why did he bring me here?

Why did he bring me here alone?

I look over my shoulder, but all I can see is black without the glow of the torch. I can't run from him. Even if I could see, I don't remember the path we traveled, and I'd never find my way back. I'd be lost in these tunnels forever. My palm jumps up to press over my heart, willing the pounding muscle to steady.

In the glow of his torchlight, his dimples crease as a grin I haven't seen in weeks spreads across his scruffy cheeks. "Mercy. I didn't bring you here to push you over the edge…at least, not in the way you think."

"Are you trying to frighten me?"

"I'm not trying to frighten you. There's no reason for you to be frightened. Though, I will admit, my intention is to spark adrenaline."

I blow out a breath through rounded lips. "You've succeeded."

"Good."

Arlo takes a step toward me, lifting his torch and placing it on a bracket fixed to the rock wall beside me. He drops his messenger bag and reaches out his gloved hand to me. I swallow the lump of residual fear and slowly lift my hand from my chest to drop my palm on top of his. His hand closes around mine, and he gently tugs me toward him. I take a careful step as he guides me closer, my eyes glued to my feet.

"Do you trust me?" His free hand floats up to tuck a wayward strand of hair behind my ear, and it sends a cold shiver down my spine.

"I don't know," I tell him truthfully.

"I'll need you to trust me during your trial."

"Why? It's my trial, not yours."

"It's your trial, but I'm going to look after you."

"I don't need you to…you should look after Delle, if anyone. I don't know how she's going to get through this."

"She's much stronger than you give her credit for. In any case, Theo will look after her. It's you I'm worried about."

There's a flurry of feeling in my belly, an odd sense of pride that he has concern for me at all. Then I wonder if that means he thinks I'm weak, and my brow furrows in scrutiny.

"Why are you worried about me? You don't think I'm strong?"

"I have no concerns about your strength. I've seen firsthand how powerful your mind is over the past several weeks. Your strength is impressive. It's your grit and your tenacity that worry me because you're the sinner my brothers truly want to punish. You've been so concerned over Delle that you haven't really prepared yourself for the fact that she's secondary in this. I don't want to frighten you, but you need to understand how my brothers speak of you."

"How do they speak of me?"

"With great anticipation to defile you. They have no respect for you. All you are to them is a sinner on her way to the grave." He takes in a shuddering breath. "They see you as nothing more than a shell of a human, fallen from God's good graces, a body they're meant to desecrate in His honor."

As he speaks, my heartbeat crescendos, and I imagine I can hear the sound of it echoing through the empty space in the cavern, each beat bouncing all around us. I watch the blue in his bright eyes swirl in the glow of firelight. I look for deception, for any trace of warning that he's only trying to frighten me. I see nothing but truth…truth and concern.

I'm suddenly overcome with awareness of how I've neglected myself, which was only partly intentional. I chose in many ways to put Delle's well-being ahead of my own because I'm so fearful for her and all she's going to face in these trials. I've focused on her to spare myself from fear. But I don't feel regretful about it, not in the least.

Yet I'm overcome with emotion by the reality of how I'm viewed by the Control. The truth is harsh spilling from Arlo's lovely lips in this strange, dark place. And being separated from Delle now, I can feel the weight of the truth I've been ignoring slowly lowering onto my shoulders, sitting heavily, and pushing me down.

A shell of a human…

Fallen from God's good graces…

A body they're meant to desecrate…

I draw in a trembling breath and all the emotions I've been shoving down for weeks come rushing out on the exhale. Tears well unexpectedly in my eyes, and when I blink, they slip down my cheeks as an echoing sob breaks free. I cover my face with my hands, trying to hide as the heavy reality tries to crush me with dread.

Then, Arlo's arms come around me, pulling me against his strong chest, embracing me as I cry. My tears stutter in their release at the surprise of him holding me, touching me, encircling me with warmth after enduring weeks of cold, lonely nights without companionship.

"Let me help you," he whispers.

I pull back to gaze up at him through a sheen of tears. His expression is somber, painted with compassion, and I hadn't expected it. I hadn't expected to see him looking at me the way he is right now—it shocks my heart. I nod slowly, agreeing to let him help me. Relief touches his eyes and I find it comforting.

His hands come up to grip my shoulders, and he dips his head, lowering his eyes to level with mine. "Will you let me bind you bare this time?"

I'd only gone as far as stripping to my undergarments in all our practice sessions before—not because I felt uncomfortable. Truthfully, I would have preferred to properly prepare myself for the first trial. I'd kept my underwear on because Delle and Theo were with us, because Delle was uncomfortable, unready, and I wanted her to feel safe.

Maybe I've done her an injustice in that way, neglecting to insist that she practice bare. She'll feel anything but safe in the trial, and now I worry I should've fought to prepare her more realistically.

And here I am again, neglecting myself in a moment Arlo has set aside for my own preparation. I close my eyes through a deep breath, letting Arlo's words float through my mind to remind myself that his brothers in God look forward to defiling *me,* not Delle. They only see me as the sinner who sparked Delle's rebellion.

A body they're meant to desecrate…

I shiver at the words in my mind, opening my eyes. I nod slowly, indicating that I will let him bind me in the flesh this time. I want to know what the rope will feel like on my skin when I wear it for seven hours in the trial. I want to be prepared. I want him to help me, and I have to let him.

Without saying a word, I reach behind to grip the zipper at the middle of my back, tugging it down to loosen my crimson gown. I push down the fabric at my shoulders, letting the long sleeves brush down my arms as they fall to my feet. Arlo's eyes lower to my chest as I unhook my bra, and my heart skips a beat at the way his light eyes darken—dark like the empty space of the vast open cavern beyond the flickering firelight.

I pull off the black bra, then bend to remove my boots before slipping off my underwear. As I rise, cool air swirls around me, and as it brushes across my breasts, my nipples harden into taut peaks. I find myself in sudden anticipation, wondering how it will feel to have him wrap the rope around my breasts, secretly hoping for a slip of his fingers brushing over the stiffened buds.

"Do you know how painfully beautiful you are?"

His words breeze past me, scattering in the darkness beyond.

He blinks and turns away before I can respond, moving to a spot on the rock wall a few steps away. I'm almost thankful that the darkness swallowed his words, that he turned away before I could reply. I don't know what I would say to that. I place a palm on my stomach, hoping to settle the flurry of pleasant stirrings in my gut.

I watch as Arlo takes a couple of steps toward the darkness, holding my breath in fear that he'll misstep and slip over the edge. He reaches up and my eyes follow his hands, stopping at the glint of metal as he tugs down a solid metal hoop. Lifting my gaze higher, I see there's a rock overhang there, like a ceiling from which the hoop hangs.

"I rigged it myself," he says, releasing the hoop. He's pulled it down far enough that it's visible in the firelight, the shiny metal reflecting the orange glow as it spins in a slow circle. "It's safe."

"What is it for?"

"Suspension. I'll put up a similar rigging for the trial."

I nod slowly, the darkness at the edge of the drop-off beckoning my glance, reminding me of a long fall with a painful death looming.

Arlo moves, stepping closer. "Trust me." He holds out his hand.

Mine is drawn to his like a magnet, my palm floating out instinctively to fill his. My skin tingles as my hand lands on his, and I realize we're skin to skin—I hadn't even noticed him remove his gloves.

I've noticed the burns and scars, but I haven't asked him about them yet, and I'm not sure if I want to. I fear that knowing vulnerable details about him will grow too strong of a connection between us—a connection I'll have to let go of when I meet my death.

The connection I fear already exists.

He guides me until I'm beneath the suspended hoop, standing behind me and positioning me where he wants me with his hands on my shoulders. I lift my head to see the metal hoop slowly spin just above me. His hands leave my shoulders, and only moments later, he begins to coil rope around my body, and though it's the same as every other time he's done it before, it's entirely different.

We're alone.

I'm naked.

I'm lost in these dark caverns, standing on the edge of a cliff.

He drapes rope around my front and ties knots along my back. I knew the braided twine would be coarse against my bare skin, but I hadn't expected it to be quite as rough as it is. It's not painful, it's just a feeling. It's a feeling that makes my pulse race to pump desire through my veins.

He twists and tugs, each small jerk of the rope threatening to drag me backward against him. I move one foot slightly in front of the other to plant my feet, to keep myself rooted to the spot because I fear colliding with him and knocking him off the ledge. I also fear feeling his warmth against my back, which will knock me off a different kind of cliff.

"Where did you learn to do this?" I ask quietly, hoping that speaking will distract me from the flood of chemicals rushing through my veins.

"From a book," he says. "There's a small library of texts hidden away on the third floor."

"A library of books on how to bind women?"

"Not just binding women. It's…" he hesitates. "There are many books there about the impulses and desires of men and ways to satisfy them. Most of them I find uninteresting."

"But ropes were interesting to you?"

He grabs my arms and brings them behind my back, forcing my elbows to bend. My forearms touch as they draw parallel lines across the middle of my back. He ties me this way, and my breaths quicken as he shifts me from relative freedom to bound and at his mercy.

If I fall, I won't be able to catch myself with my hands.

"It's not the ropes that interest me."

His hands fall away, and he's silent through several pulsing beats. I can feel his eyes on my back, and they burn my skin.

I'm almost relieved when the ropes start to move again, as he continues to twist, loop, and tug. Each drawing of the braided twine whooshes as coarse fibers rub against coarse fibers. The dangling ends whip against my flesh, each grazing touch threatening to startle anxiety and trigger another rush of adrenaline.

"It's the artwork of it that I find alluring." I feel the touch of his hand against my thigh before the rope coils around it. I look down, turning my head back to see him on one knee behind me, nimble fingers twisting a knot. "The way it twists and coils, the way it lays across tender flesh is a thing of beauty—true beauty." There's a pause. "I don't think I could ever dress another creature in bindings as beautiful as this, as natural as the way you look right here and now. The way you submit to it, with every inch of rebellion and every ounce of will that you have to fight…I'm overcome by your presence in front of me right now, Mercy."

The rhythm of his words excites me. Each panting inhale draws in a heated breath that sinks through my stomach, pulses between my legs, and slickens my cunt. Before I realize any time has passed, my thighs and ankles are knotted. I feel the heat of him move as he rises behind me, and his fingertips gently graze the ends of my hair, lifting a strand from the back of my neck.

"I mourn the length of your hair, starlight. But I'm not sorry that I cut it. I don't want any other man wrapping their hand around those perfect strands but me." He bends over my shoulder and his lips move closer to my ear. "I kept your braid," he whispers. "I couldn't bear to part with it."

A quake ripples down the length of my spine as he leaves me. He circles me, lifts a dangling end of rope that hangs from one of the many knots on my body, and reaches above me.

Looking down at myself, I find that I can see it—the artwork in his binding. The rope is so intentionally turned and twisted around my body, swooping across my chest and around each breast to cage them in, framing them as if they were paintings worthy of display. It's twirled beautifully down my stomach, spread across my hips, wrapped tightly around my thighs. I feel every inch of the crisscrossing along my back, and part of me wishes I could see it, because I understand what he means about it being beautiful.

And it isn't just in the rope itself.

Just as he said, I submitted to this. I stood still and let him position me, let him bind me in whatever way he wanted. All while standing at the edge of a cliff in a cavern so dark, I can scarcely see the opening through which we entered.

I submitted to Arlo Rainn.

I freely gave him reign to bind me, and in that, I gave him my trust.

Do I trust him?

How could I ever truly trust him?

"Ready?"

I look up at him standing squarely at my side, and though I don't know what he expects me to be ready for, I know that I am ready, regardless. With trust I didn't decide to give him—trust I'm not sure he's actually earned—I nod.

He tugs on a strand of rope at the center of my back that he must have fed through the metal loop above my head. I feel the pull of the binding as it shifts and scratches over my skin, and I yelp as my weight pitches forward with the lift. He tugs again, and I rise to my toes, calling out his name as the feeling of falling washes over me. His name echoes through the empty cavern as he works to fix a knot to hold me in place.

My body turns and sways as he works to do something, making my stomach lurch with nausea. But even the nausea draws a fear-induced desire down low in my gut.

My right leg rises as he tugs on a knot that's settled on the back of my thigh. Once my toes are off the ground, he bends my knee back, lifting my ankle from another knot placed there.

He secures me as I dangle with the toes of my left leg still dancing across stone, but then he lifts that leg, too. Within moments, my entire body is floating, suspended, laying parallel to the ground. I'm facing down and my knees are bent and parted, toes pointing toward the metal hoop that holds me up from the center of my back.

Arlo touches my hip, sending a shockwave through my body, but his touch only exists for a moment. He pushes, and I spin slowly. I make the mistake of looking out as I circle toward the dark abyss of the cavern, out beyond the drop-off. Panic overcomes me, burning through my veins like wildfire through brush, sweeping me into outright terror.

"I can't—" It's all I manage before my panicked, panting breaths overtake me.

I sense him moving, tugging, lifting, adjusting.

But all I feel is panic.

I want to clutch something, grab hold of something firm and stable, but I'm bound. The jerking feeling of suddenly falling hits me over and over again, and after several waves of it, I lose myself entirely.

"Take me down!" I shout, the eerie reverberation of my voice echoing back at me. "Take me down, I can't—"

I thrash in my bindings, trying uselessly to free my arms, but the movement only makes me swing and spin. I can't calm down, I can't relax. All I can think about is breaking free.

Then Arlo's palm lands on the back of my head, his fingers dig into my hair and grip it tight, lifting. He steadies my wriggling form with a single look as he bends to meet my eyes.

The look…

Blue fire glints in his steadying gaze, and the heat of it is unlike any earthly flame. It's something otherworldly.

Celestial.

The glimmering light of a burning star on the brink of explosion.

Eruption.

Corruption.

"Give in to the panic. Let go and give in to it, then let it be done. I've taken your control from you, and I'm not giving it back. Accept it. It's mine." He breathes out and tilts his head, narrowing his eyes with sinister, sexual, seductive intent. And with command, he speaks a truth I can't deny. "You're mine, starlight."

chapter twenty-six

Mercy

IT'S HIS TOUCH, his words, his breath against my cheeks. It's the whisper of acceptance from the shadows surrounding us that seeps through my skin, penetrates my bones, and settles me with perfect calmness.

Acceptance.

It's the peace that comes from acceptance.

I'm bound and immobile, suspended, and at his will.

I accept it.

I welcome it.

I embrace it.

Our gaze locks for moments as we share heat between us. I feel it burning from his eyes into mine and melting every molecule. It seeps through my insides and warms me deeply, sending a warm river of pleasure rippling through my core.

Arlo's grip on my hair loosens, then his hand strokes down the back of my head as a small but intense smile creeps up his lips—a smile filled with sinful intentions.

"You're mine," he says again, and I nod my agreement.

I am.

I am yours.

His fingers brush down my back, tracing over the lines of rope and slipping in between coils to touch my skin. He stops when he reaches the small of my back, his hand pressing to a flat expanse of exposed skin, rubbing a gentle circle. The ropes creak as they rock lightly in my suspension, though his hand keeps me steadily at his side.

"How do you feel?" he asks gently.

I pause, tasting my words and whether they're palatable enough to share before speaking. "I feel every molecule of existence. I feel like every atom in the universe is swirling beneath me, keeping me afloat."

He exhales heavily. "Sweet sin."

"Arlo…" I speak his name, but I'm not asking for anything.

Suddenly, I spin. His hands are on my body, turning me until I'm facing him. Then he reaches over me to grip two ropes that reach from the loop above to the middle of my back. He pushes on them, leans forward against them, and it causes my body to lift upward. He angles me so our gazes meet. His lips are parted and eyes are hooded as he lets them wander down my form.

"I've wanted to see you like this since I saw you hiding in that tree in the forest. Since the night you sinned, I've had images of you this way clouding my mind, stealing my peace, threatening to destroy my self-control. And seeing you this way now, in the flesh…it puts those images to fucking shame."

I don't know what to say, so I say nothing.

"I'm fighting sin, but, Mercy…" he pauses, leans close, and brushes his mouth over mine, "I want you to drag me to hell."

His lips are a flint sparking a flame between us, and I tilt my chin, capturing his kiss before he can steal it away from me. His pillow-soft lips press hard enough to bruise. His tongue is long and thick, sweeping past the threshold of my parted lips, tasting me with unburdened passion.

My arms twitch against my bindings, aching to wrap around him. As I wriggle uselessly, he palms the back of my head, gripping my hair and lifting my head away.

"No fighting," he pants, pressing his forehead to mine. "Be still. Practice endurance. I promise I'll give you everything your body is begging for right now."

"Touch me," I beg.

"Where shall I touch you?" he whispers, his breath hot as it breezes across my face. A playful smile touches his cheeks, tugging at the long dimples that draw such beautiful lines down his face. "Do you want my hand between your legs like it was in the forest?"

"*Yes.*"

"You'll have to earn it, then."

All at once, he drops me and steps back. I cry out with the rush of fear that grips me as I fall forward, my brain lagging in the knowledge that I'm suspended and secure, and not on the precipice of dropping into that dark abyss. The ropes snap me to a stop.

"How…how do I earn it?" I ask between panted breaths.

He grabs hold of me, stopping my body's sway. His hip presses against my side as his hands reach around my body and his palms find my breasts. I moan as he squeezes, kneading my flesh. "You earn it with patience."

I don't understand.

"Tell me how," I whimper.

His long fingers drag and dig before pinching my nipples, twisting, squeezing, turning painfully before releasing.

"Please…"

His touch turns soft, fingers grazing over the hardened buds and caressing gently.

"Stop begging." His voice is strained. "I know what you need from me without a word." His hands drag down my torso as he moves backward along my body, stopping to grip my hips to hold me steady. "But just as you'll be in the trial, I want you still and speechless right now. I want nothing more than your whimpers and moans, your acceptance of my touch."

I whimper, both as a natural response to his thumbs digging into my ass and to make it clear that I understand him.

"I'm going to touch you, Mercy." His voice trembles at this admission of his choice to sin with me. His hands drag heavily over the curve of my ass, tracing down the backs of my things. "I'm going to lick you, taste you, fuck you. I'm going to bring you to the brink of pleasure…" his hands stop at the bend of my knee and dig into my thighs, slowly pushing back up again, "over and over and over again."

His hands meet the crease beneath my cheeks and stop, fingers splaying, thumbs dipping between my legs and rubbing in small circles. "I'm going to bring you right to the cliff's edge of pleasure, and I'm going to pull you back every time before you fall."

"Why?" The single word slips out before I can stop myself.

One hand leaves me, then quickly finds me again with a sharp strike against my cheek. The slap reverberates through the darkness as it shocks me with pain, but the pain fades so easily.

"You will not give my brothers the satisfaction of your words in the trial. Do you understand me? Do not speak, do not beg for mercy, do not ask for more. If you can't control yourself, then I will gag you."

Why do I want him to control all of this? All of me?

Why do I want to give him that power over me?

He's as dangerous as any of the Control…perhaps even more dangerous for the fact that he can make me feel this way. I try to bring my shields up, to shut off the desire and lust which burns within me only for him. But trying to fight it only makes it burn deeper and hotter.

I resign myself to silence to please him, though I tell myself I'm doing it for me.

I feel him move behind me, his hands dragging down the insides of my thighs. Moments later, I feel his breath brush over the skin between my legs as he speaks.

"As much as I want to lose myself in you," fingers brush softly down my slick center, giving me a jolt of pleasure which forces a moan, "as much as I want to lose myself in this perfect pussy...*Fuck*." His warm, wet tongue touches me quickly, licking me cleanly from end to end. "I have to control myself to prepare you for this trial." Two fingers spear me, and I cry out as he sinks them deep inside. "Sweet sin. From this day until your last, Mercy Madness, you come for no man but me. You *only* come for me, starlight...and only when I tell you to."

This is something I prayed for but never imagined could be real. It feels precious to be claimed by one man and one man alone, to be consumed by him, pleasured by him...someday loved by him.

Not shared by him.

But I will be shared.

Arlo's fingers twist inside me, as if he turns the dial on my loud thoughts and forces them to silence.

There is no tomorrow.

There is no thinking about what will come in the trial.

There is only the touch of this man as he claims me as his.

Stroking, his fingers curl, rubbing with perfect pressure against some spot inside me that feels heavy as it aches and throbs. It's a spot that seems to condense every pound of my weight to that single spot. It's like I can feel his touch over every inch of my body as his fingers stroke and thump in that perfect place inside me.

My ears are filled with the echoes of my wetness as his fingers move, the creaking of the ropes as my body sways, and the reverberating echo of it all in the empty cavern.

My head drops all the way down, my hair dangling toward the ground beneath me. When his thumb curls around to rub my clit, my head snaps up again with a jolt. I have to bite down on my lip to stifle my cry, because more than anything, I want to scream out his name and beg for more.

But he said I'm not to speak, and I want to obey.

"That's it, Mercy. That's what I want from you." His voice is heavy, hot, and panting. "Get close for me, come right to the edge for me."

His fingers are expert with the way they work me, inside and out, two fingers rhythmic against my inner walls, and his thumb circling, rubbing just right. His other hand is wrapped around my thigh, holding me steady, and his warm lips trail kisses along the inside of my leg.

I feel it coming; I feel it burning and building. I'm throbbing with each stroke, aching with heat and need. My body is tense and tight and begging for release.

I want it.

I need it.

He's going to take it from me.

I pant and whimper as his stroking takes me higher and brings me closer to the edge. And just as it swells, clenching through my belly, just as my breath changes and my body stills with the anticipation of onrushing release, he takes it all away.

He pulls his hand back, his touch leaving me entirely.

I'm dangling on the edge and leaning, but instead of letting me go…he pulls me back.

chapter twenty-seven

ARLO

"NO..." SHE WHIMPERS, her head dropping forward with the disappointment of lost release.

Sitting back on my heels from where I kneel behind her, I bring my fingers to my nose and inhale.

Sweet fucking sin, this woman smells divine.

I dip my fingers inside my mouth, pressing them down on my tongue and dragging them out slowly.

It's exactly what I would imagine a fallen angel to taste like. Something so sweet it could only be forged in paradise, but so sinful it must have been cast out. Whatever kind of demon she is, she's mine, and I've never wanted anything more than this.

Am I willing to burn in hell for her?

For the taste of her cunt and a moment of bliss spent inside her?

My head aches from the turmoil of this passion for a sinner who brings such corruption to me. I fear I can only find the cure for this ache between her thighs. A demon possesses her, but it must be within me, too.

"Arlo?" she asks softly, sweetly, her voice whimpering with an edge of begging.

I pull my hand away from my mouth and press my palms to my thighs, bowing my head to take several deep breaths as I work to steady the frantic beating of my heart.

"I won't allow you to come for my brothers," I tell her. "I need you to learn how to control your pleasure, and not just when I take it away from you."

"I won't come for them," she whispers.

I shoot to my feet, rounding on her. She lifts her head high to look at me as I move to stand in front of her, straining her neck as she fights to meet my eyes. They only reach as high as my chest in her suspension.

I loosen the buckle of my belt. "What did I say about giving them your words?"

She responds with silence, and her submission screams loudly through it. It calls to me, drawing me closer.

"They're going to take you from every angle, in every way they can. I want you to know what it feels like to have your breath stolen from you while you're suspended this way." With one hand, I bring out my throbbing cock, and with the other, I tap beneath her chin. "Open for me."

Her tongue runs across her bottom lip before she tugs it between her teeth, hesitation and the desire to obey fighting between her lips. I want to give her the space to come to submission on her own, but I'm in physical pain for the way I need her lips wrapped around me. I've never ached so much for relief but in her presence.

More than that, my brothers in God won't give her a moment of mental space to prepare for their assault. They'll take from her when she's not ready to give.

The thought of it has blood boiling in my veins.

Yet, I have to prepare her.

I twist my hand so I can pinch her cheeks. "*Open*," I demand, and as soon as her lips twitch to part, I push my cock between them.

She whimpers at my intrusion, but I press forward, keeping the pressure until I'm sunk inside her, and I groan. "Fuck."

I move my hand around to the back of her head, fisting her hair and holding her steady as I force myself deeper than I should. She gags as I reach the back of her throat, spluttering around me, but I needed that protest from her body to stop me and force me to pull back—I'm so fucking lost in my hunger for her, I can hardly control myself.

I pull all the way out and she coughs. I let go of her hair and her head falls, dropping low as she sputters.

I'm about to reach out and tilt her chin for me again, but she lifts her head on her own. Though she can't raise her eyes high enough to meet mine, I don't have to see them to know they hold the force of her strength. She opens her mouth for me and waits.

Sweet sin.

"Mercy, you're killing me."

Quite literally, the lust she stirs within me inspires me to sin in ways that could lead to my death. And she'll be put to hers because she ran—she ran from the same violence and lust she stirred within Hyatt fucking Price. Jealousy and a need to claim heat me. A firestorm swirls in my gut, clenches through my stomach, and rushes blood to my cock.

I need to fuck.

Gripping her, I spin her away from me, and she cries out as I turn her swiftly and unexpectedly. I force her to face the looming darkness beyond the edge of the drop-off. Slinking my hands between the ropes that suspend her, I wrap my palms around her hips, hold her steady, and slam deep inside her.

A cry of relief bursts from her, echoing like a fallen angel's song through the dark cavern. Heaven and hell collide in our connection, in the dichotomy of celestial reward and punishment that makes this feel right and wrong all at once.

Pain and pleasure.

Sin and sacrifice.

Bliss and fury.

Tightening my grip, I push her forward, then drag her back against me, impaling her deeply with the hope she feels it in her damned, rebellious soul.

She huffs out a breath as I do it again, as I rock her away, then drag her back. I push her so she sways over the edge, dipping her starlight hair in the looming darkness, and I feel the tremor rip through her spine as the fear takes hold of her once more.

But that fear heightens her senses. I can feel the way her muscles tighten around me, the way her cunt contracts around my cock and begs for release.

I'm not giving her release.

I'm taking mine.

Push and pull, sway and slam. My pace quickens and her journey forward shortens as I pull her back to my cock with shorter, faster thrusts. I fuck her recklessly, painfully, angrily.

I'm angry.

A fury awakens unlike any I've felt before, screaming through the beat of my heart, raging through my veins.

But why?

Sway and slam. Thrust. Thrust. Thrust.

"Arlo," she says, and I feel her there, embracing my cock, trying to corrupt me with the pure, hedonistic pleasure of it all.

She's fulfilling my every desire, strung up in a dark cave with danger lurking all around us. She's submitted fully to whatever way I choose to use and abuse her. I could fall for her...I could so easily fall into this trap she's set for me. Yet, the voice in my mind calls to me, reminding me of the truth.

She's a wolf in sheep's clothing.

A demon disguised by human flesh—flesh that perfectly matches my every dangerous desire.

God is testing me.

I fuck her harder and faster. I dig my fingers into her fleshy hips to hold her steady instead of swinging her so I can give her the full force of my furious longing. Grunting and sweating, I pound into her cunt.

"Arlo," she chokes on my name, "it hurts…"

A feral growl builds behind my voice. "It's what you've earned, sinner."

I don't exist within my body. I hear my voice and the words I speak, but I feel powerless to control them. I only want the release I should have taken from her that night in the forest. I want it to hurt her for the way she makes me hurt. The longing is unbearable, and I can't have her. She'll be dead soon, and I can't even have her now without shame for what she's made me become.

"It hurts," she whimpers again.

It's as if the demon leaves her soul and enters mine, because her plea only encourages me to fuck her harder. I want to fill her deeper.

Leaning forward, I wrap one arm around the ropes at her midsection and pull back to keep her in place as I continue to move inside her. Once I'm sure she's firmly in my hold, I drag my other hand down her crack, teasing the tiny hole that makes her flinch when I touch it.

Turning my thumb and lowering it, I sneak some wetness away from her cunt and drag it upward until I reach that spot again. I should warm her up, stretch her, prepare her, but her demon tells me to claim her ass without preparation. It tells me she doesn't want to be prepared. She wants to be taken forcefully, painfully.

She wants to be mine.

But she'll never be mine, and soon, she'll be dead.

I groan with the pain of my thoughts as I push my thumb inside that tiny hole with a sharp thrust, causing her to scream and flinch, but that doesn't stop me. I press in deeper and harder. I fuck her faster, pulsing and pumping as the most painful kind of pleasure gathers in the base of my cock and swells. It throbs and pounds and begs for relief.

Dear God, give me relief.

Let me come quickly. Let this sin be over.

As if God Himself heard my plea and spurred it to spare me this pain, my release spills inside her without warning. The most intense pleasure I've ever felt tears through my soul. I shout out my anger, my shame, my absolute satisfaction into the dark void. I hope it will swallow our sins and hide them in the darkness forever.

I pant as I fight to catch my breath, still buried to the hilt inside her. It takes me far too long to come down from the high, but her soft sobbing drags me from the paradise of pleasure into the darkest level of hell.

She's crying.

She's crying because of me…because I hurt her.

I used her, and there is no full moon tonight.

If everything I've done with her before has toed the thin line that stands between my power and my duty, then this moment has been the hand on my back shoving me across it.

I drag myself out of her slowly, giving far more care than I did in fucking her. My grip on the ropes loosens gradually, and I pull my thumb from her with the gentleness I should've given her on the way in.

I stumble backward, then bend to lift my pants, working quickly to put myself back together. Her body slowly turns in my direction, as if spun by an unseen force that insists I come face to face with the pain I've caused. Her head hangs, short strands of hair dangling around her cheeks as her chest heaves with her panting.

I take a step back, then another, my spine hitting the solid wall of rock behind me as I watch her on bated breath.

And then she speaks, her voice sure and clear, but shaken with fear, and perhaps, disappointment. "Thank you." There's a long pause after those two words that stab me like a knife. "I feel very well prepared for what your brothers will do to me."

chapter twenty-eight
ARLO

I CLOSE MERCY'S bedroom door behind me as I leave her. I brought her back from the cave, cleaned her up, and tucked her into bed. She let me, and I don't imagine a day will ever come that I'll understand why.

She didn't say a word to me after I defiled her, after I used her in a way a woman should only ever be used in service under the full moon. The only thing that feels worse than her silence is knowing she'll keep my sin a secret for me. I wish I had doubt about that, but it's something I can feel. She's a woman of her word, and whether her word is sinful or saintly, I know she'll hold true to it.

"Where have you been?" I'm startled by Killian's voice as he comes down the hallway. "Theo said you were working with Mercy." His hands are lifted behind his head, retying his long hair into a knot.

"I was." I turn and walk toward him, meeting him after a few steps.

"But Delle's in bed. He said she wasn't feeling well."

"Right. And that's why she and Theo weren't with us."

Killian's eyes narrow as his hands fall to his sides. He tilts his head to regard me with suspicion. "So, you were alone with Mercy, then? Where?"

A tight grin flattens my lips. "Is there a problem? Mercy is my ward. It's my job to take care of her between the trials."

He looks down with a huff of amusement, then steps closer. An accusatory smile spreads across his cheeks as he lifts his head to look at me. "How exactly have you been...taking care of her?"

I know exactly what he's accusing, but I play dumb. "I'm not sure what you're asking. I've been taking care of her in the traditional sense. You know, feedings, cleanings, meeting basic needs. The pets need fresh air and exercise on occasion, too, so I took her for a walk."

I'm lying openly, but worse than that, I hear myself as I speak of Mercy as if she were a dog. Speaking of her that way feels like a sin greater than tying her up and fucking her.

Killian's expression turns serious. "Where did you walk?"

"Through the forest."

"Really? So Wesley didn't see the two of you coming out of the courtroom? What were you doing in there?"

Caught in my lie.

"Intimidation," I rush to cover myself. "She was being unruly, so I brought her there to remind her of her place."

He presses his lips together and nods slowly, his eyes narrowing to slits as he considers my words. "I see." He reaches out to clap me on the shoulder, hand gripping in a friendly gesture. "You should be cautious in the time you spend with her. The brothers are starting to speak of you."

"In what manner?"

"Ryker says you look at her with longing."

"And?" I shrug, causing him to drop his hand from my shoulder.

"I've noticed it, too."

"All of us have looked at her with longing; she's an attractive woman. I don't understand the point you're trying to make."

"Don't let the sinner poison your mind, brother. We're concerned for you. There's a darkness inside her, and if you're not careful, she may bewitch you into sinning right along with her."

Too late to save me now, brother.

"I'm well aware of what she is, Killian. I have my method of relieving temptation when it's present." I lift my hand, showing him my leather glove as a reminder of my own manner of self-control.

"Right," he says. "But is a single burn upon your hand enough to remove the temptation of her from your mind?"

No.

"Yes. Is there a point to this conversation? I have other matters I need to tend to. I'd like to check in on Delle."

"I'm sure Theo has his newly appointed ward well cared for."

"I'm sure he does," I cock my head, "yet, somehow, I still find myself concerned for her well-being as a member of this community, and so I'd like to check in. Are we done?"

His stare lingers for a beat, his grin contorting into an accusatory grimace before he takes a step back. "Yes, of course. By all means, go and check in on Delle."

I side-step and move past him until I've reached Delle's door just a few steps away. He moves with me and pauses at my back.

"Just remember we're here for you, brother."

I turn my head over my shoulder and grant him a tight smile before he turns and walks back the way he came. Once he's passed a couple of doors, I lift my fist and knock softly, quietly, wondering if Delle is asleep and not wanting to disturb her if she is.

But quickly, the door swings open.

It isn't Delle standing behind it…it's Theo.

He holds a finger to his lips, indicating I should be quiet. "She's sleeping," he whispers, then waves, beckoning me to enter quietly.

I follow him into her spacious room and glance across at the regal bed. Sure enough, Delle is tucked in, sleeping soundly, peacefully. The room feels somber and tranquil—a welcome reprieve to the tension I feel every moment I'm with Mercy.

Theo moves to one of the two armchairs along the wall across from her bed. I move to sit beside him, in the chair angled toward his.

"How is she?" I whisper.

"She's fine. I don't think she's ill. I think it's the stress of the upcoming trial that makes her feel unwell."

I nod. Laying my arms on the armrests, my fingers curl around the edge.

"And Mercy?" he asks after a few silent beats. "Is she okay?"

"I don't know whether she would use the word, 'okay,' but she's settled for the night."

"Did you take her to the caves?"

"Yes."

I feel his eyes on me, heavy and warning. "Do you think that was a good idea?"

I turn my head to look at him squarely, casually lifting my ankle to cross over my knee. "Why wouldn't it be?"

The lies are coming again, and it twists my stomach.

"I'm just concerned about how it looks when you're alone with her."

"And aren't you concerned about how it looks when you're alone with *her?*" I incline my head to indicate Delle, sleeping in her bed.

Theo rakes a hand through his sandy blond hair. "Perhaps I should be." His gaze fixes on her sleeping form. "I find myself overwhelmed with worry for her well-being," he admits. "I know I should distance myself. She's in the trials now, and there's nothing to come from caring about her. She's just so small and frail…so young."

"Even if she weren't in the trials, there's nothing to come from it," I remind him. "Even if she weren't a servant, you know you wouldn't be allowed to choose the domestic assigned to you at your retirement."

I need the reminder myself, though admittedly, it shocks me with a sharp pang through my chest. The Shift happens every twenty-five years in Ember Glen. It happened a few years ago, when the previous members of the Control retired, and me and my brothers in God were selected to take their place.

Three of those retiring were elected to be the new Elders. The previous Elders and the other retired members of the Control were assigned domestics and sent through the caves to the Land of Kings. There, they would live out the rest of their days in blissful retirement, happy with their domestic women and the children they bear.

No one returns to the village of Ember Glen after going to the Land of Kings. It's said the Impulse doesn't exist there—it's a holy land where no man is burdened by violent or sexual needs. And only those who have served Ember Glen as members of the Control become worthy enough to go there. Even so, they're not granted their choice of a domestic partner—that person is selected for them. One day, domestics will be chosen for me and Theo.

"I know," Theo whispers, and I hear pain in his words. I feel it, too. "The ache of compassion is a burden all men of God must carry."

Yes, he's right.

It's written in the Impulse Edict.

True men of God may feel compassion for the people they serve, but it doesn't mean that compassion has been earned by those who've sinned. It doesn't allow us to ignore the sins of our people. They must still be punished, and their pain is a burden we must carry.

Mercy must still be punished.

Regardless of my compassion for Mercy and Delle, regardless of my attraction to Mercy, my desire for her, my overwhelming need to sin with her again—*fuck*—I must recognize my compassion is a fault of my humanity and not reason granted by God.

Even as I think of this, every thought pounds with the ache of dissonance through my skull. When it comes to Mercy, all my thoughts feel painful, aching, throbbing with discordance against the harmony I held in my soul, harmony I'd earned through a lifetime of faith and acceptance of truth as it was written in the Edict.

Delle rolls in her bed, an innocent whimper slipping out in her slumber, and the sound of it returns a memory of a girl named Luna who was once my sister. We share the same mother, the same eyes and smile. She's five years younger than me, but we were always close.

I only see her in passing now. My place with the Control doesn't allow me to recognize my family as mine. I'm allowed to speak with them if we cross paths in the village, but it's rare. My role as the authority of Ember Glen requires disconnection and objectivity—the subjectivity of one's feelings clouds judgment. I feel that cloudiness when I'm with Mercy, yet through the fog of her, I can see so clearly.

She's a contradiction of my faith.

Mercy's compassion for Delle mirrors the protectiveness I had for Luna when we were younger. I used to help care for her—not because I had to, as that was my mother's role, but because I wanted to. Luna was always bright, kind, and playful. She was always laughing and joyful. I don't ever see her that way now when we cross paths in the village. She has a permanent frown etched upon her face, always chasing after one of the three children she bore as a domestic. I think she's about to have another.

As I think of it, I realize how there's such a stark difference in the demeanor of the children of Ember Glen and the women that so many of the daughters grow to become. Their joy seems to have left them, but surely, that can't mean they're unhappy.

Maybe Luna would have been happier as a servant?

The image of it strikes me, a sixteen-year-old Luna bound and strung up for my brothers in God to defile in the first trial. My stomach lurches at the thought of it. I feel nausea tear through my gut and angry tension tug at my muscles. My fingers curl around the armrest, digging into the fabric.

What if Luna had done something stupid when she was sixteen?

What if Luna were in Delle's place right now?

How can I let this be done to her?

I have to let this be done to her…don't I?

"Perhaps we don't need to carry the burden of compassion in this case." The words escape me before I even realize I've opened my mouth.

Theo's eyes narrow on me. "What do you mean?"

"Mercy pled her case to take on Delle's burden."

"And she failed. Delle must complete the trial for herself."

"Yes, she must. There's no way around that. But does that mean that you and I can't find a way to…shift the burden if we can't remove it completely?"

Theo straightens in his seat, turning and leaning toward me on his arm. "I'm listening."

"Our brothers ache to punish Mercy, and for good reason. She's older and more experienced in service. She's the true rebel we worry could inspire others to rebel with her. She's already the focal point of these trials. No one really cares about making an example of Delle."

"You're suggesting that we capitalize on that."

I nod. "It wouldn't be difficult to ensure that our brothers' excitement for the punishment be directed at Mercy. Many of them already speak as if she's the only one on trial."

He inclines his head as he regards me with confusion. "Why would you want to do that for Delle? Why would you want to do that to Mercy?"

"Because Mercy is a temptation to me," I admit, though it doesn't sit well in my stomach. "Perhaps her temptation deserves to be punished. It's women like Mercy who inspire girls like Delle toward dissension."

Theo nods and slowly turns his head to look out in front of him, gazing toward where Delle sleeps in her bed. "You're right. We'll inspire our brothers to direct their punishment toward the one who deserves it most."

This is right.

This is necessary.

I feel the ache of shame brew within me, a sense of guilt that I'm somehow betraying Mercy in this. But I'm not beholden to her, and I owe her nothing.

She'll be dead before long.

chapter twenty-nine

Mercy

SERVICE OF THE Flesh.

The first of my three trials begins in thirty minutes.

I stand facing the full-length mirror in my bedroom, still fully clothed and wondering why I even bothered to dress today. These garments will be stripped from me soon. The crimson gown made of silk, which clings to my curves but covers me so modestly with its boat neck and long sleeves. The black bra and panties I wear beneath it, the garter belt holding up my black stockings, and even the boots on my feet will be stripped away.

My fingers play across the silk at my thighs, gripping it and lifting enough to show my boots beneath my dress. All the servants wear shoes like mine, and in a way, wearing them now makes me feel bound to them, serving as a reminder of the role I was selected to serve within this community.

Perhaps I should have shed them when I entered the Homestead and worn the difficultly tall shoes left for me in the wardrobe instead. Perhaps wearing the boots as the last symbol of my servitude should make me sad.

But it doesn't.

In some strange way, the connection to the servants makes me feel stronger. They were my sisters, and I loved them dearly—I still do. They're women I care for, even if I could never understand the joy they find in service, even if I could never reconcile my changing beliefs with their own.

Regardless of what's in our individual minds, we're the same inside, and my compassion for them knows no bounds.

I recall the looks on Ellary's and Cambria's faces when I tried to speak with them at Ivy Jane's memorial. They were heartbroken, devastated, and disappointed in me for sinning—because they believed that what I'd done was truly a sin. And though I'll never agree with them on that, I don't fault them for the beliefs that have been fed to them since birth. It's not their fault they believe what they believe. I don't judge them for it, and I don't love them any less.

Still, I feel lonelier than ever in these moments before my punishment is set to begin—the beginning of the end for me—and my boots make me feel just a little more connected to the sisterhood that once loved me as much as I love them.

I hear the door at my back click open, then close again gently.

It's Arlo.

I know without looking.

I feel the pulse of him as he crosses the room, slowly making his way toward me.

I drop my dress to cover my boots, then give myself one last glance in the mirror before lifting my eyes to meet his reflection. He stops behind me, his handsome face peeking over my shoulder in the reflection, regarding me with an expression I can't decipher.

We stand this way for what must be minutes, watching each other in the mirror, each of us trying to read the other for their aching thoughts in these moments before my defilement.

He's the first to speak. "It's a shame I'll have to remove the dress. You look lovely."

I glance down, then look up at his reflection. "I don't want your compliments, Arlo."

"I didn't mean it as a compliment. It's simply the truth."

"What do you want?"

"I want to help you."

"This time is meant to be mine. Can't you allow me some moments of peace before it begins?"

"That's why I'm here."

My brows furrow as my eyes narrow, and I spin to face him, meeting the perfect blue pools of his eyes with intensity. "You're presumptuous to think I can't find peace on my own. Do you think I can find a moment's peace with you? When I look at you, all I feel is fury."

It's true that I feel something intense when I look at him, though perhaps fury isn't the right word. If it isn't, then I don't know what other word to use in its place.

"I know I hurt you," he says, his gloved hand reaching up to tuck my shortened hair behind my ear.

The mere presence of his touch coaxes my head to tilt toward his hand, and he cups my cheek. I want to lift away, but I don't—I can't.

"I went too far with you, and I hurt you. But let me help you now."

"How could you possibly help me now? Do you understand what I'm about to go through? The pain, the shame, the horror I'm about to experience at the hand of your brothers in God?"

His jaw ticks. "You sinned, and it's your penance."

Fury is certainly the right word now. I lift my head from his palm, raise my dress at my thighs to keep from tripping, and move away from him. I walk across the room and stop at the end of the bed, reaching out to wrap my hand around one of its four posts.

I feel him at my back moments later, not touching me, but there all the same. He's so close I can feel the heat of him, and my fingers tighten their grip around the post.

"It's your penance, Mercy, but I still care about you…and I want to see you through this. Let me see you through this."

I turn my head over my shoulder to look at him, but I don't lift my eyes to meet his. I'm not even sure what to say to him right now, let alone what I would do if I let myself search for sincerity in his perfect blue eyes.

He steps closer, his heat rushing into my back. Delicately, his fingers play at the zipper of my dress where it touches the nape of my neck, resting over the seven scars marking me for the trials. I breathe slowly as he draws the zipper down. I see no sense in stopping him because I'll have to undress all the same.

But also…

My pulse quickens, my spine shudders, my breaths deepen at his touch.

The dress falls open as his fingers reach the top of my underwear. With my head still turned over my shoulder, I see him work to remove his gloves, and my lips part with anticipation of his next move.

I hate him and everything he stands for.

I hate that I can't force myself to loathe him.

I hate myself for feeling anything at all in his presence.

"I know you found some moments of peace with me in the cavern."

His bare palms flatten against my back, slipping up from the center beneath the split fabric, then grazing over my shoulders and pushing the sleeves down my arms. My shoulders shrug with tension at his touch— tension for the fear of it, tension for the desire of it.

His fingers trail down my arms as he pushes off the long sleeves, his touch trailing down my skin. Then his hands fall to my hips, nudging the tight gown over my curves and shoving it to the floor.

Lifting my hand to grip the bed post again, I step out of the ring of fabric dropped at my feet, and he kicks it aside before coming in closer, closing the distance between us. I startle at the way he invades my space so completely, so quickly, his warm hands slipping up my sides and stopping just beneath my breasts.

He pulls me back against him and sweeps his nose through my hair. I feel him breathe me in, and it's as though he inhales all my tension, taking it away from me and letting it seep inside him to unburden me.

I can't trust him.

This man has hurt me. He's used me. He's sinned and asked me to keep the secret for him. Arlo Rainn is not a good man—he's just not.

So why does my pain slip away whenever I fall into his arms?

"Warden Rainn," I whisper, keeping formality to try to distance myself from him again, "the trial hasn't begun yet."

He exhales in a rush as his hands slip around me, caressing my stomach, wrapping me into a close embrace. His head comes over my shoulder and his cheek nuzzles against mine. He hugs me close, and I don't want him to let go. I almost want to cry for the way he draws me in and takes away my loneliness.

I hate him for it.

I could almost love him for it.

"My brothers in God may use you today, but you are still mine."

His.

My hand leaves the bed post, intent on pulling his arms away. Instead, my arms cross over my belly and lay on top of his where they hold me, reveling in the comfort he offers. I lean back, letting him take the weight of me, allowing him to claim me for this moment.

"I don't want to share you," he says with a broken voice, planting a kiss on my cheek, then peppering a line along the side of my jaw.

Then don't.

Keep me.

Steal me away from Ember Glen...I'd rather face whatever is beyond the mountains.

I don't speak as he kisses a trail down the side of my neck, as he stops at my nape to nuzzle and lick and nip in a way that has me drawing in trembling breaths.

"I don't want you to go into this frightened, Mercy, not fearful and tense and dry. I want to give you something to hold on to through the next seven hours." My hands fall away as his slide across my stomach, running up my sides, palms reaching around to cover my breasts. I gasp as he gently squeezes. "No one has said you aren't allowed to enjoy this."

I shove his hands and try to step forward, but I only run into the edge of the mattress. "No. I'm not going to enjoy them."

He envelops me in his embrace, pulling me back again, hands roaming and groping me everywhere. I struggle against him for a moment, but I quickly fall victim to our confusing connection, to the combustible chemistry we share. I sink in his hold as one of his palms rubs flat down the center of my stomach, reaching low between my legs, over my underwear.

"I promised you," I pant, breathless, "I promised I would only come for you."

His fingers curl and he cups my sex to claim me. "And you will only come for me. Your greatest pleasure, Mercy, your peace today, will be found in the anticipation of it."

His fingers stroke gently over my underwear, drawing out a whimper of desire I hadn't expected him to be able to draw out of me. His other hand moves up my stomach as he speaks, traveling toward my breast.

"You won't come unless I tell you to. Even if you feel it building, even if your pussy aches for release, you will not let it overtake you without my permission."

How dare he demand such a thing?

I know it's wrong of him—he shouldn't be touching me at all right now—but the way he speaks, the way he wants me, the way he touches me lulls me into a submission that I struggle to fight.

I hate this.

His fingers dance across the mound of my breast and hook over the lacy black cup. He tugs it down, exposing my nipple to the cool air, and it hardens instantly. His hand continues moving, sliding over my chest, slipping up my throat, and cupping beneath my chin. Then his thumb reaches up to brush across my bottom lip.

"Open," he commands, and I obey.

He slips his thumb past my parted lips, gently pressing inside and running the pad of his thumb over my tongue. He gathers wetness there before bringing his hand down my chest and circles his wet thumb around my nipple. His cheek is pressed to mine—every part of him touching every part of me—as he speaks with command.

"Stay out of your mind and fixed on your senses. Find pleasure in the pain, sanity in the madness." He continues to circle my nipple, causing shocking jolts of pleasure as his other hand slips down into my panties, his fingers caressing my pussy. "Focus on feeling good without the release; remain in your heightened sense of anticipation, and when you're trapped in the purgatory of need, rely on me to release you."

I'm not sure I hear half of his words, or that I even understand the ones that I do, but his sultry voice is hypnotizing, intoxicating, lulling me into pleasure in the minutes before my trial is set to begin.

His thumb circles, his fingers brush and stroke, playing without purpose or intention, simply drawing me into lust. I moan, and my body rocks to seek more from his hand, which is buried in my underwear. At my movement, his hand stills.

"Don't seek," he says. "Take what's given to you and find peace in the pleasure of it. Don't chase release...it will only bring your pleasure to an end that much faster."

I want to protest his words and his actions in this vulnerable moment. What he's asking of me is deplorable. He wants me to find pleasure as his brothers use me but for me to stave off release until he grants it to me himself. He has no right to ask anything of me; he has no right to have his hands on me right now. His sins are so much worse than my own, yet I'm the one subjected to this disgusting punishment.

But even as my lips part to tell him this, I can't force out any sound other than a moan or a whimper, and I've never been so ashamed of myself.

He makes me feel shame, yet I let him.

I don't know how much time passes as we remain this way, my weight slumped against him as he strokes below and circles above. He works faster, drawing out my quickened breaths and desperate pleas, and then he slows again, stops altogether, then starts from the beginning.

It feels like forever and no time at all when he slowly pulls his hand from my panties and covers my breast with the lacy fabric of my bra.

He lets out a breath that's like fire against my scalp as it rustles my hair. "It's time," he says, and my heart drops like a lead ball, breaking past my ribs and falling heavily into my stomach.

I turn to face him and our eyes meet. I expect to see heat, but I don't expect to see regret. The recognition of it is jarring, and it nearly makes me want to cry. I press my eyes shut and focus my attention to the wetness he created between my legs, the throbbing of my swollen clit, and the need for touch that prickles beneath my skin.

Stay out of your mind and fixed on your senses.

It's as good advice as any going into such a horrible event. My mind has always been my own worst enemy, so maybe I'll make it through the next seven hours if I keep myself out of it.

Maybe Arlo knows what I need more than I do.

He bends to grab his leather gloves from the floor, but he doesn't put them on. When he rises, he sucks his fingers clean, the regret gone from his eyes and replaced with fiery desire.

"My focus will be intent on you tonight. I'll take care of every need you have before you even know you have it. You will survive this, starlight."

My heart grows wings at the nickname.

I know I can't trust him; I shouldn't. But somehow, I have faith he will take care of me; at least, in the ways I can't fathom needing caretaking in an event such as this trial.

It's the first of three, and though I know I'll survive this trial—even if it breaks me emotionally—I also know I'll be dead soon enough, and none of this will matter.

The way he sparks lust, the way he makes me hate him, the way he makes me feel so ashamed of myself, the way he claims me...none of it matters. I'll let him have this control over me because it makes no difference to my fate to deny him.

Because somehow, I can't bring myself to deny him.

chapter thirty

ARLO

I LEAD MERCY down the grand staircase in her undergarments, still wearing her black servants' boots. My heart thumps painfully against my ribcage as I spot my brothers standing around the tile starburst in the center of the foyer. All of them are there, waiting for Mercy, except for Theo and Owen. Killian, Ryker, Wesley, and Park turn their heads, watching Mercy as I lead her like a lamb to her slaughter.

Words I never expected to think about the Trials of Dissension blast into my mind—thoughts I'd never expected I could have for the punishment faced by a true sinner.

Depraved.

Abusive.

Abhorrent.

Something primal within me roars with the need to lift her over my shoulder and run from this place, far and fast. But there's nowhere to run. Even if there were, I know what's really happening within me.

It's the demon within her. The part of her that makes her sin has embedded in my heart, and it claws at my conscience. It tells me all the things I've always known to be good and godly and true are wrong.

It lies.

It can't be that everything I've ever known is wrong. It can't be that the doctrine, the Impulse, the Edict, the laws, and rules we uphold as members of the Control are wrong.

They're not.

They can't be.

Regardless of the connection I have to her, she's a sinner and she brought this upon herself. This is the punishment she's earned. It's her penance. It's her only chance at forgiveness and for her soul to be saved.

And it's my job to see her through it.

Our feet touch the foyer and time stands still. Mercy trembles at my side while my brothers spare a look to appraise her appearance. Wesley rubs his palms together with anticipation, and Ryker's grin is alarming.

Killian steps forward, crossing the sunburst, and stops in front of us. "Mercy Madness. We're finally here. I think this has been a long time coming. No sense in delaying the inevitable." He pauses, his eyes traveling down her form and back up again. He claps his hands together before spreading his arms wide. "Let's get this started, shall we? Wesley will lead prayer and the incitement of ceremony."

Killian steps back and I touch the small of Mercy's back. She jumps, startled by my touch, and her head snaps sideways to look at me. I want to give her something, anything—a look, a nod, a smile of encouragement.

Yet I give her nothing, and I don't know why.

Her throat bobs as she swallows, blinking, dragging her eyes away from me with the loneliest expression I've ever seen. I immediately feel sick about it, but I think the emotional distance between us is good for the moment... necessary.

She moves forward, carrying herself with grace to the center of the sun. She lifts her head to look up, noting that the chandelier has been removed, replaced by a suspension system that replicates the one I'd rigged in the caves. Candles have been placed around the room to create a flickering glow around us, and though the chandelier is gone, a single yellow spotlight has been fixed to the ceiling to shine down precisely on Mercy where she'll be suspended.

Every head in the room snaps to my left when we hear the click of a door from a bedroom that's just down the hall. Owen steps into the hallway, and just behind him are Delle and Theo. Delle is softly sobbing, tears streaming down her cheeks as she clutches her silk black robe. Her eyes scan the foyer as she approaches, and as she takes in the men all staring back at her, she draws her shoulders back and lifts her chin. It's a show of strength, though it's clear her strength is waning.

Depraved.

Abusive.

Abhorrent.

I have to press my eyes shut and suck in a deep breath to force the words away. We're only doing our duty to God. I have a purpose in this, and I must serve it. I must focus on Mercy and helping her pass this trial. The only thing I can do for her is to try to save her soul.

I've already worked this out with Theo. I've already made sure that Mercy will take the worst of this trial to spare Delle as much as possible, because I know that will weigh on Mercy's mind. Delle's pain must be spared to spare Mercy an emotional burden to her compassion.

Theo stops Delle by gripping her shoulders, and he turns her to face him. Silently his lips move, whispering something to her that we can't hear. Her eyes flutter shut and her lashes catch tears as she gives a single nod. When she opens her eyes again, she moves down the hall with grace, walking forward until she reaches the foyer. Taking in a shuddering breath, she removes her robe and drops it to the floor, revealing herself in her underwear and bra.

My eyes turn away from her, though I can't say the same for my brothers. I feel something strange roil in my gut at the sight of her lithe body. Her slenderness and slight curvature indicates her young age so clearly and looking at her as we're meant to now feels...wrong.

There's no reason that it should, yet it does.

I try to rectify this odd sense of shame that ripples inside me, but I can't seem to shake it. Not as Delle crosses the room in front of me and moves beside Mercy.

Sweet Mercy.

She reaches her hand out for Delle as she approaches, and quickly takes her palm, pulling her closer to her side. Mercy gently sweeps Delle's long hair behind her shoulder, and I feel regret—perhaps I should have cut Delle's hair to avoid my brothers twisting and jerking at the strands to control her. It's too late to think of it now.

Mercy leans and whispers in Delle's ear, words I can't hear, though I know they're filled with kindness and encouragement.

Mercy's compassion knows no bounds.

My head aches from the turmoil of contradictions—the compassionate sinner with starlight hair before me.

Delle nods at Mercy, and together, they lower to their knees.

Theo and I move to take our places, standing behind our two wards on the sunburst with a spotlight shining down on us. Killian turns on a camera which is placed on a table six feet in front of us. It clicks and rolls, and within moments, it will broadcast the scene live to the village of Ember Glen. Large screens line the village square from east to west, parallel to the front of the Homestead manor. For seven hours, the villagers and servants will be able to watch Mercy serve the first trial.

Only Mercy, not Delle because Theo and I worked together to direct our brothers' excitement toward Mercy. Delle will be closed off in the room from which she entered tonight, bound and suspended the same as Mercy, used the same as Mercy, but not watched the same as Mercy....and hopefully, not as brutalized. My brothers have far greater interest in the theatrics of it all, and greater still in punishing the true person of dissent—the real rebel, the girl with the fire that could burn everything we know to ashes if she's not stopped.

Sometimes I wonder if Mercy understands the true threat she poses—I'm not even sure I have a full understanding of it. But we all know it's true that if she had the time to grow, to spread her influence with the servants of Ember Glen, she would. Her strength is only budding, and my brothers are eager to nip it.

Wesley moves with an air of ceremony, slowly working his way to stand in front of Mercy and Delle, facing the camera. His long dreadlocks are pulled together behind his back, wrapped with an elastic to keep them off his shoulders and out of the way for the night he intends to enjoy.

He rubs his palms slowly, solemnly in front of him, his head bowed slightly. A red light clicks on above the camera, indicating that we're now live-streaming in the village square, and Wesley lifts his head.

I feel no anxiety or fear pulsing from Mercy's back because all her attention is focused on Delle and providing her the comfort and strength she needs. I glance down to see Mercy squeeze Delle's hand tighter as she turns her head to look at her. I shuffle closer and strain my ears to hear as she leans in to tell her something.

"Have faith in yourself above all else," Mercy whispers to Delle. "Your strength is within you. These men don't control it, only you do. And I have faith that you'll find the best of your strength through these hours. You can endure this, and you will." They smile at each other, and an extra beat thuds in syncopation through the rhythm of my heart.

Then Wesley begins to speak.

"October sixth, twenty-one eighty-five. We gather days before the full moon to bear witness to this Service of the Flesh, the first of the three Trials of Dissension for sinners Mercy Madness and Delle Carter of Ember Glen. We welcome all who belong to the community of Ember Glen to bear witness to this trial, such that it brings awareness to the hardships that await servants who sin.

"It has been decided by the authority of Ember Glen that this trial shall be carried out by the seven members of the Control, who shall seek sexual service from the sinners over the course of seven hours. The sinners shall be bound and suspended for the entirety of the period, exclusive of two brief breaks to service their biological needs. Each break shall last no longer than ten minutes." He pauses. "Mercy Madness shall be the only sinner streamed for viewing in this intimate trial."

Mercy's head jerks up. "What?" she says with audible surprise.

"As the instigator of the events that prompted Delle to fall into sin and volunteer to participate in these trials, we, the Control and the Elders of Ember Glen, find this to be most appropriate given the circumstances."

Wesley side-steps, bringing Delle and Mercy into full view of the camera where they kneel in front of me. He turns sideways to speak to me and Theo.

"Arlo Rainn and Theo Hughes, as the selected wardens of these trial participants, please present them for this Service of the Flesh."

I step closer, close enough that I can see the way Mercy feels my presence at her back—it's evident in the way her shoulders stiffen the moment I move into her space.

"I present Mercy Madness for the first of these three Trials of Dissension. Mercy, do you enter this trial with the understanding of your sins and the means by which you are required to serve?"

She hesitates, but strongly replies, "Yes."

Theo speaks next. "I present Delle Carter for the first of these three Trials of Dissension. Delle, do you enter this trial with the understanding of your sins and the means by which you are required to serve?"

A small sob wracks her narrow shoulders, but she replies with a whimper, "Yes."

I take a step back as Mercy turns her head to the left, giving Delle a quick smile, but I see she uses it as a guise for looking back at me. Her eyes strain to look behind her, and I wish I could catch her gaze with mine.

Wesley moves in front of the girls again. "Let us share a prayer before we begin."

Clasping our hands in front of us, we all bow our heads, even Delle… but not Mercy.

Facing forward, she pulls her shoulders back as if to make it more obvious, clear that she refuses to pray. It should enrage me—and in many ways, it does—but it also impresses me. I'm not impressed by her defiance or her insolence; rather, I'm impressed by her commitment to rebellion. It's wrong and it's sinful, but regardless, it shows her strength.

I catch my brothers' stares as they notice from beneath their lashes, Killian turning his bowed head ever so slightly to look at Ryker beside him with a look of disgust on his face. He's disgusted by Mercy's show of rebellion, and that won't bode well for her in the upcoming hours.

My pulse is steady, but heavy, insistent through each beat that I have something to be concerned about with Killian.

I have nothing to be concerned about.

These are my brothers.

I swallow my conflicting feelings and close my eyes to shut them all out, to listen to Wesley's prayer and say a silent one of my own that God will find a way to remind me of what's right and true, that He'll guide me back to my purpose here in Ember Glen and take away this sinful longing I hold for Mercy.

"Our celestial creator and divine spirit, we come to You in this hour of trials and tribulations, seeking good favor in honor of our righteous choices," Wesley continues. "We bring these sinners before you, offering the sacrifice of their service in honor of the Impulse Edict, to the sanctity of Your divine word. We ask for Your righteous judgment of the souls of these sinners. Should they serve appropriately through these trials and prove themselves to be truly sacrificial servants, we ask for absolution of their wretched souls. Please grant me and my brothers of the Control the strength and stamina to carry out this trial to the greatest extent of our endurance, such that we may present these sinners with a fair and exhaustive trial for their souls. *Malo mori quam foedari.*"

"*Malo mori quam foedari*," we all repeat.

I open my eyes and lift my head at the same moment Killian steps forward to Mercy. "Say it," he demands, moving closer against her side.

She turns her head away in response, his belt buckle level with her eyes. "Say it, sinner," he demands. "*Malo mori quam foedari.*"

Bravely, she turns her head and lifts her chin high to meet his eyes. I don't have to see them clearly to know her stare has enough heat behind it to birth a thousand stars. She glares at him silently, refusing to speak a word.

This is perhaps the stupidest she's ever been. Either she doesn't understand or she doesn't care that my brothers loathe her and her rebellion. They're eager to show this woman just how wrong she is for standing against our values, against the authority they've been granted to uphold the sanctity of our community.

And she refuses now, in the moments before they prepare to take her and do vile things to her precious flesh.

I latch my fingers around the back of her neck. She cries out as I jerk her sideways, bending over her, coming in close and demanding with clear, concise insistence, "Say it, Mercy. Now is not the time to show your defiance."

I toss her forward before releasing her, and she drops to the floor, catching herself on her palms, which slap against the tile. She stays in place, chest rising and falling with her heavy, angry breaths.

Her silence continues, and my brothers close in, Killian dropping down to one knee at her side. He snatches her chin viciously in his hand, jerking her head up until she's forced to look at him. "I'll ask you one more time, sinner. Finish the prayer. *Malo mori quam foedari.*"

I know it's about to happen before it does—she's done it to me twice before. My heart kicks up in a flurry, punching adrenaline through my veins as I lunge for her, reaching out in hopes that I can cover her mouth before her furious boldness takes hold of her.

But I don't reach her in time.

She spits in Killian's face, and hell descends.

The circle closes around her as voices raise in a chorus of righteous indignation. Though I wish I could drag Mercy away and protect her, I know I can't.

Watching the rapidly shrinking circle, my concern shifts to Delle, the tiny thing who's just been knocked sideways by Ryker trying to slip around her to Mercy, blocking Theo along the way. I take my urge to protect and give it to Delle, because Mercy is beyond my help. I charge forward and pluck Delle from the floor, placing her on her feet just as Theo darts between Owen and Park to arrive at her side.

I lower my voice, though none of my brothers are listening anyway—they've busied themselves in taunting Mercy. "Take her, bind her, suspend her. Don't delay, it will draw questions." I look back at the group surrounding Mercy and nausea cuts through my stomach. "I'll encourage them to use Mercy as much as I can."

Mercy has served for four years.

She's older, stronger, braver.

And though Delle may have grown to become those things, right now, she's young and naïve, fragile, in need of care. Mercy is prepared to take this trial, and though I'm feeling oddly sick about what's happening to her right now, I know she will endure.

I'll make certain of it.

Theo nods and drags Delle away, back through the door from which they came, and closes it behind him.

I take a deep breath and turn to face the center of the foyer. My eyes behold a sight as reverent and terrifying as flickering firelight. In the center of the sun stands Mercy, naked, her shoes and undergarments already violently stripped from her body. Her fists are clenched at her sides and her head is bowed slightly as she fumes, dragging heavy breaths through her nose like a dragon preparing to breathe fire.

Sweet sin.

While my brothers look to me expectantly—ready for me to bind her and suspend her for them to use—I look directly at her.

"Mercy," I say sharply to gather her attention. I wait until she lifts her chin and meets my gaze, dark storms swirling through her gray-blue eyes. "Stay out of your mind…" I remind her of what I said earlier, to stay out of her mind and fixed on her senses.

It's a reminder that she can release her rage and try to find pleasure in this. But I can see she's already gone, lost to her anger.

And I don't know if I'll be able to bring her back.

chapter thirty-one

Mercy

STAY OUT OF your mind…

He dared to say it as if I could simply switch off this rage and allow this to happen to me. As if I could simply come out of fear and find some pleasure in this twisted rite. The men tower above me, surround me, cage me like an animal, and it's how I feel.

I'm ready to hiss and growl; ready to bare my teeth, show my claws, and scratch anyone who comes too close.

Malo mori quam foedari.

Death before dishonor. Though the men of Ember Glen speak it, it's not meant for them. It's meant for *us*—the servants. These vile creatures who call themselves men dishonor themselves and the humanity they claim to have more often than any woman in this village does. But we sacrificial servants are expected to seek death with pride, rather than sin in dishonor.

They live by the Impulse. As though women have none—as if servants have no purpose in this life but to meet their filthy needs. I desire, I rage, I feel intensely, just as men do. Yet I'm expected to repress it all for the sake of serving their uncontrollable needs.

It's disgraceful…*dishonorable.*

They should stand naked on this sun instead of me, be bound and hung, defiled and humiliated for enforcing the tenants of the vicious god they serve.

If they want to reduce the quality of their existence to being ruled by impulses, they can go right ahead. But I will not. I am more than an urge to act violently. I am more than a man ruled by his sexual needs in moments of weakness.

I am more than they want me to be.

And through my fuming rage, I know there is only one way to show it. Spitting fury, flinging words of hatred, screaming, and fighting the inevitable won't prove how much better I am. I must meet them with the dignity and grace of my entire being. I am not a raging impulse of emotion to be satiated by outbursts. I'm a woman—something stronger and far more spectacular than they'll ever be.

I breathe in deeply, and on the exhale, I force my shoulders to release their tension, my fingers to unclench from fists, my heart to calm from this passion. I search my mind for a breadcrumb of calmness I can follow along a path to serenity, and when I find it, I run toward it.

Stealing Arlo's gaze, I lower to my knees on the hard tile floor and cross my arms behind my back. "Start the damn clock."

Arlo's eyebrows flatten to a straight line and his eyes narrow to scrutinize me, his lips parting on a slow, steady exhale. Everyone's attention is pulled toward Arlo…watching and waiting. He's the one who must bind me and string me up for them. He's my warden, and his actions alone will determine when this nightmare officially begins.

Air catches in my lungs, threatening to reveal my sudden fear, but I shove it back down, refusing to show my weakness. Arlo steps slowly, his feet moving with a dull *thud* on the tile as he comes toward me. He stops in front of me, then holds his hand out at his side. "Bring me the rope," he says to everyone and no one.

Something sparks behind his eyes, something mad and powerful. I'm not quite certain if the look terrifies me or turns me on. It shouldn't turn me on, for heaven's sake. Not a single moment of this should, regardless of whether he's here. I'm enraged and horrified, and there's no room for lust. Except…the way he looks at me could easily set my insides on fire.

Someone places a length of rope in Arlo's hand, but I don't know who because I can't tear my eyes away from him. Winding the rope around his palm, his eyes skate over my naked form, drinking me in, taking his time. Then he moves so unexpectedly that it startles me, and my shoulders jump as he circles around me.

Inch by inch, he dresses me in coarse rope. Each twist, each tug, each drag of the rope across my skin cheats me into a shameful state of anticipation. It's as though he uses my anger as fuel for the fire he lights within me. I can hear his every breath as he works close to me, as he takes liberties to graze my skin with his fingers and draw sensations over my body.

I try to fight it when he jerks on a knot that tugs me backward, but his force is too strong. My lips part as I attempt to draw in a steeling breath, but it blows out shakily. I feel this way for *him*. Loathe as I am to admit it, I feel things for Arlo Rainn. I feel things that no one is allowed to feel. I feel things that are beyond the scope of reason. I feel things that could nearly restore my faith in a higher power—if only it weren't for the circumstances.

I want to fight the heaviness between my legs as my mind wanders, recalling his touch and the way he made me swell. I want to fight the pebbling of my nipples as ropes sweep across them before tugging tight around the mounds of my breasts to frame them. I want to fight the pull of tension through my core. But Arlo's voice whispers through my mind.

Moments later, it whispers against my ear. "Your strength is unmatchable. Don't let them take it from you." He speaks so softly that I have to strain to hear him—but at least I know none of the others will. He moves away from me and takes command, speaking loud enough that everyone can hear him. "Stand."

With Arlo's hand gripping my elbow, and my arms bound behind my back, I slowly climb to my feet. As soon as I'm steady, he lets go of me and begins looping the rope through one of the metal hoops dangling above me.

I tilt my head to look up at it, focusing on the rope as it moves through, trying to ignore the fact that I'm standing naked in the foyer of the Homestead with nearly every member of the Control surrounding me, staring at me, eagerly waiting for their turn to put me in my place.

My place is dancing on top of their fresh graves.

My jaw tenses as I lower my head to level, squeezing my eyes shut tightly, breathing through the heated resentment. In a heartbeat, the resentment disappears, giving way to a jolt of panic as the ropes around my body tighten, lifting me sideways from the ground. The knots that pull me into suspension are positioned along my side, just beneath my hip, and around my left ankle.

Hoisting me up, I hang sidelong to the ground. Arlo adjusts the rope so my body forms an angle, my head slightly higher than my hips. My left leg is straight, the knot around my ankle aiding in suspending my leg, and once it's secure, he reaches down, tapping my right knee, closest to the floor.

"Bend," he orders, and I do it, eager to lift my dangling leg as it hangs uncomfortably without support.

Bending my right knee and kicking my ankle back toward my bottom, he binds my leg to keep it that way, forever bent, kneecap pointing toward the floor in such a way that it keeps my thighs spread wide…

Accessible.

The familiar panic I had felt in the caves pricks in my mind, sending an electric current of frightened awareness rushing beneath my skin.

His hands leave me altogether, and I'm left to hang, settling in the ropes for a few moments. I listen to the sound of them creaking with the light sway of my body.

Then, a warm, heavy palm presses to my belly, an arm skimming along my side as it reaches around me from behind. I turn my head skyward to look behind me, and the air rushes from my lungs in relief. The hand belongs to Arlo. He's still right there at my back, running his palm down the center of my stomach.

Lower and lower he travels, and with each inch, my pounding heart beats a little faster. His fingers run down the tuft of hair before dipping between my legs.

"Let's see if you're ready for us, Mercy Madness."

My body twitches against my bindings as his fingers slip low, bending to press inside me and finding the wetness he dragged out of me in my bedroom. A low moan escapes me as he caresses, finding that wonderful spot inside and pressing against it with a perfectly pressured rhythm.

"Perfect," he mutters, catching my eyes and holding my stare.

How does he do this to me?

Damnit, how does he do this?!

Never once have I responded like this in service, not to anyone, not to a single other man.

Because none of them were him.

There is no one like him.

His lips curl in a smirk, drawing the lines of his dimples through his short beard. "This is how you serve, Mercy—with a warm, wet cunt that's prepared to take."

There's something odd about his words and the way he says them. His tone seems disingenuous. His words sound as though they're meant for his brothers, and not for me. He told me he didn't want to share me. He made me promise my pleasure was only for him. He had no right to say such things to me, but he did, and I feel they were real.

The way he speaks in front of the Control now, trying to come off as unaffected by my onrushing defilement, feels dissonant with how I know him. And I know him more intimately than anyone. He has to behave like them, speak like them, but the way his fingers move inside me whispers his truth.

He wants to help me through this.

He wants me to find pleasure if I can.

If it were only him using me, I could remain like this forever.

Then, someone else's hand touches my breast, and everything within me begs to shut down. My thighs clench, my inner walls squeeze around Arlo's fingers, but not with pleasure—with pressure to force him out. His fingers go still inside me, though he keeps them there all the same. Reluctantly, I turn my head to find my eyes level with Killian's belt buckle as he puts his hands on me.

"I'm going to enjoy painting you with cum," Killian says with a strangled voice. "I'll have you whispering the prayer you refused to speak between breaths as I choke you with my cock."

Panic pulses through my adrenaline-riddled veins, but then Arlo moves his hand again, dragging his fingers out and rubbing over my clit in perfect little circles.

I'm horrified by Killian's hand on my chest, but I can't ignore the perfect swirl of Arlo's fingers between my legs. A sickening swirl of disgust and lust storms through me, drawing me into a state of sexual awareness that begs for filth.

I hate it.

I'm sickened by it.

Yet pleasure builds in this detestable carnality.

Before long, Arlo has effortlessly stroked me toward an unwanted release.

Unwanted in every sense but physical—physically, it's needed.

He forces me up a cliff I don't want to climb because Killian's hands are on my breasts, kneading painfully, plucking harshly at my aching nipples. I can see the way his cock strains against his black slacks. When his hand falls to grip it, squeezing it through the fabric, the sparking madness within my mind combusts, burning in a blaze of misery.

I turn my head back to look at Arlo. "I don't want it," I whisper, though I'm breathless, panting, needy.

My thighs ache and twitch.

His pace and pressure remain steady, a blue flame in his eyes imploring me to finish. And just as I'm brought to the top of that peak, nearly ready to burst and tumble over the edge, he rips his hand away. He stops just before I detonate.

I cry out in frustration and confusion.

"Not yet," Arlo says, and I watch him back away.

He retreats as Ryker, Wesley, Park, and Owen close in around me.

He leaves me alone to the sound of belt buckles unlatching and zippers coming down. Five men with dark intent sketched across their faces encircle me, tower above me, strike me with fear, disgust, shame…all while the traitorous pulsing between my legs begs for a hand, a tongue, a cock—anything to put me out of my misery.

In front of me, I catch Arlo's movement beyond the outer rung of the sunburst on the tiled floor. Between Killian and Ryker's intimidating bodies, I watch as Arlo lowers to sit in a plush ivory armchair. I watch as he crosses his ankle over his knee, rests his elbows on the armrests, and steeples his fingers.

"Warden, shall we begin?" It's Killian's voice, but I don't look at him. I can't tear my gaze from Arlo and the way his eyes shift. It's like he's looking at me, but also looking past me…looking right through me.

Our connection is lost, and all that exists are the men who condemn me to be a creature used for their pleasure, all in the name of saving my soul.

In a moment of weakness—or perhaps, it's strength—I silently beg for mercy from an entity I don't believe in. I pray to a god who doesn't exist because no man will save me, I can't save myself…I'm alone in this. Even the man who promised to see me through this nightmare has stepped away, disconnected, and left me alone to endure this trial.

God help me.

Please, God help me through this.

With a brief nod, Arlo begins my ruin. "Let the trial begin."

— end of book one —

acknowledgments

Mercy and Arlo's story has been in my mind for well over a year, and I can't believe this first part of their trilogy is complete! Stepping into a dystopian world to write their dark romance was no easy feat (world building in itself is a challenge), and I wouldn't have had the determination to go for it without all the people who hold me up while I'm writing like crazy.

I have to thank my husband and kids first, as I couldn't do this writing thing without their patience and support. Hubby, I appreciate all the time you give me to work on my art, knowing how important it is to me.

To Danielle, my incredible PA and amazing friend, thank you for doing the hard work of cheering me on when I'm struggling with writer life. I know you think you don't do much, but in reality you do *so, so much* for me. I couldn't do this without you!

To Danielle and Mary for your beta reads, and Maria for your notes early in the book, thank you so much for the time you spent and consideration you gave to my story. You've always been such an incredible support system for helping me to make my stories the best they can possibly be. Echo, Amanda, and Brandy, I appreciate you jumping in at the eleventh hour to do a read through and give me some last minute notes. I appreciate all of you more than I can express!

To my street team and ARC team, I absolutely adore you. Your support and love for my books humbles me. Thank you for sharing, reviewing, and helping other readers find my books!

Najla, Nada, and the team at Qamber Designs, thank you so much for making my book look beautiful! I adore your team and the work you do is always spectacular. I can always count on you to create gorgeous covers and stunning interior design for my stories.

To my incredible editor, Silvia, you are the best! My words are pretty okay when I send them your way, and you somehow always manage to polish them to perfection. I feel so fortunate to have you as my editor!

I also want to thank Candi Kane PR, Xpresso Book Tours, and all the book bloggers who've read, reviewed, and shared my work. I appreciate you all so much!

My final thank you goes directly to you, reader. You picked up this book, you read the words I wrote, and for that alone, I am grateful. If you connected with the characters or the story and enjoyed this read, just know that you and I have met through these words, and I'm forever thankful you took the journey with me.

blaze
of
misery

EMBER GLEN | BOOK TWO

BRYNN FORD

playlist

Stream on Spotify
bit.ly/spotify-brynnford

Seven Devils by Florence + The Machine
Black Hole Sun by Soundgarden
In Flames by Digital Daggers
Love and War by Fleurie
Take Me to Church by Hozier
Can You Feel My Heart by MOTHICA
Lost My Mind by Alice Kristiansen
Just Found Heaven by Daughtry
London by Starbenders
Heaven or Hell by Digital Daggers
Can't Help Falling in Love (DARK) by Tommee Profitt ft. brooke
A Little Wicked by Valerie Broussard
Battlefield by SVRCINA
Fallout by UNSECRET & Neoni
Solitude (Felsmann + Tiley Reinterpretation) by M83

For all the women condemned by the rules of men…
Lift your chin, raise your voice,
and give them hell.

chapter one

I CALL FOR the desecration of Mercy's flesh with four echoing words. "Let the trial begin."

I expect there to be some pause, a moment's delay or hesitation before the same level of debauchery as a night of service falls upon Mercy while she's strung up in the foyer of the Homestead. But there is no delay. My brothers in God have waited for this moment to punish a true sinner, and it's evident they do not intend to waste a moment of their seven hours of torture.

An invisible fist curls around my heart, squeezing with a vice-like grip as I watch them descend upon her. I try to ignore the way that fist tugs through my chest—as if it comes from Mercy's outstretched hand, trying to drag me toward her…except her arms are solidly secured behind her back. She couldn't reach out to me if she wanted to.

Does she want to?

Or has she lost all faith in me?

Air leaves my lungs as Killian slips his palm around the back of her head. My eyes widen as his fingers tangle with her hair, tightening his grip. He jerks her head back, and Mercy cries out with a sharp, grating sound. I fight the urge to shove to my feet.

"Open your mouth," Killian demands, and her hesitation is clear.

Of course, she doesn't open for him. She holds on to the last fraying thread of her defiance as he pulls out his cock. I already feel the anger of my false possession brewing.

Mercy is mine.

She's mine, though she doesn't belong to me. She belongs to God, and we are nothing more than the men who help make our women godly.

She sinned.

She earned these trials as her punishment—her chance at redemption for her soul. Yet I'm starting to wonder how this trial proves anything at all.

I can see Mercy's throat bob as she swallows the last dregs of her refusal, then opens her mouth to meet Killian's demand.

"Good," he says, then presses his cock between her parted lips.

My body tenses and jumps at her whimper, and I nearly leap from my seat with the urge to tear him from her, to slam my fist against his jaw, and punish *him* for making her taste him. Sucking in a heavy breath, I force myself to lean back in my chair, fingers interlocking as my palms come to rest at the back of my head. I lift my eyes toward the ceiling as I work to gather my composure.

Regardless of her suffering—regardless of my *own* suffering—I can't stop this.

I *won't* stop this.

It's better they focus their efforts on Mercy than Delle. Mercy's strong; she has experienced every sexual act imaginable in her years of service, and though she's never served multiple men at once, she can do this. I have to let her—not like there's a choice in the matter.

Still, the sound of her gagging as he forces himself to the back of her throat is challenging to ignore. I drop my hands to my lap, bringing my head down to level. The way he's moved in front of her to alter his angle blocks my view of her eyes.

I want her eyes fixed on me.

I want her to remember that I'm here, that I'll take care of her. I want her to remember the way I touched her before the trial began and encouraged her to find pleasure here, any way she can.

Ryker strips naked, then steps in close against her backside. His hand slides down her lower back, over her ass, and he reaches between her legs from behind. Mercy's muscles jerk against the tension in her bindings as he roughly rubs his hand over her cunt.

I shove to my feet before I can take another breath and stomp across the tile. I come to a stop in front of her, close enough that she can see me while my brothers remove their clothing, preparing to defile her. Her watering eyes meet mine, and I've never seen such despair in her gray-blue gaze. It slices right through me—it pummels me with her aching, twists me with her anger.

Ryker's hand is moving, collecting her wetness, dragging a trail of it backward along her crack. My jaw sets with the primal need to fight him away from the prey I've claimed. Mercy yelps as Ryker's fingers play at her back entrance, and Killian pulls out of her mouth long enough to dip and grip her chin, forcing her eyes to meet his.

Killian leans close, his nose touching hers. "I hope his cock rips your insides apart." His voice is a venomous hiss.

A devious grin spreads across Ryker's cheeks as he tosses his head back to shake the dark blond hair from his eyes. Ryker lines up and thrusts, pushing inside her forcefully. Her screams intrude my ears the same way Ryker intrudes her body, and I feel her pain in the deepest parts of my soul.

Killian slaps his hand over her mouth to silence her as a tear slips down her porcelain cheek. A pained shudder ripples through me, and it causes every nerve ending to pulse with raging pain against the rigidity I must maintain to avoid interference. Mercy's expression scrunches and strains as Ryker fucks her ass with brutal force and a relentless pace.

She wasn't ready for that.

I should have had the fucking foresight to prepare that part of her body for this. I should have spread her wetness there myself, should have stretched her, played with her, loosened her up.

I failed, and now he's fucking her, and she's hurting.

It's my fault she's hurting.

Hardly five minutes have passed and it's the most torturous five minutes of my life.

How can she endure seven hours of this?

How can I?

I have to make it better.

Stepping closer, I reach out, seeking to touch between her legs and draw her back into pleasure, but her eyes snap to mine with fury. She practically growls against Killian's hand with a feral sound that halts me—it sounds like a strangled, "No."

Killian moves his hand, as if he's interested in knowing what she has to say.

Her face is puckered with rage, and she spits the words at me with fury. "Don't you fucking touch me!"

Led by her command, I yank my hand away, and I immediately know it was a mistake. Regardless of the fact that I feel things for this woman that I'm not allowed to feel—regardless of my odd compassion for her as a sinner enduring this trial—I must continue to demonstrate my authority, lest my own sins be found out.

I'm a sinner, too.

Perhaps I should be strung up beside her.

I shake my head to snap myself back to the authority I must represent. I step forward, moving in close, and before she can give my brothers the satisfaction of her angry words again, I bring my fingers to her pussy and slip them inside her. She gasps, jerking her head back. I can sense her protest as she opens her mouth, but Killian halts her words by shoving his cock between her lips again.

The weight of the world settles painfully on my shoulders.

I need to be seen as a willing participant in her trial.

I can't stop this.

I can't stop them.

I want nothing more than to end this, to end it *now* and take her back to the caves where I can hide her away from this world, where I can hold her in the darkness and bring her comfort. The only comfort I can bring her now is pleasure, and though I hadn't intended to let her come so early in the trial—though I know she has so much yet to endure—I can't help myself. I can't bear the sight of her eyes squeezed shut in misery.

Ryker and Killian fuck her from both ends with a shared rhythm that almost seems intentional—a rhythm that ensures she always feels one of them buried deep inside her without reprieve.

Though my breath catches in my lungs and my eyes burn hot, I do the only thing I can. I gently stroke my fingers inside her, coaxing her into pleasure. Her eyes snap open and her stare locks on mine, though her mouth is filled with *him*—Killian, a man I've always viewed as my brother in God, though at the moment, he looks like a fucking demon.

Maybe he's possessed by her demons the same way I am. The thought stirs jealousy in my gut. I prefer that her demons possess me, and me alone. And though it should be because I'd want to spare my brothers of the sin she inspires, it's not for that reason at all—it's because I want to be the *only* man Mercy's demons invade with thoughts of depravity.

I *am* the only man who gives her pleasure, and I intend for it to remain that way.

"Come for me, Mercy," a strangled voice demands, and it takes me moments to realize it was my own.

I sense Killian's eyes on me as I bring my thumb down over her clit, rubbing relentlessly as I stroke inside her.

The scent of her arousal swirls in the air around us, each stroke of my fingers kicking up a little bit more of her lustful aroma. It intoxicates me with desire, hardening my cock.

I hear them moving, rutting, groaning as they use her. I sense Killian's oncoming release in the way he holds her head and angles his hips, fucking her mouth faster and harder. The anger inside me has nowhere to go, so it shoots down my arm, spurring my fingers to work harder, faster, more intentionally.

"Sinner, you're going to make me come so quickly." Killian chuckles. "*Fuck*. I'm going to come all over your face, and then I can take my time to really show you what a sinner deserves."

My arm jerks involuntarily at his words and my fingers spear too harshly into Mercy. She whimpers as he pulls out of her mouth, wraps his hand around his cock, and strokes in quick, short jerks.

"Stop..." she pleads, but her eyes aren't on him...they're on me.

chapter two

Mercy

STOP, STOP, STOP, please *stop*.

I'm filled and tense, my muscles cramping and twitching as I fight the building climax Arlo tries to draw from me.

I don't want it.

I don't want his touch in this moment because it doesn't feel good. Though my inner walls clench around his fingers and a tingling pressure beneath his circling thumb tells of an onrushing orgasm, there's nothing pleasurable about it.

I feel like my insides are being ripped to shreds by Ryker, and every involuntary spasm inside my pussy makes me clench against him painfully. I've been fucked there before, but not like this—never with such relentless pounding, never so dry and unprepared. Men don't care if they hurt us in service; they only care if they enjoy themselves. The way Ryker pounds inside me makes his intention clear—he doesn't care about his own pleasure.

He only wants to hurt me.

And Killian, with the hatred in his eyes, the way he shoved his cock so deep, blocking my throat where I couldn't breathe…Now he strokes his cock, and I have the misfortune of spying the spot of pre-cum beading from the tip.

I want to scream, but I've already given them too much of my voice. I gave Arlo my voice, yelled at him to stop, yet he hadn't. His fingers remain inside me, and I never could have imagined his touch ever feeling so horrible. I don't want to tell him to stop again because it hurts enough that he hasn't already. It hurts that my gaze holds his, that our eyes are locked and he sees my pain, yet his fingers remain.

Ryker's cock swells inside me, adding pressure to the burning pain that scrapes along my insides. Killian devolves to vile thrusts against his hand and vulgar panting as he approaches his climax.

With a deep thrust, Ryker hisses and spills inside me. Killian jerks himself to orgasm, intentionally aiming and splashing his cum across my cheeks, and I pinch my eyes shut against the pulsing release. Arlo pulls his hand away—*finally*—as though he was only waiting for his brothers to finish.

He's right there, yet I feel so far from him.

Ryker pulls out from behind me, and I sense Killian's foreboding presence move away. I try to take a deep breath, to relish a moment of emptied relief before they start again. But the moment I inhale, another cock touches between my legs—a quick brush across my slickened cunt before slamming inside me. The jolting pressure forces my eyes open to see Wesley standing before me, angled between my legs, cock buried deep.

Will the next seven hours be so relentless?

How much time has passed? Minutes? Seconds?

My head rolls, seeking a place to rest in dejected exhaustion, but it only rolls aimlessly. Strung up the way I am—angled sidelong to the sunburst tile beneath my swaying body—my neck strains in all directions. I let it drop and hang sideways, gravity tugging it toward the floor. It stretches tightly through the side of my neck, causing my hair to drop over my face, sticking to the fluid Killian sprayed across my cheeks. I shut my eyes in disgust.

Then a hand slips along the side of my face to cup my cheek, easing the strain through my neck as my heavy head is lifted. My heart flutters, and for a moment, I believe it's Arlo's touch returned to comfort me...but when I open my eyes, I see that it's not.

It's Killian. He lifts his other hand to gather his cum from my cheek and swipes it across my lips with his fingers. He presses at the seam with his fingertips and urges me to open. I jerk my head toward the ceiling to try to shake free from his grasp, but he curls his fingers, tangling them into my hair, gripping the strands tightly to hold me in place.

"Open, Mercy Madness. This is what your sin tastes like." He bares his teeth with the righteous indignation that burns within him...it burns within me, too.

"Only a demon would have cum that tastes like sin," I say without thinking, my need to insult him overtaking any sense of reason.

His eyes flash with fury, and he rushes to push the sticky substance into my mouth while I'm still speaking, forcing his coated fingers between my lips. I whimper against the intrusion, and as the repulsive taste of him rubs across my tongue, I clamp my mouth shut, snapping his fingers between my teeth.

Killian curses, jerking his hand back as fury and madness overtake me. I throw every ounce of hatred into the force of it as I spit out his vile fluid. I take pride in watching it spew against his cheek, causing him to flinch as it lands.

Momentarily, I feel satisfied.

And then the satisfaction is gone, replaced by sudden, overwhelming fear.

I can't run from this. I can't fight. I can't hide…and I'm alone.

I'm alone.

Where's Arlo?

I can't feel the pulse of him nearby, and I mourn the loss of it. Without him near, I am entirely, utterly alone in this.

My breath catches as Killian's temper flares, dreadful intent glaring at me through his raging eyes. Fear grips me as sadness replaces my anger, my heart pounding out a steady, pulsing rhythm that begs for Arlo to return.

Come back.

Come back.

Come back.

Killian grips my chin with one hand, digging the fingers of the other deeper into my hair to jerk my head back. He comes forward in a rush, pressing his lips to mine, opening his mouth against mine, then biting my bottom lip, hard. He tugs at it, stretching the skin beneath my lip as his teeth sink sharply without care. He releases, and when my lip springs back into place, I taste blood…all while Wesley fucks me.

I'm weak.

All I can think about is the insistent pounding behind my ribcage, my fervent need to not be alone in this, my unexplainable need for Arlo.

Come back.

Come back.

Tears flow, sobs wrack my lungs, and I cry.

I'm horrified by my reaction. I'm showing so much weakness when I'm meant to show strength, to meet their disgrace with my grace, just as I have for years in service. Yet, I can't stop the tears that fall.

Arlo made me weak.

I close my eyes, uninterested in seeing Killian's pleased reaction to my pain, but I can hear him chuckling, feel his hand pinch my chin and angle my head higher.

"That's perfect. You're giving us exactly what we hoped for. Let every tear fall from your wretched soul and purge it of the liquid sin that runs through your veins. Perhaps if you cry enough, there will be absolution for you yet."

Absolution.

They could etch the word into my skin, and still, it would never find me.

There is no absolution for my soul. There is no God so worthy of worship that He would create a ritual such as this for one of His daughters to reach it.

So if this is God's will—if the one they worship does exist—then I dissent.

Killian moves and Owen appears before me, naked and seeking my mouth while Park comes around behind me. His hand disappears between my cheeks to find the spot Ryker had already desecrated.

With sorrow and outrage and a weakened, broken soul, I silently beg for Arlo with the painful pounding of my heart.

Come back.

I can't survive this without his presence.

chapter three

Mercy

I'M DRAINED AND dry. There isn't a single ounce of liquid left inside this body. After three hours of use, my tear ducts have dried up, my cunt is raw and sore, and the hole behind is scratched and stretched and throbbing. Of course, they were prepared for that to be the case, and have resorted to the use of slickening oils to ensure their comfort. It makes no difference to me—it all hurts, regardless.

Five men have come on me or within me—most of them have done both within the first few hours. Arlo hadn't left, like I thought he had, but maybe worse than him leaving is the fact that he sat in the armchair across the room this entire time…tense and watching. Like he was waiting for something, but I don't know what.

While Ryker finishes fucking me—coming with a groan and a deep thrust inside my pussy—I scan the room. My lax, drooping head tugs an ache through my neck as it hangs sideways, gravity pulling it toward the floor. My hair sweeps across my face and some strands stick to the sweat, filth, and bodily liquids drying on my cheeks. Ryker pulls out and steps away, releasing me. Left alone in my bindings, my body slowly turns.

I think I'm a dying star, the lonely twin of the sun painted on the tiles beneath me. I'm forever dangling, gravity pulling me toward her—it feels as though I'll never reach, as though I'll remain tethered and reaching forever. I'm burnt out, my energy draining, and all I want is to fall upon the sun beneath me and burn in her light, to drop from these ropes that bind me and burn to ashes as I fall through the fire.

For moments, I spin alone, stillness finding me for the first time since the trial began.

Am I still in the trial?

Or am I strung up in hell?

A gradually turning image of Arlo comes into view as I spin toward him. My gaze catches sight of him as he moves to rise from his seat. I don't feel anything about him as he crosses the foyer, heading in my direction. I blink slowly, my vision strained from dryness now that all my tears have been shed. He's a step closer with every blink, and I wish I felt something for that. I wish I felt comforted, that I felt some relief as he moves closer.

But I only feel alone.

He turns my body to face away from him, and his hands tug at my bindings, lightly brushing against my skin as he handles the rope. I think he's untying the knots that keep my right knee bent, loosening them, untangling them.

It must be break time.

I'm allotted two breaks during this trial—ten minutes granted as a reprieve from my misery before I'll be bound and trussed up, used and abused all over again.

Arlo pulls the ropes free from my bent leg, and my foot drops toward the floor. My muscles are tired and weak, and I think my toes would've jammed against the tile if Arlo's hand wasn't there to guide it down. My foot feels heavy, numb and tingling all at once. I don't have to put weight on it yet since the rest of the roping still holds me up, but I press down through that leg all the same, feeling relief to put pressure on my tingling toes.

Arlo moves to my drawn-out left leg, which is held straight and holds knots that keep me suspended. He loosens those knots, then gently lowers my leg to the floor. He reaches above to pull and slacken the line while shifting a hand to curve around my hip. He presses me down, encouraging me to kneel.

My body slumps, and I sit back on my heels, bending at the waist and curling forward. My head drops low in shame and exhaustion. Then his fingers graze my flesh as he undoes the knots at my back. He doesn't say a word as he unties me, freeing me from the binding that traps me in this hell on Earth.

Once my arms are freed from behind my back, they drop weakly to my sides. I hadn't realized how exhausted I'd grown when the ropes held me up, but now I feel so tired and overwhelmed, beyond ready to be done with this.

Arlo swoops his arms beneath me and scoops me up from the floor. I don't have the strength to throw my arms around his neck, so I just let them dangle, one landing across my stomach as he carries me down the hall, away from this torture.

I think for a moment that I'll be haunted by the sounds of grunting, rutting men forever. I hear the muffled sound of it along the way, but then I realize the sound isn't haunting my mind; it's coming from behind the closed door where Delle is enduring her trial alone. I quickly force her from my thoughts because I feel so broken right now that I don't have the capacity for compassion. In this moment, I'm struggling to simply exist.

I pretend not to hear it as Arlo carries me past Delle's trial room, taking me farther down the hall, then through a door into a bedroom. He takes me across the carpeted floor to a bathroom at the back. It's too bright here—much like the all-white bathroom in my suite.

Are we in my bathroom?

No, he didn't go upstairs.

He crosses the room and bends while holding me, reaching out and carefully dipping to lift the lid over the toilet with one hand. Then he lowers me, setting me down and pressing on my shoulder until I relent and drop to sit on the toilet. I don't even have the energy to feel shame as my bladder empties.

There is no privacy left for me—no common decency, no shame. I'm reduced to a soulless body and desecrated flesh, just as they had intended.

I hear the faucet running and slowly turn my drooping head to look over at Arlo. He's standing at the sink, palms pressed against the countertop, leaning forward with his head hung.

"You're nearly halfway done," he mutters, and I can hardly hear him over the running water. "You've come this far, Mercy, and I know you can get through this."

"It's not as though I have a choice." I can hear how weak and weary my voice is—it doesn't even sound like me.

His eyes turn to glance at me beneath his lashes, and then he straightens, clearing his throat, reaching down to pull open one of the cabinet drawers. He pulls out a white washcloth and soaks it beneath the flow of water. He turns off the faucet, wrings out the cloth, and moves in front of me, crouching to his haunches. He lifts the damp cloth to my face and, with gentleness, starts wiping the dried cum and sweat that smears my cheeks.

I watch as he does this, wondering what thoughts plague him from behind his tortured blue eyes. I see hurt there, and I see pain. Sadly, I don't know whether the pain is for me or whether it's from controlling his impulses while watching the debauchery as his brothers fucked me. Part of me wonders if he hasn't taken a turn with me yet because he's edging his release, biding his time.

I watch the muscles in his neck work as he swallows. "Theo and I will need to fuck you before this is over."

I scoff because the statement is pointless. I'm well aware of that fact, and it only bothers me more to be reminded of it. Honestly, I don't know how I'll shut off my feelings about Arlo when he takes his turn with me in front of the others. They can do whatever they want to me and bring me shame, but the idea of Arlo using me along with them hurts me more than

I can say.

I don't know if he'll be kind and gentle, like he's being now. He hurt me when he fucked me in the cavern—when he ignored me as I told him it hurt. With all the Control present and encouraging this depravity, I don't know how Arlo will behave. I know he feels strongly for me. I know he's claimed me, and I let him. I worry he'll lose control and hurt me again, though I suppose I can't hurt much more than I do now.

He folds the washcloth and brings it to my hair, wrapping it around a matted strand and dragging it through. "Where do you want me to…" he trails off, feigning more careful inspection of the strand of hair.

"What?"

"When I have to take my turn…when Theo has to take his…"

"Are you asking which hole I'd like you to fuck me in?"

He puffs out a breath through his nose, his nostrils flaring as he closes his eyes. "Yes." He slowly opens his eyes, meeting my stare. "It's the only choice I can give you, but at least I can give you that."

I turn my head, looking off at the white wall. "I don't care."

"Yes, you do. Tell me."

I look at him squarely. "No. *No.* You're not going to put that on me. You're not going to make me choose how you hurt me."

"I won't hurt you, Mercy, I'll be—"

"Gentle? Soft? Sweet?" I shake my head. "No. There is no way for you to make this any easier on me. Everyone in the village will be watching; the Control and the Elders will be watching you. You can't be anything less than brutal in your participation, and you know that. You and Theo both." I feel hot tears well behind my eyes, and I'm surprised since I didn't think I had any left. "Is Delle…? Is she okay?"

I'd somehow managed to forget about her in the other room. I feel guilty for forgetting, but I feel glad for it, too. The burden of carrying worry for her is too much when I can't even carry myself.

Arlo grabs my hand and pulls me to stand with him, lowering the washcloth between us. He reaches between my legs to wipe me clean, and I'm too tired to care, too weary to stop him and do it myself. He owes me care, anyway. I'm his ward; it's his job to take care of me.

Let him cleanse me.

I wish he could cleanse the filth of this trial from my mind.

"I've done everything I can to keep them focused on you and away from her," he says. "But I haven't seen her yet. Theo's still with her."

My weak knees wobble and I slap my palms to his biceps, digging my fingers into his skin to steady myself. He tosses the washcloth toward the floor and brings his arms around me, pulling me to lean against his chest while he holds me up. I turn my cheek and press my ear over his pounding heart. I close my eyes and listen, focus on the steady rhythm.

"You have to fuck her, too," I whisper.

I'm met with silence. He doesn't admit that he must, but he doesn't deny it, either. He says nothing at all, and at least the silence feels honest.

"I'm sorry, Mercy. For all of it. For everything."

"I'm so tired," I mutter.

His hand strokes down the back of my head. "I know. It's nearly done, and when it is, you can rest."

"Can I?" I chuckle humorlessly against his chest.

"Of course," he replies too gently, his voice too soft.

"I won't have rest until I'm dead, Warden Rainn. I don't think you quite understand what's going on here." Silence lassoes around us through a pause. "Maybe I'll get lucky and the next trial will end me quickly."

His heartbeat hastens as his grip on me tightens. Though we're standing still, he seems to stumble, as though something I said had bodily pushed him back. He keeps moving, walking backward and dragging me with him, until his back hits the white-tiled wall, and he hugs me closer.

Air rushes out of him, blowing warmth over the top of my head as he weakens and slumps, slipping down the wall, taking me with him to the floor. Sitting, he pulls me onto his lap and cradles me like the small broken thing I feel like I am right now.

He presses a kiss to the side of my head, holds me tight, and I'm truthfully surprised that I find warmth and comfort in his arms. I'm surprised that I'm not repulsed by any touch right now. All I wanted was to be free and as far from the touch of another as possible.

Yet…I feel nearly peaceful here in his lap. I think it's his anxiety, which pulses through his racing heart, that serves to calm me. His heart beats fast, but steady, soothing. For the moment, I let him take my burden, let his anxiety build so I can find peace in the rhythm of it, and finally rest. I close my eyes and focus on the beat of his heart, letting it lull me into a sense of calmness.

"We only have a few minutes," he mutters, his lips moving against my hair. "Tell me what you need from me before it all starts again."

Slowly, I raise my head, pressing myself away from his chest so I can look up at him. "I need you to check on Delle."

He tucks my hair behind my ear. "I'll check on Delle, but that's not what I asked. What do *you* need? I guarantee you, she's in much better shape than you are."

My eyes search his face and I'm struck by his expression—the twitch of his cheeks through the tension he holds in his jaw, the softness of his eyes, the odd downward slope at the corners of his lips in sorrow. I have the urge to kiss those corners with a strange hope that it would force them to curl up again, to cause him to smile so I can see the long dimples in his cheeks.

"I need you to be the last."

His brow furrows, waiting for me to say more.

"I need you to be the man who ends the trial. You need to be the last memory of this awful day."

His chest sinks as he sighs and his eyes fall shut. He presses his forehead to mine. "I'll try."

I lift my arms and wrap them around his neck, holding him to me, suddenly fearful of our separation.

"Why are you sad for me?" I ask, closing my eyes. "I'm a sinner and this is my penance. I deserve this, don't I?" I throw his words back at him, asking out of frustration for his emotion, but also out of curiosity about the frown and the gentleness I hadn't expected from him.

"I don't know…I don't know what to think right now."

"Don't tell me what you think. Tell me what you feel."

"I feel conflicted. I don't know what else to say."

"Do you still think I deserve this?"

He goes quiet, and I let him. I let him sit with the thought, watching as he brews over it. If I have to endure this, then he should be forced to endure the conflict within him as he draws a final conclusion about what I do and don't deserve.

If he says that I truly deserve it, then I want him to writhe in the contempt he must hold for me as a sinner. If he says that I don't, then I want him to bask in the revelation and sit with the dissonance that could make him understand me.

I'm desperate for him to understand me.

But after a minute passes and he still hasn't spoken, I start to pull my hands away, dragging them down his shoulders. His hands shoot up to snatch my wrists and he pulls them back up, latching them around the back of his neck again. My lips part to let air rush through as I suddenly feel breathless.

"You don't deserve this. You don't deserve it, Mercy."

I tighten my arms around him, pulling closer to hug him, and the way he hugs me back is *everything*. What I feel in his embrace is everything I ever wanted, all wrapped up and tied with a bow. It's warmth and tenderness, shared heartache and fear, adoration and…love.

The way he holds me almost feels like love, but I know it's not—it could never be.

I'm a sinner condemned, and he's only my warden.

chapter four
ARLO

THE TEN-MINUTE BREAK ends quickly, and I'm forced to bring Mercy back to the foyer. She kneels on the center of the hard tile sun, sitting back on her heels with her head dropped low in exhaustion.

Standing behind her, I sift a length of rope through my hands as I stare down at the seven lines my brothers and I sliced into the back of her neck to mark her for these trials. I consider how to bind and suspend her, wanting to avoid irritating the red, raw markings left on her skin from the first part of the day, but I don't think it can be avoided.

She's endured three of her seven hours, and another four remain. My hands tremble as I anxiously snake the rope between them. I've never felt so sick in my life. I'm fighting the pain of watching her endure atrocious acts performed by my brothers in God, but I'm also fighting my feelings for her.

I'm fighting my *lust* for her.

Even from the way she waits there now, naked and kneeling, submitting to her trial with such grace and dignity…

It's fucking beautiful.

Horrifying and beautiful.

Her pain hurts me, yet the sight of her, the smell of her, the anticipation of tasting her hurts me, too.

All I want is to take her away from here, wrap her in warmth, move inside her with care and passion and tender attention to make up for all the pain they've caused her…the pain *I've* caused her. Because I've hurt Mercy, too. I fucked her raw, strung up in the caves when I prepared her for this trial, moved inside her past her point of protest.

I won't ever fuck her like that again.

That's a promise I know I can't keep.

A door down the hall clicks open, and Theo and Delle appear in the hallway. His arm is around her shoulders, helping her hold a robe over her body. He turns to walk her back to the room where she's been used, bringing her back from her break. I promised Mercy I'd check on Delle, and none of my brothers have returned yet to continue their defilement of Mercy.

"Theo," I call out to him, dropping the rope and heading in their direction.

He stops to look at me, meeting my eyes with a look that reveals him to be as shaken and pained as I feel. I quickly cover the short distance between us and approach him. He turns himself and Delle—who looks shaken, sad, but not broken—to face me.

"How is she?" I ask.

He shakes his head. "Not good, but I imagine better than Mercy. They've been unusually gentle with her, which I imagine means—"

"They've been brutal with Mercy." I know I shouldn't have said that within Delle's earshot when she whimpers.

"When do we switch?" Theo asks.

It's inevitable that Theo and I will need to switch places at some point. It's our duty to engage with both Delle and Mercy—just as our brothers have done—during this trial. But only one of them is being filmed and watched in the foyer.

I have no intention of laying a finger on Delle—I still can't help but see her as I once saw my own sister—and duty or not, this is one I cannot carry through with her. It's unsettling to think of neglecting my duty, but the thought of touching Delle fills me with something like disgust.

It will be yet another sin to add to my growing list, though I know God will forgive me...

But why will he forgive me and not them?

I glance over my shoulder at Mercy.

Is she justified in questioning our faith?

"Perhaps now would be the best time." I turn back to face Theo. "We can switch again after the next break."

"Okay," Theo agrees. "But let me bind Delle first."

I nod. It's fine with me; I don't wish to touch her.

The sound of raucous laughter and the padding of footsteps behind draws my attention away. I turn to see Killian and Ryker enter the foyer. Killian is finishing off a mug of ale, tipping it all the way back before slamming it down on the side table behind the camera...but his other hand isn't empty. He turns a kitchen knife in his palm.

"Go and bind her," I rush to tell Theo as I turn away from him. I charge down the hall as I watch Killian and Ryker approach Mercy from afar, and I shout to them, "It's Service of the Flesh; no blood is meant to be drawn."

My heart hammers as I watch Killian tap the tip of the blade beneath Mercy's chin, forcing her to lift her head and look at him with wild fear in her eyes.

Killian glances at me with pure glee. "I understand the trial, brother. I have no intention of drawing blood."

Rushing into the foyer, I shove his hand and the knife away from Mercy, then I step between them. "Then what is your intent with that? To spark fear?"

"My intent is to find my own personal satisfaction. That is the point of sexual service, is it not?" He turns the knife in his palm. "Shoving the knife's handle into her cunt will satisfy me immensely, so why don't you go ahead and get her back into position so we can carry out the trial?"

I can feel my face contort in rage; heavy, heated breaths slipping in and out through my flaring nostrils in a rush. I'm so livid at the mere thought of him touching her anywhere with any part of that fucking kitchen knife that I can't hold back. Unable—unwilling, perhaps—to hide my fury, my palms land on his chest and I shove him back.

He stumbles backward, tilting sideways and catching himself against the side table that holds the camera. The table legs screech as they skid across the tile floor. The camera shakes, then falls sideways, bouncing off the tabletop before crashing to the floor. The light remains on, so I know it's still recording, but I imagine it's only filming our feet.

"You use your cock for satisfaction," I tell him, "not an object."

He rights himself, slowly bringing his gaze to meet mine. "You would dare put hands on me to spare that *sinner?* What's come over you?"

"Nothing's come over me," I falter, searching my soul for a way to calm my nerves, to correct this misstep that could reveal my sinful thoughts about Mercy. "Sinner or not, I will uphold the integrity of this trial."

"And the integrity of this trial will be upheld with our sexual satisfaction. This," he holds up the knife, "will satisfy me. You have your ropes, and I have my objects. We each have our own sexual impulses, brother. Now step aside."

I hear the sudden scuffle of movement behind me, followed by Mercy's soft whimper. In the blink of an eye, I've forgotten about Killian and his knife. Whipping around, I see Ryker yank Mercy down to the floor, covering her body with his. His hand is around her throat, and worse than anything, he's kissing her. His lips are on hers and it's all I can see.

Those lips are mine.

Her kiss belongs to me.

Killian drops the knife as I charge across the room. It clatters against the tile and slides across the floor toward Ryker, racing me to meet Mercy at her side. With his hands free, Killian grabs my shoulders and jerks me back in my rush to get to Mercy.

My eyes widen as I watch Ryker with his mouth on hers, and I struggle not to fight, trying not to tear myself from Killian's grip, rush to her, throw Ryker to the ground and beat him senseless.

Mercy's eyes are squeezed closed, creating wrinkles across her forehead and creases at the corners of her eyes. Her lips are pursed shut as she turns her head, trying to fight the kiss he forces. It's as though I can feel my ribs break, one after the other, cracking under the strain of trying to contain my pounding heart.

"Watch," Killian says to me quietly. "Watch and remember who she is…*what* she is. She's a sinner and she deserves this. I'm afraid her demons are coming for you, too. Let us help you, brother."

Dear God, what's happening to me?

I feel for her, I want her…Sometimes I think I need her, and I shouldn't. I worry God has forsaken me, letting the demons that plague her claw into my soul. But the deeper they dig and the stronger I feel them, the truer their influence feels.

I'm conflicted.

I'm afflicted.

I don't know how much longer I can fight it.

Ryker's fingers curl tighter, squeezing her throat as he sits up, straddling her waist. Her hands fly to his wrist, gripping, pulling, swatting, and her lips and eyes part wide as she fights for air. If Killian didn't grip me right now, my hands would be around Ryker's throat, squeezing just as tightly as he squeezes hers.

I know my brother is trying to help me. I know he's trying to save me from sin.

But what if I no longer want to be saved?

What if I want to be a sinner?

"I know it's difficult," Killian says as Ryker reaches to grab the knife on the floor.

If he knows it's difficult, then he knows I feel for her. If he knows I feel for her, then he may prevent me from caring for her when she needs it the most. As much as it pains me to watch this unfold, I know that I must. I must stand here and allow it to happen, even though it's shredding my soul.

I didn't know my soul could ache this way.

I shrug him off and take a step forward. "It's not difficult. I only want to ensure the rules are followed."

He moves around and strides past me toward Ryker, who holds out the knife for him. "And they are being followed. It won't hurt her." He takes the knife from Ryker. "Maybe she'll even enjoy it."

They both laugh, and I force myself to curl the corners of my lips in a fake grin because I'm failing miserably at keeping my feelings for her unknown. Ryker grabs Mercy's hands, lifting them above her head, bending over her to press her wrists to the tile floor. He raises onto his knees and Killian moves between her legs.

Mercy shakes her head frantically and kicks her legs—which is the very reason she was supposed to be bound. Each kick and thrash could make this more dangerous for her. She could cut herself on the blade as Killian moves it toward her, as he kneels between her legs, and nudges his knee against the inside of her thigh to spread them.

"You can't...Don't...No!" Mercy stammers, eyes wide, trying to lift herself against Ryker's weight pinning her down at the waist.

I told her not to give them her words.

Her words only add to their pleasure, making them more eager.

I should cover her mouth. I try to take a step forward. I try to move to her to do just that, but I can't. I can't figure out how to move if it's not to save her from this torment. I can't figure out how to bring myself to her presence, to look into her bewitching eyes and cover her mouth to keep her quiet while my brothers fuck her with the handle of a kitchen knife.

My stomach lurches without warning, some sudden sickness coming over me, and I double over, turning swiftly to grip the table beside me as my breaths turn to heavy panting that work to keep me from retching.

"If you don't hold still, you'll cut yourself, sinner." Killian's tone is so ordinary and plain, as if he's performing a procedure she had agreed upon.

"Warden...Warden Rainn..." she whimpers.

Self-hatred boils in my gut, adding to my nausea.

I squeeze my eyes shut and try not to listen.

"There you go, keep those legs open for me, nice and wide," I hear Killian say.

Tears flood my eyes and I fight to keep them back. I don't remember the last time I cried, the last time I felt pain so deep as this, the last time I felt so truly and completely out of control...

I feel out of my mind.

I raise my head, turning to look, and I instantly regret it. My gaze lands on the scene at the precise moment that Killian presses the handle of the blade against her slit and plunges it inside her. Her body twitches beneath Ryker, though she fights to keep still. And while I know I'll regret it even more, I look at her face. She watches me, her head turned toward me, tears streaking across her face and tumbling toward the floor.

She looks broken.

She looks hurt.

She looks angry…with me.

"Starlight." I don't know why the word slips from my lips, but the utterance brightens her sad eyes for a fraction of a moment.

Even in this darkest hour of her defilement, she shines brighter than all the stars in the sky. She lies there, broken, on the tiled pattern of the sun, and it's her presence that gives it light…light that breaks through the dark shadows of space that hold her down, that try to break her and take that light away.

And how dare they try to take that light away?

I rise and charge, some reckless fury overtaking me. There's a piece of me that wants to protect that light at any cost, *at all costs*, because the parts of Mercy that are good and pure—uncorrupted by the demons and sin—reside within that light. And if they take that from her, then they'll surely ruin her.

I reach for Killian's shoulder, but before I touch, two heavy hands grip the back of my shirt and yank me back. I stumble, but right myself quickly, whirling around and coming face to face with Theo.

"Go," he says. "Go to Delle." He comes in closer, lowering his voice. "You can't be here for this. Don't let her lose you to this, brother."

I blink, taking far too many moments to tear myself from my rage, but as his words sink in, I hear them. I understand. And as painful as the truth is, I know he's right.

I cannot be called out for my sins here; I cannot show my feelings for Mercy here. I must save that for behind closed doors so I can be with her until the end.

Theo turns me, shoves my back, and pushes me toward the hall. With my brother's insistence, I'm able to walk away, but Mercy's gravity tugs at me with each heavy step.

chapter five
Mercy

"I SWEAR ON all things holy, Killian Cole, if you don't let me down for a break *right* now, I will *piss* all over your godforsaken face." I hardly recognize the sound of my voice—it's filled with such fury and contempt.

"Do it and you'll regret it, Mercy Madness."

Theo has me bound and suspended in a way that's similar to how Arlo had me in the caves—suspended facedown, my front parallel to the floor with my arms pinned behind my back. My knees are bent and spread, and my height is adjusted so Killian's face is aligned with my pussy while he kneels behind me.

Killian takes his time clipping clothespins around my slit. I've counted five so far, and he's taking his damn time placing a sixth. He started fifteen minutes ago when I asked for my second break, but he insisted this "wouldn't take long" and decided to prolong my torture, simply because he could. My whole body trembles around the pinching pain between my legs, and my bladder is so full, I'm about to burst.

"Just one more," he says as if it's soothing to hear, "then I'll let you down for your last little break, sinner."

"If she pisses on you, you're cleaning it up," Theo says from where he's sitting in the armchair across the room.

I wish he'd be more insistent. He's supposed to take care of me in Arlo's stead, but I've been begging for a break for the last fifteen minutes. I honestly don't know if I'll make it to the bathroom after they untie me, but I'm determined not to humiliate myself further—though I would find a sick sense of satisfaction if Killian got too close and I drenched his face.

"I swear I'm going to—"

Killian cuts me off with the placement of a final clothespin, pinched right onto my clit. The nip of it screams through me, my sensitive, raw, overused flesh roaring against the sharp new pain. I purse my lips, holding my cry inside, refusing to give him another shriek of pain or scream of protest.

"There," he says with finality, and I hear his hands slap against his thighs before he pushes to his feet and moves around me. I lift my head so I can glare at him as he approaches my side. "You can let her down now, Theo. I can always start over after her break."

I'm so furious that if I wasn't bound, I fear I might launch myself at him. I felt broken and sad earlier in the day, but the sadness has given way to anger, and I embrace it.

"You're disgusting," I spit the words at Killian as Theo and Owen work together to bring me down to my feet.

"Slinging insults is rather undignified," Killian sniffs, doing nothing to help me down. "And there is no one in this room more vile than you, sinner. I'm so disgusted that I have to touch you for this trial."

"You could've fooled me." I'm standing on trembling legs as Theo and Owen work to untie the knots that wrap around my torso and legs.

Killian gives me a sneer that's filled with pure evil. I hold his stare, unwilling to back down from him.

I dare you to touch me once my arms are free.

He sighs, as if he's bored all of a sudden, and looks away. "I suppose I'll take a break for a while, too. Can't steal all the fun from my brothers."

"For someone so disgusted by me, you have spent an awful amount of hours between my legs." I look him up and down with hatred.

He grins, and I hate it. "You're always good for a laugh, sinner."

I let out a breath of relief as he strides past, and I look over my shoulder to watch him jog up the staircase and disappear from sight. Now if I can just empty my bladder, I can take one full damn breath.

"Please, hurry." I rush them along.

The ropes have been pulled free from my waist and legs, but the ones that keep my arms behind my back remain. They keep my forearms pressed together, drawing straight lines across the middle of my back.

The pressure on my bladder is immense, and I can feel the release about to happen. I bounce through my legs, desperate to get to the toilet. "I can't wait. Just let me go…" My feet are already moving, stepping away from them. "Can I go?"

"Okay, just go," Theo says.

With his utterance of permission to take my second break from this trial, I run down the hall with the dangling ends of the rope flying behind my back.

I turn into the bedroom Arlo had brought me into before and head for the bathroom. I lower myself to the toilet, taking care to keep the dangling rope ends out of the way, and pee more forcefully than I ever have in my life. The relief is wonderful, but as the fluid drains from my body, so does the momentary relief.

Embarrassment floods me as I realize the clothespins are still clipped—some of them, anyway. One has fallen into the toilet, and I must have lost three others on the way here. Somehow, two still remain, pinching so much flesh that their grip stays strong.

"Mercy?" I look up at the open doorway when I hear Arlo call my name. "I'm coming in," he warns, but God, I don't need him to see me this way.

"Don't," I yell back. "Don't come in."

I don't want him to see me right now, but I actually need help. My arms are still bound at my back, and I can't cleanse myself or remove the clothespins. The humiliation of it overwhelms me with such a rush that tears flood my eyes and sobs threaten to break free from my chest.

He moves into the open doorway, and the moment I see him, I drop my gaze, letting my head fall forward. "I had to go…I couldn't wait," I whisper, and it's even more humiliating explaining myself.

Arlo appears in front of me, crouching to his haunches, tapping beneath my chin to lift my head. I can't look him in the eye.

"Just take a breath," he says. "I'll take care of you."

I want to find comfort in his words, but annoyance greets me instead. It's not annoyance for him so much as the fact that I need to be cared for right now at all. He and his brothers did this to me. They declared my self-preservation a sin, forced me into these Trials of Dissension, and here I sit, embarrassed and agitated because of them—and because of *him*, too.

Anger twists my expression as I look at him, watching his eyes skim over my body. He inspects me like I'm a possession, some porcelain doll he loaned as a toy to his brothers that he expects to find chipped or cracked from their play. Maybe I am chipped and cracked…I feel fragile in my anger.

Somehow, he spots the clothespins and grips my elbows, pulling me up to stand as he rises. My fury simmers as he reaches between my legs and pinches them off, as if it's the most normal thing in the world.

He lets go of me, and I stand, waiting as he wets a washcloth under the faucet. Outrage quakes my bones as I watch him return to me, reaching down to wipe between my legs. He cleanses me instead of freeing my arms and letting me do it myself, and I've never felt so low.

I don't tell him that, though. I'm tired of speaking, tired of shouting about my rage and rights into a void. So I let him do it, silently taking note of his ignorance of my shame so I can let the anger build within me.

"You left me," I mutter, and I'm surprised that the words came out.

"What?" He finishes with the washcloth and tosses it to the floor, stepping closer, as though he's going to pull me into his arms. "What do you need from me?"

I twist my body away, staring off at the wall. "I don't need anything from you," I reply sourly.

"What did they do to you?" He gently touches my cheek, but I whip my head in his direction, meeting his eyes with heat and forcing his hand to drop. "I'm back now. I'll be with you through the end."

"Fine."

"It's almost over now, Mercy. There's only an hour left."

"Then I suppose it's your turn to have your way with me."

His jaw clenches and his gaze travels down my body, then back up again. "You know it has to be done."

"Then fuck me how you did in the cave," I tell him. "Fuck me hard and wild; take what you want from me without giving it back."

His eyes harden as he stares back at me, nostrils flaring as indignation rises through his features.

Good.

He should feel as indignant as I do.

"Is that really what you want from me, Mercy? You want me to use you like my brothers had?" He steps closer and I step back, turning my body and backing away from him.

We move until my spine hits the wall, and he closes in on me, pinning me as he aligns his body to my curves. "It's what you're meant to do."

"And I'm meant to enjoy it, but there's only one thing that gives me anything resembling satisfaction these days… " His fingers find my stomach, tracing a path up my side that makes me flinch as he tickles the soft flesh. The flinch sends a jolt of electricity straight through me. "Do you know what that thing is, starlight?"

Starlight.

Wildflowers and starlight.

Arlo had told me that my hair smelled like wildflowers, and that it was the color of starlight.

He had uttered the nickname I've come to know as Ryker held me down and Killian pushed the handle of a knife inside me. He'd whispered, *"Starlight,"* and the sound of it cut through the noise of the traumatic moment, just long enough to give me a beat of peace, a bit of hope to cling to…

I realize I'm panting, pressed between Arlo's body and the wall.

"Wh…what?" I finally ask.

His palms press to the wall on either side of my head and he leans in close, brushing his lips over the shell of my ear. "Watching you come undone."

"Don't…" I whisper. "Don't do that. I'm so *angry*. Just let me be angry," I whimper. "Please don't take that from me…"

His hands drop from the wall to the small of my back, dragging me against him as a heavy breath rushes out of me. "You want to be angry?"

I nod, though I feel warmer in his hold, my body feeling pliant and relaxed from the simple touch of him.

"Is rage what you need to hold on to while I do this to you?" I hear him swallow as he hugs me closer. "Is that what will help you through?"

Though being in his arms inexplicably calms me, it's not as though I can stand here forever, letting him hold me this way. There's still time left in my trial—time that Arlo will have to use to fuck me in front of the entirety of Ember Glen—and though part of me wants to succumb to the calm and let him take me into bliss, the stronger part of me knows that shared rage will help us both.

Fury will help us get through this. It will help him to hurt me, and it will help me to endure the hurt. It will keep suspicions of our forbidden feelings for each other at bay. Anger will save us both.

I nod with my cheek against his chest.

"Okay," he concedes. "Then in five minutes, you'll be angry with me. I'll give you a reason to be. But until then, you'll let me hold you."

He bends abruptly, sweeps an arm beneath my legs and swoops me off my feet. He carries me easily through the open bathroom door, across the room, and lowers to sit in an armchair across from the bed. He sits me sideways across his lap, rolling me toward him and hugging me close to his chest.

There's a moment when I panic as the ropes still binding my arms tighten with our movement, the immobility frightening me, but as still and quiet moments pass, the fear lessens. I can hear the beating of his heart as I settle against his chest, and the beats lull me into calmness.

He calms me, though I'm still simmering with anger.

I shut my eyes and drift into darkness.

Sleep.

I blink and feel as though I've been forcefully dragged from a days' long slumber. Last I knew, I was resting my head against Arlo's chest, listening to the sound of his beating heart, and suddenly, his hand pinches my chin. His fingers dig painfully into my jaw as he twists my head up so I can meet his eyes. I must have nodded off, but the trial is still on. I'm still on Arlo's lap in the chair in the bedroom. I had a moment's peace as I fell into sleep far too quickly, and he's dragged me from it five minutes later.

He had to…I still have to finish my trial.

He bends over me, touching his forehead to mine and staring so deeply into my soul that I think the blue flames in his eyes could burn it to ashes. "It's time to get angry with me, starlight."

I don't know why, but the abrupt shift into his intensity does something inside me. My stomach twists, my belly clenches, and my pulse thumps faster. I feel a tug of desire through my core, as if it were just me and him, alone in a room, and I've given him permission to take control of me.

Maybe it would be easier if I did.

And that's why I need to get angry.

If I'm angry, it will mask everything else I'm feeling. It will take the shame away from the inexplicable desire that exists within me. It will make it feel okay for him to take me and use me in the brutal way they are all expecting. Anger will give us both permission to let go and give into what we've wanted from each other all along—pure, unhindered carnality without judgment, without shame, without fear of being found. We have a certain kind of permission right now that we'll never find again.

My voice comes out as a breathy whisper. "Then make me angry."

The blue flames in his eyes dance across my face before landing on my lips. There's a beat of hesitation and I plead with my eyes for him to push the limit…to walk right up to that thin line between authority and abuse and step across it.

"Make me—" I start again, but he cuts me off with a kiss.

His lips land on mine and push with bruising force while he digs his fingers into my face beneath my cheekbones. I jerk in my bindings, trying to pull away from him, but at the same time, I force my tongue between his teeth, sweeping inside his mouth, eliciting a groan that vibrates all the way down to my toes.

I get one lick, one taste of his fever before he pulls back and ends the kiss. With a flick of his hand, he pushes my head sideways before shifting his arms around me. He grabs my wrists in one large hand where they touch the middle of my back, then he hoists me up as he stands, jerking me around to get my feet on the floor. Shoving from behind, he marches me forward, reaching around me to open the bedroom door before he pushes me roughly into the hallway.

He keeps pushing, moving me down the hall to the foyer. Ryker and Wesley are there waiting, chatting side by side. Ryker is seated in the armchair Arlo had occupied for much of the first part of the trial. They both turn their heads as I walk in, watching as Arlo takes me to the center of the sun.

As if I were truly standing on the surface of a burning ball floating through the heavens, I feel like my blood is rising to a boil inside me.

"Time for another round," Ryker says, pushing to his feet. "Get her strung up and the three of us can all have another go at her."

"No," Arlo snarls. "You've had your turn; now it's my time." He puts his hand on top of my head and forces me down to my knees.

"If we're all up and ready, we should fuck her together for the sake of the trial—"

Arlo's head whips over his shoulder to look at Ryker behind him, and though I can't see Arlo's eyes, I know he's staring his brother down with fury. "I'll fuck her well enough for all seven of us, now *back the fuck off.*"

My stomach flutters and flips at the way he claims me, and it doesn't make any sense.

Ryker lifts his palms in surrender and takes a step back before lowering to the seat again. When Arlo turns his attention to me, everything sinks inside, a heavy rush of heat dripping down my insides.

I've had enough today.

I've had more than enough.

Enough touching, rubbing, grating, grinding, and fucking to last me a lifetime.

Yet, on my knees here for Arlo Rainn, looking up into his eyes filled with affection and true desire for me, I cannot deny the way I want him. I'm willing to take more for him—not just willing, but strangely eager.

He removes his clothes as I look up at him, dropping his shirt to the floor and showing me his bare chest, strong and chiseled and undeniably masculine.

He unbuckles, unzips, shoves his pants and black underwear down his legs, then rises to grip his cock, already standing proud and threatening. He strokes as he looks down at me. The connection between us is daunting, all-consuming, and the longer he holds me with his eyes, the more the world around us fades into the background.

His hand lands on the top of my head and slides down the back. He curls his fingers into my hair and grips me, jerking my chin toward the sky. "I almost wish I hadn't cut off your hair. I could've braided it with rope and tied it to the ceiling." My mouth drops open on a sigh, and he bends over me. "Is that open for me?"

Yes.

I try to close my mouth, but he grips my chin with his free hand, pinching my cheeks like he did in the bedroom. "You're going to take every inch of me inside your mouth, draw all of me past these pretty lips of yours. Do you understand, sinner?" He forces my head to nod in his grip, and though I feel my pussy clench for the way Arlo so greedily wants me, the anger of our forced scenario remains. That anger heats me, boiling me with frantic energy that flows to my cunt as easily as it does through the rest of my body.

The way he angers me is erotic and chaotic, draining in a way that makes me thirst for him.

I jerk my head to the side to try to free myself from his grip, just to convince myself that I did try to fight it, but heaven knows I have no real desire to fight this.

His grip on my chin loosens, but doesn't relent as he turns my head back in his direction. Stepping closer, he lets go of my chin to grip his cock, rubbing the tip over my lips as his fingers sink into my hair. He twists and tangles the strands at the back of my head. He gives a sharp tug at my hair, and with a yelp, I part my lips, letting him press his hips forward and slip along my tongue. He sinks in deep, but not deep enough to gag me, just enough to pause and let out a breath of relief, as though he's been waiting for this moment all day.

He has.

Nervous energy tickles beneath my skin as the rush of ire floods me. I swallow anxiously and it makes him shudder. He groans and my eyes drift shut to the sound of it, to the pleasure that having him inside me brings. His taste isn't vile like the others. Though I imagine no one's cock tastes particularly good, I also don't know how else to describe it.

Arlo's cock tastes like it belongs inside me.

Firming up his grip on my hair, he slowly presses deeper, fulfilling his promise to bury every inch of himself inside me. I gag and splutter as he sinks, and when he's all the way in, he loosens his grip on my hair and his palm strokes down the side of my head.

"That's perfect, Mercy," he whispers.

My eyes fill with tears from his invasion, and I open them to blink up at him as salty tears slip from the corners. The way he looks at me is strained as he moves inside me, hardly pumping with tiny strokes, moving just enough to allow some relief of the pressure at the back of my throat.

More.

I want more of him.

He fills me in every sense, taking up all the space in my mouth, but also in my mind. With Arlo, the world doesn't exist, the pain doesn't exist. With Arlo, I don't have to think about what comes next or what came before. All that exists are him and me and this time we have together to be completely unhinged and bare, sharing our debauchery with each other unashamedly in this Service of the Flesh.

This trial requires his indulgence, and I will let this man indulge with me in all the ways that please him…because his pleasure is linked to mine. I'll never understand that, but I don't need to understand to know that it's true.

He rocks his hips, pumping slow and long over my tongue. He leisurely fucks my mouth, and my arousal grows with each stroke. He strokes until he's shuddering, and his hips start moving faster, frantically thrusting out of rhythm. Then he slams to a sudden stop, gagging me as his cock nudges against the back of my throat. He holds still as his body trembles.

I prepare to feel the splash of him down my throat, and I'm ready to swallow everything he gives me, but he doesn't come. He keeps himself there on the edge, trembling with his eyes pinched shut. I'm surprised his expression doesn't show frustration; it shows bliss.

Pure bliss finds him on the precipice of release, and he keeps himself there.

Then, without warning, he pulls out, and I cough around his absence, feeling saliva coat my lips and drip down my chin. He grips my hair again and arches me back, leaning down over me, so close that the tips of our noses touch. I gasp for air as his fingers touch my chin, rubbing across it to gather the spit from my skin and swirl it around my lips before pressing his fingers into my mouth. Instantly, I close my lips around them and suck lightly.

I find myself in some wanton headspace where this filth feels good.

I'm too lost in this, making it too obvious that I want him.

I need to feel angry again.

I bite down on his fingers, sinking my teeth into them.

"Fuck," he cries out, pulling his fingers from my mouth.

I gaze up at him, chest heaving, and lick my lips. His mouth twitches to fight the curl of a knowing smile—a grin that tells of the way he wants me roughly.

I harden my eyes, having to hide my expression of taunting, aching, pure lust. "It would be a failure on your part to underestimate me, Warden Rainn."

To anyone else, it sounds like a threat, but he knows what I'm telling him. He knows I can take what he gives me—and I want him to give it all to me.

He drops his hand from the back of my head to grip my bound wrists behind my back. Closing his grip around them tightly, he twists me around and shoves me forward so harshly that I shriek with the unexpected motion. Still on my knees, he shoves me face-first to the floor. I squeeze my eyes shut as the floor rises quickly to meet me. I can feel my breath bounce off the tile and hit my face as I come to a sudden stop.

From there, he lowers me slowly, pressing me down until my turned cheek touches tile and my shoulders are on the floor. I struggle, but with my arms behind me, I can't push myself up.

His hands land on my hips and lift, raising my bottom high. I can feel him slide closer, his legs nudging my knees apart, his thumbs circling over my cheeks. I feel like I can't breathe, waiting for him to fill me, because for the first time, I actually want it.

How can I want it?

It doesn't matter why…only that I do.

"Please," I whimper.

He groans in response, his hips jutting forward to rub his hardness against me. His hands flatten to my lower back and slowly slip along either side of my spine, fingers climbing over my bound forearms. I shudder at his touch, panting in need. His hands keep moving, skimming over my shoulder blades, up my neck, tangling through my hair. He lets go as he folds over me, placing one palm on the floor above my head to brace himself. He reaches back to tuck my hair behind my ear so he can look at the side of my face. He presses a kiss to my cheek before moving his lips against my ear, whispering so softly.

"You're going to come for me, starlight. I will make you come so hard that you'll scream, make it feel so good that it makes you cry, because I want them to see your tears. I want them to think I'm the most brutal thing that's happened to you all day, but you and I both know I'm the best."

He is the best.

He's simultaneously the best and worst thing that's ever happened to me. I loathe how much I love the feel of him against me.

I don't respond, but I don't need to. He can see my response in the way I squirm beneath him. He can hear it in my pleading whimpers. He can taste it as he draws his tongue along the line of my jaw, all the way back to my ear, causing me to shiver.

He snaps upright, his weight leaving me all at once. His hand lands harshly on my hip and his fingers dig into my flesh. I feel the tip of his cock rub through my folds, dragging wetness as he moves behind me.

He presses inside me, easing his tip little by little. Then, with a groan, he slams inside me, pushing so hard and fast that I cry out. He lets out an audible breath of relief that sounds absolutely indecent. His hand slips from my hip, up the side of my waist, tickling my skin and making me flinch. He pulls out and slams in again, shoving me forward along the tile, my body lurching forward as my sweaty skin sticks to it.

"Sweet sin," he mutters as he slowly starts to fuck me, holding on to me with one hand around the smallest part of my waist.

A guttural moan claws its way past my lips as I try to choke it down. He made no false promises—he will have me screaming from this sensation that consumes me.

He leans over me again, one palm landing on my cheek and pressing down, squashing my face against the tile. "You make sin feel so good…so fucking good," he grits through his teeth as he fucks me harder, faster, deeper.

He continues this way, thrusting into me steadily. I know I won't come like this, but it feels so good, nonetheless. I feel so full, so complete. I wonder how he's going to get me there, but he answers me without a word.

His hand moves from my cheek, and I feel him grip the knots that bind my arms behind my back. He lifts me harshly from the floor, bringing me upright while he's still deep inside me. I gasp as he arches me back against him, my head falling back onto his shoulder.

My eyes instantly drift shut at the feel of his lips brushing my cheek. He brings both arms around me, one reaching all the way across the middle of my waist to hold me in place against him, the other covering my breast, squeezing lightly.

He doesn't speak as he draws his fingers back to play with my nipple, rolling, tugging, squeezing, pinching. It all sends jolts of pleasure straight through me, making me tremble in his hold.

He doesn't say a word, but it feels like an entire conversation transpires between us as he works me up. We engage in an unspoken discussion of desire and need, of want and appreciation, of chaos and corruption. When his hand falls away from my breast and slips down my stomach, dipping low between my legs, I open my eyes and drop my head to watch.

I want to see the way he touches me.

He presses in and moves two fingers over my clit, rubbing back and forth in a quick but easy cadence that beckons me to the edge. I pant, watching his hand move, feeling his body rock slowly, his cock thumping steadily against the perfect spot inside me, over and over again.

"You're gonna scream for me," he says, and I find myself nodding, knowing it's true. He's taking me there so hard, so fast, with more knowledge of my body than I have for myself…like he was always meant to touch me.

And then I slip…He leans us forward together, adjusting the angle he hits inside me to perfection. He fucks me harder, with a steady pounding rhythm that has me clenching around him in time to match it. My clit sparks and pulses, ready to catch fire.

"Warden Rainn…" I huff out a breath and take another before I explode.

An orgasm rips through me so powerfully, so fully, that I scream, sounding a primal release from the way I feel it tingle out from my center, rushing through me in waves of pleasure.

"Sweet fucking sin," he grits.

I'm still coming as he pushes me down to the floor again, my face on the tile, his hand around the side of my neck, pressing down.

His force strengthens as his pace slows, thrusting so hard and deep that I imagine I can feel him in my stomach. His hand drifts away from my neck, finding my arms and holding tight to use them as an anchor. He pulls back on them so hard that my chest lifts from the ground while he fucks me harder, my breasts rubbing against the tile with each thrust.

I'm still pulsing around him with aftershocks from my climax. I keep expecting him to come, but he doesn't. He just groans, grinds his teeth, and keeps fucking me. It's like he's trying to drag this out for as long as he can.

Of course he is.

That's exactly what he's doing. He's filling the last of my time, so I don't have to endure his brothers again.

My chest feels a lightening flutter at the understanding.

He leaves me all at once, and I whimper at the loss of his pounding warmth, but he finds me just as quickly as he left. He grips beneath my elbows and hoists me from the floor, planting me on my feet. He turns me to face him as my legs tremble beneath me. His palms cup my cheeks as he bends to kiss me hard and fast, his tongue sweeping around my mouth as deeply and sensually as his cock was buried inside me.

I kiss him back.

But then I think I shouldn't because this isn't something I'm supposed to enjoy.

But I do enjoy it.

I enjoy it so, so much.

Our bodies move together as he walks me backward, stopping when my heel hits the marble. He releases me from the consuming kiss, and I realize we're at the staircase—the marble my heel had hit was from the bottom step.

His eyebrows lift. "Up."

Locking eyes with him, I step backward onto the first step.

"Higher."

Another step backward and up. Then another, and another, and another. He stops me there, telling me to sit, and I do. As soon as my bottom hits the marble beneath me, he crawls up the steps between my legs. My knees spread for him naturally. His sight is set on my pussy and he descends, kissing me there as feverishly as he kissed my lips.

Unable to contain the way I love this—the way I *want* it, the way I *need* it—my head falls back on a moan.

I need him so much.

He licks and laps, settling to consume me for what feels like forever, but he doesn't make me come. He groans and pulls away, climbing onto his knees beneath me. He positions himself between my legs and grips my hips to hold my ass on the edge of the step where I'm perched.

"Hold still," he warns.

I spread my fingers, trying to wrap them around the edge of the step to hold on to. Arlo thrusts, sinking deep inside me with a groan that shakes the world around us…at least, it feels that way. I feel him burrowed inside my soul, and I don't think he'll ever leave.

Never.

"This," he mutters, breathing heavily as he picks up his pace, "this is what you get, sinner." He swallows hard, reaching out to lasso his hand around the back of my neck, curling me forward so he can place his forehead against mine. His hips jerk madly as he tries to hold back, but he's too close to the edge to hold out much longer. "This is…what you get for sinning."

His eyes flutter shut, and when they open again—half-hooded—he locks onto my stare. His eyes tell me so much and so little all at once. He's so restrained, but his self-control is waning. I want to push him over the edge.

"What do I get?" I whisper, quiet enough that only he can hear. "Show me what I get, what I deserve."

I think I've lost myself because I know I shouldn't be engaging in this kind of talk with him. I shouldn't be finding satisfaction in pretending I'm the sinner they say I am, that I deserve to be sexually destroyed by these terrible men in charge of Ember Glen—that I *want* him to sexually destroy me. I know I shouldn't hold his gaze. I know I should cry or thrash or detach so completely that I'm not aware of what's happening. But I can't do any of that with Arlo, and that's why this hurts me so much.

It hurts, because I know that if what I feel between us is real, then it will only last for moments. With one breath or the next, my life will be done, and what we do or don't have between us won't matter.

But it matters right now.

"Stop fighting it…please," I quietly plead with him.

As if all he needed was my permission, he ruts chaotically, frantically pumping himself to orgasm. I feel him swell, feel him rub along my sore inner walls, and within moments, he spills inside me with a primal roar.

And then he's still.

We're both still.

Though bliss finds us for a few precious moments, it fades away so quickly. Out rushes the unexplainable connection between us, and in rushes reality.

chapter six
ARLO

I FILLED UP the last hour of her trial.

I filled *her* up for the last hour of her trial.

Killian came back and tried to take her from me, but I didn't let him. I told him, as well as Ryker and Wesley, that the rest of her trial was mine, and I made sure no one touched her but me until the time was called.

All my brothers have returned to the foyer and we've brought Mercy and Delle to stand before the camera, both wearing black silk robes, my brothers and I fully dressed. Wesley just announced the successful completion of their first trial and completes the final ceremonial prayer.

"*Malo mori quam foedari,*" Wesley says.

Mercy lets out a groan in agitation, dramatically covering her ears with both her hands as my brothers repeat, "*Malo mori quam foedari.*"

And just like that, it's over, and seemingly everything returns to normal. We disperse, and Mercy is among the first to march away, charging toward the staircase. I watch her knees wobble as she takes a single step, pausing and reaching out for the railing at the bottom of the staircase. The bindings have worn her muscles, and she's endured so much today. I go to her, ready to sweep her into my arms, but the moment my hand touches the small of her back, she flings her arm, whipping her head to the side.

"Don't touch me," she hisses. "Let me walk."

"Let me help you."

She doesn't respond. She stubbornly takes a step, then another, slowly climbing the staircase on weary muscles. I follow behind her, ensuring she doesn't tumble backward down the steps.

It feels like it takes an eternity watching her climb the stairs in her soreness and exhaustion, but she finally reaches the landing. I let her continue down the hall for several paces before my frustration at her stubbornness takes hold of me.

"This is ridiculous, Mercy." I close in and dip behind her, sweeping her off her feet, scooping her up into my arms.

She lets out a yelp. "I said—"

"Shut up," I hiss. "Just shut up for once and let me help you."

I feel her tension as her arms fling to latch around my neck. She's prepared to fight me because that's what she does. She fights. But this time she doesn't. Her tension lessens with each step, and her weight sinks into my hold as she slowly gives in.

I carry her down the hall and manage to get her bedroom door open without setting her down. I turn sideways to carry her over the threshold.

"I can walk," she says, though it's a perfectly pointless statement now that we're in her room.

I kick her door shut behind me and take her straight to the bathroom. "I know you can."

I lower her feet to the tile floor, but keep my arm around her waist, tugging her close to my side, holding her up as I bend to flip on the faucet of her bathtub. I hold my hand beneath the water, adjusting the temperature to a perfect warmth before engaging the drain block and letting the tub fill.

"I need to use the toilet," she says quietly. I start to lead her in that direction, but she halts me. "Give me a minute, *please*. I just want to be alone."

I don't want to leave her alone. I don't want to remove my arm from her waist. I don't want to step away from her for a second. I've never felt so insistently needed, even though she tells me she doesn't need me.

"Please, Arlo…Just let me have one moment of privacy."

I sigh, gradually dragging my arm across her waist until it drops free. She bends to grip the edge of the tub, letting out a breath of what seems to be relief.

Was my touch bothersome?

Was I too rough during the last hour?

A lump rises in my throat and I swallow against it, taking a step back. "I'll give you a few minutes, but I'll be back. I'll bring food."

"Go. Please—" Her voice cracks, and I know she's fighting to hold herself together, waiting for me to leave before she falls apart.

I don't want to leave her to fall apart alone. But I can't deny her the space she needs after what she's been through. I take a step back, then another, watching her fingers as she tightens her grip on the tub rim. Though it feels like the tether that binds us is made with unbreakable twine, I somehow manage to snap myself free from it to turn and walk away—because she asked for me to.

"Arlo," she calls, and I stop, whirling around to face her. She hasn't moved. "Give me fifteen minutes, but please…come back."

Her plea slices right through me, cutting a hole that immediately fills with need for Mercy—need to be near her, the need to touch her, to care for her. I'm so needy for this woman, and it's frightening.

It's wrong.

I'm not sure how much longer I can care that it's wrong.

"I'll come back. I promise." I leave before I lose the ability to pull away.

I rush downstairs to the kitchen and grab a plate I'd made for her and set aside earlier, knowing she'd be hungry after the trial. I filled it with fruits, cheese, and crackers—quick eats that didn't require time to be heated or cooked. She can start with this, and I'll make her something else myself if she's still hungry.

I bring the plate and a glass of water back upstairs, taking it into my room because she asked me for fifteen minutes, and that's what she'll get. But I don't know how to kill the small amount of time that seems like hours before returning to her.

I pace for a few minutes, crossing back and forth along the end of my bed, but as I walk, the need to be close to her claws away at my insides, scratching at my soul, and the itch is unbearable. Yet, she asked me for fifteen minutes, and I want to honor her request and grant her that time. She's earned that time alone. She deserves it.

She deserves it more than anyone.

What she's endured today is something that no man in Ember Glen could ever endure—and certainly not with the dignity and grace Mercy had showed. She championed her way through an arduous trial, passed it, and walked away from it on her own two goddamn feet.

I walk over to my desk and I lower into my chair. I unlock the drawer and pull out my journal, uncoil the leather twine and open to a blank page. I lift my pen, and the moment it touches the paper, it begins to move with the flow of poetry in my mind.

Your demons become mine,
creeping slowly through the flow of our touch.

A touch is all it takes,
and your sins bind to my heart.

Your sins pulse with the rhythm of my prayers,
prayers I repeat for the pardon of your soul.

Your soul calls to mine,
seeking light in the darkest time.

But the light in me is gone,
gone with the secrets I've asked you to keep.

You keep without contempt, endure without hope, need without
fear, yet I am not dignified in the same.

I hold contempt—contempt for the madness you've brewed within
me.

I hold hope—hope that the madness will never fade.

I hold fear—fear that the madness will be snuffed out with your life.

Your life will be taken.
Your light will be extinguished.
Your madness will fade into history...
but it will never be snuffed from my memory.

I pray my memory will be enough to sustain...to endure a lifetime
without your madness.

I slam the pen down and slap the journal shut. Panting, I huff with agitation at the disjointed and nonsensical scribbled words—a brash display of my confusion and misunderstanding of our world, our God, the truths that are proving to be lies.

Yet, after what I witnessed today, my world feels...wrong.

And the only thing that feels right is Mercy Madness.

I bind the journal with the leather strap and return it to the drawer, taking notice of Mercy's mother's journal locked in there with it. I've considered reading it on several occasions, but I haven't brought myself to do it yet. I'm afraid of what I'll find; I'm afraid that I'll learn too much about Mercy's mother and the influence she had over shaping Mercy into becoming the rebellious, stubborn, blasphemous woman I can't seem to get out of my mind. I'm afraid it will grant me too much sympathy for the woman meant to die at the end of the trials—the woman I feel too much for, the woman I'll have to let go of one day.

I shove the drawer shut and lock it, rising so fast that my chair tumbles backward. I ignore it, stepping around it, rushing toward the fireplace with the intent of grabbing a candle and burning myself to gain some sense of self-control. My eyes brush past the clock on the mantelpiece, and I quickly realize that more than fifteen minutes have passed.

I stop everything and charge for the door, opening it and stepping out into the hallway before I realize I've left the plate and water behind. I rush back in to grab both, then quickly let myself into Mercy's room. I drop the plate and water glass too heavily on the table between the armchairs. The plate clangs, and the water sloshes from the top of the glass, but I don't care. All I care about is returning to her side because I promised her I would.

I enter the stark white bathroom, but I don't see her. At first, all I notice is the bathtub full of water. It takes me a few seconds to see the nearly white strands of her short hair floating up and around her head.

She's sunk beneath the surface of the cooling water.

I panic as I rush to the tub, feeling the same fear I felt the first night she was here—when she'd dunked herself beneath the waterline, and I thought she must be trying to drown herself. I had pulled her out, and she'd told me she only wanted a moment's peace. The recollection does something to calm my nerves as I approach, as I see she's pinching her nostrils closed with one hand and her eyes are open, slowly blinking beneath the rippling water.

I know she's not trying to drown herself.

I feel the peace settling in the room, as if she's taken all of today's negative energy beneath the surface to drown it. Still, I'm ready to grab her and yank her out if she spends another ten seconds down there.

I lower to my knees, looking over the edge at her slowly blinking eyes. Her irises blend so seamlessly with the water—the same silvery blue reflected from the light against the white backdrop of the porcelain tub. Her head turns a little, and I notice the slight dip of her eyebrows as she recognizes my presence above her.

Gradually, she rises, her starlight tresses—darkened by the water—stick to her cheeks as her head moves above the waterline. Bringing her hand away from her face, she takes in a deep breath, pinching her eyes shut to squeeze the water from them. She pushes her hair up her forehead, smoothing it away from her face.

I watch the muscles in her throat work as she swallows, shifting to sit with her spine against the back edge of the tub. She casts her gaze to the top of the rippling water. "I was starting to think you'd forgotten about me."

I shake my head, reaching out to brush my knuckle across her cheek and wipe away the stray droplets of water. "If you think that's possible, then you obviously haven't been paying attention."

She turns her head to look at me and several silent beats pass. The silence pounds loudly in my mind with the echoing beat of my heart taking in the sight of an angel. She looks as though she's emerged from the heavens—bare, clean, refreshed, and renewed. A small smile even touches her cheeks, and I think it's enough to brighten the room.

Then the smile fades, as does her attention. Her head turns and her stare fixes on the faucet near her feet.

"Are you hungry?"

She shakes her head. "No." She pauses. "Yes. But I don't want to eat right now."

"What do you want?"

She shrugs, and the movement of her shoulder pushes the water, causing a ripple to fan out across the tub. "I just want you to hold me."

Her eyes turn to meet mine, and they track with such misery that it makes my fists clench. I rise to my feet and rush to remove my clothes, keeping my eyes on her to watch for protest as I prepare to climb into the tub with her. If she does protest, I don't see it in her eyes.

I strip to my underwear—deciding it would be best to leave them on—and reach down to place my hand at the base of her neck. I nudge her forward and climb in to sit behind her. I spread my legs around her hips before gripping her waist, tugging her back to rest between them.

She holds herself up, tense and rigid. Her fingers grip the edges of the tub, and I see the subtle movement of her chest as she takes in quick, shallow breaths.

What has this trial done to her?

How much did I hurt her during that final hour?

Eventually, her back rounds as her tension releases. Her grip on the tub slowly loosens, and soon, she lets go. When she does, I ease her back, sliding her against me. I snake my hands across her stomach to wrap my arms around her.

Minutes pass, and I hardly breathe until she's let herself lay fully against me, until she's calmed enough to let her head fall back onto my shoulder, and she's closed her eyes to rest.

Finally, she can rest.

There's a beautiful silence surrounding us where the only sound is the light movement of the water when one of us shifts or moves an arm. It's peaceful, at least for me, and I hope it is for her, as well.

"Did it upset you?" she asks after a few minutes, interrupting the silence.

"What?"

"Watching your brothers use me...Did it upset you?"

I sigh, taking a moment to figure out how to frame my response. "It made me feel a lot of things, Mercy."

"I asked if it *upset* you."

"Yes, it upset me. Of course, it upset me. But that's not the only thing it made me feel."

A stagnant beat hangs in the air, and when she speaks, her voice trembles, as if she doesn't really want to ask the question. "Did you find enjoyment in watching me that way?"

"Not in the way you think."

She shoots up and spins, her body easily turning to face me in the water, which splashes over the edges. "In what way, then? Tell me. Don't attempt to give me comfort without honesty."

I stay put, though my hands twitch to grab her and my arms ache to wrap around her again. "I've always enjoyed watching, and hearing, which shouldn't surprise you. On nights of service, I often sit and watch before indulging." I lift my arms from the water and lay them along the edges of the tub, afraid I'll grab her if I don't do something else with them. "I did enjoy seeing you bound and strung up, but I don't think that should come as a surprise to you. You know how beautiful you are to me in bondage."

She shakes her head subtly, slowly, sadness creeping in around the edges.

"I was excited by the sight of you, Mercy. But it devastated me to watch them hurt you." I look down at the settling water between us. "I nearly lost control when I saw Killian come out with that knife."

I hear her blow out a breath, see it skim across the surface of the water as a ripple disturbing the stillness.

"It wasn't the first time he did that to me," she says. "He used me in service before he was selected to be one of the Control." Her eyes drop to the water. "You know he always brings a knife to service."

I sit up, ignoring the water sloshing over the edges of the tub, splashing onto the floor, and touch my knuckle to her chin, lifting her face and forcing her to meet my eyes. "He's put the handle of a knife inside you before?"

She nods, her eyes gazing off in the distance rather than at me.

There's the dissonance again, the broken chords of conflict inside my mind. I'm angry that Killian has done this to her—and not just today, but during nights of service. I'm sad that she's had to endure that at all, let alone more than once.

But I shouldn't feel angry or sad about it.

I shouldn't feel anything about it at all.

It's Killian's Impulse, and she is a servant—*was* a servant. It was her duty to serve the Impulse then, and it was her penance to serve it today. It's something she and I both should take pride in.

Yet, I don't.

It feels…wrong.

Why does it all feel so wrong?

"Mercy, look at me," I demand, desperate for her gaze.

She turns her eyes to look at me, though they flicker around my face, never settling. I slide closer as I slip my fingers along her jaw, taking my palm around to the back of her head to hold her there. I press my forehead to hers and she's forced to meet my eyes.

"You can tell me how you feel," I tell her.

"No, I can't. I can't trust you. Not fully."

That hits like a lightning strike through my chest.

"You can trust me, Mercy. I promise you can."

"Don't make me promises you can't keep. I can't trust you, Warden Rainn. At the end of the day, you're the Control. Your duty is to care for me until I die…and I *will* die. When I'm gone, you'll have to go on with your life as before, and you have to protect yourself to ensure that happens. I'm disposable to you, and I always will be." Her palms touch my chest, resting delicately as she speaks. "I can never fully trust you not to take my secrets and betray me should it help you maintain your station."

Our bodies slip toward one another, slowly moving together without reason or control.

I have no control over myself with her.

"I could say the same about you," I tell her softly. "You could betray me with our secrets, with the sins I've committed with you."

Her hands slip over my shoulders and around my neck, bodies still drifting together, as if the water itself knows that nothing can keep space between us.

"I won't," she whispers.

"Why?"

Her eyes drift shut. "You know why."

"Tell me."

"Because I need you." She slips closer. "Because thoughts of the trials and death and hellfire fill my mind until I think of you."

I sink one hand beneath her knee, tugging her leg forward along the side of my hip. Naturally, she brings the other forward, too, until her body wraps around mine, straddling me in the tub. One of my hands remains at the back of her head, keeping our foreheads touching, while the other slips around her back to hold her close.

"When you enter my mind, everything else slips away," she confesses, and my heart pounds. "When I think about you, I can't think about anything else, and it's freeing."

Sweet sin.

My breathing grows heavy, but not with lust. My lungs demand more air because her confession has sucked them hollow.

"Mercy…" I have no other words. No response I can think of could ever express the overwhelming storm of emotions sweeping through me.

She lets out a sigh, as if the confession alone is freeing, and sinks into my arms, slipping hers all the way around and hugging me tightly. I hold her closer, burying my face against her neck and inhaling her scent deeply. Even in the bath, the faint aroma of wildflowers in the meadow lingers in her hair.

Wildflowers and starlight.

An image comes to mind of Mercy laid out on a raised platform, her starlight hair spread out around her head like a halo, and the scent of wildflowers surrounding her because they lie around her lifeless body at her funeral.

Will her hair still smell like wildflowers when she's dead?

Will it still shine like starlight?

A shudder rips through my chest, a lump rises in my throat, and warm tears—something I haven't felt in ages—burn behind my eyes.

My arms close tighter around her, and I press a kiss to the crook of her neck before settling into her embrace.

My thoughts are consumed by you, too, sweet Mercy.

I just can't bring myself to say the words out loud.

chapter seven

Mercy

I HAD FALLEN asleep in my bed with Arlo at my side, but I was alone when I woke. The other side of the bed had been neatly made while I slept, and there'd been no trace that he'd ever been there in the first place. I must have slept heavily because I found a tray of breakfast foods left on the table between the armchairs—he left and came back and left again, all while I peacefully slumbered.

Exhausted and overwhelmed, I pull on the long black silk robe I'd worn back to the room after the trial yesterday, and sit quietly in one of the chairs, leisurely chewing my way through a slice of toast and jam from the tray. I consider remaining in my room all day. I also consider going back to sleep because then I can avoid thinking about the trial I endured yesterday…or what's to come in the next.

But my mind flashes through the images of debauchery, the use and abuse that stretched on for so many hours. My body aches from the bindings and being suspended for so long. Spots of my skin are red and rubbed raw, and my muscles are sore from being held in a single position for hours on end.

I can manage the physical aches and pains that remind me of the trial, but I can't handle the way they make me think of Arlo and how he cared for me last night. The emotional awareness of it is daunting. He'd tended to the rope burns, massaged my aching muscles, and put me to bed. The admissions I made to him replay in my mind, and it brings me anxiety. I'd told him that he fills my thoughts, and how those thoughts of him bring me peace. I'd admitted my need for him…yet he'd said nothing in return.

He'd said nothing, that's true, but he had tightened his arms around me…he had held me closer, nuzzled his face against my neck, kissed my cheek, and gave me a kind of affection I've never known. Though a mother and father could hug their child and kiss her cheek, though a dear friend might pull you close and offer you comfort in their embrace, the moment I shared with Arlo was nothing like that…

Nothing like that, at all.

It was so much more.

Thinking of it makes my heart race, and I don't think I can handle that right now. I don't want to think about him. I don't want to think about anyone but myself. I only want to rest, but a knock at the door derails that plan.

"Mercy?" comes a sweet voice from the other side.

Delle.

I feel immediate regret for being so selfish and not going to her earlier. I rise from my seat and rush to the door, flinging it open. Delle stands on the other side, fully dressed in a burgundy silk gown that hugs her comfortably, a matching silk belt wrapped around her waist and tied in a bow at her side.

The sight of her is nothing short of surprising. I'm surprised by the color in her cheeks and the care she's taken to groom and dress today—I didn't have the energy to care for myself, but I'm glad to see her looking so well after the torture of yesterday. I reach for her, and pull her straight into a hug.

"How are you?" I ask. "Are you okay?"

"I'm okay," she says quietly.

I step aside and motion for her to come in, letting her move past me before shutting the door behind us. She sits in one of the armchairs, and I sit beside her.

As I look over at Delle, I see that her gaze is downcast and I can feel the anxiety rippling out of her in waves. Though she sits there quietly, I know there's a reason she came to me, so I remain silent and give her some space to gather her thoughts. If she wants to talk, she will. And if she doesn't, then we'll just be quiet together.

A few moments later she lifts her head and turns toward me. "You've served every month for four years, right?"

I nod.

"How…how did you do it, Mercy? How did you survive it for so long?"

I feel my forehead crease in consideration of her question, because truthfully, I don't know the answer. "I just…I just did what I had to do."

"Yesterday was…" She shakes her head and sighs. "I just feel like less of a person today than I was before."

My eyes press shut to hide the silent tears that gather for her, though I know they're not only for her. The tears also come for the person I was before I began service at sixteen. I was an entirely different person then, and I had to become someone new when I started serving. I feel like someone I don't even recognize now, knowing that my death is coming and my actions no longer matter.

"You're no less of a person, Delle. Please hear me when I tell you that. But I do understand what you mean. They took things from you that you weren't willing to give and that…that changes you."

"But in a way, I was willing, wasn't I?"

I tilt my head, regarding her with a curious expression, unsure of what she's saying, waiting for her to say more.

"I can't help but feel like I have no reason to feel this way—this sick to my stomach, this sad." She looks over at me and tears gloss over her hazel eyes. "I *chose* the trials. I *chose* to participate yesterday."

In the span of a breath, I'm out of my seat and on my knees in front of her. I don't reach out to touch her as I would have before yesterday—I don't know if she wants to be touched at all right now.

I let out a sigh. "You said it yourself, Delle. It was never a choice for you at all. You endure the three trials, or you serve every month for the rest of your days. They made it impossible to choose any life other than the one you were given. They made it impossible for you to ever truly be free."

Her tears flow as she drops her face in her hands. I remain quiet as she sobs, as she lets the pain from yesterday flow out of her with each broken breath. I stay still and silent as my own tears, so eager to fall, prick behind my eyes. I sniff and draw in a deep breath to try to hold them in just a little bit longer.

I can cry for myself once she's gone.

"Why are we the only ones?"

"The only ones?"

"Who see the truth? Who see the madness of everything in Ember Glen?" she asks.

I shift to sit on the carpet, bringing my knees to the side in a fawn position, then adjust my robe. "I don't think we're the only ones. After all, there have been trials in the past; others before us have chosen to dissent." I turn my gaze away as I drift through my mind, staring off at the door. "And I imagine there will be others long after we're gone."

"It shouldn't be this way. We should be free to choose how we live, who gets to touch us and who doesn't—"

"Who we love…" I interrupt unintentionally. I blink and turn my head, giving her my attention again. "It shouldn't be this way, but it is."

"Why can't we change it? I want to change it so badly, Mercy. I want change so much, but I don't know how that could ever be. I feel more powerless than ever." She sniffles, dragging the back of her arm beneath her nose. Then she chuckles through her tears. "Why haven't you hugged me yet? You always force-hug me whenever I cry like this."

I shake my head to draw myself from my thoughts, and give her a smile. "I'm so sorry." I rise onto my knees and hold out my arms, drawing her into a hug. "I didn't know whether you wanted to be touched."

"I don't," she breathes, wrapping her arms around me tightly, like a young child clinging to her mother for comfort, "but a hug from you doesn't count."

I let her cling to me for as long as she needs. I find comfort in her hold as much as she finds comfort in mine. "Do you want to talk about what happened to you yesterday?"

"No," she says, gently pulling back. "I want to forget it ever happened." Her brow furrows, and her eyes turn away. "Except, there was something about yesterday I did want to tell you about."

"What is it?"

"Theo…and Arlo." Her eyes meet mine. "I think it's meant to be a secret, but neither of them used me yesterday."

I blink, taking a moment to make sure I understand exactly what she's saying. "Do you mean that neither of them participated? That neither of them sought sexual service from you?"

"Theo only touched me to knot the ropes. And Arlo…"

"What did Arlo do?" My heart stalls as I wait for her response.

She chuckles. "He talked to me about his sister."

"What? He didn't touch you?"

"Only once to adjust the ropes when they were hurting me. But otherwise, no. He…he did remove his clothes, all except for his underwear, but just for a short time when we were first alone in the room. He said it would make it look like he'd just finished with me if he were putting them back on while the others came in to use me. Theo did the same thing." Her cheeks flush pink at the mention of Theo.

I'm surprised at this news…relieved. Incredibly relieved. I feel a heavy weight that I didn't know existed lift from my shoulders. I don't know whether I thought Arlo would actually use her. He was supposed to use her. In fact, by not engaging, he's failed in his duty—and Theo as well.

They willingly neglected their duty…but why?

"I don't understand." I shake my head, looking away in my confusion.

"I'm not sure I understand it, either. But Mercy, I think it's supposed to be a secret."

My eyes snap to hers. "It *is* a secret, Delle. They were both supposed to use you. If anyone else were to find out, they could be punished for it." I reach out to touch her hand. "Promise me you won't tell anyone else."

"I won't tell." She swallows visibly. "I don't want Theo to get in trouble."

"We could all be in trouble if someone finds out. I fear what you might be made to endure should it be found out that you didn't complete your first trial."

"That I didn't—" Her eyes widen with panic. "*What?*"

"The trial was to serve the sexual needs of the seven members of the Control over the course of seven hours. You endured the seven hours, but if Arlo and Theo didn't use you, then you only served five of the Control. It means…it means that, technically, you didn't complete the trial."

Her hand comes up to cover her mouth in shock. I reach up to grip her wrist and gently tug it away, clutching her hand in mine.

"You have nothing to worry about, Delle. I promise you this doesn't matter. As far as it concerns anyone else, you completed your trial. Like you said, this is a secret. And I promise, I won't tell a soul; and neither will Arlo or Theo. They could be punished for neglecting their duty. They won't tell."

"But why didn't they—"

A loud knock interrupts our conversation. I give Delle a quick, reassuring smile and a pat on the hand before climbing to my feet and crossing the room. I pull open the door to find Arlo standing on the other side, and the mere sight of him kicks my heart into a flurry. He glances over my shoulder to see Delle behind me, and my head naturally turns to follow his stare. When I turn back to face him, I catch his eyes darting to look me up and down, and it sends an odd thrill shuddering down my spine.

Then his head turns, and he looks down the hall. "Theo, she's here," he says, then looks at me again. "I need you to get dressed."

"Why?"

"The Control want to speak with you…the *both* of you."

Theo appears in the hall just behind Arlo, and I see his cheeks twitch to hide a smile as he spots Delle walking up behind me.

"What could they possibly want from us today?" I huff.

"It won't take long," Arlo replies. "Get dressed."

He steps over the threshold, nudging into my space, and I suck in a breath as he reaches past me. Our eyes meet and he holds my stare for a tense moment. I'm not sure exactly what he's doing, but he's far too close given our witnesses. Then I realize he's reaching past me to grab the doorknob. I take a step back to let him pull the door shut as he leaves too quickly. I miss him immediately, and that's difficult for me to admit to myself.

"Do you think the Control knows about Arlo and Theo? Is that why they want to see us?" Delle asks, and I turn around to find her with wide, panicked eyes.

I shake my head as I cross to the wardrobe and pull it open. "No. If the

Control knew, they wouldn't send our wardens to fetch us."

"Then what do they want from us? I don't want to see them today."

"Whatever this is about, I can tell you that what they truly want from us is a reaction. Otherwise, they wouldn't waste their time to call us before them just to deliver their messages."

And knowing myself, I'm certain they'll get a reaction from me because I refuse to keep my mouth shut any longer.

ARLO AND THEO have brought us into the dim courtroom. The spotlight shining down over the black, semi-circular table casts an eerie glow to the room, outlining the silhouettes of the Control who sit behind it in shadows.

Delle and I stand on the opposite side of the table beneath a second spotlight, which is so bright that it drenches us in heat. The three Elders are projected onto a large white screen at our backs, and it makes me feel uneasy to be so completely surrounded by the authority of Ember Glen.

"How are you feeling today, sinner?" Killian regards me with disdain.

I grit my teeth. "I'm fine. How are you?"

He scoffs, dropping his pen to the table, sitting back and crossing his arms. "I've already taken three showers today trying to scrub the filth of you from my pores."

"Well, I only took one bath last night, and I feel clean enough. Though perhaps I'm more efficient in cleansing than you are. Do the boys' teachers instruct them on how to bathe? I'm certain there was an entire unit on cleanliness and hygiene taught when I was a girl."

Arlo leans forward into the light. "Enough, Mercy," he scolds sharply, though I believe I see a hint of humor dance across his cheeks. He looks over at Killian on his left. "Would you just tell them so we can get on with our day?"

Killian doesn't look at Arlo. "Fine." He remains still, with his arms crossed, his glare focused on me. "We asked you both here to deliver this news. It's been collectively decided that neither of you will serve during the next full moon in two nights' time. I think we all agree that we've had enough filth from you." He only looks at me when he says it.

"This isn't news," I tell him, confused. "We were told from the beginning that we were sinners, no longer servants. By definition, you deemed us unfit to serve since our participation in the Trials of Dissension was decided."

Owen leans forward, tossing his head to throw back a strand of nearly black hair that had fallen over his forehead. His dark eyebrows dip toward his nose to frame his blue eyes, which always seem to cast a deliberate gaze.

He clasps his hands on the table. "It's the decision we expected to make, but we hadn't made it official until just now. We felt it most prudent to wait until after the first trial."

There's a pause, as if they're waiting for us to respond. Surprisingly, I have nothing to say to this, so I finally break the silence.

"Will that be all, then?"

"There's just one more thing." Ryker locks his fingers behind his head over his wavy, dark blond hair as he stretches back. "We're going to broadcast a special viewing of this month's purge. A live stream of the event, just for the two of you." He looks only at me, never a glance spared at Delle because none of their taunting is meant for her.

"You're both going to sit and watch it together," Killian says. "You'll view the sisterhood you left behind as they serve the men of Ember Glen with honor and pride. And since neither of you will be serving, your former sisters will have all the more work to do, won't they?" He leans forward. "You're going to watch every minute of it in your shame."

I feel bold, and speak likewise. "Presumptuous of you to assume I'll feel shame for it."

I will feel shame, but not in the way he wants me to. I'll feel shame that I can't help them; I'll feel shame that I'm powerless to save them from their fate.

Killian's expression melts into anger, his brown eyes darkening to black as his palms slam against the table. He shoves to his feet, his chair teetering. "I've never been more disgusted by a woman in my life—"

"You were hardly disgusted yesterday, Killian. I remember the pride in your cock as you shoved it into my mouth."

His chair topples to the slate-tiled floor as he shoves back and jerks sideways. He rushes around the table—behind the backs of his brothers—to get to me. I push Delle behind me, and take a step back as he advances.

Arlo leaps up, spinning and sprinting to catch him before he clears the side of the table. Arlo grabs above Killian's elbows and yanks him backward, effectively halting him. "You lose yourself to rage and we have all lost, brother."

I feel the corners of my lips snarl at Arlo's words—the way he calls him *brother*, the way he makes it sound as though they're in this together.

Because they are.

I think I'd almost forgotten that he wasn't one of them.

Killian's jaw is tense, eyes narrowed in anger, wild fury pulsing from him across the room and punching straight through me. Yet gradually, he relents and turns to face Arlo. Killian blows out a heavy breath, conceding his struggle.

"You're right," Killian says to his brother. "She's not worth it. I mustn't let the Impulse overcome me with the night of our purge so close." He straightens, brushing his hand down the front of his blazer to smooth it as he strides back to his seat.

"Right," Arlo says to him, though his eyes rise to meet mine. "Release is coming with the full moon."

My throat suddenly feels dry, and I swallow before clearing it.

"As we were saying," Killian says as he and Arlo return to their seats, "you'll both watch the service as it's streamed. Of course, we can't place cameras throughout the entire forest, but they will be placed at camp where most of the activities will be taking place."

"What's the purpose?" Delle asks from behind me, her voice meek, though striking all the same.

A swell of pride rises through my chest at the sound of her voice, though it's quickly followed by fear. I turn my head over my shoulder to look at her, and she begs me without words not to silence her, not to speak over her with my urge to protect her. Though my eyes narrow in consideration and worry, she moves around me, steps forward, and faces the Control on her own.

"Why should we watch our sisters suffer by your actions?" Delle's voice grows louder with each word. "I watched them suffer at the last service, and I suffered myself. I endured my trial yesterday. I'm already condemned for choosing to participate in the Trials of Dissension. So again, I ask, what is the purpose?"

I want to pull her back behind me so I can protect her, but more than that, I want to applaud her. I want to cheer for her. I step in closer behind her and stand silently, giving her the power of my support as she finds her voice.

"We don't owe two sinners an explanation for our decisions," Owen says calmly.

"Is that because you don't *have* an explanation?" Delle asks with a tilt of her head.

Her fingers curl at her sides and it draws notice to the trembling of her hand. She trembles, yet she still speaks, and I don't believe I've ever been more impressed by someone in all my life.

Killian chuckles darkly, and Ryker's face brightens with glee for the drama unfolding before him. Wesley looks over at Owen with furrowed brow, confusion wrinkling his forehead, as if he, too, wonders about the explanation.

"I'll say it again and more clearly this time." Owen speaks with crisp precision, emphasizing his words. "We don't owe two sinners an explanation for our decisions."

Delle straightens, pulling her shoulders back. "Is it written in the Impulse Edict? In the documentation of past trials? That participants should be subjected to witness service rather than focus their energy preparing for their own trials? I've chosen not to serve, so why must I be subjected to witness those in service?"

Killian slaps a palm on the table, the noise of it startling everyone in the room. Delle's right foot moves, as if she's going to step back. I move closer to halt her, pressing my hand to the small of her back to help her hold her stance with courage.

Killian leans forward. "You cannot *choose* not to serve. What you've *chosen* is to be a sinner. You've chosen to dissent, to defy God, to defile the values of Ember Glen in your participation in the Trials of Dissension."

Delle's head dips, but only for a moment before she lifts her chin again. "The only choice I was ever given was whether to continue my existence with a certain future in service, or to participate in the trials. I will not feel shame for making a choice for myself when I was presented with an option for the first time in my life."

I take in the most satisfying breath of my life, drawing in her strength and grace, breathing out my pride and gratitude that I've found a truly kindred spirit in Delle.

"Enough of this." Wesley waves his hand, looking to his brothers. "We've said our piece and they've said theirs. I think we're all exhausted enough from yesterday."

"Agreed," Park says from beside Wesley. "They know they'll be watching the service. Let's get on with our day."

"We might've spared the drama," Theo grumbles as he turns his head of messy blond hair in the direction of Killian, "if only we'd been allowed to deliver the message to our wards directly, rather than dragging them here."

Some voice in the back of my mind urges me to pay attention to these interactions, to take note of the way these men react to each other—and to us—in these heated moments.

Arlo stands abruptly, drawing my full attention. "I'm calling this meeting," he says with command, leaning on his palms on the table, and stirring heat in my belly. "Mercy and Delle just completed their first trial, and they need to rest to find more favorable moods. All we've accomplished here is creating a space for them to argue needlessly with decisions that have already been made."

"Well said." Wesley stands, smoothing down his waistcoat. "Owen and

I need to deliver evaluation times to some of the domestics for their children today, anyway. We have a rather large group of girls to rule on this season."

A heavy weight drops into my gut. When the girls of Ember Glen turn five, they're brought before the Control for this evaluation and ruling. Each of them will be told their future fate that day, assigned to their lifelong role in Ember Glen as either a domestic or a servant. My hand floats up to rub over my heart as anger and discomfort ripple through me at the realization that Wesley and Owen will be making those decisions soon.

"Actually," a voice from the large screen behind us booms, startling me and Delle as we both jump and whirl around—I'd nearly forgotten the Elders were here. "We need Owen to remain behind," Lawrence says. "As well as Killian and Arlo."

My head whips over my shoulder to glance at Arlo, and I find his eyes are already on me, so I turn away just as quickly, afraid someone will notice.

"We need to speak to the three of you," Lawrence says.

"I'll join you then, Wesley," Park offers.

Delle and I turn back to face the Control as they rise from their seats, breaking into side conversations as they move toward the door. Theo turns to Arlo and says something quietly to him. They both nod before Theo steps away, moving quickly toward me and Delle.

"Come on," he says, "I'll return you both to your rooms."

He grabs a hold of Delle's elbow and drags her forward, but my gaze is drawn back to Arlo. Our eyes meet and he holds my stare. I don't know the intention of the look he gives me because I find some uncertainty there, as though he's not entirely sure why he's been called to speak to the Elders.

Worry grips me as I recognize the uncertainty that he feels. I suppose I relied on that certainty to some degree before—his confidence and command, the way he can take control and I can trust him…

Trust him?

I don't think I've ever trusted him.

Or perhaps I always have, and I'm only realizing it now.

His head inclines toward the door, indicating I should go. I don't want to go; I don't want to leave him. Admittedly, I'm feeling nervous over him being called out by the Elders.

"Get moving, sinner, or I'll drag you out myself," Ryker says as he brushes past me, turning and walking backward, waiting for me to move.

I glance over at Arlo one last time, but he's already turned away, lowered into his seat, his eyes downcast to the table where he taps his pen incessantly with a gloved hand.

"Mercy," I hear Theo call for me from the hallway.

I drag myself away, though the desire to remain with Arlo is strong. I pull myself from the overwhelming urge to sit at his side, to hold his hand, to offer him the comfort of my presence. It's an urge I'm surprised I have for him, but I suppose I shouldn't be. There's compassion in my heart for him as real as there is for everyone else I care about. Yet the strength of the compassion I have for him is bewildering, overwhelming, consuming every inch of my damned soul.

It grows stronger with each passing moment, and I fear it will be the thing that breaks me.

chapter eight

ARLO

MY MIND IS lost, entrenched in thoughts of Mercy Madness, which never seem to cease—thoughts that overcome reason and threaten to swallow me whole.

Something dangerous has begun to shift within me since the trial, since her admission in the bathtub as I cared for her after. She told me that when I enter her mind, thoughts of me filled her up and freed her from the burdening fear of what's to come.

And how desperate I am to fill her up in every sense.

It's not a sin to lust after a servant, especially knowing you can use her in service under the next full moon. But it is a sin to lust after someone you can never have—a domestic, or worse, a sinner on trial.

I don't know where God is in these moments where my attention is lost. He's failing me when she's brought to stand before me, when my eyes see nothing but her starlight hair and silvery blue eyes, when my ears hear no other sound but her voice, when my nose detects no scent beyond the heady aroma of wildflowers and the sweet musk of her arousal.

I can always smell her delicious scent, even from across the room, even when her scent couldn't possibly be heavy enough to float across the space between us so strongly. It's a phantom scent which haunts me so divinely. It's as though her demons—which possess me now as fully as they possess her—manipulate my senses to the point of drawing obsession.

I'm becoming *obsessed* with her.

Worse than the obsession itself is the way I enjoy it—the manner in which I intentionally indulge myself by letting the wicked thoughts of her simmer to a slow boil inside my mind.

I had to force myself to lower to my seat in the courtroom. I had to force myself to grab my pen with my gloved hand, and I'd begun to tap it against the table to distract myself from the sight of her.

I focus on the incessant *tap, tap, tap* against the dark wood, letting the sound flood my mind. She needs to leave. I need her to leave the courtroom before I lose control entirely and chase her to her bedroom.

Drape her in rope and bind her to the bed.

Sweet sin, after all she's been through, I need to leave her alone.

The flicker of a small orange flame against a dark background enters my mind, and I close my eyes to focus on it. I imagine removing my gloves and lowering my palm over the flame, which dances atop a candle in my imagination. I imagine burning my skin, letting the fire sizzle and tear through my flesh to bring me the distraction of pain against my impure thoughts.

Eventually, the courtroom door slams shut, forcefully yanking me back to reality. I slam my tapping pen to the table and raise my head to find Killian lowering in the seat to my left, and Owen already seated on the other side of Killian. Lawrence, Edgar, and Clyde remain on the large white screen before us.

"I suppose you're wondering why we wanted to speak to the three of you alone," Clyde begins.

I nod, as do my brothers.

"I assure you the news we have to share with you is good." He smiles, and it begs my curiosity. "This is to remain confidential, as the decision will not be final until the next Shift."

There's a transition of power every twenty-five years in Ember Glen, called the Shift. The last Shift occurred two years ago when my brothers and I became the current group comprising the Control. At the same time, Lawrence, Edgar, and Clyde—who were members of the Control before us—had been officially declared the new Elders. The other four men from their cohort retired from their time served as members of the Control, sent to live blissfully-ever-after in the Land of Kings—a place where it's said the Impulse doesn't exist.

And since the next Shift won't occur for another twenty-three years, I'm confused about the fact that they're speaking to us now about a decision to be made later—more than two decades into the future.

"It goes without saying that this information cannot be shared," Edgar continues the conversation. "We need your confirmation that the information we're about to share with you will not leave this courtroom. You will not discuss it with each other, and certainly not with your brothers. This is crucial."

"Of course, you have our word," Owen says before stealing a glance at me and Killian. He looks as confused as I feel.

"You have my word," Killian says.

I turn my gaze to the Elders. "And you have mine, as well."

"Good." Clyde nods. "I'm pleased to share that you three are slated to become the next generation of Elders in Ember Glen."

My eyes widen in surprise, and my heart stops for a moment. I've just heard words that I've longed to hear for so much of my life. I dreamed of becoming one of the Elders, of becoming one of the highest and most respected leaders in Ember Glen. It's a true honor granted to so few; and only the most devout of men would ever even dream of achieving it.

Joy touches my cheeks as my lips curl into a grin, yet…my smile quickly falters. Excitement for this news that I'd only ever hoped to receive stutters and slips from my grasp.

"Really?" Owen asks with a pleased chuckle. "The three of us?"

"Yes," Edgar confirms. "We began making our observations as soon as your term began. When you're each at your best, we feel the three of you would make for a well-balanced combination of personalities to replace us when the time comes."

"This is an honor to be considered," I say slowly, cautious with my words, "but how can you make such a decision so early on in our term? The next Shift won't occur for another twenty-three years."

"That question leads us to our next point of conversation," Lawrence says slowly. "At your best, the three of you are perfectly suited to take on these roles later in your lives. But at your worst…our support for this may change."

"What do you mean?" I ask.

Clyde's eyes shift on the large screen to look over at Owen. "Owen, you're a strong leader on your best days. Others look to you easily for guidance and to bring calm reflection to stressful situations. Yet, too often, you retain your silence and allow yourself to be overlooked. You allow those with stronger voices to take charge when the situation at hand calls for the composed leadership skills you naturally possess.

"Killian, you're passionate about upholding the values of Ember Glen and are strong in representing the best interests of this community. But your passion often gets the best of you, spurring your Impulse in such a way that it may lead you to misbehavior if you aren't careful. Sin hunts you in your passionate rage, and it will find you if you aren't mindful of your reactions."

Their large eyes on the screen turn to me. "Which leads us to you, Arlo…You possess a more ideal blend of their two best qualities as a strong leader and a passionate believer. Yet we've begun to see a wavering in you, hints of ambiguity where there should be none. We've all had our moments of weakness, our own misunderstandings of God. As you come to understand Him better, and the plan He has for your future, we believe your moments of ambivalence will simply become a regretful part of your youth."

"Blended together," Clyde continues. "The best qualities of each of you will balance well to lead the community of Ember Glen, both while you remain in your term as the Control, and in the future, when you should be confirmed as the Elders of this community."

To be one of the Elders…

I'd often envisioned myself as one of the figureheads on the screen—a man with true power over his community, authority to ensure our Edict is upheld. To be privileged with the honor of accessing the Impulse Edict, to be able to learn of all the laws and history of our land, would be nothing short of incredible.

It's everything I've ever wanted.

Killian and Owen are grinning gleefully from ear-to-ear, and my lips twitch to smile the same. But something holds me back, dampens my pride, floods me with an odd feeling I can't quite name…

Guilt? Shame?

Heartache?

"And now that you know this," Edgar says, "we must discuss the Trials of Dissension. The manner in which the final two trials are carried out will have a major bearing on how we perceive your fit moving forward. At this moment, you are the three we envision as destined to become the next set of Elders. But God's will is always changing, and He may change that destiny should He see fit. You each hold the power to impress Him…or to change His mind entirely."

"You *must* regain control of Ember Glen," Clyde adds with urgency. "We sense there may be whispers among the servants. They have such great shame for Mercy Madness and Delle Carter for the choices they've made; but Mercy's ungodly wiles have bewitched those girls, making them believe she had been a compassionate and caring sister when she served along with them. They cared for her, and they express some sadness for her situation. We cannot fault them for being so weak-minded, but it is our job as the authority of Ember Glen to make them see the truth and bring them closer to God.

"We *cannot allow* their empathy, as such feelings lead to indignation, which gives way to rage, which strikes the match of rebellion. Establish your power and set them right. Your power will be found in brutality through the final two trials. You must ensure the masses know what rebellion would lead to."

"Of course." Killian nods, serious intent gleaming in his overeager eyes. "We will ensure that Delle and Mercy face punishment equal to their crimes."

"Will you?" Lawrence asks. "Because I found the first trial to be rather unimpressive."

Owen's eyes narrow as he tilts his head. "Oh?"

"Keeping Delle off camera, tucked away in a separate room? No one in the village witnessed what she faced, and she *chose* to participate, even when she didn't have to," Lawrence explains.

Killian clears his voice. "I can see how it was a misguided notion. We'll choose more wisely for the next trials."

"Of course you will," Edgar says. "After all, your future depends upon it."

Killian looks over at me, quirking an eyebrow. "Our future depends on it. Of course." He turns back to the Elders on screen. "We'll do our very best."

"Absolutely," Owen echoes.

I nod, though my mind twists and turns, swooping through a field of visions which clutter my thoughts—visions of Mercy, of wildflowers and starlight, and the softness of her touch.

"Arlo?" Owen questions, and it snaps me from the reverie.

I clear my throat. "Of course. Our very best," I confirm, though I'm not sure I believe myself.

chapter nine

ARLO

"ARE YOU COMING?" Owen asks.

Killian pushes open the courtroom door, breezing out into the hallway like a king. I'm sure he feels even more like a king now than before with his over-inflated ego—he's the last man who should've been given prior knowledge of the fact that we're slated to become the next generation of Elders.

I give Owen a tight smile and nod. "I'll be out soon."

I remain in my seat as he leaves, the room empty and the projector off. I lean back in my chair as I try to sort out how I feel about this news, contemplating what this all means for my future. There is a part of me that's thrilled, honored, excited for my future and the good fortune it holds for me. But those feelings are muddied by Mercy's presence in my mind, and the understanding that I have a future—bright with power and prestige—while she has none.

My fingers grip the armrests as I tilt back in my chair, lifting my chin skyward and looking up above me. I avert my gaze from the spotlight that hangs directly above the seat to my left, wondering if it always felt this warm to sit beneath its glow.

The dissonance in my soul has never reverberated with such intensity. This is what I wanted. It's what I've always wanted—to be shortlisted as a future Elder is an honor of the highest degree. But all I can see in my mind is a future where Mercy doesn't exist, and it pangs in my chest.

Worse than the thought of a future after her death is the means by which the Elders asked for us to achieve it. They want brutality in the trials to make an example of the sinners. To achieve the future I've always wanted requires me to ensure Mercy's brutal demise.

"Fuck," I mutter to the ceiling.

"Warden Rainn?" I sit up with a rush when I hear her call my name, the door creaking as it slowly opens.

Starlight shines in through the opening as her head peeks through, turning to search for me. I shove to my feet too quickly and my chair slips back along the floor with a screech.

"What are you doing here?" I ask.

"Everyone has left the courtroom except for you."

"And?" I snap unintentionally as unease waves through me, crashing like a breaking ocean tide.

"If you want to be left alone, just say so." She steps back, turning to leave.

"Mercy," I call after her as I dash for the door.

I fling it wide just as she turns, and I step into the hallway to grab her wrist. I drag her back, pulling her inside the courtroom with me. She whirls around when I release her, stepping backward as I pull the door shut behind us.

And then I stand there—silent and conflicted—looking at her as though an answer to a question I don't know to ask might burst from between her lips. The longer I stand and stare, the more the world fades away, the more space she takes up in my mind, forcing out the discordant harmonies that sing through my combating thoughts to make space for her perfect melody.

It's what I've come to feel more and more whenever I'm alone in Mercy's presence. And *sweet sin*, how it twists me when she looks at me like that, with that expression which reflects a perfect mixture of compassion and curiosity.

"Are you okay?" she asks, and with the slight tilt of her head and narrowing of her eyes, I can see she truly wants to know.

"No," I tell her honestly. "I don't think that I am."

"Did the Elders tell you something upsetting?"

I shake my head as I stride deeper into the courtroom, brushing past her side and shuddering with the vibration of her energy as I move away from her toward the table. "I'm not sure whether upsetting is the right word for it." My fingers come down to graze the tabletop as I walk along the curve of it.

"If you'd like to share, I'm sure I could help you find the appropriate word to match your feelings."

I chuckle, stopping at the center point of the table and turning back to look at her. She stands with her arms crossed, one hip jutted out to the side beneath the red flowing gown she wears so well—long sleeves that are cuffed at the ends, a deep V-neck with the point resting on her cleavage, cinched at the waist and flowing down around her like a crimson waterfall.

"Do you think I can tell you what they told me?" I lean, sitting against the edge.

"I think you can do whatever you want to with little risk of consequence."

"Oh?" I raise my eyebrows.

"Do I need to remind you of the sins you've committed with me?"

I swallow, my jaw tensing. "I don't need a reminder, Mercy Madness. I'm reminded of our sins every time I close my eyes."

She looks down at the floor, averting her gaze.

"Look at me."

Her eyes snap back to me in a flash. "Don't tell me what to do."

"Why are you here? Why did you wait for me?"

Her hands drop to her sides as she shrugs. "Honestly, I don't know, Arlo. I don't know anything anymore."

"Says the woman who knows everything…"

"Are we back to that?"

"Back to what?"

"Your self-righteous snark—"

"*My* self-righteous snark?" I laugh. "And what about yours?"

"*Mine?*"

"I've never known a person more self-righteous and snarkier than you."

"Then perhaps no one has shown you a mirror."

I can't help the grin that cuts across my face. "Perhaps you can guide me to one."

"Perhaps I will." She tries to remain stoic, but I don't miss the twitch of her cheek as she fights a smile.

Dear God, let her give me that smile.

My grin broadens as it slowly creeps through. My fingers curl around the edge of the table on either side of my hips, the leather of my gloves creaking with the tension, and I drop my head to gaze at the gray floor. If I look at her for too long, I might lose control of myself and take her right here in the courtroom.

"I received news from the Elders."

She's quiet for a moment before she asks, "What news?"

"I'm not supposed to tell anyone." I glance up to find her a step closer, and it kickstarts my heart.

"You could tell me."

"Could I?"

Could I tell her?

"Have I given up your secrets yet?"

"You haven't."

She takes a step closer, dropping her arms to her sides—an opening, an invitation that unwittingly tugs at my heartstrings. "Are you still worried that I will? After what I confessed…"

"After you told me that you need me?"

Sweet sin.

Hearing the words come out of my mouth is jarring enough, but it draws the memory of holding her in the bathtub after her trial, hearing them from her while she held me. I swallow hard against the rising lump in my throat.

"No, I'm not worried, though I know I should be." Confusion wrinkles my brow. "I *know* I should be worried, Mercy. I should be terrified of the sins we've committed together, and I don't know why I'm not."

"Maybe it's because we both know I'm going to die. Because you know it wouldn't serve me to tell anyone the things we've done in secret." Her head drops as her gaze lands on the floor. "Because we'd both like to have more secret moments with each other before the end."

"Come here," I demand.

I tighten my grip on the table's edge to keep myself from moving—I want her to come to me. Even when I desperately need her near, I want to see her move; I want to know she *chose* to come to me.

I want to know she chooses me.

She hesitates, but then she glides across the floor like an angel on a cloud—a dark angel in a flowing crimson gown who stains the purity with her divinely indecent sway. Each step loosens my grip on the table, easing bit by bit with each shared breath between us. And each moment where space remains between the gravity of our bodies becomes more painful than the last. Her gliding steps aren't quick enough to sate my boiling need for her.

I reach out and clamp my gloved palm around the side of her waist once she's within reaching distance, and I forcefully drag her against me. Our bodies collide with shared heat and the instant relief of finally connecting. One of her hands grips the open collar of my button-down shirt while the other drops to my waist, fingers locking on the chain that links from one button of my waistcoat to its pocket at the side.

We lock eyes, staring at each other with a soul-deep gaze that has tremors of need rippling through me. And at the same moment, we let go, wrapping our arms around each other, embracing as intimately as we did in the bathtub last night. We share an exhale in relief as we shift together, her curves gliding against me until we align perfectly, locking together like two puzzle pieces. She nuzzles her face into the crook of my neck as I slide my hand up her spine, cradling the back of her head in my palm as we strengthen our hold on each other.

"I wish it didn't have to be like this," she whispers.

"I wish for so many things when I look at you, Mercy."

"Tell me."

My fingers curl, sinking into her hair as I turn my face to press kisses to her cheek with my blasphemous lips. "I wish to understand what I feel for you and why I feel it…why my thoughts are so conflicted. Has God forsaken me to make me want you the way I do? What is this that I feel for you?"

She sighs with contentment as her hands move across my back, stroking me. "Connection."

"It's more than that."

"Lust."

"If that were all, my need for you would have been satisfied when I filled you yesterday during the trial."

She breathes out slowly, and I swear I feel her shudder. "This is something more than connection and lust for you?"

"I don't know what it is, but it's *more*, Mercy. Of course, it's more."

Her tension gives way and she sinks, her body relaxing in my arms. I rise from the table to hold the weight of her, relishing the way she relents to me. Holding her this way is divine, but my body begs for her unholiness.

I grip her hips and spin us both around, rushing her backward until her ass hits the table's edge. Her hands find my biceps and grab hold as she arches back to look at me. Our eyes meet, and her silvery blue irises flicker as they search mine beneath the glow of the spotlight over the table.

"I know it's more," she whispers. "But even that's not enough to save me, is it?"

Mercy's fate is sealed.

She is destined to die.

And there's not a damn thing in the world I can do to save her. Yet the admission that she feels something more with me—and her expression of sad acceptance—feels like a rope being drawn around my heart, a knot being tied and pulled until the beating muscle stops altogether.

I bring my hands to her face, cupping her cheeks. "Mercy, you sin—"

"Don't tell me I've sinned," she says on a rushed exhale. "Don't say I'm a sinner. We both know my sins have nothing to do with this."

Confusion creeps through my mind. "What do you mean?"

"It's about power, Arlo. It's about control. It has nothing to do with my sins, because if it did, then you'd be condemned, too."

"I *would* be condemned if anyone found out—"

"And they won't because you're allowed to sin in secret."

"Well, that's a ridiculous argument. By that logic, anyone in Ember Glen could sin in secret."

"Yes," she chuckles humorlessly, "that's exactly my point. How many men do you think are sinning in secret? And if they're found out, how many have been brought to judgment for their sins in comparison to the number of women?"

"Women bring temptation."

"Yes, of course," she rolls her eyes, "and it's a woman's fault that a man chooses to act on that temptation." Her voice twists with sardonic anger and my indignation rises to meet hers.

"It's the fault of the Impulse, Mercy. It's why we purge; it's why there are servants to satisfy those temptations on a single night so all the others can be free from the horrors brought by sex and violence."

Her hands slap against my wrists and she shoves them away from her face, forcing me to step back. "We meet those horrors monthly in service. We are *not* free from them."

"Servants sacrifice such that others—"

"Such that *men* can indulge themselves without consequence."

"And so that domestics can be free from fear, free from threats of violence, and—"

"Entirely devoid of passion of any kind? Is that what you were going to say? What kind of life do they live with nothing to fear? With no sense of urgency? Without sense of their own mortality?" She raises her hands, and though I'm expecting her to shove me away, she doesn't. Instead, they land on my chest with a half-hearted thud and remain there, drawing my breaths quicker and heavier. "Without fear, there is no drive, there is no passion, no desire…"

I step forward, crushing her to the table's edge, laying my palms on either side of her hips on the dark wood. I bend over her deeply, forcing her back to arch as my body kisses hers.

"Do you fear me, then?" I ask. "Is that what this is? Does your passion and desire for me come from your fear of me?"

"Yes," she blurts without hesitation.

Conflict swirls within my soul. I want to prove that she has no reason to fear me; equally, I want to give her something to fear, if for no reason other than to draw out her passion for me.

Heat rises within me, suffocating my lungs, making it so difficult to breathe that I pant for air. Her lips part as I stare her down. The arch in her back deepens as she places a palm on the tabletop behind her, leaning against it and jutting her hips forward. I bring one of my hands from the table to her lower back, encouraging the alignment of her body with mine.

I dip my head to bring my lips only a breath away from hers. "Do you fear me now?"

We both know what I'm really asking.

Do you desire me now?

Do you have passion for me now, in this moment?

She bobs her head with a jerky nod.

I rub the tip of my nose across hers. "Then I suppose I fear you, too, Mercy Madness."

Leaning all her weight on one hand, she lifts the other to touch my cheek, and I sigh, letting my head fall into her palm as she caresses my skin with her brushing thumb.

"I see your disbelief and the way it plagues you," she whispers. "It hurts me so much that you won't let go, that you let the conflict in your mind gnaw away at your soul. My heart wouldn't be drawn to you so intensely if it didn't know the truth hiding in yours. I just wish you could see it, too. I wish you would let yourself see me as something other than the temporary conflict that plagues you." Her eyes move about my face, studying me with such intensity that I feel burning through my skin. "Call me foolish because I must be to say this, but…I won't betray you, Arlo. I don't think I ever could, even if I wanted to. I'll take all of your secrets to the grave with me."

My eyes fall shut at the odd sense of shame I feel for her admission, because I can feel her shame for saying it rippling from her the same.

"Why?" I ask.

"I don't wish my fate upon anyone, least of all you."

"Perhaps I'd deserve it."

"It's not my judgment to make."

I drop my forehead to touch hers while she continues to brush her thumb over my cheek. "Is it God's?" The question feels strange to ask—blasphemous—but it's genuine.

"I don't know," she says. "But I know it's not mine."

I touch my lips to hers. "I haven't earned your tireless compassion."

"So earn it now. Tell me your secrets."

I kiss her softly, chastely, humming against her lips, which part gradually against mine. It's a soft, subtle movement that coaxes my tongue to slip between them. A moan vibrates through her throat as I taste her slowly, languidly swirling my tongue with hers as I shift my feet to press in closer, harder.

The kiss deepens and simmers, heating steadily, bubbling to a boil. Her hand on my cheek slips, fingers reaching for my hair and tangling through it, her grip tightening at the back of my head. Every inch of my frame is fastened to hers, our legs tangling through her long skirt as they shift beneath us, our bodies molded in mirroring arches as she curves back and I bend with her.

I'm so securely bound to the need for our bodies to exist as one that I nearly collapse on her when she turns her face away, unexpectedly breaking free from the kiss. My lips burn as though she's torn them cleanly from my face. My palm splays across the small of her back to secure my hold on her, afraid she'll squirm away from me.

Though she keeps her head turned sideways, avoiding my eyes, both her palms find my cheeks to cup them in her hold. I don't know whether she's holding me to keep me from stealing another kiss or if she's trying to hold herself away from the temptation of stealing one from me.

"Someone might see us," she pants.

"I nearly don't care."

It's dangerous for me not to care. It worries me about the state of my mind and how she's changing it, how her demons have dug in so deep that they may never climb out. But that's the thing about demons…they make you feel so good, so unbelievably alive, that you forget the higher power you follow, along with your morals and beliefs. They take it all away and make sinning feel like finding God, like dropping into paradise, like nothing could ever feel better than committing these moral offenses.

The demons are winning.

I'll soon be forever lost to these sinful delights, and my soul begs me to give into it.

chapter ten
ARLO

"STARLIGHT, I—"

"I know about Delle."

I know Mercy's only trying to change the subject, trying to break free from the sexual tension that refuses to let us go. She can try all she wants, but she can't deny how she trembles as those two syllables shake through her.

Starlight.

It's the word I use to claim her.

She turns her face to meet my gaze squarely, tightening her grip on my cheeks to hold me in place. My eyes fall to her perfectly parted pink lips, my mind stuck on the taste of them and struggling to focus on her words. I lurch for them, trying to push past the grip of her palms to steal another kiss, but she jerks her head back.

She won't let me taste her—and it's killing me—but the way she studies my features, then settles her gaze on my lips with restrained longing sends a pleasant thrill through my body.

"I know you and Theo didn't participate in Delle's trial."

The mention of the trial drags me back to reality. "How do you know that?"

"Delle told me." Her hands lower, slipping down the sides of my neck, coming to a stop over my chest, gripping my collar. "She told me this morning and I…"

"What?"

"I want to know why. I want to know how you justified it to yourself," she demands.

The sincere curiosity in her gaze implores me to speak the truth. She's given me no reason to think I shouldn't trust her with yet another secret.

"I could see her as my sister." I lick my suddenly dry lips, struck by the sobering memory of seeing Delle on display, ready for use by my brothers in God. I pull back, straightening, though I remain close with my arm around her. "I couldn't bring myself to touch her that way."

"It was your duty, and you neglected it." I hate the way she says it, with self-satisfied righteousness, but I can't deny she's right.

I sigh. "Perhaps it was, and perhaps I did."

"If they found out she didn't truly complete the first trial, would they make her repeat it?"

"No," I tell her firmly, with lifted brows, "because they won't find out."

"You're going to lie to your brothers?"

My head jerks to the side. "Are you trying to bait me into an argument?"

"I'm only asking, Arlo."

"Delle completed her trial, and that's the truth as far as anyone can see it."

"That's something I needed to know; something I needed to hear from you." She sighs in a manner of reverie. "I think there must be some goodness within you after all, Arlo Rainn."

"You think there's *some goodness* within me?" Anger shades my mind with gray clouds that threaten to storm between us as I release her and step back. "What did you think of me before? Did you think there was something wrong with me?"

Mercy pushes off the table, stepping toward me. She opens her mouth to speak, but I don't allow it. I close the distance between us, meeting her chest to chest, glaring down at her with ferocity.

"Did you think I was a bad person? Did you think *I* was the sinner?"

She doesn't back down, staring up at me with a ferocity that matches mine. "Yes. Yes, I thought you were a bad person. Yes, I thought there was something wrong with you. And, according to the Edict, you *are* the sinner. You lusted after me. You fucked me outside of service. You—"

"For God's sake, Mercy, shut your beautiful fucking mouth."

I grip her hips and spin her, turning her to face the table. I grip the back of her neck, pushing down to bend her over the edge. She slaps her palms against the hard wood, trying to press up, but I fold over her, pinning her heavily with my weight resting on her back.

She turns her cheek to press against the surface as I apply pressure to the back of her neck. "Let me up."

"You don't want me to." I reach between our bodies and press my hand to the back of her thigh, dragging my fingers slowly up toward the curve of her ass.

Her body jerks beneath me as she tries to rise. "Don't…" she whispers half-heartedly.

"Don't, what? Don't touch you? Don't prove you right in thinking I'm a sinner, the same as you?"

I'm suddenly panting as my fingers grapple with her skirt, lifting it up enough to slip my hand beneath and find her underwear taut across her cheek. She whimpers as I play with the hem, slowly nudging the fabric to bunch toward her crack.

"Someone might walk in…"

"Is that your *only* protest, starlight? That someone might walk in?" I tear my glove from my hand and land my bare palm against her exposed cheek with a light smack before caressing her skin. "Give me a more compelling reason to let you up, and I will."

Sweet sin.

One moment, I'm furious with her, and the next, I'm lost in my lust for the feel of her skin against mine.

She's quiet for a moment, still as my fingers draw along the lines and curves of her flesh. The longer her silence stews, the more pliant we become, both slowly submitting to the dominant gravity between us. The more I want her, the more my need grows. The more I need her, the more my convictions splinter. And the wedge is so deep, they threaten to shatter spectacularly.

"I don't have one…" she finally says, and my fucking cock twitches to sink inside her.

I dip my head to kiss the side of her face, her hair spread haphazardly across her cheek, soft against my lips. "I need you to give me a reason," I whisper with a trembling voice. "I beg of you, Mercy. Give me one reason to let you up before I lose control…before I lose everything."

"I'm…" Her panting hesitation reaches inside me, grabs hold of my heart, and tears it out from between my ribs.

My hips move, grinding against her ass, my cock throbbing to find some relief. My pounding heart beats wildly in her phantom grip, waiting for her to decide if she's going to encourage this or give me a fucking damn good reason to stop.

When she finally speaks, her voice is quiet, but sure. "Yesterday I was fucked for seven hours by six men I don't want, and one who I do. And though I always want you, Arlo…" She pauses, and her admission lingers, the weight of it heavy, anchoring to my lust and sinking it right down to the ground. "I always want you, but I need to heal. If you start, I'll make you finish, and it will hurt for me."

I drop my forehead to her shoulder, feeling suddenly defeated, though I can't quite sort out which battle I feel I've lost—the battle with my lust for her, the battle with my growing feelings for her, or the battle in my mind with God.

All I know is the thought of hurting her makes my chest ache, makes my spine tremor with rage— yet I'm meant to hurt her so much worse before the end of the trials.

"I wish I could erase the pain of yesterday." I stroke my palm once more down the curve of her ass, and mustering all my strength, I rise and step back.

She remains bent over the table for moments after I've left her, half of her dress hiked up, tucked into the side of her underwear, leaving her cheek exposed. And those boots—those fucking servants' boots she still wears make it so much harder to resist the ache to fill her.

With a huff, she rises all at once, tugging her dress down with a sharp hand before whirling around to face me with pinkened cheeks. "You can't. No one can. Just like you can't erase the years of pain I've experienced in service."

My instinct is to argue, to remind her that her pain in service doesn't matter, so long as she's done her duty for the men of Ember Glen. But a niggling voice inside my mind halts me, silences that instinctive voice that only concerns itself with rules and laws and godliness. She's becoming the gray that muddles my mind in the slivers between the black and white.

"Is that what service is like for you? Like your trial yesterday?"

I don't know why I asked, but I'm suddenly curious to know. I felt her pain yesterday—her moments of fear, her moments of resignation. I felt it all as though I were living it with her because of this odd connection between us. Her head ticks to the side as her expression flickers in curiosity. Perhaps she noticed the way I quelled my instinctive voice, too.

"Sometimes, yes. Sometimes it's more violent and less sexual, and sometimes it's the opposite. But focusing on one man, as opposed to several, is easier." She blinks her eyes shut, her head lowering. "Not easier, but different."

"Yesterday felt different?"

"Yes." She looks up at me. "But mostly because of you."

"What did I do?"

She shakes her head, leaning back against the table's edge, bringing her hands in front of her and wringing them nervously. "It's not about what you did, Arlo."

"Then what was it?" I fold my arms over my chest.

"It's because…it's because of the connection I feel with you." She looks down at her twisting fingers. "Having your presence and feeling it's absence are both profound."

Profound.

My arms feel heavy, and I drop them to my sides. "Mercy, I…Your presence is profound for me, too. And I imagine…" I pause to gather my words, "I imagine your absence will be, as well."

"So you think you'll miss me when I'm gone?"

Sweet sin.

Will I miss her?

Some unseen force moves me and deciphering whether it's divine or demonic in nature is pointless. It's powerful, and it barrels through me, pushing me closer to her, overwhelming me with poetic words I know I'll need to write later.

I tap my knuckle beneath her chin to lift her head. "Would the sky miss the stars? Would heaven miss an angel? Would the wildflowers in the meadow miss the rain?" My eyes skim the features of her face as I speak, finding more beauty with each line I trace. I grip her face as I step closer, aligning to her body, tilting to rest my forehead against hers.

"If God does exist," she whispers, "then He's a cruel maker to bring us together this way."

I should revolt from her words, but oddly, I feel no revulsion. I only feel agreement because it does feel cruel that I had to find her as a sinner, to know her through her trials, to want her this profoundly while she seeks absolution with her certain death looming. My resolve is weakening with each breath she takes, with each pain that she encounters. I fall deeper into her madness with each new misery she endures.

She may be possessed by demons, and they may afflict me the same now, but I'm not sure it matters to me anymore. I know that it should, yet here I am, tempting my lust once again with my mouth only inches from her parted lips.

Stop.

Pull back.

Confess your secrets in penance of your desire.

"I'm slated to become an Elder one day," I blurt out the truth, which seems less like an honor and more like a curse as moments pass—a punishment for sinning with her to get what I always wanted, yet forced to spend a lifetime without her.

"What?" She jerks her head back and I release, letting her pull away.

"It's what the Elders told us when they asked me, Owen, and Killian to remain behind. They're watching us in these trials to determine whether we've shown ourselves worthy to be the next generation of Elders."

"I…I don't know what to say." She blinks, turning her head away and gazing off at the wall, at nothing.

"It's something I've always wanted."

Her head snaps to look at me. "To become an Elder? Why?"

"To serve God by interpreting the Impulse Edict for the sake of all men in Ember Glen." I reach out to tuck her hair behind her ear. "I've always dreamt of it, of holding that power, of being one of the three highest members of authority in our community."

Her face twists with a mixture of disgust and sadness, and I can't stand it. I can't take the way she looks at me with horror in her haunted eyes. It makes my gut clench with an unpleasant ache—a feeling of sickness I only get when I know in my soul that something just isn't quite right.

So what isn't right?

Is it the way she feels about my words?

Or is it the way I feel about them?

"So you always dreamt of it," she repeats my words slowly, "but do you still dream of it now? Is that the future you desire, Warden Rainn?" There's a sharp pang in my gut at her return to the formal address. "To end my life in the trials and go on with your life as you'd planned it?"

No.

The word echoes loudly in my mind, reverberating and sending a shudder down my spine.

What do I say?

What can I tell her?

How do I find the truth in my muddled mind?

Sorrow finds its way into my soul at the reality of the situation, setting it on fire to burn me torturously in a blaze of crackling misery. I reach around her to grip the back of her head in my palm and drag her forward, forcing her to bring her forehead to touch mine.

"My life will never go on as I planned it," I tell her, letting words I haven't revised escape me freely. "I didn't plan for this. I didn't plan to find you as anything other than a sinner. I didn't plan to find your heart."

Her lashes flutter as she closes her eyes, her hand gripping my wrist where I hold her head, not to pull my hand away, but to keep me in place. "Is there any part of you that believes it's God's plan? That maybe the God you pray to wanted us to find each other…to find a better life?"

"It doesn't matter to you what the God I pray to intends for us. You're asking whether I'm willing to see a different future than the one we've been assigned."

Her head nods against mine and her eyes flicker open to meet mine, to look for the truth within my gaze, and that's all she'll find there.

"I don't believe that God could have planned to make my heart beat the way it does whenever I see you, to make my soul vibrate at the sound of your voice…" her thumb gently caresses across my wrist, "to make the ground tremor beneath my feet whenever you touch me like that, with softness and unearned compassion."

"You must believe it's the demons which plague me, then." I see her sad smile, muscles twitching at the corners of her lips.

"Maybe it's mine. Maybe I have my own demons which plague me—make me lie to my brothers, make me want to sin with you…over and over again."

I tilt my chin forward to kiss her, quickly pushing my tongue past her teeth to devour her, letting our tongues speak silently to share our fears and longing without words. The kiss breaks naturally in a moment of beautiful tension, a shared desire for more, though we both know this isn't the time or place for more.

"I'm starting to believe the whole of Ember Glen is plagued by demons, Mercy. That maybe we're all on the brink of sin."

She looks at me sweetly, a touch of concern wrinkling her forehead. "I think you're plagued by confusion, Arlo."

My forehead creases to match hers as I watch her with a serious expression. "I am." I let out a breath, finding some strange relief in the admission. "I'm so confused about everything, and I don't think I've ever felt so lost."

She nods as my hand drops to wrap around the side of her neck, my thumb absently stroking her throat. She reaches a hand forward and draws her fingers through my hair at the side of my head, tangling through the strands and rubbing my scalp in a circular motion that has my eyes fluttering shut.

"I understand you, Arlo. I've felt that confusion before, and I know it's painful. I know, and I'm sorry."

I force my eyes to open, to look at her gorgeous face and see her for what she is in this very moment—not as a sinner, and not as a woman on trial seeking absolution for a wretched soul.

How could her soul be wretched when it resonates so clearly with mine? Is mine wretched, too? Or is the lens of our judgment so smudged that we can no longer see the truth?

"The only solution is to seek the truth," she whispers, responding as though she could read my mind. "The confusion only ends when you seek truth through the madness, when you seek truth above all else."

My heart drops like a lead ball in my gut.

Right now, the only truth I know is that her last day is coming…and when she perishes, I may not survive it, either.

LATER, WHEN I'M alone, I write the truth that springs from my madness for Mercy, my hopeless longing, my ardent passion.

Will I miss her when she's gone?

Would the sky miss the stars?
Would heaven miss an angel?
Would the wildflowers in the meadow miss the rain?

Can the moon glow without the sun?
Can the snow fall without the clouds?
Can a man purge without a willing servant?

Will my lungs burn when she takes her last breath?
Will my blood refuse to flow through my veins?
Will my limbs stiffen when she becomes forever still?

Will I miss her when she's gone?
With all the brightness of her starlight hair.

Will she remember me in her damnation?
I'll never have to wonder.
I'll wreck my soul to meet her in hell...
and she'll never know the ache of missing me.

chapter eleven

Mercy

I WEAR BLACK tonight.

It's the night of service beneath the full moon, and instead of wearing red, as trial participants are meant to, I've chosen to show solidarity with my sisters, regardless of what they think of me now. I found my black servants' clothes, which had been left in my room—the outfit I'd worn the day Arlo first brought me to the Homestead—and washed them in the tub so I could wear them tonight.

The long-sleeve, form-fitting black top is more modest than the black corsets my sisters will wear, though it does bare the top of my chest with its sweetheart neckline. I brush my hands over the mid-length skirt, feeling an unexpected wave of emotion as I look down at the asymmetric tiers of black lace and the black boots I've refused to stop wearing.

It's strange to feel as though I'm traveling back in time—wearing the clothes of the servant I'd been for four years. And though I've only been wearing the elegant crimson gowns of a trial participant for a few weeks, it may as well have been decades for how different the world feels now. It's not that the world feels different so much as I feel bolder living in it, braver, more willing to take a daring stand and make my rebellious thoughts known loudly and clearly—the end of my life is quickly approaching and I have nothing left to fear.

Coming into that fearlessness is bewildering, remarkable, and at times, perplexing. It's unsettling to realize that I've accepted the fact that I'm going to die, that my days are numbered, and there's nothing I can do to change that. Sometimes it makes me feel uneasy that I've accepted it, but other times, like tonight, it makes me feel empowered.

I smile to myself, pleased with the decision to wear this, as the small act of defiance fuels me with a burst of energy. Though my sisters have turned against me, they're my sisters, nonetheless. I don't fault them for believing all the things they've been told to believe since birth. If anything, it makes me feel all the more settled in my decision to wear this tonight—to show the Control that I am still one of them, and perhaps, someday, more of them will rise against our oppression.

I open my bedroom door and step into the hallway, heading for Delle's room. Before I reach it, her door clicks open and she slowly steps out into the hallway, anxious hands running down her skirt.

Her *black* skirt.

My grin broadens as she turns to see me and lets a nervous smile touch her cheeks. I'd told her my plans to wear this tonight as my small act of rebellion and solidarity, as I didn't want to surprise her with my choice not to wear what I was meant to. But I hadn't expected that she'd choose to do the same. Truly, I *should* have expected it, with the way she's grown bolder and has begun to find her voice.

She's dressed as a servant from head to toe—a role she'd only had to fulfill once before she chose to participate in the Trials of Dissension. She looks stunning and strong in her black corset top, with thin strips of lace that drape off-shoulder. Her layered skirt is similar to mine, and of course, she has on her black boots.

I'm sure she feels relief to wear the comfortable boots since she's been wearing those awful shoes with the tall heels, provided by the Control, until now. I'm convinced those shoes were supplied for us to wear only to slow us down if we tried to run.

"Look at you," I say as she stops in front of me. "A stunning little rebel in the making."

"I like to consider myself a mini-Mercy. Just taking notes from the woman who paved the way for my sins."

We laugh together, and it feels good to smile, to joke, to share pride in our small defiance, even if the joy will only last for a few moments.

"Thank you for doing this, for wearing that," I say to her.

"I couldn't let you do it alone. I just…I want to be brave. I'm trying to be as brave as you are."

My head tilts as I sigh. "Delle, you are the bravest person I know."

"I wouldn't have been brave enough to do this," she gestures her hands down in front of her outfit, her eyes flicking down, "without you telling me you were doing it. I wouldn't have even thought of it. And I wouldn't be here at all if it weren't for you…if you hadn't chosen to run at the last service and get the attention of the Control. They brought the trials back because of you, Mercy, and it gave me a way out."

I want to remind her that she was the one who ran first that night, that if it hadn't been her first service—and if I hadn't already been labeled a rebel, chosen to run, and drawn their attention—it might have been *her* actions that spurred them to bring back the trials.

She's so much stronger and braver than she gives herself credit for. But I don't tell her that, and not because I don't want her to credit herself for her strength. I think she needs to work that out for herself to become the woman I know she'll be…even if she'll only be that woman for moments before she dies.

I'm so proud of her for choosing to fight for something better than the life she was assigned, but I feel equally broken-hearted that the Trials of Dissension are the only choice she was ever given.

Serve or die.

Malo fucking mori…

I pull her in for a quick hug, silently thanking her for seeing me as more than just a woman who sinned—more than the woman who was too scared to serve when it meant being lit on fire, who ran from a duty she never wanted nor asked for. We smile at each other as I pull back, but as moments pass, joy and pride fade.

"I wish we didn't have to watch the service tonight," she says on a sigh.

"I know. It nearly feels worse to have to watch them endure."

The faces of Ellary and Cambria come to mind. I see Ellary's bright, kind smile and her striking green eyes, her features framed so beautifully by her shiny, straight brown tresses. And Cambria, with her dark eyes and hair, her sensual pout that she liked to paint with burgundy lipstick, which always looked so stunning on her medium-brown complexion.

The sight of them in my mind lifts anxiety through my center, stress floating up from behind my ribcage and causing an ache in my chest. It was bad enough having to witness what was happening all around me on nights of service—to see my sisters hurting and in pain, and not be able to do anything about it. Yet somehow, sitting and watching it unfold on a screen seems worse.

We wait in the hallway until Arlo's door clicks open, and he appears. His foot has barely crossed the threshold when my heart starts pounding, my body turning to face his. My eyes lift, searching to lock on his, but instead, his gaze traces me from bottom to top, taking in my clothing with a frown and a wrinkled brow.

"What are you wearing?" he asks.

I pull back my shoulders. "The uniform of servants."

"You're no longer a servant." His gaze flits over to Delle, then comes back to me, once again tracing my figure, lingering at the curve of my hip. He blinks and shakes his head. "It doesn't matter. There's no time to change, anyway." He waves his hand down the hallway behind us. "Just go."

"Where's Theo?" Delle asks as we turn and walk toward the stairs.

"Setting up camp for service. He'll be back soon."

"Will you be purging tonight?" I ask, though I'm not entirely certain I want his answer.

"All men must purge beneath the full moon," he says, though I don't feel like that answers my question.

His hand closes around my wrist, halting me with a sharp tug. His body collides with my backside as he steps forward to close the distance, and he holds me in place as Delle continues on, oblivious.

He speaks against my ear, and I feel the heat of his breath across my skin. "You tempt me dressed this way, like a servant. I have only one desire to purge, and it's with you, starlight."

My stomach flips and my pulse speeds at his words, at the way his hand loosens from around my wrist and his fingers trace up my arm, leaving a trail of goosebumps in their wake.

"And if I were still a servant," I whisper, "then purging with me tonight would not be a sin."

What am I saying?

Why did I say that to him?

"Sweet sin," he mutters breathlessly. "If only I had your service—"

"Coming?" Delle reaches the staircase and turns to glance at us before descending the steps.

"Yes." Arlo quickly releases me and steps back. "Get moving, Mercy."

A shudder travels down my spine. Some vicious, wanton part of me hopes he'll grab my wrist again, pull me into a room, shut me in behind a closed door, and kiss me the way only he can. Yet, the truer part of me knows that I must keep this night in reverence. I must focus on what my sisters are about to endure, because feeling their pain emboldens and empowers me...

And frankly, I need all the boldness and power I can get.

I rush ahead, dragging myself from Arlo's inexplicable hold on me, and jog down the steps to get away from the distraction of him. In my haste, I pass Delle about halfway down the stairs. I step down to the foyer where the sunburst pattern on the tile lays mockingly, an instant reminder of my day of torture during the first trial. Then I stop and wait, turning my back to the staircase to avoid gazing at Arlo as he descends behind us.

I can no longer look that man in the eyes without giving away the obvious manner in which he makes my body sway, intoxicated by his very presence.

"We'll be down the hall," his voice echoes as he descends, "in the room where Delle's trial was held."

"Why?" Delle asks sharply. "Why in that room?" She crosses her arms over her chest, her hands coming up to rub her bare biceps.

"They couldn't have set it up somewhere else?"

"No." Arlo is terse with the single syllable.

He steps down to the main floor, circling around us and moving toward the hall. Delle and I follow him to the room where she served her first trial. The door is open and Arlo gestures for us to go inside. I move past Delle as she takes a deep breath, entering the room slowly, hoping to give her a few moments to steel herself before entering the space where she endured her own torturous trial.

The room is roughly the same size as the bedrooms upstairs, except it has no bed, no furniture to speak of, really. It's been emptied out to create a dark, enclosed space for us to sit and watch the horror.

There's nothing to look at aside from the large white screen setup along the far wall—no mirrors, no artwork hung on the walls, not even wallpaper or a lovely shade painted on the walls to draw our eyes away from the screen. There are windows behind it, but they only look out to the open village square beyond. There's nothing of comfort in here at all. Just four walls, dim lighting, and two simple wooden chairs, placed side-by-side and facing the screen.

"Take a seat," Arlo commands.

As Delle comes in beside me, we pause to share a glance. I give her a reassuring nod before I move deeper into the cold, stark room. We circle the chairs, and Delle gradually lowers to her seat, shifting uncomfortably to settle into the hard wood.

I stand beside the other chair, placing my hand on the backrest as I stare down at the seat. My nerves prickle and my pulse quickens as I'm overcome by intense and unexpected anxiety. It's not quite the same kind of anxiety I would feel just before serving, though it strikes me abruptly and harshly all the same. And it feels different—too intense for knowing that I'm not serving tonight.

Not anxiety.

A knowing feeling…A stab of instinct…

It feels as though the energy all around me is shifting and changing; as though the earth might crack open beneath my feet and swallow me whole; as though the sky might crumble and fall, raining its remnants down to destroy the world.

It feels as though everything is about to change.

"Take a seat, sinner." Arlo's voice is firm.

I look back at him, still firmly planted in the doorway. He leans his shoulder against the frame, with his arms crossed, one leather-clad finger tapping his bicep. The look of him there takes me back to the day he brought me to the Homestead, when he took me to my room, ordering me to undress and take a bath.

I remember thinking how disarmingly beautiful he was then, and I think it now, as well. His thick, wavy strands of tawny brown hair are disheveled in an intentional manner. The slightly ginger hue through his russet tresses carries through his short beard, and even through the lighter strands from his chest, hinted through the open collar of his button-down shirt.

The buttoned waistcoat serves to emphasize his stunning frame—lean and strong but not overly broad with muscle. My eyes are drawn to the silver chain that runs from one button to the small pocket stitched across the side—my fingers twitch to grab hold of it and draw him against me.

I press my eyes shut and shake my head, blinking away the image of pulling him close, his warm arms encircling me, his soft lips kissing my cheek, whispering against my ear that he'll miss me when I'm gone, that he aches for me, that he must have me now…

"Mercy," he snaps. "*Sit.*"

My eyes pop open to meet his, narrowed and strikingly blue, the intensity of his stare emphasizing the wrinkle of his brow as he watches me with a serious expression.

Confusion.

Just as I'd concluded the other day when we spoke in the courtroom, Arlo Rainn is confused, conflicted. I can see it now in the way he tries to maintain his authority, though his muscles twitch to loosen, to lengthen, to relax in my presence. In a way, it's humbling to know how conflicted he truly is. Internal conflict rises from dissonance, from seeing what doesn't make sense and seeking the truth that lies somewhere beyond.

It gives me hope for him.

I have no hope that my future will change, but it's comforting to know there may be hope for Arlo. And if there's hope for Arlo Rainn, then perhaps there's hope for Ember Glen, too.

He looks so troubled by his inner conflict that I can't help but ask, "Are you okay?"

Delle spins sideways in her seat to glare at me, curious about why I asked, perhaps surprised that I should care at all whether he's okay.

"I'm fine, sinner. Just sit." He turns his head to avoid looking me in the eyes, but I see the muscles in his throat work as he swallows nervously.

I understand why he's calling me a sinner, why he's speaking to me so curtly and keeping his distance. He can't hold me and speak to me the way he did in the courtroom a few days ago—though I long for him to do that again. The understanding of it does nothing to relieve the emotional whiplash it causes, and it's giving me a headache.

It brings about a tense frustration that burns in my chest, striking up annoyance for the way I struggle to keep up with his ever-changing manner of being. With exasperation, I turn and plop in my seat, turning my back on him and facing the screen.

"The live stream should begin in about ten minutes."

Delle is still turned sideways in her seat, looking back at Arlo in the doorway. "And we just have to sit here and watch it? For how long?"

"How long is a night of service? *That* long."

"The entire night?"

"We'll allow you breaks if needed."

I scoff, "That's more than I was ever granted in service."

Arlo chuckles. "Didn't you elect to take your own break from service when you ran, sinner?"

His tone has oddly changed, sounding so similar to the way it did during the first trial. It was forced, clipped, cold, and emotionally disingenuous in the calculation of his words. It was how he spoke to me in front of his brothers; when he needed them to know he was with them, that he felt the same outright hatred for me as they did…even when I know in my heart that he doesn't hate me.

Still, he doesn't need to speak to me so harshly in front of Delle—he didn't when we worked with Delle and Theo to prepare for the first trial.

So why is he speaking that way now?

Is someone listening?

I whip my head over my shoulder as I spin in my seat, turning sideways like Delle so I can look at him. "Are we being watched?"

His eyes find mine and widen ever so slightly, imperceptibly to someone who wasn't watching carefully. "You're not being watched tonight, sinner. You're the ones doing the watching." He turns his head slowly to hide his single nod, dragging his eyes away to look off distantly into the corner.

Of course, we're being watched.

Maybe the Elders are watching us via camera from their hiding place—wherever that may be—or perhaps we're simply being recorded as a safety measure given that it's a night of purging. The men of the Control are meant to purge, just as all the men in Ember Glen. There will be chaos outside in the forest, and perhaps they worry we might cause our own brand of chaos from within.

We are sinners, after all.

A few silent minutes pass, and then Theo arrives, his presence announced when he says, "Everything's set up. The live stream should come on in five minutes."

Delle whips her head, instantly seeking the location of his voice, finding him standing near Arlo, just inside the room. Theo gives her a tense smile and her cheeks pinken. Her obvious crush on him is still unsettling for me, though I know in the grand scheme of things, it doesn't matter. Delle's future and mine are the same.

"Where is the rest of the Control?" Delle asks.

"At camp in the forest, preparing to purge," Theo says, then tilts his head as his eyes narrow on her. "What are you wearing?"

The slight flush of her cheeks darkens. "Servants' clothes." She looks at the floor, grabbing hold of one of her long, ashen strands of hair with both hands, twisting it nervously. "For solidarity." She slowly turns back to face the screen.

I twist in my seat to look between Arlo and Theo. "Will you two be joining your brothers in the forest tonight?"

"Our brothers will enjoy the service for now," Arlo says. "They'll return in shifts so we'll all have time to enjoy the purge."

His confirmation that he'll leave to purge the Impulse conjures sordid images in my mind.

Will he use another servant to ensure his brothers aren't suspicious of him?
Are his urges so strong that he'll want to purge?
Will he enjoy it?

I'm suddenly aware that this must be how the domestic women feel when they watch their husbands leave to purge every month under the full moon—those who actually care for their husbands, that is, because truthfully, not all of them do.

A painful lump rises in my throat at the thought of Arlo using another servant, and I swallow hard against it. I swivel in my seat to face the screen again, turning my back on him.

"Then I hope you find a suitable servant to meet your needs tonight, Warden Rainn." My words come out sharply to hide the angst in my tone.

Something burns inside my chest, something like heartache, though that doesn't feel like the right word to describe it. It feels something more like…jealousy, perhaps? I feel jealous at the thought of another servant being used by him.

"I'm certain I will…" he says, and I hope it's insincerity that I hear through his clipped tone, "someone who doesn't run."

I force a chuckle to hide the jealous ache that his words cause me. "Someone who hasn't yet learned why they should run from men like you."

Men like him…or men like them?

If I believed in God, I might pray for clarity. Arlo Rainn confuses me on an existential level. He fills my waking thoughts so thoroughly, yet those thoughts are constantly bouncing around my mind, flinging from one side to the other as I try to formulate a concrete opinion of him.

He's cruel, but considerate.

He's demanding, but accommodating.

He's blessed, but broken.

He's divinity and sin, heaven and hell, a god and a demon.

I hate him and I cherish him in equal measure, though I'm beginning to feel the scales tremor as I fight to keep them balanced—all while he adds weight to the side that begs for something deeper than simply cherishing him at a distance.

"Be quiet, Mercy," Arlo says with exasperation. "Just because you have a mouth doesn't mean you should be constantly running it."

I roll my eyes, annoyed with the way he goads me…though, at the same time, it tugs an unwanted twist of the corner of my lips in amusement, and it sets off a flurry of feeling in my stomach. I hate it and love it all at once, and there's only one word I can think of that explains it. *Passion.*

Love and hate.

Bliss and pain.

Desire and fear.

Serious talks and playful banter.

The dichotomy of our doomed connection is overflowing with passion, and I desire more of it. I want passion with him in all its forms, both good and bad, right and wrong, pleasure and sin. I want to let him show me heaven before I fall hard and fast, straight through to the depths of hell.

And I only hope that when I do fall for him entirely, he'll jump off the ledge to chase me into hellfire where I'll burn for him for eternity.

A **TENSE SILENCE** settles thickly through the room as we wait for the service to begin. Though it's only a few minutes, time passes slowly. The empty room is unsettling, especially when every noise is amplified through our silent waiting. When I hear a click from somewhere behind us, Delle and I both jump.

The projector whirs—which tells me the click was the sound of it switching on—and the light from the projector shines from behind us. I hold my breath, waiting for the images to appear, wondering where they've placed the cameras and what horror we'll be forced to watch.

With a flash and a brief flicker, the live streaming of our sisters' night of terror appears on the screen, moving images filling it from corner to corner. I see the clearing in the forest where the bonfire is lit, where the servants and men will gather, where a prayer will be led, and where the events of the night will begin.

It's not quite from a birds-eye view that camp is filmed. The camera must be placed high up in the trees, such that I'm looking down upon camp from an angle, but I can't exactly see everything—some areas are obscured by the placement.

Service hasn't begun yet. I watch on bated breath as the servants of Ember Glen appear from the darkness of the trees surrounding the clearing, filtering into camp. I'm surprised that I feel more anxious than I've ever felt for a service, that nagging pang of instinct stabbing through my gut and stirring nausea.

The brightly burning bonfire appears with an eerie glow behind the scratches and tracking lines caused by the projector. The servants—all dressed in their black corsets and skirts—begin to circle the high flame, enough of them present to create two rings around it.

Wesley crosses the clearing, approaching the bonfire as the servants gather to form their circle around the flame. He almost always leads the incitement and prayer, probably because he has a pleasant yet commanding manner of speaking, that's both calm and engaging. He stops behind the outer ring of the circle of servants as they join hands, waiting with his palms folded in front of him as the remaining servants come from the darkness and move toward the light.

My nerves electrify, rushing a current of anxiety to prick beneath my skin, and my eyes pinch shut. This part of service was always the worst for me—though by all accounts, it was the easiest part for most. This is the part that required me to declare my faith and grant my consent to be used beyond my own limits and expectations. It required me to falsely declare my consent to the horror I had no choice but to endure, even when said horror meant meeting my own death. This part required me to chant our prayer and declare that I'd rather meet death than dishonor: *malo mori quam foedari.*

It always made me feel sick. It was the false declaration of my faith and honor that twisted my insides. Yet it was the waiting—the moments of standing in front of the scorching heat of the fire, the anticipation of my own desecration—that turned that sickness into outright fear.

"October ninth, twenty-one eighty-five," Wesley begins and the chattering voices fade to dutiful silence. "We gather tonight beneath the full moon to honor the Impulse. We welcome the men of our community to this night of service. We thank them all for the pain they've endured over the last month in suppressing their impulsive urges in anticipation of the right to purge tonight."

"Thank you for your endurance," the servants murmur in chorus.

When my fear would ramp up in these moments before the purging began, the rehearsed replies would sound so obnoxiously clear, so enthusiastic, reminding me of how different my thinking was from the other women. But now, in my separation from service, it sounds like a forced recitation of unwilling women. That's exactly what it *should* sound like, because that's exactly what it *is*, but I'm surprised at the clarity in which I hear it.

My fear gives way to anger, and I scoff, my eyes popping open to watch in rage as I cross my arms over my chest. A heavy hand lands on my shoulder so suddenly that it startles me, and I snap my head sideways to find Arlo at my side.

"Quiet," he commands, drawing his hand away from my shoulder, dragging it along the back rail of my chair while allowing his fingertips to graze my back.

I square off in my seat, facing forward as I swallow a mixture of swirling emotions.

"This is a night for purging," Wesley continues, and I find my heart fluttering, skittering around behind my ribcage as Arlo lowers to his haunches beside me, his gloved hand still resting on the rail near my shoulder. "Tonight, the men of Ember Glen are granted a reprieve by God's grace. As it is written in the Impulse Edict, the violent and sexual impulses of men must be satiated to allow the community to live in peace. Each month, beneath the full moon, when men are at their celestial worst, there will be a gathering of servants and men. No rules or laws shall be enforced against man in his use of servants who give themselves freely to God's will."

Give themselves freely to God's will…

If it's God's will, then how can they give themselves freely?

Yet another contradiction of faith.

Wesley begins to rattle off the expectations of service, which are simple, few, and enforced monthly. No man who's purged or woman who's served before needs a reminder, but the speech is always given for the benefit of those who are new to the ritual—that includes the sixteen-year-old girls on their first night of service, and the fourteen-year-old boys unleashing the Impulse during their first purge. They only need to know that the men can't do harm to other men, and because women must focus on effective service, they may only be used by one man at a time.

I feel Arlo shift at my side, leaning toward me, and he speaks so softly that I almost don't hear him. "I've spent a great deal of time lost in thought these past few days, and my thoughts are gray, muddied with contradictions. But I'm trying, Mercy. I'm trying to seek truth through the madness, like you said." The leather of his glove creaks over the wood where he grips the chair.

I turn my head to look at him in bewilderment. "What?"

"Face forward and lower your voice," he snaps.

I lower my arms from across my chest and press my palms against the seat of the chair beside my hips, gripping the edges while pushing myself back in the seat. I turn away and look forward at the screen as he commanded.

He's quiet for a moment, and my eyes turn to glance over at him, waiting for him to speak again. When he finally does, I have to strain my ears to hear.

"I've been thinking about the Impulse and what we've been told about it. That men have a natural inclination toward impulsivity and unpredictability, have uncontrollable urges for violence and lust."

Where is he going with this?

"As I spend time with you, I've seen you prove yourself to be impulsive and unpredictable. Delle, too. I can even remember a time when my sister was younger that she behaved the same. You've shown me your own rage and wishes for violence against those who have wronged you. More telling than all of that…you've shown your lust. You've shown me that you could lose yourself in desire as easily as I could. Perhaps it's the demons that plague you, or perhaps…"

I'm desperate for him to finish that sentence, eager for it. My breaths quicken in anticipation of his words as I quietly wait for him to finish.

"Perhaps women have the Impulse, too."

I sigh heavily, an odd relief washing through me at his train of thought for the mere fact that he's thinking…he's *been* thinking, because this couldn't be a new thought. He wouldn't share something he hadn't already mulled over.

"Perhaps we do," I whisper.

I choose not to tell him that I think the Impulse is a lie, that every urge and desire we have—man or woman—is human, and we all have the power to control ourselves through choice, without the need to purge. I choose not to say that now because I'm so in awe that he's spent time thinking about this, and I don't want to derail him from sharing more with me.

"If that's true…*If* it's true, Mercy, then servants are stronger than the men of Ember Glen." He drags in a heavy breath and forces it out. "My Impulse to have you right now is so strong that I can hardly think about anything else."

His hand moves slowly, slipping from the rail, trailing down the side of the chair back. His fingers graze secretly along my hip as they draw across the seat, coming to a stop at the heel of my hand.

Leather kisses my skin as he draws a finger across the back of my hand, and my fingers twitch where they grip the edge of the seat. He traces an invisible line over my knuckles and down the back of my index finger, which rises in response to greet him.

I can feel each of his breaths, steady and heavy, and I depend on each one to sustain me. It's as though each inhale steals all the air from the room, making me dizzy with need, and each exhale provides the oxygen that wakes me up and excites me.

"I feel you," I whisper back, and his hand clutches my fingers at the edge of the seat.

My eyes flutter shut, but then I open them again quickly, unsure of how we're being monitored—whether we're watched or listened to, whether we're recorded. His words are so faint, and his movements are so secretive that I realize the stakes.

"Be careful," I remind him.

I try to pull my hand away, but he squeezes, holding tighter. "I am. I'm trying."

"Try harder." I swallow, attempting to rid myself of the longing that rises and lodges in my throat. "You need to purge," I tell him, though I instantly regret the words.

I don't want Arlo to purge.

I don't ever want to think of him using another woman…touching her, tasting her, binding her, sinking inside her and coming undone. The ache of such a visual makes my heart pound in double time. I forcefully yank my hand from his and press it over my aching chest.

"You may be right," he mutters. "It's God's will."

There's a tense pause where I try to refocus my attention on the screen, try to listen to Wesley as he leads a prayer.

"It's God's will," he repeats again a few moments later, "but perhaps His will is no longer meant for me. Perhaps it's only meant for men who haven't tasted the holy water that drips between your thighs when you come."

I gasp, and I can't stop from turning my head as I seek his eyes. He shoves to his feet, and though I desperately try to connect with his gaze, he doesn't meet mine—he turns and walks away.

"*Malo mori quam foedari,*" Wesley recites on the screen, and the servants and men repeat, "*Malo mori quam foedari.*"

As I fight to catch my breath that Arlo stole from me, a bright white flare lights up the sky with a brilliant flash across the windows beyond the projector screen. A few moments pass, and then a resounding burst of thunder booms, causing Delle and I to jump in our seats as the vibrating sound rumbles through the walls.

I huff out a surprised breath as the crowd on screen recovers from the startling thunder with soft chattering and nervous laughter. A storm won't change anything. The service will still go on as planned in the forest, adding an extra layer of misery for the servants.

"Ladies, please," Killian shouts over the chatter. "Return to your circle so we can complete the incitement of service."

Silence among the women falls quickly at the command, and they rejoin hands in the circle around the bonfire.

Wesley clears his throat and speaks again. "Our dearest honored servants of Ember Glen. Do you enter this service with the understanding that tonight, the Impulse rules? Are you prepared to serve our men by any means necessary as they purge, such is the will of God and your duty to serve?"

"As God wills it, we give ourselves fully to serve the needs of men," they vow in unison.

They'll speak it whether they believe it or not. I repeated the same ritualized response at every service purely out of fear, knowing the outcome I'm facing right now was always a looming consequence.

They speak it because—whether they realize it or not—they have no choice.

I sense Delle's eyes on me, and it calls for my attention. I turn and meet her stare, sharing a beat of understanding for the shared pain of our sisters. I reach out my hand to her, and she places her palm in mine. In solidarity, we force our eyes to the screen, to watch the cruelty of service with wide open eyes. I give the women my attention, my acknowledgment, my reverence for the strength of their true endurance as they experience yet another night of torture at the hands of vicious men.

"As God wills it," Wesley says, "so shall we proceed. Let the service begin."

chapter twelve

Mercy

CHAOS ENSUES ON screen. Some men strip bare before quietly selecting a woman to use, while others run to grab the one they desire and drag her away from the fire. The sounds of their primal excitement are grotesque as they growl, roar, and howl at the full moon like a pack of wolves.

I'm horror-struck for the way it looks from the outside, like a festival of terror hosted by cruel men. I'm not sure whether it feels better or worse to watch it unfold from afar.

Not worse…nothing could ever be worse than serving under the full moon.

Watching it happen from a distance is certainly better than experiencing it firsthand, but it still brings me emotional pain. Distress clouds my mind, and the clouds rain down my insides with a sense of shame. I feel shame that I'm not enduring this torment with my sisters.

I know my shame is unwarranted—it's not as though my presence would lessen their suffering. This shame is born from a lifetime of indoctrination, which has taught me to believe that service is my one and only role; it's taught me to believe that service is the only means in which I provide value to my community, by which I can value myself.

And this shame is exactly what the Control and the Elders wish Delle and I will feel in watching this tonight.

I refuse.

I straighten in my seat and search my mind for pride.

I fix my eyes on the screen, turning my focus to a single dark spot in the corner where the trees appear like a black blur in the night from the hazy projection. I try to tune out the sound of pandemonium as I focus my attention on that single spot.

I'll stare at it all night if that's what I have to do.

But without warning, the spot moves.

The single rectangular block that shows us the clearing suddenly shifts on screen, shrinking and sliding to the top left corner. Then, three other rectangles materialize, and after a moment of blackness in each, new images appear. There's now a grid of four boxes, each camera showing a different angle, granting us an all-encompassing view of the debauchery in the clearing.

Overwhelmed by the movement, my eyes roam aimlessly, unable to find a spot to focus on.

Who is using Ellary and Cambria tonight?

The thought bursts in my mind, and my gaze shifts, frantically searching to find Ellary and Cambria in the chaos. I don't want to watch what they endure, but I have to lay eyes on them.

As my gaze travels across the four images on the screen, I realize I can't see into the forest beyond the tree line. We're not seeing the complete image of the depravity that occurs tonight, but that's no surprise—it would be too much to cover.

I watch for minutes before I spot Ellary, yet as soon as I find her, I almost wish I hadn't. She's not been claimed by either of the Higgins brothers as she is so often. Instead, I find her lowering to her knees before Hyatt Price…The man who set Ivy Jane on fire.

"Ellary…" I breathe out her name, fear gripping me and stopping my heart.

I turn in my seat, looking behind me for Arlo, seeking him out for comfort or reassurance—or something else, but I don't know what. I find his eyes fixed on the screen, staring, rubbing his hand down his short beard.

"Hyatt Price," I mutter, not knowing what else to say.

Arlo tears his eyes from the screen to meet mine. Slowly, he shakes his head, and I don't know what that means. I find no reassurance as he returns his gaze to the screen. I turn my frantic stare to Theo, and he shrugs, but turns away, stepping out of the room.

I turn my attention back to the screen, fixating on the box in the bottom right corner which shows Ellary kneeling before Hyatt. The glow of fire light flickers behind them, casting a dark, shadowed aura around the outline of their bodies. His fingers touch beneath her chin and lift, and she dutifully raises her head to look up at him. I can see his mouth moving as he speaks to her. I can see her nodding against his touch, a proud smile spreading across her cheeks.

And when his other hand moves, my heart finally starts again, beating wildly against my ribs in such a pounding rhythm that I worry they might break. He holds a knife, the metal blade glinting through the shadows as another strike of lightning illuminates the night. The flash on the screen is bright, temporarily washing out the images with its flare.

If I thought God existed, and that He was good and benevolent, I'd imagine that lightning strike was sent to bathe all of Ember Glen in light, to expose the true demons and bring them from the shadows. But I know the only demons in Ember Glen are men, and Hyatt is the darkest of them all—a truly evil force, a demonic darkness looming above my bright and beautiful friend, Ellary, who has been blinded against the truth.

I can see the truth…and it's horrifying.

It frightens me so much that I hardly hear the raucous thunder moments after the flash, which cracks and rumbles all around.

Delle's hand squeezes mine in an attempt at comfort. And though I wish I could give her a reassuring smile, I can't. I can't give her anything while Ellary kneels before Hyatt Price.

How can I watch this happen to her?

Hyatt moves the knife closer to Ellary, and I hold my breath. I feel like I'm standing on the edge of that very blade, teetering on the verge of my sanity. I mentally prepare for the strike, waiting on bated breath to see him stab her, slice her, cut her open…and each moment of waiting brings a new torture.

But then he turns the knife, pinching the blade to offer the handle of it to Ellary.

What…

She nods, granting him the dignified smile she always holds, and wraps her palm around the handle. She looks down at it in her hand for a moment, then lifts her other arm, turning her palm up toward the thundering sky. I watch her chest rise as she takes in a deep breath, and then she draws the tip of the blade across her forearm, near the crease where her elbow bends.

"No!" I shout. My hands shoot up to cover my mouth as thick liquid—which appears black through the darkness on screen—quickly pools and flows from her arm. I leap from my seat, moving toward the screen without any conscious thought. I think I hear Arlo call my name, but it's muffled, far away. Ellary drags another line parallel to the first, drawing more blood from herself, her chest heaving as she lifts the blade and positions it to draw another line.

"Ellary, no!" I shout, my palm touching the screen as if I could reach through it to stop her.

No one's going to stop her.

No one's going to help her.

Hyatt's lips move, speaking words I can't hear, but I know he's encouraging her, commanding her to cut more lines, deeper, faster…

He wants to watch her bleed.

He wants to watch her die.

This man is a menace in every sense of the word.

"Help her," I mutter to no one.

I search the screen, desperately looking for Cambria. My eyes widen when I spot her in the box above Ellary's. Killian has her back pressed against a tree while he grinds against her body, but I see her looking past his shoulder, eyes widening, and I wonder if she sees Ellary, too. Judging by her expression, she must. Cambria isn't easily bothered, and she finds pride in service, so the fear I see in her widening eyes tells me that she must see Ellary and the violence she's enduring. It's the only thing I can think of that might upset her.

This type of violence is rare for Ellary; the woman was gifted with such innate sweetness to go with her tempting physique that the men of Ember Glen tend to adore *and* lust after her. It's kept her relatively safe for all these years. But now Hyatt has become unhinged and unpredictable…and he wants to unleash that on sweet Ellary.

"Help her," I whisper again, internally begging Cambria, the Control, *anyone* out at camp to go to her and to stop Hyatt Price from killing another servant—my *friend*.

No one cares.

No one is going to stop him.

This is a night of purging, and these men have been granted permission to ruin these women—my sisters—in whatever manner their urges see fit.

She's alone.

She's going to die alone, and no one can save her…

I can save her.

The thought shatters my rational mind, slicing through it with urgency, with empowerment, with insistence. If I'm quick enough, clever enough, maybe I can get to her and save her.

Nothing I do will change the fact that I'm fated to die.

So why can't I save Ellary before I meet my end?

My mind swirls, swiftly rolling through one idea and around to the next, whirling with options and possibilities. On the screen, I watch as Hyatt takes the knife from Ellary, nodding and stroking a hand down the side of her head, bringing a weak smile to her cheeks…weak, because she's bleeding.

He helps her rise to her feet, and he leads her away, taking her toward the tree line, beyond the view of the camera, into the dark forest…

Run.

Adrenaline floods my veins, and I welcome it, letting blind bravery take hold of me. Without a second thought, I turn…and I run.

"Mercy—" Arlo reaches for me as I sprint past him into the hallway.

He lunges to grab me, but I jerk my body sideways to avoid his capture, moving so suddenly that he stumbles as I escape his grasp. I won't let anyone stop me—*no one*. I'm not going to stand here and wait for Ellary to die.

Heading for the front door, I sprint down the hall, already seeing the fault in my careless plan. The large, wooden doors will be locked. But when Theo suddenly appears, coming toward me from the far hall on the opposite side of the sunburst, I immediately know what I'll do.

"Mercy!" Arlo shouts. A quick glance over my shoulder shows him righting himself and chasing after me.

I rush Theo as he steps into the foyer, crossing at a quickened pace, his eyes narrowing on me. "What are you doing?"

I slam to a stop right in front of him, and we meet with divinely perfect timing. I reach out and close my hand around his wrist, tug his arm and jerk him sideways. I catch him off-guard enough that he doesn't immediately pull back or use his brute strength to halt me. With a sharp motion, I yank him as close to the door as I can, trying to bring his wrist toward the spot where I believe the locking mechanism exists, hidden in the wood.

Please work.

Please, please work.

"Hey, what are you—"

The black band around his wrist engages the locking mechanism, which whirs and clicks, telling me that it worked, filling me with equal parts of fear, urgency, and excitement.

I drop his arm, grab the door handle, and pull.

"Stop!" Arlo shouts, and he's nearly right behind me.

I slip through a sliver's opening in the door—quickly stepping out onto the landing of the Homestead—then turn back to drag it shut behind me. I pull back hard on the handle, sitting on air as my body bends to hold it shut with all my weight. I need a beat to figure out my next move. I pant, not exactly breathless, but fueled by adrenaline, which makes every working function in my body quicken.

I feel Arlo pull on the handle from the other side of the door. He gives a sharp yank and my body lurches forward, the door opening a crack. I grit my teeth and use the full force of my body to jerk it shut again, groaning as I pull even harder. I need a moment to catch my breath, to reaffirm my decision, to find my strength again before I run…because I have to run faster than Arlo.

I can do this.

I can get to her before he gets to me.

My gaze travels up the door, skimming along the intricate design of wildflowers carved into the wood. It's so similar to the flowers tattooed on the forearm of every servant.

Perhaps we servants *are* wild, just like the flowers in the meadow.

Perhaps the etchings on the door serve as a reminder of our fragile existence.

Individual flowers can be plucked easily, our lives so delicate that we're only one sharp tug away from death. The men of Ember Glen pluck us one by one, but no one cares about a single flower in the vast meadow, for it's filled as far as the eye can see with so many more.

I am only one wildflower, pulled from the earth, kept in a vase with only enough water to sustain me, though everyone knows I'm slowly wilting, slowly dying.

I've been plucked, and I'm withering.

But I will not die in vain.

I plant my feet in determination and set my mind on my sisters—on Ellary, on the beauty of those strong women who are simply trying to exist in this world. I set my sight on cutting off the hand that wishes to pluck them, for my sisters *will* greet the sunlight come morning.

I draw in a steeling breath and release the door handle, and then…

I run.

chapter thirteen

Mercy

AS I SPRINT down the stone steps outside the Homestead, I hear the door open behind me, quickly followed by the rush of Arlo's footfalls as he chases me. I don't look back when he calls my name, shouting for me to stop. I land on the gravel-covered square, turn east, and bolt toward the trees.

My layered skirt twists around my legs, but I pump my arms to aid my speed rather than hold up the fabric. Pebbles crunch beneath my boots, my feet pushing against the small stones as I run as hard and as fast as I can.

"Mercy, stop!" Arlo calls, his voice too close.

I can't let him catch me.

I let out a groan as I push myself harder, running faster than I ever have before. The world around us is silent, except for the rapid beat of our footfalls against loose stone. In the eerie quiet, another brilliant flash lights up the dark sky. This time, it's only seconds before the crashing thunder follows, the rumble vibrating through each stone beneath my feet, shaking me with urgency to push onward.

Faster.

The sound of a rushing waterfall crescendos. As I turn my eyes to the sky, I see lines of water descend. I have only a moment to realize the rain is coming before it crashes down upon us. The torrential downpour drenches me, instantly soaking my clothes and weighing me down.

I push harder, forcing myself faster as the tree line approaches. With a grunted sound of determination, I leap over the line dividing open sky from the welcome cover of lush, towering trees. The rain still pours, but the branches and the meager remains of autumn leaves ease its descent.

I trust my instincts to drive me forward, to direct my feet to camp, and find Ellary in the forest just beyond the clearing.

"Mercy Madness, *stop!*" Arlo shouts. His voice is farther away than I expected it to be.

I can do this.

I can outrun him.

I know this forest as well as anyone else. I have no fear of the dark or the trees, nor the obstacles across the forest floor that might make me stumble. If I fall, I'll roll onto my feet and keep running.

I push onward until I hear the familiar sounds of service—moaning, grunting, cries of pleasure and pain—mingling with the constant flow of rain pouring from the sky. I see the light of the bonfire through the trees, burning so bright and high that the rain hasn't taken it out yet.

I know Hyatt led Ellary away from the campfire, into the trees...

But in which direction?

I scan the clearing as I approach, and I spot bodies moving among the trees on the opposite side. Those bodies could belong to anyone. My gut tells me to turn left, to run around the edge of the clearing, so I turn, leap over a fallen branch, and push onward.

I'm nearly around to the other side when I hear the rustling ahead. Then I spot a kneeling silhouette in the dark, and instinctively, I know it's her.

There...she's there...Ellary.

Another figure towers above her, a looming shadow, a man-made monster by the name of Hyatt Price. They're farther from the clearing than I had anticipated, in a place where no one would easily find them...and his hands are on her throat.

She hardly moves, though his arms shake with the force of his grip. Her body is lax, breathless, arms loosely hanging at her sides—already unconscious. All at once, he releases her and steps back, and I watch in terror as her silhouette sways before toppling sideways.

"Ellary!" I scream, but she doesn't stir.

Hyatt's head twists at the sound of my voice, and I slam to a sudden stop, throwing my arms out to catch my balance as the toe of my boot catches in the mud.

"Mercy Madness," he croons with intrigue, turning and stepping toward me. "Is that you, sinner? Have you returned to service me and finally fulfill your duty?" He chuckles, reaching behind him, quickly drawing the knife from his back pocket—the same knife he made Ellary cut herself with.

I clench my fists as I widen my stance, mud squelching beneath my boots as I position myself for battle. Rain still spills from the sky, and I blink away the drops that catch on my eyelashes as I let the sound of the rushing rainfall embolden me. I'm prepared to welcome him, but not for service.

No. I'll welcome him with fury.

I'll meet him with all the rage of my sisters' suffering.

I'll show him the true meaning of misery.

I wait for him to come for me, but instead of stepping forward, he steps back, and an unexpected breeze sweeps past me. A force brushes against my arm and nearly knocks me sideways.

It's Arlo…and he's sprinting past me.

He didn't grab me, didn't tackle me, didn't stop me.

He didn't stop me…

He's bolting straight for Hyatt Price.

Hyatt lifts the knife as Arlo charges ahead, showing no signs of slowing or stopping.

I watch in shock, too stunned to move, as Arlo quickly closes the distance between them. Barreling toward Hyatt, Arlo reaches out to wrap his gloved hand around Hyatt's wrist, moving with such strength and speed that I can't quite say how he twisted Hyatt's arm around so smoothly. Hyatt cries out as Arlo shoves him to the ground, tumbling with him, and I can't tell where the knife is.

Did Hyatt drop it?

Is it on the ground?

Is it buried in Arlo's side?

Just then, Ellary stirs, and her sudden movement steals my attention. I dash past Arlo and Hyatt as they roll and struggle, and I rush to Ellary's side. I drop to my knees, reaching over to grip her bloody forearm, squeezing to try to stop the bleeding.

"Mercy?" Her forehead wrinkles in confusion.

"Ellary, I'm—"

"I'm okay," she says, then clears her throat against her hoarse tone.

She coughs, and the twitch of muscles in her throat draws my eyes down to the darkening spots that will surely become bruises—spots that wrap around her neck like a collar.

"The cuts aren't as deep as they look." She strains to speak after the way he choked her so violently, though I'm relieved to hear her strained voice all the same.

"There's so much blood."

She lifts her head, moving to sit up, and I help her rise slowly. "I cut carefully. The bleeding will stop…"

She was always the best among us when it came to caring for wounds, so it's a relief to hear her say that because I believe her. We'd learned how to care for each other's injuries as part of our anatomy lessons when we were younger because a servant's job was never done—we had to serve each other in healing after nights of purging.

"Mercy, I—"

"Drop it!" Arlo grunts, and my head whips over my shoulder at the reminder that he's still there, still battling Hyatt.

Why is he battling Hyatt? For Ellary? For me?

Arlo straddles him, fighting to keep his arms pinned to the ground. Hyatt flails, jerking and twisting, thrashing with violence that threatens to be a match for Arlo's strength. I watch in horror as Hyatt manages to wiggle his arm out from beneath Arlo's firm grip—and there, I see the knife. He pulls back his arm and plunges, aiming the sharp tip at Arlo's thigh.

"No!" I scream.

Arlo's head jerks sideways to look at me, and I clamp my lips shut, realizing my cry did nothing more than distract him. But just before Hyatt can sink the blade into his flesh, Arlo sees the knife. He clamps his hand around Hyatt's wrist just before the blade can slice into his flesh.

Their arms shake as they fight each other for control of the weapon. As strong as Arlo is, I distracted him, and that distraction caused him to grip Hyatt's wrist at an awkward angle. The blade lowers, inch by inch, and I'm frozen in stunned silence as I watch because I can't make sense of anything I'm seeing. The tip of the blade touches his thigh and slips, slicing through his slacks, drawing a line toward his knee that trails with crimson.

Arlo groans against the pain, against the struggle to keep the knife from sinking deeper, and his shadowed face contorts in rage. He twists, reaching over with his other hand, and though this move releases Hyatt's other arm from where it was pinned on the ground, it allows Arlo to leverage his weight.

He shoves the arm holding the knife and slams it to the ground. Just as I think Hyatt's going to flip him over, Arlo manages to wrestle the knife from his hand. Arlo flips it in his gloved palm, turns it sideways, and pushes the edge of the blade to Hyatt's throat.

Hyatt stills, chest heaving as he draws in one heavy breath after another. My chest heaves, too—from the run, from the chase…from trying to make sense of Arlo fighting this man when he should be capturing me and returning to the Homestead.

"Are you supposed to be here?" Ellary's voice startles me.

I'm quickly dragged into my own battle of shifting focus between her and Arlo.

"They're—" I stutter between the odd cadence of my breaths. "They're filming the service. I saw you with Hyatt, and I ran for you."

"You ran for me?"

"Of course." I help her move to rest her back against a nearby tree trunk. "I couldn't just sit there and watch him hurt you."

To my absolute surprise, she grants me a small smile, though it quickly fades as a familiar look of shame filters through her expression. I reach up to wipe the mud from her cheek, but her blood is all over my hands, and it only smears into the dirt that coats her face.

She speaks so quietly that I almost don't hear her through the waterfall crashing from the clouds. "Am I a sinner like you if I admit I was afraid of him?"

I no longer need to catch my breath; my lungs are filled with every molecule of meaning from her question.

"No. No, you're not. You're wonderful and good and everything God made you to be, Ellary Hill."

"What are you going to do?" Hyatt taunts Arlo from beneath the blade resting at his throat, and I look over my shoulder at the sound of his voice. "Are you going to slit my throat and kill me?" Hyatt grits. "You'll be condemned; you'll be a *sinner*."

Arlo's voice is a low rumble in the storm. "No good man would call me a sinner for ending you."

Hyatt laughs. "What are you even talking about, *no good man*? You and I are the same."

Arlo bends over Hyatt, and the blade digs into his flesh. "You and I are *not* the same," he snarls.

And he's right—they're not the same.

Arlo is not the same as he was before. Rather, he's showing what he has the potential to become. I don't know if I can withstand knowing about his potential to become more—so much more than he already is to my hopeful heart.

"Let me up!" Hyatt shrieks, bucking and twisting and kicking so madly beneath Arlo that he can hardly keep him pinned down.

Hyatt makes the choice to thrash against a man holding the edge of a blade against the hollow of his throat…and this choice is perhaps the last one he'll ever make.

Hyatt twists while thrusting his body upward, and Arlo begins to fall. As he tilts, falling sideways toward the ground, the hand which holds the blade moves with him.

Arlo slips, and so does his hand…so does the knife.

The blade slices across Hyatt's throat just before Arlo lands on his side, his hand still firmly gripping the knife that drew Hyatt's blood.

I stare in disbelief as Arlo rights himself, scrambling to his feet as his widened eyes dart frantically between Hyatt's bleeding throat and the knife held in his grip. He lifts his hand, studying the bloody blade, and then he drops it to the sodden ground.

Then, he leaps forward, bending over Hyatt, who's blood spurts from his throat, each pulse of his heart splashing with a new flood of crimson that spills down his neck, liquid racing like a river to coat the earth beneath him.

Arlo reaches over him, pressing both hands down to collar his neck, as if he could apply enough pressure to stop so much bleeding. He must know he can't. Hyatt's going to die, and if I live long enough to see him buried, I'll dance on his damn grave.

I turn to Ellary with a whip of my head, and I'm confused to find her eyes shut, her face calm, not wide-eyed with fear for what she witnessed or searching my expression for answers. I realize my kneeling body blocks her view of the scene behind me. She's tired from bleeding—which, thankfully, seems to be slowing to a stop—and from being choked to the point of unconsciousness.

"Is everything okay?" she mutters, sensing my attention on her. Her eyes flutter open and land on mine.

She didn't see Arlo slip.

She didn't see the blade slide across Hyatt's throat.

She doesn't know Arlo is the one who cut him.

A strange calmness washes over me, slowing my heart to a steady, thumping rhythm. Each beat pulses the formation of a plan—a plan that's aimed at saving Arlo from the same fate I'm facing.

He doesn't deserve to be saved…

But maybe, with time, he'll earn it?

He's just killed another man, and accidental or not, he'll be condemned for it. He'll be punished by death for this crime—perhaps burned at the stake. It doesn't matter that he's one of the Control; Hyatt did nothing in the eyes of the authority to warrant the attack. And if it comes to light that he fought Hyatt while I ran to save Ellary, then they'll say he did it for me, a sinner—and they'll call him a sinner the same.

Did he do it for me?

I look back at him, blood soaking his gloves and spattered across his shirt. Hyatt's gone still, and Arlo slowly sits back on his heels, lifting his hands from the dead man's throat. He raises his head, and our stare connects. My heart wasn't prepared to see the fear in his eyes; my soul wasn't prepared to feel such a sense of responsibility in this. I chose to run, and he chased me. He had no choice but to chase me.

It's not my fault that he chose to attack Hyatt, but I do feel responsibility for the situation I had put him in. Regardless of who is responsible for what, a much more significant and strange feeling overcomes me in this moment.

Gratitude.

I'm grateful that Hyatt is dead.

Arlo has my sudden, inexplicable gratitude for ending the man who murdered Ivy Jane, the man who came after me that fateful night—intent on setting me on fire—the man who made Ellary Hill slice into her flesh and bruised her neck while he strangled her to unconsciousness.

Hyatt Price was a menace, and he needed to be stopped. His death is a blessing to all, and Arlo delivered it. Arlo helped me save Ellary when all he had to do was catch me and drag me back to the Homestead.

I can't let him be punished for this—they'll kill him.

I can't live out the rest of my days without him.

I need him.

A quick plan forms in my mind. It's a terrible plan, a stupid plan that's likely going to backfire, but something deep within my soul begs me to carry through with it.

I turn back to give Ellary a quick once over, confirming the color is returning to her cheeks, that the flow of blood from her arm isn't heavy or worrying. "You're okay?" I ask to confirm.

She nods with a small smile. "Just need to rest a bit," she whispers, dropping her head back against the trunk and closing her eyes.

I lean in to kiss her forehead. "Stay here. And when they find you later, tell them it was me. Tell them I did it."

Her forehead creases in confusion but she doesn't open her eyes; she just nods, rolling her head to find a comfortable resting place.

I draw in one solid breath as I rise to my feet, turning and walking toward Arlo. He tilts his head sideways to look up at me as I move beside him, thankful that the roar of rainfall masks the sound of my heavy breaths. Slowly, I crouch to my haunches at his side.

"Any God worth believing in would show you grace for this accident." I speak to keep his attention away from my hand, which secretly reaches for the knife he dropped. "Hyatt was out of control, and he had to be stopped. Your God won't condemn you for this."

A twinge of pain pinches my chest for the wish that Arlo—that *anyone* in Ember Glen—would show me grace as much as I show them.

My fingers graze the handle of the knife, and I stretch them around the grip, squeezing with a firm hold to keep it from slipping through my blood-soaked hand.

"Mercy—" Arlo begins, but I don't let him finish.

With a quick motion, I turn the blade in my hand, jam the tip against his forearm, and tear a quick, sharp slice through his shirt sleeve. The blade lightly catches his skin beneath, drawing a small trickle of blood along the line I cut, just as I'd intended.

He shouts, instinctively wrapping a hand around the cut, and his moment of surprise is enough to distract him, to keep him from stopping me in what I'm about to do.

I take half a second's pause to bring my fury for Hyatt Price to the front of my mind, and it's not hard to do. I only have to think about what he's done to my sisters—not just to Ivy before, and to Ellary tonight, but all the women he hurt in his gradually increasing sadistic behavior, which escalated with each service.

I find my fury for them, but for me, as well. Because he wanted to set me on fire that night, he led me to run, and in doing so, he took my life right along with Ivy's.

My rage boils, twists my features, and I let myself feel the way it burns. With the flames of anger licking beneath my skin, I lift my arm, raise it high, then drive the tip of the blade down into Hyatt's throat.

"Mercy!" Arlo's horrified scream echoes.

He reaches out to snatch my wrist, but I move too quickly for him to catch me. I pull the knife out and flinch as more blood sprays, splashing up like a tiny explosion that spatters blood all over me and Arlo. I spare Ellary a quick glance to see her just opening her eyes—probably at Arlo's scream—and they widen as she takes in the bloody scene.

"I did it. It was me," I remind Ellary as I turn on my heel.

I take off at a run, sprinting into the darkness.

And just as I hoped he would, Arlo chases after me.

chapter fourteen
ARLO

"MERCY!" I SCREAM as I chase her through the forest.

Tree trunks seem to jump out in front of me, shifting and closing around me as I run through blankets of rain. My shoulder slams against a dark tree, and I lift my hands just in time to push off another as adrenaline floods me.

I feel lost, confused; bouncing off one tree, then another, stumbling over twigs and branches as mud squelches and leaves crunch beneath my feet. I just keep moving, chasing, desperate to catch her. The rain still falls, and though the canopy of branches slows the descent, it still soaks me in delirium…yet it doesn't seem to wash away the blood that coats me.

So much blood.

Mercy chose to wear black tonight, to show solidarity with her sisters in service, yet she's covered in red all the same. She's drenched in the blood of a man who drove her to run, the man ultimately responsible for her placement in the Trials of Dissension. I should be horrified, nauseous, sick over watching her take that knife from the ground—the knife I accidentally slit his throat with—and stab him with intent. But I'm not. I find that I'm only curious about her choice to do it.

Surprisingly, I feel no concern for Hyatt Price. He's dead, and I don't feel mournful over it; I don't feel like we lost a man horrifically at the hands of a rebellious servant. I don't care that he's dead. I almost don't care whether it was the cut I made accidentally, or the final blow Mercy delivered that ultimately ended him.

All I care about is her…

Mercy fucking Madness.

I chase her dark silhouette, watching for the flashes of starlight hair each time lightning strikes and lights up the sky. My legs slow, colliding with grass that meets my knees, the forest floor disappearing as I stumble into weeds and wildflowers. She's lured me into the meadow.

The wildflowers—which look black in the night—all sway together in one direction, guided by the same wind which blows the storm through Ember Glen.

Three strides into the meadow, and I slam to a stop. A strike of lightning bursts so brightly that the entirety of the meadow, the sloping hills and valleys beyond it, and the dark mountains in the distance appear in a flash. It's a momentary image of the beauty surrounding Ember Glen, though it's instantly cast back into darkness.

Yet before that darkness falls, I see her in the flash of light—a star shining brighter than all the universe around her.

Mercy Madness stands in the center of the meadow, her stance wide and proud, chest-heaving from the chase. She's soaked in blood from head to toe. It stains her hair, coats her face, and drips from the bottom hem of her skirt. Arms held down by her sides, she still holds the knife in a firm grip. The wind-blown flowers and tall grass violently whip against her legs.

And the rain…

It spills from the sky, bending toward her with the whipping wind in a way that could make me believe she summoned it herself.

I see all of that—all of *her*—in the single flash of light.

I'm in awe.

Another flash lights up the sky, and this time, all I see is her. Not the wildflowers that sway around her feet. Not the mountains at her back. Not the knife in her hand. All I see is Mercy, standing beautifully beneath the sheets of rain…rain that appears to cleanse her as it washes away the blood—perhaps as it washes away her sins.

Thunder crashes, rumbling through the wide-open valleys and hills beyond the meadow. I could nearly mistake the roar as a call from the heavens, from God himself, like a bursting message that His blessing circles this wild woman wielding a bloody knife beneath an electric sky.

"I killed him," Mercy shouts at me over the storm.

My feet carry me forward, slowly striding toward her dark silhouette.

"I ran, and you chased me," she says. "I ran to save Ellary, you chased me, and I fought Hyatt. I took his knife, and I stabbed him. You tried to stop me, but I cut you with the blade, sliced across your thigh, and cut your arm as we struggled."

I continue forward.

"You tried to stop his bleeding, but it was too late. He was already gone."

My heart beats faster as I listen to her spin this deceptive narrative.

"You left him behind because I ran, and you knew you had to catch me. Because it was me who killed him. You didn't attack him; you didn't slip with the knife. Do you hear me, Warden Rainn? *I* killed him, not you."

I stop two strides before meeting her, watching her blink against the droplets that catch on her eyelashes.

"That's a lie, Mercy. *I* killed him."

My words strike me as I hear them out loud, hitting me like a bolt of electricity that was meant for the sky, though it strikes my chest instead. I drop my head, scrubbing my hand over my face before I realize my leather gloves are ruined—they're soaked in blood that I've just smeared across my beard.

I look down at the red liquid, watching it streak the leather as the rain rinses it from my upturned palms. "His blood is on my hands…"

"It may be on your hands, but it's all over me," she says, and I sense her step closer. "I killed him. I did it. I won't allow anyone to believe otherwise, do you hear me?"

"Why are you doing this?"

"My fate is already sealed, but yours doesn't have to be."

My voice comes out harshly. "Why are you *doing* this, Mercy?" I step closer. "Why would you do this? Why would you *fucking* stab him and try to take the blame for an accident?"

"Accident or not, they would punish you by death. You know they would."

"And it would be my punishment to bear!"

"Well, now it's not."

"*Why?*" I shout at her.

"Because…" she looks toward the forest, staring into the dark for moments before bringing her eyes back to meet mine. "Because I finally know what I want from this life in the short time I have left. I finally know what I want."

There's a heavy pause as our breaths quicken between us.

"I want *you*," she confesses. "I want you at my side until I take my last breath. I want your strength, your comfort, the peace you give my mind in forbidden moments. I want you to take care of my needs—*all* my needs. I want you to be my true warden." She pauses and the air feels heavier, like it's harder to breathe. "I want you to sin with me until my days are done."

I fight the Impulse rising within me, the urge to grab hold of her right now and give her exactly what she wants from me. I lurch, aching to close the distance, but she raises her palm to halt me.

"And you will never, *ever* speak the truth of tonight. You keep this secret and always let them believe that it was me, that I was the horrid sinner who killed Hyatt Price. You let me take the blame and the punishment in kind, and you'll live the life they want you to lead. You'll do what you have to as a member of the Control so you can become one of the Elders, as you were meant to."

"*What?*"

"You'll become an Elder in exchange for me taking this blame for you. And when you do," another heavy, meaningful pause in her shouted words as she fights to be heard over the rush of rain, "you're going to change everything. You'll use your power to make women equals, to end these nights of service, to give everyone in Ember Glen a *choice* on how they live their lives. You'll fight for Ember Glen, for men to love women the way that you—"

She stops herself, lips parted in half-formation of the next word. Her eyes bore deep into my soul, imploring me to find the end of her sentence on my own. I don't have to search deeply for it. It's on the surface, etched into my skin, the only words that could ever describe the intense desperation and obsession I have for her.

The way that you love me.

I can't speak it because the words wouldn't be enough to show her the way I'm in awe of her. Words would never be enough to explain how she burns through my mind, sets fire to my old ways of thinking while sparking new ones to replace them. Words can't express the way she's clawed beneath my skin, seeped into my veins, altered my very soul.

In this moment, I can see her for exactly what she is…She's a brightly burning star, the kind that shoots quickly across the night sky, only existing for a short time before leaving our world entirely. Witnessing such an anomaly changes how you see the world, and it's exactly what she's done to me.

It's not demons that plague her, and it's not hell that she sprung from. She's born from the heavens, a gift from God, sent to change everything. And what an honor I will find in aiding His will. I've had her all wrong… so very wrong.

My head bobs, nodding in agreement with her plan—*His will.* I agree to her terms, her intention to burn bright and fast, to set fire to the world as it is, and ignite a new way of thinking through her death and the years that follow—years she means for me to lead. Years *God* means for me to lead.

"I'll do it. I'll do what you ask of me, Mercy Madness."

Her breath catches in her lungs, and she takes a small step back, as if she feels pushed away by the sincerity of my words.

I take a step closer. "From now until the day you die, I will worship between your legs as though you were sent to me by God Himself…because only an angel would take on such a burden to save the man meant to ensure her demise."

A strange heat and heaviness circle us in a way that makes it feel like the rain has stopped falling, though it continues to drench the world around us. I draw in the thick air between us with three shallow breaths, the last of which draws her a single step closer. It's as though she's the air I need to breathe, and my lungs beg her to come closer so they can be filled with her, can drown in her.

Her chest is only inches from my body, heaving as she takes in rapid breaths. She slowly lifts her head, blinking against the falling rain—which I can't even feel anymore—as she captures my gaze.

In her bewildering silvery-blue eyes, I can see everything she wants from me—everything she needs from me, everything she desires—and it's all a reflection of my own dark urges.

She tosses the knife with a quick lift of her arm, lets it fall, and it sinks into the tall grass. "Sin with me."

She doesn't have to say another word.

chapter fifteen

ARLO

I CHARGE FORWARD before she finishes the last syllable. I crash into her, throw my arms around her, and our bodies strike like lightning. A flash lights up the night as our lips slam together, the thunder quickly following. I feel the electricity from the sky ripple through us, and it's like a sign from heaven that this moment is divinely crafted—sacred, significant, transformative.

My hand splays across the small of her back, drawing her impossibly close as she arches against me. My other palm finds the back of her head, holding her in place so I can kiss her harder, hard enough to bruise our lips.

My hand slips over the curve of her bottom, fingers spread wide as I curl them into her fleshy cheek and grip her firmly. Arching back, I lift her from the ground, her feet dangling for a moment before she lifts them around me, climbing them up my sides. With my hand on her ass, I hoist her higher. She circles her legs around my waist, settling her weight against my hips.

Once our bodies are locked, feral need overthrows decency, a depraved manner of lust conquering our shared senses.

Mercy parts her lips to let her tongue seek mine with hunger, shoving the metallic taste of blood that smeared her cheeks into my mouth. We groan in unison, tasting the filth and fighting to lick it away faster with our battling tongues.

It's not enough to have my tongue inside her. I need to fill every open part of her, fill her so deeply that she can feel how thickly I need her…my twisted, dark, unholy need.

No, not unholy.

Twisted and dark, yes, but not unholy.

She's sent from God—it's so fucking clear to me now—and He must want me to indulge with her. If I'm to enact her will, then I should fulfill her every need, and in that way, my need for her could never be unholy.

The way I want her is destined, dark yet sacred.

Holding her tighter, I fall to my knees—a sinner kneeling in worship— surrendering to our carnal need. Her arms tighten around me as we crash to the earth. Our kiss breaks as she lands on my lap, her bottom bouncing off my tense thighs as I sit back on my heels.

The cut from Hyatt's blade burns and throbs as she drops her weight to sit on my lap, locking her legs around my middle. As she thrusts her hips forward over the cut, I imagine my blood slicking across the back of her thigh, soaking the fabric of her underwear.

My hand moves from her ass, pressing through the arch of her back as I lean forward. My gloves catch in her hair, fingers twisting through the strands as I devour her with another kiss. My skin is crawling, heart pounding, breaths swallowed up by her warm, luscious mouth.

I'm spiraling, losing control. I bare my teeth and bite her bottom lip, tugging harshly before releasing. My bite seeks the tender flesh of her neck, nipping, kissing, sucking along the curve. She pants as her hands roam my back, as her lips slip along my cheek, as she holds herself closer to align her curves perfectly with my body.

"Purge with me," she whispers. "Take me the way you wanted to the night you chased me in the forest."

Sweet sin.

I lower her, taking her to the ground as I bend over her, nestling us both in the overgrowth of grass and wildflowers.

Wildflowers and starlight…

This is the moment my poetry comes to life.

Celestial beauty and the scent of earth,
like the meadow and sweet mountain air.

Wildflowers and starlight.

I kneel between her legs, struggling to pull off my leather gloves—slippery from blood and the falling rain—and I toss them somewhere in the grass. Her bloody fingers scrape across her thighs as she gathers her skirt, hiking it up over her bent knees toward her hips.

I reach down with both hands to grab hold of the sloping neckline of her black top, which frames her breasts so perfectly. I tug the fabric sharply, yanking it down to expose her to the storm that swirls around us—the storm within us has already been raging for far too long.

She gasps as her back arches, pressing the peaks of her nipples toward the sky. The falling rain slickens her skin, painting her in a sheen of angels' tears that demand my desecration.

Slipping my arms around her, I run my tongue up the center of her chest between the thick mounds of flesh. I move one hand up her spine to grip the back of her neck as my tongue meets the hollow of her throat. I press a heavy kiss there as she swallows beneath my lips.

Tangling my fingers in her hair, I cradle her head against the ground as I kiss her deeply, devouring her entirely, consuming every bit of her.

Mercy's knees grip my hips as I grind my hard length between her legs. It strains behind my slacks and begs for the removal of all barriers.

I sit back abruptly, breaking our kiss, and she whimpers, reaching for me to cover her again. Sitting back on my heels, I pant with parted lips, staring down at her as I work my buckle, fingers twitching in the rush to free my cock from its prison.

She reaches down and pushes her underwear off her hips, raising her legs to shove them over her knees as my cock springs free. I shove my pants and underwear down my thighs and rush to help with her panties.

I lift one of her legs and stretch the elastic to get the loop over her boot. Then I let go, and her panties snap around her other ankle. I leave them hanging there, still hooked to one leg. I'm too lost to care about removing them entirely, too desperate to taste her.

I reach beneath her legs, sliding my hands up the backs of her thighs to grip at the crease where her knees bend. Lifting, I shove her knees back, forcing her body to curl as I bring her knees to her chest.

Her ass lifts from the ground as I press her legs back, her glorious cunt aiming skyward. I dip my head to kiss her pussy, licking and lapping as deeply as I kissed her mouth, tasting the darkest parts of her and willfully consuming them.

I'm in ecstasy for this moment where we can finally share our filth, our urges, our impulses. I now understand that she has the Impulse, too—the undeniable craving for sex and violence. Yet this shared craving is different from a man purging with a servant. It's different because it's mutual, delicious, *divine*.

Her hands fall to her breasts and knead while her eyes pinch shut in pleasure. I want to keep giving her that pleasure—*need* to give it—but for a moment, I have to pull back and just look at her. I keep her held in place, though I shift back so I can gaze down at her.

With the absence of my tongue, she opens her eyes and finds me watching her. I see the swirl of stars and galaxies in her eyes…the entirety of the universe in her silvery-blue irises.

"Don't stop," she pants.

I drop my gaze, letting it land between her legs, curious to see how the falling rain splashes against her flesh. "Hold your leg," I tell her as I drop one to free my hand.

Her knee drops for a second, but she quickly lifts it back up for me, her hand reaching around to grip the back of her thigh to hold her knee against her chest.

I slide my free hand between her legs, then draw my fingers over her slick center. I graze the outer rim of her opening, dipping two fingers inside shallowly, then spread them in a V to open her wide. She gasps, her stomach jerking as it clenches in surprise.

Pushing through the leg I still hold, I fold her body further, angling her just right for a stream of water to pour down into that perfect opening. Rainwater pools in her cunt, and I let it fill her all the way up.

She gasps and whimpers, jerking beneath me, though she tries to hold still. With a snarl, I bend, place my rounded lips over the pool of water that fills her pussy, and suck. I drink from her, lapping the water that mixes with the flavor of her arousal.

Swirling the heady liquid through my mouth, I swallow half the elixir consecrated by her ardent flesh. I drop her leg without warning, and her boot lands on the ground with a thump. She lowers the other, hooking the heel of her boot around my ass as I move between her legs and bend over her.

I grip her face with one hand, pinching her cheeks between my fingers, digging in at the hinge of her jaw until the pressure forces her mouth to open. I dip low, stealing her gaze, and as she recognizes my intent, she opens wider.

Sweet sin.

I spit the remainder of the filthy mixture between her parted lips. Then I release her cheeks, clamp my hand over her mouth, and bend further, touching my nose to hers.

"Swallow," I demand.

Her eyes hood with lust. I let my other hand creep up her throat, and I feel it bob as she swallows. It's so filthy, yet so divine, to share that liquid lust. Reflexively, my hips thrust forward with the need to fill her, and my cock slips right inside her, *deep* inside her, burying to the hilt. She groans beneath my hand.

I lift my palm from her mouth and find her wrists instead. Gripping one in each palm, I lift them high and slam them to the ground, stretching her arms above her head. Her hips rise, thrusting up, urgently seeking movement.

"Please," she begs. "Arlo, please."

I drag out and slam back in, shifting her body along the ground, causing her to cry out from the force. The sound of her need is drowned by the rushing rain, but it echoes in my ears all the same. It's the only thing I can hear—the only thing I *want* to hear.

I thrust, fucking her hard with a steady rhythm. Shifting her wrists to hold them between just one of my hands, I bring my other to her chest, brush my thumb across her nipple, and swirl it around the peak.

"Yes," she breathes. "Yes, yes…"

I lift her breast, dipping my head to drag my tongue over the hardening bud, sucking until she's writhing beneath me.

"Make me come," she whimpers. "Make me come. Please, Arlo."

Tugging on her wrists, I lift them, scooping my head between the circle formed by her arms. She takes the hint and grips the back of my neck with one hand, the other trailing upward to sink her fingers into my hair. My eyes fall shut at the tug on my scalp, the curl of her fingers and the way they press into my skin.

I snake my arms around her, holding her tightly as I shift on my knees and sit back on my heels. I'm still inside her, my cock sinking deeper with the angle change as she's pulled onto my lap. She gasps, curling around her clenching stomach as I splay my hand over her back.

My lips are only a breath away from hers. "Use me. Let me serve you for this moment."

I might be as surprised as she is for what I just said. Her lips are parted—panting, gasping for reason where she'll find none. Her forehead wrinkles as her narrowed eyes dart around my face, searching, exploring… but I can't stand the waiting.

I need her to fuck me.

I capture her mouth in a desperate kiss before dropping onto my back, pulling her down on top of me. She sits up where she straddles my hips, cock still buried inside her. Her body convulses as she settles herself, shifting her knees on the muddy ground and squeezing my hips. She whimpers and sighs, twitching through small shocks that hint at the explosion to come.

And when she finally starts to move, my fucking soul leaves my body. She rocks her hips, settling her weight on me and grinding heavily. She keeps me buried to the hilt inside her as she fucks me.

Dear God, the way she fucks…How could she ever be wrong?

Her hands find my thighs as she leans back and takes from me, as she throws back her head and tilts her chin skyward. She moves recklessly, wildly, *freely*, and it's pure intoxication to watch her move. Her breasts bounce lightly with the movement of her grinding hips, her chest heaving with each panted breath. The rain still falls to drench her, slicking her skin so beautifully that it makes my cock twitch inside her.

I revel in laying beneath her, watching her move, letting her use my cock. I'm in awe watching her let go, my gaze locked on her face and the way her expression twists in filthy, desperate need.

I've spent so much time thinking about the Impulse in recent days, curious in my thought that perhaps women have it, too—not just men. It's in this moment, here and now, watching Mercy fuck me with a primal energy, that confirms the truth in my mind. She's lost to her urges, feral and hungry, using me to serve her carnal need.

Perhaps we all suffer the Impulse…and if that's true, then men are weak in comparison to women. I can't look at the sensual creature riding my cock with such urgent filth without drawing that conclusion.

If it's true, then everything I know has been a lie.

The sickness of dissonance punches my gut, begging to drag me into deeper thinking. There's so much my mind aches to consider—and I will consider it all—but right now, all I want to think about is Mercy and the way she blesses me with the thrusting of her hips.

I focus on the feeling, watching her fuck me harder, sensing the monumental build of her pleasure like a volcano on the verge of eruption. She pants out heated sounds of desperation, and I feel her cunt pulse around me, squeezing out my own pleasure and mingling it with hers.

"Come for me, starlight." I grit my teeth. "Fuck me and come for me."

The pulsing of her inner walls strengthens, tightens, then releases with a vengeance. She cries out into the night and calls for the thunder as a bolt of lightning streaks across the sky, lighting up the meadow…lighting up Mercy.

She comes undone beneath the electric sky, riding the waves of pouring rain as her thrusts turn to jerking twitches—the aftershocks of her pleasure. As the satiated smile spreads across her cheeks and she leans forward to lay her hands on my chest, I'm overcome with the need to fuck her breathless.

I flip her, slamming her down against the sodden earth. I collar her neck with my hand, shift my hips to the perfect angle, and fuck her hard. I pound into her flesh as she gasps for breath beneath me. Her hands shoot up a few seconds later to lightly grip my wrist, encouraging me to let up from my unintentional squeezing at the sides of her throat.

I jerk my hand away, slamming both palms to the ground at either side of her head. I bend and smother her mouth with mine, kissing her sloppily. Her palms greet my cheeks, smearing me with dirt and blood. She holds my face to hers to kiss me deeper as I thrust my way to release.

I feel myself swell inside her, pulsing, my body on the edge of release when her lips slip away from mine. I drop my forehead to meet hers, and our eyes lock.

A thousand silent words pass between us as she gazes deeply—it's some language I know could never be learned or spoken. There are no words to describe what passes between us, how we see each other, the flames that ignite between us every time we touch. Our connection is beyond reason, beyond language, beyond the guiding laws of the Impulse Edict…

Perhaps it's even beyond God Himself.

What we share is cosmic, toxic, fated, and forbidden.

I can't fight it, and I truly don't want to anymore.

As my release begs, the rain slows to a stop. I strain with the need to edge myself, to draw this out, to stave off my release so I can remain in this perfect desperation for just a little longer.

My body trembles over hers as the rain quietens and my heavy breaths and groans surround us. I don't know if I can hold myself back; I don't know if I can control myself with her.

I know I can't.

I never really could.

But the broken parts of me still need to try.

"I want to feel it," she pleads as the storm blows away, the roar of rain dying away to give space to the perfection of her voice. "Let me feel you come inside me." Her hips buck to meet mine as I still myself, and my face twists in the agony of delayed release.

"Not yet…" I tell her, and she doesn't look at me with judgment or frustration.

She nods her head against mine and licks her lips before parting them to take in a rasping breath.

I don't know what I'm waiting for, but I know I haven't reached the pinnacle of my tension yet, haven't found the perfect moment to let go and lose myself in her entirely.

She wiggles her hips, shifting me inside her, and I groan, tilting my chin to kiss her briefly, loving the way she makes me throb for her so relentlessly.

The sounds of our ragged breaths amplify as silence enshrines us, the clouds spent and completely spilled. My jealousy of the clouds peaks, and I can't help but thrust again, slowly pumping, swirling my hips to ensure my cock rubs along every inch of her pussy. In the quiet after the rainfall, our breaths and wetness create filthy songs to fill the night.

*Sweet sin…*I can feel her gathering around me again, squeezing, pulsing, hips bucking and rocking with mine.

Please God, let me hold this moment; let me edge until she comes with me.

Please.

Fuck.

I can't…

My movements hasten and frantic energy takes me. She whimpers against the growing need throbbing between her thighs. Her back arches to tilt her hips for me, head tilting back the same, lifting her eyes to the sky. She gazes beyond me, up toward the night sky, as she pulses her hips against me, eyes widening with some strange sense of wonder.

"Arlo," she quivers through my name, on the verge, barely controlling herself, "*please…*" she begs me to come with her.

She trembles as she blinks, as she fights her own relief in favor of finding mine. But then her body suddenly stills, and a peaceful smile tugs at the corner of her lips. "I can see the stars."

Sweet sin.

Starlight above us.

Wildflowers around us.

Everything about her brings me back to the words I wrote—to *wildflowers and starlight.*

I lose all control. I fuck her harder, driving us both toward that edge. I fuck until she finally releases, crying out into the night while coming hard around my cock. Her cunt squeezes me so perfectly, begging for my cum to spill inside her. A primal growl scrapes through my throat as I fuck her through my orgasm, the pleasure of it going on and on and *fucking* on.

I gaze deeply into her widened eyes. "I can see them, too. The stars."

She looks at me with such wonder and hope—hope that should evade her for a future she won't be a part of. I know right now that if I were ever asked to identify the moment my heart opened for this woman who I called a sinner, it would be this one.

Her voice is quiet, sad, yet still filled with that hopeful longing. "I want more of this, Arlo. More of you." She wraps her arms around me, pulling me down to hug her. "I want to live long enough to see the man you'll become."

I let her drag me down. I lasso my arms around her and roll us both to our sides to lay in the tall grass and wildflowers. Neither of us care that we're covered in blood and dirt. Her leg is around my hip, cock still buried between her legs. I hold her with more intimacy than I've ever held anyone. I've never been hugged this way, and it makes me feel more vulnerable than I did while I fucked her.

"You'll have so much more of me before the end," I choke out the words.

The end…

I tighten my grip on her, bury my face in the crook of her neck. This isn't the last time between us, but one day, we will have our last forbidden tryst. Mercy's days are numbered, and I'm powerless to stop it. She'll die, but

I won't let her death be in vain.

I'll do what she asked of me. I'll cement my position in authority. I'll be whoever they want me to be in the Control until my time comes to serve as one of the Elders, and then I will use my power to influence the change God sent her to initiate.

I'll do it for Him, but more importantly, I'll do it for her…for Mercy Madness.

The life I knew before is done; I live mine for her now.

chapter sixteen

Mercy

ONCE, I WAS told of a thing called magic—some supernatural force of spells, incantations, and dark rituals we were told to fear. Making magic meant making the impossible happen, and it was always explained as something tainted and filthy. Yet something magical has happened here tonight among the wildflowers, beneath the parting storm clouds in the night sky, and the stars peeking through as those black tufts roll away.

We made the impossible happen. We found mutual pleasure in our lust, and that would seem magical enough on its own, but the truly impossible thing is the understanding we seem to be finding in each other's arms. The longer he holds me, the tighter he squeezes, the more I feel him falling into me, coming to understand me, to care for me, perhaps even to appreciate me and the sacrifice I made for him.

I stabbed Hyatt Price.

My heartbeat finds an unsteady rhythm at the reminder, but guilt and shame don't wash over me as I expect them to. Instead, I'm met with something that feels like pride…like power.

I've never had pride or power in my life, and it feels *good*.

I tug my head back to look at Arlo, and we let our eyes roam each other, watching expressions, cataloging features. His gaze falls to my lips, and he licks his before drawing me into a spine-tingling kiss. His lips are soft and wet as they push against mine, encouraging them to part.

He twists us, rolling me onto my back as he deepens the kiss in such a sensual way that I never want it to end.

I never want him to stop.

Gradually, the kiss fades, but it feels natural in the way it ends. It doesn't linger with promises of pleasure that went unmet. It isn't tinged with hatred and rage. Now, there's satisfaction found in the touch of our lips.

Arlo sighs contentedly before laying his weight on me, nudging his face to settle against the crook of my neck. Nestled between Arlo and the steady ground beneath my back, I feel smothered, covered, perfectly protected, and safe for the first time in my life.

I smile as I look beyond his shoulder at the night sky. I marvel at how quickly the storm clouds sweep across the darkness. It's only then that I feel the chill of the wind blowing over us, heavy in its weight, rustling through the tall grass encircling our bodies.

The full moon creeps out from behind one of the clouds. It's only visible for moments as another cloud passes over it, but my grin broadens at the sight of it—bright and full and more beautiful than I've ever seen it.

I think I must have feared the full moon before, but in this moment, I don't know fear. I feel invincible, powerful, *magical.*

We don't speak, lying this way for minutes in the peaceful afterglow. I know that too soon we'll have to move, and the peace will be gone and the horror of my reality will return. I'm in no hurry for this to end.

And then the strangest thing happens.

I see a blinking star moving across the sky.

"Arlo, look…" I say with wonder.

He lifts from my body, twisting to look back and above him as I point my finger from my outstretched arm past his shoulder.

"There. That's a blinking star, isn't it?"

"Oh," he says with surprise. "I think it is. I haven't seen one in years… not since I was a child."

He shifts, pulling out of me regretfully, adjusting to buckle his pants. I hate the way I dragged him from the moment, so I focus on the red blinking light skating across the sky. I'm in awe of it. I don't think I've ever actually seen one myself—only heard about them.

He shifts beside me, laying on his back. I turn my head to look at him as he gazes up, watching the star with wide-eyed wonder, the same as me. His fingers reach out to graze mine beside my hip, and liquid fire runs through my veins. Slowly, he takes my hand in his, locking our fingers together. His touch sears my flesh, and I'll wear the scars of him forever.

He rolls his head to look over at me, catching me grinning at him. He returns the smile with a broad, wonderous grin, one that perfectly displays the long dimples that cut through his cheeks.

"I don't know that I've…" he pauses, "that I've ever actually seen you smile before."

I blink at him, the weight of that thought pressing down on my chest, making my heart feel heavy.

When was the last time I smiled so authentically?

When was the last time I didn't have to fake a tense grin while gritting my teeth?

When was the last time I felt happy?

I can't remember, and it makes my chest ache. If it's truly been so long since I've been happy—since I've genuinely smiled because I *felt* like smiling—then I don't want to let the feeling go. I'll have to, I know, but I don't want to…not just yet.

I turn my head and throw my gaze toward the moon before taking in a deep breath, drawing the joy back inside me. I let the feeling exist along with the pain and fear of my circumstance. It's the best I can do, and it will have to be enough.

I focus on the feeling of his fingers between mine, the warmth of his palm, the strength of his grip. Holding his bare hand feels more intimate than the sex we just had. I don't know how that could be, but that's how it feels.

It's a precious joining of the parts of us that do so much. Our hands touch, they feel, they create, and heal. They can also curl into fists that harm, fingers that scratch, palms that hit and hurt. But right now, our hands just exist together, intertwined, joining us as one through our shared touch.

I squeeze his hand a little tighter.

Quietly, I track the blinking red light of the special star moving along in the night, looking as if it's flying over the mountains.

"It almost looks close enough to reach out and touch," I whisper.

His fingers curl deeper around mine, and the tightening sends a shockwave of pleasure straight through me. It's like I want him inside me again. It's like I'll always want him inside me after the slightest touch.

"I can feel you," I say slowly, "dripping out of me."

He rasps out a heavy breath and rolls onto his side to face me, propping himself onto one elbow, close against my side. My lungs stutter when I look at him. He's drenched from the rain, his hair heavy and dripping. Water and blood mingle in his short, ginger-tinted beard, which looks nearly black in the dark. He places his palm on the center of my chest and drags his fingers down. My back arches in natural response to his touch.

He leans over me, pressing a kiss between my breasts as his hand skims down my stomach. "I'd like for you to always feel me dripping from your cunt."

"And will I?" My mouth suddenly feels dry.

His fingers play with the curls above my sex before dipping between my legs. He trails a line of kisses over my breast, stopping to tease my nipple, playfully scraping his teeth across the bud before soothing with his licking tongue. He brings his lips to hover over mine, and he steals my final breath.

"If I have anything to say about it, you will."

My eyes flutter shut as his fingers dip, swooping so lightly to catch the liquid remnants of his release as it pools between my legs. Too quickly, he takes his hand away. He brings his fingers to my lips, tapping lightly, and I feel the sticky fluid coat my dry, kiss-swollen bottom lip. With my eyes shut, I part my lips for him because I know exactly what he wants—he wants me to taste the mixture of us coating his fingertips.

Gently, he slips two fingers inside my mouth, pushing them forward along my tongue with aching slowness. I close my lips and swirl my tongue around his fingers, sucking and licking greedily. He pulls them out and gently grabs my throat. I open my eyes to find him staring at me with hunger.

"Don't swallow that. Let me taste it on your tongue."

He descends and kisses me deeply, the raw sweeping sensuality of his thick tongue intoxicating, bewildering, purely magical.

I've never felt so much emotion for such filth. I never would've imagined I could feel something painful and beautiful and raw tugging through the fibers of my soul from just tasting the flavor of each other's cum swirling between our kiss. It tightens my belly and makes me ache to have him all over again.

But the sound of voices drags us both abruptly and painfully from our lustful stupor. He pulls away with a snap, turning his head to gaze around the meadow. "We need to go," he urges, scrambling to his feet.

He reaches his hand down and my eyes fall upon his scars. I wish we'd had another moment where I could finally ask him about them. The voices grow louder, and they steal the moment from us. Our time of bliss for tonight has passed, and I don't know when the next will come.

Sadly, I lay my hand in his, and he pulls me to my feet. He grips the top of my shirt and pulls it up to cover my chest. Then he bends, reaching for the panties still looped around my ankle. He takes hold of them, and I lift my foot to let him pull them off. I reach out my hand to take them back, but he quickly folds them and slides them into his pocket.

I meet his eyes, and he gives me a beat of his remaining filth. "I'll be sleeping with those beneath my pillow."

My thighs twitch.

He grabs my hand and walks me toward the tree line as I smooth down my skirt.

"Are you really doing this, Mercy?"

He doesn't need to elaborate; I know exactly what he's asking—whether I'm really taking the fall for him and claiming responsibility for Hyatt's death. Though there's no way to say whether my stabbing or Arlo's accidental slit was the true cause of his death, I've already made up my mind.

I'm taking responsibility.

Arlo hasn't earned this from me yet, but he will. I know he will. He'll do what's right long after I'm gone when he has the power necessary to do it—when he becomes an Elder. I know I'll never live to see him earn my sacrifice, but I can only trust that he will.

The thought of Arlo growing older, alone, long after I'm dead and gone, stabs and twists inside me like a knife. I swallow a dry lump, feeling as though *I've* been stabbed in the throat.

I shift my hand, fingers clawing for that intimacy again as they reach between his and lock together. "Yes, I'm really doing this."

"It's stupid," he tells me. "Stupid, but brave."

We walk for a few paces, meeting the trees, and then he stops abruptly. Letting go of my hand, he grips my waist and pushes my back against the nearest trunk. His body molds to mine, pressing close. His hand comes up to cup my cheek, his thumb stroking my skin.

"I don't deserve this from you."

"No, you don't," I say breathlessly as he kisses the corner of my lips and along my cheek. "Neither of us deserve our fates. Mine was chosen for me, and now yours has been chosen for you. Shall we call it even?"

His thumb catches my bottom lip and tugs. "This will never be even."

I sigh, sinking against the tree. "It doesn't have to be. Not as long as you do what you promised me."

"Remind me exactly what it is I'm promising."

"That you'll live long enough to have real power here and find a way to change things once you become an Elder."

The corner of his mouth twists. "Oh, is that all?"

"Will you really do that for me?"

The smirk fades and he leans closer, the scruff of his beard brushing my cheek as his lips find my ear. His palms tighten around my waist. "If you survive, we can do it together." He pulls back to look at me, surely finding a confused expression on my face.

"What do you—"

Voices steal our attention before I can ask what he means, if he has an idea for how I might survive the trials, or if he's just living a fantasy in his head—one where I survive and he doesn't have to do it all alone. We both turn to look into the dark woods.

"I have to take you back to camp," he whispers. "I'll have to tell them what happened—that you ran and I chased you, that Hyatt attacked you and you fought back, and that you accidentally—"

"*No*," I snap. "Not *accidentally*. You'll tell them I did it on purpose."

"Is this something you really want to be stubborn about? Your fate is sealed, yes, but things can get much, *much* worse for you before the end, Mercy. You're tempting punishment."

"I stabbed him in the throat, Arlo, and that was no accident. I had intention, and they'll know it when they see him. I would've done it myself anyway, even if you hadn't slipped with the knife first."

"Maybe you would have, maybe you wouldn't…"

"I *would* have. It's why I ran from the Homestead, to save Ellary from meeting the same fate as Ivy Jane."

"Are you sure you want to—"

"Yes, stop asking. Now take hold of me and drag me back to camp."

His eyes flash with a familiar hunger at my demand, and though I meant it literally, I imagine the figurative vision of him chasing and catching me, dragging me away for my…*punishment.*

And I'm certain now that any punishment Arlo Rainn could dream up for me would be nothing short of divine.

chapter seventeen

Mercy

ARLO HESITATES TO do what he has to do, and though the hesitation warms my heart in knowing he's no longer eager to see me punished, we both know this has to be done. The more he hesitates, the more anxiety it gives me. If I'm to be punished, I want to get on with it so I don't have to fear it in anticipation.

After all, I have enough things to fear in anticipation of the remaining two trials.

I give him a beat to move, and when he doesn't, I take action. I push him away and stomp off into the forest. I only make it five paces before he comes back to life, rushing to catch up with me.

His bare hand closes tightly around my bicep, and he jerks me back. I nearly stumble as he twists me around violently, but his hold is firm enough to keep me on my feet as he drags me in the direction of camp. I glance at his face, seeing the way it's hardened with the mask of a man in control. He pulls me along with his lengthy strides as though I were truly his unruly ward.

I still am, aren't I?

Something deeply indecent twists through my stomach, spurring a depraved kind of excitement. It's like a game we're playing—deceiving the world through a shared mission—and obscene thoughts of forbidden moments wake me with a tingling thrill that prickles from head to toe.

I can hear his breaths as he pulls me along in the darkness, as our feet squelch in the mud, and I stumble over twigs and small branches. I can begin to see the campfire's glow in the distance, now just a low flickering light since the rain had drenched it.

Without warning, Arlo flings me around by his grip and I gasp when my back slams against a tree trunk. Before I can react, he dips to kiss me with a deep, fevered rush—mouths open, tongues lashing, silently swirling with the unspoken words of shared need.

He tries to pull back, and my hands shoot up to grip his face, holding him there so I can kiss him a little longer, so I can taste him a little deeper. Too soon, his hands wrap around my wrists, squeezing tightly so he can pull back and slip out of my grip. He lowers my hands and holds them between our chests, both of us panting with need as an aching growl rumbles through him.

"I don't know if it's the full moon, the Impulse, the fucking chase…but I feel as though I can't get enough of you, Mercy. I have to stop this and take you back, but sweet *fucking* sin, I want you."

"I want you, too."

He crushes me with his body, pressing closer to kiss along my jawline and down the side of my neck. "I have to stop."

"I know," I agree, but I feel myself sink into him all the same.

He releases my hands and grabs hold of my hips instead, moving so fast that I can't resist him as he twists my body to face the tree. My palms land on the rough bark, my cheek turning to press against it, and I don't even care if it scratches my skin raw. His fingers grapple along the back of my thigh as he inches my skirt higher, lifting it above my hip on one side. He flattens his palm, rubbing it over the curve of my ass.

"I want to purge with you again, just like this," he whispers.

The echo of voices carries toward us as someone draws nearer, though we're still hidden in the dark. I clamp my lips together to trap the sound of my heady breaths as I arch my back, pushing against his palm. He squeezes my flesh, and I stifle the moan that gathers in my chest.

His touch disappears, but it returns again with force. He smacks me with a thwack across the fleshy cheek, and it echoes. I cry out against the sting, and though I hate the pain, I don't hate the way it makes me feel like I belong to him, like he claims me. I feel like I'm the only woman he's ever wanted to touch, and in a very unexpected way, it's empowering.

"Get angry with me," I hear him whisper as he strikes me again. "Make it real."

He smacks me again, harder, then again and again in rapid succession. He hits me until it hurts so badly that I'm twisting, trying to get away. He smacks until I'm fighting him, though even in the fight, my belly clenches with desire for every touch.

I have to fight that pleasant need. I have to find my rage again. I need to make it real when he drags me back to camp. I have to make the Control believe that I killed Hyatt Price on my own, out of sheer hatred, or else Arlo will meet dire circumstances.

And I can't let that happen.

He's the only chance Ember Glen has at a better future. I know that future may only be a wishful dream, one that won't even come to pass for another twenty-three years—in a decade I will never see. But it's enough for me to hold out hope.

It's enough for me to take this punishment.

I would've killed Hyatt anyway if Arlo hadn't beaten me to it.

I let images of Hyatt fill my mind as Arlo strikes me. I see his silhouette looming over Ellary while choking her with both hands. I let the rage I felt when I found them build within me.

Before he can land the next strike, I whirl around, slap my palms to his chest, and shove to nudge him back. I try to slip away, but he lunges to grab me, trying to twist me around to smack me again.

I fight, trying to keep him from hitting me, but then I'm distracted by two voices drawing nearer. A pulse of fear floods my veins, mingling with the arousal of his touch, and it makes me feel high—an overwhelming sensation that I have to pause and take a moment to revel in.

How can fear and desire exist in the same moment?

In my distraction, Arlo grabs hold of me, lassoing his arms around my waist from behind. He locks my arms beneath his and lifts me, kicking from the ground.

"Let go of me!" I shout from the fear, but secretly, I don't want him to as desire still pulses within me.

He marches me toward the glowing campfire, which gradually rises as its fed more kindling. I thrash in Arlo's arms, fully aware of the way his cock hardens against my bottom. I feel the vibration of his soul—the matching wavelengths of fear and desire—and it only strengthens my own. I can feel the way he fears bringing me to punishment as much as I fear taking it.

The shared dichotomy of our most primal fears and desires strengthens our connection in a way I never could've imagined possible. I wish I could halt time and simply exist with him, let ourselves feel the intensity of contradictions swirling endlessly between us. I can feel every emotion imaginable toward him in the span of seconds, and it satisfies every inch of my tarnished soul.

Something has awakened between us tonight—something magical has come to life beneath the rain and thunder, between the stars and the full moon. The magic is dark, but it doesn't feel wrong. The darkness of it feels so right that I wonder for a moment whether I do have demons playing in my mind—if perhaps I am born of hellfire and sent to reap destruction throughout Ember Glen.

It almost makes me want to laugh, but if that were the truth, I would welcome it, and I wouldn't deny it. It feels too good to deny. I find a twisted kind of eroticism in taking the roles given to us—the Control and the servant, the warden and his ward—and playing them out in partnership to bend the truth, to deceive so we can ultimately take what we want.

I thrash in his hold to play my part, jerking so violently that he's forced to lower my feet to the ground. The moment my boots touch the earth, I twist in his hold, breaking his arms away from my waist, and freeing myself. I whip around to face him, taking two quick steps backward before pausing, watching him for a heated beat.

And then, I run.

He chases me.

I want him to catch me…but I run faster.

I run until the light from camp shines bright enough to expose the shadows, and I sprint right past a man fucking a servant.

That used to be me.

The remembrance of being chased unwillingly strikes me like lightning, and it's instantly sobering. I slam to a stop as I'm brought back to reality with jarring force.

I may willingly play with Arlo now, but my sisters are still suffering. The small amount of power I've gained in earning his desire, his loyalty, his adoration must be used appropriately.

I must stay focused.

Arlo nearly slams into me from behind, bringing one arm around my waist as the other finds my hair, gripping and tugging back. "There you are, Mercy Madness."

"What's going on?" It's Owen's voice, I think, coming from somewhere behind us—the couple I passed who brought me back to the truth. "What are you doing out here?"

I hear the familiar sound of zippers and buckles as Arlo nudges me ahead, walking us together toward camp. Rushed footfalls pad across the ground, and in moments, Owen appears at our side.

"There's been an incident," Arlo grunts, trying to hold me steady as I fight against him. "Gather the Control."

"What kind of incident?" Owen asks.

We come through the trees, stepping into the clearing at camp. The fear in me peaks—judgment and punishment are coming, I know. The way I fight Arlo becomes genuine, because in this moment, I want to get away. I want to run, far and fast, from whatever I might face to spare Arlo.

Ahead of us, Park stands near the fire, drinking from a mug of ale. His face contorts in confusion as he spots us, and he begins to move, rushing toward our commotion.

"Let me go…" I beg quietly, and just like that, the begging is no longer a game.

I want him to let me go.

"What's going on?" Park asks.

"Mercy saw something she didn't like on camera and fled the Homestead," Arlo explains. "I chased her, but I didn't catch her in time."

"Didn't catch her in time for what?" Owen's dark eyebrows draw together.

"She saw Hyatt Price take Ellary Hill into the forest…with a knife. She ran to save Ellary, and in the process…" he trails off as I jerk against his hold. He latches his arm tighter around my waist and covers my mouth with his bare hand.

"And in the process…*what?*" My heart hammers, nausea rolling through my gut at the mere sound of Killian's voice.

He approaches from behind us, circling around into view. Stepping in close, Killian reaches out to grab my wrist. He tugs, attempting to drag me from Arlo's hold. I wanted Arlo to let me go just moments ago, but now, I fear it. I don't want to feel Killian's touch on my wrist; I don't want his arms around my waist or his voice against my ear.

Arlo's grip on me tightens. The hand covering my mouth crushes my lips as he draws me closer against him, forcing my head to tilt back onto his shoulder. "I've got her," he grits.

Killian yanks on my wrist, jerking me forward against Arlo's hold. Arlo doesn't let go, but my stomach crushes painfully against his rigid arm.

"Give her to me," Killian demands with narrowed eyes as Arlo pulls me back.

My heart flutters unwillingly at Arlo's reluctance to hand me over. It feels like protection, like care, like the love of a stubborn man who claims me at the risk of his own death. Yet, we both know he has to let me go. He has to play this wicked game as much as I do.

I stop fighting and relax in his hold. I hope he feels me relenting, giving in, and I hope that it's enough of a signal for him to know it's okay to let me go. I don't want him to ever let me go, but he *has* to right now.

My heartbeat quickens as his grip gradually loosens, and once he draws his arm away from my stomach, Killian pulls me with a sharp tug.

Being dragged from Arlo's arms feels like being pushed over a cliff's edge. It makes me think of the cavern where Arlo strung me up to prepare for the first trial. It's what I imagine it would've felt like being shoved into that dark abyss at the cavern's edge. It feels like falling into never-ending darkness, every nerve ending prickling with anticipatory fear of striking the bottom.

How far will I fall before I land?

Will it hurt?

Will I break?

Will the end meet me quicker than I anticipated?

The danger of this moment sends a deluge of adrenaline to flood my veins as Killian pulls me close. He brings me to stand in front of him, chest to chest, his hand crushing my wrist where he holds my arm down at my side. I stare up at him, meeting his scornful dark eyes with all the fear and fury that rumbles through me like thunder.

"Tell us what you did, sinner," Killian snarls.

"I killed Hyatt Price," I nearly shout, wanting the whole world to hear me. I want everyone to know that I took justice for my sisters into my own hands when they were so blinded by their faith that they couldn't do it themselves. "I took the knife he brought to service and slit his throat, then I stabbed him with it. You'll find him in the forest, along with Ellary Hill."

Killian's eyes are wild with fury, surprise, and disgust. I feel so satisfied with the look he gives me that it nearly brings a smile to my face, but I don't want to give him that.

He doesn't deserve my smile.

Not until I'm standing over him with a knife, ready to make him bleed the same.

"Go," Killian says to no one in particular. "Find him."

"You can thank me now or you can thank me later for the favor, Killian." He pinches my wrist, and I cringe against the pain, but I hold my stance and his stare. "Hyatt would've killed Ellary tonight, and then you would've lost two servants in the span of two months. Technically four, if you count me and Delle. I don't believe anyone else is coming of age to replace us in less than six months, isn't that right? How do you expect the men of Ember Glen will be served when all your servants are murdered?"

He chuckles darkly. "I could string you up again and let them all take from you to make up for the losses you've caused our village. Is that what you want, sinner? Are you such a wicked little bitch that you need to be used by all the men of Ember Glen to realize your place?"

I want to spit in his face, and I nearly do before a hand closes around my other wrist and jerks me backward, spinning me around to face the opposite direction. I slam into Arlo's chest as he pulls me close. I look up at him, brow furrowing at the way he stares down at me, lips parted like he's about to speak. But he's interrupted as Owen comes running back with shock written all over his face.

"It's true," Owen says in a rush, coming to stop beside us. "Hyatt Price is dead, just as she said."

"Fuck," Killian utters at my back.

I try to hold Arlo's gaze for comfort, but he drags it away, looking over the top of my head at Killian. "His body needs to be removed."

"He needs to be *honored*. This *fucking* whore!" Killian shouts, my shoulders jumping at the sound.

"*Stop it*," Arlo warns him with a near growl, turning us sideways so he can lean toward Killian. "Be quiet. We cannot halt service for this. Our men need to purge; it's their right, and it's our duty to protect it. We need to handle this quickly and quietly, and Hyatt can be honored another day."

"He's right," Owen agrees. "We can't halt service. It will only bring violence to the village if our men aren't given their monthly purge."

Killian looks nearly out of his mind, scrubbing a hand down his face, then smoothing both palms over the sides of his head before turning and pacing away. He turns abruptly and paces back. "Fine. *Fine*. You're right, I know you are."

"Is Ellary okay?" I ask Owen. "Did you find her?"

All eyes snap to me.

Killian charges toward us, crashing in so close against our sides that I feel his chest against my shoulder. "How *dare* you ask about the well-being of a servant in a time like this?"

Disregarding Killian's reaction, Owen answers anyway, "She's bleeding, but seems okay. She's with one of the Higgins now."

I feel some relief, hoping the Higgins brothers will take turns with her for the rest of the night, as they often do. She speaks with them sometimes outside of service, and they're kind to her then as well. Perhaps they'll have an urge to care for her rather than use her.

I won't hold my breath.

Rage darkens Killian's expression as he steps toward his brother. He places a hand on the center of Owen's chest and shoves so hard that he stumbles back. "This sinner doesn't deserve peace to know her friend's condition!"

With a quiet rage, Owen steps toward him, lowering his voice to a whisper. "We've already lost one man tonight…let's not lose ourselves in anger."

"Fuck you and your calmness, Owen; this situation *begs* for my anger."

"You need to step away from this, brother," Arlo speaks to Killian in a low, rumbling voice. "Go and purge. Your mind is clouded by the Impulse."

Killian's head snaps, eyes wide as his stare meets Arlo's. Arlo shifts me in his grip, trying to move me behind him, but the subtle movement backfires. Killian sees an opening, and he takes it. Lunging toward us, he grabs me harshly by the shoulders, jerking me back hard enough to drag me from Arlo's grip. I cry out as Killian's fingers dig into my skin, as he whips me around to face the fire, and with force, marches me toward it.

chapter eighteen

Mercy

"I SHOULD SET you on fire the way Hyatt meant to in last month's service," Killian hisses at my back, shoving me ahead toward the flames.

"No!" I shout.

I try to plant my feet, but they skid in the mud, and I stumble forward. I struggle to right myself, nearly falling, but Killian grips my hair and jerks me upright, steadying me before shoving me toward the flames again.

I will not meet my end tonight.

I will not welcome flames to swallow me.

With a scowl of determination, I try to plant my feet again, working with the mud and letting my boots sink into it—one, then the other. I firm up my stance, feet shoulder width apart, and though I brace myself for another shove, Killian's determination to hurt me matches my determination not to allow it.

He releases my hair without warning, and my weight pitches forward. Before I can steady myself, his hands strike my upper back, and he shoves me so hard that I fall. I drop to the ground, catching myself on my hands and knees. My palms dig into the pebbles and twigs as they press down upon the sodden patch of dirt that covers the clearing.

Then his hand is in my hair again, tangling so deeply between the short strands that his nails dig into my scalp. He jerks my head back so hard that it lifts me from the ground, and I rise to my knees. My dirty palms shoot back, reaching for the hand that grabs me.

My gaze lifts toward the sky, and for a moment, I can see a sliver of the bright, full moon peeking from behind a cloud. Yet the meager light from above is quickly blocked by Killian's dark expression as he bends over me, looking down with a tense jaw and gritted teeth.

"You should throw yourself on that fire for what you've done, for all the evil you've brought to Ember Glen. You're straight from hell, and I should send you back."

No.

No, no, no.

My heart races being so close to the fire with his threat to burn me. I know he could do it, that he *would*. Even if I hadn't killed one of their precious men, it's a night of service and if the Impulse urges him to do so, then he can without meeting a single consequence.

"Don't," I whisper, quietly pleading, and it makes me feel weak.

"What was that, sinner?" His head turns as he scrutinizes me, glee spreading across his cheeks at the meager hint that I might grovel and beg.

"Don't, please…" I feel instant shame for the begging words slipping from my lips.

Shameful or not, I'll beg if it might spare me. I'm afraid of Killian—afraid of the power he holds, the intensity of his hatred for me. I'm afraid of the fire and being burned like Ivy Jane was.

He releases my hair and violently tosses me forward, and I land on my hands once again.

"Crawl, Mercy Madness. Go to the flame."

I shake my head and my whole body trembles. He won't stop. He won't stop until he's hurt me, and on this night, he's allowed.

Except…

"I'm not a servant." I breathe deeply, drawing in the smokey air that wafts from the flames, and let it strengthen me, like a demon fortified by hellfire. I speak louder. "I'm not a servant; I'm a participant in the Trials of Dissension. I'm already sentenced to the ultimate acts of service in the trials, and it's not my duty nor obligation to serve your urges tonight, Killian."

"No, you're not a servant," Killian hisses. "you're a disgrace to every servant who ever lived in Ember Glen. And it may not be your duty to serve my urges tonight, but you do deserve punishment for what you've done. You deserve everything that's coming to you in the trials."

And then his voice is gone, and I feel his foreboding presence disappear. I feel him move away, and relief sinks through me. Slowly, I push back and sit on my heels. Wiping my dirty palms on my skirt, I look down at my black clothes, and the world blurs around me. Tears I refuse to shed burn behind my eyes as my mind takes me back to all my nights in service.

Four years of service.

Four years of misery and horror at the hands of men.

Four years of subjugation, and no closer to freedom.

My breath catches, and a small sob breaks free. I lower my head to try to hide it, but I can't. Legs appear at my side, and right away, I know they belong to Arlo. I can feel him there. I want to reach for him, wrap my arms around his knees and hug myself to him. I know I can't, certainly not right now.

Maybe later he'll hold me?

A few quiet moments pass, then Arlo mutters, "Fuck," and I feel the weight of the world crash onto my shoulders.

I glance up at him to see that he's looking off behind me, in the direction from which Killian left. With a sinking feeling, I turn my head to look in the direction of Arlo's gaze.

Killian returns, only he's not alone.

Cambria is at his side, holding his hand as he hurries her along. She rushes to keep up with his pace, though she still has a slight limp from the last service when Killian had broken the toes on her right foot. He brings her around to stand beside me, and I feel like I can't breathe. I lift my chin to look up at her, but she refuses to look at me—she's still upset with me for sinning, but her expression is neutral, impassive.

"Put your hand in the fire, Mercy, or Cambria will take the burn on your behalf."

My eyes snap to Cambria's, and surprisingly, hers meet mine the same way. It's brief, just a quick shared moment where I bear witness to a flash of fear so uncharacteristic of Cambria Miller that it strikes me with unease. She has always been fearless, but she's afraid of the fire, too.

Maybe all the servants are now that they witnessed what had happened to Ivy Jane. The memory of her black hair awash in flames continues to haunt me.

Cambria's throat works as she swallows, tearing her eyes away from me and casting them toward the flickering firelight. "I'm happy to serve," she says, though her voice sounds strained.

"And you always serve so well," Killian praises her. He speaks with an eerily calm voice, a doting manipulation he uses to keep Cambria under the spell of serving with pride. "It's such a shame your friend betrayed you so with her sins. Did you know she killed Hyatt Price tonight?"

Cambria gasps and her eyes find mine again, her dark judgmental gaze pummeling me with guilt I know I shouldn't feel. She always had a way of making me second-guess myself, though I don't think of it as a bad thing. When I spoke of thoughts I shouldn't, she was always quick to question me, to encourage me to question myself and to think about why I'm so stubbornly blasphemous when God's will is so clear.

As clear as mud.

She meant for the questioning to lead me back to faith, but really, I think her encouragement is what led me to sin—because I *did* constantly question myself, and it led me to the truth. I found the truth because of her constant reminders to stop and think. Cambria never could have realized that stopping and thinking meant questioning the doctrine. She wanted me to challenge my thoughts, to find my purpose through God's will…and I did. I just don't think she ever imagined that God's will for me was to find a way to change everything.

"Ellary was doing her duty in serving Hyatt," Killian continues with Cambria. "Mercy witnessed it on camera and escaped the Homestead. She's so lost to her demons that she ran into the forest to end his life."

Cambria's eyes narrow on me at the mention of Ellary.

Are they narrowed in anger?

Does she hate me even more now?

Or do I see a hint of recognition there that Ellary's life was on the line? Does she understand how dangerous Hyatt was and that he would've killed Ellary tonight?

"What do you have to say to that, Cambria? What do you have to say to your friend about the treason she shows us in committing her sins?"

"I…I don't know what to say to that." Cambria's eyes leave mine for the fire again. "I don't know what to say."

"Speechless," Killian remarks. "See what you've done to your sisters, Mercy? You've hurt them beyond comprehension. Now pay them back with your pain, and put your hand in the *fucking* fire."

What do I do?

Heat ripples from the fire before me, so hot that beads of sweat coat my face as I gaze into the dancing orange light. The crackle and roar of the whipping flames seem to crescendo as all other sounds fade around me.

It's just me and the fire, and the decision that lingers: burn my hand or watch Cambria burn hers.

It's no choice for me at all.

I'd set myself on fire to spare my sisters.

Though the choice is simple, the execution of it is hard-won and horrifying. I don't know how to force my hand into the fire; I don't know how to fight the instincts already screaming at me to back away because I'm too close to the flames.

I glance at Cambria before refocusing, and somehow, I manage to move. I shuffle on my knees, scraping along dirt and stones until I'm so close to the fire that the heat threatens to suffocate me. I lift my hand, but I'm shaking, trembling, more afraid than I've ever been before.

Cambria yelps, and my head whips to see Killian grip her wrist and drag her toward the flame. "Do it, Mercy, or I burn her, and I will hold her hand in the flame until there's nothing left but bone."

"Don't!" I shout at him. "I'll do it! I'll do it…" I slowly reach toward the fire.

I feel frantic, out of my mind with fear. The sight of Ivy Jane's floating black hair as she ran, doused in flames and dancing across the night, comes into my mind, and the image won't leave me.

I have to do this.

I have to do it for Cambria.

I can do this.

I saved Ellary, and now I must save Cambria.

A nervous half-sob, half-chuckle shudders through my chest as I suddenly think of the second trial: Service by Sacrifice. It nearly feels like the trial now, choosing to burn myself in sacrifice for my friend. I don't suppose they'll let this moment count for my trial—I know this moment will be nothing compared to what my trial might be.

What sacrifice could they dream up that would be worse than this?

I want to scream, I want to cry; I want to laugh manically through the storm of chaos in my head. I choose to sacrifice for Cambria—I *do*—but all my natural instincts prevent me from pushing my hand into the flames.

Instinct halts me, but it guides me all the same. It begs me to seek Arlo because I know he can help me. I know he *will* help me.

I turn my head and raise my chin, looking up to meet Arlo's steady gaze beside me. He's already watching me with guarded fear. With my stare, I beg him. I beg him to save me, to hurt me, to be my warden and inflict my punishment himself. I need him to help me make this sacrifice, and I just…

I just need him.

Arlo's brow furrows as he tilts his head. His blue eyes bore into mine, searching to understand the message I'm silently sharing. For moments, he looks at me with confusion, but when he receives the message, I *know* it.

His eyes widen, nostrils flare as he draws in a heavy breath, chest heaving as he fills his lungs. I nod, a brief, simple granting of my permission, telling of my need for him to help me fulfill my sacrifice.

Satisfied that he knows what I need, hoping on bated breath that he'll be brave enough to help me, I turn away and stare into the orange glow before me. My gaze tracks the small sparks of ember spewed from the crackling fire and floating away into the night. I catch on a single speck, stare at it as it flares with a small, white-hot glow. The way that it flickers and sparks steals my attention, and for a moment, my mind can drift, float away with the sparking ember until it's light dies out and it falls as ash to the ground.

I'm thankful for the moment I drift with it because it grants Arlo a moment to take me by surprise. All at once, his body presses to my side as his bare hand closes around my wrist.

Heat.

He's a different kind of heat beside me, the kind that offers warmth and peace. I feel it for a moment before he tugs, dragging me to the depths of hell.

With my arm stretched long and shoulder straining to keep myself back, he pushes my hand into the open flame. I scream as flames lick my hand, instantly searing my skin and ripping pain through my flesh like a thousand knives slicing around my hand all at once.

The pain is overwhelming, and it seems to last forever, even though my hand is dragged out of the fire just a moment after entering. A strangled scream claws up my throat as Arlo lowers beside me, falling to his knees. His fingers are still coiled tightly around my wrist. My entire arm trembles beyond control, shaking through my spine and amplifying my pain.

I need to see it.

I need to look.

I have to know how bad it is.

I dare look at my hand, and I can't stop my tears from falling. Blisters already form, but not just on my hand…they form on Arlo's fingers, too—they dipped into the flame where he held me.

He burned himself to help me.

A warped sense of gratitude for Arlo sweeps through me as powerfully as the flame licked across my skin.

I pant, trying to steady my panicked breathing, watching as Arlo slowly unwraps his hand from mine, one finger at a time. We both sigh in relief as his hand easily opens, thankful that our skin hasn't fused from the heat.

I look over at him, and he gives me a nod so imperceptible that I wonder if I saw it at all. He draws in a shuddering breath, and though his blue eyes are soft staring back at me, his voice is hard…as it needs to be.

"These scars will be yours to bear until you die, sinner," Arlo says. "Let them be a reminder of the pain you've caused our community with your sins…and as a preview of your pain to come for all you've done."

I have to turn away from him as he speaks. I know it's what he has to say, but it's still hard to know what's real. I turn my attention to Killian, looking up at him from my knees, waiting on bated breath for him to let my friend go.

Let her go.

Let Cambria go!

The seconds drag on like minutes—like hours—until finally, he lets go of her arm and releases her. Cambria rushes to step back, and my eyes widen in shock. I catch her gaze to find her eyes wide, surprised at herself for retreating—the very thing that landed me where I am right now. She comes forward as quickly as it happened, and no one else seems to have noticed. Their eyes are on me, but mine are on her. She looks horrified with herself, and I shake my head, trying to reassure her without words, though I know it doesn't work.

"You're lucky your warden is strong enough to do what's right, sinner," Killian says. "Cambria can finish serving tonight without burned flesh because your warden knows what you deserve." Killian lifts his gaze to Arlo. "Well done, brother. You did what was right."

Arlo shoves to his feet in a flash. "I'll return her to the Homestead."

"I can take her if you'd like to purge now," Owen offers.

Arlo's hand closes around the back of my elbow and he hoists me to my feet. "She's my responsibility," he says, whipping me around. "I'll return later when she's settled and secured."

Will he return?

Will he still purge tonight?

The thought plagues me, but the pain in my hand serves as a reminder of what could happen to him if our forbidden romance is discovered.

I'm lucky it was just my hand…lucky they didn't march me out into the village square and burn me to death on the spot. Maybe I was afforded the same leniency men are granted under the full moon—they still wanted their service, and they didn't want to be interrupted long enough to deliver me a swift and tormenting end. I'm spared for murder because these sordid men want to chase their lust. But spared tonight only means more to come. In the trials, they'll draw it out, the worst punishments of all.

Arlo leads me away from camp with his palm wrapped around my arm, and when we're nearly at the tree line, he whispers with urgency, "I'll take care of your hand at the Homestead. As soon as we're out of their sight, I need you to run with me. I'm sorry, Mercy."

I'll run with him, as far and as fast as he needs me to.

Who is this man?

What is he becoming?

Arlo Rainn was the hateful man who bound me, who shared me, who cut my hair, who used me.

But he's also the man who lied to his brothers, the man who held a knife to Hyatt's throat to save Ellary, who worshipped me beneath a thunderstorm in the meadow…The man who burned his own hand to help me burn mine.

He's capable of change, and that means that he's capable of changing Ember Glen.

chapter nineteen

ARLO

MERCY AND I run together through the forest and across the village square, surrounded only by the sounds of our footfalls and heavy breaths as we flee service. We turn and rush up the stone steps outside the Homestead, and she forgets for just a moment as she reaches down to lift her skirt so it doesn't catch on her feet. She hisses through her teeth as her burnt hand touches the fabric, but she shakes it off and continues onward, keeping pace with me.

We stop only long enough for me to unlock the front door, and I hurry her inside. I quickly brush off Delle and Theo when they try to stop us to ask about what they must have witnessed on camera. Mercy's hand is burnt and blistering, and taking care of it is my only immediate concern. We rush past them up the staircase, and I urge her down the hall faster, nudging her into the relative safety of her bedroom.

I slam the door shut behind us as she breezes past me with her hand wrapped tightly around her wrist, squeezing as though she fears her burnt hand might fall off if she doesn't hold on. Her face is twisted with pain, and she hisses through labored breaths.

I feel her pain, and it's so much worse than my own, but at least I know she still has feeling in her hand. I tried to pull her as high into the flame as I could—fire is fire, but I read once that flames are cooler at the top. The fact that she has pain is good. While her pain makes me shake with fury, it also means that the burns weren't deep enough to deaden her nerves.

If she's in pain, she'll heal.

It will hurt, but she will heal.

Striding past her, I head for the bathroom. "Come with me."

I head right for the vanity and turn on the faucet, adjusting the temperature until it's cool, but not cold. I pull the stopper for the drain and let the basin fill.

I turn and see her standing behind me, staring down at her pinkened, blistering flesh. She lifts her head to look at me—her face pale behind the dirt and dried blood, her expression distorted with pain.

"What do I do?" she asks with a whisper of worry under her breath.

"Come here," I tell her, though I go to her before she takes a single step.

Turning to stand beside her, I slip my arm around her, splay my palm against the small of her back, and press her forward as we move to the sink.

We stand side-by-side at the vanity, watching the basin fill, and when her head rises to look at her reflection in the mirror, I do the same. I'm surprised to find that we look…different. I suppose I shouldn't be surprised.

I *feel* different.

I feel like the world has shifted beneath my feet. Like heaven has drifted away to float somewhere among the stars, too far out of reach, and hell has risen to greet us here on Earth. And as for us…We look like the tortured souls who clawed their way up through the splintered ground.

We're both dressed all in black, hair flat but frizzy as the rain soak starts to dry. Mercy's starlight strands are flecked with mud, tangled from rolling in the meadow. Our clothes are crooked, clinging to us with remnants of dried blood and dirt coating our skin that didn't wash away from the storm.

Our eyes meet in the mirror, and I hold her stare. I allow myself to look at her—truly look at her—and in her eyes, I see everything I ever wanted. I see all the things I never knew I wanted, everything I could never have guessed wanting in my life until she was in it. My heart threatens to break my ribs as it tells me how I really feel about her fate.

How will I live when she's dead?

"Arlo?" She draws me from my thoughts.

I look down to see the sink is full, so I flip off the faucet. "Here." I gently wrap my burnt fingers around her wrist and guide her hand into the cool water—just as I had guided her to the flames.

She tenses, whimpering as I move her hand, but then she relaxes as the cool water soothes the burn. It soothes me, too. My fingertips are burnt from diving into the flame with her. It's a familiar pain for me—at least, it's one I can tolerate—but for her, it's new and undoubtedly overwhelming. Her entire hand is burnt from direct contact with a roaring flame, and I know it has to be excruciating.

"*Fuck*, this hurts," she mutters.

"I know. I'm sorry."

"It's not your fault." She turns her head to look at me, and I do the same.

There's a long pause, a moment of staring where we just look at each other. I take the time to study her features, to appreciate her beauty and commit the look of her right now to memory. She may resemble a tortured soul, but she's a tortured soul prepared for battle. She looks like a warrior— my fallen angel, like a soldier in the throes of battle, sent to save us.

She was sent to save me.

I let go of her hand so I can grab hold of her face with both of mine, unconcerned with the pain in my freshly burnt fingertips. She keeps her hand in the water as I hold her steady, bring my face closer until the tips of our noses touch.

"You're something more…so much more than I thought you were." I don't even know what I'm saying as my unstable emotions have the best of me, and they're taking control. I know that makes me vulnerable, unsafe, but I feel powerless to the way she's taken hold of me tonight.

My thumb strokes slowly across her cheek, dragging down the dried track of a tear, an imprint of the trail it made running through the patch of dirt there. Then, I kiss her slowly, taking my time to softly part her lips with mine, gently sweep my tongue between her teeth, and sensually taste her. The connection of our kiss ends naturally, gradually slowing to a stop, and I keep my eyes closed as our foreheads touch.

"Will you kiss me like that tomorrow?" she whispers.

My eyes open to find her already looking at me, our eyes so near that they're able to see straight through to our truest layer.

"Yes. And every day after until you take your last breath."

I swallow against a lump in my throat, suddenly struck by the morbid reality that the day of her last breath draws nearer with each passing second. I thought we'd both accepted that her death was coming, but now the thought of it vexes me.

Everything about her vexes me.

She's a sinner by our laws—which are meant to be the laws of God—but tonight, I knew she was more. She's an angel, a prophet, a sacrificial lamb. She's everything, yet she's nothing I can name. Whatever she is, she's mine, and I'm claiming her for eternity.

It takes too long for me to blink and drag myself from this moment of peace with her. Slowly, I lift my hands from her cheeks and sink my fingers into the cool water with hers.

"We need to soak the burn for fifteen minutes, let the skin cool," I instruct her. "Then we'll rinse it to make sure it's clean. You'll need to keep it covered to avoid infection. I'll have to go find bandages from our medical supplies…and something for the pain. It's gonna hurt like hell when we have to change the covering."

She stares at our hands in the water. "How do you know about healing a burn? Is that how…" Her head twists to look sideways at me. "Is that how you got the scars on your hands? Are they from burns?"

I hesitate. It's not something I ever planned to share with her before, but things are decidedly different now. Everything's different now, and I *want* to tell her. I want to share with her; I want her to know me, though the thought of her knowing me is terrifying.

"Yes."

"How? What happened?"

"It's not a very interesting story," I say evasively.

"I still want to hear it."

I sigh, slowly shifting my hand so my fingers come to rest above her wrist, careful to avoid her burns, though I'm eager to touch her.

"Before I came of age to purge, my urges were strong. I had to find a way to control myself, and my mental strength at the time was low. There was one night when our power had gone out," as it often does in the village, "and my mother lit candles and placed a few around the house. I was thirteen and in the quiet of night, my mind raced with thoughts from the Impulse— sexual thoughts that drove me mad with lust. It would be another year before I could purge under the full moon.

"At the time, I was still trying to understand what the Impulse was and how nights of service would help me satisfy those urges if I could just wait a little while longer to indulge. So I felt that I needed a way to control myself until then…some method to tame the urges until I was old enough to enact them.

"That night, I sat alone at the kitchen table, long after everyone else had gone to bed, and I watched the flame of a lone, lit candle dance. The firelight had me mesmerized. It captivated me, held my attention, and before long, it allowed my thoughts to drift away from impurity.

"I didn't burn myself that night. The first time was a few nights later when I had urges to defile myself. I felt so much shame that I would've done anything to make it stop."

The shame I felt back then over my sexual needs washes over me as I tell her this. It strikes me with adrenaline, making some part of me want to run from the room and pretend I never told her this, pretend it never happened. Yet something in my soul urges me to keep speaking.

"I went to the kitchen and found one of my mother's candles. I lit it with a match, took it to my room, and watched the flame, but watching wasn't enough when my needs were so strong. I wanted to touch it…so I did.

"I held my hand over the flame and let it dance across my skin. I'd nearly screamed that first time because I couldn't seem to draw my hand away, feeling as though I needed to let it burn, and burn deeply, so I let it.

"A few days later, it was a full moon, and I spied the servants leaving their homes in the village, all walking away as the sun was setting to head for the village square on their way to the forest. That was the first night I really saw the servants, recognized them as women, saw their beauty, and found lust in anticipation of purging with them in the next year.

"The lust made me sick, Mercy. It was unholy because I wasn't yet of age to have these urges, and I couldn't understand why God gave them to me if He didn't want me to purge yet." I turn my face to the mirror, seeing my brow furrowed with the internal dissonance I'm feeling over the memory.

Why would God give me urges before He meant for me to purge them? Why would He give men urges at all if it's so sinful for them to act on them outside of service?

Why haven't I questioned this all along?

Mercy meets my stare in our reflection.

I spit out the words in a rush. "I lit a fire in our backyard that night and stuck both hands into the rising flames."

She gasps, probably because she knows what that feels like now… excruciating.

"My mother treated my wounds that night." I pause. "She told me she was proud of me."

"What?"

"She was proud of me for finding a way to control myself, to suppress the Impulse until I became of age to purge. She encouraged it; she gave me candles and matches to keep in my bedroom." My gaze shifts, staring off at nothing as I hear my words out loud—how strange they sound. I've been setting myself on fire for years to combat the flames of desire sparking within me.

Why is it okay for me to burn the flesh God gave me, but not to use that flesh for pleasure outside of service?

I shake my head, blinking back to Mercy in the mirror. "That was normal for every boy my age, I suppose. We all had our vices and means of self-control when we were younger. Once I came of age and was able to purge, it lessened those urges on normal days. It made sense then, all of it. Purge monthly and the entire community benefits from our collective weakened Impulse for the rest of the month."

Silence greets me, and I let it hang until she speaks.

"I'm sorry, Arlo. You were only a child trying to do what you thought was right."

Her eyes are soft as she looks at me in the reflection, her expression compassionate, sinking a hook into my gut for the way it reels me in. She looks at me as though she were looking at a child, as though she somehow sees innocence within me, but there's none left.

"We've been told what was right and wrong every day of our lives. You were just a child and you—" She lets out a heavy sigh. "I'm so sorry you were made to feel that hurting yourself was praise-worthy. I never thought...I didn't think about the men of Ember Glen and how they were raised, how they were harmed."

I chuckle briefly and shake my head. "Why would you think of it? Why would anyone? It's just the way it is. It's the way things have always been, and it's worked. No one ever had any reason to think differently..." I pause, meeting her stare again to give her a meaningful look, "Except for you. What happened tonight was no accident. I think...I think God sent you to spark change."

Her lips fall open, her face loosening with relief at my words. She looks like I've told her everything she ever wanted to hear, and perhaps I have. Perhaps she only needed someone's acceptance and understanding to find her real strength, her true purpose.

She doesn't respond, and we let silence fill the space. I wonder what she's thinking, but I don't ask. I let her have the quiet because this day has been filled with so much damn noise. I shift closer, let our bodies touch as we soak our burnt hands—hands we burnt together in sacrifice for one another.

Sacrifice.

It's the theme of her next trial, and perhaps the entire meaning of our relationship. I'm risking everything in being so open with her, slicing open my chest and letting my heart bleed out for her. Yet at the risk of bleeding my veins dry, it's a sacrifice I choose to make for her—one I choose to make *with* her.

It's in this moment that I realize I'm going to break the promise I made her tonight—I'll be here for her through her trials, and I'll take care of her every need, be her true warden in every wholesome and depraved manner she demands. But I am not going to live my life as an honorable member of the Control so I can become an Elder and maybe effect some minor change decades in the future.

No.

I'll live honorably long enough to find a way out of this, to figure out how to take her safely away from Ember Glen, or burn the whole damn village down myself, even if it means she and I are the only two people left in existence.

And if I fail, then I'll die along with her because I can no longer fathom the thought of living without her.

chapter twenty
Mercy

THE NIGHT WAS long and painful.

Arlo cleaned my burns and wrapped my hand with sterile gauze. He covered his own with a fresh pair of leather gloves that he'd pulled from a store of them kept in his room. I was concerned about him wearing gloves over his burns, but he assured me they made a good covering to keep them clean, and that his injuries weren't nearly as bad as mine.

Once our injuries were tended to, I was forced to return to the room downstairs to watch the remainder of the service with Delle. Theo and Arlo each had to take a turn and leave us for a couple of hours— it was a night of service after all, and they were expected to purge.

Though there might have been doubt as recently as last night about whether he would purge with another servant, there's no doubt in my mind now that he didn't. Something changed between us, something powerful, as though we were struck by lightning in that thunderstorm and forever altered by the electricity.

When he told me about his scars last night, I made a decision, and it feels like one of the most significant choices I've ever made…

I chose to give him my trust.

I trust Arlo Rainn.

There's something freeing in giving him that, in choosing to assume he truly does care for me rather than fear him. It's freeing to make the choice to see the truth in him. And the truth is that he's a victim of Ember Glen as much as I am.

It broke my heart to hear how his mother praised him for harming himself to suppress his desire. I can't imagine how damaging that would be for the mind of a thirteen-year-old boy. He was just a child. He was preached in shame and guilt from the beginning, and his behavior as an adult is no wonder to me now.

It's not an excuse for all the ways he's harmed me—he's responsible for the choices he's made—but I now understand what shaped his mind in his youth, and I feel responsible for helping him see the truth. I *want* to be responsible for helping him heal, breaking down his walls, finding his compassion—not just for me, but for all the people of Ember Glen. I don't owe him that, but it's what I want for him. Before I'm dead and gone, I want him to see what I see, know what I know, feel what I feel.

The sun is rising as I stand beside Arlo in the village square. A long line is formed by the Control, the seven members stretched out across the open space and standing side-by-side. Their purpose is to thank the women for their service last night as they make their way across the gravel, heading for Sanctuary.

I bathed last night, and all the dirt and blood are scrubbed clean from my skin. I've been made to put on a red gown, as my black servant's clothes were insulting to the women who served. I've been asked to stand in line and thank my sisters for their service along with the Control because, as Killian put it, I should be showing my respect for their additional efforts to make up for the loss of me in service.

I don't want to thank them.

I want to tell them I'm sorry that they have to serve. I'm sorry they're hurting, that they're used and abused. I'm sorry that I can't save them, but I hope that one day, Arlo will become an Elder and make this place better for the generations to come.

I want to be defiant and snide, but I'm entirely too exhausted to do anything but stand here. And whatever medicine Arlo fed me a half an hour ago seems to be mingling with my system now. It's lovely because the pain in my hand is gradually dulling and fading, but it's also making me uneasy… My head is feeling lighter, freer, like my cares are slowly slipping away, and I'm looking at the world through rose-colored glasses.

What medicine is this, and why don't the servants have access to it?

We've suffered so many nights of pain, and the medicine we had was much weaker than this.

The world feels steady beneath my feet, though my body seems to lightly sway. I'm not sure whether the sway is real or it only feels as though it's happening as this powerful medicine takes hold. Either way, it's nice, like being soothed and rocked in the arms of a breeze that moves me slowly. Lulled into compliance, I quietly thank my sisters in service as they pass me and Arlo in small groups and clusters.

As more and more servants pass, my anxiety grows, creating a strange sense of nausea as it combats the calming effect of the medicine. I wait on bated breath to see Ellary and Cambria return. I stare at the forest, hoping with each new emergence of women dressed in black that I'll see them both there, walking on their own two feet.

It feels like hours have passed when I finally spot two figures emerge from the trees. As Arlo and I are so far down the line, I can't quite make out who it is yet. I lean forward, peeking around Arlo and straining my eyes because hope tells me it's them. The two women are walking side by side, and though they're slow, they're on their feet and moving independently. As they get closer, I recognize the bob in Cambria's steps, the slight limp in the cadence of her walk.

It's them.

Ellary and Cambria are okay.

I let out a heavy breath as relief washes over me. I watch their faces as they walk past the line of the Control, hoping for a moment of eye contact, a hint of recognition, some connection—however small—to acknowledge our years of friendship.

I know it's selfish, but a part of me wants their recognition of what I did for them both last night. I know it's unlikely that either of them truly understand why I ran for Ellary or why I sacrificed my hand to spare Cambria's. I know their gratitude shouldn't matter to me because I don't imagine they'll have any. I don't blame them for that—the beliefs they've fallen victim to aren't their fault.

It's just that I have so much love and appreciation for them, for all the times I spoke out of turn and they gently shushed me, for all the times I expressed my strong emotions over our fate and they calmly fought to bring me back to faith. They were gentle and kind with me for so many years when they didn't have to be.

Tears spring to my eyes as I realize how much danger I put them in, especially through my teenage years, yet they never dissociated with me. They stood by my side and tried to help me become a better servant.

Our beliefs were never aligned, but they cared for me regardless—they helped me unselfishly until they simply couldn't anymore. Perhaps I would have found my way to understand God in the way they see Him if Ember Glen had been rooted in kindness and love rather than pain and sacrifice and suffering.

"Thank you for your service, ladies," Ryker says to them from further down the line. One after the other, each man of the Control thanks my friends for suffering to their benefit as they make their way to Sanctuary.

As they come closer, my gaze drops at the hint of color in Ellary's hand, contrasting against her black clothes. She holds a plucked bundle of red and purple wildflowers from the meadow—the crimson petals match the dried blood which encircles her arm. My pulse races at the memory of last night, finding her so weak and bleeding, so afraid that she would die by Hyatt's hand.

She didn't die.

She's okay.

And Cambria's hand isn't burnt because I spared her.

Arlo helped me spare her.

I glance at Arlo, giving him a silent thank you for being my strength, for pushing my hand into the flame when I couldn't do it myself…but he doesn't look at me. He stares straight ahead, distant, cut-off, unreachable in this moment. Strangely, I understand the disconnect, and somehow, I'm not upset by it.

"Thank you for your service," Arlo mutters as Ellary and Cambria approach.

"Thank you for your—"

My words cut short as Ellary's hand opens, and the wildflowers fall, floating to land on the ground at my feet. I stare down at the bundle of amethyst and ruby, with their emerald-green stems. I'm lost in them for a moment, but soon after, I lift my gaze and find them both looking at me. I meet their eyes, sharing a brief moment of connection I've been longing for with each of them. A nearly imperceptible smile touches Ellary's cheeks, and though I see no smile from Cambria's lips, I see it in her eyes.

Gratitude.

My chest sinks as all the air in my lungs leaves me in a rush. They still have love for me, and I hadn't realized how much I needed to know that until this very moment.

As they turn away, continuing past us toward Sanctuary, I drop my head to gaze at the wildflowers at my feet. I start to bend, reaching to pick them up, but a shiny black shoe blocks my path, startling me, causing me to sharply rise and jump back. The shoe slams down to stomp on the flowers, twisting and tearing apart the bundle, petals pulling away from the stems and grinding into the gravel. I already know it's Killian before my eyes rise from the ruined bundle to confirm.

When he meets my furious gaze, he cocks his head to the side. "I guess we'll be keeping a closer eye on Ellary and Cambria from now on."

I feel the weight of his words sink through my stomach, heavy and nauseating. Though I'm so grateful for their gesture—the connection, the love shared through those flowers—I'm so regretful that they chose to do that. A shared look would've been enough for me.

But also…I'm proud.

I'm proud because they knew extending such a gesture could bring a more watchful eye to them, and they did it anyway. Not only did they do it, but they did it right in front of the Control. It makes me sick that they'll be watched more closely, but at the same time, elation swells in my chest, puffing me up with pride and making me feel all the more powerful.

"I guess you will." I stare back at Killian, hardening my expression, though the medicine in my system tries to soften me.

I hold his eyes, unwilling to look away first, emboldened by the chemicals in my system. A few moments pass where I wonder if we'll remain locked in this stare all day because I'm stubbornly resolute to hold it until he walks away—and he probably feels the same. A few more servants begin to cross the square, and Killian is forced to look away first, drawing his gaze from mine with a sharp whip of his head before returning to his spot in line to thank the servants.

The second that he moves, I feel awash with relief, and joy over the flowers from Ellary's hand creeps in with it. I draw my lip between my teeth to try and hide my growing smile as I side-step closer to Arlo.

I don't dare look at him right now—I'm too afraid I'll grab him and kiss him in this medicated state, which is starting to feel like inebriation. But I dare to let my hand float sideways, inching closer and closer until the back of my hand bumps against his leather-clad knuckles.

He flinches and jerks his hand away, but I know I only have to wait. Soon, his hand returns to his side as he lets out a sigh. His arm floats toward mine this time, repeating my gesture such that our knuckles kiss.

Though his hands are covered, I can feel him the same as if we were touching skin-to-skin. The leather gloves are a part of him as much as his scars. It's a special thing to me when he removes them to touch me, to feel me, to deliver pleasure...

And even with the barrier of his gloves between our skin, I feel everything he's feeling through our simple touch: elation, pride, hope, and fear. All of it mingles, swirling around our barely touching hands like a lasso.

As the last of the servants return to Sanctuary, and Park declares that they're all accounted for, the Control move to gather inside the Homestead. Delle and I trail along as we must. The men begin to chat, each of them moving to gather around the sunburst tile in an almost unintentional manner. Arlo whispers that Delle and I should wait by the staircase, in his and Theo's line of sight where they stand opposite the steps. I wobble up three of them before whirling around and plopping my bottom on the step, while Delle lowers hesitantly to sit beside me.

"Are you okay?" she asks.

I nod and give her a quick smile.

"We need to make a plan regarding Hyatt Price," Wesley says. "Park and I moved his body when the sun rose. I suppose we can ask the coroner's wife to begin the embalmment since he'll be resting from the purge." He sighs. "The Elders won't be happy at this loss of life."

"Mercy should be executed immediately," Killian snarls with angered conviction.

A laugh bursts uncontrollably from my chest, and Delle's hand shoots out to latch around my wrist in warning. I didn't mean to let it out—and I know the medication is to blame—but I need to control myself or they very well may execute me today.

Seven pairs of enraged eyes are upon me—even Arlo is angered with my outburst. I can't help but smile when I look at him, though. He's really quite handsome when he's angry.

"Mercy, stop…" Delle mutters under her breath, and I glance over to see the worry on her face.

The medication—I need to control myself.

I nod at her and clear my throat, forcing myself to remember the seriousness of my circumstances. Slowly, the men turn their attention away from me and back to each other.

"There's a reason she wasn't executed last night," Owen says. "As a participant in the Trials of Dissension, she's not a servant, and can't be considered as such."

Killian cocks his head. "And how should she be considered differently, Owen? She *murdered* a man in cold-blood."

"That's for the seven of us to decide together," Owen says. "Now that we've all purged and have clear minds, we can make that decision."

"I vote for immediate execution," Killian declares.

Park narrows his eyes in consideration. "But she's already a trial participant. Won't that make for a more meaningful example in her death?"

"So we're no longer pretending that one might pass the trials and survive, then?" My words fly from my mouth before I can stop them. "You're suddenly comfortable stating with abject certainty that death will meet us?"

All their heads turn in my direction, but I look at Arlo. He's fuming at me, staring me down with his bright blue eyes, surely wishing I would just keep my damn mouth shut. I nearly want to laugh, imagining the thoughts running through his head—surely, he regrets giving me a medicine which eases my pain while lowering my inhibitions.

I try to bring anger back to my mind. Shaking Delle's hand from my wrist, I cross my arms over my chest, and narrow my stare at Arlo. But everything just feels so laughable in my current state—the expression he wears is funny. He cocks an eyebrow, trying to command me with a look, but

I think he knows what's happening here because I see the twitch of humor through the corners of his lips…those thick, kissable lips and the perfect tongue he hides behind them.

Stop thinking about his tongue…

Suddenly, nothing is funny, and the air around me is *hot*. Desire for him replaces inappropriate humor at my situation, and though I'd prefer not to feel heavy between my thighs right now, it's certainly preferable to laughing out loud every time they mention my looming death.

"At this point, yes," Killian grumbles. "Death is assured for you, Mercy Madness."

"And what about me?" Delle asks at my side, her voice anxious and weary all at once.

They all look at her, eyeing her cautiously, as if no one cares to confirm the truth for her. Without another word, they turn back to their little circle, effectively ignoring her.

If the trials are crafted to ensure my death, then Delle's death will come, too—and now the hopelessness of our situation has been confirmed for her. I hear the air leave her lungs, and it's sobering. I scoot closer to Delle and slide my arm across the small of her back to hug her to my side.

"The remaining trials will set an important example for the other servants," Park continues. "It's why we chose them for Mercy in the first place. I say we allow the trials to deliver her punishment for Hyatt's death."

"If it brings about her death anyway, I agree," Wesley adds. "Today we should focus on planning to honor Hyatt. Mercy has her warden to keep watch over her and ensure she doesn't cause any more trouble." He nods at Arlo.

"Yet her warden couldn't stop her last night," Ryker snips, stealing an agitated glance at Arlo.

"That was a fluke," Theo says. "She surprised us both. She moved quickly."

"I did my best to stop her," Arlo mutters, gazing off into the distance. He defends himself, though it's clear to me he struggles with his words. I know it's hard for him to let me take the blame for this. "I lost sight of her in the storm and just didn't make it in time."

"It's okay, brother," Killian says, his voice so unusually calm and clear that it surprises me. "You did well once you caught her." Killian looks around the circle at each of the Control. "He pushed her hand into the fire to punish her when she refused to do it herself."

I didn't refuse…I chose to do it for Cambria!

I just needed Arlo's help.

"Just put it to a vote," Arlo snarls through his rising frustration. "Death today or death through the trials." His fingers curl into fists at his sides.

"Okay," Owen says. "Who wishes to move forward with the Trials of Dissension as the method of execution for Mercy Madness?"

The method of execution...

The way that phrase sucks the air from the room is striking. It's a definitive confirmation that there really never was any chance for me. It should cripple me, but I find it strengthens me instead. If death is assured for me, then the only thing I have left to lose is time.

Every man in the circle raises their hand to move forward with the trials—even Arlo does, though the lift of his arm is strained. He has to vote, and it only makes sense to vote for me to have more time.

In fact, all the men in the circle vote surprisingly to grant me more time in this life—everyone except for Killian, which was no surprise, either.

"I'm sorry," Owen says, looking at Killian. "Majority rules. We continue with the trials as planned."

"This is a mistake," Killian says, his voice remarkably steady. "I want it known that I don't support this decision."

"It's known," Arlo says.

"Don't forget that you'll have a say in how the trials are carried out," Owen reminds Killian. "Your voice will be important as we make those decisions."

"That's right," Killian says as the corners of his lips quirk into a half-smile. "Thank you for the reminder, Owen. That does make me feel better."

"Good," Owen says, "because we need to shift our focus to Hyatt Price."

"We'll need someone to go to the village and notify Hyatt's family," Wesley says. "Any volunteers?"

The room falls into silence.

"I'll go," Arlo says. "I'll take Mercy and make her explain what happened."

A few dark chuckles rumble through the room in appreciation of this idea.

"Yes, take the murderer herself to tell them of his death." Ryker laughs. "Let her know the full impact of the pain she's caused."

"I don't think it's wise to—"

"It's what she deserves," Killian says, cutting Owen off. "She must face his family's pain first-hand. Have her tell them everything she did. Have her tell his wife why she's now a widower, his children why they no longer have a father."

"I'm good with that," Theo agrees, though he casts a sideways glance at

Arlo. "It will allow us to take the time we need to meet with the Elders and make arrangements to honor Hyatt. And let's not forget that today is a day of rest for *all* the men of Ember Glen. We, too, need to recover from this purge."

He's met with murmurs of agreement while I'm left confused. I don't understand why Arlo is volunteering to share the news of Hyatt's death, but more than that, why he would want me to be the one to deliver it.

It's not safe for me to go to the village, even with my warden. The people who hate me for my sins could riot, could seize me, could drag me from his side and take me to my execution—though I suppose it shouldn't worry me anymore, knowing that my execution is assured one way or another.

"Good." Leaving the circle, Arlo cuts across the sunburst and heads for me. "We'll go now." He reaches across the bottom steps and grips my elbow, tugging me forward.

"I don't want to—"

"You should've thought about that last night when you murdered a man, sinner."

I know he doesn't mean it with his nasty tone, but the act still hurts me. It wasn't that long ago that he thought of me as nothing more than a sinner to be condemned—it would be so easy for him to switch back in his thinking.

Regardless, I've chosen to trust him, so I don't resist as he pulls me through the front door.

chapter twenty-one

Mercy

ARLO'S PALM IS wrapped around my bicep as he leads me down the steps in front of the Homestead. I'm glad for his gentle hand there to steady me as the light-headed sway makes me feel a little uneven on my feet.

"I really don't think this is a good idea," I tell him as we land on the gravel-covered square. "I'm feeling a little…off."

"I'm well aware. I knew it was a risk giving you that medication, but I couldn't stand seeing you in pain any longer."

Our feet crunch over the pebbles as we walk forward, heading across the large open space toward the village.

"I don't think I can control my mouth. I'll say things I shouldn't to Hyatt's family."

He lets out a small chuckle. "Somehow, I don't think you'll say anything they weren't already thinking. I imagine Stefanie will find relief."

"Stefanie?"

"Hyatt's wife. She was a friend of my sister's when we were younger."

"Oh." I think I'm leaning because the world feels a little sideways.

Arlo stops too suddenly and turns to face me, gripping my arms in his hands and dipping to look at me squarely. "Are you okay? Did I give you too much?"

"How would I know? And anyway, I feel incredible for a woman whose death is currently being plotted by seven angry men." I grin, unable to feel upset about the truth when my mind is so fuzzy, when it makes everything seem so much funnier than it really is.

"How's the pain?"

"Gone."

"Good."

"Will it be gone forever now?"

"No. Just until the medication wears off."

"And how soon will that be? Can I have some more?"

He pushes back on my arms, and I realize it's because I'm leaning into him unconsciously, and he's trying to keep an appropriate distance. I know we're out in the open and could be watched. I'm capable of reasonable thought; I just seem to be a little beyond my means in controlling my spoken words and my movements.

"We'll see," he says. "I'm not sure it's such a good idea for you to be in this state for too long considering you and I have secrets to keep."

"I would never share our secrets, Warden Rainn." I pull my arms from his grip and raise my hands, showing him my palms. "See? I'm not even touching you right now," I appreciatively look him up and down, "even though I'd certainly like to be."

I take a small step back, then reluctantly drag my eyes away. I bend to gather my skirt at my thighs, hoisting it up to keep the length of it from catching on my black boots. I turn and shuffle off in the direction of the village. I force myself to continue onward, trying to ignore the insistent flutter of my heart which demands me to return to him at once and beg him to kiss me.

But then a thought I can't ignore bursts into my mind, and I stop abruptly, whipping around to face him.

"Mercy!" he calls out my name as he nearly crashes into me.

Arlo grabs hold of my arms again to keep me upright as I stagger backward a step, gasping at his proximity. I hadn't expected him to follow me so quickly, let alone to be right behind me when I stopped.

Insistently, the words fly from my mouth, unbothered by our near collision. "Where do the medical supplies come from? Who makes them? How did you get the medicine you fed me, and why don't the servants have access to it?"

Why haven't I wondered about all this before?

"Slow down," he commands, his eyebrows knitting together with concern. "You're racing in every sense of the word, and it's beginning to worry me."

I make a show of taking a slow, deep breath before asking more calmly, "Where do the medical supplies come from?"

"From our medical supply store."

I huff. "Yes, I know, but where do they come from before that?"

His look of concern morphs into one of confusion—or more accurately, it's a look expressing internal conflict. "I don't know how to answer that."

"Try."

"The Elders send us everything we need in Ember Glen."

"But what does that mean? How do they send it? Where do they send it from? Where *are* they?"

"You're asking me for answers I don't have, Mercy."

"Yet they're reasonable questions that should be asked, aren't they?"

"They are…"

"Surely someone has asked them before."

"And surely no answers were given."

His hands tighten around my biceps as he takes a step closer. I'm so acutely aware of his presence, the minty smell of his breath as it breezes over my lips, the way my skin tingles beneath his touch, the way my body sways toward him so naturally. Perhaps it's some magic love potion he fed me instead of medicine which fills me with euphoric bliss.

No.

My feelings toward Arlo are natural in every sense. The things I feel for him could never be crafted or manufactured.

He lowers his voice to a whisper, though the square is entirely empty. "People don't ask questions as often as you, and most don't question anything at all. The Elders and the Control prefer it that way. There's a rule for everything, and when there isn't one that meets our needs…The Elders take time to review the Impulse Edict…and *always* return with an answer from God."

I can feel my face twist as I work through what he's telling me while combating my quickening pulse at his nearness.

"Are you saying that," I pause to gather my thoughts, trying to coordinate them with my speech, "that the Impulse Edict has an answer for everything…even when it doesn't?"

His eyes flicker as they narrow briefly, his forehead wrinkling as if speaking this to me now is the first time he's really thought of it. "Yes, I think that's what I'm saying."

"Do you think they're amending the word of God as they see fit?"

His eyes brighten with awareness and widen with epiphany, his expression softening with instant resignation to the truth. "Yes." He nods slowly. "Yes, it makes sense."

The medication is strong, but not strong enough to cloud the seriousness of this revelation. Still, I feel lighter at this heavy news because it's so telling of how willing Arlo is to change; it tells me that he must have considered these things before, that some small part of him must have wondered and questioned before I came along, and he simply prayed away his so-called blasphemous thoughts.

There is a natural goodness somewhere within Arlo Rainn's soul. It's only been buried too long, too deeply for it to find its way to the surface on its own. Maybe it's haughty to think this, but I wonder if he only needed me to find it and dig it out.

"Do you think anyone has questioned them on this before?"

"I think it's likely," he says, watching me with curiosity and consideration. "Someone must have noticed this happening before and said something about it. Or perhaps they just wondered in silence. I don't know anything for sure, but…" He looks off toward Sanctuary, getting lost in thought.

"But, what?"

His grip loosens and his hands fall away from my arms. "I've been reading your mother's journal, and—"

"You've been reading it?"

Anxiety swells. I'd nearly forgotten about my mother Mira's journal. I was reading it in the meadow the day the Control came to take me away and announced my forced participation in the Trials of Dissension. Arlo had taken the journal from me then, and we'd never spoken another word about it. My mind has been too preoccupied to think of it, but now that he's brought it up, I feel an ache in my heart for not having it through my final days.

"I want it back," I demand.

"Are you aware that there are pages missing?"

I blink at him. "What?"

"Three pages are missing. It's clear they've been torn out."

"I'm…I'm aware."

"Do you know where they are?"

"I don't understand how this has anything to do with—"

"Have you read it? Every word of it?"

"Mostly, yes, but I—"

"Do you remember the passage she wrote about her mother, and how she told her about the strange and untimely death of two members of the Control when she was a child?"

"Strange and untimely," I repeat, the two words striking my memory and bringing the passage back to mind. "Yes, I remember that. She wrote that they died within days of each other, but their deaths were labeled…" I pause, trying to draw the words from the back corner of my mind. "They were labeled 'tragic mysteries.'"

"Doesn't that strike you as odd? It makes me wonder what information they discovered—"

"Before meeting a strange and untimely end…" I nod, understanding dawning on me.

"One of the torn-out pages was right after that passage. Mercy, I have to ask you…Did you tear out those pages?"

I shake my head. "No. They were already torn out when I found the journal."

"Where did you find it?"

"I was cleaning out my father's house in the village after he died a few months ago. It was in the drawer of the table beside his bed, though it was odd finding it there."

A wave of dizziness ripples, and I feel myself begin to sway.

Arlo reaches out to grip my shoulders and steady me. "Why was it odd?"

"Because it wasn't there before."

"Could the torn-out pages have been in that drawer?"

"No. There was nothing there but the journal. I cleared out the house."

"Is there a place you can think of where your mother might have hidden them?"

I feel my forehead wrinkle. "No, I don't think so. I'd imagine the pages were destroyed. There must have been something written on them that she didn't want seen." My eyes flutter shut as a peaceful exhaustion flows through me. "You smell too good to stand so close to me, Warden Rainn."

"But she was condemned for her sins," he murmurs, almost to himself. I blink open my eyes to find his narrowed in consideration. "The Control would have confiscated her belongings." He looks at me. "Then how did you find her journal fourteen years after her death in a place where it wasn't before?"

"Hmm?"

"Do you think your father kept her journal all these years and left it for you when he got sick? He was ill for some time, wasn't he?"

I nod. "Yes, for a few years."

"I wonder who tore out the pages then…your father or your mother."

"Or someone else. Maybe someone else tore them out and kept them. Or destroyed them. There's really no way for us to know." I pause, and my head falls to the side. "Do you think those men who died knew something?"

"I think it's possible."

"And you think those three torn pages will have anything to say about it?"

"I don't know, but it makes me curious."

"The curiosity puts you at risk, doesn't it? Digging into Ember Glen's secrets. And sharing it with me is even riskier…"

I'm tempted—*so tempted*—to reach out to him, to place my uninjured hand on his chest, slip my fingers down to hook the chain that draws across from the button of his waistcoat to its pocket, and tug him closer. Remembering we're out in the open, I take a small, uneven step backward.

"It doesn't matter to me anymore. Not after…not after last night." He takes a step closer. "I don't expect I'll live long enough for it to matter anyway, and if I do, then it means I'm not held to our laws anymore."

He doesn't expect to live long enough?

"What do you mean by that? You and I had a deal, Arlo. You're going to obey and do what you have to do so you can live long enough to become an Elder and enact real change."

"Who's to say I'll have any more power as an Elder than I have now? Perhaps they're beholden to governance we know nothing about…I'm not sure of anything anymore, Mercy."

"That doesn't explain what you mean when you say you won't live long enough…What are you saying, Arlo?"

He sighs, moving closer still, though he doesn't reach out to touch me. Instead, he lets tension build between us, silently lingering in the way it has to out here in the open.

"I'm saying there are secrets being kept, and I intend to find out what they are. I intend to find out precisely what the Elders mean when they tell me that Ember Glen has been blessed by God with all the supplies and resources we need to sustain our way of life. I'm going to find out the truth and expose every secret."

He looks deep within me, catching hold of something in my soul that tugs me forward, and my body leans in his direction.

Squeezing my shoulder, he leans his head forward to speak close to my ear. "I'm going to find a way to save you, even if it kills me, because I won't live long enough to be an Elder without you. I never would've seen the truth without you."

"What did I do?"

"You questioned. You questioned everything, and it made me start to think. Because of you, Mercy, my eyes are open when they've always been closed."

I step backward, not because I want to get away from him, but because the meaning behind his words strikes me so hard that it overcomes me.

His expression hardens, and in a rush, he swoops forward, reaching out to snatch me by the wrist and tug me against his chest. "Would you *stop* backing away from me? It makes me want to chase you. Sweet sin, you're killing me."

I blink up at his blue eyes staring down at me. "Somehow I don't imagine it will be much of a chase in my current state."

A quiet growl rumbles through his chest. "That's what I'm afraid of."

"Then…you should probably release me and step back." I tell him what he *should* do, though it's not what I *want* him to do.

"Just tell me one thing before I do."

"Anything," I say too quickly.

"Is it as painful for you as it is for me?"

"What?"

"To want me now and know you can't have me until later?"

All the air leaves my lungs in a rush. "Does your question imply that I can have you later?"

He clicks his tongue. "If you can't answer my question, then I guess I don't have to answer yours."

"Yes," I blurt. "It hurts in unimaginable ways."

His eyes roam my body, narrowed in scrutiny as though he's studying me. "Does it ache between your thighs?"

I force out a whimpered breath as my body floats forward, and I sink through my weak knees trying to drag myself back.

For a moment, he draws me closer, his palms wrapping around the sides of my waist. He leans in to whisper against my ear, "I long to soothe all your aches, starlight. The ache of your hand, of your heart, of your swollen cunt—"

"You have to stop." I bring my palms quickly against his chest and try to push, but a sharp sting of pain shoots through my burnt hand. I hiss and pull it back as it cuts past the strength of this dizzying medication and the additional intoxication brought forth by his words, by his touch, by his very presence.

"You have to be careful with that hand, Mercy. It needs to heal."

"Then I need you to stop saying things that make me want to touch you."

"Oh, starlight, I doubt you'll ever stop wanting that." He smiles and those long dimples cut lines through his beard, and it sets a dangerous pace for my pounding heart.

I feel light-headed and weak again, overcome with that euphoric, pain-free bliss. My heart flutters, and my hand floats up to cover my chest as my feet stutter backward. "I think I need to lie down…"

"Not now. Come here." He turns sideways, facing the path that leads down to the village, holding out his arm for me. I slowly link my arm through his.

The tension transforms to comfortable silence as he leads me ahead, and though I imagine my mind should be swirling with questions and possibilities from this conversation, I find it to be unusually—and peacefully—quiet.

We cross the remainder of the square, and the gravel narrows to a pathway about fifteen feet wide. It gently slopes down a hill toward the center of the village, nestled in a valley below. Carefully, Arlo leads me down the path.

"Why did you volunteer to deliver the news to Hyatt's family?" I ask quietly. "And why did you bring me?"

He lets out a sigh as we walk. "To spare you, believe it or not."

"To spare me of what?"

"Of the likelihood that my brothers would come to the conclusion that all seven of us should bring you to deliver this news. It was a rash decision to volunteer, but it was a choice I made for you. I feared them dragging you through the village, parading you through town, calling people out of their homes to judge and belittle you, call you awful names and humiliate you."

I glance up at the sky. "Well, the day is still young."

I trip over my own feet and stumble forward, though I don't fall far. Arlo quickly lassoes his arm around my waist to balance me, and I can't help but laugh a little.

"I also didn't want my brothers realizing I gave you medicine that I shouldn't have, but in your current state, that nearly seems unavoidable now."

"The servants should have this…whatever it is." I have to fight the overwhelming urge to tilt my head and rest it upon his shoulder. "Why have something so potent and not give it to the people who need it most? Killian broke Cambria's toes the night I ran from service. Cut tiny marks all over her body with a knife, too. Did you know that? Can you imagine that suffering for days and weeks after service with painkillers as weak as what we're given?"

"You're meant to revel in the pain—"

"Oh, *fuck* off. You men know *nothing* of the pain we endure."

He's quiet for a few beats, but then he says, "I'm learning."

I'm learning.

The words fly straight from his mouth and strike me forcefully in the chest. They imprint on my heart in a way I wouldn't have expected them to.

I'm learning.

It's not an apology for what we've been through.

It's not an excuse for how he's contributed to our suffering.

It's nothing more than an acknowledgment that the suffering exists, yet it feels like so much more. Recognition of a problem must come before it can be addressed, and those two words express recognition in a powerful way.

I'm learning.

It's active, present, on-going.

Arlo is learning, and more importantly, willing to un-learn all the wrongs he's been taught.

As we follow the curve down the gentle slope, the village comes into view. It's a large, chaotic cluster of homes and shops built of dark hardwood. They're all crowded together in the center of a valley scooped out between large grassy hills.

We descend the slope and approach the outskirts of the village. We're not met with the usual noise and bustle of the people going about their daily business, but that's to be expected today. It's always quiet after a night of service. The men purged last night and will have the day to rest before returning to their work tomorrow, and because of the lack of ambient noise, Arlo lowers his voice before he speaks. "We'll be brief with Hyatt's family."

"What if they're angry? What if they demand my immediate execution? What if the villagers take it upon themselves to drag me away and burn me at the stake?"

"I won't allow that to happen."

"You can't control that."

"I can, and I will."

I look over at him as we continue onward, walking behind a row of houses toward the path that cuts through the center of the village. He shares a look with me, letting a smirk curl the corner of his lips.

How in the world does his arrogance twist through my stomach like that?

I'm fearful entering the village—there's a reason they've always kept trial participants separate from the people of Ember Glen. They may riot in their rage against me, gather to take my punishment into their own hands and end my life.

Strangely, the only sadness I have for the possibility of meeting my end today is the fact that I'll leave this earth so unsatisfied. I've yet to peel all my warden's layers and uncover the truest remains of his soul. I've yet to explore our forbidden cravings, my wicked thoughts and his depraved desires.

Before I die, I want all of him.

And that means I must give him all of me.

chapter twenty-two

ARLO

HYATT'S NEWLY WIDOWED wife Stefanie wraps a trembling hand around her cup of tea. She lifts it to her lips and takes a small sip before lowering it to the coaster on her small, round kitchen table. "You're sure that Hyatt's dead?"

"Yes, we're certain. I'm so sorry to bring the news of his loss this way," I tell her. "It's an unfortunate tragedy, and the Control will make arrangements for a service to honor him."

"Unfortunate." Stefanie's dark eyebrows, which match her deep brown hair, lift for a moment before she raises her cup and takes another sip of tea.

I watch her face carefully as she lifts her teacup higher, tilting her head down as she hides a twitch at the corner of her lips. My gaze narrows in scrutiny as long-held judgments fight for recognition in my mind.

Those judgments would tell me she should be weeping, sobbing, crumbling in shock before my eyes. They would tell me to take note of the way she seems to lack concern over the loss of her husband, and that we should keep a careful watch over her, perhaps reassign her to a new husband—a devout and God-fearing man who blindly follows the Edict and can lead her to a spiritual release.

Yet, as I told Mercy, I'm learning, so I fight the reflexive thoughts.

I find some strength in her at my side to help combat these habitual thoughts—she's a darkly fallen angel whose mere presence guides me. If God sent her to change Ember Glen, then he sent her to change me as well. I must learn from her if I'm meant to carry out God's will as it's shown to me through her eyes.

Is it God's will or Mercy's?

Does it matter if I know she's right?

Stefanie's three children exist in the background, making small noises with their minimal movement, but they're awfully quiet playing in the living room behind her. Their faces seem strange, lacking expression, like they've buried their feelings deep inside. They looked that way from the moment we walked in, and it makes me wonder if they always behave this way.

I can see from here that the girl who seems to be the oldest of the three—maybe nine or ten years old—is marked for service; the tattoo of wildflowers split by two dark lines encircling her forearm is distinctive. The middle child doesn't bear the mark, which means she's destined for domestic bliss, and the youngest is still toddling, wobbly on her feet. Her fate won't be decided until she's five years old.

Three girls…Hyatt had three daughters.

It's striking how distant and closed-off the girls seem to be. We've kept our voices low, and I don't suspect they've overheard us speak about their father's death, so that news doesn't explain their somber presence.

It occurs to me that it must be difficult for a man like Hyatt—a man afflicted with the Impulse to such a violent degree—to transition from vileness to family after a night of service.

The purging is meant to be a release, to quell the Impulse, such that men can do their duty as leaders, husbands, fathers…But come to think of it, I don't know whether I can say with honesty that my own perverse sexual desires have ever been fully realized from a night of purging—they always linger throughout the month. And now that I've found my desire in Mercy, it seems I may never fully find satisfaction. Every hint of her presence makes me want her, and because my thoughts are consumed by her, it's a perpetual need.

It's an obsession, one I'm now convinced God instilled in my mind so I could enact His will by meeting Mercy's.

Studying Stefanie's expression, I see relief behind her eyes. It hadn't occurred to me before to expect relief, though it makes perfect sense now. If my sexual needs are never fully satisfied after purging, then perhaps Hyatt's violence remained too overwhelming for him to control after the full moon.

Perhaps his violence bled upon his family…

The mere thought of it sends a chill up my spine.

The entire purpose of purging is to keep our families safe.

And if it doesn't work, then what's the fucking point?

"How did it happen?" Stefanie tilts her head with curiosity. "Was it an accident," her eyes flick over to Mercy, "or was it intentional?"

She doesn't regard Mercy with disdain, with hatred for being a sinner, and it's surprising, to say the least. It was surprising that she'd let Mercy step foot inside her home as it is.

Mercy glances at me, as if seeking direction. Her eyes plead with me, and I can see that she wants to speak, that she wants to tell Stefanie the truth—as we crafted it—about what happened to Hyatt.

I give Mercy a nod. "Go on. Tell her."

Straightening in her seat, Mercy gives Stefanie full eye contact. She pulls back her shoulders, and my eyes are drawn to her chest, to the dip between her breasts where the V-neck of her long-sleeved crimson gown stops.

I recall kissing that very spot last night in the meadow as the rain poured down on us, and my mind drifts at the way it stirs longing within me. I long for her, though she's right beside me.

She asked me to indulge in pleasure with her for the rest of her short days, and I will, gladly. I long to indulge *now*. Yet each time I think about her in my arms, it triggers the agonizing reminder that our days spent in each other's arms are limited. My chest tightens, my heartbeat quickens, my veins burn with misery at the thought of a future without her.

I won't have a future without her.

If I can't find a way to prolong her days, then I will lose myself in depravity and chase her into hell if that's where God means to send her.

But is she still destined for eternal damnation if God means for her to spark change?

Confusion and conflict remain ripe within me, but I feel that true clarity is near, hovering around my soul, just waiting for me to discover the truth about everything.

"I did it." Mercy's clear but quiet voice draws me from my reverie. "He was hurting my friend, and I was afraid he would kill her, so I ran from the Homestead and I stabbed him with his own knife."

Stefanie's eyes widen, then her gaze drops to the liquid in her cup. Clearing her throat, she picks up a small spoon from the table and stirs her drink—for the third time since we arrived.

"It's so…" Her eyebrows knit together as she struggles with her words. "How tragic for my husband." She taps the spoon on the lip of her teacup and places it back on the table. "You'll have to forgive me…I'm in a bit of a shock over this news."

Stefanie is doing a miserable job at concealing her obvious relief. If I were the same man I was a month ago, I would immediately call for my brothers in the Control and insist we pray for her soul before swiftly reassigning her to another family unit.

There's a twinge of pain in my gut to think about how easily I could take her from her children, give them a new mother from another family unit, and force Stefanie to care for a new husband and new children. I shouldn't feel glad that my hand slipped, accidentally slitting her husband's throat. I shouldn't feel pride in Mercy for taking the knife from me and giving him the bloody ending he deserved.

Yet, I do…because he did deserve it.

I shift in my seat at the thought I'd never expect to have for accidentally murdering a man.

Was it truly accidental?

Didn't I press down with the blade the moment I realized my hand was slipping?

"Would you like me to inform the rest of your family?" I ask. "I'm happy to relieve you of that burden."

Stefanie shakes her head. "No, Arlo, you don't need to do that. His family will be over for a visit tonight after the men have rested and recovered from their purge, so I'll tell them then. No need to disturb them now." She pushes to her feet and we follow suit with the understanding that our welcome is worn out. "I appreciate you coming by."

Such a casual thing to say after learning of your husband's death. I have a quickly passing thought of Mercy standing before me instead of Stefanie, of her as my wife, learning about my death in our home, in front of our children.

Would Mercy feel so unfazed?

Would she weep for the loss of me?

Would she suffer in grief?

I hate the thought of Mercy's pain, and it wrecks me as the image of her crumbling and crying forces its way into my thoughts. My shoulders tense and my neck strains at the image. But then my mind breaks, giving way to the image of her in a home that belongs to us, existing there as my wife, my partner, my companion—a woman meant to care for me and my needs—and I feel a warming sensation through my chest.

Yet, that's a life that could never have been.

The Control aren't assigned wives until they retire, and never if they become an Elder. And even if our fates had collided differently—if I had been a man allowed a wife and they'd assigned me Mercy—that life with her would be as unbearable as the future we face now.

I'd be unable to touch her, hold her, kiss her, devour her in passion, and grant us both pleasure through indulgence. Those carnal indulgences are only allowed for men, and only with servants beneath the full moon.

How could I spend a lifetime with Mercy without touching her?

I couldn't.

I've been thinking so much about the Impulse recently, about my lust and urges, and the way Mercy seems to crave me daily all the same. If women have the Impulse, too, then at least some of the domestics are living their entire lives suffering an itch they can never scratch.

Unless…

Unless they indulge in secret through forbidden trysts such as Mercy and I do.

Mercy's mother, Mira, was a domestic, and as I read it in her journal, she indulged her lust—and with another woman, no less. She wanted and had desire, and her thirst was so strong that she chose sin to indulge it…She had *died* for it.

I know with certainty that I would greet death with welcomed arms to quench my thirst for Mercy.

I clench my fists at my sides against the unbelievable tension coursing through me. "If anything changes," I say to Stefanie, "please let us know. Any of my brothers in God would be happy to care for you and your family in this time of tragedy."

"Thank you for delivering the news," she says politely, walking us to the door.

She pulls it open for us and stands beside it. I cross the threshold, stepping out onto the single stone step, then down to the gravel path that cuts through the middle of their front lawn. I turn to hold out my hand for Mercy to take as she steps down, but instead, I find Stefanie's hand on Mercy's wrist, halting her.

Panic grips me as I suddenly fear that I've misinterpreted the entirety of our interaction with Stefanie. She could be angry at what Mercy did, just waiting for me to leave so she could drag her back inside, lock the door, and harm her.

I place one foot back on the step and begin to rise when Stefanie whispers, "*Malo mori quam foedari.*"

The prayer halts me with confusion.

They're locked in a stare, Stefanie's eyes holding Mercy's with a significant look. There's no malice, no ill-intent, no hatred, or judgment; instead, there's peace. Peace and relief and gratitude. The prayer is intended to remind servants of their purpose, but I think Stefanie means it differently.

With a small nod, Mercy returns the prayer that she's been punished for refusing to speak in the past. "*Malo mori quam foedari.*"

Death before dishonor.

She doesn't mean this for Mercy; she means it for Hyatt, for whatever she and her children have suffered by him in their domestic life—for whatever way he dishonored his duty to protect them from harm, to provide for them, to lead them in God's will.

It's Hyatt who has been dishonorable, and her prayer spoken to Mercy was an acknowledgment that God's will has been fulfilled by the person who brought the dishonorable man to his death.

Relief I didn't know I needed to feel washes over me, loosening my tightened muscles and granting my soul a much-needed reprieve. As though last night's storm still lingers above, lightning strikes me with God's grace for ending the life of a man unworthy of the family he was blessed with.

I'm met by Mercy's grace as she turns her eyes to meet mine, showing me something I've never seen in them before—hope. There's hope sparkling like starlight through the silver pigments that brighten her light blue eyes.

Is she made from the stars?

Was her soul forged from the burning white light of the stars that touch heaven?

Did God steal the rebellious and rousing nature of a demon and mix it with her purity to craft her so perfectly?

Was she crafted for me?

I see the power she holds within her as a vessel of God…and of demons. She possesses all the compassion of a heavenly being with all the defiant conviction of a willingly fallen angel.

She certainly holds power over me.

Mercy smiles slowly, softly, and Stefanie nearly returns it. Mercy reaches out to place her uninjured palm on top of mine as she steps out, and I hold her hand as she moves down to the gravel path beside me.

She turns back to Stefanie, and her lips part to speak, but she's interrupted by a voice—a voice I'm familiar with.

"Stefanie!"

Mercy and I both look over our shoulders to see who called out Stefanie's name. It's Luna—the woman who was once my younger sister.

LUNA WALKS TOWARD us with urgency, with fear in her expression. She lives two houses down, across the pebbled pathway drawn between the homes, but I hadn't expected I'd lay eyes on her today.

I'm a little surprised to find she's no longer pregnant. She has a baby secured to her front with a wrap, one of her hands cradling at the back of its head as she rushes in our direction. Her other three children must still be at home, along with her husband, who would be resting from his night of purging. She should be there as well, taking care of him.

Shouldn't she?

Even after he's been gone all night fucking other women?

I had to go back to the forest for a few hours last night to give the appearance that I was purging, and I recall spotting Luna's husband, Archer, using three different servants, one after the other. I could have purged—I had the Impulse and the desire to seek pleasure—but no servant will ever do now that I know Mercy intimately. I'm ruined entirely by her, and it's just one of the many reasons why I know I won't survive when she's gone.

I don't think I've ever thought about nights of service from the perspective of the domestics before, and I almost wish I hadn't. Last night, Luna's husband indulged and enjoyed intimate physical pleasures, and rests peacefully today. Before me now, the kind young woman rushes across the lawn with a newborn baby strapped to her chest, looking disheveled and exhausted.

But surely, she's happy raising her family…It's something I've never asked—I haven't had a real conversation with her in years. I've had to disconnect from the family I knew before when I joined the Control in order to remain objective. But learning as I am, the palette of my objectivity has smeared, blending my black and white world into a swirling shade of gray.

"What's going on?" Luna's voice sounds on the verge of tears. "Is he taking you away?"

She brushes right past Mercy and me as Stefanie steps out of her home, quickly moving ahead to meet Luna on the gravel path. They throw their arms around each other, holding steady through several beats as Stefanie whispers, "It's okay. I'm not in trouble. Everything's fine."

Not in trouble…

There are the habitual judgments again. My mind wanders in consideration at the choice of words, and it begs me to watch this situation closely.

Stefanie's hand slips up to Luna's light copper brown hair, a messy pile of it tied on top of her head, and subtly cradles the back of her head. It's a brief slip of her hand, a moment of touch that's just beyond friendly. It's the intent in the curl of Stefanie's fingers that begs for my attention.

I don't think I would've noticed the subtlety of it before my passion for Mercy began to affect me. The way I hold Mercy, the way my hands always ache to tangle in her hair, to cradle her head, to draw her nearer—that kind of passion is too obvious to hide from someone who knows the feeling personally. Their embrace is not one that two friendly women should share.

Stefanie grips Luna's shoulders, holding her in place as she takes a quick step backward. Her eyes steal a furtive glance at me, then quickly flit away, the tendons in her throat straining as she swallows hard.

"Arlo is here on representation of the Control." Stefanie turns cold and distant again, shutting something off inside herself as she releases Luna's shoulders. "I'm afraid they had some terrible news to share with me."

Luna whips her head back over her shoulder, and I think I spy a glassy sheen of tears over her eyes—blue eyes which always looked so much like mine. "What news?"

"Why don't you go back home, Luna?" Stefanie suggests. "We'll talk about it later. I'm sure you don't want Archer to be bothered by the children."

Luna turns back to look at Stefanie, and though I can't see her face, I watch a shift happen. Her shoulders pull back, her neck straightens, and she tucks a wayward strand of unruly hair behind her ear. When she came rushing over, she looked just like the child-like version of herself that I always remember her being. But now, right before my eyes, her demeanor flips like a switch, and she straightens into adulthood.

It's an unsettling shift for me.

If I really think about it, though, that's how she always looks when I see her in passing in the village: rigid, hardened, carefully controlled. Nothing like the little girl five years my junior, who was once carefree and joyful.

As Luna turns to face us, the unconstrained expression of fear is gone, replaced by a hard, emotionless mask that disconnects her from the world entirely. She blinks, reaching down to adjust the hem of her ivory, cable-knit sweater over her long, light blue skirt, which reaches down to the top of her brown, laced ankle boots.

"I apologize for my messy appearance," she says to me with a tight-lipped smile, though she doesn't make eye contact. "I was just getting ready for my day, and I spotted you leaving here from my kitchen window. Surely, you understand how that concerned me for Stefanie."

The Control doesn't make many house calls except for handling matters of the law, so the concern for her friend is understandable—particularly seeing me here with a sinner condemned.

"Of course," I respond tersely, feeling conflicted about how to communicate with her in this rigidity. "There's no trouble here. I only needed to deliver some news to Stefanie. I'll leave it to her to share it with you as she wishes."

Luna glances back at Stefanie, who still appears emotionally distant, though she gives Luna an encouraging smile.

"When did you have the baby?" Mercy asks, and all our heads snap to look at her, surprised by the dreamy quality of her voice in this strange conversation.

Luna cradles her palm around the back of the baby's head, stroking down its notably full head of dark hair. Neither Luna nor Archer have such dark hair, though it isn't surprising that her baby does. She would've been made pregnant by artificial means, and perhaps it was another man's seed that took. Regardless, Luna can't hide the emotion in her smile as she gazes down at the tiny sleeping thing.

"I had her a week ago."

Her. A girl.

I think that's Luna's first girl, as her other three are boys.

"She's beautiful," Mercy offers softly. "What's her name?"

I'm curious why Mercy is asking, but she's fully captured my attention with the kindness she offers in her voice, the way she seems to calm my sister in showing interest. As I watch Mercy, I realize she's swaying lightly. Whatever high she's feeling from the medication I gave her seems to be peaking.

She held it together so well in Stefanie's home that I'd nearly forgotten about the way it seems to have affected her. I side-step closer, my arm tense, preparing to reach around her if she wobbles too far.

"Her name is Soleil," Luna says.

"Oh, that's a beautiful name." Mercy smiles. "Soleil…like the sun?"

Luna grins and nods.

"You and your baby are the moon and the sun," Mercy remarks with joy.

Luna and Soleil.

The moon and the sun.

A small chuckle escapes me. The choice of name is so fitting of the Luna I remember as a child—whimsical, cheerful, and light. The moon, the sun, and my starlight are all orbiting me, and the gravitational force of each affects me deeply, stretching the fibers of my soul. The way they all tug at my spirit makes the details of this moment seem significant.

It's as though this meeting is celestial, divinely crafted.

"I'd heard it as a word, but I read that it was someone's name before in a book Stefanie and I had found—"

"Luna," Stefanie bites, sharply cutting her off.

A book they found?

"What book?" I press.

All the books in Ember Glen are carefully catalogued and accounted for.

Luna's eyes briefly widen and her joyful expression falters. "I should be going. Archer and the children will be wondering where I am." She marches past us, along the path that cuts through the lawn.

"Luna," I call out as I march in her direction. This is the most I've spoken to her in two years, and I'm hesitant to let the conversation end.

She stops, hesitating in place for a few beats before she slowly turns to look at me standing just behind her. "Yes?"

"Soleil…She's lovely. Congratulations."

"Thank you."

"Are you happy?"

She jerks her head up sharply to look at me with a furrowed brow. "What?"

"Are you happy in the life you've been given? Truthfully?"

Her cheeks twitch as she forces a fake smile, lifting her eyes to look beyond me. "Of course. I'm doing God's will as a domestic, raising a family, taking care of the house and my husband. Why wouldn't I be happy?"

"Because you're not free," Mercy says, and the rest of us are struck silent.

There's a gentle touch against my back, and I tense as Mercy moves to stand at my side, splaying her uninjured palm at the small of my back. My eyes widen at the momentary shock of knowing we're out here in the village, standing in the open, and she's far too close, touching me too freely. I need to get her out of the village before she starts spilling secrets.

"Can I hold the baby?" Mercy asks dreamily, her head falling over onto my shoulder.

Sweet sin.

The way my body responds to her closeness against my good damn judgment is infuriating. Every muscle in my body hesitates to push her away, but my mind knows that a moment's hesitation could be the difference between life and death for the both of us.

I reach behind me and snatch her wrist, sharply shoving her arm away and holding it up between us, making a show of aggression with harsh movements and my hardened expression.

"Don't touch me, sinner."

Mercy's eyebrows flatten into a straight line as she narrows her eyes. "You're supposed to call me starlight."

Fuck.

Bringing her here in this state—bringing her here at all—was stupid.

My eyes snap to Luna to see her reaction, but her gaze is on Mercy's wrist where I hold it in my grasp. Bewilderment washes through her features before she finally looks at me, and when she does, her eyes widen slowly. She's connecting the dots that she shouldn't be able to see.

I never could keep secrets from her.

"I-I have to go," Luna mutters.

With that, I expect her to turn immediately and walk away, but instead, she hesitates, then takes a tentative step closer to Mercy. As I let go of Mercy's wrist, Luna reaches out to grasp the other, circling her hand around the tattoo on Mercy's forearm above her burned hand.

"It's a vicious circle," Luna whispers.

Then, she sways forward, leaning in close to Mercy, twisting sideways around the baby to bring her mouth closer to Mercy's ear. She whispers something I can't hear, and my heart hammers as I watch Mercy's expression twist and morph while she listens.

A vicious circle?

What could she possibly be saying to Mercy?

And will Mercy even remember it after the medication has worn off?

Mercy grins and nods politely, turning her head to catch my stare. And as she smiles at me, giving no indication whatsoever as to what was said to her, Luna turns and rushes away.

I could chase after her and demand answers on the authority of the Control. I could command her to tell me what she whispered to Mercy, press her about this book she and Stefanie had found—and what it even means that they *found* it. I could call her in for questioning regarding her friendship with Stefanie and the extent of their…closeness.

Sadly, I think the man I was before Mercy seeped into my pores would have done just that. I think he would have sold out his sister in the name of God, in the name of maintaining status and power in Ember Glen.

It's bizarre to feel relief wash over me when I realize I am no longer that man. I'm not the same as I was before. And it's all because of the rebel standing at my side—the lightly swaying woman so high off the pain medication I gave her that she's bound to collapse into a lengthy slumber at any moment.

"Come on." I grip Mercy's bicep and drag her along with me. Truthfully, I'd scoop her up and carry her if it weren't for the prying eyes of the domestic wives assuredly watching from their kitchen windows.

I briefly glance over my shoulder to see Luna disappear through the front door of her humble home. It was as clear as day that Luna is unhappy. There's something lost behind her eyes, which were once a brighter shade of blue, but have seemed to have slowly dulled over the years.

Luna's unhappiness and Stefanie's lack of concern for her husband's tragic passing are telling. It makes me wonder; it makes me think. As Mercy so wisely told me to search for truth through the madness, I see a sliver of it now…

Ember Glen isn't what I thought it was.

It's not a perfect community of harmony and balance.

It's terribly out of tune, and someone needs to fix it.

chapter twenty-three

Mercy

A WEEK HAS gone by since the last service and the day that Arlo took me to the village. I've mostly been in my room, sleeping or daydreaming through a drug-induced stupor. Arlo kept bringing me the medication, and I kept taking it. When it started to wear off, the pain in my hand was so unbearable that all I could do was cry. So, I chose to lose time in a medicated trance rather than endure it.

I would have preferred to lose time in Arlo's arms. He did hold me some, curled up behind me in my bed, stroking my hair until I fell asleep. But he wouldn't touch me more than that, not even when I stripped myself bare and begged him.

He politely refused.

He said I wasn't truly present, and it wouldn't feel like us.

It's a rather romantic thought now that I can clearly think back on it. No one has ever really cared before about my mental and emotional presence in sex, so long as my body was available for use.

Though there's still pain in my healing hand, it's gradually becoming more and more bearable. Yesterday, I decided not to take the medication he brought me. I haven't taken it today, either, and my mind nearly feels back to normal. I took care of myself today, bathed and dressed, and as I head for my bedroom door to go and find Arlo, I hear a perfectly timed knock from the other side.

It's him.

I always know it's him by the way he knocks—heavy-handed, sharp, insistent.

I pull open the door, and seeing him there before me lights me up from the inside. My feelings for him have grown immensely over these past days as he's taken care of me. It's his job as my warden, but it's also telling of his commitment to fulfilling the promises he made me. He promised me in the meadow, beneath the thunder and lightning, to take care of all of my needs, and he has been—save for one.

I step aside, holding the door open wide. "You can come in."

His eyes scan my body, taking me in with heat in his gaze that tugs some invisible string connected to my desire. "You must be feeling better," he says. "I haven't seen you out of a nightgown and robe for days."

"I'm much better, thanks to your care. I haven't taken the medication since the day before yesterday."

His eyes flash with recognition that my mind is clear and my body is free from influence. There's something heart-warming about the fact that he refrained from taking advantage of me in a delicate state, even though I wanted him to at the time.

"I can change the dressing on your hand—"

"No need." I shake my head and hold up my burnt hand to show him it's wrapped in a fresh layer of sterile gauze. "I did it myself. It actually wasn't all that painful this time. I think it's healing well."

He smiles, and the way his dimples cut through the scruff of his beard melts my insides. The hair seems to have grown out a touch while his focus has been on caring for me. It's just a little less perfectly manicured and a little more unruly—a physical change that reflects what I believe I see happening within his heart.

He's changing.

I sigh. Every moment that passes without being in his arms feels like torture in my limited days.

"Will you come in? Please?" I plead with him with my eyes, desperate to bring him behind a closed door.

His eyes skate across my face, then dip down to my chest where my skin is exposed from the V-neck of my wrap-around satin gown. His gaze trails down the dip between my breasts, drawing past the red tie that fastens the gown at my waist. He tilts his head to regard the curve of my hip appreciatively.

The gown flatters me, but it's also comfortable. The sleeves are long, but cinched around my wrists, allowing the soft fabric to puff out and hang loosely over my arms without slipping down to irritate the healing burns on my hand. I've worn this particular dress on a few occasions, and he always looks at me the same way when it's on—which is why I chose to wear it today.

"Believe me, Mercy…" His voice is low and quiet. "If I had the time right now to rip that dress off you and make up for every moment lost this past week, you would already be naked and writhing beneath me."

His words suck all the air from my lungs.

"And I promise you," he steps forward into the open doorway, enticing me to step closer, daring to bring my chest only inches from his, "I *will* make up for that lost time soon." He sighs, and the heat of his breath warms my skin. "But for now, I just wanted to give you this." He lifts his hand at our side, holding up a brown leather journal…my *mother's* journal.

I'd asked to have it back, and he remembered. Seeing it again rushes a wave of emotion through me that I hadn't expected. It's almost like seeing her again—like having her with me to comfort me through the remainder of my arduous trials.

"Thank you, Arlo." My eyes press shut for a moment, then open again to fully meet his. "I can't tell you how much it means for me to have this back."

"You understand that you must keep it hidden, yes?"

I nod. "Of course."

I reach out to take it from him and our fingers graze in the transfer. He huffs out a sharp, heated breath at the touch, the soft connection sparking immediate pleasure in anticipated release. His tongue sneaks across his lip as he pulls his hand back and knots of desire twist inside my stomach.

"I can't stay right now," he insists, "but sweet sin, Mercy…I can't think straight when I'm with you. When I'm with you, I can't think about anything but the way you make me feel."

"Come in and shut the door. Let me help you give your mind a rest."

"The way you tempt me…"

"Please, Arlo."

He drifts forward, his body swaying impossibly closer, drawing mine toward him like a magnet. He's so achingly close that my breasts graze his chest, sending a shockwave of delicious need right through me.

And then he steps back.

"I can't. Not right now. I have to meet with the rest of the Control and the Elders in fifteen minutes about your next trial. I need a clear mind."

I turn sideways to clear a path for him. "So come in for fourteen minutes and let me give you a clear mind."

He pinches his eyes shut and his fists clench at his side. "Mercy…"

"Warden Rainn."

His eyes snap open and his blue stare is brimming with passion. I draw in a hopeful, shaky breath as his gaze falters in desire. I hold his stare, challenging him to come forward, to meet me with his need and use me to satisfy it…to satisfy us both.

He tugs on my arm and draws me close, wrapping his arm around my waist to embrace me as he gazes down at me. The way he looks so deeply into my eyes makes my breaths quicken. I want him to kiss me right here, in the doorway of my bedroom. I want him to sneak it away from me in a passionate rush before someone sees us.

I lean in, hoping he'll mirror me. But then he jerks back, closes his hand around my wrist, and drags me behind him into the hallway.

Still clinging to the journal, I rush to keep up with his quick steps. He slams to a stop in front of his bedroom door, unlocks it, and shoves it open. He whips me through the doorway, flinging me forward across the threshold.

I stumble in and whirl around to face him, smiling from ear to ear in anticipation of a few lustful moments with him. If mere minutes is all he has right now, then I'll gladly take them.

He slams his door shut, but instead of coming to me, he turns and goes to the set of drawers near the door.

My smile falters as he pulls open a drawer, unsure of what he's doing or why. But then he pulls out a length of rope, and my breath gets caught in my lungs. My heart stops for a moment, then starts again in a rush, pounding heat and lust through my veins.

Yes, I want him to bind me.

He's after me in a hurry, meeting me quickly as I step toward him. He reaches down to grip my wrist as he storms past me, dragging me behind him to the bed. "Sit," he orders, stopping beside it.

I plop down on the edge of the mattress without question. He starts to wrap the coarse rope around my uninjured right wrist, knotting it expertly before drawing out the length of it, attaching it to the post at the head of the bed.

Once I'm secured, he moves in front of me, coming in so close that I have to spread my legs to make room for him, that I have to tilt my head skyward to look at him. His knuckle swoops beneath my chin to hold me there.

"Fifteen minutes isn't nearly enough time to begin all the things I wish to do to you, starlight. If you truly want to give me a reprieve from the torturous thoughts I have muddling my mind, then you'll wait right here for me in agonizing anticipation. Tell me you'll think of me while I'm gone."

"You know I will, Warden Rainn."

A smirk brightens his expression as he groans. "Volunteering to be your warden was the best decision I ever made."

"It was." I nod.

My chest is heaving from the desire, from the heat of his proximity.

Slowly, he bends, his body folding forward at a creeping pace, lowering his lips to meet mine. Even more slowly, he kisses me, a soft press of our lips that would ordinarily seem so chaste, though it feels profane in its simplicity. Too quickly, he pulls away and leaves me there, sitting on the bed, my right arm bound to the bedpost. With a last glance, he shuts the door and locks it behind him, leaving me breathless and wanting…*waiting.*

I lift my arm and pull it away from the bedpost, dragging it across my body to test the slack. He's left several feet of slack so I can move my arm freely, which I appreciate since my other hand remains useless in its healing.

As I test the rope, I see I still have my mother's journal clutched in my bound hand. I loosen my grip as I realize just how tightly I was clinging to it.

Relief to have it back washes over me again, and I smile at the leather-bound journal as if it could smile back. I don't know how long Arlo will be gone—it could be ages if they're working on the details of the second trial. A lump rises in my throat and I swallow hard against it.

I can't just sit here doing nothing while waiting for him to return. I'll go mad—either from the dreaded anticipation of learning how I'll soon be tormented, or obsessively wondering about Arlo's plans for me now that he has me bound to his bed.

I've been wanting to go back and read some of what my mother wrote, so I decide to entertain myself by flipping back through the journal. I turn and raise my legs onto the mattress before scooting all the way back, straightening my spine against the headboard.

I open the journal and lay it on my lap, using one hand to flip to the very first page. For a few moments, I simply look at it, tracing the lines of my mother's handwriting with my gaze, memorizing the way her letters swoop and dance with each other. She had beautiful handwriting, and while I think mine is similar, it's not exactly the same. I can see the difference in the notes I scribbled in the margins.

I spend some time flipping through the pages and re-reading all the passages I've read before. It's my second time through, and I'm spotting new details, things I don't remember seeing the first time. It's just bits and pieces of her life—so much of it that happened before I was even born—and it brings a smile to my face to read about some of the joyful moments she had.

At the end of the passage I'm reading, I flip the page to find rough edges of parchment peeking out of the spine, remnants of a page that was torn from the journal. Arlo mentioned the three torn pages before. Truthfully, I have no idea what might have been written on them. I don't know whether they still exist, hidden away somewhere strange, or if they've been destroyed. It seems most likely that those pages are long gone.

I find it surprising that I recall Arlo mentioning it to me. I was on the medication then, and I'm struggling to remember all the details—except for the moment I stripped myself and begged him to fuck me, as that embarrassing moment is crystal-clear in my mind.

The other details are muddy...details like *vicious circle.*

I remember Luna saying those two words to me outside of Stefanie's house, and I wish I could remember the context. I know she whispered something to me, and I remember it made me feel like I wasn't alone. Yet I can't place the feeling with context because I don't remember exactly what she told me. I know Arlo's curious about it—he's asked me twice, but I have nothing to tell him other than *vicious circle.*

There's something else here, covering the text of my mother's next journal passage. Folded pieces of parchment have been tucked in and laid to rest together here, either as a placeholder or...as something for me to find.

Did he find the missing pages?

My heart nearly stops.

But then my shoulders slump as I realize the folded pages are a different shade of parchment and couldn't have come from this journal. I tug the folded pages from where they're nestled in the spine, setting them in a pile on the bed beside my hip. Then, I pick up the first one and open it.

It's handwriting I don't recognize, yet I know at first glance who it belongs to.

Arlo.

A nervous flutter of curiosity ripples beneath my skin.

What has he written inside these pages?

Did he place them here intentionally, or was it an accident?

Of course, I know it wasn't an accident. Arlo would never be so careless. He meant for me to find them, but I nearly feel sick to my stomach to think of what they might say. My hand twitches and begins to shake as I thumb open the first page.

Breathing you in is sweet sin,
transgression worthy of fire and brimstone.

You are heat.
You are flame.
You are smoking ash which floods my lungs with each delicious breath I take.

Burn, sweet sinner, and I'll bathe in flames with you.

I will disintegrate to ash at your feet.
And my remnants will beg for your grace, your sin…your mercy.

Mercy.
Sweet, sweet Mercy.

Send me to hell, you demon of delight.
Burn with me.

It's poetry, a string of beautiful words all tied together with such elegance.

And the words are about me…

Mercy.
Sweet, sweet Mercy.

My heart thuds, sending a rush of emotions to flood my veins. A prickling, electric feeling shudders beneath my skin. I want to read the words a thousand times over, but I want to read what's on the next folded page even more. I reach for it and open it.

Light of the universe,
starlight in human form.

Celestial beauty and the scent of earth,
like the meadow and sweet mountain air.

Wildflowers and starlight.

Stunned at his words, I gasp.
Wildflowers and starlight.
He'd used those words to describe the scent of my hair, the nearly white shade of the strands that remind him of the stars in the night sky.
Wildflowers and starlight.
Those words belong to us.
I read them and think of the meadow, the way thunder rumbled through the mountains and lightning struck us with moments of bright light that kept the darkness at bay. I think about our promises we made to each other.

I think about the way he kissed me, the way he touched me, the way he gave me more pleasure than I've ever known as we lost control together among the wildflowers whipping in the wind.

I take my time to read each delicious word on the page, and then my fingers are scrambling to set it aside and move onto the next. Unfolding the third page, I read slowly, letting each word seep inside me and melt in the simmering blood rushing through my veins. I feel something unexplainable flowing through me…and by the time I finish the third page, tears spring to my eyes.

Your life will be taken.
Your light will be extinguished.
Your madness will fade into history…
but it will never be snuffed from my memory.

I pray my memory will be enough to sustain…to endure a lifetime
without your madness.

A sob breaks through my chest as the warm tears which flood my eyes begin to spill down my cheeks. There's a fire burning inside me, flames encircling my heart, and his words only make it burn brighter, hotter, faster.

The pain of it awakens me to the truth, to the somber reality that I have so little time left. It awakens my soul to recognize that I would selfishly squander my last days alive in blissful denial of the world around me if it meant I could spend all my days and nights wrapped in his arms.

Like flowers need the rain, I need this man.

I'm desperate for him, foolish for him, selfish for him.

More than that, my heart is broken for him.

I'll be gone, and he'll have to live without me.

I want to push the pages aside and sob into the pillow, but instead, I pick up the last page and read the words to myself out loud.

My dark angel…
crafted in the sky,
the only light in a vast obsidian void.

A stellar explosion…
ashes of light,
she was speckled stardust over an onyx canvas.

An envious God…
stolen cinders from the sky,
heaven forged from the embers of her starlight corpse.

A demon's delight…
annihilator of bliss,
set fire to paradise, and her ashes fell.

Her light darkened…
the will of a demon,
starlight trapped in human form.

Her celestial embers…
the universe within,
the heaven I strive for contained in her flesh.

My suffering found…
untouchable divinity,
flesh of my dark angel formed by her demons.

Her outspoken rebellion…
mistaken for evil,
the truth of her origin hidden in her warmth.

Nirvana thrives inside…
sweet, parting thighs,
spread like the gates of heaven to beckon me home.

My spiritual awakening…
where holy water flows,
my thirst is sated in the kindling of her arousal.

A celestial roar…
her truth ignites,
the universe exists within her cresting pleasure.

Clarity is found…
my eternity in bliss,

she and heaven are one in the same.

My beloved starlight…
my mortal universe,
her death will bring the end of all things.

Yet…
my love for her is immortal,
and suffering will haunt my mortal flesh eternally.

She is paradise.
She is endless.
She is mine.

This man…He's everything to me.

I've felt every possible emotion toward him, and the most painful of all is love. Deeply, truly, unexpectedly, and profoundly, I've found so much love in my heart for Arlo Rainn.

There is no other way to describe what I feel for him.

I love him.

I love him in a way I've never loved anyone before, and I didn't even know that was possible. I love him intimately, passionately, with the kind of desperation that begs for me to give him all that's left of me.

The love I feel for him is the kind that's seen as rare and precious in Ember Glen—something found by luck or miracle or divine intervention because no domestic woman chooses the husband they receive. And yet, our rare and precious love doesn't feel lucky or miraculous or divinely conceived. It feels like punishment because I'm destined to die, and he's sentenced to live with a broken heart.

I sniff back my tears as I neatly fold the pages, piling them beside me again. Then, strangely, I hear my mother's voice in my mind, softly saying, "I'm glad I loved." It's not a memory of her saying that to me, but I do remember reading those words in her journal.

I'm glad I loved.

They seem to have stuck with me, and I feel compelled to find them. I flip to the back to re-read her last few passages, somehow recalling that I had read the words that day in the meadow, when Arlo took me as his ward for the trials. It's a passage where she wrote about the woman she loved in secret.

I'm glad I loved that incredible woman while I could. My hand shakes as I write this—the words are blasphemous, I know. But what does it matter now that I'm sentenced to death and my soul is already damned?

As I read the words, I notice something…something scribbled in the margin. I wrote many notes in the margins, but this one isn't mine. I never had a chance to write anything on these last pages before Arlo took the journal from me. It's the same handwriting as the poetry—the scribbled notes are from Arlo.

If Mercy's soul is damned, then so is mine.
Our souls are tethered eternally.

There's another note from Arlo further down the entry, but before I read his scribbled words, I read the passage from my mother beside them.

I regret everything.
I regret our stolen fates.
I regret our carelessness.
I regret that we didn't spend more of our numbered days together, sinning in secret.

And then I read Arlo's thoughts.

We could sin in secret daily, and it still wouldn't grant me enough memories to survive without Mercy. I would still regret that I couldn't save her. I don't know if I can go on without her.

My heart stops and starts chaotically at the acknowledgment of the memories he wants to create with me and the regret he'll hold after my death.

I don't want him to regret that he can't save me.

I know he can't.

I thought I had accepted my fate, and I had—for myself.

How could I ever accept the way he might hurt when I'm gone?

I know he wants to try to save me, but I don't believe it's possible. I hold some hope, but it's not strong. The reality of my timed existence and the weight of his words bring fresh tears to my eyes.

I love Arlo Rainn, and his pain belongs to me.

I want our remaining days to be filled with memories for him to hold on to when I'm gone. It's all I can give him, and I resolve to do just that.

I fold the pages neatly and tuck them back into my mother's journal, closing it and setting it on the nightstand. And then I wait, remaining tethered to his bed, bound to him through my numbered days, ready to grant him memories of us that will last.

chapter twenty-four
ARLO

I'M DRAINED, EMOTIONALLY wrecked in a way I didn't know was possible. I'm physically exhausted from the drawn-out meeting and the mental whiplash I've suffered in all the back-and-forth discussions about the second trial. The entire ordeal was chaotic, frustrating, and for me—a man whose heart is bound to the participant meant to endure—it was torturous.

I thought the discussion of the second trial would be straightforward. Yet the moment we rested in our seats in the courtroom, Killian decided to throw in a wrench. He questioned the integrity of the trial if the wardens were aware of what would take place and able to share it with their wards. I was immediately confused by his questioning because we were told by the Elders that trial wardens were always meant to provide some preparation to the participants.

The Elders confirmed that yes, that's what they had told us before, but they were open to making a change. More and more, I'm coming to recognize the ambivalence when it comes to the Elders' rulings. They alternate between rigidity and flexibility in God's word, and their only consistency is in their support of tormenting women.

I'm beginning to think that divinity is absent entirely from these Trials of Dissension, that perhaps absolution can't be found for participants through these ultimate acts of service. With the way rules and circumstances are constantly changing, it makes me wonder which parts of it were in the original Impulse Edict.

Which parts came from God and which parts came from men?

Owen and Park argued against keeping the trial a secret, debating alternatively that it seemed unnecessarily cruel to make the participants wonder and fear—the trials themselves are punishment enough for sinners. Of course, Theo and I both argued the same. I need to know what Mercy is meant to face. If I can't figure out how to avoid putting her through the second trial, then I need to prepare her for it fully. I need to know what she'll be asked to do so I can prepare her to survive.

After some debate, a compromise was reached—one I'm not happy about, but one I'll have to accept. The compromise is for wardens to be told one detail, one single aspect of the trial for which the participants could prepare. But without the details, I could never fully prepare Mercy. I know how psychologically tormenting Service by Sacrifice is meant to be.

To think of it makes me sick to my stomach, and not knowing the details makes it feel even worse. I can imagine a thousand ways to punish a sinner. It wasn't all that long ago that I dreamed of ways to punish Mercy for her sins—though I can admit so many of those punishments in my mind led her from pain to teeter on the edge of pleasure.

The meeting stretched on for two hours, during which Theo and I were ushered in and out of the courtroom as they worked out the details of the next trial and decided what they would share with us.

And I only know one detail.

One horrifying detail.

My nerves are shot just thinking about it and all the ways in which this could play out. My mind is trained for debauchery, and I can imagine so many wretched scenes they might lay out before her. Adrenaline-fueled tremors tear through me as it floods my veins.

I don't know how I'll tell her, how I'll prepare her, but I'll think of all that tomorrow…or maybe the next day. The trial is set for ten days from now, and I could lose her then.

I could lose her.

I fight against my fear, struggling to push it from my mind as I jog up the staircase and race down the hall, knowing the only thing I can do for her right now—the only thing I can do for myself—is to sin with her in pleasure as I had promised her.

For all I care, God can damn us both to hell if this is the fate He's chosen for us. I'll sell my soul to demons and burn for eternity, so long as she and I stand together in the same flame.

Regardless of everything that weighs on us so heavily, I realize I've left her tied to my bed for two hours, and I feel bad for it. I didn't expect to be this long. I quickly reach my door and rush inside.

"I'm sorry I was gone so—"

My words cut short as my eyes land on her, still on the bed where I left her, curled on her side, quiet…asleep.

Sweet sin.

She is the most divine angel and the most wicked temptress. She's an agent of God and demons, the human representation of all that's good and all that's forbidden, and she's bound, waiting for me in my bed, finally unhindered by the medication that muddied her mind and slurred her speech.

I want her eyes open, her lips parted, her chest heaving as she pants through the pleasure I give her. I want her moans, her gasps, her sweet begging voice in the way she says, "please," and asks me for release.

I undress, stripping myself bare in the physical sense, but each item of clothing I remove feels like shedding a piece of the man I was before. Each discarded item casts off a part of the man who prided himself as an authority figure, as a future Elder, as a man who blindly followed the laws of God without any physical proof of the words He meant for us to adhere to.

I bare myself in every sense as an offering to her.

Though habit momentarily guilts my mind into believing her a false idol, everything else within me tells me she's worthy of all the ways I wish to worship her. I feel it instinctually, pounding through my heart, rushing through my veins, tugging at my soul, and prickling across my skin.

I walk softly across the carpet, each peaceful breath she takes drawing me nearer. I approach her at the side of the bed where she's curled up on her left side, facing away from me. Her right arm, which is still coiled in rope and bound to the bedpost, rests comfortably in front of her with the several feet of slack I gave it. Her fingers are curled loosely into fists, and her porcelain cheeks hold no tension at all. She appears so unusually calm, so relaxed, so peaceful.

I reach down with my bare hand to brush my knuckle down her cheek with a gentle touch. She doesn't stir, doesn't move, doesn't wake. She's as peaceful as I've ever seen her sleeping here in my bed.

The blisters on my fingers that I burnt in the fire with her were surprisingly mostly superficial and have all but healed—it's almost as though her skin touching mine when I thrust her hand into the flame offered some sort of miraculous protection. I kept my hands covered from her all last week while we both were healing, so touching her now, skin to skin, feels electric, shocking me with a jolt of pleasure that makes my cock twitch.

I draw my knuckle up her cheek again, turning my hand to catch her hair in my finger and tuck it behind her ear. A small moan escapes her as she shifts on the pillow. I should pull my hand away and step back, leave her to sleep. But I can't look at this woman without feeling the overwhelming need to touch her. I stroke my palm down the side of her head, and though it makes her stir, I don't regret it. If she wakes up, I'll wear her out enough for this peaceful slumber to find her again later.

She sighs out a heavy breath and her fingers twitch before she shifts her hand, drawing my attention to the knotted rope around her wrist.

Sweet sin.

The sight of her bound in my bed twists my insides, dragging out every sordid desire of the flesh I have for this woman. One moment, my eyes are tracing the slackened line of rope between her right wrist and the bedpost, and the next, the end of the rope is untied from the bed and knotted around my own right wrist. I hadn't made a conscious effort to bind my hand to hers, yet it happened.

Reaching down with my tethered hand, I drag my palm down her shoulder. My fingers trail along the silk sleeve covering her arm as I watch her slowly rouse to my touch. I slip into bed behind her and press in close, curling my body around her backside. I prop my left elbow on the pillow, and lean my head against my hand, watching her slow, soft movements as sleep slips away from her.

My movements are slow and soft, too, but filled with indecent intent. If she's going to awaken to my touch, then I want her filled with pleasure in her awakening. I spread my palm over her belly, tugging her closer, and though she's still gripped by her slumber, her back is arching, intensifying the pressure of her ass against my steadily thickening cock. I sigh as her body subtly shifts as she grows more aware of my presence, naturally tilting to lean back against my frame.

Slowly, I run my hand up the center of her body, slipping through the valley between her breasts, flattening my palm over the bare skin of her chest exposed from the deep V of her gown. I feel her chest rise against my palm as she draws in a deep breath, back arching deeper with tension, and then she lets out a whimpered sigh—a sound that's so peaceful, it brings me an unexpected moment of sadness.

Has she ever felt such peace before?

Has she ever lived a moment of her life without fear?

The thoughts ache as they take up residence in my chest, laying heavily on my heart. But I don't let the sadness of such thoughts consume me; instead, I let them fuel me in pursuit of granting her continued peace through her numbered days.

I let my hand rest there for some time, feeling the rhythm of her heart, the way it's slow and steady at first. Then it crescendos, gradually quickening, pumping more insistently as sleep slips further from her grip.

I can see her face clearly now that I've tucked her hair behind her ear, and I watch as her lips faintly twist from peaceful to blissful. The look of her desire is becoming familiar. It's apparent in the faint flush of her cheeks, the tension of her body as it subtly squirms against mine, the slight parting of her pink lips as her lungs demand a deeper breath.

The beauty of her face in this rare moment where passion meets serenity is overwhelming. It begs my hand nearer, an unseen force tugging my hand to glide up her chest, my palm circling her throat gently as it slips up to her chin. My thumb reaches to brush across her bottom lip, gently tracing the subtle curve of her smile that curls more deeply with each sweep.

I watch as she blinks her eyes, batting away drowsiness with her lashes. My thumb begs to press between her lips, to feel her warm, wet tongue glide over my flesh. Her body curls deeper, the thick flesh of her bottom pressing against my cock with a slight wiggle of her hips, and it urges my hand to move, to touch her in all the places that will make her beg for me to slip inside her. My cock thickens at the thought of her begging, the way she says "please" when she's on the edge.

Drawing down the center of her chest, I turn my hand and slip it inside the deep V of her neckline, seeking her breast and groaning when I find it bare—no bra or corset—beneath the silk. Her eyes flutter shut again as I gently move my palm, softly touching her skin and trailing my fingers over her nipple.

The way the tiny peak hardens with each brush of my thumb is intoxicating. I keep at it, teasing with the gentle touch for what must be minutes, until it's clear that Mercy is fully awake, aroused and needy.

Her hand raises sharply and lands on my arm, her palm curling around the rope knotted to my wrist. "Wait," she says.

I can't stop myself from pinching the hard bud and rolling it quickly between my fingers. She gasps and tenses, tilting to lean back against me, and her head rolls against the pillow. She looks up at me as I stare down at her, my eyes narrowed with intensity.

The strength of my passion doesn't frighten her, even when I feel like it should—when I feel like I'm feral, barely holding on and teetering on the brink of losing control to the Impulse.

I've never felt the Impulse so strongly as I do when I'm with her. The way I feel it with Mercy makes me wonder if every time I thought I felt it before her was just a lightly passing urge. The real Impulse lives and dies with her.

And that's not the way it's supposed to be.

The Impulse is a faceless, nameless plague on men. An uncontrollable need for violence, sex, and depravity. But in this moment with Mercy Madness, I feel it more profoundly than I've ever felt it before…yet, I wait.

I pause.

I control it because she asked for me to.

Fuck. Is the Impulse a lie?

Is the Impulse an excuse for vicious indulgence with impunity?

Dormant shame stirs, shaking through my shoulders, pricking an urge beneath my skin to add new blisters and scars with a flame against my palm. With the shame comes a strange exhaustion and my propped arm drops onto her pillow. I slip it quickly beneath her head, settling my arm under her neck as I fall to lay my head down beside her.

She leans back heavier against me, craning her neck to look at me. When her bewitching silver-blue eyes steal my gaze, guilt halts me, and I start to pull my hand away.

But she surprises me…she's always surprising me.

Her arm moves and her hand shifts, turning to slip beneath mine. At first, I think she's only creating a barrier against access to that sweet, hard peak of pleasure. But then her fingers thread between mine. The moment I realize she's taking hold of my hand, I lock my fingers with hers, gripping so tightly that every inch of our palms kiss. Then, she turns, rolling to lie fully on her back. I stay tight against her side, molding myself to her curves.

I feel the way her eyes stay on mine, even when I glance to see our hands locked together above her chest. My heart stutters as I take in the absolutely stunning view of our fingers interlaced, the same strand of coarse brown rope wrapped around each of our wrists to tether us entirely.

Some unmeasurable amount of time passes this way in silent watching, as we grow in quiet understanding that regardless of whether it's painful, shameful, or filled with heat and desperate need, this moment is ours and ours alone.

Right now, she's mine and I'm hers.

My heart belongs to this woman, whether God wanted her to have it or not.

"I found the pages," Mercy says quietly.

She still holds my hand, and her thumb brushes my knuckles. The comforting touch tugs at my mind, insistent upon its full presence and awareness. The urge to burn my hand is still present as I live here on the edge of indulgence, but I tuck the thought away, shoving it far back in a dark corner of my mind, knowing I can always satisfy the insistence later.

"I read the poems." Her eyebrows knit together as her expression turns thoughtful.

"I meant for you to."

My words are true; I had meant for her to read them. But having confirmation of it now makes me nervous in a strange way I can't say I've ever really felt before. My poems were always for me, never meant for another soul to read, and I never shared a single word of them with anyone before. No one else even knows that I write them.

She squeezes my hand, dropping hers back to rest against her chest and pulling mine down with it. My eyes flutter shut in reverie of the way she affects me. I sigh, letting the tension held through every inch of me loosen all at once, and I relax into the mattress. Letting my head fall deeper onto the pillow, I brush her cheek with the tip of my nose, breathing in the wildflower scent of her hair as I nestle my face against the side of hers.

"I have so much to say to you, Arlo. I don't even know where to begin."

I'm struck by a wave of unease, suddenly fearful that she didn't like the poems, that the meaning of my words was mistaken, that she simply didn't like that I've spent time writing about her while being so cruel to her. Regardless, I have to know. I need to hear her words and know what's on her mind, what's in her heart.

I let out a sigh. "Then just speak and let the words come."

Though my eyes are still shut, I feel the rise and fall of her chest beneath our hands and how it quickens in pace and pitch. Her fingers tighten their grip between mine as she whispers, "I'm bound to you."

My eyes pop open at the words, darting down to look at our hands, tethered by rope. We're literally bound, but I know that's not what she's saying. The deep expressiveness in her tone tells me her words mean so much more.

A few seconds pass as she silently fights through her panted breaths. I'm not sure if she's on the brink of shedding tears or if she's growing so heavy in lust that the desperation steals her breath.

"My heart is bound to yours, Arlo."

Now my breath is stolen by her words. It rushes out of me all at once, my body sinking into hers. I squeeze her hand and kiss her cheek, turning my head to draw the tip of my nose along her face, nuzzling into her hair, inhaling deeply.

Wildflowers and starlight.

"Against all odds, I've fallen in love with you," she continues, "and I don't want to waste another moment of my finite existence trying to fight it or trying to pretend that I don't love you."

Her voice becomes a heady drug, stirring new affections, rousing my every desire for her with the vibration of her words alone.

"The poetry…your words were everything to me. I know who you are beyond what you've been told to believe. I know who you were before you were broken. I know who you're meant to become, and I'm watching you become that man slowly, bit by bit, growing closer to everything you could be with each passing day.

"I'll love you when you become that man, but I love you just as well now. I think I even loved you before, even in your cruelty. Because I think you were right…that our souls are tethered. We're cosmically bound by a tether that can never be broken. I want to give you memories to last your lifetime if you can't—"

Jerking my head up from the pillow, I lean over her to cut her off with a kiss. I need her to physically feel the way her words resonate within me… but also, I can't bear to hear her finish that sentence.

I kiss her with rough sensuality, with pressure but not force. I sweep my tongue across the seam of her lips and she opens eagerly, seeking a taste of my tongue with a sweet brush of hers. I worship her mouth with mine, giving praise to the way her spirit grips me, overwhelms me with divinity and light, with sacrilegious pleasure.

The kiss becomes our unspoken words, a tangible exchange of everything we feel for each other existing in a space that's beyond words. Our kiss becomes the discussion of our indecipherable needs and unexplainable emotions. Yet the kiss alone isn't enough to express it all. I need to use every part of her, and I need her to use every part of me.

With agony, I drag my mouth from hers, pulling my head back to look at her. The skin around her parted lips is flushed pink, soft and wet from our kiss, and it makes me wonder if the flesh between her legs is flushed and wet, too. Desire floods my veins, rushing blood to my center, hardening my cock, which pulses with the insistent demand to fuck her.

She shakes her hand from my grip and pushes it down her body, the rope that binds us trailing her hand. Her fingers grapple at the silk fabric over her thighs, bunching and gathering until it's lifted above her hips.

There's no barrier against her perfect pussy, no underwear to be removed. She was ready for me hours ago, and the evidence of it is clear in the slick sheen that coats her flesh. Her right knee bends slightly, pressing against my thigh at her side as she parts that heavenly gate, opening up for me so freely and insistently.

Yet, before I can reach for the divinity between her thighs, she stretches her arm and reaches for it herself.

My eyes are glued to her nimble, delicate fingers as they rub down her flesh, gently circling her clit before dipping lower and curling inside her. She moans as they sink, shifting her hips to sink them deeper. At the sound of her enjoyment, my gaze is drawn to her face, eager to see the expression of pleasure painted across her features.

Her eyes are already fixed on me, dancing across my face as if it brings her even greater pleasure to watch me.

"You were gone for so long," she whispers. "I read your words over and over…" Her fingers move, and I can hear the wet stroking of her digits over drenched flesh. "I needed you…I needed relief."

My hand snaps down, my palm instantly clamping over her knuckles as I halt her movement. "Did you touch yourself, starlight?"

The man I was only weeks ago would be horrified at the thought of a woman stroking herself in pleasure. Women aren't meant to satisfy that unholy need—the only exception occurring beneath a full moon when a man's Impulse demands it of a servant. Yet the man I am today finds it unbelievably arousing. Everything we do with each other is forbidden, wrong, sinful…and I want to commit every sin imaginable in her presence.

She nods. "I did."

"Did you find relief?"

She rolls her head against my arm, turning her face to press a soft kiss to my shoulder. "No."

"Did you try?"

She kisses my shoulder again before meeting my gaze, letting the corners of her lips curl ever so slightly. "No."

"Why?"

"It wasn't worth it to me without you."

I snap my fingers down between hers, reaching through her hand to lightly brush against her slick folds, a teasing brush that makes us both force out a heavy breath at the same time.

"Tell me what you did." I bend to sweep my lips over hers. "Were you on your back? On your knees? Which of these fingers brought you the closest?" I tighten my grip, bending my roped wrist deeper over her hand, rubbing all our fingers through her wetness.

Her eyes hood and she pants through her words. "Don't you wish to tell me what a sinner I am?"

I kiss her, a quick, heavy press of my lips to hers, followed by a quick drag of my tongue across her bottom lip. "You do enjoy being wicked, don't you?"

"I'm a wicked woman, Warden Rainn. It's what they all say."

"A wicked woman, indeed." I let go of her hand just so I can smack it away, and I spank her swollen cunt with my hand. "*My* wicked woman. My sinner." I kiss the corner of her lips and along the line of her jaw until I reach her ear. "My fallen, forbidden angel."

I spear two fingers inside her, burying them as deeply as they'll go before the rest of my hand strikes the barrier. A rough moan claws out from her throat and her hips thrust up to greet my touch. The sound strikes me with impatient hunger for her pleas. I stroke my fingers inside her, pressing up to rub hard and fast over a ridged spot of flesh inside her.

I bend my arm beneath her neck to tug her closer to me, locking her head against my shoulder to ensure she can't escape me. Her face turns toward my shoulder as she pants, as her hips buck and writhe against my hand. I clamp my thumb over her clit, and press my fingers harder, stroking faster.

She lets out a sharp cry and I tighten my grip around her head, encouraging her to fully press her face into my shoulder. I feel her teeth grazing, like she needs to bite, but she's holding back.

"Do it," I growl as my fingers work harshly inside her. "Sink your teeth into my flesh. Let me know how good it hurts."

She whimpers, but then her bite closes, and her teeth clamp hard around the curve of my shoulder.

"*Fuck,*" I hiss at the burn, then groan at the ache that follows, but my fingers never falter.

"Arlo," she pants my name, "I need…" Her thought trails off as her body rolls toward me onto its side. Her hips rock, fucking my hand while she licks the flat of her tongue over the bite mark on my shoulder. I shudder beneath the drag of her tongue, wondering if she likes the way I taste.

I live for the way she tastes.

I'm hungry for it, suddenly feral with the urge to tear my fingers from inside her and lick them clean, but that won't do. I want to taste all the subtle flavors of her wetness through each moment of her rising pleasure, through the peak of her climax and the blissful fall that follows.

I'm thirsty, and the only thing that will sate me is the divinely unholy nectar between her thighs.

chapter twenty-five
ARLO

I TEAR MY hand from Mercy's cunt to the dreadful sound of her disappointed whimper, though I won't leave her disappointed for long. I grab her hand and quickly thread my fingers through hers to secure my grip. I stretch our tethered hands above our heads, and as I roll on top of her, I slam them down hard to the pillow.

She gasps as I settle my weight on her, as my hips roll and my cock teases between her thighs. The warmth, the wetness, the way she parts her legs and bends her knees, bringing them up to grip my hips…Every sensation vibrates through my soul and insists that this is where I belong.

I dip to kiss her with heavy lips and a thirsty tongue, coaxing a moan from her chest, and swallowing it whole. Her breasts crush to my chest as her back arches from the bed. By the time I manage to tear myself from her delicious lips, we're both beyond desperate, heated, and needy.

Mercy's half-hooded eyes lock on mine, and the look she gives me is so intoxicating that I get stuck there, watching her watching me as her hips writhe beneath me in heat.

Sweet fucking sin.

I need to taste her…I need the flavor of our forbidden craving to coat my tongue and drip down my throat.

I tighten my grip between her fingers as I bring my other hand to the curve of her waist. With a quick flip, I roll us both, twisting onto my back while I bring her on top of me, causing her to gasp at the sudden change of position.

Eagerly, she pushes through our locked fingers to rise on her knees, settling her weight against my heavy, thickening cock. She carefully holds her healing hand near her waist, and it strikes me with pain when I realize how careless I was in rolling her over on it.

With my free hand, I reach out to wrap my fingers gently around her forearm, covering the tattoo of wildflowers she's had since she was a child. My gaze narrows as I turn to meet her eyes, silently asking if she's okay. She answers with a bob of her head as she sits down heavily over my cock.

Fuck.

I groan as she moves, pressing down, gliding her hips forward and back to rub her wet pussy along the length of it. Her crimson gown cascades around us, spreading the silk over our bodies and spilling onto the mattress. It hides the filthy way she slickens my cock.

Red is the color of blood and sacrifice, and its why the trial participants are made to wear it—because they have to sacrifice pieces of themselves through the ultimate acts of service.

I could almost be fooled into thinking Mercy has willingly cut herself open for me, dousing me in her blood and painting it across my cock with her raging, righteous cunt. She demands her pleasure fulfilled, regardless of my own...and she deserves it.

She deserves to take from me.

I would sacrifice my pleasure for eternity if it meant she could have hers. Yet she tells me with her eyes that she wants my pleasure as much as she wants her own. My heart hammers at the way she wants to give me things I don't deserve. As she slickens me further with each glide of her hips, I feel anointed in her righteous blood.

I slip my untied hand from her waist, around to her back, and tug her down to bend over me. With only one hand able to hold herself up—and those fingers locked firmly with mine beside my head—she's forced to settle her weight on me, and the pressure against my chest feels fucking incredible. Her short strands of starlight hair fall forward around her face, tickling against my cheeks as her face drops close to mine.

"I want to taste you, starlight."

"Please..." she hums.

"I want you to lay on me just like this, but turn around so I can fuck you with my tongue. Bury me beneath this red silk and smother me with your delicious cunt."

Her mouth descends and she kisses me with a rumbling moan, tasting me as though she's showing me with her tongue how she wants her pussy to be kissed.

She doesn't need to show me.

I already know what she wants.

She sits up and releases my hand so she can maneuver. She brings her right leg over me to kneel at my side, then twists toward me, spinning her body in such a way that the rope draws across the front of her rather than hanging behind her.

I'm about to correct her, to sit up and help her turn from the other direction to untangle the rope before she straddles me. Yet again, as she always does, she surprises me. She lowers her arm to settle the slack against my chest, so when she climbs over to straddle me, she straddles the rope, as well.

The tether connecting our hands now runs between her legs, and I can't think of a more perfect place for it to be.

I have a perfect view of her ass and pussy as she scoots backward, her skin shadowed in red as the silk fabric of her gown shrouds my head. Before she settles, I twist my hand around the slack in the rope, and tug. She yelps as it jerks her hand down between her parted thighs and I tug until I can see her fingers wiggling beneath her sex.

"Move back," I command. "Give me your cunt. Let me devour you, starlight."

"Arlo," she breathes.

Her hips wiggle, but she doesn't move back. Instead, I feel the rope tug sharply where it's coiled around my grip, and my hand shoots forward toward her ass. Still hovering, I watch as she drags the rope over her flesh, angled to glide over her clit, and she groans as the harsh fibers roughly rub over her sensitive flesh.

"Sweet sin, Mercy…"

I pull back on the rope, tugging up to drag it over her again. Mercy gasps, tensing at the sensation, the pain of the coarse rope mingling with her wet, desperate desire. She pulls it forward; I drag it back. We fuck her needy flesh together with the tether that binds us until she's shuddering, tensing, needy for my tongue to lick away the ache.

I uncoil the slack and let go of the rope, letting her pull it all the way forward through her legs. With a gentle hand on her back, I push her forward, encouraging her to bend and lay down on me. Her hair tickles my stomach, causing a jolt of tension through my muscles. Then I feel her lips kiss a trail down my stomach, making me shiver when I feel them press just inches from the base of my cock.

I groan, grip both her ass cheeks in my palms, and squeeze as I swipe my tongue up the length of her pussy.

She whimpers and loosens all at once, knees spreading further to lower fully against my face, her body falling to lay on me with her full weight. The way she sinks to our depravity sends shockwaves of bliss through my body. I feel the softness of her cheek rest on my stomach, her bound hand coming to rest at the same spot on the opposite side of my jutting erection.

I'm suffocated in her heady, delicious scent, and my face is slickened by her arousal. And the way she lightly thumps her hips up and down against my tongue threatens to undo me entirely. I feel beads of pre-cum at the tip of my cock, and she hasn't even touched it yet.

Her hair drags across my skin as I feel her head lift, and without any warning, I feel her tongue lick across the tip of my cock.

"Sweet sin," I growl against her cunt.

Her fingers wrap around the base, and my hips jerk off the bed, rising to meet her perfect lips as she opens to draw me into her mouth. She envelops me in warmth, slowly taking me in along the flat expanse of her tongue. I falter, a full body tremor shuddering through me as I tense against the premature eruption that threatens from her slightest touch.

I close my eyes to revel in the power she holds over me, the celestial energy she exudes which calls for my satisfaction. I've never felt anything like her in all the years I've indulged my urges with servants on purging nights. The simplicity of Mercy sucking my cock while I lick her pussy is the most spectacularly erotic moment of my existence, which is nearly unfathomable given the breadth of my sexual experience.

She takes me deeper, then gradually begins to work me in and out with a slow, steady rhythm. I almost wish I could see her starlight hair bouncing with her bobbing head, but the view I have, nestled tightly between her luscious thighs, is more than enough to satiate my visual cravings.

She moans and it vibrates around my length, making my muscles twitch and my hips buck beneath her. Only Mercy could ever make me feel this lustfully insane, this wickedly sinful, this demonically divine. I could spend an eternity right here beneath her, finding all the sustenance I need. She sates my thirst with her arousal. She nourishes me with her ethereal energy. She grants me spiritual salvation as I serve her every need.

I want to serve her.

I want to serve this woman until I take my last breath.

I can't fathom ever denying her again.

With a long sweep of my tongue, I lick her from end to end and back again before swirling around her clit. I tighten my grip on her perfectly curved bottom and shake my head side to side, rubbing my entire face through her folds, washing my beard in her sweet nectar.

"Move, starlight," I mutter against her opening. "Fuck my tongue until you come."

She shudders, her hips sinking as the heft of pleasure weighs her down. I hold my tongue out—long and flat—and let her slide her pussy across it. She squirms at first, shifting her hips side to side as she plays against my mouth to test the sensation, but soon, she finds her rhythm, dancing forward and back as she presses herself down onto my tongue.

She manages to keep pace for a minute or two, bobbing her head to match the rhythm of her hips. But it's not long before she falters, finding such overwhelming sensation in riding my tongue. Her lips smack as they pop off the tip, and she pants warm breaths against my erection, beginning to move at a brutal, insistent pace.

Her forehead taps lightly against my stomach before she rolls her head with a moan, then turns to rest her cheek there instead. Her breaths turn to short, panting whimpers as her hips work. Then she's working her bound hand between our bodies, shoving it down until I feel her fingers brush the tip of my tongue at her clit.

"Arlo…" she whispers, and it's the sweetest sound.

Soon, she's writhing, twitching, and fucking toward her rushing orgasm. Her fingers curl, pressing hard against her clit. Her hips press down, angling in a way that nestles my nose snuggly between her cheeks. I groan in pure delight. If I should suffocate here through the force of her climax, I would die a happy man.

I want it.

I *need* it.

I have to taste the way she comes undone for me.

Give it to me, Mercy.

Use me and take your pleasure.

Let me be your servant.

These are all words I want her to hear, sentiments I want her to know, feelings that would grant her strength and comfort in knowing where she stands with me. She stands on a pedestal that rises high above me, and I'll gladly kiss her feet if that's all I can reach.

Mercy gives me her precious flesh freely, lets me taste her, lets me be the conduit for whatever spell this is that she weaves through my mind.

Not a spell…it's only her madness.

Madness I'm glad to be afflicted with.

"I'm…I…" she stutters through her speech as her body does the same, jerking against the same spot on my tongue as she presses down, as her fingers work frantically against her clit.

I dig my nails into her fleshy cheeks to spur her onward, encouraging her movements, her moans, her desperation. I tell her with a deep rumbling groan to come for me. Her body twists and jerks while fucking my face and her fingers.

And when she comes, she breaks apart—all the pieces of her shattering and bursting outward into the universe. It's as though I can feel her bursting into flames, burning to ashes, her stardust embers floating in the dark night sky as the remnants of a stellar explosion. It's like the words of my last poem come to life.

My dark angel…
crafted in the sky,
the only light in a vast, obsidian void.

A stellar explosion…
ashes of light,
she was speckled stardust over an onyx canvas.

I can't see beyond where my face is buried, but I feel the beauty of her entire being through such a powerful climax. She stifles the sound of it, pressing her lips to my stomach, gasping and moaning as she crests.

And then she falls.

Her body collapses onto mine, lax and spent.

Smoothly, I flip her onto her back, quickly twisting myself around to face her. She places her burnt hand above her head to rest on the mattress, and I watch as she pants, eyes fluttering shut though she tries to keep them open. As I rise to my knees, she spreads her legs for me, and I shift to settle between them.

She blinks her eyes open as pure satisfaction etches itself across her cheeks. She watches me as I swipe my hand across my face, intentionally gathering her wetness onto my fingers and bringing them in front of me to watch the way it shines as it glides between my fingers.

She lifts her knotted hand, drawing my attention to it, and I watch as she twists, coiling the rope around her palm to quickly shorten the slack. She yanks, and I fall for her.

I fall for her over and over again.

My hands land on either side of her on the mattress, but she continues to coil, further shortening the slack. She keeps pulling, tugging at my wrist until I relent. I drop to lean on my left elbow so I can lift my right hand and let her pull. She tugs at the rope, bringing my hand in front of her face, guiding my fingers to her mouth.

She wants a taste.

Understanding what she wants, I push two fingers past her pink lips. She closes her eyes as she sucks them in, taking in a deep breath through her nose in appreciation of the shared lust between us.

"Mercy."

Her eyes flutter open and meet mine as I slowly drag my hand away, catching my fingertips on her bottom lip. I trail my fingers down her chin, over the hollow of her throat, making her back arch as they draw a line down the center of her chest.

I sweep my hand right, pushing away silk to expose her breast, then sweep left to do the same with the other. Still leaning on my elbow, I dip my head to lick her nipple, to swirl my tongue around it as it hardens, to suck it into my mouth. I play until she's squirming again, arching her back and begging.

"Please," she pleads, and I think I might come from the sound of that word alone. "I need you inside me. Please."

My hand snaps to latch around her throat, pressing against her chin to tilt her head back. "Do you need me, starlight? Do you need me desperately, the same way I need you?"

"Yes."

"Tell me again that you love me."

Tension finds me with a sudden fear that maybe she didn't mean it when she said it before—that maybe she changed her mind now that I've given her some relief from the overwhelming urge to come.

Her eyes flicker, narrowing for a moment, as if she senses my fear. Then her gaze softens, and I feel her compassion slip between my ribs, blanket my heart, and comfort me in a way I didn't think was possible from a single look.

"I could say that I love you again, and you would hear the words," she says softly, "but if you need to feel that it's true, you only need to kiss me. Put your lips on mine, Arlo."

Put your lips on mine.

It's a command I don't hesitate to fulfill. My lips are on hers in a flash, pressing with bruising need. She lets out a whimper beneath my rough kiss that begs me to ease and let her lead this connection. Easing back, I lighten my pressure to a feather-light brush.

Gradually, she guides me by feeling alone with subtle movements of her lips against mine. Slowly, she coaxes me to deepen the kiss, drawing us both into a slow burning heat that simmers between us.

She parts my lips with hers, gently slips her tongue between my teeth, and sweeps across mine with unspoken words. Her silent words intensify, mingling with my own as our tongues tangle. I can hardly breathe with the way she devours me so sweetly.

She kisses me in the same way that I fell in love with her—languidly, imperceptibly, intensely, and entirely. I didn't know what love was, and I certainly didn't know it could be felt through a kiss, yet I feel it. I feel it from her so spectacularly.

My forehead drops to rest against hers as the need to catch my breath ends our kiss. "I felt it, Mercy," I admit. "Did you feel it from me, too? The way I love you beyond reason?"

Air catches in her lungs, and she stutters through a breath, nodding her head against mine. "Yes."

I need her. Now.

I shift my hips as my hand comes down from her throat to grip my cock. I line myself up against her, and with a steady thrust, I sink deep, nearly faltering to the sound of her gasping whimper. With my forehead still pressed to hers, I hold her stare as I bring my hand up to cup her cheek, to brush her lip with my thumb.

I fuck her slowly, deeply, ensuring she feels every inch of me inside her. Every movement is electric, hot, and sparking with fire I want to ignite. Each thrust is a strike against flint, sparking hotter, burning brighter. Soon we're panting and frantic, bodies jerking and writhing, seeking more, harder, faster.

"Fuck," I mutter as I rush toward the edge, and I know there's no use in trying to stay there when the sparks are flying so intensely.

"Come inside me," Mercy pants. "Please, Arlo."

The flames ignite, blazing through every inch of my body as I spill inside her. As if the universe celebrates our union, she comes with me, my release spurring hers. She starts to cry out, and I kiss her hard to silence her.

I would scream for her if I could; I would let the fucking world know how good it feels between her thighs. I would claim her away from any other man for all of eternity.

I collapse against her, spent and fighting to catch my breath. I shift to press my ear to her chest, listening to the beat of her heart. With each breath she takes, her chest rises and falls, lifting and lowering my head in a gentle rhythm.

Her breaths are heavy at first, but they gradually slow. Though I wish I could let them lull me to sleep while I'm buried inside her, they drag me back to reality. The reality is that soon, a day will come that I might lay my head upon her chest and find it cold and still, with no heartbeat, no breath, no life.

Ten days.

That day could be just ten forbidden nights away.

With each of her breaths, I'm struck with an ounce more dread for the second trial and what she'll endure...whether she'll survive.

She has to survive.

Time is fighting against me.

We need these moments together, but we have so little time to waste, and I need to prepare her for the next trial.

Minutes pass this way as we hold each other in the quiet. Yet gradually, I feel her tension rising, increasing with my own as my mind leaves bliss behind to formulate a plan.

"I've lost you now, haven't I?" she whispers.

I raise myself from her chest, propping my elbow on the mattress and leaning toward her side. I cup her cheek, rubbing my thumb along her jawline to soothe her.

"You haven't lost me."

She smiles, but it's tinged with sadness. "You're thinking about the end now, aren't you?"

My eyes fall shut, but I force myself to open them again, giving her a subtle nod.

"What…what did you find out about the second trial?"

I sigh. "The Control and the Elders decided it was best for you and Delle to enter blindly. I don't know what your trial will be, and neither will you."

"You don't know anything at all? Nothing to prepare us?"

"I do know one thing. They agreed to share one detail so we can do something to prepare you, but…I haven't figured out how to prepare you yet. It's more of a hint than a detail, really."

"Tell me." I see fear flicker behind her eyes, but it's quickly washed away, fading into determination. "Tell me what you know."

I'm hesitant to tell her—not wanting to cause her fear or worry until I have a plan—but she looks at me so expectantly, so insistently, that I know I can't deny her. Still, I fear saying the words out loud, knowing it will firmly end our blissful moment, and we'll be dropped head-first into the terrifying reality we're about to face.

My eyes narrow, studying her features, hating that I own responsibility for the anxiety that creeps into her expression. The question I ask next effectively sweeps away the anxiety to make room for outright dread.

"How long do you think you can hold your breath?"

chapter twenty-six

Mercy

A FEW DAYS ago, Arlo asked me how long I could hold my breath. Today, he and Theo lead me and Delle down the stone steps through the hidden passage from the courtroom.

"I don't recognize this path," I say to Arlo in front of me, leading the way with a burning torch in hand. "Where are we going?"

"Watch your head," he says. We turn left and he leads us through a narrowed passageway cut naturally through the stone. The arched ceiling hangs lower through this tunnel, forcing us all to trudge ahead with our heads dipped to avoid striking it. "I'm taking us to a place where you can practice holding your breath."

Those words alone steal my breath from me.

A surge of adrenaline pulses through my veins to think of what the second trial might be. I'm honestly a little frightened to think of where Arlo is leading us and what his plan is for preparation.

I don't know how we could ever fully be prepared when we don't know what's going to happen during the trial. There's any number of methods of torment that could steal away my breath—and every horrid scenario that comes to mind adds to my daily growing anxiety. Part of me is itching to retreat, to run back to the Homestead, crawl into bed, and slip into my nightmares, because at least I know I would eventually awaken from those.

I think I would rather know nothing about the trial than to have this tease of knowledge. Knowing I might not be able to breathe is frightening, but if I knew what to expect, then I could at least prepare my mind. Instead, I'm overcome by stress from the questions that plague my thoughts.

In what manner will I be asked to sacrifice myself?

How will they steal my breath? And for how long?

Will I be trapped somewhere? Drowned? Mouth and nose covered? Is it a false clue to induce anxiety?

Delle's voice trembles as she speaks from behind me. "You really don't know anything at all? Nothing more than the fact that we…that we might be breathless?"

"That's all we know," Theo grumbles from the back of our line.

Theo's been rather sullen since the meeting that decided our second trial, and he's put up an obvious wall against his interactions with Delle. It's noticeable, and I can feel the tension it creates with her. Though I wished for him to put up those walls before—against her obvious crush on him—I hate that he's putting them up now because she needs him. I see how near the end is, and I don't want her to be alone.

A twinge of guilt twists my stomach. I haven't been there for her. I've been sinning with Arlo, indulging with him as often as we can manage, knowing my final days are coming. I've been distracted by lust—he and I both have. We've lost sight of the fight, of trying to seek the truth, because we've been lost together in our passion. Delle deserves a better friend than I've been.

Still, the reality of death looms, and every passing moment feels wasted if I'm not spending it with him. Every day, I think to myself, "What if this moment were my last?" And every time I ask myself that question, my answer is the same—I'd choose to spend my remaining time in his arms.

My last moments, my final breaths belong to him.

"Almost there," Arlo says.

He leads us ahead through an opening into a taller passage on our right, and I'm thankful to be able to straighten to my full height as we pass through it. Then we make another turn and head through a tunnel that gradually widens.

At the end of it is a broad, circular opening, and I can see the cavern bathed in light—sunlight, not just from the glow of Arlo's torch. The stagnant scent of rock mingles with a new, gradually thickening aroma—the fresh, clean smell of mountain air after a rainstorm. I realize that the air feels thicker here, too, like when the clouds are full of rain and ready to burst.

There's water nearby…I can feel it.

I can see it, too. Not that I can see the water itself, but rather, I can see ripples of sunlight dancing along the rock walls of the open cavern ahead, reflections of gently flowing water.

I hesitate as Arlo continues forward, passing through the rounded opening cut with jagged edges through the rock. Delle moves around me, continuing ahead to follow him, and Theo pauses at my side.

"Go ahead," he urges with a tilt of his head.

I look over at him, his face visible in the light streaming in from the opening, though the flames of the torch held in his hand make shadows dance across his expression, darkening his features.

"Is Delle okay?" I ask him quietly, careful to keep my voice low enough that it doesn't echo.

"Are you?" His eyebrows draw into a straight line. "Are any of us?"

My expression mirrors his. I can't quite formulate a verbal response to that, so I shake my head slowly.

"Yeah, well…" he turns his head, looking through the opening where Delle and Arlo have their backs turned to us, "at least you and your warden have a distraction."

He knows…

I'm struck solidly in the chest by fear, my eyes widening with my stare locked on his face. Every muscle is rigid with worry as my mind races to formulate an appropriate response.

Do I deny it?

Do I admit it?

Do I beg him not to tell?

Does he know because we've been too obvious? And if we have, who else has figured it out?

His head turns back slowly, and he meets my eyes. We stare through a few beats as fear continues to pulse through my veins.

What do I say?

"I'm more observant than my brothers, Mercy. You don't need to worry."

"Please don't—"

"Your secret's safe. You're already a sinner condemned, so what does it matter to me if you sin through your final days?"

"I don't care what happens to me if our secret is found out. It's Arlo… He needs to be okay. I need to know he'll be okay when I'm gone—" My voice cracks with sadness, and the sound echoes. I clamp my hand over my mouth to silence myself before unexpected tears fall.

Theo grabs my wrist and gently pulls my hand from my face. "I can't promise you he'll be okay because I know he won't be. But it won't be because of me. You've kept the secret for me that I didn't participate in using Delle in the first trial, and I owe you, keeping this secret in exchange. I just…" He sighs and lets go of my wrist, and I let my arm drop to my side. He blinks, shakes his head, tries to smile, but it falters into a frown as he shrugs. "Sometimes I wish I could have the same with Delle."

"You've never—"

"I've never, Mercy. Not even the night she ran and I chased her. I did hurt her…" his gaze turns, looking off into the cavern through the opening, "the lashings on her back. She's just too…" He seems lost for the right word.

"Young." I fill in for him.

He bobs his head. "Innocent. Or at least, she was before the trial."

"She's still innocent. She's still young. And now she'll never have a chance to grow—"

"Don't say it, Mercy." His head snaps to give me one final look, and though his tone is firm, his expression is filled with pain. "I know what she'll never have a chance to be." He turns and stalks through the opening, heading into the cavern after Delle and Arlo.

My heart aches for him. Theo is like Arlo in many ways—a man with goodness buried deep, hidden beneath layers of trauma and shame and a lifetime of brainwashing.

Our exchange is too much for me to process right now. I need to focus. I need to try to prepare myself for this trial, not because I think I'll survive them all—I know it will be rigged against me. I just have hope that I might survive this one, hope that I might extend my limited days with Arlo for just a little longer.

So, I take a steadying breath, and force my feet to move, refocusing my thoughts on the preparation ahead.

Passing through the round opening, my gaze traces the flat expanse of solid rock beneath my feet, finding that the slab of bedrock stretches out to my left maybe twenty feet or so along a wall of rock. At the end of it, water pours from a dark opening about halfway up the rock wall, filling a basin that stretches out in front of me from left to right, parallel to the rock wall at my back. The basin is the size of a small pond, the cavern wall at the opposite side encasing it.

I'm mesmerized by the gentle but steadily pouring waterfall that glistens in the sunlight, which shines through an opening at the ceiling of the cavern, at least two stories above us. My gaze traces the rays of light shining down over the pool of crystal blue water that fills the basin. It's so beautiful here that I can almost ignore the autumn chill.

"How on earth did you find this place?" I ask in awe.

"Lots of exploring," Arlo replies.

I turn toward his voice, watching as he takes Theo's torch and places it on a black bracket fixed on the rock wall. I notice his own torch is still burning brightly from another bracket, and the messenger bag he brought with him rests on the slab beneath it.

I have to assume he placed the brackets himself—he'd done all the rigging in the other dark cavern where he'd strung me up and prepared me for the first trial. A shudder tears through my spine at the memory, which was equally good and bad. He'd hurt me that day, but I also recognize that my pain had driven a wedge through his version of the truth, and it had started to splinter then.

"Are you going to—"Delle starts, her arms crossed over her chest, hands rubbing over her biceps. "Are you thinking of having us go in there, under the water? I can't swim…" She backs away, her path curving toward the broad circular opening in retreat.

Theo rushes in front of her, blocking her from my view. I see him cover one of her hands with his. "I can swim, and you know I would never let anything happen to you."

"Well, that's a lie, isn't it?" Delle's voice rises in pitch, tension creeping into her words. "It's your job to ensure I make it to the trial where terrible things will happen to me. You've let all kinds of awful things happen to me already!"

Theo's hand drops away and he takes a step back. It's an immediate cue for me to step in, to share some strength for her, especially as I've been so absent as of late.

I rush to her before she even finishes speaking, slipping between her and Theo. She starts to move away from me, but I halt her, reaching out to grip her cheeks, though she doesn't immediately give me her attention—her eyes fixate beyond me toward the water.

"Look at me, Delle." I wait until she lifts her worried eyes to meet mine. "I know this is frightening…I'm frightened, too. But Theo isn't going to hurt you here. He's trying to help you. If you don't want to prepare, that's fine. No one is forcing you to do anything today. But you *will* be forced to face the second trial, and preparing your mind to endure panic now will only help you later."

I sigh, loosening my grip. I keep one hand on her cheek, while the other strokes over her hair, down the side of her head. "You can choose to do as much or as little as you want to prepare for your next trial. If you want to sit over there with your back against the wall and watch me prepare alone, you can. If you want to go back to the Homestead and do nothing at all, you can. Right now, you still have control."

Her eyes flicker around my face as I speak, fear etched into every twitch of her expression.

"Remember that you chose this, Delle. And it's still your choice how much you want to fight for survival. I wish you would fight with everything you have. If any woman would be the first to survive the Trials of Dissension, it would be *you*." I know neither of us will survive, but it doesn't matter. Delle needs hope to fight, and I'll say whatever I have to say to give that to her.

She deserves to have hope, even if mine is lost.

I pull my hands away and step backward, giving her space to choose whether she'll move forward or retreat. "Theo wants to help you, and I hope you'll let him. Don't forget what he and Arlo did for you in the first trial. They couldn't spare you from all pain, but they did everything in their power to protect you as much as they could. They mean us no harm; they're as bound by duty as we are by service in these trials. Don't forget that, Delle."

I watch as a single, silent tear slips from the corner of her eye, tracking down her cheek. "I'm so…I'm terrified, Mercy."

"I know." I nod slowly. "I am, too. You're not alone in fearing this, but we still have to fight, Delle. We can't give up just yet." I reach out and wipe the tear from her cheek with my knuckle. "The more you expose yourself to your fears now, the more prepared your mind will be for whatever we'll face in the next trial. And who knows? Maybe it won't be so bad as what we imagine. Maybe whatever Arlo and Theo have planned for us here will be worse, and the trial will feel easier."

She scoffs, crossing her arms in protective defiance, and sniffing back her tears. "I doubt that," she says, rolling her eyes.

A grin twists at the corner of my lips. "You stood before the Control and the Elders not so long ago and despite your fear, you spoke your mind freely. You can do anything, Delle. And you can do this."

"*You* can do anything; *I* can't."

"If only you knew just how weak I was, you'd know that you're so much stronger and more capable than you give yourself credit for."

She huffs out a heavy breath, forcing agitation to the sound of it, though her fear is masked behind it. "Okay. Fine. I hear you. I'll try whatever they have planned today, but I'm not promising I'll do it again."

"That's good enough for me." I smile and nod in acceptance before turning to look at Arlo and Theo behind me. "So, what's the plan? How will you prepare us?"

Arlo's arms are crossed over his chest as he takes a step forward. "Service by Sacrifice is meant to test your willingness to sacrifice yourself for another. Sacrifice is one of the ultimate acts of service because servants must give parts of themselves to satisfy the needs of men."

I quickly fall into fascination listening to him speak and watching his body language as he tells us of the second trial. It's fascinating because I can see the way he's changing—I can hear it in his voice, in the way he says the words he once would've recited without feeling. He says them now with a hint of disdain and disbelief, and it gives me such hope for the man he'll become, for the changes he could make in Ember Glen long after I'm gone.

"This trial could be designed in any number of ways," Arlo continues. "It's impossible to predict exactly what our brothers have planned, but since we have this one hint, this morsel of knowledge that it might in some way require you to hold your breath or be deprived of oxygen, then we can at least exercise your lungs and work on extending the time in which you can hold your breath. It's something…

"Beyond that, we also know that the trial will hold a psychological component. It's meant to involve a difficult choice…one where you'll have to choose to sacrifice yourself, but the choice isn't meant to be an easy one, so I don't think that practicing holding your breath alone is going to cut it. The next two trials are meant to be arduous, brutal. An element of fear will likely be involved, so conditioning your mind will help prepare you, as well."

"So, we are going in the water, then?" I ask.

Arlo nods. "That's my plan, yes." His throat bobs as he swallows nervously, and it strikes anxiety within me, as well. "Theo and I will go in with you to ensure you're safe, but also to ensure we're preparing you well. You'll fight being underwater for too long, and you may need to be subdued."

That's the moment it hits me, a punch of adrenaline racing so fast through my veins that I can feel it tingling in my toes and through the tips of my fingers in mere seconds. "You're going to subdue us underwater…" I say to clarify my understanding of the events about to unfold.

"Yes, for however many times you want to try. We'll slowly increase how long you're under, both to prepare your mind and your lungs." Arlo drops his arms and takes a step toward us. "I know this trial won't be easy. Most participants lose their lives by the end of the second trial, and I'm not going to mince words about it. This trial will be dangerous and likely terrifying. If some form of oxygen deprivation is involved, then panic will bring you to a swift end, so figuring out how to calm your mind through your fear will be crucial. And now is the time to figure that out."

My head bobs slowly in understanding and agreement, though my mind tries to disconnect from the raging fear that pulses through me. My eyes lose focus, shifting to look somewhere beyond him as I fight to bring myself back to the present, to keep myself fully aware and in the moment so I can do what has to be done to prepare.

I'm terrified, but determined.

I need to pass this trial.

I need more time with Arlo.

I blink and take a deep breath, then turn my head to look at Delle. "Are you ready to do this?"

She looks at me, fear widening her hazel eyes. She straightens to her full height and pulls her shoulders back, though her jaw tenses from fear.

"Okay." She nods. "I'm ready."

chapter twenty-seven

Mercy

I'M BURIED BENEATH the surface, entombed in a water-filled coffin. Arlo's fingers dig into my shoulders as he presses down, holding me under the water while I struggle against him.

I need air.

I need to breathe.

The edges of my vision are blackening from the deprivation of oxygen and panic is taking control.

Don't panic. Be still.

No matter how many times I repeat those four words in my mind, I can't help but lose myself in a frenzy of fear, wildly thrashing for the surface. I fought so hard the last time I went under that I asked Arlo to bind me and force me still. I needed him to tie my legs to stop me from kicking at him and thrusting myself away, but he couldn't bring himself to do that. At least he was willing to bind my wrists this time.

Still, my frantic thrashing continues, and it almost feels like it's worse now than it was when my hands were free. I can't grab him, I can't pull his hands from my shoulders, I can't squeeze his palm, or give him a physical signal that I've reached my breaking point. With my hands tied in front of me, panic rises faster and sharper than it did before.

Let go of me!

Let me up!

I scream inside my mind as my muscles twitch, instinct telling me to open my mouth and take in a deep breath. I have to fight through the urgency in my mind that begs my body to take over.

I made Arlo promise to hold me down for ten seconds longer, no matter how much I fight. I can keep fighting the unavoidable and make this harder on myself, or I can focus my energy into finding some pathway in my mind that leads to peace and calm.

Don't panic. Be still.

Don't panic. Be still.

I can't! I need to breathe…

Just as my panic peaks, Arlo's hands fall from my shoulders and slip beneath my elbows. He yanks me up, and I crash through the surface, water splashing and rippling away from me as I break into open air. I gulp in a desperate breath as he moves to hold me up, snaking his arms around my waist.

Seconds later, there's another splash beside me, and I turn to watch Delle break from the surface. Delle gasps for air with her mouth open wide, fear dousing her expression.

I blink the water from my eyes as I look away from her while panting to catch my breath. She's above the surface again, and that's all I have the capacity to concern myself with at the moment. My head feels light and wispy. We've done this over and over, and it's starting to drain me. My muscles feel listless from the repetitive oxygen-deprivation exercises. It's only been short bursts beneath the surface, but we've done it so many times that it's starting to catch up.

My hands are pinned between my body and Arlo's, and I have to fight the urge to lift them, loop them over his head, and lean my cheek against his to rest. Instead, I ask him, "How long?"

"Forty-five seconds," he says.

"Forty…forty-five? That's it?" I draw in a deep breath to fill my lungs fully, then blow it out slowly. "I told you to keep me down for fifty."

He shakes his head. "I couldn't."

"I need you to be stronger than me—" I start, but Delle's shaking voice cuts through.

"I can't! *I can't.* I can't do this anymore!" Her fingers have a death grip on Theo's shoulders. "Take me out. Now!"

Arlo and Theo are both able to stand on the rocky bottom of the pool. The surface comes up across their chests, nearly drawing a line across their shoulders. I could strain on the tips of my toes and tilt my chin high to keep my face out of the water, but I wouldn't be able to do it for long. Instead, I rely on Arlo to keep me up because I don't know how to swim, and neither does Delle. So, when she demands for Theo to take her out, she has to wait for him to move, which he does right away.

He takes her to the edge, and she reaches out to place her palms on the stone, which is level with the top of the pooled water. Her hands are unbound because she was too panicked at the thought of being tied, so she's a little bit braver in letting go of Theo than I think I would be in letting go of Arlo.

She struggles as she works to pull herself out, still panting and fatigued, but she doesn't struggle for long. Theo grips her waist and hoists her up, twisting her around to sit her on the edge.

Her eyes widen as she looks at him, quickly reaching down to tug her gown across her bare legs. There's a strange, tense pause between them, but then she blinks, huffs in frustration, and drags her legs over the edge. She maneuvers to her feet and takes a few heavy breaths as we all remain still, waiting.

"I can't do anymore of this today. I'm done," she says.

"Fair enough," Theo replies easily, and lifts himself out of the water.

He shakes his hair, flipping the wet strands from his face before stalking across the stone slab toward Arlo's messenger bag. He pulls a dry gown from it and takes it over to her, holding it out. "Here. Go back through the entrance to change." He indicates the broad circular opening we entered the cavern through at her back. "I'll wait here while you dress."

Delle gives him another look that makes me feel sad for her. I don't know what she feels about him. She has a crush, that's certain, but I had many of those when I was around her age—though that was all before I began service.

It brings to memory the way we were encouraged to develop these little crushes and attractions for the men in Ember Glen while we trained to be servants. It was regularly discussed in school when I was fourteen and fifteen-years-old, on the brink of age to serve. We were taught that men like to be longed for, adored, pursued.

Domestic wives are forced into celibacy, so men certainly aren't allowed such longing from them. Yet it was no harm at all for servants to look, to long, to even go so far as to innocently and appropriately let a man know that she would find honor in serving him under the next full moon.

It was all a ruse, though. It was a part of their control. They had us convinced that we would enjoy our nights of service, that under the full moon, we would be able to seek out and serve the men we longed for…as if it would be romantic. Service could never have been romantic in the way they wanted us to believe. It was never enjoyable and it was never consensual.

Delle peeks around Theo to look at me, still held up in the water with Arlo's arms around my waist. "Are you staying?"

I nod. "I'm going to try a few more times. You don't need to wait."

I hope she doesn't wait.

I do want to practice again, but I'm also eager for time alone with Arlo. Though what we're practicing here is anxiety-inducing, the beauty of this cavern—the sunlight, the waterfall, the gentle bobbing of the water that blankets us in our embrace—calls for a memory to be made here.

Delle nods and rushes out through the entrance, turning to move out of sight so she can change.

"You want to try again?" Arlo asks.

I look at him squarely, seeing in his eyes that he also feels the call for memory-making. His palm splays, fingers stretching wide across the small of my back, subtly encouraging me closer.

"I do," I tell him. "But give me a minute to catch my breath."

I lower my hands between us, curling my fingers into fists, pushing lightly. I get that Theo knows, but it makes me uneasy, and I don't want to risk it all falling apart with so little time left. The trial is just a week away and that could be the end.

We wait in the pool as Delle returns in a dry dress, waiting while Theo steps out to change. I make a show of deep breathing, trying to make it obvious that I'm only waiting to catch my breath and ready my mind, and not just waiting for them to leave.

This forbidden love has turned me into a liar. We've all become liars because so much of what we want and need is forbidden. Perhaps that's why it's so difficult to find the truth.

Theo returns in dry clothes and takes one of the torches from the rock wall. "Be mindful of your time," he says to Arlo. "It looks suspicious when you're both gone for too long."

Delle's eyebrows knit together as she looks at Theo, trying to decipher his words. I don't dare look her in the eye for fear she'll figure it out, too. I think somewhere deep down she probably knows, but as I said to Theo, she's still innocent in her thinking, and I only hope she hasn't connected the dots.

I don't know how she would react.

Arlo gives a nod in response.

Delle and Theo disappear through the tunnels, leaving me and Arlo alone in the water beneath the shining sun. We wait in stillness until we can no longer hear the echoes of their voices, until the last hint of light from Theo's torch fades into shadow.

At the same time, our heads turn and we look at one another. Our eyes meet, and an involuntary flash of heat sparks between us. A breath passes, then Arlo's eyes fall to my lips. He lurches forward to capture them in a kiss, but I stop him with my fists against his chest. Before we lose ourselves, I need to try, just one more time.

"Keep me down for sixty seconds, no matter what." I take a deep breath, pinch my eyes shut, and sink beneath the surface.

The muffled roar of water fills my ears as he lets me go, his arms drifting away from me as I fall under. I'm calm for the moment. His hands aren't on my shoulders, gripping tight and forcing me down. He hasn't touched me at all yet, and I think he must be waiting until he sees me fighting for the surface.

Seconds pass before a hint of anxiety creeps in, and I know I need to get ahead of it. I bring the meadow to my mind and imagine I'm there, lying on my back in the sunshine.

In my mind, bright sunlight warms me.

Tall green grass tickles my skin.

My lungs are filled with the scent of wildflowers.

Shades of ruby and amethyst surround me with vibrancy.

My daytime dream is peaceful and calm, but conjuring an image of the meadow also reminds me of the heated night Arlo and I shared beneath the full moon.

The moon, round and bright white.

The flash of lightning and the rumble of thunder that vibrated across my skin.

The rush of pleasure that passed between us.

The starlight appearing behind the clouds.

And the rain—the unrelenting rain that drenched us, soaked us, drowned us…

No…it didn't drown us that night.

But I'm drowning now.

The images and memories I conjured to calm me disappear as panic rises, and I realize Arlo's hands still aren't on my shoulders. He's not holding me down, and I could get my face above the surface if I really wanted to.

But where is he?

A rush of fear concerns me that something's happened to him, and my eyes pop open at the worrying thought. And there I see his crystal-blue eyes blending so spectacularly with the crystal-blue water. He's right in front of me, sunk beneath the surface, and right here to feed my strength.

His hand moves slowly in the water, reaching out to grab hold of the rope that binds my wrists. He tugs lightly and our bodies are drawn nearer, floating together like two celestial bodies moving through space. His other hand floats up, and with two fingers, he points to my eyes, then turns his hand to point to his own, silently urging, "Watch me."

I nod slightly as I fight the urge to let out a bit of the air I'm holding in my lungs.

I fail.

Bubbles shoot out from my lips as I let go of my breath. Arlo drifts closer, his grip on the rope solid and unyielding. He has the same grip on my soul, meeting my eyes with the intensity and strength I can feed off of.

I'm not doing this alone.

Arlo's doing this with me, and it feels profound.

Moments pass as my lungs begin to ache, screaming for me to let go of the air inside so that I can draw in another breath. I let it escape with one small puff at a time, trying to hold it for just a little longer between each release, though the relief of letting go feels so good.

The tension builds within me, painful aching in my chest as my lungs beg for the movement of air. Pressure builds behind my nose and mouth as every single human instinct insists that I stop fighting the urge to take a breath. It becomes so painful that I squeeze my eyes shut, scrunching my face, trying to fight against the urge to breathe because it will only let the water into my lungs.

And then my arms rise.

I open my eyes to see Arlo lift them, ducking into the loop formed by my bound wrists. I let them fall around him, then I pull back on my hands until they catch around his neck. I tug him toward me as his hands find my waist and he pulls, our bodies drifting together with ease.

The urge to rise and breathe is etched across his face, but he fights it with his eyes on mine. His arms slip around my waist, and he holds himself against me, gripping as panic slips through his features. Slowly in the calm, clear water, he brings his face closer to mine until our foreheads touch, and we hold there, our eyes locked and determined.

We're both determined to fight through these last seconds, and I know if we share our strength, we can. He gives me his, and I think I give him mine, too. I have to give him mine when he starts to struggle, when he starts to let out too much air from the breath he's holding and a rush of bubbles trail from his nostrils.

He hasn't gone under once today and now he's trying, struggling to match the time I've been building up to. I feel the way his anxiety greets him, twitching through his body, causing him to jerk and kick his legs as though he wants to leap for the surface.

I want to leap, too.

I can hardly hold on any longer, but I know the time is close.

So close.

Just a few more seconds.

His eyes shut as his face tightens, fighting against the need to breathe, and I know I have to bring him back to me. My chin tilts and I press my closed lips to his. His eyes don't open, but they don't have to. I see a fraction of the tension sneak away from his features. His arms hug me closer. And there's the way his head tilts so slightly, as though he wishes he could part his lips and deepen our kiss.

I lift my legs to wrap around his middle, settling my bottom against his thighs, crossing my ankles behind his back to tighten my hold. One of his hands slips down from my back to curve around my ass, holding me up and keeping me close.

A few more seconds…

Our embrace tightens, our lips press harder.

Almost there…

His palm curves, his fingers dig into my flesh.

Now!

As if Arlo can hear inside my mind, knowing the exact moment when I truly can't bear a second longer, his feet drop to the bottom of the basin, and he launches us toward the surface.

Our kiss breaks as we burst through the waterline, both of our mouths opening wide as we gulp for air in thick, heavy breaths.

But he doesn't let me go.

We're still tangled together.

I blink rapidly to rid my eyes of excess water as we battle to take ownership of the air between us. Our eyes meet as we gasp and pant, the rush of water from our break slowly fading to calm. His eyes dance around my face, narrowing with a scrutinizing gaze before settling on my lips.

And just as I think of how much I want him, how much I need this moment to become a memory of fierce passion, his head tilts and his mouth descends, lips crashing against mine. We share a breath between us as powerful relief strikes, as our lips eagerly part and tongues quickly slip. I sigh as my back arches, and I tighten my legs around him to pull myself closer.

I haven't fully caught my breath, and though my lungs are aching, I find the ache easy to ignore. Every cell inside my body vibrates with pleasure and passion, and it's more demanding than the need to breathe. Maybe it was the desperation of breathlessness that spurred such intensity, our pretend play at suffocation devolving us to our primal needs.

Breaking free from my lips, Arlo kisses across my cheek in a fevered rush, skimming over my jaw, pressing his lips to my neck. "I want you so much that I'd die for this." His large hands curve, fingers digging in to grip my bottom cheeks firmly. Keeping me snug against him, he steps forward, taking me backward to the edge of the pool until I feel the rock touch my spine. "I'd let you steal my last breath. I'd let you end me for a moment of warmth between your thighs."

I pant, letting my neck roll back against the ledge as his lips skate across my throat. "Then find warmth and meet your end, Warden Rainn."

A growl vibrates from his chest, and I feel his teeth scrape across my skin. He pins me to the rock wall with his weight, lowering his hands, fingers scrambling to reach beneath my skirt and hook the fabric of my underwear. He tugs them over my ass and down my thighs. I tighten my arms around his neck as I lower my legs, kicking to help him tug them off over my bare feet. He lets them float away in the water, and I don't care about getting them back.

In a rush, his hands find my waist, and he hoists me up out of the water. The unexpected lift makes me yelp in surprise as he seats me on the ledge in front of him. He grips my knees to spread my legs as his gaze drops, then his palms slowly slip up my thighs, taking my dress up with them. It's clear he's intent on devouring me.

I scoot closer to him as he slips his hands over my hips, reaching around to grip my ass and hold himself against me. I tilt my hips down to teeter on the brink, hanging off the edge and ready to fall for him.

He gives me a quick glance with his sultry blue eyes before his face disappears between my thighs, and he kisses me there as though he'll never taste me again. My bound hands land on the top of his head and my fingers tangle through his hair.

He inhales deeply, drawing in my scent, and the way he groans makes my stomach clench and wetness rush to my center. He licks and laps, curls his tongue to dip inside me, then swirls it around my clit. My head drops back as I revel in the way he makes me feel so alive, even while I'm living my last days so close to death.

I hum in appreciation at the way he worships me while I tighten my grip on his hair. "I love the way you taste me."

"And I love the way you taste," he groans against my skin.

I lower my head to look down at him as his eyes raise to meet mine. I see them light up from his sinful grin as he rubs his tongue over my clit. Then he closes his lips around the swollen spot and sucks with a light, pulsing rhythm.

"Arlo..." I breathe his name.

My back arches, my body twisting in beautiful tension. My eyelids flutter with the ecstasy he brings, but I don't want them to close...

I want to see him.

I need to watch him there between my thighs.

I need to see the way he tastes me so boldly.

I want to watch him give me power I was never granted before as he gives me pleasure absent his own—not entirely absent his own, but certainly, he gives it freely. His face is buried between my legs, fervently worshipping the part of me that was used and abused by the men of Ember Glen for so long. He adores the flesh that was meant for service, yet instead of serving him, my warden serves *me*.

He gives me power freely with each swipe of his tongue. And the more powerful I become, the more his need for me grows.

Arlo turns feral between my thighs, licking, sucking, pressing into me so deeply that his beard tickles and scratches my sensitive flesh. I squeeze my thighs against his ears as he works, tasting every inch of me for minutes or hours or however much time passes in pure ecstasy.

I'm swollen with need, aching pleasantly with the urgency to come. He holds his tongue against my clit, pressing hard, turning his head side-to-side to rub it with an insistent, heavy pressure.

"Arlo…please," I beg as my head falls back.

I'm so close, so heavy, so filled with need…I'm about to fall off the edge into a dark void of pleasure that never ends.

But just before I fall, he stops.

He reaches above his head to grip the rope between my wrists with one hand as the other curls around my waist. The backs of my thighs scrape painfully over the rock ledge as he jerks me forward. My body drops into the water with a splash, and a rush of panic hits me as he takes me off-guard. But the panic swiftly turns to excitement as his arms close around me.

My legs float instinctively to wrap around his waist, and I drag myself against him. He ducks his head into the loop of my arms, and I hold myself there as his hands slip between our bodies. His knuckles bump against my sex as he works to unbuckle his belt, unzip his pants, and bare his cock.

I shift my body with urgency as he juts his hips forward, the tip of him nudging my entrance. I whimper at the tease, but he eases my suffering as his arms wrap around me, grabbing my ass in one hand and splaying the other across the small of my back to hold me steady as he sinks deep with a sharp thrust.

We gasp together.

We sigh together.

We find a strangely frenzied sense of peace together.

I'm overwhelmed with pleasure from the way he tasted me, need lingering from the way he brought me to the edge. I'm desperate to jump from that cliff, to let myself quickly fall back into the dark pit where nothing matters except for the thrill he gives me. I dig my heels into him, thrust my hips, and ride his cock as he holds me in the water.

His lips part as his eyes darken, watching me as if it's the first time he's ever had a woman, and the look of it only intensifies the throbbing between my legs. His eyes dance across mine, delving deep, seeing something in me beneath the surface.

It must be something deeply erotic, feral, powerful, and needy, because that's how I feel. I feel strong; I feel like I own my sexuality in this moment, taking from him with my rocking hips. I feel like he would let me use him to find my own pleasure without seeking any for himself.

His forehead touches mine in the way he always does it, and it makes me sigh. "Use me," he says with a shuddering breath. "Take it from me, Mercy. Stake your claim in corrupting me. God only knows that corruption is my fucking salvation."

"Arlo…"

"Take it. Take it all from me. Make yourself come undone so spectacularly that I can sense no other god in existence but you." Each word he speaks is a match strike between my legs. "Fuck, Mercy. You've become a god to me. Let me be your only disciple, and I'll worship you forever. Sweet *fucking* sin," he growls the last three words, tightening his grip on me, thickening inside me.

I slow my hips to a sensual rhythm, rolling my body in waves that ripple the water around us. I lean in to kiss his cheek, to brush my lips across his skin and whisper against his ear, "Is this your prayer between my legs?"

He shudders, holding me tighter. "More than prayer, deeper than worship…This is my *service*."

Service—my only role in life, the torture I unwillingly endured at the hands of men, and he gives his service to me freely now.

"I'm your servant, Mercy." His voice shakes as he makes the admission, and it ripples through me. It shocks me with pleasure so consuming and joyful that my eyes burn hot with the threat of tears.

He tilts his chin and kisses me softly, wetly, sweetly. Then he nips my bottom lip between his teeth and gives it a playful tug before releasing it. "Promise me forever."

"I promise." The words rush out of me, and there's an instant shift, a jarring switch from desperate sex to an aggressive, feral, all-consuming need.

I need to feel every inch of him.

I need to fuck him harder.

I need to come so roughly that I feel the ache of my release for days.

My rocking thrusts become frantic pulses, my mouth dropping open in anticipation of my release as it builds. With each beat, my pleasure coils tighter in my center, twisting and turning me until I can't think of anything else.

Nothing exists in the world but our writhing bodies.

"How close are you?" he pants.

"Close…" I barely manage the word.

"You'll come for me?" One of his hands slips between us, sliding up my chest, over my throat, curling around to grip the back of my neck.

My head bobs.

His lips curl into a smirk. "Then, I need you to hold your breath one more time for me, starlight."

"What?"

"I'll let you up when you shatter around my cock. Now take a deep breath, Mercy." His grip on the back of my neck tightens. "*Now.*"

His lips fall on mine, pressing as hard as his fingers dig into the back of my neck. It nearly takes me too long to make sense of what he's saying, what he's about to do, but then I quickly take in a short, sharp breath through my nose. Then his hand on my ass squeezes to firm up his hold, and the way it shifts my hips strikes me at the perfect angle.

I cry out into his mouth at the shockwave that sparks my climax, and my deep breath is spent. My orgasm crests, but we descend. Arlo bends, laying me back on the water, sinking me beneath the surface with his lips attached to mine.

He buries us in a liquid coffin, sinking us toward a watery death I would welcome a thousand times over if I knew it would always feel this good. A jolt of adrenaline from being forced under floods my veins, and it drives my climax faster up the peak. My thighs squeeze as I continue to rut my hips breathlessly through my release.

The bliss shatters spectacularly, and my body twitches through aftershocks as he sinks us deeper, kneeling on the rock floor beneath our feet, lifting me upright in his lap.

I want to watch him come.

My eyes open against the water to see my hair floating around me in slow-moving waves. The pressure of water filling my ears is a low roar that dulls all other sounds, making it seem like we're in a world all our own. His wavy hair floats away from his scalp, and I imagine seeing him floating in space, surrounded by the light of the stars.

His beauty is otherworldly, and in my euphoria, I see him as an ethereal savior.

Could this man still save me?

Arlo moves his hands to hold my hips, and he thrusts, fucking me with short, shallow thrusts, fucking me quick and hard to take himself over the edge in a matter of moments.

I watch without breath as he comes undone. His pleasure meets me with a beautiful calmness. There's a perfect, serene bliss under the clear waves as we float together in the gentle sway with our spent bodies still joined.

How long have we been under?

Less than thirty seconds?

More than forty-five?

It doesn't matter. I know I would take the ache and fear of having my breath stolen if I knew it would save this man still sunk inside me. In truth, that's exactly what I have to do for him. I have to carry his secrets to my grave to save him.

I like to think there's some version of the world where Arlo and I could have been together, that some civilized place might still exist out there, somewhere beyond the mountains, where we could choose who we love and how we love them. Some place where partnerships weren't selected by those in power, but instead, by the people themselves. Some place where loving a servant like me wasn't forbidden. Some place where my mother could've been with the woman she loved. Some place where love was stronger than hate, and hate wasn't encouraged by a spiteful god.

Maybe that place exists somewhere.

Maybe it exists nowhere.

Maybe it can only ever exist in these stolen moments between us…and maybe it dies when the men of Ember Glen take my breath from me for the last time.

chapter twenty-eight
Mercy

RED.

I'm swathed in the color of blood, cloaked in the shade of sacrifice.

A crimson corset cinches my waist, and though the vertical boning is rigid—nearly too tight in the way it's fastened—the fabric is soft against my skin. A sheer tulle allows the porcelain shade of my skin to peek through the spaces between the lacy flower appliques across my waist. My chest is exposed above the sweetheart neckline, formed by the rigid cups which cage my breasts.

Sheer sleeves cling to my shoulders, sewn with elastic to keep them from slipping with the weight of the long sleeves which drape loosely down my arms, secured with more elastic that's uncomfortable around my wrists.

I gaze at my profile in the mirror from where I stand in the foyer of the Homestead, beneath the chandelier.

Red.

Sacrifice encases me and blood flows in waves of fabric all around me.

My eyes leave the mirror, tracing down the layers of the gown, sighing at the beauty of the dress that may be the last one I will ever wear. I suppose if I should die today, this would be the most fitting attire to wear while taking my last breath.

The dress is truly stunning. Layers of the same sheer fabric as the sleeves float down from where the skirt is secured with a red silk bow around my waist. A chilled autumn breeze sweeps in from the wide open front doors, rustling the layers and making the appliques of floral lace dance like the wildflowers in the meadow.

Red.

Everything is red.

Blood-red.

It's the color of a servant's ultimate sacrifice—blood spilled from the violence of purging.

My blood won't be spilled today—they'll save that for the next trial, Service from Bloodshed. But today, I will sacrifice. I will be tested emotionally, psychologically, asked to choose some form of torment for myself in exchange for…something. I don't know what I'll be asked to sacrifice myself for yet, but the fear of it is already torment enough.

I glance at my reflection again and lift my gaze from the dress, meeting my eyes in the mirror. One corner of my lips twitches in the direction of a smile, though the motion doesn't carry all the way through.

The Control had called a special meeting yesterday with me and Delle. They'd been firm and insistent that they wouldn't tolerate us wearing servants clothes like we'd both done when we were forced to watch the last night of service under the full moon.

They were very clear that the only color we were to adorn was red, because we were no longer worthy of wearing black like our sisters. I'd put on the red dress they wanted me to wear, but if they thought I'd so easily take to their demand, they were sorely mistaken.

I mixed all the colors in the palette of make-up in my room until the powders turned a hazy shade of black. Then I painted it across my eye lids, sweeping the dark shadow up to my eyebrows. I drew a thick outline of black liner around each eye, and the way it frames my gray-blue eyes reflects my world as light surrounded by darkness.

The recklessly applied onyx is my quiet defiance, a silent reminder of who I am—the rebel they can't control.

I've vowed to myself that I won't let this make-up run down my cheeks today. I won't shed a single tear; I think I shed them all last night with Arlo, anyway.

I close my eyes at the memory of the last words he spoke to me before I fell asleep…before I chaotically fell into a restless slumber that I'd fought for hours in his arms. His embrace had tightened before he whispered the words that chased me into my dreams, "Whatever happens tomorrow, I promise, I won't leave you alone. Alive or dead…I'll follow after you, starlight. I won't let you go."

His words gave me comfort in the moment, but now, they threaten to force tears from my eyes, and I promised myself I wouldn't cry today. I fear that if I die, he'll break his promise to me. I fear that if I die, he'll chase me into the afterlife instead of staying strong, learning to lead, growing older to become an Elder who could enact real change in Ember Glen.

There's a lonely part of me that selfishly hopes for just that. It hopes for him to follow me into death and chase me to hell, or heaven, or wherever our souls may find themselves. But if he did, then suffering might remain in Ember Glen forever, and I can't have hope for that. I have to hope for his strength to remain.

I force my gaze from the mirror and look out through the wide open front doors of the Homestead to the sound of feet padding down the staircase at my back. It's Arlo and Theo. I know it from the way the air has shifted, the way it feels like it's all swept away and pulled out the doors, sucking every last hint of oxygen from the room. I stifle a gasp at the feeling of change, knowing that it's all about to begin.

Or end.

I steal a quick glance at Delle at my side, but her eyes are downcast as her chest heaves, as she fights for each breath in her rising fear. I quickly look ahead because the sight of her struggling through her panic is too much for me to handle.

I hear their feet come down on the landing, and there's a pause, a beat of silence in not knowing exactly what's coming next. My breaths quicken, though I fight to remain steady and calm. I know this is only the beginning of this awful day, and I can't let panic get the best of me now.

A minute of anxious silence passes.

And then there's movement.

Arlo appears, walking along my side, and as he moves past me, he draws a long red veil over my head, holding it delicately in his gloved hands. A long, sheer layer of crimson tulle floats down in front of me as he drops the veil, cloaking my vision in red. The veil is speckled with the same flower appliques that appear on my corset and down the skirt of my gown. They line the hem of the veil, giving some weight to keep it down.

It's beautiful.

It's stifling.

It shrouds me in terror.

This is it…

This day could be my last.

My vision is obscured by the flower appliques, and everything I see is marred with red. Arlo appears as though he's tainted by my blood as he steps in front of me. My heart stops beating at the sight of him—his jaw set, his expression hardened to hide his emotions, though he can't hide them from me. His downcast eyes lift to meet mine beneath his lashes, and he falters, just for a moment, just long enough for me to see how broken and fearful he feels today.

This can't be the last day.

It can't be.

I have to survive this.

"I can't," Delle whispers from just a few feet away. Theo stands before her, lowering her veil. "I don't think I can do this…"

Internally, I scream, and every part of my soul screams with me against the horror of this moment.

I have no words for her now as I did before the first trial. There's nothing I can say to bring her comfort or give her strength, because I have neither today. We may face death, and there's no reassurance I can offer against it.

"You can do this," Theo whispers. "I know you can. Just stay calm, okay?"

Emotion overcomes her and she starts to cry. Theo jerks forward, almost as though he was going to hug her, but quickly stops himself. He grips her shoulders instead. "Okay, let it all out right now. You have ten seconds, Delle, and then you need to stop. You can't carry this emotion with you to the trial; it won't serve you."

I appreciate that he's trying, but I'm frustrated by his words. It's not possible to leave emotion behind. I'm carrying the weight of the strongest emotions I've ever felt with me to this trial.

I feel so heavy, yet I also feel the way I'm beginning to shut down inside. I feel the dial turning the intensity of my feelings down, gradually easing me into a state of numbness.

Arlo's bare hand touches mine and my attention snaps to him, wondering why he removed his glove. My gaze narrows on him as I feel him place something small in my palm.

"Hold on to it. Take it if you panic. It will calm your nerves and slow your breathing. You have to stay calm to survive."

His fingers slip away from mine as he drags his hand away and quickly puts his glove back on. My fingers curl to grip the small object in my hand, and I quickly realize what he's given me. It's a single pill—the medication he gave me when I burnt my hand and the pain was too great to bear.

"Does Delle—"

"No." He shakes his head. "There was only one left and I…I need you to have it."

I swallow a rising lump in my throat and give him a small nod before turning my gaze to look beyond him. I curl my fist around the pill to hold it tight, grateful that he wanted to try to help, but unsure of how I feel about using it.

Outside, Owen, Park, and Wesley stand side-by-side halfway down the stone steps leading up to the Homestead. They face out toward the village square where a row of four large projector screens are set up. There's a space between the middle two, allowing a wide gap at the bottom of the stone steps for us to pass through. The villagers are gathering to watch our processional as we leave for the trial, throngs of men, women, and children filtering across the large gravel-covered square to bear witness.

I feel the veil move as Arlo adjusts it. It doesn't need adjusting; he's just anxious and needs the distraction of busying his hands.

"You just couldn't help yourself, could you?" he asks, and a weak smirk tugs at the dimple in his cheek.

"What?"

"The black around your eyes, Mercy. You just had to do it, didn't you?" There's a hint of teasing amusement in his voice, and the sound of it gives me a moment's relief.

"I can't follow *all* the rules, now can I?"

"No. You can't." He sighs. "You look—"

"Wicked? Sinful?"

"Powerful…Otherworldly."

Words fail me at the way he looks at me, with awe and longing, though it's tinged with fear and heartache. Tears well in my eyes, and I fight feeling anything in favor of numbness.

I blink away from him, glancing around to see Park turning to walk up the steps toward where we stand just inside the Homestead. The processional to the site of the trial is about to begin. My heart kickstarts in a chaotic rhythm, and my gaze darts back to Arlo, seeking him with urgency.

"Warden Rainn, I—"

"Don't say it." He shakes his head sharply, silencing me. "No last words."

My breath catches in my lungs at the way his eyes narrow and flicker across my face, skimming down to take in the full sight of me. He draws in a deep breath and I see the way his shoulders shake. If he breaks, it will break me, too.

I have to look away.

Park steps across the threshold, stopping a few feet in front of us. "It's time."

I swallow hard, my throat suddenly dry. I don't suppose anyone would give me water if I asked for it.

Water.

Will I be under water today?

I've wracked my brain trying to think of all the methods of torture one might use to steal another's breath in a test of faith and sacrifice. Water is the best I could come up with on my own—it's how we practiced holding our breath and taming our fear.

Yet it seems too easy, too simple.

Whatever it will be, I'm afraid for it.

My head turns, tracking Arlo as he moves to stand beside me, my mind urging me to take a final look at him before fear takes hold of me and makes me forget the world around us.

The first thing I search for is the crystal-blue of his eyes. They're always so striking, enchanting, able to hold my attention through my darkest moments—even now. His thick hair is a little messier than usual, which matches the way his beard remains untrimmed and unruly. I like the way it looks on him compared to the perfectly trimmed and polished way he was before. It makes him seem a little more rugged, a little feral, less rigid, and more flexible…more like the man he needs to become.

Still, his attire is sleek in comparison. He wears perfectly pressed dark gray slacks beneath a black, knee-length overcoat. The black coat is unbuttoned, revealing the gray waistcoat he wears over a crisp, white button-down shirt. A familiar silver chain links from one of the fastened buttons of his waistcoat to the pocket stitched at the front of it.

With a final sweeping glance, I draw in the complete picture of the imperfect man I fell in love with.

I fell in love with him.

Beyond reason, beyond sense, beyond the will of God, the universe, demons, or men, I fell for a man who was impossible to love…and now I have to leave him.

Air rushes from my lungs in a huff of awareness.

This day might be our last together.

"Are you wearing the boots?"

I nearly leap out of my skin. Arlo whispers the words, but the silence in my mind is so loud that his voice is startling. He holds out the crook of his arm for me to take, side-stepping closer. Slowly, I hook my arm with his.

We look at each other, and he gives me a secret grin. "Well? Are you?"

Though fear shakes through us equally, I want this moment. I want to give him one last smile before we go, one last memory of my rebellion. I kick my foot out to the side as I reach down to lift my dress and show him that, of course, I'm wearing my black servant boots.

When our eyes meet again, I give him a small smile.

"Good. I would have been disappointed if you hadn't worn them." He briefly returns the smile, though it quickly falters with his shaking voice as he looks out toward the village square.

He subtly side-steps closer, tugging through our linked arms like he's afraid I'll let go.

"Alive or dead, I'll follow after you, starlight. I won't let you go."

"Alive or dead…" I mutter, and I feel the air move as his head whips to look at me. "I won't let you go."

His jaw twitches as he tenses. A glossy sheen appears over his eyes, making perfect oceans of blue that might just drown me in heartache.

I force a small smile against the overwhelming sadness that claws its way up from the depths of my soul. I fight my tears as I squeeze my eyes shut, shake my head, and turn away from him.

"Wildflowers and starlight," he whispers, and my heart shatters.

Those words mean more to me than any other three words he could ever speak. *I love you* isn't ours; it never really could be. I don't want *I love you* when we have *wildflowers and starlight*.

Park gives a nod, then turns away to lead us forward. I drop my hand to quickly link my fingers with Arlo's. I squeeze, and he squeezes back. I try to tug away so we won't be seen, but he holds me for a beat longer, a moment past reasonable risk.

How do I let go of him?

With a lurch in my stomach, we move, following Park through the open front doors as Arlo's grip slowly loosens, as we both have to fight to let go of one another. As I link my arm in his again, we take our first steps onto the stone staircase to begin this procession of our suffering.

chapter twenty-nine

Mercy

COOL AUTUMN AIR swirls around us as we descend the stone steps, sending a ripple of goosebumps up my arms. The long sleeves do nothing to protect me from the chill given that the fabric is sheer, and neither does the veil. I can feel the impressive length of it trailing behind me, flowing like blood down the staircase from the Homestead.

Arlo and I lead as Delle and Theo follow behind us. I hear Delle crying as Arlo guides me, but I don't look back. I can't look back. I can't let the last time I look at her be like this—dressed in that red gown, covered by that loathsome crimson veil, crying through her fear and heartache. She's breaking, and I can't bear to witness it.

I'm breaking, too, but I have no tears to shed. The well is dried up, every drop boiled and evaporated by the flames of suffering that flicker within me, a fire so hot that it threatens to burn all that's left of me in a painful blaze of misery.

Park meets Wesley and Owen ahead of us as he steps down to the gravel. The three of them proceed ahead between the gathering of villagers, a group of them on the left and another on the right, leaving a wide aisle for us to pass through as they watch.

"Where are Killian and Ryker?" I whisper, feeling the need to know so I'm not taken off-guard at their sudden appearance.

"At the site of the trial."

We reach the final step, and our feet land on the small pebbles that cover the square. Then, we pause.

I hate the pause.

It prolongs these dreadful moments, allowing tendrils of fear to coil around my veins, squeezing to intensify the looming panic.

Worse than my own panic is hearing Delle's as they stop behind us. She fights to get control of herself, whispering, "It's okay. It's okay. I can do this," as she sniffles, trying to find the strength to stop her tears.

I know she feels weak, but I wish she understood just how strong she is.

I wish they all understood how strong they are—my sisters in service.

They don't even recognize the value of their worth beyond serving the men of Ember Glen, and no one can blame them for that. It's what they've been told since they were babies. But part of me wonders....

What if?

What if they knew their strength?

What if they knew their worth?

What if they knew there could be more than painful sex and unprompted violence?

What if I die today, never knowing what could be if they only knew?

My stomach lurches. I bend forward around the awful clench in my gut, the knowing of terror to come, the harrowing realization that I could be marching to my death at this very moment.

Arlo whispers beside me, "Don't give them this, Mercy. Don't let them have the satisfaction of your fear in this moment."

I'm too afraid to open my mouth to speak in fear that I'll spew the contents of my stomach and give them all such a glorious image of my final moments to laugh over when I'm gone. A tremor tears through me, breaking into a full body shiver that shakes through me uncontrollably.

But somehow, I force myself to stand.

I link my shaking arm with Arlo's, and together, we leave the dreadful pause. I lift my chin as we walk, my black boots—hidden beneath the length of my red gown—crunching over the small stones and pebbles beneath our feet.

My eyes scan the crowd as we walk, searching for Ellary and Cambria in hopes I can make one last connection, give them a silent goodbye. My stomach twists in knots as I search for them, my heart pounding out of control. As adrenaline rushes through me, I struggle to track individual faces in the crowd. They all blur together as I'm brought to walk before them in the shame and disgust they have for me.

"*Malo mori quam foedari.*"

The prayer is spoken, words fleeing mouths and catching on the breeze, swirling all around me. They're not spoken in unison; they come from the individuals who wish to see me die for my sins, the people of Ember Glen who are so lost to their faith in God that they think I deserve death for fleeing that one night of service. It feels like so much time has passed since that night, and nothing in Ember Glen has changed.

Arlo will change it.

I have to keep my faith in him.

The prayer is spoken over and over as we proceed, following Owen, Park, and Wesley.

"*Malo mori quam foedari.*"

Over and over and over again until…

"*Circulus vitiosus.*"

The two words are spoken by a single, unsteady voice, and the procession comes to an abrupt halt. Owen turns to look at Arlo with a confused expression as Park and Wesley glance at each other the same.

Another voice cuts through the odd silence, "*Circulus vitiosus.*"

I feel Arlo tense at my side in the confusion. The Control in front of us scan the crowd, searching for the voices that spoke words I've never heard before. They don't have to search too hard; someone's arm shoots straight up from the center of the crowd at our right, drawing everyone's collective attention to the sight of it.

It's a woman's arm, palm open wide with fingers splayed, and when the words are shouted again, it's clear they're coming from her. "*Circulus vitiosus!*" The words break through the quiet confusion, bursting loudly and clearly in such a way that I can feel it vibrate through my bones.

The blade of a knife rises sharply to the woman's bare arm, stretched high above the crowd, and we all watch in silence as she draws the tip of it straight across the back of her forearm, slicing through her flesh. A line of blood pools and drips, soaking her skin in crimson. All of Ember Glen watches in shock, frozen by the surprise of this moment.

For me, it's a moment of unexpected peace to witness this brutal action that feels so much like solidarity. For the Control, it's a clear act of protest—one that will need to be stopped immediately.

Circulus vitiosus…

What does it mean?

The crowd begins to shift, and voices rise, but the woman with the bleeding arm shouts one final time as Park and Wesley begin to move toward the crowd. "*Circulus vitiosus in aeternum!*"

"Sinner!"

"Stop her!"

"Someone take the knife."

The men in the crowd begin to turn on her as one of them reaches for her arm, circles his hand around the dripping line of blood. Wesley and Park drive their way through the crowd, and the people part to make way for them as they join four or five men from the village who've taken an active role in subduing this woman.

Someone takes her to the ground, pinning her arms behind her back, but she's not fighting, not struggling, like she's already accepted this consequence because she knew it was coming…like she had planned for it. It's not until she turns her head, pressing her cheek to the ground, that I realize who it is.

Stefanie Price, Hyatt's newly widowed wife.

"Fuck. Where's Luna?" The words rush from Arlo's lips as a terrified whisper. I look over at him to find him scanning the crowd, tension tightening his features.

I search for her, too, wondering if she's part of this with Stefanie, worried as I'm sure Arlo is, that she may do something to get herself in trouble. If she does, I know Arlo will react, and selfishly, I don't want that. I need him. *I* need him because I know that nothing will stop this trial from happening today.

More than my selfish need for him, he's kept promises for the future of Ember Glen that require him to maintain control. I cannot allow him to lose focus, to lose control of himself. He has to become an Elder when it's time for the next Shift. So when I spot Luna ahead of us, standing beside her husband, with Soleil strapped to her chest and her other children beside her, I tell Arlo right away.

"She's there, up ahead. I see her."

"She's going to—"

"She's not going to do anything."

He fears she's going to act as Stefanie did, but I know she won't. I can see horror on her face, the surprise and utter shock. Tears stream down her cheeks as she watches Park and Wesley lift Stefanie from the ground. Her palm cradles the back of her baby's head as her other hand tightens its grip around her son's palm where he stands at her side. She may be unhappy with her domestic life, but she clings to her children, and I know she won't risk leaving them.

It makes me wonder for a moment why Stefanie chose this, knowing it would take her from her children. Though I suppose now that Hyatt is gone, she doesn't need to be there to protect them from him. They'll be assigned to another domestic family unit, and any home they're placed in would surely be better than the one Hyatt ruled.

Owen appears in front of us. "Move, *now*," he tells Arlo as I watch Park quickly bind Stefanie's wrists with rope behind her back. He takes hold of her arm and drags her toward the aisle where we stand. "Keep the processional moving, we can't draw further attention to this."

Owen abruptly turns on his heel and marches ahead, expecting Arlo to follow…but he doesn't move.

Arlo's frozen, rooted to the spot, his eyes fixed on Luna, watching with blue blazing fear. He's afraid for her, afraid she'll follow Stefanie and speak those words that seem to be blasphemous, words of protest or solidarity…

something I don't know or understand.

Circulus vitiosus...

Circulus...Does that mean circle?

Are they saying vicious circle?

Those are the two words I remember Luna saying to me, but I have no idea what they mean or whether that's really how *circulus vitiosus* translates—I can only guess. Yet, even in my confusion over what's happening and the meaning of the words, my heart flutters with wonder and a strangely optimistic flurry of hope. Whatever the words mean, it's clear to everyone that these are words spoken only by sinners. And in Ember Glen, sin is our only weapon in the fight for freedom.

If there are murmurs of rebellion among the women, if there's a chance that my sins have sparked a war, then my death may just set it ablaze. Arlo must survive the loss of me to stoke those flames, to guide the so-called sinners to the corrupt so they can burn them to ashes. He needs to remain strong, in control, an influential member of the authority. He has to survive, regardless of whether I do or not.

I take a step forward while he remains frozen, and my arm tugs against his, pulling until he moves with me. "You promised me, Warden Rainn."

I stare straight ahead, but from the corner of my eye, I see his head turn in my direction. I can feel the intensity of his eyes as they fix on me, but I don't turn to meet his stare. I focus on what must be done for Ember Glen, following as Wesley rejoins Owen ahead of us and they lead us through the crowd.

"You promised you would maintain control, that you would solidify your place as an Elder so you can bring change to Ember Glen. You promised me you would do what it takes to set sinners free and end the corruption and violence." I grit my teeth against the rising indignation that settles with a heavy weight in my chest. "You will *not* break that promise to me now, not ever. Whether I survive this day or not."

His gaze leaves me, but I feel the unease ripple through him, humming from his aura, mingling with my righteous anger in a way that makes me tremble.

"Luna...What if she—"

"You can't control her any more than you can control me. You will *not* break your promise to me, Warden Rainn—" My voice cracks and I fight to steady my emotions as we reach the end of the aisle between the gathered villagers. We follow as Owen and Wesley turn, leading us east toward the forest. "When this trial is done, regardless of what happens to me, you have to talk to Luna and ask her about vicious circle. If it's the start of an uprising, they'll need your power, your influence…they'll need your guidance. Do you understand me? Promise me right now that you'll do right by me. That you'll fight for my sisters and make this a place where choice and love and freedom can exist." When he doesn't respond right away, my voice trembles through the word, "Please."

He whispers so faintly, I can hardly hear him, "A place where you and I could have loved freely forever…"

He sighs, and I feel his understanding in that release of breath. I feel acknowledgment shiver through him. I feel his promise in the way he drops his head, staring at the ground in resignation.

Silence cages us together with our shared sorrow as we enter the forest… and not a single word is spoken between us for miles.

OWEN AND WESLEY lead the way, maneuvering around tree trunks and stepping over fallen logs as we march through the forest. The day is overcast and dreary, and we're surrounded by chilly air that only makes my shivering that much worse.

We proceed this way through the forest for what feels like an eternity. We're approaching the second hour of walking this rough terrain, and I'm exhausted.

During the first fifteen minutes of our trek, our veils continually snagged on twigs and leaf stems as they dragged across the ground. It was slowing us down, so Owen insisted they be removed, and he carries both of our veils now. It makes me wonder whether there was a point to having us wear them at all, or whether they were just meant to be the shroud that draped us in terror, knowing our trial was about to begin.

My arm is no longer linked with Arlo's. Instead, I hold the front of my dress up with the heels of my hands resting against my thighs, fighting my way through each step of this endless processional.

I glance behind me to check on Delle as she walks side-by-side with her warden. Theo carries a pair of red shoes in one hand—shoes with tall heels they expected us to wear on this hike through the forest. I'm glad I didn't, but I feel sorry for Delle because clearly, she's barefoot now. The ground is rough and cold, and it adds another layer of torment to the suffering in this trial.

Twenty minutes ago, the ground began to gently slope upward, and each uphill step becomes more tiresome than the last. The trudge up the incline slowly siphons air from my lungs. I'm already panting in my anxious state, and it makes me angry. I'm angry that I have to exert myself just to be tortured and tested.

Another twenty minutes pass as we travel up the never-ending slope, and I can feel the air is changing. It's growing colder, and I hear the gentle autumn breeze crescendo toward a vicious howl as a sharp incline approaches. A mass of greenery and wild overgrowth conceal the ascent, but looking up and beyond, I can see the bases of tree trunks jutting from the ground ahead, which is high above us.

Owen and Wesley shift, moving one behind the other as they come upon a narrow path beaten into the dirt, the end of which disappears between a cluster of tall bushes.

This is it…

The instinctive clench in my gut tells me we've reached the site of the trial.

I stop, loosening my grip to let my hiked-up skirt fall and skim the dried leaves beneath my feet. I quickly clench my fist again when the small white pill slips, reminding me of its presence in my palm. I'm not even sure how I've managed to hold on to it this entire time.

If the trial will begin beyond this path, I know now is the time to take the medication. Yet I've already decided that I won't. There are two of us participating in this trial, and only one pill. I can't take it for myself if there's none for Delle. She struggled far more than I had in preparation for this trial, and I'm truly terrified for her. Giving her this pill is the last thing I can do for her, my final parting gift, knowing that the odds of both of us surviving—of *either* of us surviving—are low.

Arlo stops to look at me, questioning me with a tilt of his head. I meet his eyes for a moment, then turn to look at Theo as he and Delle catch up to us. "Could I have a moment with Delle?"

Arlo and Theo glance at each other, but Arlo gives a small nod. He turns his head to look behind him and calls up the path, "Owen."

A few seconds pass before Owen appears from the overgrowth, his eyes narrowed in confusion. "What is it?"

"Our participants would like a moment with each other before the trial."

Owen looks between us with a surprisingly severe expression. "Fine, but only a moment." He takes a step forward and crosses his arms over his chest, watching, waiting.

I hold out my empty hand to Delle. She drags her wide eyes away from where they were fixed on the narrow dirt path to look at my outstretched hand instead. It takes her a beat to blink away from her outright fear, but then she finally swings her arm forward and places her hand in mine.

I drag her a few steps away, staying close enough that Owen will feel secure in knowing that we're not trying to run, but far enough that none of the men will hear my whispers. I turn to face them and tug on Delle's hand to move her in front of me, making sure her back is turned squarely to them.

"Give me your hand," I whisper once she's facing me.

Her forehead creases with confusion, but she lifts her hands between us. I flatten my palm beneath hers—the one that holds the pill—before turning our hands over. Then, I slowly slip my fingers down to her wrist to keep her hand right there in front of her between our bodies, concealing it from the Control at her back. She looks down at the pill now resting on her palm.

"Take this," I whisper, "right now. But don't let them see. Swallow it down, quickly."

With trust I don't understand, she nods, and my fingers fall away from her arm. She pinches the pill between her finger and thumb, quickly and sneakily bringing it up to her lips, then popping it into her mouth.

I watch her throat bob as she harshly swallows it dry. "What is it?"

"It will calm your nerves, trick your mind into euphoria. It will help to ease your panic."

"You already took one?"

"Yes," I lie.

"Is this…" Her bottom lips trembles as she shivers against the chill while simultaneously fighting tears. "Is this it?"

I sigh, reaching out to tuck a strand of hair behind her ear, and tears threaten to well and fall—tears I promised myself I wouldn't shed today.

"This is it." I nod sadly, but I force a small smile for her. "I'm really proud of you, Delle. You've become the woman I always knew you could be."

"Mercy, I want you to know that—"

"Stay strong and fight for it, Delle." I had more to say to her, but the moment she said my name, I splintered. She said my name, and for whatever reason, that was the thing that drove a wedge into the crack, breaking through my remaining strength with force. I have to get away from her before it crumbles and falls to pieces on the cold, hard ground.

I lift the front of my skirt and rush around her, pushing past Owen, Arlo, and Theo, trudging ahead up the narrow dirt path. Just a few steps in and greenery surrounds me. My boots dig harshly against the ground as I push my way up the steep incline.

The howl of wind intensifies with each step, beckoning us forward with its ominous roar. Lifting my chin, I look ahead up the path, and in less than a minute, I can see the end of it opening up again to the forest.

Some part of me wants to stop, pause, and take a breath. That part wants me to turn back and run away. It wants me to leap into Arlo's arms and beg him to take me far, far away from here.

Yet I know I can't.

I can't run from this fate; I can't hide. The cowardice of fleeing won't inspire change, but my participation in this trial just might. This path is steep and hard to climb, and though I hate it with every molecule of my existence, I cannot stop. This is a path that must be traveled to the end once the first step has been taken…and I took the first step the night I chose to run from service.

I push harder through the final inclined steps, and as I come out from the bushes, the ground levels out. I can finally take a full breath. Arlo's not far behind me; I feel his presence pulsing at my back as I slowly move forward between the trees, yet I don't turn back.

My eyes are fixed on the sight before me.

Twenty paces ahead of me, the forest comes to an end. The colors of autumn dissolve into bleak and desolate shades of gray; the brown soil, yellow and orange fallen leaves, the emerald- and hunter-green hues of the evergreen shrubbery all fade into solid, drab rock. The forest ends to give way to a gray slab of rock, which stretches from the tree line across a vast, semi-circular clearing.

And at the end of the clearing, the world ends, dropping off into nothingness at the edge of a cliff. Beyond is open air, empty space that's filled with dreary fog. I see the jagged outline of gray mountains in the distance, clustered together and rising menacingly toward the sky. My heart skips a beat before wildly thumping against my ribs.

I falter as I step back, instinctively wanting to put as much distance as possible between myself and the edge of that cliff. Arlo's palm wraps around my forearm, gripping tight and halting me. He spins me around to face him, dragging me closer, but I can't look at him with my panic rising—meeting his bright blue eyes will only make it worse. I turn my head away to avoid his stare, and my gaze drops to the forest floor.

I quickly find that looking at the ground is no better for my anxiety. My gaze follows a trail of flattened leaves beside us, the crunched and leveled remnants which show a path that someone has recently walked parallel to the tree line. My head gradually rises as I follow the trail to its end, and fear punches through me as broken leaves fade into disturbed soil.

Two large piles of soil rest as mounds behind two side-by-side trenches dug into the earth, nestled between the trees. The trenches are slightly longer and wider than the wooden boxes hovering on platforms above the empty, dug out pits—wooden boxes long enough and wide enough to fit a body.

Coffins.

Graves.

"No…" I gasp, the word sneaking out from between my lips.

Movement from beyond the graves steals my attention. I turn my head toward the motion and see people coming out from the forest, crossing the slab of stone, and making their way to the precipice.

Black skirts whip in the wind, and my heart drops into my stomach. Ellary and Cambria walk toward the cliff's edge with their hands bound in front of them by rope…and Killian leads them there to stand on the precipice.

My body jerks into action, twisting to run after them, but Arlo stops me with both of his hands painfully squeezing my biceps. It aches as he digs his fingers into my flesh, but he'll have to grip tighter if he wants to keep me away from them.

"You can't go to them." He struggles to keep hold of me as I fight against him, twisting and jerking. "Mercy, *stop!*" He shouts so loudly that his deep voice bounces off the trees, carries into the clearing, and echoes through the void beyond.

I freeze, going still at the harsh sound of it, gritting my teeth against the cold, the fear, and the anger, which all make me shudder. My lips fight a snarl, a primal urge to hurt the man in front of me to avoid feeling the hurt within me.

He didn't do this.

Arlo didn't choose this for me.

He huffs, tilting his face closer to mine. "The only way you can save them is by sacrifice. It's your trial, Mercy. It's your friends who you have to sacrifice yourself for."

My eyes dart madly about his face before finally settling on the blue of his irises. He grabs hold of me with a look that encircles me. It feels as though he coils his rope around my body, twists and knots it, tightens it to force me into calmness, stillness. Slowly, I nod, coming to understand that Ellary and Cambria will be okay; they won't be harmed today because I'm going to make the choice to sacrifice myself to save them.

And just as I begin to steady myself, Delle's scream tears through my soul, vibrates so harshly through my bones that they rattle and threaten to break.

She saw the graves…

Arlo's grip loosens, and I turn just in time to see her take off toward the clearing. I lurch, but Theo is already moving, already chasing. He swiftly closes the distance, throwing his arm to bring it around her, his forearm crossing her chest so he can drag her back against him.

As Theo pulls her back, I see what she was running for. In the clearing beyond the forest, Ryker moves with two others, walking them out to stand beside Ellary and Cambria, who are far too close to the edge.

Don't fall. Please, don't fall, don't fall, don't fall.

Four people—two for me and two for Delle—are brought to stand shoulder-to-shoulder on the edge of the cliff. Each pair of wrists are bound with rope and all of their faces are etched with fear. Ellary and Cambria are brought to be the ones I sacrifice for, and I shouldn't be surprised by that.

But I'm shocked to see who stands for Delle.

I recognize them both, though I don't know either one well. One of them is a servant in training—a fourteen-year-old girl, not even a woman of age to serve—who Delle had a close friendship with. And the other…the other is Delle's seven-year-old brother.

I clench my fists as fury takes me. I drag in a breath, and every particle of it bursts, exploding in my lungs and erupting from me with a vicious scream that slices through the trees, tears across the void, and makes the mountains quiver. My fists punch down toward the earth as the scream draws every ounce of energy from my body, tensing every muscle and vibrating through every bone.

How dare they bring an innocent child into this?!

The flames of rage engulf me, setting me ablaze with righteous indignation. These men know no bounds, no decency; they show no respect for the same innocence and purity they pretend to treasure for their domestic women and children. They know nothing of sacrifice, yet claim that women should dutifully and unquestionably sacrifice for them.

What have the men of Ember Glen ever sacrificed for us?

I turn back to Arlo, stepping closer, letting him see the flames burning behind my eyes. "I have a vow to make, Warden Rainn. Today is *not* the day my life will end. I will survive this trial," I promise through gritted teeth. "I'll survive this, and you'll no longer be held to the promise you made to me."

"Mercy—"

"We're not going to save this place; there's no redemption for the vileness of these men. We're going to destroy it. You and I are going to burn Ember Glen to the ground."

chapter thirty
ARLO

MERCY SCREAMS, AND the power of it makes the mountains tremble. The image of her stuns me. Sheathed in red with her mouth dropped open wide, the dark sweep of eye shadow across her lids and the thick black liner, which frames her ethereal silver-blue eyes, makes her appear otherworldly, like a furious fallen angel shouting her disgust of the way the world has turned.

She leans forward to project her anger. Her fists are clenched as she powerfully slams them down at her sides, and I swear I feel the ground shift beneath my feet, as though the force of her fury shot out from her fists and punched through the earth.

Watching her lose herself in this moment is horrifying, troubling, yet inspiring. Her rage is a thing of beauty.

All I can manage to do is stare at her when she moves in front of me. "We're going to destroy it. You and I are going to burn Ember Glen to the ground."

I know I can't kiss her, but oh, how I want to. The strength she found in the blink of an eye—horrified one moment and coldly determined the next—has my heart beating wildly, making the ache in my chest that's existed all day feel more profound.

I can't speak.

I'm so in awe of her that I'm lost in her stare, so humbled by her power that my words refuse to share space with hers. Slowly, I nod, telling her with my eyes that *yes*, she will survive this, and *yes*, we will burn it all to the ground.

We'll do it together.

I won't have to do it alone because she's not going to die.

She can't die today.

"Wesley, let's get started," Killian calls from across the clearing, and Wesley moves, walking out of the forest and into the open space beyond.

I grab hold of Mercy's shoulders as she fumes with fury, her shallow breaths rapidly lifting and lowering her chest. Mercy and I share a final look—a beat of acknowledgment that we suffer the same anger, that we both want the same war. There's a child standing out there at the edge of a cliff, his life threatened for the sake of asserting our power over sinners.

No, they aren't sinners.

Mercy didn't sin.

It's for the sake of asserting our power over *women*.

I tell her silently that I'm with her, yet I turn her to face the clearing and nudge her forward to her potential death.

I can't stop these events in motion.

I can't spare her from this trial.

But I know she'll fight hard for each and every breath; she'll fight harder than I ever could to survive this, because her work in this life is not done yet. The people of Ember Glen need her…

I need her.

Wesley stops about halfway between the tree line and the cliff's edge, turning to face us as we move among the trees. He rubs his palms together, blowing a huff of breath between them to generate heat. "Wardens, please bring your trial participants forward."

I loosen my grip on Mercy's shoulders and move to walk beside her, lowering one hand to the center of her back to urge her forward as we move between the trees. She marches gracefully, powerfully toward the clearing, her anger carrying her toward the danger faced by the innocent ones standing at the ledge.

She vibrates with the hum of willing sacrifice—a low, eerie sound that ripples through me and tells of her willingness to face death for the lives of those being threatened.

The lives of innocent women and children.

Wind whirls around us as we step from the tree line, coming to a stop before Wesley in the center of the clearing, where he readies himself to begin the trial with the incitement and prayer.

We wait for Delle and Theo to come and stand beside us, and the waiting is dreadful. It takes them minutes, which pass with excruciating slowness. Delle cries and protests the start of her trial. It's not just the cold that makes me shiver, but the sound of her fear, her misery, her distress. It's the tension from Mercy at my side as she fights to ignore Delle's pain that makes it even worse.

Gradually, Delle calms. It happens so evenly that it's almost like she's falling asleep. When Theo is finally able to bring her to stand beside us, I glance over and notice that Delle is loosening, relaxing, almost in a way that seems…artificially forced.

I look over at Mercy and find her eyes on Delle. She looks relieved at

Delle's state as she seems to calm, loosely hanging onto Theo's arm. Mercy sighs before she looks at me, telling me without words what she did, and that she's not sorry that she gave Delle the little white pill.

Though I had grappled with the choice, I wasn't able to bring myself to give the only pill to Delle. In hindsight, I probably should have. Mercy seems to have found some peace in her fury, though Delle found none on her own, and I should have anticipated that. Without thinking of it consciously, maybe I knew deep down that Mercy wouldn't have kept the only pill for herself when she was able to give it to Delle. She sacrifices daily for the benefit of others.

"October twenty-seventh, twenty-one eighty-five," Wesley begins, lifting his chin as if he's speaking to the treetops, where I assume at least one camera is placed. "We gather on this day to bear witness to Service by Sacrifice, the second of the three Trials of Dissension for sinners Mercy Madness and Delle Carter of Ember Glen. We welcome all who belong to the community of Ember Glen to bear witness to this trial, such that it brings awareness to the hardships that await those who sin.

"It has been decided by the authority of Ember Glen that this trial shall be conducted in a means representative of the severity of the sins committed. This community cannot thrive without our nights of purging beneath the full moon, and our servants must be committed to making the ultimate sacrifice in God's name, such that our community will remain a safe place for all. Mercy Madness chose to flee death, and as a result, one of her sisters in service lost her life."

Who does he mean…Ivy Jane?

Hyatt would have set a servant on fire that night whether Mercy had fled or not. It's taken me a long time to see this, but I understand it now…It wasn't Mercy's choice to flee that resulted in Ivy Jane's death; it was Hyatt's choice to set her on fire that ended her life. Hyatt alone is responsible.

"Delle Carter teeters on the brink of corruption. She chose to participate freely in these Trials of Dissension when she was under no such obligation, even though she, too, fled during a night of service. Though we hold hope that she'll find absolution through these trials, her actions must also be met with consequences representative of the severity of her sins."

Wesley pauses, adding tension to the moment as we wait to hear exactly what this trial will entail, as the wind whips around us all, making hair and skirts dance sidelong to the current of air.

"This Service by Sacrifice will be achieved through the live burial of each of our trial participants."

"What?" Mercy snaps.

"No, I can't—" Delle starts, but Theo silences her.

I don't look at Mercy, I can't. If I look at her right now, I'll fall apart entirely. She needs me strong. She needs to see me strong so she can find her own strength in this.

Buried alive?

How long can someone survive being buried alive?

Our training was pointless. She doesn't need to hold her breath...she'll slowly suffocate.

Fuck.

Fuck!

I falter, my head dropping low as I take in a trembling breath. I struggle to lift it again, but I do. Pulling back my shoulders, my pointed gaze rests firmly on Wesley.

"In a symbolic gesture, the participants will volunteer to sacrifice their own life to save the lives of two others. Standing behind me are Ellary Hill, Cambria Miller, Juniper Holly, and Adam Carter, the dearly beloved of our trial participants. We've brought them here to stand on the precipice of death, a touch away from toppling over the edge. We put their lives in the hands of our trial participants today."

Wesley looks between Mercy and Delle. "Participants, you each have a choice, and it is yours to make freely. Your first option is to walk to your grave, climb into your coffin, and close the lid. If you make that choice, your coffin will be lowered into the ground, and you will be buried alive. You'll remain inside for an amount of time to be drawn at random. When that time has expired, you'll be exhumed, which may or may not be before you suffocate and die. If you choose this, the lives of your beloved will be spared. The moment the lid of your coffin is closed, their hands will be untied and they'll be sent home, unharmed.

"Your second option is to spare yourself. Walk to the edge and stand before your loved ones. Tell them you choose your life over theirs, and then you must push them over the edge. Perhaps the fall will kill them, perhaps it won't. But that's certainly something to consider in making your choice. Could you stand before them if they survived and look them in the eye, satisfied with the choice you made?

"Both options involve facing the uncertainty of death. Either choice is a sacrifice...for others or for yourself."

There's no choice in this and they know it. Even if Mercy or Delle were cruel enough to push their friends over the edge to save themselves, what would happen then? It wouldn't be enough to pass the trial, which by the very definition, requires the sacrifice of *oneself* in the service of *others*. It's intentional by design. Mercy and Delle have no choice; they must climb into their coffins and allow my brothers to bury them alive.

My stomach lurches and I fight the urge to double over as nausea takes hold of me.

"Arlo Rainn and Theo Hughes, as the selected wardens of these trial participants, please present them for this Service by Sacrifice."

A full body shiver moves through me, rattling my nerves and shaking away my strength.

How do I do this?

Just as I begin to fear losing myself—just as my knees weaken and threaten to give way, bringing me to kneel in sorrow—Mercy's voice cuts through the madness of it all, and her enigmatic strength helps me find mine.

"I present *myself*," she grits. "I will sacrifice myself for every woman and child standing in this clearing. I will sacrifice myself for all of Ember Glen." We each turn our heads to look at each other at the same time. "Take me to my grave, Warden Rainn. I'm done with this. I won't allow the fear of those innocent people standing at the edge to be prolonged any further."

She holds my gaze for beats longer than I should allow, but I'm stuck there in her gaze, in the knowing that she is something so much more than I ever expected her to be. And though I feel like my insides are melting—like my organs are liquefying and creeping slowly through the cage of my bones to drip toward the earth—something in her eyes gives me the strength I need to speak. To say my rehearsed part and move forward through this nightmare…

The only way out is through.

"I present—" I falter, then pause, clear my throat, and begin again, "I present Mercy Madness for the second of these three Trials of Dissension. Mercy, do you enter this trial with the understanding of your sins and the means by which you are required to serve?"

"Yes," she replies, with no hesitation, no fear…only fury.

Theo speaks, but his voice is weak, sad, and broken. "I present Delle Carter for the second of these three Trials of Dissension. Delle, do you enter this trial with the understanding of your sins and the means by which you are required to serve?"

"Okay. Yes," she murmurs softly, though it's hard to hear her with the whipping wind rushing through the empty space beyond the cliff's edge.

It's the medication that calms her, that makes her more complacent. It seems to be taking hold of her much more quickly and stronger than it had with Mercy, and I fear for a moment that maybe it's because her body hasn't matured enough to handle it, that maybe she can't withstand the strength of it, and it will do damage.

But what does it matter when she's about to step into her own coffin? Fuck.

I hope it's strong enough to give her courage, to keep her relaxed, to bring her into a quick sleep so she doesn't suffer.

No.

They're not going to die.

They're strong; they will survive this.

"Let us share a prayer before we begin," Wesley says, and I sharply turn my head to watch as he bows his head. "Our celestial creator and divine spirit, we come to You in this hour of trials and tribulations, seeking good favor in honor of our righteous choices. We bring these sinners before You, offering the sacrifice of their service in honor of the Impulse Edict, to the sanctity of Your divine word. We ask for Your righteous judgment of the souls of these sinners. Should they serve appropriately through these trials and prove themselves to be truly sacrificial servants, we ask for absolution of their wretched souls. Should these sinners choose selfishly, we ask for You to grant the innocent ones with quick and peaceful passages into the afterlife such that You may welcome them with Your eternal grace."

The boy, Delle's brother Adam, begins to cry, and the echo of it carries through the void beyond the cliff to echo against the mountains in the distance. "I'm scared," he whimpers.

"No." The single syllable from Delle is strained, crawling out of her throat along with the sob she tries to subdue. "Don't cry, love. Don't cry. I won't let anyone hurt you." Her head twists and rises to look up at Theo. "Take me to the coffin. I'll get in." She looks back to Wesley, who still has his head bowed through the unfinished prayer. "Bring him away from the edge...Please..."

Wesley continues, "Please grant me and my brothers of the Control the strength and peace of mind to carry out this trial with the uncertainty of whether lives will be lost today, such that we may present these sinners with a fair and exhaustive trial for their souls. *Malo mori quam foedari.*"

"*Malo mori quam foedari,*" I hear my brothers repeat, but I don't hear the words come from my mouth...I don't think I hear them come from Theo, either.

Wesley lifts his head and looks at Delle. "Delle Carter, we've selected you to choose first." Strangely, Wesley seems to falter, shifting his eyes away for a fraction of a second, his throat bobbing as he swallows hard, before digging deep and bringing his gaze back to Delle. "Tell us of your choice. In this trial of Service by Sacrifice, do you choose to sacrifice yourself or do you choose to sacrifice the lives of your innocent loved ones?"

"Myself..." Delle whispers. "I choose to sacrifice myself."

"Very well." Wesley turns, holding out his hand as Ryker approaches, carrying a small black fabric bag. He hands it to Wesley, who tugs the drawstring to open it before holding it out to Delle. "There are ten pieces of parchment inside this bag, each with a different duration for your live burial before you are exhumed. Reach inside and draw your time."

I look away, gazing out into the distance at the gray backdrop of this living nightmare. I don't want to watch as Delle reaches inside that bag. I hold my breath to hear how long she'll be buried beneath the earth, trapped in her own grave, slowly suffocating. I hear her hand rustle through the pieces of parchment in the bag, and my gaze is drawn back to Wesley as she hands her selected page to him.

Slowly, he unfolds the small piece and reads aloud, "You've selected one hour."

He turns the page around to show us in confirmation, and my chest sinks with relief. Delle could survive an hour, especially with the medication to keep her calmer than I know she would've been without it. The relief I feel is visceral, but the nightmare isn't over yet.

Wesley looks at Mercy. "Mercy Madness, tell us of your choice. In this trial of Service by Sacrifice, do you choose to sacrifice yourself or do you choose to sacrifice the lives of your innocent beloved ones?"

"Myself," she fumes.

"Very well," Wesley replies, holding out the bag to her. "Reach inside and draw your time."

She doesn't hesitate and she doesn't take her time. With rushed and forceful movement, she reaches into the bag and quickly selects a piece of parchment, handing it to Wesley. He unfolds it and reads, and it happens so quickly, that I'm not sure whether I heard him correctly at first. But when he turns the page around to show us, my eyes confirm the truth.

Four hours.

Four hours, in a coffin, buried beneath the soil.

My brain stutters, stalling as it tries to wrap around that measure of time and whether there would be enough oxygen buried with her in that coffin to last for four hours...and truthfully, I don't know.

I don't know if she'll survive.

Voices speak around me, but I can't hear what they're saying. They all blend with the wind circling around us as faded echoes, whispers of spoken sounds without discernible words. The sound fades into an empty howl behind my ears. Space and time warp, stretching me apart into oblivion, making everything appear as though it's happening in slow-motion.

I'm unaware of how Mercy's arm has come to be linked with mine, how I've managed to unconsciously put one foot in front of the other, how the distance is closing rapidly between us and the two graves nestled in the trees.

At some point, we stop moving, and I'm still lost to the dull roar created by every sound in existence blending into one. It obscures the world in such a way that Mercy has to turn to face me, move into my space, and dig her fingernails into my bicep just to get my attention.

My eyes shift through the haze to find her giving me a stern look, but the moment I meet her eyes, the world harshly falls into focus. Sounds separate, my vision sharpens, and emotions flood my veins from my rapidly beating heart.

"Do you hear me?" she snaps, her eyes narrowed on me.

My head tilts in confusion because I hadn't heard a word.

"Mercy, I can't—"

"You can, and you will. The moment I'm inside, you will close the lid, lower that damn coffin, and bury me yourself. I will *not* allow you to let my friends die because you're too weak to do your duty."

"If wanting you to live makes me weak, then I am the weakest man who has ever walked this earth." I have no conscious thought of my words—they simply slip out.

Her eyes remain narrowed on me, but the harsh line of her eyebrows twists and softens. "This must be done, Warden Rainn. It must. And you have to ensure it. If I'm not buried, they will kill Ellary and Cambria. You know they will, even if I refuse to push them myself. You have to do this." Mercy's nails dig deeper into my flesh, and I savor the pain of it. If it's the last touch we ever share, I'll revel in the pain of it forever.

But suddenly, the beautiful ache is gone. Her hand has fallen away, and she no longer stands in front of me. She moves to her grave, and as I watch her walk, I have no awareness of anything else happening around me. I'm frozen in time as I watch her reach to lift the lid of her coffin. I'm stuck in place as the layers of her red gown shift and move, as she lifts her leg over the side of the coffin and climbs to stand inside it.

My chin lifts to look up at her eyes, finding her face etched with a myriad of expressions all at once. She straightens, pulling her shoulders back to stand tall and proud as she faces the clearing.

"I sacrifice myself for all the women in Ember Glen," she shouts, and the world around us falls silent. There's no roaring wind, no rustling leaves, no voices or footsteps…only silence and the piercing sound of Mercy's powerful voice. "I sacrifice myself in the name of all things deemed unholy. I sacrifice myself as a willing catalyst for *war*." Her jaw sets and she grits her teeth, spitting the last words with fury. "May the women of Ember Glen cut out the heart of every hateful man and deliver his soul to demons…And may those demons show no mercy in delivering their penance for our suffering."

She lowers. She sits. She closes her eyes.

"Warden Rainn," she calls out to me as she starts to lay back, "do your duty. Shut me in and bury me. Let it be done."

I suddenly find myself at her side, not knowing when I moved or how I got here. I lean over to see her laying in her coffin, her eyes squeezed shut, her black-painted lids appearing as eyeless voids. Her red dress takes up so much space in the coffin—space that oxygen might have filled.

Red.

The color of her sacrifice…

The time for it has arrived.

"Please," she whispers, as if she can sense how near my presence is without looking. "Before I lose my nerve, shut the lid, Warden Rainn. Shut the fucking lid…" her voice trembles, "and make sure they're all okay."

This woman, this warrior, this goddess or mystical being…Whatever she is, I'm in awe of her, bound to her, tethered to her for eternity. She gives her life so others may live. And her speech—her incitement of *war*, her declaration of her willingness to die in hopes it will spur others to rebel in the name of their freedom to live as they wish—gave me strength. It gave me power. It gave me the determination I needed to fight through this moment of true horror with my eyes set on the future and what must be done.

Rebellion.

An uprising.

An unholy war.

I will lead that war in her honor if she can't lead it herself.

She will *lead it herself.*

She'll survive this.

I reach over her to grip the lid, the leather of my glove creaking as I fold my hand around the edge. Then, I bend, dipping close enough to whisper, "Steady breaths. Don't panic. Be still."

"Arlo." Her eyes twitch to open but she fights it, and I imagine it's because she knows as well as I do that if our gazes meet, fear and sorrow will grip us both. She slowly lets out a breath, relaxing her features, trying to bring herself to calmness before she whispers, "Wildflowers and starlight."

My pulse speeds, racing through my veins with equal parts anguish and elation.

The last words are for me.

Her last thought is of me.

It's humbling and gut-wrenching, and the only thing I can do to survive this is to act.

I tug on the lid, preparing to lower it swiftly, but before I do, I tell her what she needs to hear in plain and simple terms—no holding back, no secret phrases or substitutions of words to hide their meaning from others.

"I love you, Mercy Madness," I whisper. "I love everything you were, everything you are, and everything you will become when you survive this. And you *will* survive this. You and I have a rebellion to lead."

A strained smile tugs at the corners of her lips, and that's it. That has to be enough. I open my hand to drop the lid, and it slams shut with a thump that bounces off the trees and echoes into the clearing. I step back, moving quickly to the head of her coffin, and press the button at the side of the platform. The mechanism whirs as the coffin begins to lower.

I have to hold the button down to keep it running, and my hand trembles with the urge to let go, but I can't. The moment that lid closed was the moment I trapped her with all the oxygen she'll get to take with her into her grave. The sooner she's buried, the sooner her time will start, and the more likely she'll be to survive.

She'll survive.

She'll fucking survive.

I lift my head and look out into the clearing, needing to focus on something other than the whir of the machine that sinks my Mercy—my love, my wildflowers and starlight—into the earth. I can't look as I force her descent into her grave.

I look at Delle's loved ones at the edge of the cliff, watching as Ryker unties their hands. Her brother Adam runs for the trees the moment his hands are freed. If they're being freed, then it means Delle's coffin is closed, but I can't bring myself to look over. If I see that Theo's expression mirrors my agony, it might just break me.

I watch Killian carefully as he moves, first untying Cambria's hands. She steps away from the edge and waits for Ellary, turning to watch as Killian moves in front of her. I assume he's untying Ellary's hands, but the way he stands blocks my view of what's happening between them.

It's why confusion washes over me when Cambria screams, "No!" and lurches forward.

Abruptly, Killian whirls around and looks at me, but my eyes are quickly drawn away. I can only sense the curling of his lips in a vicious smile because all I can see is the widening of Ellary's eyes—the moment of panic in her expression—as she tilts backward, black boots teetering on the edge as she fights to maintain her balance and step forward.

Mercy's coffin lands at the bottom of her grave.
The whirring stops as the machine cuts off.
And I watch helplessly as Ellary falls.

— end of book two —

acknowledgments

I have completely fallen in love with Mercy and Arlo's story, and I feel so grateful that I'm able to tell it. Though writing is a solitary process, I wouldn't have the time, energy, confidence, or perseverance to put words on the page without some amazing people who—for some unknown reason—want to see me succeed.

Chris, your patience and encouragement keep me going. Every time I think about giving up, you remind me why I started writing the words in the first place. I literally couldn't do this without you. *Wildflowers and starlight.*

To the woman who took a chance on reading a debut novel from someone she'd never heard of before and ended up becoming an incredible friend, consistent supporter, die-hard fan, and personal assistant, thank you for being you, Danielle! I've told you before, but I'll tell you again, I might have given up on this long ago if it weren't for you, and I'm so grateful that you keep me going. You really are the best!

I have the most amazing beta readers! You lovely ladies cheer me on, give me life, help me find and fix my mistakes, and just generally make me a better writer. You're also amazing people, and I'm so glad we connected through my stories. Danielle, Mary, Echo, Brandy, and Amanda, you are incredible. I can't thank you enough for the countless hours spent reading my chapters that I send to you in agonizing bits and pieces with terrible cliffhangers. I appreciate you so, so much!

I'm so grateful for my Street and ARC team and for everyone who has read, reviewed, or posted about this series. Seriously, *thank you*. I don't know if you understand how much you mean to me for taking the time to read this story and share your thoughts about it. Truly, I appreciate you more than I can say!

Najla, Nada, and the team at Qamber Designs, thank you so much for making my book look beautiful! I adore your team and the work you do is always spectacular. I can always count on you to create gorgeous covers and stunning interior design for my stories. You all are amazing!

Silvia. Let's chat for a minute about how awesome you are. Not only do you somehow manage to make my words sparkle and shine, but you put up with my crazy schedule when this book got the best of me. Your flexibility was literally my saving grace as I fought through writing this book. Thank you so much for making my words the best they can be!

My final thank you goes directly to you, reader. You picked up this book, you read the words I wrote, and for that alone, I am grateful. If you connected with the characters or the story and enjoyed this read, just know that you and I have met through these words, and I'm forever thankful you took the journey with me.

embers of mercy

EMBER GLEN | BOOK THREE

BRYNN FORD

playlist

Stream on Spotify
bit.ly/spotify-brynnford

Landmines by BELLSAINT
Born To Die by Euphoria ft. Bolshiee
Detached from Reality by MEJKO ft. Arkane Skye
Where the Lonely Ones Roam by Digital Daggers
Reaper by Glaceo & RIELL
The Calling (EPIX Remix) by The Rigs
Breathe by Parah Dice & Brianna
Marble by Neptunica & Shockz & Rebecca Helena
Lover. Fighter. by SVRCINA
MIDDLE OF THE NIGHT by Elley Duhé
Unstoppable by Sia
Where We Rise by Neoni
Royalty by Egzod & Maestro Chives ft. Neoni
Ember by Katherine McNamara
Alpha by Little Destroyer

For all the women who are struggling to rise…
Dig deep, have faith in yourself,
and begin with a single step.

chapter one

ARLO

I'M STUNNED, PARALYZED, rooted to the spot.

A whip of black lace from Ellary Hill's skirt catches on the wind before following her down into the abyss, dropping into the empty space beyond the cliff's edge. Her sudden descent is silent—no scream escapes her—and I'm horror-struck.

A stunned beat of silence passes.

My soul has sprouted deep roots that snake into the earth beside Mercy's grave, keeping me motionless despite the horror unfolding before my eyes. My heart, which I tore from my own chest and gave her freely, is trapped in the coffin with her, resting at the bottom of a hole dug six feet deep. But when Cambria screams, breaking through the eerie silence, the rest of my consciousness leaves my heart and soul behind.

We all feel the collective pull, as though Ellary's fall drags us all down with her. My brothers and I run to save the servant who's already fallen, already gone. Cambria runs for the edge, but Killian grabs her wrist and snaps her backward into his hold.

Wesley is the first to reach the edge, but his focus is set on Killian. Coming up behind him, Wesley grabs Killian's shoulders with a firm grip and jerks him back so hard he stumbles. Killian loses his grip on Cambria as he whirls to face Wesley, whose face is tense with rage. The moment she's released, Cambria runs for the edge in a panic.

I sprint ahead, skidding toward the edge, barely stopping in time as I lasso an arm around her waist and tug her back. In her frenzy, she nearly met the same fate as her friend. I stumble backward as I drag her, drop my weight to sit, and pull her down with me to anchor her to the solid ground.

She turns her head back to look at me with dark, teary eyes. "He pushed her…he pushed her…"

"What the fuck did you do?" Wesley's voice echoes, calling for our attention. I glance over to see him stepping up to Killian, grabbing his jacket collar, and jerking him closer.

Killian slaps Wesley's hands away as Owen approaches, coming in close. "*Shut up*, both of you. Everything is being streamed to the village right now."

"There's a ledge!" Theo calls out from where he carefully leans out, looking down. He glances back at us. "She's there, I can see her!"

I release Cambria and scramble to my feet, quickly telling her to stay put, then rush to join Theo's side. Cambria ignores my demand, and I see her moving from the corner of my eye, but she's down on all fours, crawling slowly, so I'm not as fearful she'll accidentally leap to her death to chase after her friend. While I lean out to look over the edge, she flattens to her belly, creeping forward to do the same. We wait and watch as the rolling fog clouds over everything, then gradually clears.

At first, all I can see is the gray rock forming the ledge Theo spotted, maybe twenty or thirty feet below. But then a gust of wind blows, pushing the clouds and revealing a morbid palette of black and red splatters against the gray rock canvas. Ellary's black skirt whips against her unmoving limbs, waving over the blood spilling from beneath her lifeless body.

Lifeless?

Is she dead?

"Ellary…" Cambria's voice has turned calm against the chaos. "How do we get down there? You have rope?"

I feel her looking up at me, but my gaze is fixed on Ellary's chest, watching it closely, hoping to see a rise and fall. Ellary is so still, flattened against that rock, and her left arm is twisted at an odd angle as the bloody pool beneath her steadily grows.

Truthfully, I don't know if she's alive or dead.

I don't know if this kind of fall is survivable.

Seeing her laying there is grotesque—an image that will no doubt haunt my dreams—yet I stare all the same. I suffer the image to fix my gaze on her chest, to watch for a sign that her lungs still draw breath.

"You must have rope with you," Cambria says again, pressing her palms to the ground and pushing to her feet. "Tie it to my waist."

"What?" I look over at her.

"Tie your rope to my waist and lower me."

My brow furrows, and I shake my head at her before wrapping my palm around her wrist. I turn—dragging her away with me—and stalk away from the ledge to where my brothers have gathered in an ever-shifting cluster of pandemonium.

Wesley shouts at Killian.

Ryker shouts at Wesley.

Killian goads them both.

Ryker lunges at Wesley, and Owen grabs him by the back of his shirt to stop him.

"That's *enough*. Start filling the graves," Owen commands as he shoves Ryker. "Wesley. Wesley!" He waits for Wesley to tear himself from the argument with Killian to face him. "We need you to make a statement. Get control of the situation, assure the village that Ellary's fine, and that the trial will go on as planned."

"But Ellary's not *fine*." My tone is clipped, harsh. "Let's end the trial. Mercy and Delle made their choice; they made their sacrifice, and a beloved servant fell off a cliff on *our* watch. That's enough death for one damn day."

"She's not *dead!*" Cambria jerks against my hold, and I tighten my grip around her wrist. "She landed on a ledge! She might be…she could be okay…"

"Did you see her?" Owen asks me.

I nod. "I can see her. It doesn't look good. I don't know if she's alive or—"

"Okay," Owen huffs, raking a hand through his hair. "We'll see if we can figure out how to get to her. If anyone can figure out how to rig something up, it's you."

"I told him to tie rope around my waist and lower me." Cambria's voice rises desperately. "I'll do it. I'll go over the edge for her."

My grip on her wrist tightens in frustration. I'll leap over the edge myself before I let Mercy lose both of her best friends on my watch. I need Mercy more than I've ever needed anyone in my life, and though I know she needs me too, I also know she needs them more.

"I'll go," I volunteer.

My adrenaline is already spiked, and I need a distraction from the dull thud of each shovelful of dirt that lands on the coffin. Ryker is quickly shoveling in soil from the mound behind Delle's grave, and the sound echoes through my mind. I already know it's a sound that will haunt me for eternity—it's a sound that calls to me, begs me to act, to make it stop.

I can't make it stop.

I want to. I need to. But I can't.

Mercy Madness is a symbol for change, a martyr for her cause, a catalyst for rebellion, and the greatest dishonor I could do her is sully my own name in trying to free her from her coffin. It wouldn't serve either of us. The Control would only take me under arrest and bury her again, and then I'd be powerless to help her when she survives this.

Because she will survive this.

She has to survive this.

"Let me go to her." Cambria's voice softens as sorrow and sadness drag tears from her eyes. "Please, she needs me." She tugs against my grip, but it's weak and she breaks into sobs. "She's all I have…Ellary and Mercy are all I have."

"All you have?" Killian snaps, tearing himself away from Wesley. He pushes between me and Owen, then charges toward Cambria.

She flinches, but she stands her ground, like a good servant would. She knows that retreat would ultimately get her thrown into a coffin and buried alive like Mercy. *For God's sake.* I tug, pulling her into my side as Killian moves to loom above her.

"How *dare* you say in my presence that she and *Mercy* are all you have? How *dare* you speak of that vile sinner so fondly?" He wears a disgusted scowl, a look of betrayal as he spits his words at her with fury. "What has she ever done for you besides bring you torment? What has she done besides disappoint, hurt, and abandon you and her sisters in her sins?"

"I don't…" Cambria stammers, averting her eyes and shaking her head. "I'm sorry."

What is she sorry for?

I release her arm and raise my hand to Killian's chest as anger greets me, slipping between them as I push him back.

"She owes you no explanations or apologies. She just stood on the edge of a cliff to serve as a potential sacrifice and watched her friend fall." I feel my lips snarl with the building rage, and my voice lowers to a gritty growl. "You pushed her over the edge, Killian Cole. I know you did."

I stare him down, eye to eye, expecting to see something, anything that would confirm my suspicion—the shadow of guilt flicker across his brown eyes, the twitch of his jaw, perhaps the bob of his throat as he swallows nervously. Yet I see nothing, no sign of weakness or faltering.

Instead, the side of his mouth lifts in a self-righteous smirk, and he simply says, "Prove it."

In my mind, I grab him by the collar, shove him back to the edge, and push until he falls. I used to see him as my brother in God, my equal, a powerful leader in our community.

And now…all I see is the truth.

I see a demon standing in front of me—if such a thing even truly exists. The demons I once so stupidly believed to possess my Mercy were never within her. Nothing vile or evil could ever exist within that perfect woman's soul.

The evil is within *us*—the Control, the men of Ember Glen. We are the evil that made these women kneel and serve. We are the demons who whispered threats in their ears, who denounced them in their unwillingness to serve our every manic impulse. No man could serve these women in the way they've so dutifully served our vileness. We threaten them—*manipulate* them—into believing what we tell them to, and they pay the price for our sins again and again.

Mercy's strength, her power, her hard-won love broke me. She broke the part of me that believed the dark lies, and with her brightness, she brought light on the truth.

For all she's done for my soul, I will not let this overwhelming urge to end Killian overcome me. It wouldn't serve her if I lost myself now. I cannot let her suffer for my mistakes in vain. I made her promises, and I intend to keep them.

"It will be proven, I assure you." I return his challenging smirk with one of my own. "The footage that's livestreaming to the villagers at this very moment will tell us all we need to know."

He tilts his head to the side. "Will it?" He takes a small step closer and lowers his voice. "Are you so certain the cameras are angled appropriately to show what you *think* happened?"

"Are you so certain they aren't?"

A tense silence lingers through a beat, a quiet transference of understanding that he and I are no longer brothers in God.

His grin gradually widens, then he claps his hand against my shoulder. "I suppose we'll find out, won't we, *brother*?" He nudges me sideways as he moves around me, taking hold of Cambria's wrist and dragging her toward the forest. "I'm taking her back to the village so she doesn't get any bright ideas, like hurling herself over the edge to save Ellary."

"Are we letting him get away with this?" Wesley nearly shouts, glancing around at us in search of support. "He *pushed* her!"

"He did," I agree. "I know he did. We need to—"

"What we *need* to do is complete the trial," Owen demands. "It's our duty, and it *must* be finished. Whatever Killian did or didn't do will be judged later. This is our job...our *duty*. Let him go and let's finish our work here. We'll deal with him later."

"Deal with him later?" Wesley scoffs, brow furrowed over his dark eyes and indignant expression.

Owen sighs, finding a gentler tone. "We'll bring Killian in front of the Elders, review the footage, and cast our judgments, but it will have to be done later." He steps closer to Wesley, placing his hands on his shoulders in camaraderie. "I promise, Wesley, we will evaluate the circumstances together after this day is done. When our minds are clear and capable of seeing the truth. Decisions should not be made in rage, such as the state you're in right now."

"Stop!" A small, but mighty, voice carries in the quiet, and we all turn to see Adam, Delle's younger brother, standing beside her grave. "Stop it!" he yells at Ryker. "My sister's in there!"

Theo turns and runs full speed toward the grave while Ryker continues shoveling soil onto Delle's coffin, unaffected by the horror of the child's cries just feet away from him.

"Get back!" Theo shouts at Adam as he closes the distance.

The child bends his knees, leaning forward with intent. That's when we all move, running after him as we shout our protests. But none of us reach him before he jumps, disappearing into Delle's grave.

Theo gets there first, hopping in without hesitation. Ryker pauses his shoveling with an annoyed huff, as if this is a mere disruption to his work and not a terribly traumatic scene.

I slam to a stop beside the grave. Beneath my feet, Theo struggles to get a hold of Adam as he fights for his sister. Theo's feet slip out from under him, and he falls backward on his ass. He's down just long enough for Adam to move away, his small hands searching along the edge of Delle's coffin.

He finds the lid, and his fingers curl to lift it, raising it a mere inch before Theo rises, slaps his hand against the top of the lid, and slams it shut before wrapping his arms around Adam's waist.

"No!" Adam cries out.

But his voice isn't loud enough to drown out the sound of Delle's harrowing cries from within her coffin. "Stop! Adam, stop! Please, just go!"

Air catches in my lungs, a swell of swirling, twisted emotions filling every empty space within me, and it aches. I fall to my knees, desperate to pull this child from the grave, and spare him and Delle both from further heartache.

"Here," I call for Theo's attention, reaching a hand down.

Theo twists him around and lifts him to meet me. I grab hold of him and drag him up. He struggles so much that he knocks me sideways onto my hip, falling with me into my arms. I tighten my grip, though he fights. I feel sick subduing this innocent child, stopping him from saving his sister.

This child's pain burns hot enough to melt my heart. Though my hold on him is firm, my touch softens. I cradle his head in my palm, stroking to soothe him as a mother would her child.

"She'll be okay," I whisper. "Delle will be okay."

He continues to fight me for what feels like hours—though I know it's only moments that have passed—before I feel him being tugged away from me. Theo kneels beside me, his face and fine clothes covered in soil, and plucks Adam from my arms, forcing him upright. He grabs his face, forcing him to meet his eyes.

"You cannot save her," Theo says firmly. "You cannot stop this, Adam. It must be done. Do you hear me?"

"I'm scared!" Adam cries out. "*She's* scared! Don't hurt her!"

"She chose this." Theo's stern eyes flicker with dissonance, flitting away from him for a moment before he steadies his gaze again. "Delle chose to sacrifice for you because she loves you. And if you love her, you will let her do what she must in your honor."

"No!" Adam stills, but cries.

We can hear the muffled cries of Delle's tears, of her demands for us to, "Take him away…take him away from here!" coming from behind her closed coffin lid.

"Go," I tell Theo, then scramble to my feet. "Take him back to the village, and make sure he remains until Delle comes back."

I'm urgent to move away from these graves, from Delle's cries. My ears strain against my will to listen for Mercy's cries, drawn into concern for the fact that I don't hear them at all. I don't hear her cries or her voice. I have no idea if she can hear what's going on outside her coffin, though I think she must. If Delle can hear it, if she can hear her brother's cries, then so can Mercy.

What must she be thinking?

Is she horrified?

Fearful?

Lost in panic?

"I can't." Theo's alarmed gaze meets mine. "I can't take him. I need to be here for Delle. I have to be. Because I'm her warden," he adds the last sentence in a way that makes it feel like an afterthought.

I move in front of him, Adam crying between us. "*Go.* Take him for Delle's sake. He shouldn't be here; he should never have been here. She cannot endure her trial if she knows he remains."

His gaze shifts around the clearing as he lowers his voice. "I-I can't leave her, Arlo."

I flash back to the first trial, when it was time for me to leave Mercy behind to endure my brothers without me. I'd been on the verge of losing control, ready to attack Killian as he turned a knife on her and threatened to push its handle inside her. I would have laid hands on him. I would have hurt him, and in turn, it would only have hurt Mercy more. They would've taken me away from her then, and she would've been alone. She would've had to endure her remaining trials and all the days between without me.

But that didn't happen.

It didn't happen because Theo knew what I was fighting.

He grabbed me and forced me away.

He saved me.

He saved *her.*

And I owe him the same now.

I gently grip one of Adam's small shoulders with one hand, gripping Theo's shoulder in the other. I force them both to turn away from Delle's grave, and I urge them ahead.

"Take him back," I demand as I push them away, leading Adam to move in front of Theo. "Walk, and don't look back."

Theo grips Adam by the shoulders, and I put a hand on Theo's back, pushing them along until we reach the hidden path from which we emerged from the forest.

At the top of the path, Theo turns to look at me. "I promised Delle—"

"You promised you would help her. It's your duty as her warden. And this is the only way you can help her right now."

His eyes skip past my shoulder, peering beyond me toward the graves as though Delle might emerge at any moment.

"I will not let anything happen to her," I assure him with a steady voice. "I will dig her up myself and ensure she returns to the Homestead, alive and well. I promise, Theo. Now go."

He nods slowly as he finds his resolve in my reassurance. With a strained intake of breath, he reaches to take Adam's hand and drags him away, disappearing down the path where Killian and Cambria have already fled.

When I turn back, I find that Wesley stands once again in the clearing, facing the tree line, speaking through his barely controlled anger, delivering a message through the broadcast as Owen urges him to continue from a few feet away.

"…a full investigation into the leadership of the Control and the Elders. We urge your calm and patience in the meantime. A memorial honoring the sacrifice of Ellary Hill will be arranged and held before the next full moon."

Memorial?

We don't know whether she's alive or dead yet!

"We will now be ending the livestream here at the cliff's edge to allow privacy in our..." he hesitates, glancing down at his hands as he rubs his palms together, "privacy in our retrieval of the honored servant, Ellary Hill. We will now switch over to livestream the remainder of this trial at the burial site of Delle Carter and Mercy Madness. Their time begins as soon as their graves are filled." He clears his throat. "*Malo mori quam foedari.*"

The moment he finishes speaking, Wesley stomps off toward the tree line. He bends to pick up a shovel near the graves with an angry huff, then scoops from the pile behind Mercy's grave and tosses it into the hole.

Mercy.

Sweet Mercy...what have we done to you?

My legs beg me to run to her, to Delle.

Owen grabs another shovel, and along with Ryker, begins to bury Delle. I stand still and watch as Wesley shovels dirt over Mercy, each heap landing with a thud against the top of her wooden coffin, a sound that reverberates in my head.

Thud...Thud...Thud...

"Arlo!" Owen calls, and I'm pulled from the trance of that horrifying sound. He waits until I look at him. "The sooner they're buried, the sooner we can be done."

He's calling me to come and help bury these women.

I have to help bury them.

I have to help bury Mercy.

Sound dissolves into an echoing roar inside my mind. Somehow, my feet begin to move beneath me, carrying me toward the graves. Somehow, my body bends and my hands wrap around the shovel's handle. Somehow, I turn and scoop soil onto the blade, turning to toss it onto the coffin.

Somehow...I bury Mercy.

Thud...Thud...Thud...

I'm numb, lost, so broken by this day, that my movements become rhythmic, automatic.

Thud...Thud...Thud...

And then the descent into my most horrific nightmare begins.

The lid of Mercy's coffin rises, pushed open from within. I feel her terror slip out from the crack, rushing out like some dark and terrible magic was trapped inside for centuries, begging for release. It flows out and strikes me hard in the chest with a sickening feeling of horror unlike anything I've ever felt before. And as her fear rushes out, soil falls to fill the empty space inside her coffin that it left behind.

Dirt pours from Wesley's shovel mid-toss, and I see a flash of white, her starlight hair shining at me like a beacon.

Starlight.

Wildflowers and starlight.

I still feel lost, as though my mind hovers in a gray and dreary purgatory while I suffer through this dark nightmare. But the flash of her starlight hair reminds me that everything I do is for her. She made me promise to do this, and though it's tearing me apart inside, I must.

Black soil dusts her starlight tresses as it slips through the crack, and I can't bear the sight of it.

How dare the earth sully such perfection with filth?

How dare the earth try to swallow her whole, to fill her coffin and steal what little air she has left to breathe?

Mercy screams and it's a siren song, calling me back to her light, her love, to my duty to ensure her rebellion is led and her revolution is won...

But more than that, her panic calls me to be her reason, her sanity, and to ensure she survives this trial.

Her oxygen is limited, and more escapes her coffin each second she keeps the lid open. It must be shut.

God, it has to be shut.

I have to keep it shut...

I shift my grip on the shovel and slam it down hard, the blade hitting the wooden lid and forcing it closed. Mercy screams again and my stomach lurches. I swallow the rising bile and press down harder as I feel her push against me from the inside. My jaw clenches against the nausea of her terror, against the pain of her fear ripping through my soul and shredding it to pieces.

I have to hold her down.

I have to do this to keep her alive.

I close my eyes and press harder as Wesley buries her.

Thud... Thud... Thud...

chapter two

Mercy

THUD…THUD…THUD…

Is that the echoing sound of my pounding heart?

The tempo of my heartbeat is so quick that the beats fade together in a rushing whir that vibrates painfully through my chest. I wonder if the panic alone might end me long before the air runs out.

Because the air will run out.

I'm going to be trapped for hours.

There's no way out.

There's no air to breathe.

A long, slow suffocation.

Fear grips me firmly by the throat, its icy cold fingers squeezing, making it that much harder to breathe. My lungs are desperate to fill as fully as they can before the light of day is gone, before my coffin is fully covered with soil, truly buried. My chest sharply rises and falls with each rapid breath. I know I should breathe slowly, but I'm fighting madness here, and I just *can't*. Each breath heightens my panic, reminding me that I may draw my very last one today.

I have to be calm.

I have to be still.

The lid is closed, and soon, I'll be buried beneath layers of soil, trapped with only the oxygen that swirls around me at this moment…and there's so little space.

My arms are pressed tightly to my sides, palms on my thighs, legs tangled through the fabric of my gown. The soles of my boots press flat to the end of the coffin, and the top of my head is only inches from the top.

It fits too perfectly, as though they built it to match my height and width. There's only just enough room to make slight adjustments, but every adjustment brings further discomfort and greater panic—my movements are so restricted that each one reminds me that I'm trapped.

I'm trapped!

Four hours…

Two hundred and forty minutes…
How many seconds is that?
Would counting them help pass the time? Give my mind something to focus on?

No…it will only remind me how slowly time is passing.
Four hours.
Four hours…
Four hours?!

Every muscle twitches at once as a collective tremor tears through me, begging me to move, to stretch, to take up more space. And when I realize I can't, my body thrashes with urgency through the panic, through the desperate need to move.

I have to move!
Don't panic. Be still.
Thud…Thud…Thud.
I can do this.
I can do this.
I…I can't…
I can't!

Conscious decision and rational thought are gone.

My determination to sacrifice myself in the name of revolution has fled my spirit, forced out by the rising cowardice which quickly fills me. It's like a rising tide washing away my strength in this moment, in this terror, in this living, waking nightmare.

My arms creep up my body, twisting until my palms press to the lid above my chest. A small voice screams inside me not to do it, that there's some reason I shouldn't open this coffin right now, but I can't remember why that is. That small voice is drowned by a much louder voice, screaming for me to get out at any cost, and I can't fight it.

I push, expecting the lid to rise immediately, but it's heavy, and I can't seem to remember why it should be. I can't make sense of anything. I'm all action with no thought, and my only motivation is to escape. I shove hard, with all my might, and the lid rises slowly.

Blackness rains, dark soil trickling in through the space I created by cracking the lid open.

There's light beyond…
I'm not entirely buried yet, but I will be soon.
I'll be buried soon.

A mangled scream claws up my throat, escaping from my lungs and leaving a burning trail of terror in its wake, like a fire that snuffs every ounce of oxygen from my tomb.

I'm terrified, desperate, more frightened than I've ever been in my life. I push harder, but I'm weak through my fear, weak as tears well and sobs break free. And just as I find a moment's strength, a moment's resolve to push as hard as I can to escape this certain death, the lid slams shut, and a weight from above holds it down.

No…

No!

I push, but it doesn't budge. The soil was heavy, but this is something else, something forced—perhaps someone holding it down to ensure my entrapment.

I need to conserve my oxygen; I can remember that, at least. But remembering does nothing to persuade my panic against forcing another scream to burst from my soul.

I'm trapped.

There's no way out.

Soon the meager light begins to fade as my grave steadily fills.

Shrouded in darkness, helpless, *buried alive,* I close my eyes and force my mind to drift to another world where peace exists, where women are safe and where love is open. I think of a world where I wouldn't be buried alive for my sins…and the man who loves me wouldn't be forced to shovel the soil.

chapter three
ARLO

"ARE YOU ALL right?" Owen asks.

His voice startles me, and my head rises from my hands to look up at him. For a moment, I falter, unable to register what he's asked me or how I should answer. I force out a sigh, then drop my head to fall back against the tree where I sit. My elbows rest on my bent knees as I wring my sweaty palms between them.

"I'm okay," I manage, though my voice is unusually quiet. I clear my throat and press my eyes shut, then try again, a little louder. "I'm fine."

"Are you sure?" he asks. "If you're sick—"

"I said I'm fine, Owen." I open my eyes and meet his, trying to reassure him with a tight, forced smile.

I managed to help Wesley fill Mercy's grave about halfway before sickness overcame me. I dropped my shovel and ran for the trees with the overwhelming urge to vomit, but on an empty stomach—knowing what would come, I couldn't bring myself to eat or drink this morning—I was launched into a fit of dry heaving that went on for minutes.

Guilt, heartache, terror, grief.

A swarm of emotions roils in my gut, and they keep me in this horrid sickness. I don't hate it; I'm glad for it. I deserve it.

What kind of man allows the woman he loves to be buried alive?

What kind of man holds her coffin shut so she can't escape?

I deserve to feel sick.

I deserve to remain in misery before meeting an appropriate, horrifying end.

"You're shaking," Owen points out, though I don't need him to. I feel the way every muscle twitches, how my bones quake with fear for my starlight encased in darkness, buried beneath the soil. "I've never seen you ill before." His brow furrows. "Perhaps you should return to the Homestead when Park arrives to take Ellary back to the village."

Once we'd buried Mercy and Delle, I kept my ailing mind focused by anchoring rope to the stone cliffside before repelling down with my brothers' assistance. Ellary had a pulse—it was faint, but it was there. The moment I lifted her from the ground, she screamed in pain, awakening suddenly and horribly. One leg and one arm were bent in ways they shouldn't be, but I feared more urgently for the potential of a shattered pelvis or broken ribs that may have punctured organs.

We're so far from the Homestead, from medical supplies and medicines. We had to call for Park to return after ensuring Stefanie—who'd protested at the processional—was securely locked up.

Killian isn't wanted here by any of us at the moment, and Theo needs to keep watch over Delle's brother. So Ellary's broken body lies in wait near the pathway hidden by brush. She's unconscious again, and that worries me because the pain of such a fall should have her veins so flooded with adrenaline that rest evades her. I fear she's in shock, slowly drifting toward death—a death she most certainly didn't deserve.

There's a strange fondness that many men hold for Ellary Hill. She's always had such a pure and kind energy about her—a sweetness and docile demeanor that brings calmness around her, even during violent nights of service. There will be men outraged over the loss of her if she dies.

They should be outraged over the loss of *any* woman, but it seems hypocrisy is rooted in Ember Glen, my own running the deepest roots into the earth beneath my feet.

"I'm not going anywhere," I affirm.

Regardless of how much I want to help Ellary, I can't. I can't leave Mercy behind, even knowing that she'd want me to take care of her friend.

Owen gives a quick nod of acknowledgment as Wesley calls out, "Five minutes."

I scramble to my feet with the notice of Delle's remaining time, rushing to her graveside, and picking up a shovel. I'm prepared to work hard and fast to dig her out the moment Wesley calls her time. She'll be alive, I know she will. She only had to survive an hour, so she'll be okay, but I will not let that girl suffer a moment longer than necessary.

I shouldn't have let her suffer at all.

Guilt threatens to make me heave again, but I swallow it down and pull my shoulders back, forcing myself to feel the ache of it in my gut, the nausea of shame that ripples and runs through every inch of me.

It feels like hours pass as I wait. Owen appears across from me on the opposite side of the grave, lifting a shovel from the ground. Wesley paces, watching the black band permanently attached to his wrist. Ryker stands nearby, casually leaning against a tree with an expression of boredom on his face—and I have the urge to knock it off of him with my fist.

"That's it. That's time," Wesley finally says.

I dig before he even finishes speaking. I work quickly, pushing myself past a reasonable pace for my waning strength and through this guilty sickness which consumes me.

At first, it feels as though I'm doing the job alone, but soon I find my brothers matching my pace and urgency, and it's nearly strange to find a moment of solidarity with them. It's not an altogether foreign feeling; before I began to see the world as I know it now, I shared many moments of brotherhood and solidarity with them. It only feels strange now because I hadn't expected to share a collective determination with them in digging Delle from her grave, in ending this trial we've orchestrated ourselves under the religious law we enforce.

Maybe—*just maybe*—they see the absurdity in this ritual, too.

Minutes, hours, I don't know how long it takes before my shovel scrapes the wooden coffin. I hasten to push away the soil, brushing it off the sides and down toward the end. When I see enough of the coffin cleared—enough to know I'll be able to raise the lid without raining soil over her face—I drop my shovel and leap into the grave.

I shift to stand precariously on the sloping soil filling in the space between the side of her coffin and the grave wall. Crouching, I swipe away the last heaps of soil with my gloved hands. As soon as I can get my fingers under the lid, I raise it up to free Delle.

She lies still inside her coffin, stiff, every muscle tightened though twitching from fear. Her hands are balled into fists beneath her chin, her elbows tucked in tight against her chest, and her eyes are forcefully squeezed shut.

"Delle," I say as a warning before I grab her wrists.

She's so gripped by fear that she hasn't even realized she's being freed. When my fingers touch her skin, her eyes pop open and she jolts in surprise. She's so tense from the horror that her upper body rises with her hands, as though her arms are fastened to her chest, though that at least helps me pull her out faster.

"Is it over? Is it done?" Her voice is nearly inaudible, though it's tone is frantic, quick-paced.

"It's done," I reassure her quickly. "You're done, Delle. You completed the trial."

All at once, she cries. She loosens, throwing her arms around my neck and clings to me. She kicks her bare feet, scrambling to get out of the coffin. Inadvertently, she presses me backward, trying to climb me like a ladder to escape her grave. My feet slip along the inclined soil, angled toward her wooden tomb.

Sliding over loose soil, I lasso an arm around her waist and hoist her up against my side to keep us both from falling into the coffin. I reach above me with my other arm, fingers clawing for a grip at the edge.

"Give me your hand, Delle," Wesley says as his hand appears, reaching down to help.

Delle doesn't respond, lost in her panic to escape. She only continues to scramble and claw, trying so hard to climb out, though it's to her detriment—every time she pushes to try to climb me, we slip deeper into the hole.

"Delle." I try to get her attention as she fights, but she doesn't seem to hear me. I firm up my voice, and snap, "*Delle!*" She turns her eyes to mine and gives me a moment of her attention. "Give him your hand."

She blinks, taking a few seconds to bring herself to the present—I think her mind is still trapped in the wooden box at our feet. Eventually, her gaze turns to spot Wesley's outstretched hand, and eagerly, she reaches for it. He pulls her up as I lift, and she falls over the edge onto the solid ground above me. I watch from below as she scrambles to her feet, and Wesley helps her stand.

I move my feet, trying to climb up, but the dirt beneath them shifts. I slip with the soil and stumble backward, catching myself as my feet slam against the wooden bottom of the coffin. The strike of my shoe against wood and the fall into the lowest part of the grave brings about an explosion of reality, a bomb of aching truth detonating in my mind.

Surrounded by black walls, I lift my head to look up at the gray, cloud-covered sky, visible through the looming tendrils of nearly bare branches. A dark brown leaf slips from a branch and slowly falls, floating back and forth on the autumn breeze, drifting downward like it's slowly dying and seeking the grave.

Down it falls, and before long, it lands at my feet. But the landing isn't gentle. The small leaf strikes the wood coffin with the force of a lead weight. It shakes through the dirt walls and makes the earth shift beneath my feet. I feel as though the world has flipped, and I'm tumbling from the grave, falling upward, forever upward toward a heaven I'll never see.

I'm hurtling through space, tumbling eternally through a dark sky, forever seeking that point of light in the distance—the forever fading starlight that's slowly dying, out of reach, too far for me to touch and too far for me to save.

"Starlight." The word whispers from between my lips.

"Arlo." Owen's voice sounds so far away. "Take my hand and let me pull you out before you pass out down there."

"He looks sick," Wesley says.

I hear them both, but all I see is darkness behind closed eyes—the darkness of a night sky with a single, fading star calling to me in the distance…

Wildflowers and starlight.

She calls to me across space and time.

She calls to me from her grave.

Suddenly, I'm hoisted upward. My soul snaps back into my body as I open my eyes, drawing in a gasping breath to fill my lungs because for moments, I'd held it. There's an ache in my chest so strong that it brings tears to flood my eyes.

Does Mercy's chest ache this way?

Can she breathe?

Panic shakes through me, and adrenaline floods my veins. As Wesley and Owen hoist me up, I turn and climb. I bend onto solid ground and swing my legs up to follow, rolling away from the edge before shifting to all fours. I crawl forward and climb to my feet, moving quickly with my sights set on Mercy's grave…and then I see Delle.

It stops me dead in my tracks to see her, bending to wrap her shaking hands around the handle of a shovel, sobbing as she moves toward Mercy's grave.

"She can't breathe," Delle mutters through her tears. "She can't breathe. She can't breathe."

Weak from low oxygen, from panic, from the drugs still flowing through her system, Delle barely manages to puncture the earth with the tip of the shovel, though she tries. She tries to do what I should have done from the very beginning…*save Mercy Madness.*

My brothers run to stop her, and their movement kickstarts me into action. I sprint past them and reach her first, wrapping my hands around the handle and lifting the shovel between us. Tears stream down her cheeks and she grits her teeth as she tightens her grip, pulling back with all her might.

"*No.* Let *go!*"

I jerk the shovel from her weakened grip and swivel back to face Mercy's grave.

Dig.

It's my only conscious thought.

I drive the blade into the soil, scoop, and toss.

Dig, scoop, toss.

Dig, scoop, toss.

"Arlo, stop," Owen demands.

"What are you *doing?*" Wesley asks.

I don't stop; I keep digging.

I dig until Ryker knocks into my side and we tumble to the ground. He lands heavily against my side, trying to twist me to face down so he can wrestle my arms behind me.

I won't allow it.

I can't let them stop me.

I tighten my grip on the shovel and swing it in his direction as I roll toward my back to hit him. He rolls away, just missing the strike, and that's enough for me. It's not my goal to harm them, but I will if I must.

I will *not* be stopped.

I fight to my feet, rush to her grave, and I dig.

Dig, scoop, toss.

Hands grip my biceps from behind, fingers digging into my flesh and jerking me backward. "Stop!" Owen shouts.

"Get *off* me!" I demand.

My voice sounds like it's coming from someone else, someone feral and lost.

But I *am* lost.

I'm lost to my love for her, and I have no desire to ever find my way back.

I twist and jerk, shaking Owen off.

Dig, scoop, toss.

"You have to stop," Wesley's voice calls from somewhere behind me, calmer than the others. "Arlo. You have to stop."

Dig, scoop, toss.

Dig, scoop, toss.

Someone grabs my arms again, and another grabs the shovel. I'm being pulled and twisted, and though I try to keep my grip on the handle, they eventually tear it from my grasp, tossing it away.

Wesley stands before me, dark eyes fixed on mine as he lowers his voice. "The cameras are on," he hisses. "This is livestreaming; everyone in the village can see you right now."

Delle's soft crying floats to my ears from somewhere nearby, and it tugs on the last thread of sanity remaining in my mind. And when she hiccups through her words, whispering a broken refrain, "She can't breathe. She can't breathe. She can't breathe," she snips that thread, and all my control is lost.

With fury and fear, I fight for Mercy.

I lunge, and Owen grabs my shoulders from behind. "I *can't*," I grit through my teeth, swinging my arms around to knock him off. "I *won't*. I won't stop."

Ryker tackles me from the side again, and we tumble—rolling, twisting, fighting. I manage to get on top of him and slam my fist into his face, watching blood spurt from his nose, as his head turns sideways from the force. Then Owen's at my back, tugging at my arms, and in our struggle, we fall. I scramble to get away from him, but he grabs my leg. I jerk to get out of his grip, and unintentionally kick him in the gut, hard enough that he grunts and rolls away.

I crawl, racing to Mercy's grave on my hands and knees. I claw at the black soil, scratching and tearing my way through the earth to Mercy. My only goal is to free her, to draw her into my arms, to wrap her in warmth, and to carry her away from this place forever.

"We can't do this anymore…" I mutter mindlessly as I dig. "We can't hurt them anymore. We can't do this…"

I pause just long enough to rip off my gloves and toss them away, needing the freedom from restriction to scoop the soil away faster.

The Control doesn't speak; they don't grab me and try to stop me. Eerie quiet loops around me, the absence of sound except for Delle's soft crying, her soft chanting, "She can't breathe. She can't breathe."

We're broken.

We're all broken from this madness.

And I know I won't be whole again until I feel Mercy's heart beating beneath my palm, until I see her chest rising and falling, until I feel the press of her lips against mine.

I claw with my hands until something hard and heavy collides with the side of my head…

I fall sideways and snap into darkness.

chapter four

Mercy

CLARITY IS FOUND…
my eternity in bliss,
she and heaven are one in the same.

Arlo's voice recites poetry inside my mind. Anguish draws from my memories, seeking things that brought me joy, forcing me to recall them in these dreadful moments, and causing me further pain.

Arlo's words are plucked from somewhere hidden within my subconscious. I'd read his words over and over in my final days, but I hadn't intentionally memorized them—but the words are there all the same, imprinted eternally.

My beloved starlight…
my mortal universe,
her death will bring the end of all things.

Yet…
my love for her is immortal,
and suffering will haunt my mortal flesh eternally.

She is paradise.
She is endless.
She is mine.

"I am yours…" I whisper into darkness.

Panic had overwhelmed me for some time, but gradually, a sense of calm has slowly begun to wash over me. My slow breaths feel unsatisfactory, and I'm growing tired…*so tired.*

I try to fight the calm.

I try to hasten and deepen my breaths.

I try to remain angry, panicked, anything other than *calm*.

Calm means tired.

Tired means breathless.

Breathless means death.

It's coming.

I can feel it coming.

Should I welcome it?

I think I can hear the scythe of the grim reaper himself, cutting through the earth to get to me so he can steal my soul. It's a faint sweeping, scraping sound as he digs down to find me…*No.* He must dig from below, creeping up from hell as a demon to take me away for my eternal punishment.

The sound grows louder, and though it seems clearer at first, it quickly crescendos into a sonorous, clashing echo inside my mind, bouncing around with all my strange thoughts, with Arlo's voice reciting poetry, with the voices of a thousand men calling me a sinner. And I'm trapped with them all, trapped in my mind as much as my body is trapped in this coffin.

I'll never be free from this tomb!

No man nor angel nor demon will ever break my soul free.

Even if they pull my physical remains from the coffin, my soul will stay right here, trapped forever in this purgatory—

.

.

.

.

.

.

Wake up!

My body jolts as I force myself awake, and my arms fly out, colliding with the sides of the coffin. I open my eyes wide, blinking rapidly against the heaviness of my lids, which threaten to close again so quickly.

Will I miss her when she's gone?
With all the brightness of her starlight hair.

Will she remember me in her damnation?
I'll never have to wonder.

My eyes…they're so heavy.

I fight them as they will to close, as the time between each blink gradually lessens and the peace of slumber calls to me. I'm exhausted, weak, and tired from fighting to stay alive.

I let out a long, slow breath, willing the last bits of air to leave my lungs, sadly hoping there won't be another to fill them again because I'm so tired…

So damn tired.

I'll wreck my soul to meet her in hell…
and she'll never know the ache of missing me.

I'm losing the fight.
I close my eyes.
And maybe it's for the last time.

.

.

.

.

.

.

I drift through the darkness of space as a lonely star, yet I feel the presence of his being floating out there, somewhere in the vast emptiness, searching for me. The gravity of my heart reaches for him, draws him near, pulls him into my light.

And before I fall into my final slumber, he appears. I see his face behind my lids. The bright blue of his shining eyes, his devilishly charming grin, and the disarming dimples that chisel through his short beard, creating such uniquely distinctive lines through his handsome face.

He's beautiful bathed in light, just as he is in the dark.

I love you…

Arlo, I love you.

I love you. I love you. I love you.

I know I'll find myself in hell the next time I awaken, but I won't have to wait long for him to chase after me. I know I'll awaken to find him right there with me, prepared to suffer our damnation in tandem, and we'll burn together eternally.

chapter five
ARLO

GOD, PLEASE...

Dear God, please let her live…let her be alive.

I stare at Mercy's grave with wild eyes, adrenaline racing through my veins as the Control finally—*finally*—works to dig her out. I've been intently watching the soil that traps her for hours, praying for a miracle from the cruel God who's forsaken us both.

Perhaps I should call upon demons to save her.

I'd sell my soul in a heartbeat…

The Control—no longer my brothers because I can no longer consider myself one of them—had bound my hands at the wrists using my own damn rope. The side of my head still throbs where I was struck with a shovel, though I still don't know which of them hit me. I didn't ask, and I don't really care. It was the only way they ever would have been able to stop me during my mad rush to scrape away the soil, to free my starlight from the darkness of this wretched land.

I kneel at the foot of her grave, watching as my brothers dig, tossing away the dirt one shovelful at a time to free her now that her time has been called.

Four hours.

She has to be alive…she can't be dead.

If she's dead, I'll lay with her in that grave and let the Control bury us both.

I'm gripped with maddening fear, my body trembling as I watch helplessly.

"Arlo," Delle whispers, and it startles me, making my shoulders jump.

The world disappeared when they started to dig, and everything but Mercy was forgotten. I forgot that Delle was there, standing beside me. I forgot that she sat with me all these hours as we waited. I forgot how I let her lean on me to share my warmth. I forgot about the few times she drifted to sleep, but woke again with a start, with a scream for help to free her from the grave where her mind was still trapped.

Delle lowers to her knees beside me. "Do you think she's…" She doesn't finish the question, and I'm grateful that she doesn't because I wouldn't know how to answer her.

All I can do is shake my head.

I don't know.

I don't know if she's alive or dead.

I don't know if she's dead.

If she's dead…

A thud signals that someone's shovel strikes hard wood, and my pulse races.

They've hit her coffin.

They keep shoveling.

My body tenses, lurching forward with the instinct to leap into her grave, to wrench the lid of her coffin open by force against the remaining dirt that still weighs it down. Urgency ripples beneath my skin, and I shove to my feet, stumbling sideways in my rush.

Delle rises with me. She reaches for me, her hands grabbing hold of my biceps. With an impressive grip for such small hands, she twists me around, turning me to face away from the grave.

I start to turn back, but then she snaps out my name with a sharp bite, *"Arlo."*

Her insistent tone halts me as she glances over my shoulder, probably finding my brothers lost in focus as they dig behind my back. And then her small hands fall to the rope around my wrists. She works frantically at the knots, her nimble fingers moving quickly to free me. A sigh of relief escapes me as she pulls one end free from a loop and keeps going.

"Hurry," I whisper.

"I'm trying," she says.

We share a chaotic energy between us, both of us caught in our desperation to save the brightest star in the sky. Though I selfishly want Mercy to shine for me alone, I could never deny the fact that her light belongs to the world.

Delle finds the last knotted thread and tugs it through to free me. "Just get her out," she whispers urgently.

The moment the rope falls away, I move.

I turn and jump into her grave to the sound of protests from the Control. I grab the end of someone's shovel as it slices into the final layer covering her coffin, and I wrestle it from his grip. I think it's Ryker's because I hear him shout something as I tear it from his hold.

Turning the shovel in my grip, I sweep and scrape—sweep away the dirt, scrape against the wood. The sound of it is haunting because I don't know what I'll find when the sound stops, when the soil is all swept away and I finally open the lid to her coffin.

Please, please…let her be alive.

Before long, I toss the shovel aside, press my foot into the dirt, letting it slip between the sodden grave wall and the side of her coffin. I curl my bare fingers, wedging the tips into the crevice where the lid meets the frame. I feel fingernails bend and break, scraping along the wood as I wedge them deeper.

When I'm finally able to slip my fingers deep enough to try, I lift with force, grunting as I raise the lid against the heavy soil that still covers the coffin where her head and feet lie. Slowly, it rises, and I shove harder, pushing it up entirely, then leaning it to rest against the grave wall.

Without taking so much as a moment to steel myself, my gaze drops, and I look down into Mercy's coffin.

There she rests…*my Mercy.*

Pale, except for the flecks of dirt smeared across her cheeks.

Silent, still, the crimson fabric of her dress unmoving.

Her eyes are softly shut.

Her expression is neutral, impassive, like she's asleep.

She looks like she's asleep…

"No!" Delle screams from above, and the punching sound of it strikes my gut.

I drop and reach for Mercy, shifting awkwardly in this wretched space. I feel out of my body, out of control, animated only by the desperate need to get her out.

She'll be okay once she's out.

She'll breathe once she's out.

I struggle to slip my arms beneath her, to circle them around her waist. I raise her motionless body from the coffin, dragging her into my embrace. Her weight shifts against me, and I lean back to avoid dropping her into the coffin, falling back to sit. I drag her with me, shifting until she's cradled on my lap.

She's so cold…so fucking cold.

Her head rolls, falling limply to the side. There's no tension straining through the muscles in her neck, no consciousness.

"Mercy…"

Nothing.

Not a word, not a movement, not a breath.

Delle screams and cries, and the Control speak in rushed and urgent voices above me, but it's all just noise. The only sound I want to hear is Mercy's voice. I'd settle for a sigh, a puff of breath escaping from her lips, *anything.*

"Mercy." My voice is commanding, insistent on having her attention. "*Mercy!*"

Nothing.

I shift her on my lap, hoist her higher, hug her closer.

"Mercy..." My commanding voice lowers to a pleading whisper that I breathe against her ear, my palm cradling the back of her soil-speckled hair. "Starlight, open your eyes. Wake up." A lump rises in my throat and I swallow against it. "It's over. The trial is done. You can wake up now." My voice catches and I hiccup through my words as liquid glazes over my eyes, making them burn.

I hold her tighter.

I kiss her cheek.

I curl my fingers and comb them through her hair.

I tremble, fighting against the voice in my head that tells me she's gone, the voice that begs me to feel the pain of losing her, that pushes me right to the edge of falling apart. It tells me she's not responding, she's not moving; it reminds me that she's been buried for four hours and there wasn't enough oxygen for her to survive.

"No. *No.* Mercy, no...wake up. Wake up, *please.* Just wake up."

She can't be dead...she can't!

My chest stutters, rising sharply as I draw in a deep breath, and then tears fall.

I cry as I hold her.

I bury my face in the crook of her neck and cry against her cold skin, losing myself entirely to a pain more intense than anything I've ever felt. I thought I was broken before, but I wasn't. I know that I wasn't because I'm breaking *now*, my soul shattering into a million pieces, scattering in the soil, never to be pieced together again.

I cannot exist without her.

If her soul is gone, then mine has gone with it.

I weep over Mercy until silence falls around me. When all that exists are the black walls of the grave around me, the coffin beneath me, and the gray, dreary sky above me.

I press a kiss to her neck, then another, and another. And then I crush my lips to the spot again, using her cold flesh to hide my sob, pouring my sadness through her veins from the gentle *thump, thump, thump* of her pulse—

Her pulse...

I turn to stone, focusing hard on where my lips touch her neck. I feel it as sure as I feel her body in my arms—a faint *thump, thump, thump* beats in a slow, but steady rhythm, pulsing against my lips.

I sink my fingers deeper into the strands of her hair, gripping her head, tugging back to tilt her face toward the sky so I can look at her.

Skin still pale, eyes still shut.

I move my other hand between us, pressing my palm to her chest, desperate to feel the beat of her heart beneath my palm.

I wait.

One of the Control calls down from above, "Arlo, she's—"

"Wait!"

I push harder against her chest, and in the stillness, I can feel it. I can feel her heart beat slowly in her chest.

I bring her face to mine and kiss her cheeks, her chin, her forehead. "Open your eyes, Mercy. Open your eyes. It's done. I'm here. It's all over, and I'm here with you."

I kiss her lips, tender, soft, lingering.

I don't care anymore.

It doesn't matter who sees, who knows what I feel for her. All I care about is bringing her back to life, consequences be damned.

Let them see me kiss her.

Let them bring me death so long as it brings her life.

I feel the warmth of a shallow breath ease from her nose, breezing hope over my skin. She's still limp, asleep, but she's breathing and her heart is beating.

"Starlight."

I kiss her again, and a faint moan vibrates through the connection of our lips. I lift away to look down at her, watching the muscles in her face twitch to life as she makes another soft sound.

I sigh, tension releasing, my weight sinking in relief. Her head turns slightly against my hand, and I splay my palm wider to hold her steady.

I lift my head to allow my shout to echo beyond her grave. "She's alive!" I bend to kiss Mercy's forehead. "You're alive," I whisper, feeling the tug of a grin at the corners of my lips.

"Mercy?" I hear Delle and look up to see her on her hands and knees, peeking over the edge with tears streaking her cheeks. "She's…Is she—"

I nod, smiling. "She's alive."

"Oh, God," Delle sobs. "Thank God!"

"How dare you thank God, you little sinner?" Ryker wraps his hand around Delle's hair and forcefully jerks her back from the edge.

I need to get out of this grave.

I hoist Mercy up, moving her to sit on my lap, though she's still limp, her body still slumping heavily against me. "I need you to wake up now," I tell her. "I know it's hard, but I need you to wake up. Delle needs me. She needs *you*."

Mercy hums, slowly awakening. I can feel the way her soul fights within her, begging her mind to wake up, imploring her limbs to move.

I shift beneath her, trying to get to my feet, though I don't exactly know how to lift her out of here without help.

"Arlo," she whispers, and it halts me. Her head turns against my shoulder. She sighs, blinks against heavy eyelids before losing the fight, then fades back to sleep.

"Here." Wesley's voice startles me, and I look up to see him reaching down. "Lift her up, and we'll pull her out."

Owen appears and reaches down to help, as well.

"I'm gonna get you out of here." I promise Mercy before moving again. With all the strength I can muster, I pull her up with me as I stand, struggling against the soil which constantly slides and slips beneath my feet.

Somehow, the three of us manage to lift her out while she's unconscious, and gratefully, they pull me out after her. I wouldn't have been surprised if they'd left me here to die—they saw me kiss her, I know they did, and the sin won't go unpunished.

Mercy is laid on the ground beside her grave, and I move quickly to kneel at her side. Her fingers twitch before her hand briefly lifts from the ground, floating up, then falling back down again.

"Where are you?" Mercy asks dreamily as her head rolls sideways, caught between sleep and waking. "Arlo...love...I need you..."

"How far has it gone?" Owen asks softly at my side, and I look up at him, meeting his eyes, which are wide with concern. "How far across the line did you go?" He sounds as though he doesn't want to know, and of course, he doesn't. I'm supposed to be his brother in God—a man of faith, upheld to the highest standards in our community.

And I've just shattered that illusion.

I'm not that man anymore, though I suppose I never really was—and now they all know.

They saw me share physical affection with a woman—a servant and my ward, no less. And they heard her call to me with *love*. I am her love, and I no longer care if it brings me death for them to know it.

"The line was thin," I mutter, recalling a conversation I had with Mercy when she first became my ward, a musing about the thin line we both saw between asserting my authority and abusing it, "and I broke it long ago."

There it is.

The truth is out, and there's no reeling it back in.

I turn away from Owen's judgment to give the woman I would die for my full attention. I bend over her, cradle her cheeks in my hands and watch as she slowly opens her eyes, her gaze searching until she locks on mine. I smile at her because she's alive, and the joy I find in that simple fact is all that matters to me.

"I'm here," I tell her. "Mercy, you're alive. You survived the trial."

I kiss her forehead, then move my hands to her waist to lift her into my arms, but I see panic cloud over her bright eyes as my arms close around her, caging her in to my embrace.

Her face contorts in fear and she jerks into motion, her hands gripping my arms and shoving them away, her legs kicking as she fights to break free from my confining grip—she's fighting to break free from the coffin that no longer traps her.

I let go of her, fearful that holding her will only further her distress. She rolls away, pushes to her hands and knees through a burst of adrenaline, then scrambles to her feet. She steadies herself quickly, though her panic holds her hostage. Her head turns frantically, looking all around her with wild eyes as she seeks to make sense of her situation.

"Mercy," Delle softly cries.

Delle.

Her voice reminds me that she needed me, that I saw Ryker violently pull her from the edge of the grave. I whip around to find her face down on the ground with Ryker's foot pressed to the back of her neck, holding her there.

Fury sharply rises, chaos rippling through my veins because I am *done.* I am over this hypocrisy; I'm finished with the violence against these women who have done *nothing* to earn it.

I'm forever changed by Mercy Madness, and I'm glad for it…*grateful* for it. In her name, I swear, I will never be the same again.

I look back at Mercy, catching her gaze for a beat. She's clearly trapped in her panic, yet I can still see the heart of her through her bewitching eyes— the fury of injustice still lives there, burning as brightly as ever, and I let it catch me on fire.

I've already lost favor with the Control. My death certificate is all but written now that they know the extent of my sins. I no longer have a reason to hold back, so I take Mercy's righteous anger, stir it with my burning rage, and let the fiery mixture take hold of me.

With the force of all the pain Mercy and Delle have suffered at our hands, I turn, charge, and barrel into Ryker.

chapter six
Mercy

MY MIND DRIFTS between dark and light—asleep and awake. My body bobs in the cadence of a slow walk as it drifts through space. I fight to wake up, to lay eyes on Arlo so I can see for myself that he's safe and well because I fear for him.

I think I heard someone accuse him of crossing a line with me. And I think I glimpsed him charging Ryker near my grave before I grew weary, before the world once again went black from my breathless exhaustion.

Maybe it was all a dream—I *hope* it was a dream. If it wasn't a dream, then he's not safe, and he needs me.

I have to wake up.

I say his name, though I don't know if I'm saying it out loud, whether I speak in reality or in this semi-conscious void.

"I'm here." It's Arlo's voice, and I know it's real. I know he's really there, trying to drag me from exhaustion. "You're okay, Mercy." He sounds near and far all at once.

He says that I'm okay, but is he?

Blinking slowly, I force alertness through sheer determination. Peering straight through my half-hooded eyes, I see branches…bare branches cutting across a gray, cloud-covered sky. They seem to be moving, dark brown limbs scratching across the gray as they roll away behind me. Except, it's not the branches that are moving, it's *me*. I'm floating through the forest, looking up at the autumn sky.

The more alert I become, the more that I *feel*, my senses awakening from stagnancy. My neck feels strained as the muscles stretch, my head dropped back and dangling, jostling from the motion of whatever unseen force pushes me through the woods. My left shoulder aches as gravity tugs my swinging arm toward the earth. The cold air sweeps over me, and I shiver. Goosebumps prickle all the way up my right arm, and my hand twitches, making me aware that my arm is bent across my waist as I feel my fingers move on my stomach.

I'm being carried.

But by whom?

Arlo would never carry me this way, and I'd feel warmth if I were in his arms. He'd cradle me against his chest and hold me close to him—I'd feel safe.

I don't feel safe at all.

I don't feel like a woman loved by a man.

I feel like a package that's being delivered.

I try to lift my head, but my neck muscles are strained, as is my voice. "Arlo?"

"I'm here. I'm right here." There's an anxious timbre to his voice, and it's tinged with sadness. "I'm sorry." The odd sound of it overwhelms me, and immediately, I feel like crying.

"Don't speak to her." Ryker's voice is loud, though I don't think he's the one carrying me. "You're already walking toward a painful end; don't force our hand in silencing you before you meet it."

Fear strikes me, and it triggers the flow of adrenaline through my veins. I feel it rush through my limbs, twitch through my muscles, and violently jerk my body into full awareness. My eyes snap wide, and I manage to lift my head against the aching muscles in my neck, turning against the pain— which, thankfully, quickly fades in the chemical rush—to try to spot Arlo.

But all I see are trees and gloom.

"Ar...Arlo!" My lips quiver from the chill, from the buzz of adrenaline as it floods my system.

I raise my heavy arms, twisting my body against whoever is carrying me, and try to push away. I don't care if I fall; I just want my feet on the ground. I just want to move, to look, to find Arlo and run to his side.

I could have died today...I should be dead right now, but I'm *not*. I'm alive, I survived, and being with him is all I want.

"Put her down!" Arlo shouts. "Let go of me!" I hear the sound of flesh colliding with flesh, of fists slamming into muscle, of Arlo groaning in pain.

My hands find fabric, and I curl my fingers to grab hold, tugging myself up against the chest of the man carrying me. My gaze skips across blue eyes—blue eyes that certainly don't belong to Arlo—and quickly sweeps over his face. I happen to notice his jet-black hair and realize it's Owen.

It doesn't matter who it is, I just need him to let go of me.

I kick, trying to get him to drop my legs. I jerk, twist, thrash, move any way I can to get away from him, though he fights to hold on. "Let *go*!"

I have to get down.

I have to get to Arlo.

"Put her down!" Arlo's shouts. "Let her down; let her walk!"

As if he suddenly realizes that trying to subdue me isn't worth the effort,

Owen finally drops my feet. My boots hit the ground with a light thump and the brief crunch of dry leaves beneath them.

My hands come up on instinct to push Owen away, landing on his biceps and shoving him back. I push him, yet he doesn't move…*I* move. Weak and unsteady on my feet, I stumble backward. I plant my feet and lean forward, bending at the waist. My arms fly out, prepared to catch myself, but I don't fall. Somehow, I steady myself on shaking legs, and slowly, I straighten to my full height.

I keep my lips closed though they beg to part so I can pant through rushed, heavy breaths. Instead, I force the quick breaths in and out through my nose, trying not to show them too much of my weakness.

Because I've never felt weaker.

I've never felt so exhausted while simultaneously feeling so alert, so fearful, my mind preparing my body to flee or fight.

"Easy," Owen says as he steps toward me slowly, one palm raised as if to show good intentions.

Fear punches my gut, and I take a step backward. My eyes nervously dart around, seeking, searching, taking stock of my surroundings. I see Owen right in front of me and Wesley a few yards behind, slowly closing in with a concerned expression.

I see Delle off in the distance toward my right, crying silent tears as she hugs herself. Her stare is fixed on me, watching me with such pain in her expression that it aches inside my chest. She slumps sideways to lean her shoulder against a tree.

I hear a hit, a groan, and my eyes shift focus to Arlo and Ryker, about halfway between me and Delle. I find Arlo in time to watch as he doubles over in pain, Ryker pulling his fist away from his gut. Still bent, Arlo's eyes raise to meet mine from beneath his lashes as pain contorts his expression. But we lose the connection when Ryker moves directly in front of him, digging his claws into Arlo's biceps to jerk him upright.

Then Ryker turns, but one arm remains behind him. His hand grips the rope between Arlo's wrists—which I'm just noticing are bound together— and drags him with a sharp yank as he stomps toward me and Owen.

I naturally take a step back as Ryker moves closer.

He stops beside Owen, releasing Arlo long enough to release a length of rope from his belt—*Arlo's* rope. My lips snarl with an oddly placed sense of outrage that any man other than Arlo should hold that rope, never mind the fact that they've *bound* him with it.

Owen takes the rope from Ryker and turns to face me. "Don't run." He takes a step closer. "That will only make things worse for both of you."

"Worse than *what?*" Fury takes hold of Arlo. He moves swiftly between me and Owen, facing him squarely. "She already faced death. Can you imagine any fate worse than being buried alive?"

"You and I both know there are deaths far more painful than being buried alive."

I take another step back on shaking limbs, muscles weak from lack of oxygen, my knees already threatening to buckle beneath me.

Arlo's head cocks to the side. "And is that the fate you intend to push for us to meet? A more painful death?"

Owen steps forward, bravely standing chest-to-chest with Arlo. "It would be the fate you've chosen with your actions, *brother.* The sins you've obviously committed with her are atrocious...unforgiveable."

Arlo's voice lowers, but his cadence remains steady. "I've come to a different understanding of that word than you have."

Unforgiveable.

"There is no misunderstanding here," Owen says. "You admitted to crossing a line with her. I watched you; *we* watched you put your lips on hers, as if you've kissed her a thousand times before—"

"I *have*," Arlo declares with open defiance, straightening to his full height. "And I don't regret a single moment of our indiscretion."

My legs finally give way with a brief spell of faintness that makes me feel as though my heart has stopped pumping blood through my veins...like my heart is skipping beats. Leaves crackle as I fall to my knees, then drop forward on my hands as my vision blackens around the edges.

"Mercy..." Arlo is quickly at my side. I think he's kneeling beside me as I work to slow my breathing.

My mind feels blurry, on the verge of tumbling back into unwanted slumber. Everything seems fuzzy except for the situation we find ourselves in; the only thing that's truly clear to me right now is that Arlo has let our secret loose into the world—and it puts him in danger.

He's in danger now that they know about our shared sins of the flesh. Yet, strangely, instead of fear, I find relief washing over me.

The secret is out.

And though we both may soon face deadly consequences, in this moment, I don't care. I can't think of the future. All I feel is relief that I no longer have to hide what I need—and what I need right now more than anything is my warden, my keeper, the man that I love.

I can let go now.

I can stop pretending I don't need him desperately.

I can seek him for comfort.

And I do.

Tears rush to the surface and pour down my cheeks as an unexpected sob bursts free. I let myself collapse, tilting sideways to fall against him, knowing that he'll catch me, and he does. He drops back to sit on his heels, and I let myself break apart, falling into a heap on his lap. Though his hands are bound, he uses them to comfort me, fingers grazing my cheek as he tucks my hair behind my ear.

He doesn't speak; he only strokes my cheek with a tenderness I didn't know I needed until he touched me. I cry on his lap and he comforts me, both of us losing any remaining dignity in the eyes of the Control.

As if they know the first thing about dignity.

For moments, nothing happens, no one speaks. It's just a stagnant, broken moment in between one horror and the next.

"You know what?" Owen sighs. "Fine. I could use a damn break, too. I've been carrying her for nearly a mile." Through my tears, I see him sit down, leaning his back against a tree.

"What? We don't have time for this," Ryker says impatiently. "We need to enact punishment immediately."

"Punishment will be enacted whether we take a break or not, and I *need* a break if I have to carry her all the way back to the Homestead."

"I can walk," I mutter quietly.

My voice sounds so weak.

Has all my strength left me?

Did it die? Was it left behind in my grave? Buried, and never to return?

"I'll carry her if you can't," Ryker says, taking a step toward us.

Wesley stops him, coming up to place a gentle hand on his shoulder. "A ten-minute delay won't harm anyone. I could use a short rest after all that chaos, anyway."

Arlo shifts beneath me, moving to sit on the ground as Ryker shrugs Wesley's hand off his shoulder, spins, and paces away. Wesley watches Ryker for a few beats, then, satisfied he's given up, leans his back against a nearby tree. Arlo stretches out his legs and shifts me between them, bringing my head to rest on his thigh.

I hear movement near our feet, and I sharply lift my head to see Delle slowly lowering to the ground with her back to a trunk. Our eyes connect, and we share a moment of silent misery, a beat of camaraderie in our shared mental anguish. She and I were buried alive today, and we survived. We were pulled from our graves, but pieces of our souls were left behind—pieces we'll never get back.

No words need to be spoken.

The way we've been damaged screams between us.

I should go to her, hug her, try to give her some comfort. Though my love for her insists I should give her whatever compassion I have left, I realize I have none left to give. I feel a sudden ache in my chest as this dawns on me—it's like a chisel has been driven into my heart, forming a crack right down the middle, and it hurts so much that it makes me sob.

Of all the things they've done to me, this trial has stolen my compassion, and losing that is the worst thing of all. I turn and press my face into Arlo's thigh as I cry.

"I'm *disgusted.*" Ryker's voice curls with disdain and I feel his eyes on us. "This is *disgusting.* Are we just going to allow them to touch each other so… *inappropriately* in our presence?"

"Give it a rest, Ryker," Wesley says.

"It doesn't matter." Owen's tone is somber and distant. "Their time left is short, and they're both damned eternally. Let them do what they want. I need to rest my eyes."

I would laugh at that if I could, as if he's so weary from the events of his day. Not a single man in this forest—in the entirety of Ember Glen—could withstand the impossible trial I just passed.

I passed.

I passed the second of the Trials of Dissension.

Yet they said our time left is short…

"What's going to happen? What happens to us now?" I'm not sure whether I've spoken loudly enough for anyone to hear, or whether anyone would care enough to respond to me if I had.

"Don't answer her." Arlo's tone is clipped, sharp, a quick command to silence anyone who should dare try to tell me what our fate is going to be.

Somehow, I manage to raise my weary head from his thigh, rising to sit sideways between his legs. "I want to know." I meet his eyes. "I want to know what's going to happen to us."

"I'll tell you what's going to happen, sinner." Ryker chuckles. "You're going to—"

"*Stop,*" Owen cuts him off. "*Enough.* This isn't a moment worthy of gloating." He gives Ryker a stern look. "Our brother has fallen. This situation is mournful and I feel *sick* about it… and so should you."

Owen rakes his fingers through his dark hair, then brings up his knees where he rests his elbows. He turns his head to look at Arlo with narrowed eyes, though he doesn't look angry—his stare is filled with confusion, betrayal, maybe even sorrow. "Why have you done this? Why have you let her drag you into sin? Have you lost your convictions, your love for God and your loyalty to uphold His word? Why would you give up your entire future to lose yourself for mere moments in sin with *her*?"

I look at Arlo, watching him as the weight of Owen's judgment settles heavily on his shoulders. I see the way his expression flickers, the way it hurts him to answer to them this way. A small part of me is fearful in this moment where he faces their questioning, where one of his brothers in God has boldly asked him to justify what he and I have done in our secret sin. That small part of me is fearful he may waiver.

His response is crucial; this moment is pivotal.

I stare at Arlo with wide, tear-soaked eyes as I wait for him to speak. Before he responds, he turns his eyes to meet mine instead of theirs. No dishonesty or deceit exists in the small, sad smile that lightly lifts the corners of his lips.

He responds to Owen, but his loving gaze is fixed on mine. "Our moments of sin were filled with more love, more joy, and more passion than a lifetime of dutiful worship to an unseen God has ever brought me."

"Fuck," Ryker interrupts with his disapproval.

Arlo continues on as if Ryker never made a sound. "The God we've been called to worship is one I no longer wish to follow. If He exists in the ways we were told, then He's a hateful, spiteful creator for deeming that we should have pride in what we've done today. I would sooner follow demons than the creator who compelled us to bury these women alive."

Arlo's bound hands close around one of mine. "I'm sorry, Mercy. I am so sorry for all we've done to you, to Delle. I'm sorry for saying all of this now because I know this seals my fate, but if you have taught me anything, it's that my future is worth nothing if it's not a future found in truth, in passion, in love.

"As you would die for your cause, I would die for *you*. I choose death over a future where you're not with me. I choose hell over serving a God who insists upon your pain. I choose you." He briefly glances at my lips. "I feel no regret for telling them now that I love you, Mercy."

Tears spill down my cheeks as I nod, unable to speak, stunned by his admission and overwhelmed by everything that's happened.

His grin broadens for a moment as he returns the nod, then turns to look out at his brothers. No, they're no longer his brothers in God, as he's just renounced his faith. They are the Control—the men who will punish him—and nothing more.

"You asked me why I would give up my future for her," Arlo says to Owen. "The answer is simple, yet you'll all fail to understand it if the only voices you hear are those of men. The simple answer is that I fell in love with a woman who refused to be silenced. She demanded to be heard, and somewhere along the line, I chose to listen. I should have listened long ago, and I've failed her in that way, but I won't fail her now. Hear me when I say she has my heart; I am in *love* with her. Her love is greater to me than God's has ever been. My faith is in *her*, and though loving her leads me to death, I'll choose to take that walk every time."

Owen huffs, closing his eyes for a beat as righteousness takes hold of him. "Falling in love doesn't *work* that way," he says before he opens his eyes, then looks squarely at Arlo. "Love is for the lucky, for the rare partnership between a man and his assigned domestic that God has deemed divine. And he would never sully such a perfect partnership with the physical intimacy meant only for servants to perform.

"I hear you say you fell in love with her, but I don't think you understand what that means. If you do love her, then you would never kiss her, never touch her. If you were truly blessed by God to have found love with her in a divine partnership, then you would have *honored* it. So tell me…just tell me because I have to know. Have you used her in the ways a man would purge with a servant? Have you lost yourself to the Impulse, such that you've mistaken it with love? I need to know the extent of what you've done with her."

"You already know what I've done with her," Arlo replies. "You've already decided that I'm damned, and you already know what my punishment will be."

"Nothing has been decided." Wesley pushes off the tree where he leaned and steps forward.

Owen combs his fingers through his hair again before laying his forehead in his palms. "You know as well as the rest of us that Arlo's fate is sealed. A member of the Control has to be held to the highest standards— it's in the Edict. He's condemned to meet his end with—"

"Meet his end?" I snap.

Wesley speaks slowly, calmly. "I fear you'll judge me for asking this, brothers, but I think it must be asked. Where…" he hesitates, "where is the line between God's will and our own if we were selected by Him to lead this community?"

Wesley is met by a heavy silence, one where all eyes are upon him, watching and waiting for him to go on.

Owen lifts his head from his hands to look at Wesley. "I'm not sure I understand what you're asking."

"If we were chosen by God to be the leaders of Ember Glen, then shouldn't that mean that…well, that we've been chosen to lead? Shouldn't that mean that we could choose a different interpretation of His word? God chose us to lead, and there must be a reason for that. He must want us to exercise some flexibility in the enforcement of His word. Forgiveness is a pillar in His rule, is it not? The Control must be held to the highest of standards, I understand that, but how were these standards selected? And couldn't we alter those standards such that the highest of them are more reasonable for us to attain? We are only human, after all."

"I should hold you in *contempt* for speaking such blasphemous thoughts." Killian's voice echoes outward from the endless cluster of trees.

My anxiety instantly spikes at the sound of his voice, and nausea twists through my gut as he appears through the fog, his lips twisting into a proud sneer. Last I saw him, he was standing at the edge of the cliff beside Ellary and Cambria, watching me climb into my own coffin to sacrifice myself for them.

Where are Ellary and Cambria, anyway?

Did they return to the Homestead?

"What the fuck are you doing here?" Wesley spits, turning to face Killian. His long, black braids slipping over his shoulders as he turns and marches to meet him.

Killian and Wesley come to a stop directly in front of each other as they square off, fuming. I don't quite understand what's happening between them, but there's anger and animosity rippling in waves, sweeping around all of us.

"I came to help my brothers," Kilian says.

"Right off a cliff, you'll help us," Wesley snorts.

"If that's supposed to be an insult—"

"*Stop.*" Owen climbs to his feet, walking over to them. "Enough of this fighting between us," he glances around, "all of us. It's been a long damn day, and we all need to get some rest before we speak to one another again… before we tear ourselves apart and lose control of this community. Domestics are rebelling openly, and if we start fighting against each other, we'll never be able to fight against a rebellion."

Is there truly a rebellion brewing?

My heart beats a little faster at the thought of it. Stefanie's outcry at the processional before my trial had been a loud and clear act of rebellion, even if I hadn't understood the words she shouted.

Circulus vitiosus.

Circulus vitiosus in aeternum.

I think it might mean *vicious circle*, but I still don't know what that means. Arlo's sister, Luna, had whispered something to me about *vicious circle* that day we went to the village, when Arlo had given me a pill that had taken away all the pain of my burned hand and had made me feel so blissfully high that I couldn't recall the exact events, or whatever else Luna had said to me.

And then women had started to shout *circulus vitiosus* from the crowd before my trial. Stefanie had cut her arm in protest, and the Control had taken her into custody.

But why had she cut her arm?

It was the same arm which servants bear the tattoo—an image where two black lines slice straight across the middle of the forearm, wrapping all the way around to form circles which split the image of wildflowers.

So she'd cut her arm in the place where a tattooed circle wraps around mine… Is that the vicious circle? The tattoo?

That doesn't make any sense.

Despite Owen's attempts at finding peace between his brothers, they continue to bicker, voices rising to shouts as they speak over one another, entirely distracted.

Arlo slowly shifts his feet, twisting them beneath him and moving into a crouching position. I look at him, but he's watching the Control—the men so lost in their need to be heard that they aren't even paying attention to us. His hands close around my bicep, and he gives me an encouraging tug as he slowly rises, gives me a quick sideways flash of his blue eyes to make sure I'm rising with him.

Inch by inch, we rise to our feet, and Arlo shifts sideways to stand in front of me. He looks at Delle, shifting his arms slowly in her direction, giving a wave of his fingers to beckon her. She moves slowly, rising, taking gentle steps to move beside us.

With his arms swung out to his side, he nudges the back of his hand against Delle's stomach, urging her backward. I reach out and wrap my hand around her wrist, taking his cue to move her, and I drag her behind me.

I stare at his neck in confusion, wondering why he wanted us to stand and move behind him. Then he takes a slow step backward, forcing me and Delle both to move back as well. He takes us back another step, then another…

Killian says something that must prod Wesley, because Wesley's voice rises to a shout, and all attention is held on them.

Arlo turns his head over his shoulder, and just loud enough for us to hear, he quickly says, "If you don't run, you die. This is your last chance. When I turn…"

"We run," I whisper, finishing his sentence.

I lean forward to press a soft, silent kiss between his shoulder blades. He shudders, and then I see the slow nod of his head.

Mid-shouting match, Killian turns his back on Wesley, and Wesley lunges for him, rushing him on the attack. Owen and Ryker race to stop the fight that threatens to become a brawl, and I know this is it. I know this is the moment where Arlo will turn and we'll run. It's our chance to get a head start before they realize we've fled.

Perhaps it's useless to even try. I'm fast, but I'm exhausted from a trial that nearly killed me. Delle has been walking on her own, but I'm sure she's exhausted as well. I already know we aren't going to win this race, and I imagine Arlo knows it, too.

Yet all the same, I understand why Arlo has made the decision for us to try. It's the same decision I made that night in the forest when everything changed—when Hyatt Price set his sights on me after lighting Ivy Jane on fire, and I knew his intent was to do the same to me. That night, I chose to take a step back. Despite the consequences I knew I would meet for running, I still chose to run because the choice was *mine*. It was the only choice I had the benefit of making, and so, I made it.

I chose to try.

And I choose to try now.

So, when Arlo turns, Delle and I turn with him, and together, we run.

chapter seven
ARLO

WE RUN. WE try. But I don't think we'll make it far. I have to try now because I didn't before when I should have, when we might actually have stood a chance at fleeing this godforsaken place.

The Control knows it all now. They know that my allegiance belongs to Mercy. Death will soon find me, and the thought of her laying witness to it burns inside me. They'll make her live without me before killing her as viciously as they'll kill me.

And there is no doubt, it *will* be vicious.

The Elders will push for brutality in the third trial, and not just because of what Mercy has made herself to the women in this community—a rebel, a saint, a martyr. They'll blame her for ruining me because she's a sinner. They'll be more inclined to hurt her in retaliation for the way she corrupted me. But she didn't corrupt me; she opened my eyes to the truth, but that's not how they'll see it.

So, we run.

Leaping over a large, fallen branch, Mercy stumbles when her foot twists beneath her. Helping her with my hands bound is challenging, but I grip her elbow in my hands and try to steady her all the same.

Delle stops, turns, and Mercy yells, "Go! Run!"

Delle waivers between coming back to help her friend and running from certain death. She never gets to make the choice for herself as Ryker sprints out from the trees at a rapid pace, barrels into her, and takes her down. Mercy sprints after her, running straight for Delle, and I chase after Mercy.

I only make it a few steps before someone collides with my back. My weight pitches forward and I fall, landing face down so hard that the air is knocked from my lungs. Two of the Control are on top of me within seconds, and with my arms pinned between my body and the ground, I know it's over for me.

I turn my cheek to look for Mercy, and see her fighting with Ryker, trying to wrench Delle from his grip so she can run. I want her to help Delle, I do, but more urgently, I want her to help herself. Selfishly, I need Mercy to *run*…with or without us.

"Mercy, *run!*" I shout, and instantly, I regret it because my plea doesn't urge her to move. Instead, it draws her attention to where I'm pinned to the forest floor.

She sees me and stops.

She turns toward me and takes a step.

With anger in her eyes, she runs to me.

Mercy rushes to attack whoever is on my back, to save me, though I don't deserve to be saved by her. Yet before she can reach us, she's stopped short, tackled to the ground by Owen.

Once Mercy is down, that's it.

We tried, and it's over.

We tried, and we failed.

We are all defeated, and none of us can be saved now.

chapter eight

ARLO

"I'M BEYOND WORDS for how far you've fallen, Arlo Rainn." The Elders fume at me from the projector screen in the courtroom. I've been brought to kneel before them beneath the spotlight. My wrists are still bound. I'm covered in dirt and scratches from the tussle in the forest, from trying to escape.

I failed to save her…again.

I keep fucking failing her.

They took her from me the moment we crossed the threshold into the Homestead, and I don't know where she is. I don't know if they've hurt her. It's all I can think about, and it's killing me to stay here on my knees, to face their unwanted judgment when every part of me is screaming to find her.

"We had such *hope* for you!" Lawrence shouts at me through the screen, his fist pounding against an unseen tabletop. "How could you betray us like this? How could you turn your back on God?"

"Don't speak to me of God; you know nothing of true divinity." My words are unfiltered, as are my thoughts. My mind has never been clearer since the events of this awful day.

I'm met by raised voices all around me, everyone shouting their judgment all at once. Killian rushes to my side, lashes his hand against my throat and twists my head sideways to force me to meet his eyes.

"You make me *sick.* I trusted you as my brother in God. We had faith in you as a leader in this community, and all for what? For you to betray us just to get your cock sucked by that filthy sinner?"

His expression is so serious. The hypocrisy of him holding this anger against me for loving a woman at the same moment he faces his own judgment for pushing another off a cliff is so absurd that it makes me chuckle.

"Are you concerned, *brother*, that I didn't return the favor for her? Because I assure you…I did. And believe me when I tell you that I found God right there, between her thighs—"

Killian spits on my face, making it abundantly clear that I've lost his favor—as if it weren't clear enough before. He releases me with a shove that knocks me sideways, but I catch myself with my fists against the ground.

"Let's not forget that you're facing judgment here, too," Wesley says, gripping Killian's shoulders and shoving him down to his knees beside me.

Killian snickers. "I'm facing judgment for what you *think* you saw. We *know* what Arlo has done; the entire village knows. We watched him kiss her!"

"And I watched *you* push Ellary over the edge," Wesley bites back.

"Prove it."

I look over at Killian. "You're a coward. At least I'm man enough to admit to my sins."

His face twists in rage as he lunges for me again, though Wesley pulls him back. Owen moves quickly to stand between us, facing the Elders on screen.

"Give us guidance," Owen pleads. "How do we judge our own brothers for their sins?" His voice is strained as he struggles to come to terms with my betrayal—and there is no doubt my betrayal for loving Mercy is seen as far more horrible than Killian pushing a servant off a cliff.

Guilt weighs me down with my acceptance of the truth—with the recognition that Mercy has always been right, and I have always been wrong. It's painful because I can never see this world the same as I did before. I can never see these men as I did before. I can never forgive myself for all the choices I've made that have caused so much harm.

I don't deserve Mercy's love.

My head drops forward, hanging with sorrow for how I've hurt her, how I've failed her, how I've *used* her.

I put her on trial. I strung her up to be fucked by these men who are so *lost*—as lost as I've been my entire life. I cut her hair in the name of removing a temptation that I couldn't control myself against. I let her take responsibility for a murder that *I* committed—it was no accident that the blade I held slipped across Hyatt's throat that night. I walked her to her own grave, stood by and watched her climb into her own coffin. I closed the lid and allowed her to be buried alive.

And the one time I tried to run with her, to *save* her, I failed. I should have tried before. I should have tried every day. I should have loved her sooner...I should have loved her *better*.

"Only one of your brothers should be kneeling for our judgment right now." I hear Edgar's voice, though I don't look up at the screen. "We've reviewed footage of the broadcast when Ellary fell, and we can't clearly say whether she was pushed. And what would it matter if she was? She's a servant, and she stood as a sacrifice for the trial. Mercy might have made the choice to push her over the edge herself rather than be buried alive, and we would have allowed it—"

"Are you saying…" I lift my head to look at him on screen with narrowed eyes, "that it doesn't matter if Killian pushed her because she was chosen to serve as a pawn in this twisted game?"

"I'm saying that she was selected to serve as a potential sacrifice for Mercy's trial, and we all knew that could result in her death. In fact, most of us expected it would. We all thought Mercy would choose to sacrifice her sisters in service to save herself—it's what we'd hoped for. We wanted the servants to see her push her dearest friends over the cliff's edge and squash this rebellion once and for all."

I scoff. "You are so out of touch with the truth, it's astounding. Mercy is more selfless and compassionate than any one of you could ever dream of becoming. She would *never* harm another to save herself, and the fact that you don't know that is so telling of how ignorant you truly are.

"I hope the servants heed Mercy's words and bring war against you. I hope they turn their backs on the god you crafted to control them. I hope they renounce the Edict and break every law you twisted to fit your narrative in the name of God. They should bring all men to kneel before them and force us to endure the same brutality we've forced upon them, because we have earned it. We *deserve* it.

"I am no longer one of you. I no longer recognize your sacred laws." A prideful smirk twists the corner of my lips. "I'm a sinner, and I hold the name proudly in honor of Mercy Madness. She and I are unholy, and I'll gladly burn in hell with her."

"And burn, you *shall*," Edgar snarls.

"I refuse to hear more of this," Lawrence adds. "I presume we all agree on the fate of Arlo Rainn after that vulgar speech. He's clearly possessed by the same demons who possess Mercy Madness."

"There are no *demons*." I laugh. "There's only truth and clarity, and thank *fuck* she's opened my eyes so I could find both."

"Arlo, stop." Owen's hand lands on my shoulder, fingers digging in harshly. "I can't bear to hear another word of your blasphemy."

In a strange way, I feel bad for Owen. A part of me feels that he could find the truth if he found someone who called to his soul the way Mercy calls to mine. He's the man I was before her, and it's difficult to acknowledge that now—to see myself as I was at my worst in the man standing beside me, calling my own words blasphemy, just as I called hers.

"I move for Arlo Rainn to be burned at the stake in penance of his sins," Ryker says as he steps forward. "He's aligned with sin, and his corruption will only embolden those who seek rebellion."

"I second the motion," Killian says—a murderer with the right to say I should die for my love while he should live for his honor.

"*Malo mori quam foedari,*" I mutter with disdain, and their voices rise around me again.

Edgar's booming voice shakes through the room as he shouts loud enough to cut across the noise, "We will not waste another moment discussing this. There will be no vote. Death is your sentence, Arlo Rainn. By ranking decision of the Elders, we declare it."

"*Death* for his indiscretion with a woman?" Wesley asks in scrutiny. "And what of Killian's judgment?"

"Let it go!" Edgar's outrage is clear. "We saw no definitive proof she was pushed, and regardless, her death is of no consequence."

"Wait," Theo says, "is she dead? I thought she was still alive?"

"She was close enough to death when I left her in Sanctuary," Park says quietly.

"You *left* her in Sanctuary?" I twist my head around to glare at him. "Is she alone? Is anyone assigned to care for her?"

"Silence!" Edgar shouts. "Our word is final. Killian is absolved of any blame. We need him as a leader now more than ever—a strong man of God to lead this village back to the light. But you, Arlo Rainn," he chuckles darkly, "you will be made to suffer from this sunset to the next. And with the rising dawn that follows, you will *burn*."

I huff, resigned to meet my fate. "So be it."

"Hear me now." Edgar's eyes shift around the room, looking at each member of the Control. "You men are tasked with delivering his death publicly. Burn him with Stefanie Price in the village square, and let all see what deviation from God's law will bring them. Let them see that no man or woman is immune from our judgment."

"Then we should burn the trial participants with them," Killian adds. "Let Mercy and Delle burn before the eyes of the village to reassert God's will."

"No," Lawrence snaps. "No. Let Arlo burn, knowing that Mercy will live her final days in misery. Let him know she'll watch him go up in flames, that she'll witness his death. Let him see her in his final moments, knowing that she'll suffer until she meets her own brutal end."

"Hurt him," Clyde adds. "String him up by his own rope and lash him until he bleeds. Bring him pain before the morning of his death. Make him suffer, knowing what you'll do to Mercy in her final trial. Make it known how you will punish her in Service from Bloodshed. Let him go to his death with fear for hers."

My breaths are heavy and quick, my eyes wide with anger that pulses hot through my veins. I'm outraged at their use of Mercy to hurt me, but perhaps I shouldn't be. I should've known how quickly they would turn against one of their own in the name of God.

And before Mercy, I would have done the same.

I'm furious, and I'm frightened. I'm guilty and filled with shame because it's my own actions that will ensure her pain after I'm gone. I'm the one who lost control at her gravesite; I'm the one who showed all of Ember Glen the truth of our forbidden love. She would have been strong enough to hide it.

For my actions, I will burn…but she will suffer.

Even in my death, I don't deserve her.

chapter nine

Mercy

A SUNSET. A sunrise. Another sunset. That's how long I've been locked in my room since the day of the trial, the day we tried to run and we failed. I haven't seen Arlo since we stepped inside the Homestead and they pulled us apart, when they dragged me away from him and locked me here.

Before they left me alone in my room, I'd demanded answers, insisted that they tell me what would happen to us next, but they refused to speak a word. I cried forever when they left, sitting with my back pressed against the locked door and sobbing until my tear ducts ran dry. And then, too easily, I slipped into numbness. I sat motionless for what must have been hours, my gaze unfocused as I dissociated from reality.

Gradually, sensation crept back in, and I was quickly overwhelmed by the feeling of filth caked onto my skin. I looked down at my red gown and the sight of black soil sullying the fabric startled me back to life.

I had to get away from it.

I had to take the dress *off*.

I had to get clean.

I needed to scour every last speckle of dirt from my body.

In a panic, I tore off the wretched gown—the dress that was meant to be the last article of clothing I would ever wear. I drew a warm bath, and with a washcloth, I scrubbed every inch of my body until my skin was raw and pink. Yet even now, it feels as though the soil from my grave has seeped through my pores, like it runs through my veins and has clogged my heart.

My heart...

It stutters and starts through alternating beats of fear and pulses of joy. Fear of what comes next; joy from Arlo's confessions—and for the fact that I survived what should have killed me.

Maybe it should have killed me.

Every moment of my survival since the trial has been torturous. It still feels as though I'm drawing in speckles of soil with each breath I take, and the thought of it keeps me teetering on the edge of panic.

I'm exhausted from balancing on the brink, but I don't dare close my eyes for too long. The darkness behind closed lids only takes me back to my grave, so dark and cold buried beneath the earth.

And I thought hell would be bright and hot from the eternal fire.

I was trapped in that darkness, just as I'm trapped now—alone with my thoughts. This room is only a larger coffin, and every slowly passing moment piles a new shovelful of soil on top.

Will it always feel as though I'm being buried alive?

I have the sense that I cheated death in my trial, and now it's chasing me. Truthfully, I know it's always been chasing me. It's just running faster now—and because he chose to run with me, it's chasing Arlo, too.

Where is he?

Is he safe?

Is he alive?

Does he know that I'm okay? That I love him? That I'd give anything to hold him right now?

I'm fully dressed, awake and aware. I put on a burgundy velvet dress with long sleeves and a sharp V-neck. It fits comfortably with the way the fabric stretches, though it snugly hugs my curves. It's tight to my body until it reaches my hips, but then the skirt flares out from my thighs, cascading to cover my black boots. The sleeves are just a little too long for my arms, but the way they hang over the heels of my palms gives my fidgety fingers something to play with while I pace the carpet in front of my bed.

It's a gown in which I could run, in which I could fight. Of course, I could run and fight better if I wore pants like a man does, but I don't have that option. I'm prepared to flee at a moment's notice, knowing that it would be unwise to get too comfortable here.

It's the middle of the night, but I can't sleep. I've dozed off for brief naps here and there, but nightmares awaken me, and then I remember that I don't know where Arlo is or whether he's okay. I don't know what punishments he'll face for his confessions, for doing things with me that he was never allowed to do.

Punishments for wanting me, for needing me, for loving me.

They're going to hurt him for loving me.

Air catches in my lungs as a sob tries to break free. I press my hand over my heart and draw it back inside with a deep, steady breath. I can't cry anymore. I don't want to. I don't want to waste what little time I have left in this life in sorrow.

I march over to the tray of food placed on the table beside the armchair, and I snatch a handful of blueberries from the small bowl. I pop them into my mouth one at a time, chewing them slowly as I return to pacing, working out my nerves through my gnashing teeth.

I suppose I should be grateful the Control didn't entirely forget that I was a human being who needed sustenance for survival. They brought me a tray of food twice since they left me here alone, and I've been anxiously grazing.

I pace back and forth, eating one blueberry at a time from the small pile in my hand. I pluck another berry from my palm, but the lock on my bedroom door snicks, and I freeze in surprise with the morsel held there against my lips. I stare at the door, waiting, holding my breath as the knob slowly turns.

I step forward as the door creeps open, then stops, and a sudden, jolting fear that it will close again rips through me. The blueberries tumble from my hands and plop onto the carpet. I rush forward, lunging to grab the door. I grip the side of it and wrench it open wide.

I hardly have a moment to register his presence as Theo rushes into my room. He hurries to close the door behind him, then presses his back against it. I feel my forehead scrunch in confusion as my head tilts to the side, waiting for him to speak.

He lets out what seems to be a long-held breath. "This is probably a bad idea."

I close the space between us, coming nearly chest to chest so we can speak in hushed voices. "Where is Arlo? Is he okay? What have they done to him?"

"Mercy, he's… He's not well."

"What do you mean? Where *is* he?"

"He needs you."

"Then take me to him." I reach for the door, but his hand shoots out to the side, easily bumping mine away. He shifts to position himself so he stands between me and the doorknob.

"If I let you out and you're found, the consequences for me would be dire. And by association, so would Delle's."

"Then I won't be found."

"You might be if I let you go to him."

"Where *is* he? Theo, please, tell me what's going on."

He sighs. "He's in the foyer."

My face twists in confusion. "The foyer?"

"He's bound, Mercy. Strung up in the center of the foyer just as you were for Service of the Flesh."

A hard knot in my throat forces me to swallow. "Is he hurt?" Tears I said I would no longer shed burn hot behind my eyes. Fear thrusts between my ribs like a knife, stabbing me in the heart. "Is he hungry? Can he rest? Is he able to sit?"

My mind races through memories of being suspended above the starburst tile during my first trial. I remember the ache of my muscles after seven hours of straining against the rope, the panic of having no control.

What would they do to him?

How long has he been bound there?

"Theo, I can't—"

Unexpectedly, he draws me into his arms, pulling me into a warm, heavy-handed hug that I didn't know I needed—and I do need it. Yet the warmth and kindness are too much for me, insisting that I let go for just a moment and lose myself to sobbing heartache.

No. No more crying. No more tears.

I put my hands on his chest to push away from him as I step back. "Just tell me. *Please.* I need to know everything."

His expression is somber. "He's hurt, Mercy. He hasn't eaten. There's enough slack in his bindings that he can sit, but I doubt he can truly rest." His head drops as he swipes a hand over his mouth. He looks down at the floor, his forehead wrinkling in confusion. "How could he ever rest away from you like this? I couldn't rest away from Delle knowing—"

"Theo, please," I stop him before he says something that will only further break my heart. "Why are you here? Why did you come to me?"

He meets my eyes. "Mercy, he's a wreck. I don't know…I thought maybe I could sneak you out to see him, but—"

"But nothing. Do it. Take me to him."

"If you get caught… If *I* get caught—"

"I won't get caught."

"He's out in the open. If any of them wake up and wander downstairs, you'll be found."

"Is it dark? Are the lights out?"

"Yes."

"Then I'll have plenty of time to hide if someone comes."

"If they find you, and they realize that I'm the one who let you out, it won't just be bad for me. If they strip me of being her warden—"

I step close and grab his face. "You already know that I would *never* do anything to jeopardize Delle's well-being. I will *not* get caught, and no one will know you let me out. I promise you, Theo. I swear. I know she needs you. But right now, Arlo needs me more." I release him and step back, giving him space to choose, to open the door for me—because I know he will. "You wouldn't be standing here right now if you didn't know that."

He sighs and his shoulders slump. Slowly, he nods and takes a small step toward me. "I'm going back to my room. I was never here. And you *will* be back in this room when I return with breakfast in the morning. You'll be here before sunrise."

I nod. "I understand."

He turns and reaches for the knob.

"Theo…Thank you."

"I haven't done anything," he whispers, pulling open the door to reveal the unlit hallway. "Nothing at all." He reaches over to flip off the light in my room, and we're cast into darkness. I sense the shadow of him slip out of the room and walk away.

chapter ten
Mercy

IN MY MIND, I count to ten before stepping into the hallway. I'm surrounded by shadow, entombed in the pitch-black darkness. Not a single light is on, and the entire manor is asleep. It's eerily silent and unusually still, even the air around me feels particularly stagnant.

I take a few steps, moving in the direction of the staircase, but I find that whether I move or stand still, everything around me looks the same—like dark, black night. It looks like I haven't moved at all. It looks like I'm pushing against a never-ending wall of darkness, and I feel trapped by it, condensed by it, like it closes in all around me, and I can't escape.

Just as I couldn't escape my grave.

Suddenly, I'm back in my coffin.

I gasp. I stop. I double over, placing my hands on my knees as I fight to breathe.

I can't breathe.

My lungs ache. My chest is tight. My heart is pounding.

I have to get out of here.

I turn to go back to my room, eager to flip on the light, but then a pained groan echoes from ahead, and it halts me…It calls to me.

Arlo.

I hear his pain, and it pulls me from my grave.

I push against the crushing darkness and rush down the hall. I reach out with both hands, sweeping them in front of me as I seek the banister. Relief washes over me to see a trace of moonlight peeking in through the window downstairs. It's faint, but it's enough light for me to follow. It's enough light to keep me from being swallowed by the darkness.

I find the top of the staircase, and with my palm wrapped around the banister, I pause. My gaze sweeps down the dark steps, and at the bottom, I find Arlo. I can see his shape, outlined by shadows in the foyer beneath me. A true sense of urgency takes hold of me, and nothing matters but being near him. I turn at an angle to grip the railing with both hands, rushing so I can get to him as quickly as possible.

I descend, moving closer to the window where the moon sends us its meager light. My heart thuds against my ribs, urging me to get to him, to put my hands on him and give him comfort.

I finally step down onto the tile floor, and I reach out my hands toward his silhouette. "Arlo," I whisper as my fingers graze his bare back—his skin is warm, though I expected it to be cold.

He startles, jerking his arms, which I think are bound above him with ropes around each wrist. I flatten my hands against him as I press in closer, and it takes me a moment to work out his position. My touch rests between his shoulder blades, but they only reach the height of my hips so, he must be sitting on the floor.

"It's me," I whisper.

"*Mercy…*" All the air rushes from his lungs in relief. "You're okay?"

"I'm okay." I let my hands slip down his back as I lower to my knees, but his skin isn't smooth as I would've expected. It's rough, and there's dampness in spots.

He's injured. Is this blood?

His muscles twitch, jerking away from my touch. I quickly move my hands away from his back and around his torso. I stop my palms on his chest as I kneel beside him. Shifting closer, my knee bumps against his thigh. His legs are stretched out in front of him, though the bindings around his wrists keep him sitting upright on the floor. I reach up to grab his face, but the angle is odd. I need to be closer.

He needs me closer.

I hurry to shimmy up my skirt and raise it to my hips. I climb over him, straddling his lap before placing my hands on his cheeks, lifting his drooping, weary head. I kiss him first, before another word is uttered, before another moment passes us by.

"What did they do to you?" I ask, dropping my forehead to meet his.

"It doesn't matter."

"What happened to your back? Does it hurt?"

He doesn't answer right away, but eventually, he says, "Yes."

"I'm sorry. I'm so sorry. Am I hurting you? Should I move?"

"Don't move," he says quickly, and I'm grateful because I instantly regretted the offer. "Stay close. Stay right here with me."

"I'm with you. I'm always with you."

I tilt my chin to kiss him slowly, and though I intended it to be chaste and comforting, he insists that it be *more*. He parts my lips with his, beckoning me to deepen the connection. I melt into him, bring my arms around him, and hug myself close.

He pours love into my soul, feeds me affection with each swipe of his tongue. He strips me of my armor and lowers my defenses. He draws each of my emotions to the surface—even the ones I'm trying so hard to fight. An unexpected sob leaps up my throat, and it breaks our kiss. Though I try to stop the tears from flowing, they insist on being shed. I drop my face to his shoulder and I cry.

"I wish I could hold you." He turns his face to press against my cheek. He draws in a deep breath as the tip of his nose nudges strands of my hair, brushing over my skin until he reaches my ear. "You still smell like wildflowers. Wildflowers and starlight…I wish I could see you better."

My tears slick his skin, and I feel ashamed for it. He's bound and hurt, and here I am crying when I should be comforting him. I kiss the crook of his neck, letting my lips linger as I fight to steady my emotions, waiting until I feel like I can speak without sobbing. Then slowly, I lift my head from his shoulder, blinking away the remaining tears so they no longer glass over my eyes, but drip down my cheeks instead.

"You said they hurt you." I swallow against the lump in my throat. "What did they do?"

"I don't want to talk about that. I don't care." He draws in a shaky breath. "I was so afraid for you, starlight. You're okay, and that's all I care about. It doesn't matter what they did to me."

"It matters to me. Tell me."

"It's nothing."

"What did they do?"

"Mercy, don't—"

"*Tell me.*"

"They whipped me, Mercy." His voice turns harsh, agitated, even in our hushed speaking. "Do you really want to recount the details with me? They tortured me slowly, a few lashings here and there from one night to the next. I've been bound here and tortured since the night we returned from your trial, and it ended only hours ago."

I don't know what to say to him. My heart hurts for what they've put him through. Yet there's a selfish part of me that feels some vindication to know he's experienced a fraction of the torment I've endured for years as a servant.

Now he knows my pain firsthand, and strangely, that makes me feel closer to him than I've ever felt before—when he could only hear my words and imagine what it was like to serve. But now he knows because he lives it. It hurts me that he lives it, but this pain connects us deeply.

After moments of my silence, he speaks again, and his quiet voice is gentler this time. "I'm sorry. Mercy, I'm so sorry for what we've done to you, for what *I* have done to you. You were right all along—right about how wrong things are in Ember Glen. I was so blinded by my faith that I couldn't see it on my own. I couldn't see it until you showed me and I'm so sorry for all the pain—"

"You don't have to do this," I cut him off because I forgave him the moment 'I'm sorry' slipped from his lips.

"Let me finish. I need you to hear me. I won't take unspoken words to my grave."

His grave.

To hear him speak of his own death is jarring.

I speak slowly, softer than a whisper because I'm afraid of saying the words out loud. "Arlo, tell me the truth. Have you been sentenced to die for your sins with me?"

Silence.

Tense moments of painful, honest silence.

"I have."

I gasp at the admission, though I expected it. We both expected it, yet knowing it's been decided is shocking in a way I couldn't have imagined.

"I regret nothing, starlight. I need you to know that. I would choose to sin with you all over again, even if it meant dying a million painful deaths. I hurt you. I failed you, time and again. And yet, you loved me. I'm grateful for you. I'm grateful for every stolen moment, every breath, every whisper, every heartbeat. They may burn me at the stake come morning, but my love for you is fireproof. They can never truly take me away from you."

"Come morning?" A tremor moves through me. I strain my eyes against the dark, willing them to adjust and let me see the blue of his eyes.

'They may burn me at the stake come morning...'

My hands are moving before I even form a coherent thought, slipping along his arms, over the ropes tied around his wrists. I'll untie him. I'll free him. We'll escape over the mountains; I don't even care what exists on the other side of them.

"Mercy, stop."

"I'll untie you and we'll go. We'll run together, one last time."

"You can't untie me."

"Yes, I can, I—"

My voice cuts short as I realize it's not just rope. There are metal cuffs around his wrists, which are attached to chains that are tangled with the rope in such a way that they don't make a sound. I could free him from rope alone, but I can't undo these chains.

"Theo already tried," Arlo tells me. "And even if you could get me free, we can't get out of the Homestead. They've deactivated the band."

The black band that all the Control wear. The one that's latched around their wrist, permanently affixed when they take their oath at the Shift and become one of the Control. It's the black band that unlocks all the doors in the Homestead. The one they wear with them to the grave.

If it's deactivated, then we can't get out.

If it's deactivated, then it's…it's over.

"But I—" My thoughts stutter. "I need a warden for my final trial."

It's a stupid, selfish reply to everything he's just said to me, but my mind feels broken, and I'm grasping at straws. I can't fathom living without him. I can't comprehend the reality of this.

I was supposed to die first.

I was meant to die in these trials.

And now he's telling me that this is the last I will ever see him.

"Even if they showed me mercy and allowed me to live, do you really think there's any scenario in which they would allow me to remain your warden?" He chuckles a little but there's no humor in it. "I confessed to committing atrocious acts with my ward, with a true sinner on her way to death. Not only did I fuck a woman outside of service, but I fell in *love* with her. They don't want love in Ember Glen because it makes you too bold, too powerful, too idealistic—and the Elders can't have that."

He pulls himself up, sitting taller, leaning into me. "Though, I have to be truthful with you, starlight. I think I might have found their forgiveness when I faced judgment if I'd been willing to show some humility. Instead, I committed the worst offense of all." His lips brush my cheek on the way back to meet my ear. "I showed no remorse for any of it."

I shudder at the touch of him, at his nearness, at the warmth of his breath against my skin.

"They asked me to repent for the sins I committed with you, and I refused." He kisses the spot just beneath my ear and my head tilts naturally to open more for him. "I would've used my last breath to refuse it, Mercy. I would've let them kill me rather than lie. Because what we are, what we've done, who we've become…it's greater than God, bigger than the universe. We're beyond death, starlight. You and I are eternal."

"I love you." The words rush out of me just before I turn to capture his lips, and I kiss him with more passion than I ever have before.

I sweep my tongue inside his mouth and he hastily meets it with his, licking me, consuming me like I'm the most delicious thing he's ever tasted. My back arches, my body molds to his, my hands slip up the sides of his neck to hold him steady as I grip just beneath his jaw.

"You taste so sweet," he mutters against my lips. "What did you eat?"

"Blueberries," I reply, and then I slump, realizing he hasn't eaten in at least a day. "I'm sorry, I should have brought you some." I start to shift off his lap. "I'll go get—"

"Don't you dare move from my lap, Mercy Madness. The only thing I need to consume right now is you. Let me taste you. Let me love you." His voice is sultry, filled with heat and need, but it wavers when he says, "Let me have you one last time."

One last time...

"One last time?"

The deep sorrow over our fate threatens to devour me, to break me into a sobbing mess, crying on the floor until all my tears dry up. But I know that wouldn't be right. I would regret losing myself in sorrow instead of losing myself in *him*. I have him now, and I'll be damned if I let sadness take this moment from us.

One last time?

"This won't be the last time, Warden Rainn. They could end us both right this moment, and I'd only find you again in hell." I press my lips to his as I shift my hips forward, settling my weight so he can feel me. "And I would do things to you that would make the demons threaten to cast us out for depravity."

I feel his lips move against mine as he smiles, groaning softly. "And you know I would welcome it."

He captures me in a rough kiss that quickly turns frantic. We easily devolve into lust-driven fools who risk everything for another forbidden moment, another filthy and beautiful memory of physical love to hold on to in our final days.

I've faced death already.

I've accepted my fate.

And though I thought Arlo would last—that he could bring change to Ember Glen—there's something darkly comforting about knowing that he'll join me in death if it's going to find me, anyway. If there is an afterlife—if hell really does exist—there's a twisted sense of comfort in knowing that we'll quickly find each other in the flames.

And we'll burn together eternally.

chapter eleven

ARLO

MY SANITY HAD been slowly slipping away from me before she descended, before Mercy crept from the darkness surrounding me—my starlight in the endless black universe.

The end is coming for both of us and there is no hope of changing that. Yet somehow, in this moment, I find that I don't care. There is no space in my mind to think of the future or of death. My only need is to exist within her.

I'm lost in her rough, urgent kiss, enchanted by her touch, enthralled by her very presence. She fuels me with raw, undeniable passion, spurring a visceral need that was inevitable from the moment she arrived at my side.

I am so in love with this woman.

In all my years of purging and debauchery, I have never known such pleasure as what I feel with Mercy. I never felt satisfaction before her. Purging has kept us at arm's length from true bliss—it disconnected our souls from the physical acts we committed with servants.

If I had known—if *any* of us had known—how incredible it feels to fight for mutual release, to seek shared pleasure in tandem, then Ember Glen would've crumbled long ago.

My hands feel like they've been set on fire, like my scars have been freshly lit by a flame that could only be extinguished by the touch of her flesh beneath my palm.

Yet I'll find no relief for my scarred hands—hands I've used to punish myself for having desire outside of service. A lifetime of self-mutilation, of burning my own flesh to distract myself from the pangs of lust...

And all for what?

If I'd known how essential lust would be—if I'd known that I would find peace, harmony, and acceptance in our mutually feral cravings for one another—I would've given into her from the beginning. I would have given myself to her freely and without restraint.

My burning hands fight for relief, my arms jerking against my bindings. I'm bound at the wrists, and there's only enough slack to allow my elbows to bend at shoulder height. They could have just bound me with the chains and metal cuffs around my wrists alone, but Killian is a fucking demon disguised as a human, and he took great pleasure in using my own rope against me.

I hope he dies a slow, brutal death.

If the situation weren't so dire, I'd have to laugh at the irony. I'm strung up by my own rope, bound by my own rigging. I'd secured it to the ceiling myself for Mercy's first trial so that men as vile as me could desecrate the woman who had freed my soul.

And it serves me right.

I deserve to be strung up this way in penance to her…or perhaps, in this moment, as a gift for her.

Turning my wrists, I stretch my hands and wrap my palms around the braid of rope and chain that tethers me. I grasp firmly, using my grip to lift myself, to sit just a little taller, to hold my form solidly, and give her what strength I have left. She stifles a moan as my chest flexes, rigid against the softness of her breasts pressed against me in her tightening embrace.

"Pull down your dress. Take them out for me," I growl against her lips. "Let me bite and suck that soft flesh until you're dripping wet for me."

She leans back just enough where I can make out the movement of her dark silhouette, the motion of her pushing down one sleeve, then the other. She lowers her gown to free her perfect breasts, and I only wish I could see them more clearly in this damn darkness. Her weight against my lap lessens as she rises onto her knees. She leans into me, and I nearly come undone as I feel the mound of her flesh bump against my cheek.

If only I could lay my hands on them…

I can't touch her, but I can taste her. I turn my head to brush my lips over her skin.

"I'm already wet for you," she whispers. "But I want more. I need you to make me drip with desperation."

I groan at her perfect filth as my lips graze her nipple, already peaked, hardening easily in her desire. I flick my tongue over the nub a few times until she's huffing with sweet, desperate little breaths, her body twitching, muscles clenching with each swipe. And when I finally suck the peak between my lips, she melts.

Mercy leans into me as she arches her back. Her arms are wrapped around my head to hold me there as I rhythmically suck, drawing out the desperation she asked me to give her.

I'll make her desperate, but she doesn't need to be.

I would never leave her unsatisfied, unrelieved.

Except my hands are bound and I can't touch her.

I scrape my teeth over the sensitive nub, kiss it, bite into the side of her thick mound before I move to the other one. I kiss my way along the inside toward the peak and mutter against her skin, "It kills me that I can't touch you."

"It kills me, too," she agrees sadly.

"Use your hands where I can't use mine, starlight." I play with her nipple using my teeth and tongue. "Put your hands between us. Stay close to me, and let me feel your fingers slip down our stomachs together." Another lick, a hard suck that draws her nearer. "And when you reach between your legs, sit heavy on my lap so I can feel your hand move as you touch yourself."

It's quiet between us for a few beats as I continue my pleasure-filled assault on her breasts. Then, gradually, her grip loosens. Her hands land softly on my shoulders before slipping down my chest. She drags her palms down my stomach, her back arching to keep herself firmly pressed against me. She's so close, and I imagine she feels the same drag of desire pulling down her stomach. Where I feel it through her palms, she must feel the same at the backs of her hands.

She pauses at my belt, her fingertips curling to slip behind the elastic of my boxer briefs. She tugs at the fabric, teasing me, but she doesn't free me yet. Letting go, she gently rakes her fingertips over the bulge trapped beneath layers of fabric. She does it again and again—teasing me so sweetly—until my entire body is trembling with need for her.

Her palm cradles my cock, lightly squeezing, and I draw in a sharp breath through my nose to avoid calling out her name in desire. I lean in to press my face between her breasts, deeply inhaling the sweet and heady scent of her skin as she rhythmically squeezes my cock.

"I want this," she whispers. "I want you."

"Sweet sin," I mutter, turning my face and sinking my teeth into the side of her breast.

"Arlo," she gasps.

"I wish I could feel your warmth on my fingers." I sigh. "Feel it for me, starlight. Touch yourself. Sink your fingers inside you."

She shifts, bringing her hips closer. The back of her hand falls to rest against my hardening cock. Her knees slide further apart on the tile as she lowers, and her fingers move between our bodies. I can feel her hand stretch and flex as she starts to play. I know the moment her fingertips graze her sex because she huffs out a small breath of relief—relief, though she trembles with a greater need still unsatisfied.

She teases herself through heavy breaths that make me harder, thicker. And then she gasps at the same moment her body sinks, impaling herself on her fingers. Her weight pushes her knuckles down, heavy against my cock, almost painfully in the way they dig into me. Yet I welcome the ache because it feels so good when it's delivered by her touch. Only Mercy could make pain feel like pleasure.

She moans, forcing out a heated breath that sets me on fire, makes desire burn low in my stomach, and draws pleasure down to my twitching cock.

"Fuck your fingers." My voice is deep and feral, though I fight to keep quiet in the dark. "Do it for me. Let me feel you move. Fill me with the sweet sound of your whimpering desperation until you're ready for me to fill you."

Her free hand grips the back of my neck, holding me close as she drops her forehead to mine. "I'm ready," she pants, her hips rolling forward with short, smooth thrusts. "I'm ready for you now."

"No, you're not. You want to be…but you're not."

"I'm always ready for you," she protests with another gliding forward thrust, then back.

"No. I want you more than ready. I want you *frantic* with need. I want you pulsing, swollen, aching for relief before you fuck me. I want you so ready that you nearly come the moment I'm inside you."

She shudders at my words as she continues to move forward, then back. "I could come on my fingers right now. I don't want to, but I could."

As if to prove her point, she hastens the pace of her rolling hips. The back of her hand rocks with her body as it pulses against my bulge, making her knuckles dig in harshly. She fucks her fingers like she's riding my cock, and I'm so damn hard that it hurts.

"Tell me…" she pants as she moves. "Tell me you need me now. Tell me to take out your cock. Tell me how much you need me to make you come."

"Sweet *fucking* sin," I growl as I tilt my chin to kiss her deeply.

I didn't want to rush this…I wanted us to take our time.

I know she can't stay here with me all night. I know it will only lead to more misery for her if we're found together, and I can't be the reason she's met with more misery.

This one moment is it for us—the last we'll ever feel each other. I wanted to draw it out; I wanted to make it last because the thought of it ending is too much for my mind to take. Though perhaps it's not the length of time spent in this physical affection that would make it perfect…Perhaps it can only be perfect because it's fleeting.

"*Please*," she begs, her parted lips brushing mine.

The way she wants me—the way I need her *right this fucking second*—overcomes me. "Do it. Take my cock out and fuck me, Mercy. Let me inside you." Suddenly, I'm panting. The slow burn I tried to maintain has burst into flames within me, lighting me on fire.

She pulls her hand from between us and sits heavily. I groan at the feel of her pressing her pussy down hard, soaking my slacks with her wetness. She flexes her hips, grinding slowly, driving me wild.

The heady scent of her arousal draws nearer—I can smell the intoxicating scent of her before her slickened fingers find my lips, slowly dragging across them. I open my mouth and capture her fingertips with my tongue, licking from knuckle to nail. She pushes them inside my mouth, encouraging me to taste her again, and greedily, I do. I swirl my tongue around them, lick and taste and suck her fingers until she tugs, pulling them away from me.

For seconds, she's stark still, silent.

"I hate this," she whispers.

Her words strike like lightning.

I try to bring my hand to her cheek, but my arm only jerks against my bindings, reminding me that I can't touch her. *This* is the worst form of torture.

"I hate it, too," I admit.

In one swift motion, she slides back to sit on my thighs while her hands drop to my belt, quickly working at the buckle.

"I hate them. All of them. *Everyone*." Her voice is odd—curt, frantic, angry, and sorrowful all at once.

She unfastens the button and pulls down the zipper of my slacks. I grip my bindings, pulling against them to lift my hips for her. Her nails claw my skin as her fingers curl, hooking into the elastic of my boxer briefs. She grabs hold and harshly tugs, dragging my pants and underwear down to my thighs.

"I hate this place. I *fucking* hate it," she grits through her teeth.

She rises onto her knees, moving closer again. She lowers her body just enough so her wet warmth teases across the tip of my cock as she puts herself in position.

"Mercy," I groan.

She shifts her hips, taking me inside her no more than an inch. "I have hated every moment of this awful life that was chosen for me until you became my warden…And then I hated it even more."

She chuckles darkly, wiggling with me barely inside her. The way she teases me is agonizing. I'm panting, throbbing, *dying* to be buried deep inside her.

"I hated it," she says, "and then you made me love it. With no warning, Arlo Rainn, you took every moment of hatred and twisted it into something I could never have. I could never have had you—" Her voice breaks, and my hands are on fire again, burning with the need to touch her.

"They would never let me have you, and the proof is here, twisted through the ropes that bind you." Her palms touch my cheeks. She grabs hold of my face, bringing her forehead down to touch mine. "They never wanted us to have each other because they know how dangerous we are together. They think they can tear us apart, but they don't understand, my love. They can't separate us now, not by putting me behind a locked door or binding you with ropes and chains. They can't even separate us in death, because even there, I will find you."

With a shared moan that shakes violently through us both, she lowers fully, sinking me all the way inside her. She tremors against me, both in pleasure and in sorrow.

"I will find you again," she promises.

She presses a kiss to my lips, lingering sweetly before a sob breaks free. I feel like chiseled stone, cracks rippling throughout my soul at the sound of it. She cries freely, wrapping her arms around me and hugging me close as she nuzzles her face into the crook of my neck. And while she cries, she moves—a gentle rocking of her hips, forward and back.

"We'll find each other," I promise, turning to kiss the side of her head before nuzzling my nose through her hair, letting myself become overwhelmed by the scent of wildflowers that's present each and every time I breathe her in.

Each gentle motion draws intense pleasure through my cock, but *sweet sin*, the way she clings to me, the way she needs me, the way she *loves* me… there's a pleasure I've never known radiating through my soul.

Her crying gradually fades, lessening with each sweep of her hips as they rock. The hiccups that shook her while tears slicked the curve of my neck become slow, heavy breaths, breaths that hasten with each passing moment. Her panting, her small, sweet whimpers tell me how good it feels for her, despite the fact that her heart is breaking.

And my heart is breaking with hers.

Though a part of me wants to fight the pain and be strong for her, I know I can't. This hurts too much. And if she feels a fraction of the pain I feel, then it's too much for me to let her bear alone. So, I let myself get lost in the ache of it, let myself shed tears with her for the perfection of this moment on the brink of our demise.

We share tears as she moves me inside her, and gradually, surprisingly, the pain begins to change. It twists, blending with the overwhelming physical pleasure of our bodies, morphing into pure bliss for sharing something with her that I can only describe as *more*.

She's not just holding me, it's *more*.

She's not just fucking me, it's *more*.

This is what they're trying to keep us from finding. This is love in a very visceral way. It's dangerous, terrifying, brutal, and beautiful. It's finding that we still have strength, even in our weakest hour.

I have strength to face the end because of her, because she gave me truth and peace and *this*. She gave me this love when I did nothing to earn it, all because she saw me and all she hoped I could become.

An absolutely unholy tremor tears through my spine as the truth strikes me—that she and I crafted this passion between us. Together, we created a connection that was never meant to exist, and it changed the course of everything. She and I are making this love together, adding to it with each touch, building upon it with each breath, making it grow with each slip and stroke of our bodies. Our hearts are pounding through the pain of our fates, and our bodies grant us all-consuming pleasure in reprieve.

I let my lips brush her ear. "Wildflowers and starlight."

She shudders, and her movements hasten. Her cheek stays pressed to mine as her hands climb up my arms. Her palms touch mine, and I quickly lace our fingers together, clamping my hands around hers to hold them tight so she doesn't let go.

She fucks me wildly, refusing to slow her pace until she's panting, chasing release, her inner walls squeezing and pulsing around me. Her lips brush my cheek as they quickly seek my lips, and I silence her with a kiss as her explosive release barrels through her. Her brutal, beautiful motion and the sensual sweep of her tongue over mine spurs me to come inside her.

She feeds me unspoken words through her deepening kiss…

I love you.

I need you.

I'll find you again.

Her rocking hips slow and her eager kiss softens. Her grip on my hands loosens as her palms brush down my arms before she wraps them around me, clinging to me like she'll never let go. She lovingly kisses my cheek before resting her head on my shoulder.

My heart feels light and heavy all at once.

Mercy sighs, settling herself in this embrace, holding on to me as though she'll never let go.

"Wildflowers and starlight," she murmurs against my skin.

The words circle around my head, floating in the air, forever lingering in the ethereal space that surrounds our souls whenever we're joined.

Fresh tears slip down my cheek, and I don't fight them.

I can't fight what her love has done to me.

I don't want to.

Loving her is what brought us here. It's the reason why I'm facing my death now, but I wouldn't change it. I could never regret falling in love with Mercy Madness.

My only regret is that I didn't love her sooner.

chapter twelve

Mercy

THICK FLAKES OF white snow tumble softly from the overcast sky. The air is cold and stagnant, still and silent. The world around me seems unreal, as if I'm already dead, a ghost haunting this plane of existence, trapped in this purgatory where peace evades me.

Theo leads me out through the front door of the Homestead, his hand wrapped firmly around my elbow. Delle is on my other side, but she's withdrawn, distant, broken. Her arms are crossed tightly over her chest, and her gaze is downcast—she hasn't made eye contact with me yet. The trial stole something from her soul that she'll never get back. I know what it stole from me, but I wonder what she lost.

Her innocence?

Her peace?

Her hope?

Perhaps she lost them all.

I've lost my compassion, and I've lost my instinct to help. I've lost my strength, my willingness to try, my hope. It's all gone, shed with the ocean of tears I spilled last night, alone in my room.

Arlo and I were lucky we weren't caught together in the foyer, though it's not like either of us truly cared if we got caught. It's not as if they could worsen our onrushing fates—I didn't care about that at all. But as sunrise neared, Arlo reminded me of what I'd told him, that Theo had let me out of my room to be with him, and we both knew he would be met with severe consequences if found out—and that meant consequences for Delle, too.

I suppose I still had some selflessness and compassion remaining; my love for Delle is something they could never take away from me. I knew she still needed someone strong like Theo at her side because I'll have no strength left for her once Arlo is gone. But now my empathy seems out of reach…and if it's not gone entirely, then it's buried too deep within my soul for me to grasp.

I feel numb.

I feel lost.

I feel like Theo is moving me through an illusion of reality, a hallucination, a waking nightmare about to unfold.

His grip tightens on my arm as we move toward the stone steps that lead to the square. I turn my head, dropping my gaze to look at his hand. His fingers are wrapped around my red velvet sleeve—the same dress I'd hiked up over my hips last night so I could straddle Arlo and sink him inside me.

I blink, forcing myself to focus on the present. I see just how hard Theo's fingers are digging into my flesh, like he's expecting me to fight him for freedom at any moment now. When I look up at his face, I find his expression is tight—jaw clenched, eyes hard and fearful all at once.

What does he have to be fearful about?

"Wh-what's going on?" Delle asks with a frantic voice, and my head whips to look over at her. Her eyes are wide as she stares toward the square at the bottom of the stone steps.

My gaze hadn't even traveled that far yet, completely lost in the cascade of softly falling snowflakes. It's beautiful, yet it's haunting. It seems too early for snow here in the final days of October—it seems to fall as an odd distraction, brought in by the cold air that settles heavily all around me, that feels stifling in its stillness.

I feel like I can't move against the stagnant air, can't breathe through it. It nearly takes my mind back to the grave, but then my eyes catch the snowflakes again. They're large, resembling tiny tufts of cloud falling from the sky, and my foggy mind is mesmerized as I watch them slowly float toward the ground.

A distraction…

I'm forcefully hauled into reality with a sharp and sudden sting that slices through my heart, as if someone's just taken a knife and thrust it into my chest…only there's nothing there. I don't know where the pang comes from, but it hurts. It hurts so badly that I feel tears well behind my eyes.

Something compels me to track the line drawn by Delle's eyes, following the path of her fearful confusion until I'm looking out at the center of the village square…and my heart violently drops into my stomach.

"It's not for you," Theo reassures Delle, though his tone is sorrowful. "It's not for either of you."

Two piles of brush and logs sit in the center of the square. The piles are arranged intentionally—brush, thick around the base with logs angled to point upward toward a pole fixed at the center and staked into the ground.

No…No!

I step backward, and Theo pulls. I bend my knees, using my weight to pull against his grip with all my might. I grab at his hand, trying to pry his fingers, to loosen his grip.

"*No*," I whimper, twisting, pulling, fighting. "It's not for him…" I grit my teeth, clenching my jaw with determination as I claw at Theo's fingers. I drop my weight hard, nearly falling to sit, though his grip on me is strong enough to yank me back to my feet. "Say it's not for him, Theo!"

"Don't do this, Mercy," Theo's voice lacks conviction, but his hold on me is strong. He jerks me closer, facing me squarely as he grabs both of my arms. "Let him—" his voice cracks. "Let him go with some dignity left."

Dignity?

"There is no *dignifying* this!" I fight even harder to get out of his grip, and he struggles to hold on to me through my violent thrashing.

"God," I hear Delle mutter softly. "Oh, God, *no*. What are they doing?"

The sound of her fearful voice cuts through the madness taking hold of me, and somehow, it brings my fighting to an abrupt end. I freeze, overwhelming panic washing over me, turning me to stone. With wide eyes, I look past Theo's shoulder, casting my stare down the stone steps and out toward the center of the square. My hesitation gives Theo pause, too, and his head turns over his shoulder to follow where Delle and I both watch with dread.

Stefanie Price is brought forward, positioned to stand on a small platform affixed atop the angled logs, facing the Homestead. The crowd of villagers and servants who have come to watch are gathered near the bottom of the stone steps, facing her—facing the two stakes that are meant to go up in flames.

Before the trial, she protested in a clear act of rebellion. And for that, they've sentenced her to die. So quickly, so easily, they've chosen to end her life for having a voice and using it.

Circulus vitiosus in aeternum.

I don't know what it means, but I don't have to know to understand the intent. It was a shout against the Control, against the Elders, against the whole of Ember Glen.

I slowly step forward and Theo moves with me. I take a single step down the stone staircase without even realizing it, but then I feel too weak to take another. My body slumps, lowering to sit on the top step of the staircase. Theo releases me—perhaps he's satisfied that I'm no longer on my feet and fighting to run—but he remains close to my side.

I'm transfixed, unable to look away from Stefanie. I watch with wide eyes as her arms are brought behind her back and tied to the stake with rope. It's hard to tell from this distance, but I think her eyes are shut. Even if they are, she looks strong and powerful, with her chin tilted toward the sky.

They're going to kill her.
They're going to light her on fire.

I fall back into a trance, my eyes unfocused on the scene laid before me, focusing instead on the white tumbling snowflakes.

I hear the voices of women in the crowd—the voices of domestics, no less—screaming, crying, openly calling out for Stefanie to be given another chance. Their voices seem disembodied—there, but not—faded into the background of my gradually detaching sense of reality.

Though my distressed mind begs me to remain in this trap of dissociation, it's the men's voices that draw me away from detaching entirely. The men shout, raising their voices with anger above the women. I force myself to regain focus and see husbands grabbing their wives, jostling them violently within the crowd, shaking them, telling them with force what they should feel about this, what they should think, and what they should believe.

The men want to see Stefanie burn.

They wanted to see *me* burn, but instead of a quick death, I was given this drawn-out torture through the trials. I'm a dead woman all the same.

My pulse thrums, my heartbeat quickening as I feel a sudden shift. The stagnant air moves, grabbing my attention. A breeze that's barely existent draws my gaze away from the crowd, away from Stefanie, and shifts my focus to the second stake.

The noise from the crowd gradually fades, one voice after another falling silent until the world is so quiet that you could hear a pin drop, and then…

I stop breathing.

My heart stops beating.

Arlo steps from the crowd.

Killian and Ryker flank him, bringing him forward before the stake. A cold current rips through my body and causes me to tremble. I shiver violently, eyes open wide and unblinking. I can't look away as he steps up onto the platform. He turns to face the Homestead, his head bowed, looking down at the ground as Killian and Ryker work together to bind him to the stake.

Slowly, his chin rises. His gaze scrapes beyond the crowd as if they don't exist between us. He finds me without searching, locks in on me beyond the distance and obstacles between us, and I don't think I can—

I can't breathe.

They're going to burn him alive.

They're going to kill him today.

My soul snaps, instantly breaking apart the protective illusion and casting me back into my horrifying reality.

My body moves without thought. I shove to my feet, and before Theo can react, I *run*. I charge down the stone steps, running faster than I ever have before. My boots land on gravel at the bottom, and I don't hesitate to shove my way through the crowd. I slap away the hands of men who try to stop me; I stomp on their feet, and I use my nails like claws to force them away.

"Let her through!" I hear a woman's voice.

Then another rings out, "Let her go to him!"

Through the chaotic crowd, a path gradually emerges, a sea of angry men splitting as my sisters in service—donned in their black clothes—fight them away. Black boots skid on small stones as the servants push back against the men they're beholden to serve; they fight to make a path for me to get through…to help me get to the man I love.

It makes me pause.

I thought they hated me.

I know they all saw the trial as it was broadcasted, which means they also saw Arlo lose control. They watched him openly show his love for me after digging me out from my grave. I just thought that would make them hate me more.

Yet forming before me are two walls of black, two unyielding rows crafted by these incredible women. It's a show of solidarity I never would have expected; one I never would have asked for.

They hold strong through my brief pause as I stare in awe of their kindness. But then the walls buckle at the hands of the men who push back, and for a moment, the path narrows, but only for a moment.

They strengthen again as the domestics turn and join the servants, pushing back at their husbands, and the path widens again. Tears drip down my cheeks at the sight of it, my heart heavy with appreciation and awe of their stance. A gentle hand touches the small of my back, and nudges me forward.

"Go," Cambria says. I glance to see her at my side, her eyes filling with tears, the same as mine. "Just go to him, and don't look back."

My eyes sweep the area quickly, looking for Ellary because she's always with Cambria. But I don't see her now, and I didn't see her lining the path, either.

"Go!" Cambria shoves, and I stumble to catch myself as I lurch forward. I give her a quick nod, a brief lock of our eyes in gratitude.

And then I run for him.

chapter thirteen

Mercy

I BURST THROUGH the path made by my sisters moments before it closes. I sense the chaos devolving behind me—a cacophony of shouting voices, shuffling feet, fighting, and colliding bodies.

The commotion serves as ample distraction—which will at least keep the Control away from me—but it's easy enough for me to ignore. It's all happening behind me, and my singular focus is in front of me. They're going to light a fire beneath the man I love, and I will *not* let him burn alone.

My boots skitter across the gravel as I slide to a quick stop, nearly falling forward onto the brush and logs beneath the small platform where Arlo stands.

"Mercy," he calls down to me.

I don't reply.

I don't pause to look up at him.

I plant my foot against the slanted logs, and begin to climb.

I glance up, looking for something to grab hold of to hoist myself up with, and I spot the rope they've wrapped around his thighs to tether him to the stake.

"Get down!" Arlo shouts at me. "What are you doing? Get *down*, Mercy!"

I grab hold of the rope at his thighs and pull myself up, climbing onto the platform. I have to position myself quickly because there's barely enough room for us both to stand. All at once, I lasso a hand around to grip the back of his neck, the other rising from the rope around his thighs to hold on to the one around his waist. I shift my stance, moving one boot between his feet, while the other is bumped up against the outside of his shoe. My body is pressed tightly to his, and I cling to him, unable and unwilling to let him go.

If I let go, I'll fall…and I can't fall without him.

I lift my chin to look at him and find tears streaming down his cheeks, fear in his glassy blue eyes as they dart wildly across my face.

"Mercy, what are you—"

Bang. Bang.

I startle, strengthening my hold on Arlo as two loud bursts explode through the chaos, met by shrieks and screams and voices calling out their confusion. I turn my cheek against Arlo's shoulder, looking in the direction of the sound, and unsurprisingly, I find Killian at the source.

He stands between the posts that secure Arlo and Stefanie, facing the crowd, his arm stretched high above him. And in his hand is something black, metal…

His fingers move over the item in his hand.

Bang.

Another burst of sound makes me jump as a small explosion erupts from the barrel-shaped end of the black metal object.

Is it…is that a gun?

I know what they look like from photographs, but I never imagined I would see one in Ember Glen. We knew they existed; that the Control could be given access to them, but they were only meant for the most dire of circumstances.

Guns were what wars were fought with.

Guns were for violence against the masses.

And if Killian has one now, then it means the Elders have called for that kind of violence against their own people. If the Control has been given access to guns, then it means…

Then it means the Elders have called for war in Ember Glen.

"Quiet!" Killian bellows toward the crowd, his chest heaving with fury that radiates off him in waves. "We will have order or blood will be spilled!"

Beats of heavy silence pass, and slowly, Killian lowers his arm.

"Get down," Arlo whispers. "Get down. Please, get down…"

He can't compel me to move, and I only cling to him tighter.

"Men of Ember Glen, if you cannot control your wives, then they will be stripped from their duty to care for you and your children, and reassigned as servants! And servants, mind your place. Remember…the men you stand against now are the same men you *serve*. Should the Impulse compel them to retaliate against you under the next full moon, then your actions today will have *earned* it."

Killian is more furious than I've ever seen him, and it's frightening. He's dangerous with empty hands, but now his palm is heavy, holding a tool meant only for murder. "This community has shunned God's grace, invited demons to tear us away from what's right. The Elders have called for order to be restored by any means necessary, and we *will* find that order *immediately*.

"Stefanie Price has acted in rebellion, citing ancient and forbidden texts—*unholy texts*—that call for the destruction of our morality in Ember

Glen. Our way of life is *right*. Our way is *good*. Our way is *Godly*. And any word, written or spoken against it, will be seen as a violent attack against all things holy. It will be seen as an attack against God Himself, and it will *not* be met with tolerance. We no longer grant grace in your humanity when your humanity threatens the very fibers of our existence.

"Arlo Rainn," Killian lifts his chin, turning his head to look over at Arlo, "a man I thought was my brother in God has betrayed us all more brutally than anyone." He raises his gun, pointing it at Arlo through his outstretched arm, and we both flinch from fear of his aim. "This man committed sexual acts against his ward. He fell victim to her demons and he went to her bed, time and time again, using her in ways a man should only ever use a servant on nights of purging. He has defiled himself in the *filth* of a sinner, for this woman who doesn't even hold the dignity of a true servant. And worst of all, they claim to have fallen in *love*."

He spits at the ground in rage. "Only demons could claim to have found something so divine outside of a marriage. Mercy Madness and Arlo Rainn are *possessed*." His dark eyes meet mine, looking straight at me. "And if you mean to stand there and burn with him, then we'll gladly let you."

"Get down," Arlo tells me frantically, speaking before Killian has said the final word in his tirade. "Get down, get down *now*. Mercy, get—"

Bright orange heat roars to life in front of Killian, a flame rising high from a torch held by Ryker.

My eyes are wide.

My heart is pounding.

The air is sucked from my lungs.

My scarred hand throbs with the memory of being burned when I was forced to thrust my hand into the campfire to spare Cambria from doing the same. I don't fear death…but I do fear the pain that flame will bring.

I let go of the rope around Arlo's waist and wrap my arms around his middle. I embrace him fully, press my face to his chest, and squeeze my eyes shut, shaking as terror grips me.

"No!" Arlo screams, his voice strangled, panicked. "Get *down*! Ryker… Ryker, stop! Wait! *Mercy*, get *down*!"

"No," I tell him.

"Please, Mercy. Get down…let me go…"

The sound of his voice twisting from panic to sorrow brings me to tears. I sob into his chest, crying as he begs me to leave him. I lift my head, place my chin on his chest, and look up to meet his eyes. My tears run like rivers down my cheeks at the sight of his own.

"*Please*," he begs one last time.

He wants me to climb down, but I can't. I won't leave him to face this alone. I can't fathom surviving a single day after watching him be burned alive.

There's no choice for me but to burn with him.

"I'm bound to you, Warden Rainn. In this life and the next."

His eyes fall shut as he cries, as screams and raised voices surge from the crowd. "You don't have to burn for me. You don't have to do this. There's still a chance for you."

"There's no chance for me…there never was." I force a smile to lift my cheeks against the tears that drench them.

I kiss him, ignoring the shouts of angry men who protest our love—love that changed us, love that gave us strength as much as it made us weak.

I speak softly against his lips. "If you burn, I burn with you."

"Starlight…"

Chaos crescendos from the crowd behind me.

"Set them on fire!"

"No!"

"Don't hurt her!"

"Burn them!"

"Get her down!"

A scream of absolute horror startles me, and I hold Arlo tighter. I suck in a sharp breath, bracing myself in the anticipation of flames engulfing me, waiting for the worst pain I'll ever know to wash over me…the *last* pain I'll ever know.

"*Circulus vitiosus!*" A single voice rises from the crowd.

Then another. "*Circulus vitiosus!*"

Twice more I hear it, and there's a sharp descent into pandemonium.

The roar of a new flame being lit echoes through my ears, igniting and crackling to life, but the flames don't rise around me and Arlo…

Stefanie screams.

I look over in time to see Ryker lift the torch away from the branches bundled at her feet.

"No!" I cry out.

Ryker snaps his head and glares at us with intent. I flinch as he turns, rushing toward us with his torch held high. He's coming to end us now, and in a strange way, I welcome it. I'm tired of the fighting, the waiting, the fearful anticipation.

Let him come.

Let him set us on fire.

Let this wretched life be over.

And just as I find acceptance, someone collides with Ryker, striking him hard around his center, brutally knocking him to the ground. The torch falls from his grip, landing on gravel, the orange flames still whipping violently from its end.

But the flames from the torch are nothing compared to what climbs the brush and logs surrounding Stefanie. My gaze tracks upward, as it's not just the flames that climb to reach her. A domestic woman clambers up the pile, bravely stepping onto a log that hasn't caught fire yet.

There's another running to help—a servant tearing at her black skirt, as though she could possibly use that to smother the roaring flames.

And then I see Luna, fighting her husband with all her strength. She's kicking, screaming, *fighting* to get out of his hold so she can get to Stefanie… just as I'd fought through the crowd to get to Arlo.

My sisters helped me; they fought for me. They made a path for me where there was no path before, because I'd done the same for them the night I ran from Hyatt's flames in the forest. I chose to run that night rather than accept my fate, and it brought us here—to this moment of rebellion, this fight that's for love as much as it is for freedom.

They're fighting for each other.

The women of Ember Glen are finally fighting…

It's something I never imagined seeing in my lifetime. The women— domestics and servants—fighting *together* against a fate chosen by the Control and the Elders.

Unexpected hope fills my heart and floods my veins.

I have to fight with them.

It's not the end. I have to stay, and I have to fight with them.

I look up at Arlo, and my lips part to say something to him, though no words come out.

What can I even say to him?

I don't have to say anything at all. My entire body jerks as Arlo startles me, his palm suddenly landing at my elbow. I look down at my arm to see it with my own eyes, and that's when my gaze tracks the movement behind him. They've come to help us, too. Two domestic women have already freed one of his hands, and they continue to work at the knots binding him to the stake. I look up to meet his eyes.

"Go," he says, squeezing my arm, prying it off from around his waist. "Do what you were meant to do, Mercy Madness. Go and fight with them, and don't look back."

His other hand is suddenly freed, and he grips both my arms. He wrenches me away from him, still bound to the stake by the ropes around his waist and thighs. My hands are balled into fists as he lifts them between us.

"Arlo, I—"

"Go," he demands, and shoves me backward, forcing me off the platform.

I try to twist on my way down, but I fail. I land hard on my ass, rolling onto my back, my spine crashing into gravel. Before the back of my head slams to the ground, I roll, flipping onto all fours, and shoving to my feet.

Don't look back.

Gratitude for my love, for his strength, ripples through me. He knew what I had to do—he understood it—but more than that, he gave me the push I needed to let go of him so I could do what has to be done.

I want to look back, to make sure they're still working to undo the knots that bind him to the stake. I want to look back to make sure that Ryker hasn't recovered, doesn't have the torch, and isn't on his way to set Arlo on fire.

But Stefanie's fearful scream claws through the stagnant air and steals my attention. My focus renews to rescue her from the climbing fire that's meant to silence her—the fire that's meant to silence us all with fear.

I will help Stefanie, but I know I'm not the one who will save her. Instead, I turn and run to free Luna from her husband's grip, because I know it as sure as I know my love for Arlo that there is no one more determined than Luna to save her.

chapter fourteen
Mercy

"PLEASE, *PLEASE*!" LUNA shouts at Archer. "Let me go!"

"I can't let you do this!" he shouts back at her as she twists and tugs, pulls and fights him to get free. "We'll lose *everything!*"

I nearly collide with Archer as I skid to a stop, small stones crashing together with a crunching sound beneath my boots. I reach out and close my hand around his with the intention of prying his fingers from her wrist.

Bang.

A gunshot startles us all. I duck my head on instinct as my shoulders lift toward my ears. I can't gauge where the gunshot came from—I don't even know whether it's Killian who still has the gun.

Is he the only one with a gun?

Do the other men of the Control have them, too?

Though I'm afraid of what a gun might do in the wrong hands—in *Killian's* hands no less—I have to push my fear aside and focus on getting Luna free from Archer's grasp.

"Let her go," I grit, clawing my fingernails into his flesh, and he flinches, letting go of one of her arms to swat at me. I take a step back, then rush forward, slamming my palms to his chest and shoving back. Luna pulls as I push, and with a quick twist of her arm, she snaps free from his grip. She stumbles backward and falls on her bottom, but she quickly scrambles to her feet and backs away, palms raised to ward him off.

And then there's a pause—a moment of standing and staring, an exchange of something that seems rooted in mutual kindness between them.

"You can't do this," he mutters, stepping toward her.

Luna quickly steps back. "Just let me go, Archer."

"Think of the children…"

Luna's eyes are glassy with tears. "I *am* thinking of the children. They… they'll be okay, I promise."

I hadn't noticed before, but I notice it now—there are no children here today, not with Luna, not with anyone. I feel relief for that, but it also confuses me. There are always some children left behind in the village when there are gatherings, but not many and not often. When the children stay behind, it means that some of the domestics have to miss the events to stay behind with them. But there's not a single child here for this, and though I'm thankful for it, it doesn't make sense.

Bang.

"Mercy, let's go!" Luna shouts, rushing forward to grab my wrist and tug me along as she runs.

I can't make sense of anything, but it doesn't matter right now.

We sprint toward Stefanie, and I'm in awe of the scene before me, how quickly the events have changed in the few moments since Arlo pushed me from the platform. A circle of women—domestics and servants alike—has formed around the burning brush that surrounds Stefanie.

It reminds me of nights of purging when servants were made to gather around the bonfire in the clearing. We were forced to give our open consent to be used, abused, brutalized in any manner of choosing by the vicious men of Ember Glen. The women surrounding Stefanie now don't join hands as we would before service, but the visual of sisterhood is the same.

They've formed a circle around this fire, not one where they join hands in collective service of men, but one where they've turned outward to fight back against them.

It's beautiful.

It's heart-wrenching.

It's divine.

It's a vicious circle of women…

The circle opens just enough for me and Luna to pass through, and we rush toward the fire. A few of the servants have ripped fabric from their skirts, trying to smother the growing flames—it's useless, but it's the only thing they can try, and it's humbling to see that they did.

The flames are roaring, climbing, and I don't know what to do. My mind stalls, searching for a solution, looking for a path untouched by flame that I might climb, but there isn't one.

"Stefanie!" Luna shouts up at her. "Jump!"

I look up and see the women who climbed have managed to untie the knots. They edge the platform, searching for the clearest spot from which to leap, but there isn't time for searching, for thinking. Flames are going to touch them no matter what they do.

"Jump…just jump!" I yell. "Now!"

It feels like hours pass while they hesitate in fear and we shout at them from the ground. Then finally, they leap, flames brushing the ends of their skirts as they fall toward the ground.

"Down!" I shout at them as they land, screaming as orange dances around their ankles. "Lay down! Roll on the ground."

I grab the shoulders of one, who panics, and I shove her down, telling her to roll. Others come to help smother the flames, and we make fast work of putting them all out.

Luna is on her knees beside Stefanie, gripping her arm as she sniffs back fearful tears to help her sit up. I move to Stefanie's feet, quickly lifting the tinged and smoking fabric of her skirt to check her legs for burns. I'm thankful to find she's wearing beige leggings beneath. They're singed, burned through in a couple of spots that expose slightly reddened patches of skin, but nothing that looks severe.

"She's okay," I say, then look up at Stefanie. "You're okay." I stand, reach my hand to her, which she takes, and Luna and I pull her to her feet.

Bang.

A man cries out in agony, and the sound is unmistakable.

It's Arlo, calling out in pain.

Expecting to see the worst, I look over at the stake, at the platform where I left him behind. My mind imagines flames rising to meet him, engulfing him, swallowing him whole.

Yet there is no fire, there are no flames.

The ropes that held him dangle free.

He reaches across his body, gripping his left arm with his right hand, standing alone on the platform. His body sways sideways, feet teetering on the ledge. And just before he falls, I see the sleeve of his button-down shirt beneath his hand is soaked with dark crimson…

He's been shot.

"Arlo!"

Bang.

A woman from the circle who stands in front of me drops heavily to the ground. She's strangely silent as she lands on her back, eyes wide with fear and one hand covering her bloody stomach.

Shocked at the sight, I quickly tear my eyes away, looking back at the breach in our protective circle. And through the gap, Killian appears, aiming his gun at me through his outstretched arm. A streak of blood drips down the side of his face, and it frames the rage in his expression as a nasty smirk lifts the corner of his mouth.

Stunned by overwhelming fear, staring down the barrel of this horrible, violent tool of brutality he holds in his hand, the only action I can manage is to take a step backward.

And then he shoots.

I flinch, my eyes slamming shut.

Nothing happens.

I only hear a click, and then shocked gasps from the women around me—some speaking my name in a way that nearly sounds…*reverent*? No less than three women rush him, attack him, take him down to the ground before more men come to forcibly remove them. Then someone tugs on my arm. My head turns and I find Stefanie at my side.

"Come on, we've got to get you out of here." Stefanie speaks with an oddly calm voice, given she was nearly just burned alive.

I glance around for Luna, but I don't see her. "Where's Luna?"

"She's fine, she's coming." Stefanie tugs, turning and dragging me as she moves away from the crowd.

The vicious circle of women has broken away, the flames now roaring too powerfully, climbing high around the lonely stake. A group of domestics break free, sprinting across the square, heading for the path toward the village.

One of them calls back, "Stefanie, Mercy, come on. Run!"

"Mercy, I need you to run with me. *Now.*" Stefanie's grip on my arm is steadfast, unyielding.

My feet have no choice but to move beneath me as she runs, pulling me along with her. We've nearly crossed the pebbled square, and she's already released my arm when the guilt of running overcomes me.

I stop, yelling ahead at her and the other fleeing domestics, "Wait, we have to go back…We have to help them!"

I turn my head over my shoulder to look back and sorrow washes over me. This battle is nearly done. The men have their conditioning for brutality and brute strength on their side. The women who fought are gradually being brought to heel, overpowered by men who believe in their right for total dominance over women.

More heartbreaking than that is seeing the women who didn't fight helping their men; the women who are still poisoned by the untruths they've been fed in the name of holy righteousness. I know some of them are just afraid, and I can't blame them for that.

"Go ahead," Stefanie tells the others, stopping to face me, taking a single step toward me as they continue down the path to the village. "Mercy, I need you to come with me. I need to get you away from here."

I waiver. I've never felt so hesitant or indecisive in all my life.

"Mercy!" she snaps at me. "We have to go. *Now.*"

I look back and see a group of servants break off from the crowd, sprinting across the square toward Sanctuary—a place no man is allowed to enter. Ryker and two other men chase after them, catching one or two of my sisters and drawing them back.

We're losing this battle.

I glance toward the Homestead, and my heart drops to my stomach. I see Delle in her red dress being dragged backward up the stone steps. She's kicking and thrashing—probably screaming, though I can't pick out her voice from so far away—as Park and Owen carry her away.

It's Delle who makes up my mind for me. I can't leave her behind. I turn and run back toward the crowd.

"No!" Stefanie yells after me. I hear her footfalls on the gravel as she runs after me. "Come back!"

I run hard, scanning for a clear path through, wondering if I can get to Delle faster if I skirt around the throng. But I never get the chance to decide how I'll get to her. I don't even see it coming. I collide with a wall—Theo's rock-solid chest—and bounce back. I nearly fall backward, but he grips my upper arms and harshly pulls me in front of him.

"You have to go with her," Theo tells me. "Go with Stefanie."

"But Delle—"

"I'm going back; I'll look after her, but you have to go." He rushes to get the words out, shaking me in his grip. "They'll kill you on the staircase if you come back, so get the fuck away from here. Now fight me off and make it look real. They have to trust me so I can be with Delle."

I can't just go…I can't leave Delle behind in this.

What if they place their rage on her in my stead?

If they don't have me, Delle will be their example. They'll destroy her to get the women back under their control.

I press my hands to Theo's chest, and I shove—not to make it look like I'm fighting back, but because I need him to let go of me. I have to go back for Delle. Theo hardly budges, and I shove again, kick at his shins, beat my fists against his chest.

"Good, keep fighting," he murmurs, thinking I'm doing this for show so anyone who sees will think he tried to stop me.

It's not for show.

I fight him. I twist in his grip as my fear for Delle rises, bringing tears to my eyes. "Let go…let *go* of me. She *needs* me!"

A fist comes from nowhere and collides with the side of Theo's face. He jerks sideways on the impact, releasing me so quickly that I stumble backward as he falls.

"Come on," Luna suddenly appears, grabbing my arm to help steady me, "We have to go."

"What are you—"

It wasn't Luna who hit Theo hard enough to fall. I look up and find Arlo before me, his face contorted in pain as he unclenches his fist. I shake Luna off and run to him, but he steps forward with force, forcing me to stop.

"Turn around and run." He steps forward, forcing me to step backward.

"Delle needs me—"

"No, Mercy."

"I'm not *leaving* her!"

"Yes, you are." He moves faster, his chest bumping mine as he forces me backward.

"No, I'm—"

He dips, wraps his arms around my waist, hoists me up, and tosses me over his shoulder. He groans in pain as I yelp, and he starts to move, running with me toward the village.

I bounce against his back as he runs with me, lifting my head so I can look back. I watch in horror as the front door of the Homestead opens, as Delle is dragged across the threshold, and it closes with her behind it.

"Put me down…Let me go back for her!" I shout. "What are you doing?"

"What I should've done the first time you ran from me in the forest," Arlo grunts through his pain, through the strain of carrying me as he runs. "I'm taking you away from this godforsaken place."

chapter fifteen

ARLO

THE CONTROL FAILED to set me on fire, but my arm burns all the same, throbbing in waves of pulsing pain from the bullet. I feel every step I take, thudding against the gravel as we run.

Mercy's weight over my shoulder intensifies every sensation, cycling through alternating rounds of numbness, then agony. Though it hurts to carry her, I'm afraid to put her down. I'm afraid she'll try to run back again, that she'll try to rush toward a goal she can't achieve…

That she'll run away from me, and I'll never get her back.

Delle is locked in the Homestead, and Mercy cannot help her. Going back would bring Mercy to a quick, but brutal, death. I fear I'd see them put her on the stake—the very spot where my charred and lifeless body should be at this very moment—and burn her in my stead.

She came to me.

Mercy was willing to burn with me.

I'm still stunned that she ran to me, that she climbed onto the platform and was ready to *die* with me. I'm in awe of the way she loves me; I'm humbled and inspired by it. She was willing to be set on fire with me just so she wouldn't have to live a single day without me.

And as much as I hated it, as much as it terrified me to think of her enduring that unimaginable horror just to die with me, I understood it. I'm not as brave as she is, but if I were, I would have climbed into that damn coffin with her at the trial and let them bury us together. I would have let them steal my last breath to avoid living without her.

Yet, I didn't—I *couldn't*—because I'm weak. I could never match the strength and bravery of Mercy Madness. No one ever could, and no one ever will.

So, I'll happily suffer this paltry ache in my arm to save her, to carry her away from certain death and give her a chance at another day, a chance at even one more moment of bliss in each other's arms before everything implodes.

I follow Luna and Stefanie all the way to the village, realizing as we approach the homes of the villagers that I don't know where we're going, whether they have a plan, whether anyone is following us at a distance.

"Let me down," Mercy demands. "Put me *down*. I know I'm hurting your arm."

"My arm is fine, but you won't be if you run back there."

"I won't run back there; I'll come with you. Just put me down."

I ignore her and keep moving, following as Stefanie leads us behind a row of homes that provide some cover from being out in the open.

"Arlo, please put me down," Mercy begs. "Your blood is soaking my clothes. It's warm…" Her voice lowers to a whisper, unease touching her tone. "I can feel it, and I really don't want to feel it."

Fuck.

That guts me.

Immediately, I stop, loosen my grip, and let her slip down in front of me until her boots touch the ground. Her eyes fall immediately to my arm, and they widen. She lifts her hand as though she's going to touch the wound, and it makes me flinch. She stops, her hand hovering above my arm as my muscles tense, sending a shooting pain rippling outward from the wound. I feel my face contort in pain.

"Oh, love…I—"

"I'm fine."

I try to convince her as much as myself, though I'm fearful of what I'll find when I finally gather enough strength to look at the wound. Truthfully, I'm terrified to know what it looks like, to see how much damage has been done. At least I can be thankful the bullet didn't strike me in the chest, or the stomach, or my head. There were others struck in the chaos who were far less fortunate.

"We need to keep moving." I reach out with my right hand to snatch her wrist. I turn to follow after Stefanie and Luna, dragging Mercy with me before she can protest, breaking into a run. "Come on."

Mercy runs along with me, quickly and easily matching my pace. After a few strides with no resistance against my grip—assured that she's not going to try to slip away from me and run back to the Homestead—I let my hand slip down her wrist, wrap around her palm, and lace our fingers together. There's a pulse of relief from both of us, comfort striking as our entwined fingers lock us together.

We run until we arrive at the outer edge of the village, where there's a short row of three houses nestled together, their backs facing the rising hillside beyond. We circle around behind the row, and I'm confused as we make our way to the one on the end because I know who this house belongs to. Luna creeps right on up to the backdoor as if she's been here before.

"What are we doing here?" Mercy asks. "What are we doing at my house?"

This is the home Mercy's father owned—the one where she was raised, the one where she stayed all alone after he died. Other than the weeks she was required to remain at Sanctuary after nights of service, this is where she lived, alone—no mother, no father, no siblings.

It was always such an unusual thing, her family. Most family units had several children. It wasn't entirely unheard of for a family to bear only one or two children, but it was unusual. The Madness family had always been unusual in that way.

But what's truly unusual about this moment is watching my sister locate a key that seems to have been buried in the rocks lining the outer edges of the home, as if she always knew it was there.

Luna gives a brief, wary glance over her shoulder, flashing an apologetic look at Mercy. "We'll explain everything once we're safe, but we have to hurry."

As Luna reaches forward to slip the key into the lock, the knob turns and the door opens gently from the inside. We all gasp, startling easily with the adrenaline flowing through our veins. One of the domestic women I remember seeing run away from the crowd ahead of Stefanie and Mercy—Enid, if I recall her name correctly—peeks out through the crack in the door.

"I saw you coming," she says quickly, then pushes the door open and steps back, beckoning us inside. "Hurry. The others have already gone through."

Luna nods, quickly returning the key to its hiding place among the rocks before she and Stefanie rush inside.

Stefanie turns back when we don't immediately follow. "Come inside, quickly," she says, waving her hand to beckon us forward.

Mercy glances over at me, and we share a puzzled look. But then she steps forward, her hand tugging mine as she moves inside. Stefanie skirts around me to shut the door behind us, and she locks it from the inside. All the lights are off, and no one makes a move to turn them on.

"This way," Luna says, following Enid past the small kitchen table.

They turn and head toward the living room. I glance at the space as we pass through, noting an ordinary room that somehow sparks my interest. My mind instantly wanders to thoughts of Mercy living here, all alone with her thoughts.

Where would she sit?

Did she have a favorite spot?

Was it in this room where her mind first wandered toward thoughts of dissension and rebellion?

She grew up without siblings, without a mother. Perhaps it was all the time she spent alone that gave her mind the space to think. Most of the family units in Ember Glen are crowded with children who fill days with noise, disruption, and activity. For most, there's a lack of time and space to be alone with your own thoughts for too long.

If only I had taken the time to consider my own thoughts and feelings about God, our laws, and the ways of Ember Glen. Maybe then I would have seen all that was wrong with it sooner. Perhaps more of us would be like Mercy Madness if we'd just taken more time to think for ourselves.

Who am I kidding?

There is no one like Mercy.

And maybe that's the way it had to be for us to see the truth.

Mercy's choice to run from service—the choice that started all of this—acted like a chisel that's slowly chipping away at our harshly dichotomous ways of thinking. Bit by bit, the events that brought us from that fateful night of service to the acts of dissension today have steadily chipped away at the exterior. Perilous cracks have been made to the collective, and when Mercy emerged as a symbol for a movement of change, she delivered the final blow to that indoctrinated façade.

Indoctrination.

That is the best word—perhaps the *only* word—to describe our upbringing in Ember Glen. It's a word that was used to teach us about the evil that existed in the world before a great civil war tore this country apart.

We were told that people were indoctrinated by those who wanted freedom from God's law and order. We were told of the ways those freedom seekers wanted to denounce God—that they wanted to be free to choose whether they believed in his existence, whether they followed his word. We were told they were indoctrinating their children to believe they had the right to choose if they believed in God at all.

And because of Mercy, I see the truth now. I see it with my own understanding, rather than seeing it as I was always commanded to see it. I see that we—the people of Ember Glen—are the ones indoctrinated. And I'm so affected by my own indoctrination that it makes me feel sick for admitting that to myself, the dissonance of growth still lingering in my gut.

Mercy squeezes my hand, drawing me from my thoughts and back to the present. We continue to follow Enid and Luna past the living room and down the hallway, with Stefanie behind us. There's a door open at the end of the hallway and Enid disappears inside.

Mercy halts. "That's my father's room. What are you doing in my father's room?"

Luna pauses, turning to face Mercy. "I am so sorry. I know this is all so confusing for you. I promise, we will explain everything soon, but first, we have to get you to safety."

"In my father's bedroom?" Mercy's brow furrows in her confusion. "This isn't a safe place. The Control are smart enough to think of looking for me here—"

"It's difficult to find something when you don't even know it exists..." Luna replies cryptically. She gives Mercy a soft smile before turning and moving inside the bedroom.

Mercy hesitates for a moment, but then she follows, and I walk with her. Once Stefanie has stepped into the room behind us, she shuts the door and locks it. By all accounts, it appears to be a normal bedroom. Wooden floors, a bed with two end tables on either side, and long, rectangular rugs running along each side of the bed in a drab shade of green.

Enid stands at the rug on the far side of the bed. "I closed off the entrance after they went through, in case the wrong people showed up, just like you told me to." She lowers to her knees, grips the end of the rug, and flips it back, folding it over itself before standing and stepping back.

I half expected to see something obvious there beneath the rug, but all I see is a plain wooden floor—the same wooden floor that runs throughout the bedroom.

Luna kneels near the spot where the rug laid before Enid flipped it back. Mercy lets go of my hand to move closer to Luna, and instantly, anxiety spikes. I rush to follow, feeling that need to be close since her presence is the only thing that puts me at ease.

Mercy crouches, watching as Luna digs her fingernails into the crack between wooden planks on the floor, and before I can make sense of what she's doing, she pries up the edge of a plank. She lifts it from its spot and sets it aside. Then, she scoops her fingers beneath the plank it was nestled against and lifts. An entire section of the floor rises on a hinge.

"Wh-what is this?" Mercy asks. "How did you find this?"

Luna glances back at me, then looks at Mercy beside her. "It's a long story, and I promise I will tell it, but we need to go through first and get to safety."

I look past Mercy and Luna, and I spot a haphazard hole chiseled through the foundation, creating a chasm that leads into darkness.

"It leads to a tunnel," Stefanie says as she comes up beside me. "It's a narrow drop in, but manageable. The surrounding walls are sturdy. It's as safe as anything else in Ember Glen."

A narrow drop, indeed.

The chaotically carved hole appears just wide enough for a single person to slip through at a time. I suppose if it were any wider, it would be harder to hide. As it is, I would have had no idea that anything was hidden here beneath the floorboards—the planks are lined up so perfectly, fit together as neatly as the rest of the floor.

What is going on here?

This revelation has happened so quickly. My mind is lagging, struggling to make sense of how we got here, what's happening in this moment, and what might happen next.

"Where does it lead?" Mercy asks.

"I don't know how to describe it," Luna says, lifting her chin to look at Mercy. "You just…you have to see it all for yourself. We just need to get you there and keep you safe."

Luna smiles, and though her expression is still tense with fear, the smile is bright and optimistic. She has that look in her eyes that she used to have as a child when she was caught in a daydream—a look I haven't seen from her in a very long time. The hope my sister lost has returned, and it only strengthens as Mercy turns her head and connects with her through her compassionate stare.

"You're the author of this rebellion," Luna tells her, "and we need you to finish our story."

chapter sixteen

Mercy

I'M BEWILDERED BY this dark space carved into the earth beneath my father's floorboards. I'm entirely perplexed about how Luna and Stefanie somehow managed to find it.

How on earth did they find this?

I've lived in this house my entire life, and I've never stumbled across it. I've lifted the rug that covers the wooden floor; I've swept and mopped the planks that hide this opening to a dark world below. I've never had so much as an inkling that there was anything out of the ordinary hidden here. I have so many questions, and I just hope they have the answers.

The chiseled opening is just wide enough for a single person to slip through it. Enid goes first, lowering her feet into the hole, scooting forward, then slipping into the darkness. Her entire body drops through the entrance, and she disappears.

"One at a time," Luna says. "Follow me."

Luna goes next, following after Enid in the same manner, dangling her feet first before slipping through and disappearing beneath the ground. I stare down through the opening, and my heart pounds with a fury at the sight of the darkness below.

A hand gently touches my shoulder, startling me. "Your turn," Stefanie says, gesturing toward the hole.

I give her a slight nod, though I feel panic clawing inside me. It scratches at my soul, teasing me with awareness that it's always present— forever lurking, ready to pounce at the slightest hint of my fear.

I have to fight it.

Drawing in a deep breath, I shift, lowering my feet into the open void. They dangle as I contemplate asking how far the drop is, whether it's a few feet or if it's more. Ultimately, I think it's better not to know. I scoot forward, letting my thighs teeter on the edge as my knees lower beneath the surface. Deciding it's best not to think too much about it, I close my eyes, shift my weight forward, and let myself plummet into the black abyss.

I drop heavy and hard, but my feet quickly slam to solid ground. The only light in this dark space comes from above, from the hole through which I slipped, which is nothing more than the meager light of day that peeks through the edges of the closed curtains in my father's bedroom.

I gradually straighten to my full height as I look up at the entrance, noting there's little less than a foot of clearance between the top of my head and the ceiling of this open cavity. I feel a tremor through my arms as I realize I can't climb back out. There's no way I can pull myself out of here and the darkness all around me.

"How do we get out of here?" I ask in a rush.

Arlo looks down at me through the opening, and I find some comfort in his blue eyes, though it's difficult to make out the shade of them with so little light.

"There's a step stool." Luna's hand taps my forearm, and I jump, whirling around to try to find her in the dark. She moves in close to me, enough that I can see the outline of her, and I reach out to grab her wrist. "I've moved it out of the way, but it climbs high enough that it's easy to pull yourself back out. Elijah really thought of everything."

Elijah…

My father.

I can't wrap my head around any of this.

"Come on." Luna places her hand over mine, where my fingers have curled to grip her wrist so tightly that I'm surprised she hasn't tried to pry me off yet. She has a gentle way about her. She calmly strokes my forearm, and the simple gesture reminds me to take a breath. "Move aside so they can follow. Watch your head."

I nod and move with her away from the entrance, deeper into the darkness. We stop and wait, watching as Arlo drops in next, quickly followed by Stefanie. Luna pats my hand to get my attention, waiting for me to release her wrist before she leaves me.

She moves beneath the opening, bringing the step stool she mentioned out of the darkness. There are three steps to climb up the stool, and when she reaches the top, she's high enough through the opening to clear her arms and shoulders.

I move closer, looking up through the hole to watch as she reaches for the wooden plank she'd removed and set aside before. She nestles it back in its spot. Then, she reaches up to grip a small, silver handle fixed to the underside of the hinged set of planks. She pulls it halfway closed before reaching out with her other hand, somehow managing to maneuver the rug so it will fall flat over the wooden floor once she closes it.

Then she pulls it shut, cutting off our only light, our only exit.

We're trapped.

I'm trapped.

I'm being buried alive again…

I stutter through a breath as a shockwave of adrenaline punches through my veins. I instantly feel dizzy, like I can't draw in a decent breath, and the faint feeling threatens to take me to the ground. I double over, hands pressed to my thighs as I fight a wave of nausea.

I know I'm not alone. I can hear them all moving around me in the darkness, whispering in words that seem blurred and foreign in my panicked mind. I'm here with them, but it feels like I'm not. It feels like I'm entombed, like the air is running out and there's no way to escape.

"I can't—" I gasp, trying to suck in a breath, though it feels like my lungs have closed.

"Mercy?"

Arlo's arm slides across my back, but instead of giving me comfort, it startles me. I rise too quickly, bringing myself a light-headed rush as my feet move me backward into the dark.

"I can't…" I barely manage the words. "I can't breathe…"

They all start speaking at once, and their voices blend into a dull roar that echoes in my ears. Every sound is streaming, rushing, bringing a vision of soil pouring steadily through the hole above, covering the cavern floor, rising to my ankles, my knees, filling this space until I'm buried, and—

There's no way out…

"Get me out," I pant.

I hear the strike of a match and the hiss of fire as it ignites, a small flame casting haunted shadows across the inner cave walls.

I feel like I can't breathe, yet at the same time, I'm breathing far too much, far too quickly. Air rushes in and out of me, but it doesn't fill my lungs.

"She's panicking," Stefanie says. "We need to get her out of here."

"We can't go back out there," Arlo says.

"We're not going out," Luna says. "We're going *through.*"

"Through where?" Arlo asks.

My knees go weak and I drop to kneel, catching myself with one hand on the ground in front of me as I bring the other to press over my pounding heart.

"Get me out…*please,*" I beg as Arlo drops in front of me. "Please, dig me out. Dig me out…"

"Oh, God," Luna's voice cracks, and it makes me worry that maybe it's real…That maybe she's afraid because there really is soil pouring in all around us, filling in this small cavern, burying us alive. "She thinks she's in her grave again. That trial must have done *awful* things to her mind. What do we do?"

"You said it yourself," Stefanie says. "The only way out is through. Arlo, she has to crawl. The tunnel is only about thirty feet long, but it's hands and knees all the way. She'll be okay once we get her through it, but…somehow we have to get her through it."

"Show me," Arlo says, then he disappears.

I sit back on my heels, pressing my eyes shut, willing myself to calm down and come back to reality.

I'm not alone.

I'm not being buried alive.

The trial is over and I'm safe.

I'm alive.

"Fuck," Arlo mutters, and it sends a shiver down my spine. "Thirty feet?"

"Just thirty feet. Luna, go first with the lantern to give her some light. And Arlo—"

"She's going in front of me, and I'll push her through myself if I have to."

"Good," Stefanie says, and she sounds so much stronger than me. "I'll go in front of her then, and I'll pull her if I have to."

I hear movement around me. Panicked at the sound of wordless motion, I open my eyes. The meager light that formed dancing shadows before begins to drift away, and it frightens me.

"Arlo!" I cry out for him.

The single source of light shrinks, diminishing as it moves into an opening in the cavern. As darkness closes in, my love finds me. His palms touch my cheeks and his eyes catch mine, wide and fearful. I latch my fingers around his wrists, desperate to hold his touch against my skin as the light continues to fade.

"I need you to crawl with me, starlight. Hands and knees. You're going to follow the light into the tunnel, and I'll be right behind you."

My head shakes furiously against his hands, though I don't mean for it to. I mean to be strong, to be brave, to go fearlessly into the unknown, yet I feel weak, broken…

That godforsaken trial has broken me.

"I-I can't…" I hiccup as sobs threaten to take hold of me. "I can't."

Arlo's forehead touches mine. "You *can* do this. You *will* do this. There is no choice here." He takes a deep breath, and I'm envious of it, because I wish I could do the same. "Forgive me, Mercy, but I have to make you do this."

A fearful sound screeches out from my throat as his hand snaps around the back of my neck, snatching me in his firm grip. He twists me around and pushes me down, groaning as if it pangs him to move me by force.

He holds me down on my hands and knees as he shifts to kneel behind me, his knees straddling mine. His hips press to my bottom as he shuffles closer. His fingers dig into the sides of my neck, using his grip to encourage me forward. His other hand slips between our bodies, flat against my ass, and he pushes hard. "Crawl," he commands, and I have to.

Because if I didn't, I'd collapse under the weight of him shifting over me, and the thought of being pinned on the ground in the quickly darkening cavern sends anxious shivers through my entire body.

Arlo pushes me through a small entrance into a narrow tunnel. He has to force me because every muscle in my body is tense and rigid, pushing back against him to fight moving into an even smaller space.

"Don't, I can't—"

"You must," Arlo grunts as he shoves me hard, forcing my entire body through the opening and into the tunnel.

He hisses as his touch disappears and he releases his grip on me. His body is no longer against mine, and I cry out in fear of his absence, turning my head to look back over my shoulder. He blocks the only exit, his shadowed form painted across a pitch-black canvas of darkness behind his back as the only light bounces away from us down the tunnel. There's just enough light cast across his face to show me his features are twisted in agony as he clutches his arm.

His pain washes over me, rinsing away bits of my fear, cleansing me of my panic just enough to allow my compassion for him to creep back in.

His pain reaches out like two hands that shove against my panic, begging it to leave my mind because he needs me. I catch his gaze, and when he meets my eyes, he slowly smiles. He lets go of his bleeding, wounded arm, trying to pretend like it doesn't hurt.

"No need to worry, starlight. I'm coming right behind you. I only needed a moment to appreciate the sight of you on your hands and knees in front of me."

I hear Stefanie groan in annoyance.

Luna laughs, and the playful, echoing sound is strange in the way it cuts through my panic—strange, though it seems to help, like a vibration that cracks the walls of fear.

"That fall really must have hurt," Luna says from ahead as Arlo slips in through the opening and reaches out to grip my ankle.

"What are you talking about?" he asks.

"When the mighty fall from grace, they fall hard, don't they?" Luna laughs again, and I feel the way it tugs at the corners of my lips.

Arlo grins, and it washes over me. It bathes me in warmth and douses me in comfort. It's a rising tide that crashes against the cracking walls of fear with promises to tear them down.

"You should remember from our childhood, Luna; I don't do anything halfway. I'm in the grace of demons now."

Stefanie snorts, "Welcome to hell."

His eyes scan my backside before turning to meet mine. There's a heat there, a passion for me that always burns blue in his eyes. It further chisels at those walls of fear, weakening their stronghold around my peace.

"I like the heat." He gives me an encouraging smile and squeezes my ankle. "Get moving, starlight."

With Arlo's grip firm on my ankle, somehow, I find the strength to push ahead. I still feel the ripples of anxiety coursing through my veins, but some courage has found me, just enough that I can crawl, reassured by the calm movement of the others with me.

Because they're with me, not against me, and it makes all the difference in the world.

It's not long before we reach the end of the tunnel and climb out, one by one, into another cavern. Luna holds a lantern that offers just enough dim light to show us how high the rock ceiling is above our heads. There's so much space above us, I feel a snap of relief inside my chest, and suddenly, I'm able to draw in a slow, deep breath.

Another breath.

Then another.

Gradually, the panic lessens. I don't know if it will ever fully go away, though I'm thankful it loosens its grip on me enough to be present and aware of what's going on around me.

Glancing around, I spot three stone passageways. The passages remind me of the cave system beneath the Homestead, and I have to wonder if they're all connected somehow.

Luna seems to know exactly where she's going, turning left and heading through a long, dark passage, and we follow her lantern light through. There's a junction splitting off into two stone hallways, and we take the one leading left. The anxiety starts to creep back over me the longer we walk without an end in sight. But almost as quickly as panic strikes, we come to the end of the winding passage.

The meager light from Luna's lantern gradually becomes unnecessary as the end of the passage makes itself known to us, bright with all the light of day. My heart beats with excitement, rather than fear…with the anticipation of finding out what lies ahead.

The air around me feels damp and heavy, unusually warm as we move closer to the light. The smell of water clings to each breath I take. The autumn chill fades as a pleasant warmth envelops me.

Luna glances over her shoulder and smiles at us before stepping through the opening, and we follow. With Arlo's hand in mine, we step into a glorious cavern, wide and open, flooded with light from a circular opening in the rock ceiling—an opening that exists directly above a large, clear pool of water.

Steam rises from the pool where the cool air from above meets the warmth that radiates from the water. The pool is serene, clear, a shade that reminds me of the color of robin's eggs. But even more enchanting than the sight of this grand cavern and warm pool of water is the sound of children laughing. I blink away from the pool and take in the sight around me.

The children of Ember Glen are all here—safe—and a group of domestic women are with them in their care.

"What is all this?" I ask in awe.

I hear Luna sigh happily as her hand lands softly on my shoulder. "This is what you've done, Mercy. This is what you started when you chose to run that night of service. This is the rebellion your bravery has sparked."

I look at her where she stands at my side, tears springing to my eyes at the look of gratitude in her expression—gratitude she has for *me*.

"Mercy," Luna grins, "these are all the people you're going to save."

chapter seventeen

Mercy

THESE ARE ALL *the people you're going to save.*

I'm speechless.

Luna and Stefanie lead me and Arlo into the vast cavern, leading us across the expanse of bedrock, where people gather in front of the crystal pool. I'm vaguely aware of how tightly Arlo's hand squeezes mine, can sense the unease that pulses through his grip, but the rest of me feels numb in my shock. I'm stunned by this scene and more confused than I've ever been.

I don't understand how these women and children are here; I don't understand *why* they're here. I suppose the children have been brought here for safety, but I don't understand how they were brought here so quickly after the fight at the Homestead.

Unless they were brought here before…Did the domestic women plan the fight?

"What happened at the gathering?" a woman asks, her hands on her child's shoulders who stands in front of her.

"That's Mercy Madness…" another woman says in awe. "Oh, thank God. Tell us what happened. How did you save her?"

"Mercy Madness!" someone else says with relief.

"Stefanie!" Another woman runs up and throws her arms around Stefanie, pulling her into a relieved hug. "You're alive…They did it! I can't believe they did it!"

A smiling, laughing, joyful group of children run full force toward Stefanie and Luna, who crouch to greet them with eager, open arms. Three little girls and three little boys crash into them at near full force, effectively knocking Luna back on her bottom. Her precious boys tackle her to the ground in a fit of laughter. It's such a beautiful interaction—a joyful reunion between innocent children and the mother they love—and it brings tears to my eyes.

Though Stefanie's daughters greet her in a much less obvious manner than Luna's sons—lively little boys who climb all over her, hug her, tickle her, and make her laugh with pure joy—their expressions show how thrilled they are to see their mother. They cling to her like they're afraid she'll slip away from them if they let her go.

The girls are so calm and quiet in their greeting that it feels restrained—like a learned behavior, like vigilance in self-protection. Being calm and quiet probably kept them safe from their father, Hyatt Price. I have no doubt that man carried his violence with him daily. No single night of service could ever be enough to satisfy the bloodlust of someone like him.

Stefanie's oldest daughter—I think her name is Heidi—has a glassy sheen of tears forming over her eyes. I notice it when she looks over Stefanie's shoulder while hugging her close, her tearful gaze tracing the features of my face before she meets my eyes. I hold my breath while she confidently holds my stare. There's resilience and curiosity shown in her beautiful brown eyes, which are framed by thick, dark eyebrows that resemble her mother's.

I smile as she watches me and the curl of my lips somehow beckons her. She breaks free from Stefanie, slipping around her and walking straight for me. Unexpectedly, she collides with my middle, throwing her arms around my waist and hugging me close. She squeezes, and a sudden sob escapes me.

My hand falls from Arlo's grasp as I drop to my knees, my arms wrapping around Heidi to give back a fraction of the comfort she gave me in her unrestrained hug—unrestrained and *brave* and filled with warmth and care.

When she decides to release me, she takes a small step backward. She stops and regards my face, searching my expression, reading my character from my features before deciding I'm worthy of her trust.

She blinks, then looks down at her left arm as she swings it forward, holding it out between us. She pushes up her long sleeve, revealing the tattoo that marks her for service, the same as mine. I mimic her, holding out my left arm and pushing up my long sleeve. Her arm looks so small next to mine, the tattoo so cumbersome on such a tiny frame.

I always hated the image before—not because it's ugly, but on the contrary, because it's beautiful. The artwork of the wildflowers is stunning with its graceful lines, striking a perfect balance between small and large florals from a variety of different flowers clustered together, so elegant in the diversity of petals and shapes.

But then that beautiful image is broken in half by two lines that encircle the arm—lines that separate one cluster of wildflowers from the other.

Separate…like domestics and servants.

Perhaps separation was the only way Ember Glen could survive for as long as it has, with one group living complacently in relative peace, while the other fights for survival from one month to the next. Today I saw how strong we could be when we fight together as a collective group of *women*, not as separate and distinct groups of servants and domestics.

Our lives may be different, but our hearts are the same.

We all just want freedom to live as we choose, to love who we want to love, to say *no* to a man and have it mean something.

"Mom says you saved me." Heidi's sweet, innocent voice reminds me that she's only a child and not a woman who's already been hardened by forced service to men. "She said you were strong and brave, and that you wouldn't serve my dad, and that might mean I won't have to be a servant when I'm older. She said you were changing things." Her head tilts to the side as she regards me with curiosity. "Is that true?"

A heavy breath rushes out of me.

Is it true?

What do I say to that?

"I-I'm trying," I stammer. "I'm trying to change things. I don't really know what I'm doing, but I'm going to try my very best to change the future for you."

Am I? How?

How could I possibly change the future of Ember Glen?

Heidi smiles sweetly, appearing satisfied at my answer. "Mom always says that the only thing you can do is try. I think that's why she yelled and got in trouble when they were taking you to your trial. Your dress was really pretty."

"Thank you." I smile, swiping a knuckle beneath my eye to drag away my tears.

"You look really pretty in red, but I liked it better when you wore black and it matched your boots. Mom said black is the color servants wear, though. I like how it looks, but I don't want to wear it because I don't want to be a servant."

I swallow against the lump in my throat. "I don't want you to be a servant, either. I never wanted to be one myself."

"You didn't?"

I shake my head. "No, but I didn't want to be a domestic, either."

Her brow furrows in confusion. "But there isn't anything else."

"Not in Ember Glen, not right now, but I always thought that maybe, someday, things could be different."

"Is that why you ran from my dad? Because you wanted things to be different?"

I pause as a swell of tears fill my eyes, and then I force my lips to curl into a tight grin. "Yes. That's why I ran. They didn't want me to run, but I had to make a choice for myself, now didn't I?"

A shy, restrained smile tugs at the corners of her lips and she nods. A chorus of questions from the gathered women quickly fills the cavern with voices, effectively ending our conversation. I give Heidi another smile before I rise to my feet.

"Where are the others?" someone asks. "Where are all the women?"

Luna has managed to untangle herself from her boys. She's tying a fabric wrap around her body, taking her baby girl, Soleil, from another domestic woman who must have been caring for her while Luna was away.

"Why is *he* here?" someone else asks. "Are we safe?"

I glance over at Arlo and see him tense. I reach out to grab his hand and he quickly laces our fingers together, holding firm.

Luna sighs, looking flustered as she finishes tying the wrap that holds Soleil against her body, cradling the back of her head in one palm. Luna's head hangs for a moment before Stefanie places a hand on her shoulder. Luna lifts her chin to look over at her, giving her a small smile. Stefanie's hand rises from her shoulder to her cheek, tucking a fallen strand of hair from Luna's messy updo behind her ear.

"Everyone who was able to get away is here," Luna says, dragging her gaze from Stefanie to look out at the women and children. "Everything became so chaotic. Everyone fought so hard to save Stefanie, and by a miracle, we did." Luna glances at her, and though I can only see one half of her face in profile, the complexity and depth of her feelings toward Stefanie are profoundly etched in her expression.

"You should know that if it wasn't for the servants, Stefanie wouldn't be here right now. *Mercy* wouldn't be here right now. We underestimated the violence we would meet for fighting back today. But the servants took a stand with us—entirely unexpected—and now Mercy Madness is safe. She's here and she's safe, and we should be happy about that."

"Danielle hasn't returned," one of the domestics says. "Neither has Echo."

"Mary's not here," another says.

"Brandy and Amanda aren't back, either."

Distress is clear in their voices, and I feel the energy of it ripple through me. I squeeze Arlo's hand.

Luna lets out a small breath. "I don't think anyone else is coming back here. Everyone who could get away from the chaos did, and the rest were stopped by the men. I have to tell you that the gathering today was brutal. The Control have guns now."

There's a flurry of gasps and shocked whispers, words spoken in abrupt fear.

"Is that what happened to his arm?" someone asks.

We all turn to look at a woman standing near Arlo, staring at his blood-soaked sleeve. Her eyes are wide, glued to the sight of his injury, and the horrified look on her face makes nausea roll through my gut at the thought of his mangled flesh.

"Yes," Luna says firmly. "But before they shot him, they tried to burn him at the stake. They tried to burn one of their own for the offense of loving someone, for loving a *woman*…for falling in love with Mercy Madness!"

She says my name like I'm important, like it means something to speak of me, but I don't feel it. I don't feel like I'm important. I don't feel like I've done anything meaningful. I'm simply surviving.

"So it's true then? About Mercy and Arlo?" someone asks.

Luna looks at us over her shoulder. "I know what I saw today, but I think everyone would like to hear it from you."

"From us?" My eyes narrow in confusion. "Hear what?"

"Is it true that you've fallen in love?"

Arlo and I look at each other, sharing the same expression of confusion over the fact that they want to know, that they care, that this information is important in some way.

Of course, it's important.

Loving each other is what brought us here.

Luna turns sideways and takes a step back, opening the space in front of me like a curtain, putting me in a clearer view of the crowd. "We all saw the livestream of your trial, Mercy. We all saw with our own eyes that Arlo held affection for you…the kind of affection that's deemed blasphemous by the laws of the Impulse Edict. We saw how you broke, Arlo." She looks at him with empathy and sorrow. "We all witnessed you trying to dig her out early. The way you clawed at the soil on your hands and knees until they knocked you out…I can't speak for anyone else, but it was one of the most heartbreaking things I've ever seen."

He did what?

I watch Arlo's expression as it morphs, cycling through several emotions as Luna speaks. Pride, sorrow, heartache, regret—it's strange how I can identify each feeling from the slightest flicker of his blue eyes or a subtle twitch of his jaw.

"We saw how you fought for her, how you cried for her…the way you held her when you thought she was dead—" Luna's voice breaks.

The way she speaks of these events sends a shiver up my spine that radiates with hope, love, and warmth. I knew he'd been caught in displaying his feelings for me—it's the reason they intended to burn him alive today. Yet I didn't know exactly what had happened after the lid of my coffin fell shut, in the time between my burial and waking up in Owen's arms as he carried me through the forest.

I didn't know Arlo tried to dig me out early. I didn't know the village had witnessed him holding me, showing me affection without a care for who might bear witness. An odd sense of relief washes over me, knowing my burial hurt him, spurring him on to try to dig me out early without a care for his own judgment.

Somehow, I feel lighter in knowing that. I hadn't realized it before, but I can feel it now—there was a part of me that had held some resentment for him, some anger for the fact that he didn't risk everything for me sooner. There was a lingering hurt that he hadn't fallen for me faster, that he didn't understand how much he loved me before the first trial so he could have saved me then.

Hearing Luna tell of how he clawed at the soil on his hands and knees, trying to save me in desperation before my trial was complete, gives me such relief. Knowing this unlocks a door in my heart that I didn't know was still closed to him.

It's freeing, and my love for him deepens.

"We all know you're in love with her, Arlo," Luna says to him, then looks at me. "And Mercy, I think those of us who witnessed you today, running to join Arlo at the stake, ready to *die* with him…I think we already know the answer.

"But the women here who didn't see what happened need to hear it from you. We all need to know, because as strange as it sounds, hearing you say it out loud would give us such hope…Hope that even the worst of men," her eyes flicker to Arlo, "that even the misguided and lost are still capable of seeking truth, are willing to accept it and change for the better."

She smiles at me. "We have faith in who you are, Mercy. The author of our rebellion, our leader of change. If you tell us that you've fallen in love with Arlo Rainn—that he's made himself worthy of your love—it would give us the hope we need to fight for change."

Luna watches me with equal parts hope and fear. She hopes her brother is a good man—a man who's worthy of our trust and someone she could love again, too. Yet she's fearful that he's not.

She takes a slow breath. "Are you in love with him, too, Mercy? Does he have your heart?"

Yes.

Unequivocally, irrevocably yes.

I clear my throat, hoping my voice won't break as I make this solemn and cementing proclamation, sharing the secret that Arlo and I had to keep between us all this time. "He has my heart." At that alone, the women react in whispers and grins, a wholly unexpected joy filling the cavern—it fills me, too, fueling me as I speak. "It was hard won, but he earned it fully. I trust him. I love him."

I turn my head so I can look at him, and I find he's already gazing down at me, his blue eyes showing the same relief I feel for lifting the burden of secret-keeping from our shoulders. "Arlo listened to me; he learned from me, and when he finally opened his eyes to the truth, he made the choice to change."

I can't stop myself from smiling at the way Luna's face brightens. The unrestrained joy in her expression is so innocent, so idealistic, so child-like. I can almost see the hope filling her soul, lifting some undefined burden from her shoulders. Her eyes meet Stefanie's, finding her with a peaceful, silently hopeful expression.

There's a wordless connection shared between them, and though it appears intimately unique, the pulse of their shared energy is familiar—reminiscent of the electricity that passes between me and Arlo whenever our eyes meet.

A strange swell of emotion overcomes me, tears filling my eyes again, though these tears aren't from sorrow—these are tears of peace and contentment. It's so fulfilling that I don't hear what Luna and Stefanie say to the others before the crowd gradually disperses. I only see their smiles, feel their hope, and hear the laughter of children as they run off to play.

I've been surrounded by hatred for so long that I'd forgotten what it felt like to exist in peace—truthfully, I'm not sure I ever knew what that felt like.

It feels like this.

For a moment, I'm surrounded by love and not hate.

"There's something we need to show you," Stefanie says as she and Luna appear before me, "and we don't think it should wait." Her dark eyes have shifted so quickly into urgent gravity, and Luna's expression has fallen, too, reflecting the same.

The sudden shift sparks a quick-burning fire in my soul, and in a flash, the peace is gone.

chapter eighteen

ARLO

"ARE YOU SURE you're all right?" Luna asks me again. "I know it must be painful."

The gunshot wound to my arm *was* painful—overwhelmingly so—yet the burning has given way to an odd tingling sensation, the injured spot teetering on the edge of numbness. I'm not sure whether that's a good or a bad thing.

Thankfully, it seems to be nothing more than a flesh wound. I think the bullet grazed my arm rather than pierced it, and though it currently looks like my bicep exploded from the inside out, Mercy thinks that the tattered remnants of my flesh can be stitched back together.

I didn't want her to look at it as closely as she had; the thought of seeing her wounded that way pierces my heart more painfully than a bullet ever could. I didn't want that for her. Yet she was insistent on making sure I was okay before she would allow us to go with them for answers, and I was eager to find out what the fuck was going on here.

I didn't bother to remind Mercy of the injuries on my back, the lines of fire across my skin from the lashings I endured at the hands of the Control. Pain from the welted stripes was not as intense as the initial strike from the bullet, but it's a pain that remains no matter what I do, consistent fire across my back without relief. At least I can hold my arm still to lessen the pain there.

I'm exhausted, hungry, possibly on the verge of collapsing as the adrenaline from our escape begins to wane. Yet I push myself past the fatigue because I need to know what's happening as much as Mercy does.

Luna and Stefanie lead us by lantern-light through winding, dark tunnels—passageways cut through rock that seem so similar to the caves beneath the Homestead.

"I told you, I'm fine," I reassure for the thousandth time. "I'd rather have answers than medical care."

"Then you might get an infection and *die*." Luna sighs dramatically.

The exasperated tone is something familiar, like the way she'd speak to me when we were younger, whenever I made decisions she thought were ridiculous. I can't help the grin that touches my cheeks. When I became one of the Control, I'd closed myself off from my past so completely that I hadn't even realized how much I missed her. I missed my sister, and I'm glad she's here, that's she's safe and alive.

"I think I'll push my luck today," I return in a playful tone, "given that I should already be dead."

"It's only a flesh wound," Stefanie says, "and it's covered now. It won't take long to show them, and then Mercy can stitch him back together."

"If her hands aren't shaking with rage after she sees this," Luna mutters, then suddenly stops.

Mercy nearly collides with Luna's back. I tug her against my side to keep her upright, but I continue to hold her there for her warmth.

"Maybe we should go back." Luna turns to face Stefanie squarely. "Let her stitch him up now, get some rest, and we can show them later."

"No." Mercy's voice is firm. "Please. I won't be able to rest without answers. And as much as I want to tend to Arlo and stitch his wound, I trust that he's okay for now if he says he is."

"And I've said it a dozen times already. I'm *fine*. I should be dead right now, but here I am…a breathing, walking miracle. I'm suddenly wary of spending my minutes wisely, as clearly one never knows when the next will be their last. So face ahead and walk, Luna; show us what you know." My mind is processing my words as I speak them, realizing that I *am* alive when I should be dead, and I feel my pulse quickening with the strange sensation that awareness brings. Worried my tone has come across harshly, I add, "Please."

Luna nods, "You're right…you're right, Arlo. I know we can't waste any more time." She says it convincingly, but I see the way she anxiously chews her bottom lip, her face shadowed in the meager glow of her lantern's light.

I remember her doing that when she was younger and nervous about getting in trouble—it's a tell I'd completely forgotten about until this very moment. It makes me wonder what else I've forgotten about the people I cared for before the Shift. It makes me feel shame for the man I let myself become.

I'm not that man anymore, and I never will be again.

We walk down the dark passageway. Mercy remains close, our arms pinned between us and fingers interwoven. She holds my hand tightly, sending two squeezing pulses through her grip as a silent reminder that she's here with me.

Mercy walks beside me in the darkness. I can't help but feel as though we're chasing the creeping shadows along the cave walls into hell.

I can feel the change coming. I can sense the onrushing pain of acknowledging truths we'd rather deny.

I fear it.

I fear I'm too weak to accept further dissonance, too weak to admit I was wrong again, too weak to grow more than I already have. Yet, I follow the truth as we march onward…and I'm willing to confront it for Mercy.

Stefanie and Luna share anxious whispers as they lead us through the tunnel. I can't make out what they're saying as my mind races through all the possibilities of what they might be leading us to. It's not too much farther ahead before they stop, and I see an opening in the passage wall just in front of them on our right, a small alcove through it.

Stefanie gently takes the lantern from Luna, crossing to the opposite side of the opening in the rock wall. "In here," she says, gesturing for us to move inside.

Luna leads, and Mercy and I follow. I expect to see something grand, an obvious revelation, but instead all I see is a small cavern—small enough that I can cross the space with three long strides.

"Is this what you wanted to show us?" I ask, turning around to face Stefanie as she moves into the alcove behind us.

"No." Stefanie moves through the small cavern until she reaches the back wall, and then she crouches, bringing the light down with her to reveal a boulder—big enough to reach my knees—sitting against the wall.

"Your father led us here, Mercy," Stefanie says.

I feel Mercy's grip loosening. I feel her drift toward the boulder and away from me in her curiosity. I want to cling to her and drag her back, but I know I cannot hold her back anymore. Though it's painful, I let her hand leave mine, remain still as she steps forward.

"What do you mean?" Mercy asks.

Stefanie sets down the lantern, dropping her knees to the ground and placing her hands on the side of the rock. She glances up at Mercy. "Help me push? Luna has the baby, and Arlo's arm is useless right now."

Mercy doesn't hesitate. Nodding, she steps forward and lowers beside Stefanie. Together, they push the boulder, straining to make it scrape along the solid bedrock beneath. I want to help, but a twinge of pain in my arm reminds me it's useless. Still, they make impressively quick work of it on their own.

As the boulder moves, they reveal an opening in the rock wall behind it, a low tunnel through which one could crawl. My attention immediately flicks to Mercy, remembering the way she panicked when we had to crawl through the tunnel into the main cavern.

Stefanie must be thinking the same, as she grabs the lantern and quickly lifts it to the rounded opening. "It's not a tunnel; it's just like a small doorway, see? Quick in, quick out."

I crouch to my haunches to look through, trying to hide my wince as a searing pain burns across my back, and I see there's another alcove on the other side. It's still shrouded in darkness beyond the lantern's light, but I have the sense that the room is larger than the space where we currently stand.

I also spy some opaque slate blue plastic bins on the ground. A lid covers each bin to protect their contents—whatever those may be—and some of them are stacked on top of each other.

What's inside them?

How many fill this small cavern?

The bins are rather ordinary-looking storage containers but seeing them here gives me an unsettling feeling of foreboding. It jumpstarts my heart, and I feel a new wave of anticipatory adrenaline punch into my veins.

These containers are buried beneath Ember Glen, hidden away in the dark, where they were likely never meant to be seen...and perhaps their contents will answer questions we never thought to ask.

"What's in there?" Mercy's voice is soft, quiet.

Stefanie looks at her, waiting until their eyes connect. "The real story of Ember Glen."

There's a stagnant pause.

A haunting silence wraps around us.

The real story of Ember Glen?

A new battle begins in my mind, a sharp clash between the man I was before and the man I am now. My natural instinct is to balk at the insinuation that there's a story we haven't been told—a story that's true, a story that will reveal the lies upon which we've based our lives. And yet, I already feel the wavering in my soul, the unease of dissonance. I can feel the whole of Ember Glen teetering on the brink, and there's something in that room that's going to bring it all crashing down.

"Show me," Mercy demands. "Tell us everything."

She feels it, too.

I know it.

Her soul is resonating with mine, vibrating on the same frequency of hope and fear.

Stefanie nods, then crawls through the opening, taking the lantern with her. She sets it down once she's inside, and holds out her hand, beckoning Mercy to follow. I expect her to panic, but she doesn't. Her need for this information must be stronger than her newfound fear over small, dark spaces—a fear we gave her by burying her alive—as she crawls right in.

I turn to look at Luna. "How will you get through with her?" I indicate baby Soleil, strapped to the front of her frame with a fabric wrap.

"I always manage," she says, moving in close to the entrance before lowering to her knees.

She cradles the back of Soleil's head with one hand, crawling through the opening on her other hand and knees. Stefanie reaches out from the other side, her upturned palm hovering beneath the baby's head for additional protection. Once Luna is inside, Stefanie grips her arm to help her to her feet.

Forgetting about the wound in my arm for a split-second, I drop to my hands and knees to follow, and I'm quickly reminded of the pain. The moment my weight presses down through my arm, I hiss, flinch, reflexively jerk my left arm from the ground as I let out a groan in agony.

"Arlo…" Mercy appears on her hands and knees in front of the opening, worry wrinkling her forehead. "Are you okay?"

I rush to slip through the opening with only one arm. "Fine. I'm fine," I mutter, climbing to my feet.

I'm not fine, but she doesn't need to know that.

I hear a click, then a whirring sound, and a bright light comes on from the center of the room. It shines across the space toward the back wall, across from the entrance, concentrated on a white screen that rests upon a black stand—the light coming from a running film projector. Though it spotlights the white projector screen, the light is strong enough to illuminate the center of the bedroom-sized cavern, casting shadows around the outer edges to reveal stacks of the plastic containers lining the walls.

"How…What *is* this?" Mercy's tone reflects my own bewilderment. "How did you find this?"

I watch as Luna moves past a set of stacked bins, lowering to sit on a thick pillow placed against the wall. "The projector and screen weren't set up when we found this place; everything was packed up in these bins." She waves her hand, indicating the stacks of slate-blue plastic totes all around the room.

Mercy slowly turns, her eyes catching mine with a quizzical look before she completes her rotation, glancing between Stefanie and Luna. "What's inside the boxes? How did you *find* this place? You said my father led you here…but how?"

"I'm not quite sure how to start," Luna says, stroking the back of her baby's head.

Soleil whimpers and whines, preparing to cry. Luna anxiously chews on her bottom lip as she loosens part of her wrap, adjusting her clothing so she can nurse.

Stefanie leans sideways against the wall at Luna's side, crossing her arms. "She's hesitant about sharing some parts of our story…how we came to find the pages from Mercy's father that led us here."

"The pages?" Mercy asks at the exact moment my eyes shift to look at her, my attention immediately drawn to those same two words.

The journal of Mira Madness—Mercy's mother—was missing three torn pages, and we had no idea what was written on them or whether they still existed.

Is it possible those pages still exist?

Is it possible my sister somehow found them?

"What pages?" I ask carefully.

Luna shifts on the pillow where she sits, settling in to nurse Soleil. "Pages we found in Mercy's house." She sighs, staring at her feet. "I'm going to tell you everything—what we found, how we found it, the horrible truth about everything—but I need to start at the beginning. I need to start with an admission, knowing you may judge me for this, Arlo. I'm not the God-fearing domestic woman you've always thought me to be."

I'm struck silent by her words, by the guilt that overcomes me, knowing she's hesitant to speak with me. It's a hesitancy I can't fault her for having; I've given her every reason in the world to believe I would judge her—and judge her harshly—for any sins she may have committed. However, she knows I'm no longer a threat to her, no longer in favor with the Control or the Elders.

"I'm no longer with the Control," I remind her. "I can't punish you for any sins you've committed."

Her head rises, gathering my full attention with the intensity of her blue eyes on mine.

"I'm not worried about you punishing me for my sins, Arlo. I'm afraid of the way you're going to look at me, the way you're going to *see* me. I fear your judgment because you're my brother. You've always been my brother, even after the Shift, even after you joined the Control and had to distance yourself. You put up walls and you shut me out, but I never stopped loving you. I never stopped caring about you. You chose power over being my brother, but I never got to make a choice."

She sighs, averting her eyes. "It felt like you had died, and I had to grieve the loss of you…It was like you were dead, but then Mercy brought you back to life. I'm just afraid of losing you again. I'm afraid that when I tell you who I really am, that you'll judge me, hate me, shut me out like you did before."

It feels like the air has been sucked from my lungs. Shame settles heavily in my chest, making my heart ache. I turned my back on her for *them*, for the men who meant to kill me today for loving a sinner.

I feel Mercy's eyes on me, but I can't look at her. The weight of my guilt is so heavy, and I'm afraid that if I look at her, she'll try to help me carry it. It's *my* guilt to carry, and I have no right to put that on her.

"I want to know who you really are, Luna. I'm not..." I pause, struggling to put my thoughts into words. "I don't want to judge you. And I'm not really in a place to judge, now am I? I'm a sinner condemned, after all."

An uncomfortable silence settles as I wait for her response; the stillness made eerie by the whir of the idling projector and the flickering shadows its light casts on the rock walls surrounding us.

Luna still avoids my gaze, though she slowly nods and says, "Okay." She draws in a deep breath to steel herself as she looks down at Soleil, stroking her head.

Then softly, she begins to speak, starting her confession from the very beginning.

chapter nineteen

ARLO

"I'M SURE YOU remember that Stefanie and I were friends when we were children," Luna begins. "We met on the day of my evaluation when I was five. Stefanie had already gone through her evaluation since she was nine years old at the time.

"I was really nervous that day. I thought for sure they were going to evaluate me as a servant, and I knew I didn't want to be a servant. I didn't understand exactly why back then. It all seemed so much simpler when I was young." She gives a sad smile. "I just knew I wanted to have children, and you can't have children if you're a servant.

"I can't recall all the details from my evaluation, but I vaguely remember one of the Control telling the others that I was a good girl who followed rules well, and that would make me an obedient and dutiful wife." Luna's eyes narrow as her brow furrows. "And then another argued that *because* I was a good girl who followed rules well, I should be made to serve, because I would never say no.

"That's the only part I remember before they decided I would be a domestic. I was so thrilled with the decision that I skipped away and ran right into Stefanie, who was waiting with her mother outside. I accidentally knocked her over, and she started to cry. So *I* started to cry, thinking that I'd hurt her. I hadn't hurt her, though. She was upset because she'd just found out they'd decided her little sister would be a servant.

"I didn't understand at five years old why she would be upset for her sister. I might have been upset if I'd been evaluated as a servant, but only because I knew I wanted to be a domestic. I didn't understand why she would be upset about *someone else's* evaluation. After all, maybe her sister really wanted to be a servant, and she was happy about it. Lots of little girls wanted to be servants.

"But Stefanie told me that she'd heard some bad things had happened to servants during the full moon, and she was scared that bad things might happen to her sister. I gave her a hug and tried to reassure her that she'd be okay." Luna chuckles a little, smiling to herself. "Maybe this is just something

I made up in my head and not an actual memory, but I think I was a little in awe of her when we met that day…I thought she was pretty, and I really wanted to be her friend."

"You didn't make it up in your head." Stefanie's voice is quiet and her grin is subtle, but it's there. "And you didn't just think it. You told me that day that I was the prettiest girl you'd ever seen and asked if I wanted to be your best friend."

Luna smiles up at her. "I did?"

"You did." Stefanie nods.

As they speak, Mercy moves in front of them, slowly lowering to her knees just a couple of feet in front of Luna. She presses her palms to her thighs as she sits back on her heels, leaning in to listen as if she's a child who has come to gather for story time. I'll admit, I'm rather absorbed in the story myself.

Luna fights her overwhelming smile, dragging her eyes away from Stefanie. "I'm sorry, I'm entirely off track here, and I said this would be quick."

"It's okay," Mercy says. "I like this story."

"Well, Stefanie and I became friends after that day. It was strange how easily we connected, given that she was four years older than me. Our age difference was so much more pronounced back then, but even so, she was easily my best friend. And that's all we were to each other, the very best of friends, until…" She pauses, her eyes losing focus, staring across the space at the opposite rock wall.

"Until I turned sixteen, and they made me Hyatt's wife," Stefanie says, and our collective attention shifts to her, though she only steals it for a moment.

Luna blinks, and I can see how she actively drags her mind back from some past memories that haunt her. She continues speaking as if she never paused. "I was only twelve when it was time for her to become a wife, and I struggled for a long time trying to figure out what that would mean exactly. It was the first time I saw her with Hyatt that I knew what I felt in my heart— though I was too young to fully understand it or find a word to express it." Luna looks over at me, meeting my eyes with intention. "It was jealousy, Arlo. I was *jealous* of Hyatt."

She doesn't have to say another word.

She doesn't have to finish this story for me to know the nature of her confession, and why she fears my judgment. I think I knew it before; I probably knew it all along but wouldn't allow myself to acknowledge the truth.

Luna and Stefanie have become…something more than friends.

I blink, shifting my gaze from Luna as old judgments fight for power in my mind. I can't bear to look at her as I struggle against habit, feeling too vulnerable as I battle my conditioning and fight to keep my mind open for her truth.

"Right," Luna says with a regretful sigh.

I don't mean for her to think I've turned away in judgment, but I hear in her voice that it's exactly what she thinks.

I wish I could offer her reassurance that I'm struggling with *myself* and not with *her*, but I can't bring myself to speak. The appropriate words evade me as this war of obedience versus truth rages in my mind.

"Anyway, that's when I first started to feel…discordant? I can't think of a better word for it. The whole world just started to feel so wrong to me. I missed my best friend. I *hated* Hyatt—and that was before I even knew what a vile human he would turn out to be. I only hated him then because he'd just become the center of Stefanie's life. She didn't have time for me anymore because she was a wife…and a soon-to-be mother within a few months. Our friendship faded when she became a mother, but she never left my heart. We just…she went on with her life as a domestic, and I went on as a child preparing to become the same.

"Years went by where we only said hello to each other in passing in the village. Then everything changed again when I turned sixteen and became a domestic. I'd been assigned to Archer, of course, and by all accounts, he's a kind husband and a loving father." A pained look flickers across her eyes as she looks down at Soleil.

I wonder if Archer knows she's here with his children. Perhaps the pained look is an indication that he doesn't, and she feels some regret for that.

"I never felt any fear with him," Luna says. "At least, not in the way Stefanie did with Hyatt. I had some fear for Archer's strict thinking, but I felt that with everyone in Ember Glen once I worked out the source of my confusion and accepted the truth about myself. I felt things I wasn't supposed to feel for anyone, and worse than that, I felt them for another *woman*.

"I had to accept this truth about myself when it literally came knocking on my door, and it came only a week after I became Archer's wife. Stefanie came to my house late one night after we'd gone to bed. Archer was sound asleep, but I was wide awake, spending yet another night wondering why I didn't feel happy yet. I thought I'd feel happy all the time once I started serving my purpose as a domestic, but I didn't…" Luna falters, closing her eyes as she swallows hard.

When she opens them again, she tilts her chin to gaze up at Stefanie as she slowly lowers to her knees beside Luna. "You came over in tears," Luna says to her. "Do you remember that night? I know there were so many other nights just like it, but that first time you came to me after he hurt you will always be locked in my mind."

My heart feels constricted, my chest tight with a familiar ache that resembles the pain of watching tears fall down Mercy's cheeks. I glance over at her at the same moment she looks back at me, and it pains me further to see her eyes are glassy with tears of her own.

"You were sobbing when I opened the door," Luna goes on. "It nearly broke me to see you that way. You could hardly catch your breath enough to tell me what happened."

"I remember," Stefanie says calmly, maintaining an energy that perfectly contrasts Luna's—a perfect balance. She reaches forward to tuck a wayward strand of hair behind Luna's ear. "You gave me exactly what I needed. You invited me in, you let me tell you what Hyatt had done to me, and you listened without any judgment. But I felt so guilty for putting that on you when you were still so young, when you'd only just married Archer."

"You shouldn't feel guilty," Luna replies. "You kept it to yourself for so long."

"I couldn't burden you with that before you were assigned to someone, before you were married," Stefanie says. "I didn't want to make you fearful of what it would be like when you became a domestic. You'd had such high hopes for it when you were younger."

"And I'd been wrong to have that hope at all." Luna's shoulders slump with her sorrow.

"Hyatt hurt her, Arlo," Luna says my name so emphatically that I have no choice but to meet her stare directly. "That's what the purge is supposed to prevent, isn't it? It's for the men to let out all their violent and sexual urges so their wives don't ever need to fear them. But you probably didn't know all the ways he hurt Stefanie. You probably didn't know that she's been his domestic *and* his personal servant for ten years. Because if the Control knew, they'd surely have done something about it, right?"

I swallow hard. "I didn't know."

I probably should have known, but I didn't.

"Hyatt did everything he could to hide it," Luna says. "He'd been so intentional about it, only causing injuries in places that were hidden by clothing. That first night she came to me...He'd hit her hard enough to break a rib."

Stefanie shifts uneasily, slowly rising to her feet again.

"Her back was bruised so horribly that she winced with every movement.

I went to her house every day for weeks afterward, just to help her care for Heidi and Hattie."

"Hattie was just a baby," Stefanie adds, crossing her arms over her chest, her body rigid and tense.

"That wasn't all he'd done to her." Glancing up, Luna asks Stefanie, "Will you show them?"

There's a long pause, but then Stefanie nods. Pushing off the wall, she steps past Mercy on the ground, moving to stand between the light of the projector and the screen at her back. She lifts the hem of her cream-colored sweater, and with her other hand, hooks her thumb into the waistband of her modest skirt to pull it down. She exposes a patch of skin on the lower right side of her waist, just above her pelvic bone, revealing an old white scar in the shape of the letter 'H.'

Fuck.

I let out a heavy, audible breath, swiping my hand across my beard.

"He hurt me for years," Stefanie snaps, covering her scar as she brings her sweater and skirt together again with a sharp motion. "I couldn't tell anyone. The Control couldn't have helped me; no one could. Hyatt told me he'd kill me if I told the Control, that he'd do it before they could take action against him. And then where would my daughters be? He was *cruel* to them. It was only a matter of time before he started to hurt them physically, too. Heidi would have been next."

Mercy rises sharply, and in a flash, collides with Stefanie, throwing her arms around her to embrace her with clear compassion. For a moment, Stefanie's frozen in surprise, but then she welcomes the hug, letting out a heavy breath and hugging Mercy around the middle.

I have to turn away to compose myself as an array of emotions overcomes me. Most prominent is shame because I should have known. It was my job to punish sinners, and that vile man sinned against his wife for years. Hyatt Price denied everything I stood for each time he placed his hands on her.

"You saved me from him, Mercy." I hear Stefanie tell her. "I'm grateful for what you did to him."

"It wasn't just me," Mercy says. I turn to see them untangle and stand at arm's length from each other. Mercy glances over her shoulder at me. "I want to tell her. Can I tell them what you did that night?"

I'm so lost in my racing thoughts that I don't know what she means at first. I nod because I don't care what she tells them.

She turns back to Stefanie. "There's something I think you should know about the night Hyatt died."

Stefanie's dark brows slant toward her nose, her head tilting at an angle.

"Hyatt selected my friend Ellary to serve him that night…"

Ellary…Fuck.

I haven't told Mercy that she fell.

She doesn't know that her friend is in Sanctuary, grasping at tiny threads of life that can easily slip through her fingers.

She may be dead now.

"I escaped the Homestead and ran to save her," Mercy says. "Arlo chased me, but it wasn't to catch me. He went straight for Hyatt, and he was the one who attacked him first. Arlo took Hyatt's knife and held it to his throat, but then his hand slipped and—"

"My hand didn't slip, Mercy."

All eyes fly to look at me.

"I was in control of the situation. I didn't consciously decide to do it. I don't remember a moment where I thought I wanted to kill him, and I don't recall making an active decision to end his life." The words fly out of me, as if this room was meant for sharing secrets and draws it out of me. "But what I do remember is making a decision to press down on the blade when he moved beneath me, and I knew exactly what would happen when I did."

Mercy's chest rises sharply, then falls slowly as she exhales, her gaze dripping down my body before drifting back up to my face.

"I took the knife from Arlo." Mercy's voice is suddenly deeper, slower, like something in my admission effectively altered her mood, and the subtle hint of longing in her voice alters mine just the same. "It's true that I delivered the final blow, but we both had a hand in Hyatt's death. I wouldn't allow Arlo to take the blame, though. I chose to take responsibility for it to spare him," she says to them before she turns to me. "I wanted to spare you."

"And you did."

Stefanie asks, "Is that true?"

I nod, though my gaze is fixed on Mercy, watching her, watching me. "It's true."

"Then I have to thank you both," Stefanie says, "for ending my misery."

I don't know how to respond to that, but saying, 'you're welcome,' in response to being thanked for killing someone's husband seems inappropriate. Though I suppose there are many things I once found to be inappropriate that I no longer see as such. The way Mercy looks at me right now is *entirely* inappropriate under the standards I held before, but now I consider the look to be expected, necessary…*wanted.*

"For what it's worth," I tell Stefanie, "I'm glad for what Mercy and I did to him now that I know it ended your suffering."

"So am I," Mercy whispers, her eyes flickering over my face as a grin pulls across her cheeks. She draws in a deep breath, then turns back to Luna. "So, you were telling us that you and Stefanie…that you feel for each other the way that Arlo and I do?"

Luna blinks her glassy eyes, tugging her bottom lip between her teeth. "Yes. And I first realized it that night she came over. I wanted to be with her. I wanted to comfort her and take care of her. I wanted to be her partner, her *wife*, the mother to her children. I wanted to be the domestic who cared for her, made a home for her…"

Luna drops her head, eyes focusing on a spot near her feet. "And I wanted more than that. I wanted…I had desire for her in the way a man has desire for a servant. I felt sick over it for the longest time; I prayed about it nightly. I kept my thoughts a secret for years until I simply couldn't anymore. That day came shortly after Stefanie's youngest daughter, Hollie, was born two years ago."

Her head snaps up and her eyes lock with Mercy's as she cries, "I kissed her, Mercy. I couldn't take it anymore. I just grabbed hold of her and I kissed her. I thought for sure that was the end for me—that she would report me and the Control would kill me for this sin—but instead, she kissed me back."

Luna smiles, though tears drip down her cheeks. "She kissed me back, Mercy, and it didn't feel *wrong*. It felt…it felt like the world had been gray before, but it all turned to color the moment our lips touched. Maybe that doesn't make any sense, but—"

Mercy lowers to her haunches, resting a wrist on her knee. "It makes perfect sense to me, Luna." She smiles at her, reaching out with her other hand to touch Luna's knee with compassion.

"Stefanie and I have sinned, over and over again. Sins of the heart, sins of the flesh…" She sighs with relief. "I never thought I'd be able to say that out loud."

"But you did." I can only see Mercy's face in profile, yet her genuine smile radiates all the same.

Her natural grace always strikes me hard, but I feel it especially now in the way she shares her kindness with Luna so easily. I feel a ripple of warmth blanket me, vibrating through my limbs. I feel light-headed…

More than light-headed, I feel dizzy, suddenly faint, and the room seems to tilt sideways.

"Arlo?" Mercy's voice echoes oddly as my vision blurs.

Does she feel the room tilting, too?

No…it's only me.

I've hit the wall of exhaustion, and my body's shutting down.

"Arlo, sit down!" Mercy commands as the room turns.

I stumble sideways, seeing the blurry vision of her rushing over to me. I slump to the floor at her command, but before she reaches me, my exhausted mind shutters to blackness as my body collides with solid rock.

The world goes black.

chapter twenty

Mercy

ARLO COLLAPSED NEARLY two hours ago. I stare at his chest, watching the gentle rise and fall that reminds me he's still breathing. Every so often, I nudge him, just to make sure he responds with a groan or a wince, so I'll know he's all right.

He's exhausted after the torture he endured by the Control—the sleepless nights bound to the foyer ceiling while suffering the pain of being lashed across his back. And then there was the chaos at the Homestead this morning, where he faced his death at the stake, where the crowd battled, and he was shot in the arm.

That would be enough to make anyone collapse from exhaustion, but I also have no idea when he last had something to eat or drink.

When he collapsed, he'd toppled sideways, landing on his right side—thankfully, not landing on his wounded arm. I knew we needed to turn him onto his stomach so the wounds across his back from the lashings wouldn't be further irritated by the rock-hard ground.

I asked Luna and Stefanie to help me remove his shirt first, as I wanted to clean his injuries while he was resting. Then, we rolled him onto his stomach, turning his head to rest his cheek against the pillow Luna had been sitting on earlier. He groaned and muttered as we moved him, so at least we knew he was okay—he was just beyond exhaustion, entirely succumbed to his need for rest.

Luna and Stefanie left, and in their kindness, they brought back food, water, and some medical supplies. They left me with two lanterns and some matches so we could leave the space later.

Both lanterns are now lit, resting on the ground a few feet away. I told them I would come back to the main cavern to find them later.

I still have no answers about how they found this place through my father's house. I still haven't been told the 'real story of Ember Glen,' as Stefanie had promised would be revealed in this room. I'm beyond anxious to know, but I don't want to know before Arlo. I want to learn these secrets together because I don't know if I can handle learning the truth on my own.

It all just feels so overwhelming.

I've turned off the projector, worried the light would wake Arlo. Though, I must admit, there was something comforting about the sound it made when it was running. The way the light filled the space made it feel less like a tomb where secrets were buried, shining a light on them instead.

I'm beginning to face exhaustion myself with this cycle of fear that keeps repeating. The small, dark space reminds me of being buried, so my panic rises sharply. I'll push it back down, forcing it away somewhere deep in my soul, but it can only lie in waiting for so long before the panic rises again.

The cycle is wearing on me.

But I refuse to leave Arlo's side, even if he doesn't realize I'm here with him.

I need him.

I don't ever want to be apart from him again.

Sitting beside him, I stroke my palm down the back of his head. I laid beside him for a while—even dozed off for a bit—but now I'm wide awake.

He groans in his sleep, drawing in a deep breath before letting it out again. "Starlight…" he mutters.

There's an extra thump between heartbeats, another pulse of life through my veins at the sound of his voice.

"Mercy," he whispers in a gravelly voice. "Come back to bed."

"I'm here, love. You can rest."

The wrinkles on his forehead deepen at the sound of my voice, then his eyes flutter, slowly blinking open. "Mercy?"

"It's me; I'm here." I curl my fingers to drag them through his hair as I continue to stroke the back of his head.

He groans. "Where are we?" He opens his eyes fully, slowly lifting his head from the pillow.

"You don't have to get up. We're safe here. You can rest."

He pushes himself up into a sitting position. "I don't need to rest…I'm fine." He reaches up to pinch the bridge of his nose, his face scrunching against the pain.

"Please don't lie to me, Arlo. Don't tell me you're fine when you're not. You collapsed."

He blinks as he drops his hand. "Where's Luna? I need to tell her—"

"We're alone right now. I told them to go while you rested. You've been out for nearly two hours."

"Two hours?"

I nod. "You needed the rest."

"I don't need rest." He places his hand on the ground, shifting as if he's going to push himself up. "I need answers."

"I need them, too." I grip his right bicep and wrap my other hand around the side of his neck to hold him in place. "Trust me when I tell you how much I need some answers. But it was foolish of us to rush after what we've been through."

I let my hand drift down the side of his neck, lightly brushing over the curve of his shoulder, stopping there to avoid touching his gunshot wound. "I need to stitch this up, disinfect it, and cover it. After all we've survived, Arlo Rainn, wouldn't it be ridiculous for you to die from an infection we could have prevented?"

I smile at him, hoping to ease some of the tension that naturally exists in this small, dark space.

His head inclines as he watches me, his gaze fixed on mine. "You're right. You're always right." It's strange that I can see just how blue his eyes are in this dim lighting.

A small flame sways and waves in the two lanterns nearby, making shadows dance on the cave wall behind him, appearing like dark ghosts which haunt him.

He looks haunted.

But at least he's alive.

I swallow hard against a rising lump in my throat, the same one that rises each time I remember that he could be dead right now. If the women hadn't chosen to fight back today, Arlo would be dead. I would be entirely without him. I'd be crying alone, locked in my room at the Homestead, grieving the loss of this man who won my heart.

The mere thought of it is unbearable.

I shove to my feet and move away as tears rise behind my eyes. "Let me just put on the projector for light, and I'll stitch your arm." I put on a cheerful tone, though I have to force it. "There's food and water there beside you. You need both to get your strength back."

I flip on the projector, and it whirs to life, the light brightening the center of the room as it shines on the white screen in front of it.

"Come here, starlight."

I turn to find him watching me, his bare chest lifting and lowering with each deep breath he takes. I expect to see some heat behind his eyes with the way he called me back to him, but I didn't expect to see them so somber, shining at me with gentle longing.

"Look," he says, reaching over to pick up a glass of water from the tray Luna and Stefanie had brought back. "I'll drink." He takes two long gulps. "I'll eat. Just come here and be close to me."

I bend to grab the small kit with medical supplies before making my way to Arlo. I step in close, placing one boot on the ground between his slightly spread legs, the other on the opposite side, before I lower over his knee.

I settle my feet beneath me and shift forward on my knees to straddle his thigh. I sit, landing heavier than I'd meant to. His flesh is warm, pressed firmly between my legs, and impossibly, I feel desire for him now. I have to ignore the feeling, though, so I can focus on his arm.

I glance down at the wound, and the sight is instantly sobering. I don't even know how to describe what I see, but I'm so damn thankful that the bullet merely grazed him. This particular injury will be a challenge, but I know how to stitch a flesh wound. I wouldn't know where to begin if a bullet had burrowed inside him. I tremor at the thought of it.

"It's only flesh and blood…That's nothing to be afraid of." Ellary's voice is clear inside my mind. *"It's injuries of the heart and soul that make me uneasy."* That's what she'd told me once when I asked her how she was so good at managing gruesome injuries.

Ellary is such a natural caregiver, truly gifted with medicine and healing. She would be so much better than me at stitching this wound, and I wish she were here right now to help me.

I just hope that she and Cambria are safe.

I didn't see Ellary at the gathering this morning. I know some were grabbed by men, while others were chased by the Control as they ran, and I don't know who was caught or how they'll be punished.

I hope they ran early and that they thought to seek safety at Sanctuary. It's naïve of me to think that any rules designed in the favor of women are sacred in Ember Glen, but perhaps the men will honor the one that prevents them from stepping foot inside Sanctuary without the unanimous permission of every servant within.

Perhaps if they stay in Sanctuary, they'll remain safe…at least until the next full moon.

I open the medical kit and twist to place it on the ground beside me. Arlo's hand touches my cheek, and it stills me. A wave of loving energy flows from his palm through my entire body, the warmth of his touch reminding me that it was only last night that I thought I'd never feel his touch again.

His thumb brushes my skin, and all the emotions I've been suppressing rise against the dam wall I've built, threatening to break through and flood me. I shut my eyes and inhale slowly, trying to steady myself as my head drifts naturally into his palm. When I open my eyes, I find him watching me with a small smile, and my lips curl in response.

There's a beat of peace now that we're alone, away from all the world and safe for the moment…I should be happy, and I am, but I'm also intensely aware of how broken I am from the events over the last few days.

I feel tears prick my eyes, but I don't want to cry anymore.

I'm so sick of crying.

I sniff them back and force a brighter smile through my expression. His hand falls from my cheek when I turn away from his touch to reach over and grab some rubbing alcohol from the kit. I pour a small amount on some fresh gauze, then begin to clean the area around his wound, disinfecting while scrubbing away the dried blood in preparation for stitches.

Silence surrounds us, and it begs to be filled.

The one truth I don't want to acknowledge gnaws at the inside of my cheek, grinds through my teeth, then sneaks out past my lips the moment I let them part…

"You almost died today."

It's a thought that has me twisted up in knots on the inside, though the words sound so ordinary, as if I'm engaging in small talk and this is a normal topic of conversation.

Arlo remains quiet as I work, and just when I start to think he's not going to respond at all, he quietly replies, "Almost."

I swallow against a thick lump that's risen in my throat, blinking a few extra times to bat away the tears dotting my lashes. I finish making a clean circle around the wound, then pick up a new square of gauze from the kit and pour more alcohol so I can clean the wound itself.

"This might hurt," I warn before gently working to cleanse the injury.

It's a canyon dug into his flesh, raw and open, reminding me just how fragile we are—how easily their bullets could tear us all to shreds. All I can do is close the wound by stitching the broken flaps of skin together, seal it from infection, and hope his body knows what to do to repair itself in time.

I work gently but quickly to disinfect as much of the wound as I possibly can. I try to focus on the whirring of the projector, to tune out the sound of him hissing and groaning in pain. When I finish, I discard the blood-soaked gauze. Before I reach for the needle, I drench my hands in alcohol, rubbing them together to disinfect my skin thoroughly.

"You promised you would eat," I remind him as I clean the needle, then work on threading it.

"Were you really going to burn with me, Mercy?"

My breath stutters in my lungs at the question, and for a moment, I'm frozen.

"Yes," I whisper.

My hands are suddenly trembling. I stare at them intently while struggling to thread the needle, trying to avoid his gaze. But then I realize that I need him to know clearly, without a doubt, that it was my intention to die with him when I climbed onto that platform and stood with him at the stake.

I meet his eyes. "Yes, I was going to burn with you, Arlo. I was ready to die with you."

Arlo sighs. "Starlight…I wish I could find a way to put my thoughts into words."

I grin, looking down at my hands again, finally managing to work the damn thread through the loop. "The poet is at a loss for words?"

"A complete loss. A blank page."

What does that mean?

Does he think I'm weak?

Does he think less of me for choosing to die with him rather than face the final trial without him?

I don't know what to say, and he's quiet again.

The silence festers between us.

Letting out an anxious breath, I bring my hand to his shoulder, turning my palm above his wound to get a good grip. I shift closer and bring the needle to his arm.

"This will hurt," I tell him.

From the corner of my eye, I see the motion as his head bobs in understanding. I can feel him staring at me. I know he's studying each twitch of muscle through my tense jaw, watching every subtle shift in my demeanor.

"Do you regret it?" he asks.

My head turns with a snap, and I quickly meet his eyes.

"If you had the choice to make again, not knowing that my life would be miraculously spared today, would you still choose to run to me? Would you still choose to burn and die with me?"

"Arlo, that's…it's an impossible question to answer."

He glances at my lips before returning to meet my eyes. "Then give me an impossible answer."

I don't know how to answer his question, though it's not because I don't know the answer. It's because I'm afraid of what he'll think of me once he knows the truth.

He leans forward, pressing a sweet kiss to my shoulder. "Please. Tell me the truth, starlight."

My body softens as he drops his forehead to my shoulder, turning his head to nuzzle his face into the slope of my neck. His breath is warm as it breezes across my bare skin, softly dripping heat down my body.

He melts me.

My skin prickles and my muscles release their tension as every part of my body begs me to relax into his touch, to find comfort in his nearness. Yet I know comfort can only be found with the truth, and so I have to speak mine.

I let the words drip from my lips. "The impossible answer is yes, Warden Rainn."

His head rises from my shoulder, and our eyes connect deeply. I didn't intend to call him Warden Rainn, yet the honorific came out so naturally. His blue eyes give me clarity, reminding me of who he was, who he is, and all he will become.

Arlo Rainn has always been, and will always be, my warden. Not the warden assigned to ensure my punishment in the trials; he's the warden of my heart, the jailor of my soul, the captor of my desire, and only because I *choose* him to be the keeper of every part of me.

"You can ask me this question a thousand times on a thousand different days," I whisper, "and my answer will always be the same. Forever, my answer will be yes. Forever, I would choose to die with you, to burn with you."

His chest sinks. "Forever…I would burn with you, Mercy." He leans closer to kiss my neck, trailing his lips up to my cheek. They skim along the line of my jaw until he reaches my ear and whispers, "I would die a million deaths for you."

My lips part, letting out a breath of relief, releasing all the fear I held that he might think less of me for my answer. Of course, I should've known he wouldn't, because in my heart, I knew his answer would be the same.

My parted lips draw his gaze to my mouth, and the promise of his kiss hangs heavy in the air between us.

"I need to stitch your wound…" I remind him.

Arlo slowly nods. "Go ahead."

His fingers brush over my cheek before they comb into my hair. A tremor runs up my spine as they curl and flex, fingertips gently rubbing against my scalp as he indulges in his obsession with my hair. My eyes flutter shut at the soothing feel of it.

I swallow, my mouth suddenly dry. "Do you want me to give you a warning or just begin?"

"Starlight," he whispers. "There is no warning you could give that would sufficiently prepare me for your touch."

I open my eyes to find his gaze roaming across my face, touching every feature, slipping through my hair, tracing the curve of my neck. His eyes could easily be his hands, because I feel every sweep of them over my skin.

"Arlo."

His eyes shift to meet mine. "Go ahead."

His thumb moves back and forth, gently rubbing a spot on the side of my head, and it calms me.

I need to focus.

I need to stitch this and get it covered.

"You're not going to make this easy for me, are you?" I squeeze my hand over his shoulder, leaning in and preparing to sew.

"I just need to touch you. I don't mean to make this harder on you than it is." He continues to stroke my scalp and play with my hair.

It feels so good; I want to drop my head into his palm and let him touch me like this forever. It's so soothing, so loving, so calming, yet arousing all at once. Perhaps I can give into it once the stitching is done, but it has to be done now.

I wait until I feel his fingers draw through my hair again, and when they're halfway through the strands, I whisper, "Hold on tight."

Then I plunge the needle into his flesh.

He tenses, groans, and just as I told him to, his hand closes around a tuft of my hair, holding on tight. My head tilts back slightly as he pulls a little too hard, but he quickly relents, loosening his grip enough to allow me to lower my head.

"I'm sorry," he says. "Did I hurt you?"

"No," I tell him breathlessly.

I feel awake.

I feel alive.

My scalp tingles from the pull, prickling like tiny bursts of lightning all around my head.

"You don't have to let go," I tell him.

I sew another stitch.

His groan is feral.

His grip is tight.

He tugs my hair so hard that my chin aims skyward.

I gasp at the feeling of pleasure that ripples through me, surprised at its presence, heat touching my cheeks with the awareness of desire coursing through my veins.

I feel the tremor through his arm, though he doesn't release me. My hands are still, holding the needle at his arm, waiting for him to let go. His lips graze the hollow of my throat and I shudder, letting out a whimper.

The tease of his touch—of feeling him *alive* when only hours before we were both preparing to die—makes my eyes fall shut in ecstasy.

Gradually, his grip loosens, though he doesn't entirely let go.

"Don't stop," he breathes the words along my collarbone. "I've felt so cold. I've felt so lifeless since your trial, since I found out what it would be like to lose you. The pain of you sewing me back together is *divine*, starlight."

His hand shifts to find a stronger grip, to sift more of my hair between his fingers from the base of my skull. His hold on me is possessive, and I cherish it, crave more of it. A rush of warmth drips down the center of my body as liquid heat stirs my lust for him.

I let out a breathy moan as my body loosens to his touch. I sink heavier against his thigh, and he flexes, shifting the hard muscle beneath me. He groans as my hips drive forward, rubbing myself along his thigh.

"Please," he begs, his voice soft with desperation. "Mercy, *please*. Let me feel you. Give me pain. Make me feel alive."

He lets me loose enough to drop my head so I can see what I'm doing. I line up the needle for the next stitch, and a rush of anticipation overcomes me.

I want his hand in my hair, gripping tight, pulling hard.

I press the needle through his skin to make the next stitch.

I nearly cry out with how hard he jerks my head back.

"*Mercy…*"

The way he says my name makes my thighs clench.

My head drops forward and I tug the thread through, taking a split-second to make sure the line I'm stitching is straight. His injured arm moves slightly as I inspect my work; he reaches forward to grip the smallest part of my waist, his other hand still tangled with my hair.

I sigh, arching my back. "I missed your hands on me." My hips drift forward to drag my pussy shamelessly along his thigh.

He groans, his hand squeezing my waist before slipping down my hip. "I thought I'd never touch you again."

"Touch me now." My hips move back and forth, grinding down hard. "I need you."

He holds my head steady, then dives in to kiss me, bruising my lips with the pressure of his. I open for him, begging to taste him with a moan he eagerly swallows. His tongue sweeps heavily against mine, taking command, tasting me exactly how I need to be tasted.

I cannot control myself, though I wish I could. Wanting him this way, desiring him *here*, in the midst of this brewing rebellion, feels wrong, like something only a sinner would do…

And that makes me want it all the more.

I can't stop rocking my hips.

His sweeping tongue forces heat down my throat that sinks straight through me, melting my core and dripping wetness between my thighs.

I pant as he drops his mouth to the hollow of my throat, licking and kissing a sensitive trail that travels up the side of my neck, along my jawline, right beneath my ear.

"I want to be inside you while you mend me. I want you to make me hurt while I make you come."

I don't even know how he manages it, but in a swift motion, he sweeps me up, lowering me quickly on my back. I lose my grip on the needle, and it dangles from his arm, miraculously hanging onto the thread. I reach for it, but he pulls back, rising onto his knees between my spread legs.

"The needle…" I warn.

He ignores me, staring into my soul as he unbuckles his belt.

The dangling needle puts me on edge. I'm anxious to grab hold of it before it falls, before it accidentally punctures his skin somewhere unintended, yet he remains entirely unconcerned.

I'm almost bothered by it until he grabs my skirt with both hands, shoves it up my thighs, then slaps his hand over the wet spot soaking through my underwear. He circles his fingers, rubbing me over the fabric, and all rational thought spills with the rush of wetness between my legs.

I reach down to slip my underwear over my hips, lifting my legs so I can kick them off, tossing them away somewhere, forgotten forever.

"Lay down; let me take care of you." I try to sit up, but he quickly bends over me, placing both hands on the floor to cage me in. "You're going to hurt yourself." He slowly smiles at me as I speak. "Sit back down the way you were and I'll…"

I'll…what?

What was I going to say?

The full length of his dimples slices down his cheeks, and his divinely unholy grin shuts me right up.

His hips move forward, and I feel the tip of his cock rub against me. He shifts until he's perfectly aligned to enter me, and with a slow, steady stroke, he sinks inside me.

My eyes slam shut, my back arches off the floor, and I suck in a sharp breath. He's as deep inside me as he could possibly be, and it feels so perfect that I don't care if he moves. I don't care if he fucks me; I don't care if he makes me come.

The feeling of him inside me is all I need.

"Starlight," he says, and I open my eyes. "Stitch me up."

The needle still dangles from his arm, literally clinging to him by a thread. It takes me a few seconds to regain enough focus to reach out for it, plucking it between my fingers. Arlo remains still as I shift beneath him, reaching up, aligning the needle with his flesh, and then I pierce him.

He hisses through his teeth, his eyes clamping shut.

I watch his face as I slowly tug the thread through behind the needle. As I drag the thread, he drags his cock, pulling out of me at a speed that matches mine.

I twist the needle around to position it for the next stitch.

And at the moment I pierce his skin, he slams deep inside me again, making me gasp at the rush of it as my back arches from the ground.

I pierce and pull.

He thrusts and drags.

Arlo fucks me in time with the movement of each stitch.

It's a tease, a game, a gradual build-up of need.

By the fifteenth, and final, stitch, we're both panting, throbbing, needy to have our hands on each other.

"Wait," I tell him before he moves again, reaching over to grab a strip of clean gauze.

Quickly knotting the stitches, I wrap the clean strip of gauze around his arm as he pulses inside me, making my hands shake as I hurry to finish the task.

I tie a knot in the gauze to secure it around his arm, and the moment I tug it tight, he adjusts the angle of his hips. The tip of his cock thumps against a perfect spot inside me as I let my hands fall away, dropping to the ground on either side of my head.

His hand collars my throat, and I gasp at his touch. One of my hands comes up to circle his wrist as I watch him fuck me. He thrusts deeper, moving with a steady rhythm that lets me feel every inch of him slip along my inner walls.

"Can you feel the way I need you? How hard I am for you? Can you feel how desperate I am to come inside you?" He slams into me so hard that my body slips backward, grinding against the rock floor.

"I want you to." I reach up to grab his cheeks and he thrusts again. "Always inside me."

"Always. *Sweet sin*, the way I love you."

He kisses me and it hurts.

It hurts because he's deep inside me, filling me entirely, yet it doesn't feel like enough.

I need more of him, desperately, but more isn't possible.

I've never known such pleasure as what he gives me. I didn't know it was possible to desire so deeply. It's physical, but it feels emotional, too…it feels *spiritual.* Rushed and desperate as it is, we're connected in every way, and it's beautiful.

This is more than sex, more than using each other physically to chase an impulse for release. I won't deny that we're both chasing that release—of course, we are—but more than that, this is a reminder that we're both *alive.*

Our hearts beat.

Our lungs burn.

Our bodies beg.

I feel every part of him, and he feels every part of me.

We're alive, we're together, and we're in love.

It's an act of rebellion so blasphemous that it makes me hot, like my warden is fucking me in hell. My stomach clenches at the thought of it, and a devilish grin lifts the corners of my lips.

My hands slip along his cheeks, his unruly beard scratching my palms. I comb my fingers back through his tousled strands, tugging at the ends.

"I love you," I whisper, and with a sigh, he drops his forehead to rest against mine. "I love every version of you…dark and light, angel and demon, saint and sinner."

"Sweet sin…you're *mine.*" A demonic growl rumbles through his chest, and he fucks me faster.

My stomach clenches against the flurry of pleasure building through my core, both from the way he moves inside me—as though his anatomy was crafted for the sole purpose of making me come—and for his words, his voice, and the vulgar, intoxicating sounds of his desire.

The hand around my throat slides around to the back of my neck, fingers climbing up to sink into my hair as his palm cradles the back of my head. He holds me tight so he can pound me hard, dragging his nose up my cheek, drawing in a deep breath to inhale my scent along the line of my hair.

"Wildflowers," he mutters. "Wildflowers and starlight."

Those words will never fail to kickstart my heart, and I wrap my arms around him, hugging him as tight as I can. We hold on to each other desperately as he fucks us toward oblivion. He's so heavy against me, every inch of our bodies kissing. I angle my hips just right to feel his body rubbing against my clit while he moves inside me. His cock is so hard, so beautifully thick, and it pulses with his onrushing release.

"*Sweet sin,*" he groans. "Come with me. *Fuck.* Come with me, starlight. *Please.*"

It's not as though I could ever come on command; it only works because his timing is exquisite. He pays such careful attention to the way I move, the sounds I make, the way my pussy clenches around his cock. He holds off his release until he knows I'm near mine, edging himself until he's sure I'm ready to come hard on his cock.

And I'm there…ready and needy.

Three perfect thrusts bring me to release. I come so hard, it's silent. So hard that it freezes me in stillness, traps me for seconds that feel like hours in the stagnant tension that holds him tightly inside me…and then the pleasure crests, crashes like a tidal wave against the shore, breaking to release its hold on me.

He pumps into me twice more before the grip of my cunt squeezes him to his own spectacular release. He bites my shoulder to stifle the sound of his groan as he spills warmth inside me, spurring another small aftershock of pleasure that twitches through my insides.

We fight together to catch our breath. Still held close in each other's arms, he rolls us to our sides, and though the ground is painfully hard, I don't care. My head is cradled in his arm wrapped around me, his fingers splayed over the back of my head. Our hips still rock lazily as we come down from the high.

"I love you," he whispers. "I love you more than my own life."

"And I love you more than mine."

I work my hand up between us, my fingertips playing through the overgrown hair of his untrimmed beard.

He grins at me. "That makes us dangerous, you know."

"I know. You and I will be the most dangerous threat to ever rise against Ember Glen."

"Of course. That's why they want us dead."

"Well, they already tried to kill us, and they failed, didn't they?" I press a kiss to his perfect lips.

"If only they knew what they were really up against with you, Mercy Madness." A smirk curls one corner of his lips. "A woman who evades death *and* can stitch a man's gunshot wound while he fucks her across the floor? They don't stand a chance."

"And that doesn't even speak to what I can accomplish when I'm on top."

"We'll have to explore that once my back is healed."

"Are you in pain?"

"Mercy, I just came inside you; that's all I feel. Ask me again in ten minutes."

"Okay, I will."

And I fully intended to ask him again in ten minutes, but I hadn't realized how utterly exhausted I was. My attention had been given to everyone else, and I neglected myself.

But I think Arlo knew.

Despite his injuries, he laid there beside me, gently playing with my hair until I drifted into sleep.

And through the hours, I was trapped in nightmares of blood and fire, battles fought and lost, women kneeling before violent men.

There was nothing I could do to help.

I couldn't escape my own mind.

The only way to end it was to burn it all down.

The only way to end the nightmare was with fire.

chapter twenty-one

Mercy

IT'S DARK ASIDE from the lantern's light, and everything feels so quiet, so still…except for the low moan of pain from Arlo beside me. I find I'm still curled against his chest as I awaken, his right arm beneath my head to give me a pillow against the hard ground.

I breathe in and his scent fills me, instantly bathing me in comfort. My hip aches from the rock beneath it, but I feel well rested, calm, and more at peace than I have been in a very long time. It's because I'm with *him* and we're together freely, unburdened by the fear of being found out.

My lips curl up into a grin as I press them to his chest. He stifles a groan, leaning away from me, though I don't get the sense that he wants to. His left arm is tense, ramrod-straight, resting on top of his hip.

I untangle myself from him and push to sit up, gently laying my hand on his forearm. "Are you in pain?"

"Yes," he hisses, tilting toward me.

I shift back on my knees, giving him some space to roll onto his stomach. "You could have moved."

"I didn't want to wake you."

I reach out to stroke the back of his head, hoping to ease him back to sleep, but my fingers slip down the back of his neck as he unexpectedly pushes to his knees, then sits back on his heels. He hangs his head, pressing his palms to his thighs as he blows out a heavy breath.

"What can I do?" I ask.

His hand floats out to the side, and without looking up, he catches my fingers and pulls my hand onto his lap. "You're already doing it."

I scoot closer, reaching up with my other hand to sweep an untamed strand of hair across his forehead. He tilts his face toward me, granting me a small, pained smile.

"I wish I had one of those little white pills to give you now."

The medication he'd given me after Killian made me push my hand into the bonfire had effectively ended my pain, and how I wish I could give Arlo one now. I wish I could do anything to end his pain.

Arlo's brow furrows. "Even if you had one, I wouldn't take it."

"Why?"

"Because I deserve the pain."

"You don't—"

"How much pain have servants suffered at the hands of men? How much suffering have I caused? We forced pain and granted no relief. We have medicine that ends pain, yet the servants who need it most don't have access to it. We hurt them in service, and then we just send them to Sanctuary… injured, alone, in pain…" His blue eyes darken.

Air rushes from his lungs, the feeling of dread slipping out with it, and I'm forced to draw it in with my next breath. "Mercy, I need to tell you something."

"Okay…"

"I don't know how to tell you this because it's going to break your heart." His eyes flick away from me.

"What is it?" I move closer, placing my hands on his cheeks, turning his face toward mine.

He's quiet for a moment as I search his eyes.

"Just say the words, Arlo. Whatever they are."

"I should have told you last night in the foyer, but I didn't think it would matter then. I thought I would be dead by now, and that you would be soon after…I just wanted that time with you; I didn't want to cause you more pain."

"Arlo…"

"Something happened at your trial," he hesitates, and his reluctance agitates me.

"A lot of things happened at the trial. Can you be more specific?"

"Cambria and Ellary were meant to be set free once you were in your grave."

"Right," I pause, "and they were. I saw Cambria at the Homestead."

"Cambria was there, yes, but Ellary…"

"But Ellary, what?"

His chest sinks as his warm breath quickly fills the space between us. "Ellary fell from the cliff."

My hands drop from his cheeks and they land on my lap. I sit back on my heels as my eyebrows knit together, my head inclining as I watch him.

"I don't understand…What do you mean?"

"Ellary fell, and she landed on a ledge. The drop was twenty or thirty feet."

I hear what he's telling me, the words he speaks, but somehow, they aren't making sense to me.

A lump rises in my throat, and I blink as I swallow against it. "W-What are you saying?"

"Mercy…" He reaches out to touch my cheek.

I slap his hand away reflexively. "What are you *saying*?" My voice sounds angry, though I don't mean for it to be.

His eyes harden, hiding his gentleness from me so he can spit out the truth. "Once you were lowered into the grave, Killian pushed Ellary over the edge. She fell as much as thirty feet and landed on a ledge. We had to bury you and Delle first, but then I went over the edge to retrieve her. She had a pulse, but she was near death. Park took her back and left her alone in Sanctuary, and that's the last I know. I don't know if she's alive or…"

Alive or…dead.

.

.

.

.

.

Arlo is in front of me, but I don't see him.
My eyes are unfocused.
Everything's blurry.
My mind is a blank void.

.

.

.

.

Arlo speaks to me.
His hands are on my cheeks.
His forehead touches mine.

.

.

.

It's dark all around me, and I'm lost in empty space.

.

.

Liquid runs hot down my cheeks.

.

His arms close around me.
I'm warm.
My body forces me to breathe.

I smell him.

Instead of drenching me in comfort like it did before, it shocks my senses and awakens me, brings me back from the dead.

I'd rather be dead.

I want to return to nothingness.

This sudden pain in my chest, this sob bursting out of me, these tears that burn like fire are too much for me to bear.

"No…" I think the word came from me, though I'm not sure.

I didn't think it.

I didn't choose to speak it.

All I know is pain.

"She's okay," I mutter against his chest. "She's okay. She's not dead. She wouldn't die. She couldn't."

"I'm sorry. I'm sorry, Mercy."

Sorry?

I jerk back, my palms on his chest, shoving. "Don't be sorry. There's nothing to be sorry about. She's fine." I feel tension through my forehead, misplaced anger touching my expression. I sniff, willing the wells of my tears to dry up as I blink rapidly to bat the remaining droplets away. "She's *fine*. I survived being buried alive, and she can survive a fall."

"Starlight—"

"*No.* Ellary's alive. The servants will care for her in Sanctuary. She'll heal and she'll be fine."

If she's alive, she's certainly in pain.

Are her bones broken?

Did she bleed?

I meet Arlo's eyes for a moment, but he looks at me with pity and despair, and I have to look away. I reach around him to grab the one lantern that's lit and start crawling toward the exit.

"Where are you going?"

"To find Luna and Stefanie. I want answers."

"Right now? After what I just told you? Take a minute, Mercy, you're—"

"Shut *up*."

His hand grazes my ankle as I reach the opening, but I jerk my leg away.

He groans in pain, and a twinge of guilt passes through me. I hesitate for a moment, but only just. I reach through the opening to place my lantern on the other side, but just as I duck my head to crawl through, Arlo's hand clamps around the back of my knee, and it makes me jolt with surprise.

"Let go!" I turn my head over my shoulder, looking at him sternly as I reach back to grab his arm.

"Stop. Come here." He tugs at my leg, and it makes me furious.

Fine. I'll be furious, then.

Anger is better than heartache.

Rage is better than sorrow.

Action is better than stillness.

I let go of his arm just so I can smack it hard. "Don't *touch* me!"

Conviction shadows his expression with darkness, and his grip tightens. My leg rises from the ground as he pulls hard, dragging me backward toward him. I try to crawl forward, but he unbalances me, and the shin of my opposite leg—still planted on the ground—grates against solid rock.

"Stop!"

I drop on my hip as I twist, then sit my ass on the ground as I bring my arm around, aiming without thought to slap his cheek. He snatches my wrist just before it lands…and I'm glad he did.

I don't know what I'm doing.

I don't want to hurt him.

Was I trying to hurt him?

Was he trying to hurt me?

"I'm not trying to hurt you," he says as though he can read my mind. "I don't want to hurt you. Just let me hold you."

He huffs as our eyes meet, and it settles me to see his own heartache ripple through the blue. I go still, blinking up at him with wide eyes.

"You can't run from the pain," Arlo whispers, his grip on my wrist gradually loosening. "Don't run from me." He moves over me, his other hand slipping around my waist to splay across my back. "If you go through hell, then I go with you." He lifts, slowly bringing me against him.

I'm trapped by his gaze as he holds me there, chest to chest, eye to eye. The longer we stare, the more the pain grows, the faster misery fills me like a rising tide of anguish that drowns the world until the black waters of despair are all that's left.

And as his forehead touches mine, I cry.

Ellary is my best friend; she means everything to me. They knew this, and they made her walk to the cliff's edge to serve as a sacrifice for my trial.

And I sacrificed for her.

I did what I was supposed to do to save her. I climbed into my own coffin, let them *bury me alive*, and it was all for nothing. Because they pushed her anyway.

Killian pushed her. Killian fucking Cole…

I'm going to learn the truth about Ember Glen, and then, I'm going to murder Killian Cole.

He owes me a debt in blood, and I'll make sure he pays.

I weep in the sanctuary of Arlo's arms until there's nothing left, until I'm an empty black void and the only thing that can fill me is rage…

The only thing that can fuel me is revenge.

chapter twenty-two

Mercy

ARLO'S ARM IS around my back, hand curled around the side of my waist to keep me close to his side. I hold the lantern as we navigate the dark passages back to the main cavern. Even with the lantern's light, we can only see a few feet in front of us as we move through the black-as-night corridors.

Arlo navigates the way for us so easily, especially considering how dark it is. I can remember it always seemed so effortless the way he took us through the paths and tunnels in the cave system beneath the Homestead. I suppose he just has a good general sense of direction, and I'm grateful for it because I think I'd be lost on my own right now. It's hard for me to think straight with the chaotic swirl of emotions muddling my thoughts, keeping me in a constant state of anxiety.

Will this sense of unease live in my soul forever?

I grip the back of his belt, holding on so he can't slip away from me. "I don't remember it being so dark when they led us through before."

"It wasn't, but night must have fallen." He squeezes the side of my waist and guides me to veer right. "This way. This is the main cavern."

The sunlight that filled the space when we first entered has faded, leaving only the soft ring of moonlight that outlines the circular opening far above the pool.

"Did we sleep the entire day?" I whisper. "It's so quiet."

"It seems that way."

We creep forward into the wide-open space, and it almost feels like an intrusion.

"Should we just go back?" I wonder. "Try to find them in the morning?"

"That would probably be the polite thing to do."

"I've never known you to be particularly polite." Despite the disquiet in my mind, he was just asking for a response like that, and I grin as it slips out so effortlessly.

He stops us, turns his head to look over at me. "I used to have very good manners, you know. It earned me quite a bit of power…" his mouth curls up on one side, "but it certainly never got me beneath your skirt."

My grin broadens, though I force my eyes to roll. I feel heat flush my cheeks. I don't know if I'll ever understand how he affects me the way he does. I suppose it doesn't matter why; it only matters that he does.

Despite thinking it may be best to head back, he leads me forward anyway, on a slow walk through the dark, and it's peaceful. I might even venture to say it's serene, despite the horrors that haunt us. Yet any serenity we find is soiled by the invisible fragments of each trauma we've faced, like speckles of stardust which constantly trail behind us, pulled along by the gravity of our dark souls.

Even so, there's something ethereal about this place in the quiet night—I half expect to see tiny flakes of starlight following behind us as I glance over my shoulder, the dark remnants of my pain lit up bright and sparkling in this safe space as I drag them behind me.

I feel open here…I feel free.

Free to feel joy.

Free to feel pain and heartache.

Free to exist as I am, even when it hurts.

In a strange way, this place reminds me of Sanctuary. The week we were required to spend in Sanctuary following a night of service was always filled with pain and suffering. Yet there was freedom found in just existing there with my sisters.

Though I couldn't speak freely with my dissenting thoughts, I was free enough to let myself *feel* them—free to cry, free to scream, free to sit quietly and drift into my own mind without interference. Those were the only weeks I felt safe, and in that safety was my freedom.

No man is allowed to enter Sanctuary—not ever. The only exception is the Control, and even so, they can only enter if every single servant within agrees to *allow* them to enter. And I don't think that happened once in my four years of service.

Although…

Arlo said Park took Ellary back and left her alone in Sanctuary.

Did he leave her outside, on the landing?

Were some of the servants inside, and they agreed to let him in?

Did they take Ellary from him and bring her inside themselves?

I shake my head, forcing it from my mind. If I think of Ellary again and what happened to her, I'll fall apart entirely. She is family to me, and the thought of her suffering, dying—perhaps already dead—will break me beyond repair. So I tell myself that she's fine, that she's alive, that she's not suffering, even if I'm only lying to myself.

I force myself to think of Arlo's fingers at my waist, the comfort I find in feeling his touch and having him near me. I feel his warmth against my side, though the warmth isn't just from him—I feel it radiating from the pool as he leads us nearer. Stefanie had told us that the water was warm, a natural hot spring or something.

We stop at the edge of the water, standing still in the silence. Without the sunlight shining through the opening far above, the water appears glossy black. Warm air from the water rises against the cool air from the night sky above, with soft, nearly translucent clouds of steam rolling in the space between. My gaze tracks the steam, following it upward until the night sky steals my attention.

A clear, black sky.

A sliver of moon glow from the waxing crescent.

Bright white lights speckling the dark canvas.

"Starlight," Arlo whispers.

I glance over at him, thinking he's calling for my attention, but I only find him looking up at the same night sky, marveling at the beauty of it.

And I marvel at the beauty of him—he's war torn and battered, but he's alive.

And he's mine.

"I thought I'd never see the stars again," he mutters. "I thought I'd never see you." He looks down at me, and even in the dark, I see the depth of his love.

True love is a divine thing—they had that much right. But Arlo and I would never have found it if we'd lived the way they wanted us to. It wouldn't have been some celestial blessing from God that we miraculously found as assigned domestic partners; it came to us as a sinner and a self-proclaimed saint.

We had to choose it.

We had to fight for it.

There's a light splash somewhere in the water and our heads turn at the same time to search for the source. Holding out the lantern, I don't see anything in the pool before me, but I'm certain I heard the ripple of waves…

And then we hear it again, followed by a muted whimper.

What if a child has fallen into the water?

I step closer to the edge, and Arlo grips my dress, bunching the fabric in his grasp to tug me back.

"Careful, Mercy…"

Leaning forward, I look out as far as I can, but it's all just dark, black water. There's a moan, and I'm fearful again that someone needs help.

"A child might have fallen in," I rush, tugging myself from his grip as I walk to the edge of the pool.

"Mercy…"

I stop about halfway to the outer edge of the main cavern, noticing there's a path that cuts across the water. Trusting my instinct, I turn and follow it.

The farther I go, the more my light reveals—there's an arched opening up ahead where the path continues through on the left side, water flowing through into a smaller pool on the right. My pace hastens when I see the flicker of firelight emerging as I move into the alcove, growing from shadows from around a bend that cuts left up ahead.

I move slower as the light grows brighter. That odd feeling I had before washes over me—like moving through these caves at night is an intrusion.

Yet, I'm still worried someone might be hurt. It would be too easy for a child to fall in if they decided to wander at night.

So I creep ahead, and turn the corner, revealing another cavern, as large as a house. The path I'm on continues in front of me, opening into a wider expanse of bedrock that reveals a baby sleeping comfortably, tucked safely into a corner, laid on piles of soft blankets.

I'm almost certain it's Soleil, and I lift my foot to rush to her.

But then I stop abruptly when my eyes scan right.

No one has fallen in.

No one needs help.

And I have most certainly intruded where I shouldn't be.

My hand comes up to cover my mouth as I'm frozen there in surprise, stuck and staring.

The water here is shallow enough for Luna and Stefanie to stand. It only reaches the middle of their waists, revealing both of them bare-chested and tangled in each other's arms. Luna's head falls to the side and Stefanie's lips land on her collarbone.

I should go…

I know I should turn and walk away, but I'm completely stunned by what I'm seeing.

I fully comprehend the nature of Luna and Stefanie's relationship—she made it very clear in her admission earlier, though I'd already suspected it before.

Yet it still stuns me to stumble upon this intimate moment despite the debauchery I've been privy to from my four years of service. I've never seen a domestic be physically intimate in any way before, let alone like *this*—domestics are meant to be modest and humble.

Though I know that's not all they are.

After all, I was never what they wanted me to be.

I need to step away quietly, go back the way I came and walk away... But a twinge of curiosity gets the better of me, and for just a few moments, I watch.

I'm not sure how I ought to feel seeing two women together this way, but I feel a little in awe of this moment. They're entirely lost to each other, unaware of my presence, and that's something I'm familiar with. It's the same way I get so lost in Arlo when he loves me in that physical way.

A trace of desire whispers low in my belly, and that feels wrong. Shame quickly rises, threatening to take hold of me, but then that feels good, too. Ember Glen gave me that shame, and my mind somehow knows it shouldn't exist.

Why should I feel shame witnessing beauty from love when I feel none witnessing beauty from nature?

I can lie in the meadow among the wildflowers and watch the stars at night, feeling a different kind of pleasure and warmth at the beauty that surrounds me, leaving me in awe. Witnessing the love they share is no different.

I give myself permission to let go of the shame because I understand that the desire I suddenly feel isn't desire for them—it's desire to feel the way they're feeling, to have the touch of the person I love, and share pleasure with him.

I should go.

They don't want to be seen.

I take slow, careful steps backward, though my eyes are still fixed on the scene. I watch them kiss and touch, I see the way they hold each other. I watch for moments too long and witness the shift from slow exploration to urgent pleasure-seeking...

And every second of it is beautiful.

I'm intruding.

I force myself to turn and softly pad back along the path the way I came. I'm surprised Arlo isn't already right behind me, surprised still when I don't crash into him along the path across the water in the main cavern. As I near the end, I see him standing there, waiting in the dark for me to return to him.

He looks at me quizzically as I hasten my pace, reach out to snatch his right hand, and drag him with me as I move away from the pool, back toward the passage we came through.

"What did you—"

"Quiet."

I don't speak a single word until we've crossed the main cavern and entered the dark tunnel.

"Are we being polite, then?" he asks. "Waiting until morning?"

"Yes," I whisper.

I stop abruptly, turning to look behind me, as I'm suddenly so flustered that I can't remember if we turned left or right.

"To the left," he says, and I pause to meet his eyes. "Are you all right? Did you see something?"

My face heats. "It was nothing. You should be resting, anyway."

He inclines his head. "If there's something I need to know—"

"Trust me, you don't want to know about it."

"And now that you've said that, I'm certain I *must* know." He takes a step toward me. "Tell me."

"Don't press, Arlo."

As if in direct defiance, he presses forward, moving me backward until I collide with solid rock against my spine. "It's in my nature to press, especially with you." He plucks a short strand of hair that hangs in front of my cheek, dragging his finger slowly down. His body kisses mine in a manner that's achingly indecent—he takes the trace of desire and magnifies it until I feel it through my entire body.

"Tell me, starlight."

The way I always ache for him…

How does he do that?

I lift my hands to his chest as he leans in and pins me in place before kissing my cheek. He sighs as he slips his one uninjured arm around me, splaying his fingers over the small of my back. "Why is every part of you so tempting? So distracting? Sweet sin, I want you so much…but I don't think I have the strength right now."

"You don't, and you shouldn't."

I wish he did.

I wish he could.

"If you saw something sobering, Mercy Madness, now would be the time to share."

I swallow both my desire for him and my apprehension for telling him what I saw. And then I tell him, anyway. "I saw your sister…"

"Luna?"

"And Stefanie. In the water."

He pulls back slightly and looks at me, perplexed.

"They were sharing an intimate moment."

"What do you mean?" He looks genuinely confused, and for some reason, that amuses me.

"Arlo…" I grin at his continued confusion, "surely I don't need to put two and two together for you. They were seeking pleasure together."

His brow furrows, and though the confusion fades from his features, a serious consideration of what this means filters him instead.

"Are you upset?" I ask.

"I'm…not sure."

"What do you feel?"

"Conflicted."

"What is there to be conflicted about, love? They care deeply for one another. They share a passion for each other, similar to what you and I share. Shouldn't they be able to indulge as we do without judgment?"

"Everything I've been told my entire life has led me to believe that it's wrong for a domestic woman to seek pleasure, and least of all, with another woman. It's sin—"

"According to the documents of God's word written by men. Documents we've never seen, and documents that probably don't even exist."

"I understand, Mercy. I know. Give me some grace." All at once, his hold on me loosens, he steps back, and turns away. His hand scrubs over his beard when he faces me again. "My mind is…it's my greatest enemy now, and everything is changing so quickly." His voice is pained. The strain of conflict and confusion pulls at his features, so I remain quiet and let him speak.

"I was one of the Control. I was a man of God in all manner of speaking, and I learned to be faithful to the Edict. I know it's all wrong now. It *has* to be wrong, because I'm fated to be yours. I will *always* be yours. That's a simple truth I know in my soul that can't be refuted or denied, even if the Edict says we don't belong together.

"But knowing what's true doesn't help my mind escape the conditioning any easier. I cannot help that there's a voice in my mind that rushes to judgment of my sister's choice, even though I know it's hypocritical of me to pass judgment on anyone now."

He glances down with a shake of his head. "She's my *sister*. I've always cared for her; I've always wanted her to be happy. If Stefanie makes her happy, then I accept it. Deep down, I know that's all I feel about it. Acceptance. Just a fact about her life. But that *voice*…"

I step forward, laying my hands at the sides of his waist.

"That voice keeps trying to sway me, and I fear it will always be there. I'm fighting to silence it. I promise that I am." He bends to press his forehead to mine, reaching out to cradle my cheeks. "Please be patient with me, even though I know I don't deserve it."

"I have patience for you, Arlo." I hug myself against him, careful to avoid the wounds on his back. His arms close around me, and I let out a long-held breath. "I know the voice…I still hear it sometimes, too."

"Do you?"

"Yes. I think we all do, and I think we all *will*. I think it's always going to be there. Our minds don't always tell us the truth, not at first. Sometimes they tell us what we need to hear to protect ourselves. Even when that old, small voice has to tell us a lie for self-preservation's sake."

"But you learned to ignore it, didn't you? How?"

"Truthfully, I'm still learning. It's there sometimes, telling me that I'm wrong, that I'm a sinner, that I should feel ashamed for what I've done and who I've become. And sometimes I feel the shame for becoming the woman I am."

Admitting that out loud nearly brings me to tears—something I hadn't expected—and I bury my face in his chest.

"That kills me, Mercy. Knowing that is more painful than any physical wound. The voice of your shame is…it's *mine*. It's *my* voice you hear whispering in your mind, isn't it?" He squeezes me as though his loving embrace could put me back together, as if it will mend all the pieces of my heart and soul that he played a role in breaking.

Arlo has hurt me in so many ways.

It's a fact that can't be denied.

It's a fact that demands to be acknowledged.

"I've laid so much guilt upon you," he continues. "I've called you a sinner more times than I can count. I've told you it was all your fault, that you deserved the punishment of the trials, that you deserved to *die* for your sins…"

He releases me and paces away, leaving me so abruptly that it feels as though he's sucked my soul from my body and has taken it with him. I pause for a quiet moment and watch him stop a few feet away with his back turned to me.

"The voice is my own," I tell him gently. "At least, it sounds like my own voice. I know it's not really mine, but Arlo, I know it's not yours, either. It can't be because we both know that the words you spoke to me in judgment didn't really belong to you, either."

Arlo turns to face me.

"That voice," I continue, "the one that sounds like your own, the one they try to make you believe is your conscience, or the voice of God trying to lead you down the right path, the voice that brings you shame…That voice wasn't born with you; it was created.

"They put these so-called morals in our minds, told us what was right and wrong to believe before ever giving us a chance to figure it out on our own. And it's why we feel such shame with that voice, because it isn't *ours*. It doesn't match the truth that we know in our souls.

"We feel shame for not being true to ourselves, and fear for our disobedience against the voice all at once. It's troubling. I've felt troubled all my life. And I'm willing to bet there is no person in all of Ember Glen who can say they haven't felt the same."

His chest rises as he takes in a deep breath, then lets it out heavily in a rush of relief that I can feel as it leaves him. He hurries to close the distance between us, touching his forehead to mine the way he always does as he pulls me into his arms.

"Mercy Madness," he whispers my name with a sense of honor and pride. "I'm in awe of you…perplexed by the way your curious, brilliant mind works, and completely, *madly* in love with you."

chapter twenty-three
Mercy

"BEFORE WE SHOW you the real story of Ember Glen, I think we should tell you how we found this place," Luna says.

Arlo and I waited the night to find Luna and Stefanie again, but now that the sun has risen, we've made our way back to the hidden space with all the plastic bins and the projector.

Stefanie brought more pillows back with her, which she drops on the ground, then glances up. "You might want to sit."

Her expression tells me I should take her seriously, so I do, lowering to sit on a small, square throw pillow. I'm about to order Arlo to do the same, given how weak he is from his injuries, but he has the good sense on his own to sit beside me this time, probably wanting to avoid another fainting spell.

Luna hands Soleil—who's sound asleep—to Stefanie. She brings the baby against her chest to snuggle her close with a soft smile, appearing as natural with her as Luna.

A few feet in front of me, Luna bends to snap open the lid of one of the plastic bins on the floor, setting the lid aside. She doesn't take anything out of it. She straightens and looks at me, wringing her hands together in front of her.

"I feel like we owe you an apology, Mercy." She bites her lip as her eyebrows knit together.

"For what?"

"Your father's home—*your* home—was left behind, empty, when you were first taken to the Homestead for the Trials of Dissension. When Stefanie and I found out that Hyatt had…that he'd set a servant on fire during service, we were horrified. He'd done a lot of terrible things, but setting someone on fire…?" Her face scrunches with disgust. "How evil must his soul be to have such an impulse?"

"Anyway," her eyes cast downward, "I was scared for her, and of course, she was terrified of him. We both…Well, we needed to find some comfort. We needed to be with each other. We needed time together, in a safe place, to take care of one another."

Luna glances back at Stefanie, who gently sways with Soleil in her arms. She briefly meets Luna's gaze before Luna turns back to face us with a tense grin.

"We knew that your house was empty, unwatched. We went there to be together, and Mercy," she sighs, placing a palm over her heart, "we were finally free in your home. We could finally love each other without fear. We only meant to meet there once, but then we just kept going back. I'm sorry. We used your home without your permission to *be* with each other. And with everything you were going through—"

"Stop." I gently lift my palm. "Luna, it's okay. You don't need to apologize. I'm not upset."

"You're not?"

"No. For all that you've done—finding this place, bringing the children here to safety, bringing domestics together in rebellion—how could I be upset? I understand the need for comfort, especially when you're going through hell."

I glance down as I rub my palms over the velvet soft fabric of my red gown, suddenly wondering if it would be worth the risk of going back through the secret space to my father's home to find something black instead. I want to wear black for my sisters, for Ellary...

No, no, no. Don't think of Ellary.

I draw in a cleansing breath and lift my head. "When Arlo and I stopped hating one another and started to find love, it was all I wanted— finding comfort in his arms, being alone with him every moment I could before death found me." I glance between them. "I understand the need. No apologies are owed."

Luna drops to her knees and reaches out, dragging me into a hug. "Thank you. I didn't know I needed to hear that, but I did. I felt so awful."

I already have a deep fondness for Luna. Her natural kindness and concern for others are so genuine, so endearing. She's a lot like Ellary in that way.

Stop...

My breath stutters as I fight rising tears, and I quickly grip Luna's shoulders to push her away. Heartache looms behind my appreciation of Luna's kind nature. Holding her at arm's length, I grant her a smile, hoping she doesn't see the tears glassing over my eyes.

"So," I redirect, hoping I don't sound entirely depressed, "you and Stefanie were meeting at my house. But how on earth did you find the way here? I've cleaned those floors a million times, and I never noticed anything that would ever make me think I should try prying up a floorboard."

Luna smiles, and for a moment, it brightens the shadowed space. "Of course. Who would think to do that?"

She pushes to her feet again, turning to pace away. She reaches into the bin she'd opened before and pulls out a black leather journal, bound by a black leather strap.

"What is that?"

Luna looks at it with a conflicted expression, etched with pain as she draws her fingers down the front cover. "We didn't know what it was at first…Odd scribblings, ranting and rambling passages that were difficult to read, and none of it really made any sense. There's a list of names at the front, and it's actually where I saw the name Soleil." She glances back at Stefanie and smiles at her baby.

"The rest of its contents didn't make sense to us when we first found it, and it wouldn't have made sense to your father, either. He couldn't have known what it was; you should know that. But when we found out…" She grips it in one hand and holds it out to me. "This is the Impulse Edict."

I look over at Arlo, and our eyes lock in shared confusion, apprehension, anticipation, and outrage. I tear my gaze from his to look at the journal, hesitating for a beat in knowing that everything is about to change.

Luna must be wrong.

The Elders are supposed to be the keepers of the Impulse Edict—the only ones who have access to it and know the laws of God.

Slowly, I reach out, grip the journal, and take it from Luna. I hold it and stare, running a finger over the leather cord that secures it shut.

"We were in your house one night, and there was something I wanted to write down before I forgot it." Luna chuckles a little. "Actually, I did forget it. We were trying to find some parchment and a pen when I went into your father's room. I sat on the bed and pulled open the drawer on the nightstand."

My head snaps up.

I'd found my mother's journal in the nightstand drawer beside his bed.

"It was empty," Luna says, and my forehead creases in confusion. "At least, I *thought* it was empty. I was about to close it when I saw what looked like the corner of a page sticking up through the bottom. I was only able to tug it out about halfway, and I could see it looked like a letter or a journal entry that someone had written. I actually thought that if it was something from your father, then maybe I could find a way to get it to you; though, of course, that was a foolish thought. Still, it seemed important, so I called Stefanie in to help."

"We couldn't pull the page out." Stefanie speaks in a hushed tone, mindful not to raise her voice too loud over the sleeping baby against her chest. "I didn't want to risk tearing it, so I figured I'd try prying up the bottom of the drawer so we could pull it out carefully. It was surprisingly easy because it was meant to be pulled out—the drawer had a false bottom."

"That's where we found this." Luna points at the journal in my hands. "The page that was peeking out must have been from a different journal, though—it was smaller and a slightly different color. There were two other pages with it, all laying on top of the journal."

"There were three? Three torn pages?" I frantically look at Arlo.

"Mercy found her mother's journal in that drawer after her father died," Arlo explains. "She'd never seen it before then, like perhaps her father had left it for her to find? Three pages were torn from it, though…missing."

"Oh." Luna's head tilts, giving us a quizzical look. "I'm surprised by that."

Stefanie shares the same expression. "So am I. It seemed clear that he meant for you to find those pages."

"Eventually, at least," Luna adds.

"You read them?" I ask. "What do they say?"

Luna nods at the black journal in my hands. "I tucked the pages inside the cover. Open it."

My heart races as I eagerly uncoil the leather cord, impatient to see what's written on the three pages—equally nervous that I may learn something I wish I hadn't. I lift the black leather cover to open the journal, and there they are…

Three torn pages, the same size and color as the pages of my mother's journal. I let out a breath as I stare down at the page on top, my eyes unfocused as I search for courage to move boldly forward. I search for the courage to read them and learn the truth I've been searching for my entire life.

"What do they say?" Arlo nudges.

I turn my head to stare into his blue eyes, knowing I'll find strength I can borrow from him—and I do find it. Then I look down at the journal placed on my lap.

With trembling hands, I slip my fingers beneath the three pages and lift them from the journal, easily recognizing my father's handwriting.

I steel myself and read the words of the first page aloud.

Buried beneath Ember Glen,
secrets below soil found in corridors of stone.

Tunnels weave through layers of hell,
from mountain to mountain,

forest to forest,
and into the great beyond.

Beyond…the place where fabled hostility still reigns.
Yet, it reigns no longer.
Peace was won.
Though we are lost in Ember Glen.

Hostages.
Captives.
Unwilling savages.

Everything is buried.
The truth is beneath us.
The only way out of hell is through.

Dig.
Burrow.
Bury yourself alive.

Seek hell beneath your feet,
and should the demons show you mercy,
you'll find the path to the truth.

Peace.
Harmony.
Freedom.

It's all beyond…

Copied from the "lost" journals of E.K. and T.W.

My eyes narrow, fixed on the page. "I don't think I understand…"

"Neither did we," Luna says. "At least, not at first. Flip it over."

I glance up at her briefly and she gives me a nod. I turn the page and look at the other side. There are a few lines of text at the top, still in my father's handwriting.

It's right in front of you…the way to hell.
Lift the rug.
Pry the floorboard.

A crude map is drawn beneath the lines of text my father wrote. I stare at it as Arlo moves closer to view it with me. He seems to work it out almost immediately.

"This shows the way we came," he says. "The tunnel we crawled through," he reaches out to trace the path with his finger, "the passages we followed. And here's the main cavern where the water is."

I nod, starting to see the familiarity of it as he draws along the corridors, and the strange verse of text on the front of the page begins to make sense…

Buried beneath Ember Glen,
secrets below soil found in corridors of stone.

"These are the passages we took to get here, and this," he circles a spot with the tip of his finger, "is the alcove we came through on the other side of this room."

"It took us longer than it should have to figure out that we needed to move the boulder," Luna says with a grin.

On the map, it appears that the corridor we traveled to get to this room extends past the alcove, branching off into several different paths. And those paths branch off into even more before the page comes to an end.

It appears similarly on the other side of the page, paths extending out from the opposite side of the main cavern—tunnels leading to more tunnels that end with the paper's edge. And my father scribbled a note in the blank space between lines that outline a path, at the spot where one path diverges into three.

The way out?

"The way out?" I speak his words aloud, glancing up at Arlo, then looking at Luna and Stefanie. "What does that mean? The way out…of Ember Glen?"

"We think so, maybe. But that page is the only map we've found. Those paths can lead anywhere. They can be dead ends, or they can extend for miles. It would be so easy to get lost if you didn't know exactly where you were going. I think your father was trying to figure it out, or at least, leave behind enough information for you to do it."

I blink at her, my lips parted because I want to say something, I just don't know what.

"But over here," Arlo says, and I glance down to see him point to a spot on the map that's closer to where we are on this side of the cavern. Another note is scribbled where the path diverges.

Homestead?

"I wondered…" Arlo looks over at me. "I've been thinking perhaps these caves connected with the ones under the Homestead."

"You knew about these caves?" Stefanie asks with an accusatorial air.

Arlo meets her gaze directly. "There are caves under the Homestead, and I knew about those. Theo and I took Mercy and Delle there to prepare for the trials because it gave us privacy. I've been exploring them carefully for two years since the last Shift when I became one of the Control. All the Control know they exist, but mostly, they don't seem to care. I might be the only one who's done any exploring down there." He nods, turning his attention back to the map. "It makes sense that it's all connected."

"I don't understand. Why would my father be trying to find a way out? And who are," I pause to flip the page back over, then read the last line aloud, "Copied from the lost journals of E.K. and T.W. Who are E.K. and T.W.?"

Luna shrugs. "We don't know."

"E.K…" Arlo mutters, and then his face tenses with recollection. "Ethan Kaine?" His head snaps up with recognition. "It's Ethan Kaine and Tucker Whitler. I recognize the names from the record of the Control." He looks at me pointedly. "Do you remember what we talked about the morning after the last service, when your hand was burned and I had you take the medication before we went to deliver the news of Hyatt's death to Stefanie?"

"Vaguely…bits and pieces, I suppose. I was so high on that little white pill you gave me."

"We talked about the three pages torn from your mother's journal. One of them was torn out right after a passage that told of the strange and untimely deaths of two members of the Control when your grandmother was a child."

"Right," I nod, "I remember that. The deaths occurred only days apart, and the Control and the Elders had just labeled them as tragic mysteries."

He nods. "Yes. I never told you this, but while you were healing from your burns, I went to the Control's library on the third floor of the Homestead and did some research. I looked back through the records denoting all previous and current members of the Control and the Elders, dating back from the very beginning. Ethan Kaine and Tucker Whitley were both listed as deceased in the same year. It was…twenty-one forty, maybe forty-one?"

I quickly do the math in my head. "That would've been around the time my grandmother was a child. That could be who she was talking about."

"It makes sense," Arlo agrees. "If they were on to the secrets being kept—if they knew about the caves and that maybe there was a way out of Ember Glen—then it wouldn't surprise me at all to learn the Elders had orchestrated their deaths."

"Wasn't that…" Stefanie starts, then stops, eyes turning up toward the ceiling in thought before a realization changes her expression. "That would have been when the last Trials of Dissension were held. Forty-five years ago, right?"

"Yes, I think that's right," Arlo confirms. "So, during the last trials, two members of the Control learned things the Elders didn't want them to know, and they had them killed. This," he points at the page, "could be the only remaining record of the secrets they learned."

"It's not…" Luna's voice is soft.

Arlo and I both look at her.

"It may be the only record of what *they* documented," Luna says, "but what was copied on that page led us to this room. And this room holds a history of Ember Glen that's…"

"Disgusting," Stefanie finishes for her. "The history of Ember Glen is disgusting."

chapter twenty-four

ARLO

THE HISTORY OF Ember Glen is disgusting?

"Mercy, I think you should read the next two pages," Luna says gently. "It's a letter…from your father."

Mercy blinks, tearing her eyes away from me to look down at the pages in her hands. She seems to hesitate, as though the idea of knowing more is painful.

"Do you want me to read it?" I offer.

Her head turns in my direction, her face blank, lost, overwhelmed. But then she nods. She lifts the pages and hands them to me, fixing her eyes on my face as I take the first page from the pile of three and set it aside. Quickly turning them over, then back again, I see with a glance that these two pages are filled with text—a complete letter from her father.

I give Mercy a cursory glance, lifting my eyebrows to ask if she's ready. She responds with a quick bob of her head, watching me as I read the letter out loud.

My dear Mercy,

I don't know how to begin this letter. I suppose I should start by telling you that I'm a coward. I didn't have the courage to tell you what I was doing, that something had been eating away at my mind since your mother died. I didn't have the courage to confess all the ways I failed you as a father, though I'm certain you're aware of them all the same.

I'm the reason your mother is dead.

The guilt of that has chipped away at my sanity since she died, and I think it's what has slowly been killing me.

I need you to understand something; I was in love with your mother. I loved her from the moment we were married. I thought she and I were divinely blessed in our assigned domestic partnership. I confessed my love to her when you were only three years old, and she denied that she felt the same. I thought in time she would come to see what I knew—that God had blessed us. But as you'll know by now, having read your mother's journal, she would never come around.

She eventually entangled herself with someone else.
Another woman.
They'd been sinning in secret.

I reported her indiscretions to the Control when I lost myself to a jealous rage. And Mercy, please know that I have regretted it every moment of every day since. Had I understood then what I understand now, I would have loved her better. I would have helped her find a way to be with the woman she loved, if only to make her happy.

Instead, I sentenced her to die. I took her away from you. I forced you to live a life without Mira Madness, and I can say from experience that a life without her is misery.

I am so sorry.

I thought it was the right thing to do when I made the choice, but since the day I stood and watched her go up in flames, my relationship with God has changed. It's been gradual, so slight that I didn't even notice the changes happening myself. I didn't dare speak of them with you. I didn't know your mind, and that's my own fault. I was not the father I should have been.

But now, in my final hours, none of it matters. I have been so sick lately, and I feel the end is coming. I wish I were brave enough to give you this face to face, but I'm not. I just hope you find this before the Control does.

I found the journal entries of E.K. and T.W. a few years before you started service. It was in a box of books that had been taken during a raid by the Control—books that were meant to be destroyed. I couldn't just take the journal—they'd already catalogued all the books and were taking inventory before throwing them in the flames.

I'd been carrying your mother's journal with me everywhere back then. I was always afraid it would be found if I left it behind. Even as I write that, I'm not sure I can say exactly what I was afraid of...only that I was afraid. It was all I had on me, so I flipped to the first blank page I could find, and quickly copied the text and map into her journal.

I didn't understand what it was a map of, and it took me forever to figure out the text. But once I did, I began chipping away at the stone beneath our feet, and I've been chiseling into the ground for years...burying myself alive to find my way to hell.

I became ill before I could explore much beyond the map for myself, but I can proudly say that I finished cutting the way through for you. Hopefully, the tunnels will lead to somewhere special, somewhere new...perhaps to freedom.

You were not born to be a servant of men, Mercy.
You were born for something more.

The nearer I come to death, the more vividly I see you—your compassion, your strength, your unyielding nature...
You are so, so much like your wonderful mother.

And so I leave you with this, hoping your curiosity leads you beneath the surface, and you find what I couldn't...I hope you find the path to truth.

I love you, Mercy.

I watch Mercy as I lower the pages. Her silvery-blue eyes are unfocused, looking off into the distance.

"I…I don't understand," she whispers.

Luna crouches in front of her. "Your father dug beneath your home. He chiseled through stone to make the tunnel we crawled through. He cut the way through to these passageways. This is where the *tunnels weave through layers of hell, from mountain to mountain, forest to forest, and into the great beyond*," she quotes from the secret message left by E.K. and T.W.

"I can't believe this," Mercy says slowly. "I can't believe *him*. Why didn't he bring me here before he died? Why didn't he just *tell* me?"

Luna shrugs, glancing at me for help in responding, but I have no response that will offer Mercy any comfort. I can already feel the electric current of anger flowing through her, making the hairs on the back of my arms stand up.

Mercy's voice is quiet, but the tone of resentment is clear. "He could have brought me down here. He could have protected me, kept me hidden away so I wouldn't have to serve," she huffs and her expression twists, the anger clear through her slanted eyebrows.

She tears the pages from my hand. "Why bother to write me a damn letter just to remind me that he's the reason my mother is dead? That he's a coward who can't stand face to face with me and speak his truth? I don't *want* this." She balls up the letter and tosses it aside.

I'm hesitant to speak against her anger because it's fully justified, and I understand it. But I also think I understand her father. Though I don't care to defend a man I didn't know—a man who has clearly hurt Mercy so deeply—I want to service her compassion. She's at her best, her strongest, when her empathy is triggered, and I have a feeling this is only the tip of the iceberg.

She's going to need her strength.

"I agree; he was a coward," I tell her calmly. "He even admitted as much himself. But I think he was also afraid. You understand what fear does to you, Mercy. You were so afraid that you served for four years while hiding your dissenting thoughts. You had to in order to survive."

Her head snaps in my direction, as does her voice. "Don't you *dare* speak to me about the things I had to do in service. My father was too afraid to speak to his daughter; I was afraid for my *life*. It's not the same thing, Arlo Rainn, and you know it."

"You're right," I concede. "But so am I. Fear is the same for everyone, Mercy. When fear finds you, it takes control of you. It clouds your judgment. It doesn't matter what the fear is from, whether it's from a threat that's real or a threat that's perceived. It alters your decision making.

"Your father made a terrible choice to hide this from you, only hoping you would find it. By all accounts, you, me, and Stefanie should be dead right now, and those pages should still be hidden in the false bottom of that drawer, trapped there forever, never to be found.

"I'm angry at him, too. I'm furious that he hid this from you. He *is* a coward for avoiding you, but he had at least one moment of clarity. He had just enough courage, for just long enough to write the words on paper…and that may be an even more courageous feat than speaking.

"Writing requires bravery. It requires acceptance that your thoughts are printed eternally, acceptance that whether you're right or wrong, your words might be read by anyone at any time—perceived and accepted for what they are, or twisted and used against you in judgment.

"And you must see that your judgment of your father is also a judgment you hold over *me.* I was a coward, the same as he was. I have to accept that, and I do. I was too afraid of my feelings for you when they were first forming. I couldn't say them to you, so instead, I wrote them down. I never intended for you to find the poetry you inspired, but I always knew it was possible. It took me a very long time to find the courage to give you those pages.

"Perhaps," I pause to collect myself as I process my own truth, "perhaps it's time for you to recognize that you are gifted with more courage and strength than any of the rest of us could ever hope to have."

"I don't want to be strong," Mercy whispers, and saying the words brings tears to her eyes. "I don't want to be brave. I just want to be…I don't know. I just want to be angry."

She starts to cry, and it guts me. I put my arm around her, but she shrugs me off.

"No. Please, just let me be angry." She looks at Luna. "Tell me the truth about Ember Glen and let me be angry at someone other than my father."

Luna seems to hesitate. "Maybe this is too much all at once. Maybe we should wait—"

"*No.* No more waiting, no more delays. I want to know about vicious circle. I want the real story of everything, and I want it *now.*"

"Okay." Luna nods, slowly rising to her feet before she turns and goes back to the open bin. She reaches in and pulls out a video reel for the projector. "A lot of archived videos seem to be stored in these bins—hours upon hours of them—but we only need to show you five of them for you to see the truth." Luna pauses, then asks, "Are you sure you're ready?"

Mercy nods. "Yes."

Luna moves toward the projector to set up the first reel. "Then I'll let the footage speak for itself."

video record one
Instigation

March 31, 2032
One Year Before the War

THE REEL BEGINS with a black screen. White text fades into the upper left corner to reveal the video has been catalogued with a title and a date, this one is revealed to be 'Instigation' on March thirty-first, twenty thirty-two.

The video begins to play with a flurry of noise—a large crowd cheering with loud music in the background. The visual is confined to the shape of a rectangle in the center of the screen, the longer edges running from the top to the bottom. There's a brief flash of text to indicate the video was recorded on the personal cellular phone device of someone named Violet Clare.

A throng of people are packed together in an outdoor space, continually moving, swaying, and dancing to loud music being played by a group of people on stage. It's nighttime, and bright overhead lights artificially illuminate the space. Many of the people raise their hands and cheer, singing along with the song that must be familiar to them.

The recording device is clearly held in the recorder's hand—Violet Clare. Violet's voice—clearly the voice of a happy young woman—is the loudest as they cheer and sing along.

Violet pans the crowd with her device as she sings out of tune. A couple of rows ahead of her is a woman with both arms raised, her right arm adorned with bangles and bracelets. But more notably are the two solid black lines encircling her forearm. The tattooed bands are about two inches apart.

"Hey, hey!" Violet shouts with excitement, her voice loud near the microphone of her device. "Vicious Circle!"

"Oh! Where?" asks another female voice nearby.

"Over there!" Violet's left arm stretches out to point, and we see a glimpse of the same two-banded black tattoo on her forearm. "Vicious Circle!"

The woman with the bangles turns her head over her shoulder, and when she spots Violet recording from rows behind her, she smiles.

She can't be heard over the crowd and the music, but her mouth moves and it appears as though she shouts, "Vicious Circle!" as emphatically as Violet had while waving her left arm.

She taps the shoulder of another woman standing beside her, and that woman looks back. They look friendly in a way that might suggest they see someone they know, though it doesn't seem Violet knows them.

The women being recorded both raise their left arms, revealing that both of them have the same tattoo. Violet and what sounds like three or four other loud female voices beside her all scream excitedly, having found a common bond with strangers.

There's a clear sense of camaraderie.

Violet pans her device to record the people next to her, scanning across the faces of six women to her left that wave and cheer, or sing dramatically along to the song being played on stage. It's clear they're all friends who are attending this concert together, and when they move their arms, we can see they also have the same tattoo.

"Hey!" a male voice from somewhere behind Violet bellows, and she must whirl around to face him with the way the recording spins with her. A man with anger etched on his features stands closer to Violet than he needs to be. There's a close-up of his face, showing his dark eyes and light hair. "Cover that up or put your fucking arm down. No one wants that VC bullshit here."

"Excuse me?" Violet says from behind her device, an attitude of annoyance detected in her voice.

"I said, put your *fucking* arm down."

"No. Fuck off."

"Fucking bitch."

"What did you just call me?"

"I said, you're a *fucking bitch*. Is it too hard to hear me over the music, dollface?" He raises his voice. "All of you are *fucking bitches*, and your little *Vicious Circle* camaraderie is dumb as fuck."

"Do you realize I'm recording you?"

"I don't give a shit. Record me." The man moves into her space, and the recording shakes as Violet is forced backward.

"Get your—hey!" Violet shouts, as other voices rise around her. "Get your hands *off* me!"

The video is a jittery blur as Violet fumbles with her device, but it all steadies when she drops it and it lands on the ground. The perspective is now that of someone lying on their back, looking up at the sky. However, the sky is merely the backdrop for a chaotic visual where several sets of hands are pushing and grabbing while contradictory shouts of protest and encouragement are flung violently through the brawl.

"Fucking trash," the angry man mutters.

Though, truthfully, with so many people speaking and shouting all at once, it's difficult to tell if the voice belongs to him or to another of the men who seem to have joined in.

"You want rights? Then act like a goddamn lady."

"Don't touch her!"

"Fuck off!"

"Where's security?"

The voice of the woman singing stops mid-chorus, and her spoken words echo through the speakers. "Hold up. Cut it, guys. Hey, cut it off…" The music stops discordantly, with individual musicians ending at different times. The disharmony lends to amplify the sounds of the fight, and the tone is unsettling. "They need help back there. Hey! Get my girls some help back there! Where's security?"

A woman's dark brown hair whips across the screen as she falls over the camera. Her feet—adorned in black, lace-up ankle boots—fly up as she's knocked sideways, landing on the concrete.

It's difficult to make out the words over the scuffle, but it sounds like "…snap your fucking arm in half right between those lines…"

A man's foot lifts over the camera, then comes down hard on the other side of it, out of sight. At the same moment, a subtle, yet harsh, sound strikes, and it's reminiscent of a twig snapping in half.

The fallen woman screams, "My arm!" The voice is easily recognizable as belonging to Violet. Her pained sobs are distressing as they echo through the recording.

Some people wearing bright yellow coats appear, moving into the middle of the brawl, and they nudge the two conflicting groups apart. One of the yellow-coats crouches toward the ground, asking Violet if she is all right..

end of video

video record two
National News

April 17, 2032
Eleven Months Before the War

THE VIDEO FILLS the entire screen, displaying two women sitting on tall chairs that are angled toward each other. The image is bright and clear, slowly zooming in as music fades out, and a red banner appears across the bottom of the screen with text that reads, "Exclusive Interview with Violet Clare."

The same white text that appeared in the first video fades in at the top left corner of the screen. This time it reveals the title as 'National News,' dated April seventeenth, twenty thirty-two.

The woman on the left side is dressed in a cream-colored blouse that's tucked into a bright red pencil skirt—and her attire matches her serious expression. Her blonde hair is styled in a perfect sweeping wave that frames her face, and her make-up is done impeccably.

"We are live in Denver today, here with an exclusive interview with Vicious Circle activist and recent alleged assault victim, Violet Clare," the blonde woman says with an even, practiced cadence to her voice. "Better known to her social media followers as Vicious Vi, she's recently garnered the attention of news outlets across the country with her video of a brawl at an outdoor concert that resulted in a broken arm for her, and broken faith in humanity for her following." She makes a show of turning to face Violet directly. "Violet, thank you for joining us today."

Violet gives the blonde woman a tight grin. "I appreciate you having me, Lindsey."

Everything about Violet's appearance is in direct contrast to Lindsey's.

Violet's dark brown hair is pin-straight, stopping just at her shoulders, and her precisely trimmed bangs draw a straight line across her eyebrows.

The neon green cast on her left forearm brings out the color of her striking green eyes, which are noticeably bright against her tan skin. Aside from that, and the deep burgundy shade painted on her lips, the rest of her clothing is dark. The black T-shirt makes the perfect canvas for the bright white letters displayed across her chest.

The words *Vicious Circle* are printed in all capital white letters, and the Latin—*circulus vitiosus in aeternum*—is printed directly beneath it in lowercase cursive. Her dark jeans are faded gray and torn in spots, and she wears the same black boots she was wearing in the first video.

"Violet, your video of the assault has stirred up quite some controversy online."

"It's not exactly controversy, Lindsey. Right and wrong are clearly defined in this situation. If you want to call the online attacks launched against me and my followers since I posted that video 'controversial,' I suppose you can, but it's not the correct term. Controversy implies there's an argument to be made for each side of a debate, but I think it's pretty clear from that video what happened. My friends and I were assaulted, and that's not really up for debate."

"Hmm. It seems there's a rather significant portion of your online following that disagrees, but your stance is that their opinions don't matter. Well, I have to say, Violet, your position on this seems rather…*controversial*." She laughs to herself, as if she believes she said something truly humorous. "So, if controversial isn't the right word to describe what's been going on, then what word would you use?"

"What word would I use to describe the cyber bullying and stalking instigated by Ian Cole and his friends? Hostile. Aggressive. Repugnant. Any of those would be better. That significant portion of my following you mentioned—the ones who seem to disagree with the *fact* that this was a bias-related assault—aren't my followers.

"I had eighty thousand engaged and respectful followers before I posted that video, and within three hours, I'd surpassed a hundred and fifteen thousand. At least half of those new followers were in *support* of Ian Cole and his friends and their assault against me and mine. He was praised for, and I quote, 'Putting a VC girl in her place.' There were thousands of new comments on nearly all of my videos, and they were hateful, disrespectful, targeted, and outright disgusting. I won't even mention the emails, phone calls, and the attempts at doxing me."

Lindsey turns her head away from Violet, looking straight out from the screen as if she's speaking to the viewers directly. "Ian Cole, the son of presidential candidate Frederik Jay Cole, has been named as the alleged perpetrator in the assault." She shifts her attention back to Violet. "Now, Violet, some have said that you're capitalizing on the attention this video has received to increase your following."

Violet shakes her head. "No, I didn't want to increase my following of misogynistic men who feel the need to be heard in situations that don't involve them. Their comments on my videos and the videos of my loyal followers have been atrocious."

Lindsey's forehead creases as she nods with a tilt of her head. "Yes, we actually have a few of those controversial comments here." She lifts her hand to indicate a screen on the wall behind Violet.

Violet turns her head to glance at the screen, but quickly snaps back to look at Lindsey. "I'd actually prefer it if we didn't show those comments. I'm not here to give a larger platform to men who hate women. I'm actually here today to talk about Vicious Cir—"

"Let's take a look at this comment," Lindsey cuts her off as a white box containing text comes up on screen.

"So sick of these VC girls and their bullshit.
So concerned about their rights, but these
bitches don't give a shit about men's rights."

"What's your take on that comment?" Lindsey's voice can be heard, though all that we see is the comment on the screen.

"What's my…I'm sorry, did you just ask me what my *take* is? Can you even show those words on the news?"

"This is a privately operated news station."

After an unusually lengthy pause, Violet speaks again. "Okay, then, my *take*, Lindsey, is that men like that commenter are so privileged that they've lost their ability to empathize with the female experience in this country, especially over the last decade, where our rights have been so subtly stripped that most women don't even realize it's happening.

"It started with our right to access appropriate health care, our right to make decisions about our own bodies, and these changes have been happening ever since. Just last week, the federal government introduced a bill that makes it *legal* for employers to require female applicants to sign a disclosure as a part of their application, stating whether they plan to get pregnant in the first five years on the job. And if they get hired, and become pregnant within those first five years, the company has full rights to *terminate* her employment without cause."

"Wouldn't most of those women be planning on taking a maternity leave, anyway?"

Violet's eyes widen, gaping at Lindsey. "Is that a serious question?"

"Well, wouldn't they?"

Violet blinks. "Sure, Lindsey. Sometimes, when women get pregnant, they take maternity leave. But typically, they value the right to take that leave by choice—maybe even with pay—and *certainly* with the option to return to their jobs. Instead, they're being punished for having a uterus."

Lindsey leans in as her head inclines. "So, you view this bill to be… what? Detrimental? Wouldn't you agree that employers have a right to know that information when making hiring decisions?"

"*No.*" Violet glances around, her gaze stopping straight ahead, as though she's looking straight out through the screen. "Is this a joke? Really, is this a prank show?"

Lindsey chuckles. "I assure you it's not, Violet."

"Then let me be clear; the proposed bill is most certainly detrim—"

"Let's take a look at another comment," Lindsey cuts her off again.

"VC girls should all have their arms snapped
right between the lines tattooed on their
precious little arms. Nice work, Ian C."

There's a long beat of silence, then Lindsey says, "Give us your take on this one, Violet."

Violet glances down at the neon green cast on her left forearm, then with a hard expression, she simply says, "No."

Another pause.

"Okay, then let's take a look at this one."

The comment on screen fades out and a new block of text appears.

"These sluts couldn't even come up with
their own name. You know who did? A man.
So fucking dumb. Next time you open your
mouth, you'd better be on your knees so I
can shut you up, Violet Clare."

"Are you kidding me?"

"Now, this has always been a controversial point of discussion surrounding the Vicious Circle, hasn't it? What's your take on this?"

Violet sighs, leaning her elbow on the wooden armrest of her chair. "You keep asking me about my *take* on these hateful comments, Lindsey, but I guess I'd like to hear *yours*. Given the shocking manner in which you skipped over this man's flagrant insinuation that he'd like to 'shut me up' with a non-consensual sexual act, I'd like to know…Is there a take on rude comments from hateful men that *isn't* absolute disgust?"

Lindsey leans her elbow on her armrest, then delicately places her fingers beneath her chin. "You seem angry, Violet."

Violet's face scrunches as she tilts her head with a sarcastic expression. "Do I?"

Lindsey gives Violet an inquisitive look and waits for her to respond. When she doesn't, Lindsey continues, "Is the commenter correct about the source of the name for your activist group, Vicious Circle? Did a man come up with it?"

Violet huffs, "Fine, let's talk about the name if it will steer us back in the right direction, because frankly, I'm not a big fan of the direction we're heading here, Linds. When my girlfriends and I—"

"*Girlfriends*…Can you clarify what you mean by that? It's often been speculated that all the women who support Vicious Circle are lesbians."

Violet claps her hands together, leaning even closer to Lindsey and looking at her sideways. "Do you think I'm a lesbian? Is that a question you'd like to ask me?"

"I'm certain our viewers would like to know."

Violet bobs her head with a look of disbelief, sitting forward and looking directly at the viewers. "Viewers, let me be very clear about this. *My sexual orientation is irrelevant*; the sexual orientation of the women who've chosen to associate themselves with the Vicious Circle is irrelevant. Our activist group celebrates all sexual orientations and preferences, or the lack thereof, and that's all I'm saying on the subject."

"Could you—"

Violet sits back, turning to look at Lindsey. "That's all I'm saying on the subject. Now if you'll allow me to speak…"

Violet waits for a cue from Lindsey, or to see if she'll cut her off again. When Lindsey doesn't speak, Violet goes on, "As I was saying…When my *girlfriends* and I started protesting together nearly a decade ago, we had no intention of forming an activist group for women's rights. We just wanted to bring awareness in honor of our friend Kendra, who died well before she should have at only eighteen-years-old.

"She died because the teaching assistant in her freshman biology class decided that he wanted her, and she didn't have the right to tell him no. She died because that man just couldn't control himself, because he decided to follow her home from class and insist that she say *yes*. And when his insistence was still met with her refusal, he beat her, raped her, and left her bleeding beside the dumpster behind our dorm…in broad daylight.

"My friends and I were heartbroken, but we wanted to take action because accepting what happened to her was unfathomable. So we went to a women's rights protest because that's what our safety boils down to—men's perception of whether women *should* have rights. The right to safety, the right to bodily autonomy, the right to say *no*."

Violet pauses, and miraculously, she isn't interrupted by Lindsey. "Anyway, the name came from the first protest we went to after Kendra's death. While we were preparing, we were trying to think of a way to honor her at the event. We were talking about her and who she was, and remembered the way she always had two elastic hair bands on her arm—always two, and always black. She would joke it was because she always wanted to be ready to throw her hair up and get in a fight to defend one of us."

Violet gives a small smile, lost in her story. "Really, it was just because she was always too warm to keep her hair down for long, and she had very thick hair, so the ties were always breaking. But we couldn't think of Kendra without those two black bands around her arm.

"One of my friends got the idea that we should all wear two elastic bands as our way of remembering her at the protest, and we did. At the end of the event, they had a moment of silence, and we didn't plan it, but me and the six other girls found ourselves forming a circle together, our arms wrapped around each other in comfort.

"Kendra's death was still so fresh, so raw then, and I don't even know why…I just felt compelled to reach out to her. Like I wanted to show her the bands on my arm so she'd know I'd always remember her. So I reached my arm straight up toward heaven, and before long, the rest of the circle did, too. The photo that was taken of that moment is what started it all."

A photo fades in to fill the screen. A circle of seven women together on a city street as dusk falls, a traffic light shining red nearby. A crowd of mostly women fills the background, but they're blurred. The focal point is clear—the circle of young women, all wearing matching pale pink windbreakers. Their left arms are all raised, their fingers splayed, and each arm is adorned with two black bands outside the long sleeves of their matching jackets.

"It was a really powerful moment for us. After that, we started going to every protest, every activist event for women's rights." The photo fades as Violet speaks, returning to the view of her and Lindsey sitting on the two tall chairs. "Eventually, we started organizing our own events. It was at one of the events we organized that a drunken group of white guys decided to start spreading hate.

"Our security staff were talking to them, trying to get them to leave, but one of them just kept arguing, so I came over to help. That man told me that all women were vicious and vindictive, and that our event was proof of it. Now I'm all for free speech, but he was spewing a lot of hateful comments and badgering protesters. And when he grabbed one of my friends and snapped one of the black bands on her arm, we had to call the police to intervene.

"It was after that event that we decided we'd all get tattoos of black bands around our arms so men couldn't go around snapping them. And that spread like wildfire. We were kind of shocked with how many women across the country started getting the tattoo to honor their own female friends and family who were victims of violence. It's like wearing a name badge or club pin—we can find each other easily, spot solidarity in sisterhood from a simple mark.

"So that man at the protest was arrested for drunk and disorderly conduct, and as they were putting him in the police car, he started yelling nonsense about how we were vicious, vicious women, and how we should all stand in our vicious little girl circle like we were in the photo. We had a good laugh about it and started calling ourselves a vicious circle as an inside joke… but then it sort of just stuck.

"We took what this man had intended to be an insult and made it ours. We took ownership of being a vicious circle of women who would not stand by and watch our friends die at the hands of men. We're proud to be considered vicious if it's what we have to be to make sure no other circle of friends has to go through what we went through."

"Wow, I'm…Thank you for sharing this story," Lindsey says. "I'm sure that was a difficult time for you and your friends."

"Yes, it was." Violet appears pleasantly taken aback by Lindsey's response.

"But just to go back to the comment, you are verifying that a man at one of your protests came up with the name for Vicious Circle, and your group has taken credit for it ever since?"

"That's…Is that what you took from everything I just said?"

"I'll take that as confirmation. Why don't we move on?"

Violet's jaw visibly tenses. "*Yes.* Why don't we?"

Lindsey looks out at the viewers. "As we're committed to unbiased reporting, and we've provided Violet with ample time to speak today, we also have a special guest joining us for this exclusive interview to talk more about the alleged assault—"

"Again, it's not *alleged* if it's on camera…" Violet chuckles humorlessly.

"Ian Cole is here to tell us more about the events of that night. Ian? Why don't you come on out?"

Violet's eyebrows shoot into her hairline as she leaps anxiously from her seat. "Ian is here? *No.* If he's here, I'm done. I have a personal protective order against him for cyber stalking…"

Violet freezes, staring wide-eyed with fear as a clean-cut man in his mid-twenties steps into view. Though he has a pleasant expression on his face, he's clearly the same angry man who started the fight with Violet at the concert. He wears a pressed, pale-blue button-down shirt tucked into his khaki pants. His blond hair is styled neatly, and his brown eyes appear dark as night on screen. Not dark in color, but dark in expression…dark with ill-intent.

"Violet, let's just talk about this calmly," Ian says, holding up a palm. "I know we can find common ground on our differences."

Violet nearly stumbles over her own feet, rushing to take a step backward. She raises her hand, pointing a finger at him. "You…you're in violation of the protective order and the terms of your bail."

"I just want to talk about this," Ian says. "Let's come to an agreement on dropping the charges."

Ian steps forward and Violet steps back.

"Violet, be reasonable."

He takes another step.

Violet turns, runs, and disappears off screen…

end of video

video record three
The Edict

May 14, 2032
Ten Months Before the War

IAN COLE APPEARS on screen as he lowers to sit in a chair behind a desk. The wall at his back is light-gray and bare—no picture frames, no shelves, no indication that this is a space where someone frequently spends their time. His sandy-blond hair is swept neatly across his head, styled intentionally in a clean-cut manner that suggests his outward appearance is important.

There's a brief flash of text to indicate the video was recorded on his personal cellular device, which must be propped up somehow, as the video is clear and steady. He sits centered within the rectangular frame created by his device, and the familiar white text fades in at the upper left corner of the screen, revealing the title of the video to be, 'The Edict,' and dated May fourteenth, twenty thirty-two.

He sets his arms on the table, folding his hands in front of him, his expression contrite and reflective. Turning his gaze downward, he sighs.

Slowly and softly, Ian begins to speak. "I tried to reach out to Violet Clare again today. She just doesn't seem to understand how sorry I am for what happened at that concert; that all I want to do is apologize to her and her vicious *fucking* circle of friends." When he cusses, his palms slap the table with a jarring snap that shakes his perfectly styled hair out of place.

Gradually—*eerily*—a broad smile draws across his cheeks as he presses slightly forward on his palms, and his sinister grin displays straight, white teeth. He lifts his eyes to look directly at the camera, as though he's staring at the viewers.

"Violet Clare," he begins quietly. "Violet, Violet, Violet. Vicious little Violet. If she had any idea what's waiting for her, she would keep my *name* out of her fucking *mouth*."

He leans back in his seat, then combs his fingers through his hair, drawing in a deep breath as he stares straight ahead.

"This is what I'm here to talk to you about, my brothers—my most loyal, faithful followers. This situation with Violet Clare has reached an impasse, and the time has come for action. The cushy little plea deal Violet's lawyers offered me? It's gone. They took it off the table yesterday when they realized the pretty little bundle of flowers she'd found on her doorstep were from yours truly."

He throws up his hands. "It's what I get for trying to be a gentleman with a woman who *refuses* to be a lady. Let that be a lesson to you, brothers. Treat her how she deserves to be treated, how she *demands* to be treated. I've tried to be nice, but Violet has affirmed time and again that she doesn't *deserve* nice." His dark eyes narrow. "So she's not going to *get* nice from me anymore."

He begins to unbutton the cuff of his long sleeve shirt, working to roll it up his forearm as he speaks. "Without that plea deal, I've been assured that we're going to trial. And though my father could easily find a means to sway the jurors, that alone just doesn't satisfy me. You see, my inclination toward Violet Clare is…" he pauses, glancing up at the ceiling as he searches for the exact right word, "*obsessive*. And gentleman, I don't think I will ever get these fantasies of her crying face pressed to the ground beneath my polished leather shoe out of my mind. Not until I act on them. So what exactly am I telling you?"

He moves on to the other sleeve, unbuttoning it at the cuff, working to roll it up his forearm. "Well, I'm telling you that I'm leaving. I'm going away for quite some time. My criminal record isn't exactly clean, and my father's lawyers have assured us both that there's no way I'm walking away from a trial by jury with less than five years—and that's if I'm lucky. Felony assault, bias-related hate crime, stalking… They say it's astonishing that I'm out on bail right now given my past. I think it's astonishing that they seem surprised by how easily the system can be bought."

He pauses mid-twist of his sleeve and looks straight out at the camera. "Well, not *all* of his lawyers are surprised, of course. Certainly not my father's dearest friend, Waylon Creed. He's actually the one helping my father—the one and only Frederik *fucking* Cole—to hash out this plan of ours. Spoiler alert: they're going to buy me a playground and help me…*disappear* before my trial."

Ian stops talking long enough to finish with his sleeve, then he folds his hands on the tabletop. "In case you didn't know it by now, my father is the filthiest fucking politician to ever grace these glorious states. Everyone knows that, even the people voting for him know that. But none of you know just how filthy he is because he's so *precise* in his manipulations, so practiced, so clean.

"You see, I *am* my father's son...an apple that certainly didn't fall far from his tree. But I'm not quite as polished as our dear elder Cole has been with his own little obsessions, not nearly as neat and clean. I've been learning, I've been growing." He waves his hand like this is a normal topic of conversation. "But with my criminal record, and this latest blow from vicious little Violet, I'm afraid my time for learning and growing has come to an end. So, as my father would say, it's time to purchase ourselves a solution.

"And oh, what a beautifully twisted solution it is. I don't want to give away all the details just yet...I think I'd rather show you when the time comes. But allow me, if you will, to give you a little preview of what my disappearing act is going to look like."

He reaches off camera, and when he pulls his arm back, he holds a black leather journal. He uncoils a leather strap from around it, then drops it on the tabletop in front of him before flipping open the cover. He straightens in his seat and brings the side of his fist to his lips before dramatically clearing his throat.

"*This*," he begins, turning his palm toward the ceiling and floating his hand over the open pages, "will be my gift for Violet Clare. A gift she'll receive when she's finally brought before me on her knees, where she fucking belongs. Call it my playbook, my manifesto, my Bible, my *edict*...my written documentation of the feral *impulse* I have to destroy her."

He strokes his hand down the pages. "It contains the details of every terrible thing I plan to do to her in my new playground, but I've left a lot of blank space, spots that she and I can fill in together as I ruin her."

He flips a page and slaps his hand down on it. "Here is a list of fourteen names. Mine and Violet's names are the two at the top, of course. I even drew a little heart in between just so I could scribble it out. But what are the names of the other twelve? Well, half of them are *your* names, my brothers. My father and I have chosen six of you to join me—six of you connected to very powerful men in this country who will help us keep this secret safe. You're going to help me keep our playground secure and our playthings under control. Because *we* will be in control.

"And the other six names...Can you guess who those names belong to? I'll give you a hint. The name beneath Violet Clare is Jada Johnson." He pauses and waits, as though he expects an actual reply. "Another hint, you say? Well, I'll tell you that name number three is…" he drums his hands on the table to build anticipation, "Soleil Garcia."

His head inclines with a self-satisfied smirk. "Catching on now, aren't you? Violet and her six besties—those bitches who started Vicious Circle—are coming with us when we disappear, though of course, they don't know it yet. Violet and I are going to have a surprise reunion at the new property—our new playground—where I'll have free rein to show her *precisely* what I think of her.

"Now *this*, gentleman, is the secret project that my father, Waylon Creed, and our favorite corrupt Senator Bright are working on to get me out of this mess that vicious Violet has put me in. Right as we speak, they're searching for the perfect property upon which we'll build this playground of ours—a *community* where we can *finally* be real men again.

"Somewhere hidden away, so deep that no outsider will ever stumble across it. Somewhere far enough that it's treacherous to reach, impossible to leave, yet near enough that our dear elders—Cole, Creed, and Bright—can continue to funnel in the resources we need for survival and debauchery for however long we need to exist apart from this world…this *fucking* world that wants us to sit down, shut up, and let the Violet Clare's speak their heinous thoughts of men.

"And, of course, the collective wealth of our founding fathers…did I call them 'elders' before?" He tilts his head and chuckles to himself. "Actually, I like that."

He sits back and spreads his arms wide before dramatically bellowing, "Our *glorious* elders!" He laughs again before gradually bringing his arms down.

"They have so much wealth between them that they'll be able to keep this secret for years…decades. *Fuck*, even generations of Coles if it's what we want. We'll finally be free to exist how we were born to be—as brutal, savage men who *take* their power and maintain it with violence. We won't be held to the laws and standards of the world around us. *No.* It's time for us to return to the days where men held all the power and the women existed to serve our needs."

He leans forward, pointing his index finger out at the viewers. "Men rule, and women do whatever the fuck they're told, and that means *you*, Violet Clare. I'm coming to get you, dollface." He slowly grins and whispers, "You better be ready for me…"

end of video

video record four
Day One

September 19, 2032
Six Months Before the War

THE SCREEN IS black.

The darkness creates a disturbing background to the sound of distressed whimpers, soft crying, and pleading. The voices of several young women are amplified in a deeply unsettling manner without a visual to provide context.

It remains this way for mere seconds, though one might feel as though they stretch into hours, like a looming threat about to fulfill a sinister promise. The only place to focus one's visual attention is the upper left corner of the screen, where white text fades in, displaying the title of this record to be 'Day One,' and the date as September nineteenth, twenty thirty-two.

Just as the darkness begins to settle as familiar, the camera abruptly switches on to reveal another cellular device recording. The camera is aimed at the gravel-covered ground, revealing the toe of a man's polished leather shoe peeking out from beneath his clean, pressed black slacks.

The fearful crying of several women continues as the man holding the device slowly pans upward, and our view gradually rises. The camera adjusts as the light changes, a bright-white flash of sunlight filling the rectangular frame and momentarily obscuring the scene. But quickly, the flash is gone—the sunlight returns to its single point in the sky, becoming mere backlighting as the camera refocuses, revealing a frightening scene.

Directly in front of the man holding the device are seven women, all on their knees upon the gravel, and each placed a few feet apart from each other. Their hands are bound behind their backs and black hoods are pulled over their heads.

One woman's head is hung low in fear.

Another's shoulders shake while she sobs.

The next rocks back and forth as she mutters, "Please…"

And another is stark still, like a kneeling statue.

The subtle clack of a man's dress shoes against concrete draws attention. The man holding the device turns slightly to the right, revealing Ian Cole as he slowly descends a set of stone steps from a grand manor that rises from behind them.

He steps down onto the small, gray stones, and he pauses, taking his time to adjust his cufflinks beneath his sharp, black suit—it fits him precisely, as though it was tailor-made. He smooths the lapels of his jacket, then slowly lifts his chin.

Ian turns his head—scanning the line of women to his right, then to his left—and satisfied with the sight before him, he lets his grin spread. He takes a step forward, and the sound of his sleek shoes crunching over the shifting stones seems to startle the women. They take turns whimpering fearfully, flinching at the sound of dread approaching as he steadily stalks toward them.

He finds the woman kneeling at the center of the line.

He stops directly in front of her.

He looks down at her, appraises her…

And then his grin broadens.

Five other men move to stand behind the line of women—all looking perfectly pleased with themselves—and there's also the man who's filming. With Ian, that brings the count of men to seven.

Seven men.

Seven women.

The fourteen names written in Ian's journal.

Ian reaches forward to grip the black fabric covering the head of the woman who kneels directly in front of him. He glances up and gives a nod to the other men. "Take them off."

Each man tears off the black hood of the woman kneeling in front of him. As their hoods are tossed aside, the women are brought into overwhelming sunlight—they blink and twist their heads, turning away from its source. As they begin to adjust, batting their eyes against the bright light, they begin to glance around at their surroundings, at each other, trying to make sense of it all.

And that's when they begin to recognize one another.

"Jada?" It's the girl kneeling in the center of the line—the one directly in front of Ian Cole—who says her friend's name…

It's Violet Clare.

"Soleil?" says another woman, recognizing a familiar face beside her.

The collective suffering crescendos as they realize this harrowing experience is shared, not just with other women, but with their closest friends.

Ian steps in close to Violet, and she lifts her head, squinting and blinking against the light, trying to make out who stands before her.

"Hello, Violet…" Ian says.

It seems to be his voice that triggers her instant recognition.

He reaches out to snatch her by the back of the neck as she lets out a gut-wrenching scream. With force, he slams her down sideways onto the gravel. He presses his palm to the side of her head to hold her down, though he rises just enough to replace his hand with his shoe.

Violet's friends scream, shouting and crying for him to stop.

Yet it doesn't seem to faze him.

Instead, a look of relief relaxes his features.

He straightens to his full height, unaffected by their pleas. His eyes fall shut as his leg pushes down, squishing Violet's cheek to hold her in place beneath his foot.

Her body thrashes.

Her bound hands are useless.

Ian's head rolls back on his shoulders as he draws in a deep breath. Then he grins as he opens his eyes, dropping his head forward again.

He looks down at Violet—his new plaything.

His expression could be described as hungry, and Violet Clare will be his favorite meal.

"There you are," he croons, "*finally*. Right where you belong."

His foot begins to twist…

THE VIDEO CUTS to black, and there's a beat of darkness before a new clip appears on screen. The device is laid on the ground, camera pointing straight up to show the clear night sky. It's a black canvas spotted with white dots of starlight. The angle is just wide enough to reveal a bright, full moon.

The sound of a woman stifling her cries—trying to choke down her whimpers while fighting to catch her breath—crescendos just before the top of her head comes into view over the camera. Inching forward, presumably crawling on her hands and knees, she continues forward until her entire face is centered within the rectangular frame of the device. Her eyes are closed as she fights through fear, and her dark hair dangles toward the camera.

"Right there, stop," Ian Cole's recognizable voice commands. "Don't move another inch, my vicious little Violet. Open your eyes and look down."

With dread painted across her face, Violet Clare obeys, and she does it easily. A conclusion about the nature and length of her suffering on this night could surely be drawn by her quick compliance alone. Yet it's the distant echoes of her friends—screaming and crying from faraway places spread across the property—that serve as true evidence that they've been drawn into a nightmare.

Blinking open her eyes, Violet looks down at the device, and her gaze burns a hole straight through the screen. She stares into the unseen faces of the viewers on the other side.

Someone's finger reaches out in front of her eyes, seeming to tap the screen of the cellular phone, and a light from the device switches on. She squints, slightly turning her head against the shine that brings unwanted clarity to the injuries marring her face.

With eyes clenched shut, she cries out as a hand lashes out, tangles in her hair, and twists her head to bring her face fully back into the frame.

"*Violet*. I told you to open your eyes. Now do it. Take a good fucking look at yourself."

Trembling against his grip, she slowly opens her eyes and looks down… and the image of her face is haunting.

Bloodied with scrapes.

Covered in dirt.

Darkening skin from fresh bruising.

Bloodshot, weary eyes.

Though no tears presently spill from her eyes, clean streaks cut like riverbeds down the layers of soil and blood on her cheeks.

And despite all that grime, her green eyes remain vibrant and striking.

"Don't you look pretty now that your face is all made up? *Fuck*, I wish I could put you on live with your followers. I wish they could see you just like this…Sadly, this recording is just for me."

Violet Clare continues to stare straight down—straight out toward the viewers—as Ian speaks. Her breaths are heavy, drawing rapidly through her lightly flaring nostrils. One might think she's restoring her strength as she watches herself reflected in the self-view. Another might think her strength is restored in knowing that someday, someone will see this, and know what really happened to her…They'll know Ian Cole for the monster he truly is.

The slight quirk of one corner of her lips—a brief twitch that shows a smirk for no more than a second before she hides it again—is telling that it's the latter.

"It's not like I could send it, anyway," Ian goes on. "No Wi-Fi out here, so far away from the world. No cell phone service either, in case you were thinking of trying to steal my phone. Dear old Dad has his own private satellite that only three people on the outside have access to.

"Now don't worry, dollface. Even if you did manage to get a hold of my phone without me realizing it—which is next to impossible because it's always on me—you'd have to know the password to access the satellite cellular. And if your tiny little brain managed to figure that out—*and it won't*—there are only three people you'd be able to call. Can you guess who those three people are, Violet?"

Rage creeps into her expression, like a filter slowly making its way up from chin to forehead, scrubbing away at the fear. When humanity is lost, and all seems hopeless, passionate fury may lead the only path away from fear.

And Violet Clare is traveling that path.

Without hesitation, and without inflection, Violet simply replies, "Your father."

"Yes!" Ian says. "That's one. The *obvious* one. Anyone could have guessed that. Why don't we play a little game for you to guess the other two?"

Her eyes briefly shift to glance sideways as a sneer flattens her lips. "A game…"

"A *game*," he repeats. "It's very simple, VC girl. You guess the names of the other two people who know this place exists—the last of our three glorious elders, if you will—and I won't fuck you so hard in the ass that you bleed for days."

Her eyes widen slightly as fear tries to drag her back, but she lets them fall shut briefly as she takes a deep breath, bravely refusing to let it take her.

"So, are we going to play? Or should I just skip to the good part—"

"I'll play," she says, nearly interrupting him as her eyes snap open.

"Oh, this should be interesting. A little game of 'How Much Does Violet Know About Ian Cole.' Fuck, if you win, I might just force you to come for me as a fun little treat for you. Because let me tell you, Violet, that would get me *right* the fuck off, knowing you've been paying such careful attention to me."

Violet can hardly hide the look of disgust.

"Okay. So, one down, two to go. Who else do you think is involved? Ten seconds on the clock, Vi."

Her brow furrows, creasing her forehead. Her eyes dart around as she searches her mind, but then they brighten a little, perhaps as she latches onto an idea.

"Five, four, three…" Ian counts. "Two—"

"Bright!" she shouts. "Senator Bright..."

"*Violet*, you sneaky little thing. You have been paying attention to me." Then he mutters, "Fuck, that gets me hard."

She sprints the path from fear and reaches passionate fury in an instant.

"Your father is a fucking presidential candidate. I haven't been paying attention to *you*; I've been paying attention to *him*, you dumb fuck. I've been actively campaigning against that sick son of a bitch all year!"

There's silence for a moment, and it's filled with tension.

"No, go on," Ian urges with an eerily calm tone. "Keep talking, dollface. Talk yourself right into another broken bone."

A flicker of fear shows in her eyes, and she presses them shut, huffing it out with a heavy breath.

"I almost don't even want to finish the game now, Violet. You hurt my feelings, and it makes me want to hurt yours." He sighs. "Though, I suppose fair is fair. I did lay out the rules, and the rules are meant to be followed, so we must continue with this game to determine what happens to you next. So, let's see if you can get out of the most brutal ass fucking you've ever had. Tell me, baby, who's the third person? You have ten seconds."

Violet's head shakes with such a slight subtlety that it can probably only be seen by the viewers. As moments creep past, her eyes seem to shift away, less and less focused, and it becomes clear that she doesn't know the answer.

"Five more seconds. Come on. Make it fun. Take a guess."

"I-I don't remember his name," she mutters.

"Who's name?"

"The...his lawyer. Your father's friend."

"Oh. This is getting interesting. You've almost got it. Three seconds. Come on, now, throw out a name...any name..."

The urgency strains her features. "Reed?" She quickly guesses. "Is it Raymond? Raymond Reed?"

"*Raymond Reed?*" Ian laughs.

Her eyes widen a hair as something seems to click. "No! It's *Creed.* Raymond *Creed*..."

Ian is still laughing. "No, Violet. It's not Raymond Reed, and it's not Raymond Creed. It's *Waylon* Creed."

She sighs, distress taking hold of her expression, eyes darting wildly. "But I said Creed...The second time, I said Creed..."

"And sadly, time was already up, buttercup. But good effort. I'm truly impressed that you figured it out, even though you got Mr. Creed's name wrong. Well, rules are rules. I'm gonna have to fuck you now. We can do this the easy way or the hard way. It's up to you."

"No!" Violet screams, her dark brown hair swinging as she crawls forward, her head moving away, up the screen.

But then her face rushes past in the opposite direction, entirely awash with fear as she's violently jerked backward…

THERE'S ANOTHER JARRING cut to black, though it only lasts a moment. The video jumps around the screen as Ian Cole fumbles with his recording device. He appears to be indoors—somewhere with fluorescent lighting—and there's a pervasive buzzing sound in the background.

"Just a second, doll," he says. "I want to record all your cute little whines and whimpers."

The video stills when he places his device on a flat surface beside him. He appears sideways within the rectangular frame on the screen, and the view peeks up at him from below.

"I don't want it," Violet quietly cries. "Please…" Her voice is unusually soft, weak. "Did…did you put something in the water?"

"Of course, I did. I can't have you squirming and messing up my artwork."

Ian leans over the camera, looking down at his device with dark eyes, and raises his hand above it to show that he's holding a tattoo machine—the source of the pervasive buzzing in the background.

"You'll ruin it," Violet pleads. "You can't…It was for my friend; it was for Kendra. Ian, *please*…"

He brings his free hand to his heart. "Violet, *please*. If you say my name like that and beg so sweet, I'm gonna have to stop and fuck you again."

"Y-you can. You can stop. Just…don't draw over my tattoo and I'll let you. I'll let you, Ian."

He looks down and rolls his eyes at the camera, as if he's glancing over at a friend to share a look.

"Of course, you'll let me, Vi. You're gonna let me do whatever I want to you forever, because you don't have a *choice*."

Violet cries. "Please…"

"Shh. Quiet now. I want to make sure you understand why I'm doing this before you fall asleep. It's funny actually, because you could've prevented all of this from happening. There was a plea bargain on the table for the charges you had brought against me, and I was fully prepared to accept it. I would've accepted it, and you and I would've continued on as we were, sharing our sexy little aggressions toward each other in secret—"

"I…I never shared…" Violet's voice is fading.

Ian continues as though she hasn't spoken. "I would have kept messaging you, and you would've kept blocking every new account I made to follow you. But do you know what happened to that plea deal? Of course, you do, because *you* were the one who told them I'd come by your shitty little apartment and left those flowers on your doorstep.

"Those were a *gift* for you, Vi. I was being a gentleman. But you went and cried to your lawyers and they pulled the deal, so it's kind of like *you* made a decision that would send me to prison. I wasn't going to go to prison; my father was not going to allow that to happen. So I need you to understand that this game we're all playing here now…it's all your fault."

"It's…not…" She's barely audible.

"So because you wouldn't accept my flowers, VC girl, I'm going to make you wear them forever, right here on your forearm with your stupid little black bands. Now, there's no need to worry. I know how to use this. And if you bothered to learn anything about me, you'd know that I'm actually a rather talented artist—a tortured soul, if you will—and I will make this the most beautiful bouquet of wildflowers you've ever seen. I promise, you're going to love it."

He sighs. "It's just rather poetic, isn't it? I've plucked you from your meadow, my little wildflower, just so I can watch you wither and wilt and slowly decay…Violet?"

Ian's head turns, and he looks down at the camera. "Oops, she's asleep." He reaches out to tap the screen with his finger…

end of video

video record five
New World

March 31, 2033
The Civil War Begins

AN OLDER MAN with salt and pepper hair appears, centered within the rectangular frame on the projector screen. A bit of white text fades in briefly to indicate that this is a recording from Ian Cole's personal cellular device. His face appears within the rectangular frame as well, but it's confined to a smaller rectangle in the upper right-hand corner.

"Mr. Creed," Ian says from the smaller box, his face visibly tense and his voice clearly strained. "I was expecting my father to call. Where is he?"

"I have to say, I'm rather surprised to hear you ask," Waylon Creed responds—the man who appears largest on screen. He's well put together in a sharp gray suit, but he looks tired, stress clear in the tone of his voice.

Ian's head tilts to the side. "Why? Do you think I don't care about my father? Of course, I fucking care, *Waylon.* He's my father, and he saved my life with this property. So where the fuck is he? I'd like to know he's safe."

"He's safe, Ian. He was gone before the worst of it came through. Intelligence had already predicted an attack; they just hadn't expected a group of women to be so—"

"*Vicious,*" Ian finishes for him, turning his head over his shoulder to look behind him. "See what you did, Vi? You had those angry little VC girls wound so tight before you disappeared that they just couldn't play nice anymore, could they?"

"What?" Violet's voice is quiet from somewhere in the background. "What do you mean? Did something happen?"

Ian snaps, whipping sideways, "*Yes,* something happened, Violet! Your

Vicious Circle followers have started a goddamn *war* over you! Went into D.C. today, guns blazing—*literally*—because they think my father had something to do with your disappearance."

There's an odd pause where everyone seems to wait for the obvious to strike.

"And yes,"Ian says a touch more calmly,"I'm aware he *did* have something to do with your disappearance. But that doesn't stop me from being angry about what your girls are doing, Vi, so don't give me that goddamn look like you think I'm stupid." A pause. "I'm fucking serious. Fix your face or I'll tie you to a damn tree again and leave you for days." Another pause. "That's better." Ian turns to face forward again.

"Ian,"Waylon begins calmly. "You do understand that their motivations are more complex than you're making it seem, right? The Vicious Circle has coordinated attacks across the country in all the places where your father facilitated the stripping of certain women's rights. This isn't just a VC protest for a proper investigation of Violet and the other girls' disappearance. I'm not trying to be condescending, Ian, but it's incredibly important for me to know that you have a clear understanding of the nuances and complexities of this situation before I give you the power I'm about to give you."

Ian's demeanor switches from self-righteous anger to calm and collected in an instant. The change is harsh, rehearsed, disingenuous…He puts on a charming façade that's reserved for the outside world, one that's necessary for politics and deception. It's a mask he likely destroyed six months ago when he made the property his new home.

Ian folds his hands on the desk in front of him and speaks deliberately— deceptively. "These events have been rather difficult for me to process, and my fear over what this world is coming to got the better of me. I apologize for the outburst, Waylon. I regret you saw me in a moment of weakness. Yes, I understand the complexities of this situation."

He lifts his eyes toward the ceiling, as though he was going to roll them in a sarcastic manner but fought the urge mid-roll. Then he sighs and bows his head, casting his eyes downward.

"It's tragic that these women have felt the need to resort to violence. While I certainly appreciate why they might feel afraid and confused as we work to change our laws for the greater good, I see these attacks as their attempt to…to cry out for help.

"They need guidance from men, solid leadership and great care as they come to terms with these changes. It will be difficult for them, but these women of the Vicious Circle are simply victims of Violet Clare, brainwashed by her hate and hostility, and they've become cult-like in their mentality. We must grant patience to those willing to change, but violence shall be met with violence when they leave us without a choice—"

"All right, Ian," Waylon says flatly, with an annoyed expression. "That's enough."

Ian switches back to his former—and truer—persona, dropping his palms to the table as he leans back. "Thank fuck."

"I'm glad to know you can still turn it on when it's necessary. We've all been more than a little concerned about your ability to do that. Frankly, we hadn't expected you'd be capable of attempting to take this role until you were much older and we had more resources in place—"

"You're talking around the point, Waylon. Let's get down to brass tacks."

"Are you recording this call?"

"Of course."

"Good, because we have a lot to discuss and you may need to review this later. Just remember the protocol. Immediately convert to reel, then make a duplicate. Store them properly for longevity, place them separately for security—"

"And wipe the data clean. Yeah, I've got it down to a science."

"Good. It's important because at some point soon—far sooner than we were thinking due to the recent attacks—we're going to need you boys to go dark on all devices. For good."

Ian's brow creases as he straightens in his seat and leans forward on his elbows. "I'm listening."

"When we purchased this property we had two goals. The first was to get you out of the impossible situation you'd gotten into with Violet Clare. Actually, your father and I had already foreseen that something like this would be coming, so we'd been discussing it off and on for years. I don't need to explain to you why we've both had concerns for your…proclivities."

"I live with my *proclivities*, Waylon, so I think I have a good understanding of your concerns," Ian says with a proud grin.

"This is serious, Ian. Your father is being targeted by the Vicious Circle, and it puts all three of us at risk. And if we're at risk, then all of you at the property are at risk without the appropriate infrastructure in place."

"Okay, I hear you. So what's the plan?"

"Senator Bright is making arrangements for the three of us to go into hiding, and he's handling the press on that. And we've decided that we will be in hiding for a very long time. The VC have made it abundantly clear that they do not intend to stop fighting until their rights are restored and your father is thoroughly investigated regarding the disappearance of their founding members."

"Well, shit." Ian combs a hand through his hair, leaning back in his seat.

"The situation is dire. The VC are increasing their numbers as we speak, and they've declared their intent to engage in civil war if their demands aren't met. That was the purpose of the recent attacks…to demonstrate on a small scale what they're capable of. Intelligence has confirmed their growth, and they're recruiting men, too—their weak-minded husbands and brothers."

"Waylon, seriously, tell me. Is this a joke? We're really talking about a bunch of angry women who were followers of Violet? *My* Violet? Did anyone think to wait a week and see if it's not just collective PMS hysteria from their cycles all syncing up at the same time? Christ. Give them a week to finish bleeding and maybe they'll all go home—"

"This is serious, Ian. It's not just women associated with the Vicious Circle who are involved…it's women from *our* side, too. This was our fear. It's one thing for them to be stupid women, but an entirely different thing when they start brainwashing the good ones—our obedient wives and demure daughters. *I* have daughters, and I don't want to see them get dragged in by VC rhetoric."

"Okay." Ian nods. "Okay, I get it; you're being serious about this."

"Things are going to have to change. They were always going to have to change…we just thought we'd have more time to prepare. We thought we'd have years to plan and prep, but we have to move quickly."

"So what's your plan?"

"This is the second goal we had when we purchased this property—creating a community that serves the needs of men like us; a community committed to serving the needs of *men*. But it requires a beginning with the right people: those who are already committed to our beliefs, and those who are susceptible enough to commit under the right circumstances. And there are seven 'right circumstances' already living on the property."

"You mean, me and my friends."

"Precisely."

"Sounds like the perfect job for my father. Why doesn't he come live here himself? It's probably the safest place in the world."

"It probably is, but only because we've worked very hard to make it that way. And as soon as we've finalized the selections for the first generation, we'll have them delivered to the property. Once they've arrived, it will be your responsibility to ensure the community is built properly. Once they've arrived, we'll have to shut down all communications for a while—at least a month, maybe two."

"Stop. You're going to bring more people to the property, which means more mouths to feed and more resources used…And then you're cutting off communications? How the fuck am I supposed to keep them alive, Waylon? Where are they supposed to live? The boys and I are *not* giving up the mansion, and there are only three houses in that little village area down the path."

"We'll do a major supply drop along with the first generation—everything you'll need to get started—and then once a month thereafter. And we're selecting the population *carefully*. You'll have people who can plan and build, people who can heal, people who can teach. Women who can care for their homes and children…women you can breed."

"Go on."

"You know you can't make wives and mothers out of those heathens there with you now. And you *certainly* shouldn't be breeding with them—which reminds me of another item you'll need to resolve."

Ian's face hardens. "You're not taking away my plaything, Waylon…*our* playthings. My father promised me Violet Clare, and I will be keeping her for as long as I choose. It will be *my* choice when she fucking dies and no one else's. Do you understand me?"

"No one is trying to take away your playthings. They'll be an important part of this new community. You know as well as I do that men don't just need subservient wives and dutiful mothers for their children; we need sex and violence. It's a primal, natural need that we've all been suppressing for far too long…and we need women upon which we can unleash."

"So how the fuck am I supposed to unleash on the mother of my children?"

"You're not. Are you suggesting that Violet Clare should be the mother of your children?"

Ian glances off screen. "No."

"Good, because I just told you that she and her repugnant friends aren't fit for breeding. Are you listening carefully, Ian?"

"*Yes.*"

"There are good, faithful women we are bringing to you, and they must be treated differently than the others. They are perfect to breed a future generation of domestic daughters from. Those daughters will be the first generation born and raised on the property, the most important for ensuring that this community will continue on for decades to come."

"And what makes you so certain these women will be willing to have those daughters?"

"Because your brilliant father has already convinced them that *God* has chosen them for this task."

Ian chuckles. "He is fucking brilliant that way."

"Oh, he is. He's convinced them that—"

"*Circulus vitiosus,*" Violet whispers from somewhere off screen.

Ian's head snaps toward the sound.

"*Circulus vitiosus in aeternum.*"

"The *fuck* did you just say?" Ian's eyes widen as he looks at something we can't see, then abruptly rises to his feet. "Violet, put that down. Put it down right this goddamn second…"

"What's wrong?" Waylon asks.

"Violet, stop…*Stop*…I swear, if you try to slit your wrist one more time, I will fucking murder you. *Violet!*" Ian bursts forward, instantly darting off screen.

There are sounds of a struggle happening off camera—grunting, fighting, skin hitting skin.

Waylon pinches the bridge of his nose.

"I will *always* be with the Vicious Circle." Violet's soft, sad voice drifts through the speaker. "VC forever…*circulus vitiosus in aeternum.* No…*No!*"

"Let *go,*" Ian grunts. "Give me the knife, Violet!"

Silence falls, immediately following the reverberating sound of skin slapping skin. There's a clang, like the sound of something hitting the floor. Then further struggle as Violet whimpers—

chapter twenty-five

Mercy

I DON'T REMEMBER standing.

I don't remember screaming.

I don't remember shoving the projector to the floor.

Yet I do remember glancing at Arlo, and I remember seeing him with his legs bent, his elbows on knees, his forehead against the heels of his hands, and his fingers tangled in his hair.

And I remember his silence…

He hadn't said a word as we watched, but that's not the silence I recall. It was the silence of his soul that I remember, a silence so deafening that it will haunt me forever.

It felt like moments where he ceased to exist.

It was the revelation of the truth that broke him.

It broke me.

It broke *all* of us.

And I had to make it stop.

The projector is on the floor, but the video still plays, the sound still surrounds us, and the echo of Violet Clare's broken whisper, *"Circulus vitiosus in aeternum…"* brings me to my knees as I sob.

And I whisper the words *with* her.

chapter twenty-six

ARLO

I DON'T KNOW who I am.

Everything I believed was a lie.

Everything Mercy went through was for nothing.

I let them hurt her in the name of a god who doesn't even exist.

I hurt her in the name of a god who doesn't exist.

I am nothing.

My life has been meaningless.

Meaningless until Mercy…

The haunted past of Ember Glen demands atonement, and my soul rips itself apart, offering the pieces of me as payment. I'm in pain, and I don't mean in the physical sense. I can't feel the wounds on my body while my soul is being shredded in this excruciating manner.

I exist in the shell of my body, trapped in this spiritual agony, and my only earthly awareness is of Mercy—my starlight—the strongest woman I've ever known. She had sensed all along that our world wasn't right, that something didn't fit, that we were all broken. I should have listened to her sooner, yet I resisted—and for far too long.

My resistance brought her here, to this place where she was forced to witness the *disgusting* truth she feared.

I brought this misery of humanity upon her.

My head is planted firmly on the heels of my hands, fingers gripping my hair and pulling so tightly it aches. I don't realize Mercy has moved until I hear the projector crash to the floor, and even then I'm frozen.

The sound of her sobbing doesn't just surround me, it *fills* me.

Where my soul is shredding, hers has been lit on fire.

Where my misery is quiet, hers is loud.

Where the void of my mind's entrapment is cold, hers is blistering hot.

The truth has set Mercy on fire.

Though her flames roar with pain too unbearable to fathom in this moment, I know that soon she'll burn to ashes only so she can rise renewed.

But the sparking embers of Mercy's soul will always remain…at least, I hope they will. I'll forever need the shock of her embers setting me on fire to ensure I never forget this moment when we learned the heinous truth—this moment where I realized that without her, I am nothing.

I was a soldier before her, blindly following orders.

And now, I am *hers*—a broken man willing to kneel before the fire's glowing truth while she burns for us all.

chapter twenty-seven

Mercy

NOT A WORD has been spoken about what we saw. I don't know how long I sat and sobbed. I've been left alone here, and I don't know where they all went. I know comfort was offered, though I can't say for sure by whom.

I couldn't stand to be touched.

I couldn't bear to listen to a single word that was spoken.

I shrugged off a gentle touch on my shoulder.

I covered my ears when someone asked if I was okay, if there was anything I needed.

I wanted to scream at them…

There's nothing you can give me that will make it right!

But I couldn't even bring myself to speak—no words had meaning. None except for Violet's dying whisper…

"Circulus vitiosus in aeternum."

Did Violet die that day?

Did she survive, only to suffer more in the days to come?

I suppose it doesn't matter. It was a century-and-a-half ago, and they're all long since dead now.

It almost feels like nothing matters…

My tormented thoughts want me to believe that, and I'm trapped within that belief for the longest time.

I allow myself to believe it as I sit alone, my back to the wall of stone that encloses the projector room. It must be hours that I wallow, that I remain in silence, encased in hopelessness and despair.

Yet eventually, a moment comes where I realize that a decision has to be made.

I have a choice to stay here. I could sit still, refuse to speak, refuse to eat or drink…I could decide that nothing matters and there's nothing left worth fighting for…I could lay down and wait for death—and I hate to admit it to myself, it's a choice I'm tempted to make. My heart hurts so much that I think it might give out, stop beating, and make the choice *for* me.

But then a realization dawns on me, a sudden understanding that I was missing before—the lesson I was meant to learn from watching the video records.

"I *have* a choice." The words tumble free from my lips, the first words I've spoken since learning the truth.

"Starlight?"

I turn my head toward the sound of Arlo's voice, sneaking in through the low entrance to the projector room. He must be out there in the alcove, maybe waiting for me, and I didn't even realize he was near. I've been so lost that I hadn't even sensed his presence.

"I thought you left."

"No," he says from the other side. "It was clear you needed to be alone, but I couldn't leave you. I wouldn't."

It's a relief knowing he's there. I needed the space, and the fact he recognized that warms my heart. As I crawl out from the depths of my mind after the initial shock of it all, I can feel the vibration of his existence flow through me, and my senses feel renewed. I find enough clarity to know I can't process this alone—and since I'm not alone, my thoughts easily tumble out of me.

"I'm horrified, Arlo. I never would have guessed that was how we came to be, and it makes me feel lost. A part of me wishes I didn't know the truth, but now that we do, I realize that it gives me a choice. We have a *choice*. The way we lived, the way they meant for us to die…we never had a choice before. We were forced to live the way we have because following the word of *God* was the only option. We were told there was nothing for us beyond the mountains. That leaving was impossible, that even if you *could* leave, there's nothing good out there.

"They told us we were safe in Ember Glen because we had rules and laws and were governed by God. But this God they spoke of was nothing more than a man who scribbled his violent obsessions in a book—a book we were told the Elders had possession of, yet it was here in Ember Glen the entire time. Everything they told us was made up; it was fiction. Every rule was just a game."

I pause to take a deep breath against my building anger.

"They told us we were lucky to be born here, but we weren't. Our ancestors were lied to, and those lies trapped them here—it trapped *all* of us here. We would've died by their lies, never knowing what was real. But the truth gives us a choice. We can take what we know and run…or go back and fight like hell to end this madness for good."

I could just be imagining it, but I can almost feel him drawing in a deep breath. "So tell me your choice, Mercy."

"You know my choice."

"I do."

"But you want to hear me say it."

"I'm not…I don't want to make assumptions about anything anymore." His tone is contrite. "I thought I had all the answers, but I was wrong. I was so…I was so *wrong*, Mercy." His voice breaks, and I hear him take a stuttering breath. "And you were right…"

It's unmistakable that he's crying. His heartache quickly brings me to my hands and knees, and I crawl to him. I move into the alcove through the low opening connecting the spaces, and I find him directly beside it, sitting to my right with his back leaning against the rock wall. He's cast in shadow with the light of a lantern on his opposite side, but when he looks at me as I move through, everything stops.

I've never seen such pain in his expression.

For a moment, we're both still.

And then he reaches for me.

I launch myself into his arms, and we hold on to each other stronger than we ever have before. We shed tears together from the agony of knowing the truth.

"I doubted you for so long," he mutters against the side of my neck, his tears slicking my skin. "I'm so sorry. I'll never doubt you again."

"None of this is your fault. It's not your burden. You were told what to believe; we *all* were."

He draws his arms back and reaches up to grab my cheeks, gently tugging to bring our faces together, leaning in to touch his forehead to mine. He peers into my soul, his blue eyes faded in the dim light.

"We wouldn't be here right now if it weren't for you." Arlo's tone is resolute. "You need to know that. None of this would've happened without you. We would never know the truth, and this choice wouldn't exist. All of this is happening because you chose to run from service, and if you make the choice—if you say the words—then Ember Glen ends with you. Say the words, Mercy, and we will *all* be with you. Say the words, and we'll burn this place to the ground."

My choice was already made, but his encouragement emboldens me further. "We're going to war, Arlo. We're going to take control of Ember Glen, destroy anyone who gets in our way, and leave the ashes of this wretched place behind us for good."

chapter twenty-eight

Mercy

"I FEEL LIKE I have more questions than answers," I tell the others, and I'm met with sounds of agreement.

All the women—save for a few with the children—have gathered in the main cavern, and we sit together near the crystal blue water. It radiates a pleasant warmth that rivals the cooler air of these underground spaces. The afternoon sun fills the cavern, and I'm so grateful for a clear day where the light can reach us.

The warm water was soothing against my skin when I took a quick dip before we gathered. Luna had showed me and Arlo to the shallow point of the pool so we could finally get clean. That shallow point happened to be where I'd accidentally witnessed her and Stefanie together, though I wouldn't tell her that.

One of the women, Silvia, brought us fresh clothes. For Arlo, she had some items from my father's room, and for me, she brought black outfits from my closet. Strangely, I find comfort in wearing black again. I'm no longer in red; I'm no longer a trial participant. Dressed in black, I feel solidarity with my sisters.

Though I was grateful that Silvia brought us clean clothes to wear, I expressed concern that she compromised her safety when it wasn't necessary. She explained that she's still in good graces with her husband, that she and two other younger domestics—wives who haven't yet had any children to worry over—had volunteered to go back and forth between the caves and the village. They hadn't engaged in the fight at the Homestead, and they've been supplying everyone here with all the resources they need for survival. Secretly, they've also been able to collect information about what's going on above to help keep everyone down here safe.

The three of them are young—only sixteen and seventeen years old, and brand-new wives—and their bravery is inspiring. They remind me of Delle, who I often think has been the true unsung heroine throughout our nightmare journey. I imagine Delle's choice to participate in the Trials of Dissension would have inspired other young women her age to *think*, to challenge their thoughts and beliefs.

I'm told that Delle's still alive, being kept within the Homestead. It's a relief to know they haven't made movement on her third trial, yet I know that decision could come any day now.

I swear I will save her before they hurt her again.

I will not leave Delle behind.

"Every day I have a new question," Luna agrees. "I still wonder where the Elders are, whether they know the truth about Ember Glen's founding. But they *must* know…"

"Not necessarily," says Enid, the woman who guided us into my house when we fled the Homestead. "They might be hidden away from the rest of the world, too. And maybe Ian Cole had, at some point, created the true version of the Impulse Edict—something that wasn't nonsense like his black journal. They could be in the dark about the truth just as much as we were."

"Perhaps," says another woman named Willow. "I might be able to believe that if *all* the Control become Elders and they go to the same place at the Shift, but only *three* of them become Elders. So, maybe those three could be hidden away from the world and sealed off from the truth. But then that means the retired Control are, too. How could there possibly be three secret locations that no one from the outside knows about? How could they keep everything a secret from all the people in Ember Glen, all the Elders, *and* all the retired Control?"

"But we know the place where the retired Control are sent. They go to the Land of Kings—the place where the Impulse doesn't exist. The retired Control are assigned domestics and sent to live there, where they are finally allowed to have a wife and children, their happily-ever-after…" Enid tilts her head with a puzzled look, trailing off as if she's just realized something. "Though…how do they have children with their domestics in the Land of Kings without seed from a donation? Who would be there to perform the fertilization?"

"No one." Arlo's voice is loud and clear, every head turning to look in his direction. He enters from the arched entryway that leads to the tunnels. "The Land of Kings doesn't exist."

I stand and rush to meet him as he moves into the cavern. "Where have you been? You said you'd be gone ten minutes, and it's been nearly two hours." I throw my arms around him as we collide, and though he groans in pain, he hugs me back. "Where did you go?"

I release him and step back, though I reach out my hand for him to take. He quickly latches onto it, locking our fingers together, and lifting our hands to kiss my knuckles.

"I wanted to test a theory," he says.

"What theory?"

I lead him back to the gathering of women, and we sit together on the ground beside Luna and Stefanie.

"I had a theory about where one of the passageways would lead, so I followed it. It led me to a forked path and I'm almost certain it's the one I was looking for. If it is, then I think I know the correct path to get to the Homestead."

"You *think*?" Luna chides.

"As I said, I'm almost certain."

"Certain enough that it's worth the risk of getting lost forever in the winding tunnels?" asks Luna.

"Sure." He shrugs, giving a dismissive look.

It gives me the urge to throttle some good sense into him—and Luna shares the same look of frustration.

"What did you mean when you said the Land of Kings doesn't exist?" Willow asks.

"I have no evidence to say whether I'm right or wrong, but my gut tells me it doesn't exist," he says.

"I suppose a gut feeling is as useful a measure as anything else when you have no measuring stick," Stefanie says.

Arlo nods. "Right."

"Did you…Did the Control know anything about the Vicious Circle?" a woman named Kinsley asks Arlo.

He shakes his head. "I didn't. Though I do remember Killian saying something odd about it at the Homestead before we were freed. Do you remember the speech he gave while holding the gun? He said something about Stefanie having cited ancient texts, *unholy* texts that were forbidden, which, of course, isn't true. It's a great way to twist the narrative in their favor to ensure the people would see Stefanie as unholy before setting her on fire. I think the Elders just told him to say that without offering further explanation. He would've done what they asked without question."

"That wouldn't surprise me," Stefanie says.

"Nothing surprises me anymore. Nothing ever really did…" My eyes drift to focus on a spot far away. "A new violent encounter every single month, and no way to escape it…"

There's a beat of quiet.

Then Kinsley speaks slowly. "Arlo…Do you think Killian knows the truth?" She pauses, and when he doesn't respond right away, she continues, "Killian Cole *has* to be a descendant of Ian Cole, don't you all agree?" She's met with nods and whispers of agreement. "Maybe the Coles have known everything all along…"

Arlo's brow furrows, his head tilting slightly to the side as he considers it. "I don't know," he says slowly. "Anything is possible at this point, but…no, I truly believe that he doesn't know anything."

He looks out at the women gathered. "I can't think of a single interaction I've had with Killian that suggests he might know more. I think the history of Ember Glen was buried intentionally. They wanted this to become a community to last generations, and the only way to achieve that goal would be to maintain the secret until it naturally died out. They would have had to stop telling their children.

"And maybe…maybe it's only revealed to the Elders. They would be the only people who need to know the truth, and they *only* need to know to ensure our survival, to ensure resources from the outside world are delivered."

"And how do they deliver those resources?" Kinsley asks. "I've honestly never even thought to ask, and it seems so silly now that I haven't. I guess in my mind I'd always just assumed that we were mostly self-sustaining."

"That's what they told you to believe, and why would anyone question it?" Arlo replies. "Our community has done well in creating many of the things we need for daily sustenance, but some things come from the outside, too. I don't know exactly how they arrive, but about once a month, the essentials are left for us to collect. We never know when or where the boxes will be left until they've already arrived, and then we go and collect them."

He chuckles humorlessly, glancing down. "They told us that *God* provided our supplies, and I'm embarrassed to admit that I never thought twice about it. The supplies came from *God*, and it's all I thought I needed to know."

There's another lingering silence that surrounds us, though I'm certain no one's mind is quiet.

"Do you think it's safe out there beyond the mountains?" Luna's question cuts through the silence, and all heads turn to look at her, though she's looking at the ground. "Do you think it will be better than it is here in Ember Glen? I just don't know what to think, and I'm…afraid.

"They always made the Civil War seem like it was so devastating across the entire country, like the world beyond the mountains was cast into an apocalypse. But maybe that was a lie, too. Maybe the Vicious Circle won their fights, and there's a place out there where women have rights and freedom. Some place that maybe even Stefanie and I could just…*be*."

"I don't think we can trust anything we were told," I tell her. "I think we have to question all of it." The wrinkle of her brow suggests she's not quite satisfied by my response. "I think anything's possible now, Luna. But the only way to know is to find out for ourselves…and we will."

She turns her chin to glance at me with a smile, and I'm glad that something I said gave her some hope. She deserves to have it.

"So, what do you think we should do, Mercy? What's the plan?" Enid asks.

I shrug. "I guess I don't really have one…not yet. I just know that we need to fight for control of Ember Glen and save as many women as possible before we find a way out."

"How are we going to save *anyone*?" a woman sitting farther away asks.

"If we leave these caves," Willow says, "the men will capture us the moment they see us, and there's no telling what they'll do. They put you through the trials just for turning and running from service. What are they going to do to us for fighting against our husbands at the Homestead? For taking their children away and hiding them here?"

"That's the point of fighting," Stefanie says. "You would have to be willing to end the life of any man who tries to take you."

"But that's not really fair, is it?" Enid says. "Not all the men want to see their wives punished. Some of them are only living the way they're told to live. They might even be on our side if they knew the truth. How can we fault them for falling victim to the same lies *we* fell victim to? This has gone on for generations, and no one knew. We can't just kill anyone who tries to stop us from taking control."

"But how do we know who's with us or against us until we fight?" Kinsley asks. "We can't know that *any* of them would be with us just for knowing the truth. There will undoubtedly be some who are still unwilling to relinquish control, some who may fight harder to keep it. We don't know their hearts and minds. And because we can't know which men are safe, we have to assume *all* men are dangerous."

There's a flurry of agreement from the women.

"But how can we justify faulting every man without giving him a chance to choose? If we do that, where do we draw the line?" Enid asks. "Should we go after the domestics who chose not to join us in the caves as well? The wives who turned to help their husbands fight against us at the Homestead? They're all victims of these lies, the same as us, aren't they?"

"So, what do we do?" Luna asks. "How can we give them a chance to choose when they don't know the truth?"

"I have an idea," Arlo says, and all eyes land on him. "I don't know if it will work, but I'd like to try."

He glances over at me, and I nod, encouraging him to speak.

"Inside the Homestead, there's a door that leads to a system of caves, which I believe are all connecting with these tunnels and passageways. If I can successfully navigate my way through, and sneak in through that door, there might be a way to show everyone the truth."

"How?" I ask.

"Theo Hughes has always been good with the technologies we have. He's set up all the broadcasts and livestreams, all the cameras and projections for the trials. He connects us for every call we have with the Elders, and I think—I *hope*—that maybe he can help us. If I can find my way into the Homestead with the reels, then perhaps he can broadcast the videos across Ember Glen."

"What makes you think he'll help?" Willow asks.

"I don't know if he'll help," Arlo replies. "But I have a feeling that he will. He's shown kindness and care toward Delle as her warden, and I believe he grapples with conflict over his role with her. I have great hope that once he knows the truth, he'll help us."

"Okay," Willow says. "Then let's say for argument's sake that your plan works, and the entire village sees the video records all at once. What do we do then? Domestics will be with their husbands; servants will be in their homes with their fathers and brothers. If the men choose to turn a blind eye to the truth, or if they simply don't believe it, then they'll keep the women from leaving and we won't be able to save them, anyway."

"That's true," Stefanie agrees, "but I think there's a way around that. And it will give us the time we need to plan this well. The full moon will be in nine days, and we all know there will be a short period of time where everyone is separate before service begins.

"The servants will gather in Sanctuary before heading into the forest. At the same time, the domestics will be left alone in their homes. And, of course, the men will have to make their monthly deposits to the Bank before heading out for the purge. If the timing is precise—if the videos broadcast at just the right time—there would be enough separation for everyone to have a moment to reflect. There would be just enough time to let them make a choice."

She's right…

I hadn't thought about that, but it would certainly allow time for everyone to make a decision. I'd nearly forgotten that the men would first have to gather at the Bank to make their monthly deposit. All the men of Ember Glen who *can* produce viable seed *must* provide it—and it can only be done on nights of service, on the only night pleasure is allowed.

I nod in agreement with Stefanie. "That would help us know the men who are with us and the ones who are against us. Those who still want to purge will have proven they don't care about us. I don't know about the rest of you, but that's enough justification for me."

"But what about the…" Kinsley begins, then lowers her voice as if the word itself is taboo, "*guns*? Killian had one at the Homestead, and we all saw the damage it did. Are there more guns? Will the Control have them?"

"There's no way for us to know. We were trained in how to use them at the last Shift, but they're only to be used in times of rebellion and war—something none of us ever really expected to see," Arlo explains.

"There's one gun for each of the seven Control, and our bands are required to gain access to them, though mine has already been deactivated." He twists the black band still affixed to his wrist absentmindedly. "No one person can access all seven guns—each of us has access to only *one*. And they can't be accessed without permission, which the Elders control electronically with a certain activation in the bands.

"It's possible that Killian may be the only one of them with a gun…" he says, "but it's equally possible that they all have. And given that the children have been taken, I wouldn't put it past the Elders to ask them all to be prepared to…take action as needed."

"And this is why I'm not…I can't just leave my children to fight," Willow says. "I refused to go the first time because it was too dangerous to try to rescue Stefanie. But this? There *will* be bloodshed over this. You know there will be."

"Yes, there will be bloodshed if we do this," I say honestly. "But there will be bloodshed all the same if we don't. Maybe I'm asking too much of you all to try to understand what the servants go through on nights of purging. Maybe it's unfair of me to ask anything of you at all.

"But the fact is that we are all *so* lucky to be here right now. We're free to speak openly about this, free to choose what we do next. But the women left behind are up there right now, and I beg of you to think of them as you would want someone else to think of you. You would want someone down here to think you deserve a chance. You would want someone to come back for you. You would want someone to fight for you. And we're the only ones who can fight for them."

I pause and take a deep breath. "We don't all have to go. We'll need some to stay behind with the children. And no one is going to force anyone to do something they don't want to do. But the more of us who are willing to fight for this, the better our chances will be. It's a game of numbers, and we won't know which side is outnumbered until the truth is revealed to everyone. I just…I can't stand by and watch my sisters endure another purge.

I *won't*. And I'm asking for your help."

Tears well in my eyes, and I glance down as I shake my head. It feels like hours slip by as I wait in silence for someone else to speak.

"So, this is the plan." Luna speaks with finality. "On the next night of service, Arlo will go through the tunnels to the Homestead. He'll find Theo Hughes and convince him to broadcast the video records just before it's time for the servants to leave Sanctuary. Once the videos are broadcast, we demand that the purge be canceled. The men who still insist on seeking service after learning the truth will have made their choice."

"And we should hold no remorse for shedding the blood of those men," I add. "By choosing to purge after they know the truth, they will have proven that they'd show no remorse for you."

I hear Arlo's sharp intake of breath, but I don't have to glance at him to know the look of pride in his eyes. I can feel the way he looks at me, his gaze reflecting his desire to praise my bold declaration.

And then I wait, unsure of exactly what might be said next.

Then finally, Enid stands and glances around at the others. "Well, it sounds like we have nine days to prepare, so we may as well get started on gathering the supplies and resources we'll need. I don't know about the rest of you," she says, "but I'm done living a life that was chosen *for* me. I'm ready to fight for freedom."

chapter twenty-nine
ARLO

"IT MUST BE difficult to write by lantern light." Mercy's voice surprises me.

I'd expected she'd come looking for me soon, though I didn't know exactly when. I lift my head from where I've been staring down at a blank journal in my lap, one in which I hoped to pour my thoughts onto the pages with new poetry…something to give to Mercy in case we're not able to retrieve the ones left behind in the Homestead.

It seems odd that the words evade me, though I have to wonder if it's due to the fact that I've had ample time to whisper my words of desire directly into her ear. Instead of flowing from my mind to the pages, my poetry has spilled directly from my lips and splashed inside her mind. Perhaps that's why it's difficult to write—because I haven't needed to leave anything unsaid.

I smile at her as I close the journal, placing it and the pen on the floor beside me. I straighten my legs from bent knees, then gesture for her to come to me.

"I wanted the quiet more than I wanted to write," I tell her as she crosses the dark enclosure—a hidden alcove we found together while exploring the caves.

"That makes sense," she says, lowering to sit sideways on my lap. She settles against me with her head on my chest. "The children were particularly chaotic today…I could nearly see your headache forming when you left."

I smile at that. "They can't stay down here much longer. All that energy has to go somewhere."

"I don't think it does. I think it just bounces off the walls and then goes right back into them."

"How's Adam?" I ask, wondering how Delle's brother is doing. Witnessing his sister being buried alive has obviously done something terrible to his mind.

Mercy sighs. "I wouldn't say that he's well, but I did get a small smile out of him today. So, it's progress, at least."

"That's great progress," I tell her. "You've done a lot for him over the last few days."

"It feels like the only way I can help Delle right now."

"Speaking of…"

"I know," she mutters. "I heard."

Silvia—one of the younger domestics who is secretly moving back and forth between the caves and the village—had come forward with news earlier today.

Delle's trial date has been set.

Service from Bloodshed—the final trial—is set to take place on the next night of service, which is the day we've chosen to fight for control of Ember Glen.

"At least the timing of it works out in our favor, don't you think? It should work for our plan…" Mercy's palm slides up my chest. "If they plan to set her up to begin her trial at the start of service, then we'll be able to find her easily. We'll be able to save her once the videos have been broadcast—maybe *while* they're being broadcast. We'll make sure she's freed before anyone lays a hand on her."

I rub my hand over her back as I place a kiss on the top of her head. "She'll be fine."

"What do you think they had planned? How do you think they mean to…kill her?"

I sigh. "I'm not sure I want to speculate on that too much. But if they arranged it to take place at the start of service, then I think it's safe to assume they mean to involve all the men of Ember Glen in her trial."

"All of them…and with the intent to make her bleed. I don't want to think about it." I can feel a tremor ripple through Mercy, and it's followed by a beat of quiet. Her fingers curl, gripping the open collar of my button-down. "It's so strange to think of it now as something separate from me. I never dreamed there would be a way out of it. I was prepared to die in the trials, right along with her. And I don't know what to make of the fact that it somehow feels *worse* to think of it happening to her than it does to think of it happening to *me*."

"I don't think that's strange, Mercy. I can empathize with the feeling."

She lifts her head to look up at me, reaching up to wrap her arms around my neck. Her forehead wrinkles as her eyes narrow on mine, giving me a serious expression. "If I had to help them bury you alive—stand by and watch it all happen while pretending I was okay—then I…I wouldn't have been able to do it."

"It was a waking nightmare, but it was *nothing* in comparison to what you went through. I won't allow you to minimize it just because you have compassion for me. That compassion is your greatest strength. It's one of the reasons I fell so hard for you, but I don't want you to misplace the use of it on me. I hurt you as much as any other man in this village, and I don't ever want you to forget it."

"Do you think I could ever forget? Arlo, I've forgiven you for every pain you've caused me, but none of them will ever leave my memory. They've left scars on me—the same as every other pain I've endured—but the scars you left are the only ones I *want*."

"Why would you *want* them?"

"Because they remind me of yours."

She draws her arms back from around my neck to lift my hand away from her waist, bringing it up between us as she presses her palm flat against mine. With her other hand, she traces the lines and ridges of the old burn scars across the back of my hand.

"You were only a child when you started to burn yourself, punishing yourself for urges, which I'm now certain we all have. You were praised for seeking pain instead of satisfying your need—a need you were told could *only* be satisfied by a servant once a month when you'd reached a certain age.

"And that was all for nothing. Now that we know what Hyatt did to Stefanie, we know the purges haven't done what they were intended to do. We know that whatever rules we were made to follow were arbitrary, made up by the original founders, who were doing nothing more than playing a game with money and power.

"We've both been scarred by this place, Arlo. You hurt *me* because they hurt *you*. And that doesn't make it right; it's not an excuse for anything… it's just the truth. But you should know that when I think about the hurt you've caused me, I think of your hands, too. When you hurt me, your hands belonged to them…but now they belong to *you*."

I lean my forehead against the side of her face, letting my eyes fall shut as I breathe her in. I bring my fingers between hers to lock our hands together before she pulls our shared grip against her chest.

"I won't hurt you with them again." I brush my nose across her cheek, nudging her hair away so I can whisper near her ear, "Not unless you ask me to."

She lets out her breath, sinking into my hold. I kiss her cheek as her eyes drift shut. "I could be convinced to ask you to…"

"No, starlight. I won't try to convince you of that. I'll only give you that when you beg me for it on your own."

"Then don't give me pain, Warden Rainn. Use your hands to give me *relief* instead. Take care of me." Her head turns and with her eyes still shut, she plants a whisper-soft kiss on my lips. "And then, perhaps, I'll beg you for it."

I groan with the visceral shift in her energy, and it rumbles through our lips as she kisses me again—it's light, gentle, teasing with soft pecks that seduce me to open for her. Mercy's tongue sneaks past my lips, deeply yet delicately licking against mine with soft sweeps that drag me under her spell.

So easily, I'm lost in her.

Every fear, every ache, every worry fades away.

I could stay like this forever, with her close against me and feeding me love through her delicate kisses. I still don't feel I've earned what she gives me, and this kiss feels too sweet for a man who doesn't deserve it…yet it's because she gives it so easily that I *want* to deserve it.

I want to be the man who deserves Mercy Madness.

Her grip on my hand tightens, and I feel her entire body tighten with it, holding my hand firm to her chest. I deepen our kiss, feeding my tongue so deeply that it takes her breath away. She gasps, breaking the kiss, and I take the opportunity for my lips to draw a trail across her cheek.

"Tell me what you want from me, starlight. How should I make you come?"

"Love," she says, twisting her head to look at me. She fully captures my attention with her silver gaze. "I can't believe you would ask me *how*…" My head inclines as I watch her, trying to work out what she's saying. And then her lips curl up at the corners. "You should be asking how *many*."

I'm on her in a flash.

Ignoring the ache in my arm, I wrap both around her to ease her landing, lowering her sharply to the hard stone floor. She lets out a yelp on the way down.

"Awfully bold of you, Mercy Madness." I grin at her as I plant one elbow on the ground beside her head, tracing my fingers down her throat.

"You like it when I'm bold," she says as a matter of fact.

I bend to follow the trail of my fingertips with my lips, dotting soft kisses down the line they draw from chin to chest. "I *crave* your boldness, at least as much as I crave these curves." I lift my head to watch my fingers glide up the slope of her breast. "So boldly tell me what you want from me. Ask me for anything, and you'll have it."

Moments pass as her chest rises and falls. I get lost in the motion of her curves as her breaths quicken, but my eyes are torn away, called back to her face when she finally speaks. "I want you to undress me…"

That doesn't seem like a very bold demand, so I look at her expectantly, waiting for her to say more.

"Strip me bare…"

She looks so serious that it draws my face closer to hers, and I wait. Looking deep into her eyes, I know there's something more to this that I'm just not understanding.

"You and I have never been fully undressed together. Every time we've come together, one or both of us has been at least partially dressed."

I nod, realizing she's right. "It was always in secret or in a rush…"

Her hands find my face, thumbs brushing my cheeks. "I want to feel your skin against every inch of me. No barriers between us, no rushing." She lifts her head from the floor as she pulls me closer, brushing her lips over mine. "No secrets. Just my skin against yours."

Sweet sin…

That sounds like the most provocatively *perfect* thing I could ever give this woman.

I force her head back to the ground as I kiss her hard, and she moans into my lips. Her fingers sink into my hair and tug, triggering a shockwave of need that makes me shiver. I sit up sharply, pulling out of her grip to the sound of her whimper. I sit back on my heels between her spread legs and grab her left ankle, moving it in front of me. I drop the heel of her boot into my lap and start to untie the laces, my eyes locked on hers as I remove her boot and sock. I toss the shoe over my shoulder, and it lands somewhere behind me with a heavy thud.

Lifting her leg up with my hand at her ankle, I lean in to kiss the side of her knee. I raise it a little higher and kiss the back of her leg, where it creases behind her knee. She startles at the touch of my lips, drawing in a quick breath, so I kiss her in the same spot again, eliciting the same response, which gives me absolute satisfaction.

Grinning down at her with my lips pressed to her skin, I start to nip at the inside of her thigh, watching as her stomach visibly clenches. My cock twitches at the sight of her pink lips parting to gasp before whispering my name. I repeat it all with her other leg—removing her boot, kissing behind her knee, then gently nipping along the inside of her thigh.

I cross my arms before grabbing her hips, and with a quick twist, I roll her onto her stomach. She plants her palms on the ground as she lifts onto her knees, only just enough so she can shift her body backward through her pressing palms, ass pressing toward me, back arching like a cat.

I reach forward to unzip her layered black skirt, then slip my fingers beneath the waistband—beneath the underwear, too—and slowly drag both barriers away. I bend over Mercy to kiss her skin, covering each exposed inch with my lips.

Slowly, sensually, I bare her hips and the breathtaking curve of her gorgeous ass. I ease the fabric down to her knees, and she lifts each leg so I can remove it entirely, tossing it aside.

I take a moment to appreciate the beauty of Mercy on her hands and knees in front of me, hips squirming, back arching, already so needy for my touch.

When she whimpers, desperation punches through my gut, and I absolutely *must* taste her. I cup her cheeks in my palms, squeeze and spread as I shift my knees back. I lower my head behind her and dive in to taste her. Mercy rewards me with a gasp and a moan, pressing her ass back to bury my face as my tongue finds her pussy.

I lick until she twitches, spending minutes right there with my face submerged in the delicious rising waves of her lust. I get lost in her perfection, obsessed with her taste and scent. My hands are around her thighs, fingers digging into her flesh to hold her still as I try to satiate this never-ending thirst.

This—right here between her thighs—is my favorite place in the entire fucking world. I would move mountains for a single taste.

"I'm…" Mercy pants. "Love, I'm…*Oh…*"

Her hand swings back and smacks my forearm, and the strike is enough to bring me back. I promised her I would never hurt her with these hands, yet my fingers are sunk so deep into her fleshy thighs that I know they must *ache*.

All at once, I release, and her body launches forward, but I quickly grab her hips to drag her back and steady her. The hand she smacked me with reaches back again, her palm covering the back of my hand on her hip. Her head hangs as she fights to catch her breath.

How long was I there between her thighs?

"I'm not ready to come yet…" Her fingers curl and her nails dig into my knuckles. "You nearly made me come and I'm still half-dressed…"

I blow out a breath, knowing I have to pace myself.

I let go of her hips, slowly bringing my palms over the curve of her cheeks. I slide my hands up her back, then slip my fingers beneath the hem of her black lace top. I move in close behind her on my knees and drop my hands along her sides, slipping around to the front of her to palm her breasts beneath her shirt.

I fold over Mercy's back, molding to her body as her head rises, the back of it touching my shoulder. I nuzzle my face into her hair, brush my nose across her cheek…I kiss along her jawline, lick down her neck, paint her skin with her scent which coats my tongue.

Closing my arms around her waist, I lift her as I rise on my knees, keeping her flush against me as we kneel together on the bedrock. She raises her arms as I peel off her shirt and toss it away, then pull off her bra beneath.

She sighs the moment she's bare, relieved, letting her weight fall back against me.

"Take off your clothes," she whispers as my hands roam over her body. "Let me feel you hard against my back."

I squeeze her breast, drawing my fingers back slowly across her nipple to tease her. "Move forward, starlight. Put your hands on the wall and wait for me."

I guide her forward, moving until she can flatten her palms against the stone wall when she bends. I have to force myself to back up with the way she arches so beautifully, but I hastily remove my clothes because it's what she asked me for.

And I'll give this woman *anything* she asks me for.

As soon as I'm naked, I press in behind her, nudging her knees apart with mine between hers. I reach over her head to wrap my hands around her wrists, her palms still flat against the rock wall that rises before her. She whimpers as I dip to kiss the back of her neck, making sure she feels my hard cock just begging to force its way between her cheeks.

"Sweet sin, Mercy. I'm so hard for you right now. So fucking hard…"

"Fuck me," she commands. "I want to feel how hard you are when I come."

I lasso one arm around her waist and angle her hips. My fingers slip down over her curls as I eagerly reach for her clit, and I know I've found the right spot when her entire body jumps at my touch. I find an easy, gentle rhythm with my fingers, and I continue until her belly is clenching, twitching against my arm, her entire body trembling.

"Arlo…I can't…I want…."

"You want my cock?" I kiss her shoulder.

Her head bobs in a jerky nod.

"Are you trying not to come right now, starlight? Are you letting me edge you until you have me buried deep inside you?"

Again, a tense bob of her head.

I rub harder, faster, and then abruptly, I stop.

"No…I need…"

"What do you need?"

"Inside me…"

"Fast? Hard? Gentle? I want you to tell me."

She hangs her head, gasping, steadying her voice. "Fuck me hard. Make me come fast, even if it hurts."

I drop my head onto her shoulder. "Sweet sin."

I flatten my palm over her curls to draw her body back, encouraging her to arch deeper, to angle her hips for me to enter. I bring my arm around behind her so I can fist my cock and run the tip along her slick folds. I thrust inside her in one long, deep stroke, and we groan in unison at the shared relief of being connected. I hook my arm beneath her waist again to find that swollen nub, rubbing in a steady rhythm that quickly draws her into tension.

"Yes. Warden Rainn, *yes*…I feel you…every inch…"

Just as she wanted, every inch of my skin is touching every inch of hers, and *fuck*, it feels so perfect.

She feels so perfect.

I turn my face against her shoulder, press it into her neck and whisper, "Wildflowers and starlight."

She gasps, as if it's my words that cause the full body tremor down her spine and not my fingers on her clit or my cock deep inside her.

I start to move, giving her fast, hard strokes that have us grunting together with every slap of our bodies. We move with pure carnality, letting our bodies take control. Our movements are utterly indecent, vulgar thrusting in physical desperation. Yet each motion is driven entirely by our deeper connection—our spiritual devotion, our unconditional love. The physical need for one another couldn't exist on its own; sex would *never* feel this perfect without the guiding passion from our souls.

I plant my palm over Mercy's mouth as she cries out with her release, keeping my rhythm steady with my cock and my fingers to draw it out as long as I can.

I don't stop until she's shaking—until she reaches back to *make* me stop—and when I settle to be still inside her, she lets out a small chuckle. She turns her head slightly over her shoulder, not enough to fully look at me, just enough to get my attention.

"That's one." Through her profile, I can see her smile. "I want more."

Sweet sin, she wants more.

And because she demands it, I give until she's spent.

And I'll give her so much more once we've won this war.

"PROMISE ME YOU'LL be careful," Mercy whispers into my ear. She rises onto her toes to wrap her arms around me tighter.

It's when her fingers slip up from the back of my neck, tangling in my hair, that I feel it—the pang of saying goodbye once again. My arms circle her waist, pulling her closer as I draw in a breath filled with the wildflower scent of her hair.

"When all of this is over," I whisper, "promise me we'll never say goodbye again."

She nods, her cheek brushing mine as she gives a final squeeze. "I promise."

Reluctantly, I let her go, let her slip from my arms as she gradually releases me. I stand still and stare at her as Luna hooks her hand through the crook of Mercy's arm to drag her back—as if she knows there's no escape for me if Mercy isn't anchored.

"You really should go," Luna says. "You'll have to find Theo without getting caught, and even then, he'll need enough time to set up the broadcast without the rest of the Control finding out."

"I know. I'm going, just..."

Sweet sin, just one more.

I reach out to snatch Mercy's wrist and yank her from Luna's grip. I drag her straight into my arms, cradle the back of her head in my palm, and kiss her hard.

Hard, but not long because time is running short.

I drop my forehead to meet hers. "I know I'll never convince you to run if this all goes sideways, so I won't bother trying. I'll just tell you that I love you, Mercy Madness, and I need you to survive." I sink my fingers into her hair, hold her in place, press my cheek to hers, and whisper in her ear, "I haven't spent nearly enough time with my face between your legs, and I won't be able to rectify that if you get yourself killed."

I pull back to look at her, and find a grin on her face, her eyes fluttering open to meet mine. "I can't think of a better reason than that to survive," she jokes. Her chest rises, then her shoulders drop as she exhales. "I love you, Arlo Rainn."

I plant a heavy kiss on her forehead.

I nearly give into the urge to lift her over my shoulder, to drag her away with me through the tunnels to avoid this rapidly approaching battle for freedom.

Yet I know I can't do that.

This fight is hers, and I have to let her lead it.

I force myself to release her, then sling the messenger bag with the video reels over my shoulder. I take a step backward, and she lurches against Luna's hold. I know it was unintentional—a natural urge she has to be with me. I know it because I feel it, too.

There's a painful tension through the invisible rope that binds us, and my muscles strain to fight it. I force myself to take another step backward.

"You're the sinner we all needed, starlight." Another step. "And you're the only one who can lead us out of hell."

With all my might, I turn away from her, flinching as the imaginary rope snaps, untethering us as we separate on the brink of war.

With a quick pace, I head into the dark passageway to leave for the Homestead, charging out of sight because I'd never be the man who deserves Mercy Madness if I didn't fight for her…and fighting for her means fighting for what's right.

So tonight—beneath the light of the full moon—we fight for freedom.

chapter thirty

Mercy

THE SUN HAS nearly set, and the full moon will be rising soon. The last remaining glimmer of daylight gives way to the falling night, crushed beneath the descending darkness. The way the light fades beneath our feet feels visceral, like our steps are stomping out the final embers of the dying sun.

Most of the domestics have arranged themselves around the village in smaller groups, spread out and ready to fight. We know there will be some men—and probably some women, too—who will reject the truth when it's revealed to them. We're prepared for those who reject it to react in one of two ways.

Our hope is that they'll recognize their part in our suffering—that they'll stand down and step back. But that's not the reaction we expect; that's not the reaction we've prepared for.

Tonight is meant for the purge, and the men are primed for violence.

The men see this night as divine, a night that's *owed* to them after the month-long suppression of their depraved urges. Yet we're going to stand before them once the truth has been revealed, demanding that their one glorious night of debauchery be canceled immediately, insisting that we be granted freedom from service and forced domesticity.

We already know this will end violently.

So, we're prepared to meet them where they stand.

It looks like most of the men have already arrived at the Bank to make their deposit before the purge—a few here and there crossing the way to enter. The servants have already gone to Sanctuary and have been there for a while now. The domestics are home alone, and the Control could be anywhere.

My goal is to be at the center of the action because these women are looking for me to lead. Though it's terrifying, I'm committed to this fight, and even if I don't survive, maybe some of the others will see freedom come morning.

And the thought of that is worth risking *everything* for.

Stefanie and Luna make their way with me behind the houses, winding through the village in shadowed spaces that provide good cover in the dark. It's not a challenge to make it from my home to the backyard of the house nearest the sloped path without being seen. But it *will* be a challenge to make it across the open village square to Sanctuary.

We can make it soundlessly up the sloped path that leads from the village to the square—grass lines the edges of the gravel path, which will keep our steps muted. But once we reach the top and the ground levels out, the gravel beneath our feet will surely give us away, and there's no way around it. And of course, there's the possibility that they might simply *see* us running across the square. It's a vast open space without any spots to hide.

I turn to Luna and Stefanie behind me and speak in a quiet voice. "We just have to make a run for it. When I move, you follow. Don't stop, don't look back, just *run*."

"We'll be right behind you," Luna says.

I look out to scan the path and find it's all clear.

The opportunity is now…and I decide to run.

We take off, running single-file up the narrow patch of grass that lines the upward-sloping gravel pathway. As I approach the top of the incline, I steel myself against the fear of being seen, not knowing if the Control may be in the square or watching from the Homestead. Though truthfully, it doesn't matter if we're seen—we have to push onward all the same.

The square opens before us, and my boots land on gravel. The sound seems so much louder than I anticipated, and it's further amplified by Luna's and Stefanie's footfalls as they follow. The slipping stones beneath our feet only serve to slow us down, so we push harder, running as fast as we can across the square.

Sanctuary is in sight…

We can make it.

We're halfway across the square when bright lights switch on at the exterior of the Homestead.

"Hurry," I urge. "Faster."

"Mercy…" Luna's voice holds a tinge of warning.

"Go!" Stefanie shouts, and the volume of her voice alone suggests that we've already been seen.

And Killian Cole's booming voice only confirms it. "I see you, Mercy Madness!"

I glance right, watch as he charges down the front steps of the Homestead, and panic strikes me.

"Mercy, *stop!*" I see Owen running out the front doors of the Homestead, and he chases after us, too.

My lungs ache, my calves tighten as my feet slip over the shifting stones, but I keep going.

"Open the door!" I cry out, hoping the servants in Sanctuary will hear me, that one of them will let us in. "Please, open the *door!*"

Luna and Stefanie shout with me.

We run, we scream, we *hope.*

I reach the bottom of the stone steps that lead to Sanctuary, and the moment my boot lands, one of the two heavy wooden doors swings inward.

"Mercy?" It's Cambria at the door.

"Let us in!"

Her forehead wrinkles, but then she must spot Killian charging after us because her eyes widen.

She steps back. "Hurry!"

I reach the landing and stop, turn sideways to usher Luna and Stefanie through first. "Come on!"

Luna enters first, closely followed by Stefanie.

And Killian's halfway up the steps.

Cambria grips my arm.

I turn as she pulls me, then sprint across the threshold and slam to a stop just behind her. We turn together and see Killian crash to a halt. His hands come up, slamming against the closed door on one side and the frame on the other, bracing himself in the opening.

"You can't come in." Cambria hastily steps forward, blocking the way, holding the door open with her hip.

Killian cocks his head to the side. "Cambria—"

"You can't come in," she repeats. "You don't have permission from me, so there's no way you'll get permission from *all* of us."

I gape at her, stunned at her boldness, especially with Killian.

"I don't need to come in, Cambria. I just need *her* to come *out.*"

Maybe I only see it now because I know the truth about his ancestor, but Killian and Ian Cole share the same darkness in their eyes, the same penchant for obsession, control, and violence.

I move to step in front of her, but her hand swings out to stop me, her eyes never leaving Killian.

"Ten minutes." She grips the side of the door and starts to push it shut.

Killian sticks his foot out to stop it, the toe of his polished leather shoe slamming into the wood.

Cambria's head drops to look down at his foot, then she slowly drags her gaze up to his face. "Killian Cole, remove your foot from our Sanctuary *at once.* You're a man of *God* and you need to behave as such. This night of service has not yet begun, and until it *has,* I suggest you control your Impulse."

He drops his head and chuckles darkly before looking up at her from beneath his lashes. "Cambria Miller, you're testing my *fucking* patience."

"And I'm sure you'll test mine for the remainder of the night, so let's call it even. *Ten. Minutes.*"

This time, she moves behind the heavy door and shoves, forcing his foot out before she slams it shut. She spins to face me, and for a few moments, we only stare at each other. Then, we move at the same time, and throw our arms around one another.

She exhales heavily, her body sinking just before she releases me and steps back. "That was terrifying," she says. "I thought he was going to force his way in. What are you doing here? Where have you been?"

"There's so much I have to tell you, and I will." I glance around, seeking Ellary, expecting to see her lying broken in a bed. But the beds are all empty, so she must be doing better—yet I don't see her among the servants gathering around us. "Where's Ellary? I need to see her. Where is she?"

Cambria's lips part, but she doesn't speak, and her relieved expression melts into something somber. "Mercy, she—"

"Where is she? I know she survived the fall; Arlo told me she did. And she's had all this time to heal…Is she walking? Is she moving without trouble?" The words all come out of me in a rush, filling time, delaying her from telling me what the glassy sheen over her eyes implies.

Cambria's head falls with the weight of the truth. "No, Mercy." She lifts her head again to look at me as a tear streaks down her cheek.

My eyes shift, drifting away to peer at a faraway spot, my vision becoming unclear and unfocused. My eyes feel warm and wet, but I can't be crying…

Because there's nothing to cry about.

I blink and shake my head, forcing my gaze to refocus as I look squarely at Cambria. "Where's Ellary?"

Cambria shakes her head.

"Where's *Ellary?*" I insist.

"She died! She's gone, Mercy. Ellary's *gone.*" Cambria gasps as she looks at me, and I don't know what she sees in my expression, but she hurries to close the distance between us, grabbing and pulling me into a rough hug. "Ellary died. She's dead, and they didn't even hold a remembrance. No honor or gratitude was given." She grips my shoulders as she pulls back, looking directly into my eyes, waiting until I meet her gaze. "Mercy?"

"I thought she was okay…"

Her hand touches my cheek, her thumb brushing beneath my eye as if she's brushing away a tear.

Am I crying?

"No. No, she wasn't okay. She never even woke up."

"When did she…"

"Six days ago."

"Oh…*no*…" Tears fall like rivers down my cheeks.

"I know," she mutters sadly. "I know…"

"Where…where is she?"

"You can't see her, Mercy."

"But where *is* she?"

"They burned her after she died. All that's left of her are…ashes."

"I-I can't see her?"

Cambria shakes her head.

"So, she's just…"

"She's gone."

Ellary's gone.

"Killian did this," I mutter.

Cambria nods. "He did. He pushed her; I know he did. Mercy, I'm afraid. I'm afraid to go out there tonight and face him. We're *all* afraid."

I look up to find my sisters have gathered around us, and every face is awash with fear. I turn my attention back to Cambria, giving her a questioning look.

"I don't know where you've been or what you know, but things in Ember Glen have turned for the worse," she tells me. "The Control, the husbands… they're so angry that the children are gone and that half the domestics have disappeared. Their rage has been building since the incident at the Homestead, and we don't know what will happen to us tonight in service. We have to serve—we know we do—but how can we walk out there and offer ourselves freely, knowing how angry they are tonight? And what if the Control brings their guns? What if their Impulse is to use them against us?"

Their fear surrounds me, consumes me, triggers my compassion so strongly, it's sobering…and it reminds me why I'm here. I have to take my despair over the loss of Ellary and box it up, wrap it tightly, and store it away somewhere deep inside my mind. Ellary is gone, but these women are still here and they need me.

I press my eyes shut. I allow myself to endure a single sob that twitches through my gut, let out the cry that claws up my throat and forces its way out from between my lips. And then I straighten my spine, pull back my shoulders, and lift my chin as I open my eyes.

"A plan is in motion—that's why we're here. And I'm going to tell you *everything*," I begin. "But know that if everything goes right, none of you will serve tonight. None of you will ever have to serve again."

chapter thirty-one

Mercy

"WHAT'S HAPPENING, MERCY? I don't hear anything playing yet." Cambria's ear is pressed to the door. "The men are out there. They expect us to be in the forest already for the purge. What do we do?"

I told the servants everything. I told them about the video records, and the real story of Ember Glen. I told them about the plan for Arlo to engage Theo's help in broadcasting the videos. They listened to me, and many of them seem to believe me.

The ones who don't believe me insist upon proof, and that's understandable. Yet I don't know when that proof will be unveiled because we're still waiting for the damn videos to broadcast.

They're late…

What's going on?

Is Arlo okay?

What am I supposed to do?

"Let me think," I tell Cambria as I pace the floor.

"The longer we wait to serve them, the worse this night will be," says Phoebe, one of my sisters in service.

"You said there was proof," Ruby says. "I want to believe you, but if there's no proof, then we *must* go out and serve. It's our duty."

I whirl around to face her. "It's not your duty to serve those men, Ruby. I swear to you, it isn't. Everything I told you is true. I just…I don't know what's going on with the videos. Something must have happened to delay them."

They're delayed…

What would delay them other than being caught, captured, or killed?

"We've seen the videos," Luna says in my defense, gesturing to indicate herself and Stefanie. "I promise you, it's real. What Mercy told you is true. Service is not God's will for you; it was the will of *men*."

Phoebe points at the door. "And those men out there have provided for us. We owe them our gratitude for that…We owe them our *service*."

"Those men have done *nothing* for you. They are not the providers in this village. Our providers are right here." I point to where Luna and Stefanie are standing. "The men do *nothing* in comparison to what the domestics do. Domestics are the pillar on which our community stands, and truthfully, they should be named the same as us—*servants.*

"We may serve the men's brutality once a month, but domestics serve their husbands daily in all other manners of speaking. Those men who purge with us go home when the sun rises, and their domestics take on the burden of caring for the remainder of their needs for the rest of the month." I glance over at Stefanie. "And some of them have served in violence."

Stefanie gives a brief nod, then steps forward and raises her shirt, pushing down the waistband of her skirt to reveal the letter 'H' that Hyatt had carved into her flesh.

"What is…" Phoebe steps closer, staring. "Is that a scar?"

"Yes," Stefanie says, covering it again. "My husband gave me that. You recall Hyatt Price? The man who set your sister Ivy Jane on fire. Sadly, her *service* that night was meaningless since he hurt me when he returned from service that morning because his breakfast wasn't ready. Violent men are violent, whether during a purge or in their homes with their wives. You will not spare the domestics from violence and fear by serving those men tonight. I'm sorry to tell you that you never have."

Cambria looks around at the servants. "I feel like my eyes were opened when Ellary was pushed. Killian's Impulse to shove her from the cliff proves that his violent urges were not satisfied from the previous purge. I think what Mercy's telling us must be true. I think the Impulse is a lie. And given how angry those men are that so many of us helped Mercy when we were gathered at the Homestead…I fear that some of us will die tonight in service."

I smile watching Cambria as she speaks, my heart beating wildly to hear her, of all people, speak those words. *Cambria*—the woman who always wanted to feel the pain from her service in reverence of how dutifully she served.

Her eyes are open…*finally* open.

"I have faith in Arlo…faith that he and Theo will succeed. You will have your proof tonight, Ruby." I turn to Luna and Stefanie. "I think we have to stall. The timing is all wrong. We expected everyone would still be separate when the videos were broadcast."

"You're right," Stefanie agrees. "The men won't wait forever."

"And by the sound of it," Luna says, "they're growing angrier the longer the servants make them wait."

"What if Arlo fails?" Phoebe asks.

"Arlo won't fail, not with this." I pause to take a steadying breath, then I turn to face Cambria. "We need to stall the men. We need to give them a plausible reason for why you're all making them wait, and I think I have an idea. I need you to open the doors, and I need you to speak to Killian."

"What? Me?"

"Yes. He listened to you before, and he'll listen to you now. You need to convince them that the servants *want* to come out, convince them that you're all planning to serve tonight."

"No, I can't—"

"Cambria, *listen.* Tell him that you all want to serve, but you're afraid of retaliation for what happened on the day that Arlo and Stefanie were meant to burn. Draw him into a negotiation."

"But what am I supposed to negotiate?"

"Tell him…" I pause to gather my thoughts. "Tell them that you want to negotiate certain restrictions for tonight's service; that you want to limit certain acts of violence."

She shakes her head. "They would *never* go for that. And even if they agreed, it wouldn't matter. Any acts they commit against us tonight will be forgiven by God. They could lie and say they agree, then commit those acts anyway."

"That doesn't matter. It's not the point. *No one* is serving tonight—that will happen over my dead body. The point is to stall until the broadcast comes on. You can do this, Cambria. Just keep him talking…for as long as you can."

She's hesitant. I can see the muscles in her neck working as she swallows hard. Her eyes cast around the room, but finally, they land on mine.

"You swear that it's true?" she asks me. "Can you swear to me that everything you told us is true and there are videos to prove it?"

"I swear it, Cambria. On my own life, I swear."

Slowly, she nods. "Okay. I'll try."

THE DOUBLE DOORS to Sanctuary are open wide and Cambria stands between them. She remains inside, just a few feet back from the threshold. Though I know the men believe that entering Sanctuary is a sin against God's will, it's still unnerving to see her so exposed. The crowd of men are gathered outside, and their voices rise in anger and frustration.

Killian slowly approaches, moving away from the gathered men to cross the gravel-covered square alone. He comes to a slow stop at the bottom of the stone steps, and for a beat, he watches Cambria. Then, he raises his arm to demand silence.

As the voices of men fade toward quiet, I see something I hadn't noticed before. I'd been so focused on getting to Sanctuary when we ran that I must have missed them. Two screens are set up in front of the Homestead on either side of the staircase, and what they show makes my blood run cold.

On screen is a livestream from within the forest—from the clearing where the bonfire roars high and hot. Delle is positioned away from the fire, her wrists bound in rope. The ends are tied to trees on opposite sides of the clearing, stretching her arms out and up. She stands barefoot on the ground, wearing no clothes except for underwear and a bra on this cold November night.

Seeing her like that—alone, shivering, and frightened—sends anxiety tearing through me.

Why haven't they broadcast the truth yet?

"Cambria," Killian's voice is deceptively gentle. "Would you please enlighten me as to what the fuck is going on in there?"

"We have some demands before serving tonight."

Killian chuckles. "My apologies if I'm a bit confused. I thought there was a full moon tonight." He turns his head, lifting his chin skyward, spotting the full moon as it's revealed from behind a gray cloud that's sweeping away. "Yes, there it is." He turns back to look at Cambria. "And under the full moon, it is your *duty* as a servant to come out to the forest and *serve*. So I'm going to need you to be very explicit with your words, if you're capable of such articulation, because none of us understand why you're all in *there* when you should be out *here*, asking how you may serve our needs."

It's subtle, but I see her pull her shoulders back. "On the day Arlo Rainn and Stefanie Price were meant to burn, some of us behaved in ways that were…inconsistent with our role as servants. Naturally, we fear retaliative acts being performed against us out of spite for our actions that day. And for us to serve such retaliative acts would be beyond the scope of our duty. We are beholden to serve the needs of men by their *Impulse*, not by their acts of aggression in revenge. Now, if you would kindly receive our requests in good faith, and grant us certain reassurances for this night, then we will gladly come out to service you all." Cambria pauses. "Was I explicit enough with my words? Or should I find a way to be more *articulate*?"

Killian shows a tight grin, glancing down at his feet as he takes a single step up the stone staircase. "Quite articulate." He looks up at her. "Let me grant you the reassurance that no retaliation is sought *tonight*. The men you are beholden to simply want to purge, and it is their holy right to do so. Now, tell me what must be done so you will all come out and serve God's will."

"No guns," Cambria says.

Killian cocks his head to the side, watching her.

"You will not allow guns at service, tonight or any night hereafter."

Slowly, menacingly, Killian climbs the steps without speaking a word. He stops on the landing, looks at her for a beat, then takes a single step forward. He stands right at the edge of the threshold, though thankfully, he doesn't cross it.

He lowers his voice. "Are you asking me to deny my Impulse to make you come around the barrel of my gun? Surely, you don't wish to deny us both such *fun*, Cambria Miller."

Her neck works as she swallows, eyes widening slightly, though she manages to hold her ground. "That's precisely what I'm saying, Killian Cole. Guns are tools of war; they were never meant to be involved with service."

He nods, pursing his lips. "Perhaps you're right." He reaches behind him, lifts the bottom of his jacket, and pulls a gun from his waistband. "I'll make a deal with you. In good faith, from *both* sides, we'll relinquish one gun per servant. I'll put down this gun, and you send out a servant. *Or...*" He stretches his arm, aiming his gun at me. "Send Mercy out to service us all, and we will relinquish every gun immediately, banning them from use in service forevermore."

I fight the panic that sharply rises, keeping my body still and steady.

"No. She's not coming out," Cambria says. Killian turns his arm along with his eyes, pointing the gun at her instead. Her eyes press shut for a moment, but she doesn't falter, quickly opening them again. "Put down your gun, and I'll come out."

His eyes scan her face, and he looks pleased with her response.

I'd been so busy watching the gun that I hadn't noticed Owen charge up the steps with Wesley right behind him, each holding two guns—one in each hand.

"Hand it over," Owen demands as he climbs onto the landing.

Killian glances over at him. "I have this situation under control."

"You most certainly do *not*," Owen says. "Their request is fair. Our guns were never meant to be involved in service. Any one of us might mistake the power we feel when holding one as an Impulse that must be satiated. Half the domestics have already disappeared. Would you like someone to accidentally plow through half the servants as well?"

Accidentally?

How would one accidentally *fire a gun at multiple servants?*

I'm outraged by that statement alone, but by sheer force of will, I bite my tongue. Cambria is stalling successfully, and any time we can buy is necessary.

Owen tucks one of the two guns he holds into the back of his waistband, then holds out his empty hand to Killian. "If you want to purge, hand it over."

Killian turns sideways, facing Owen fully. "Are you really suggesting that we leave ourselves and our men unprotected right now? Do you see who's here?" He points back at me. "Mercy Madness has crawled straight out of hell and barged back into Sanctuary like nothing's changed. And she brought *domestics* with her, no less! Clearly, she's been keeping them captive somewhere and poisoning their minds—she's probably poisoning the minds of the children, as well!"

"The only ones who have poisoned our minds are the men of this community," Stefanie says, and all heads snap in her direction.

"And that one should already be dead!" Killian bellows.

"Once the servants are out," Owen says, "we can deal with them, and we will. But our men need to purge, and that *must* come first."

With a sneer, Killian points his gun at the ground, swings his arm forward, and hands it to Owen.

Owen looks over at Cambria after he takes the gun from Killian. "There. The guns are gone. We'll take them back to the Homestead right now."

Killian huffs in frustration, turning to face Cambria again as he lifts his palms to show her his empty hands. "There. See? You got what you wanted. Now, will you *kindly* exit your Sanctuary and do your duty?"

Where is the damn broadcast?

Cambria looks over her shoulder at me, and I know she doesn't know what else to say.

But it doesn't matter because Killian crosses the line a moment later. He shamelessly charges into our Sanctuary—a space no man is allowed to enter—and snatches Cambria around the waist.

"No!" I shout as he lifts her from the floor.

He backs out of the open doorway, dragging Cambria in his arms. He swings her around in front of him, sets her on her feet, and shoves her forward. She tries to stay on her feet as she's flung toward the steps, but she trips and falls, rolling as she lands sideways on the gravel at the bottom.

"Gentleman," Killian announces. "You've been given permission to enter Sanctuary and take your selected servant by force." He gestures toward the wide-open doors at his side. "By all means...help yourselves."

Cambria climbs to her feet and backs away as a sea of men rush toward Sanctuary. Killian chases her down the steps as the wave swallows her whole, and then, she disappears...

This is not what we had planned.

This is not how this will end.

I shout at the others to shut and barricade the doors, but I don't stay to help them. Instead, I run full speed after Killian Cole.

I fight the hands of desperate men as I shove my way through the crowd, force my way past them down the steps, and rush out into the open space of the village square.

I leave the sound of pandemonium at my back, forcing myself to ignore the servants' screams, and I dash across the pebbled-ground chasing Killian as he chases Cambria.

"Cambria!" I yell after her, hoping she'll stop. If she stops, then I can catch up, and when I get my hands on Killian, I will *end* him. "Cambria, stop!"

She must hear my voice because she slows, then whirls around to face me before taking a few staggering steps backward.

I expected her to stop.

I *wanted* her to stop.

But I didn't expect Killian to do the same.

He slams to a halt.

He turns to face me.

He grins.

The unnerving look forces my feet to stop, and they skid across the stones as I slide to a halt.

He chuckles darkly. "You're so predictable, Mercy Madness. And you're late for your final trial."

Did he pull Cambria out of Sanctuary just to lure me out?

Anger rises, burning hot in my chest.

I'm going to kill him.

I charge, slamming into him so hard that it knocks the air from my lungs, but I also manage to knock him off his feet. I fall on top of him as he falls backward, but he's ready for it. He grips my waist and rolls us both, slamming me to the ground, my spine crushing against the gravel.

I try to kick up my foot, reaching for the small, sharp knife that's sheathed in my boot—a leather holster some of the domestics sewed in for each of us before this battle. But he's over me fast, straddling my waist, heavy as he pins me to the ground…and I can't reach it. His hand closes around my throat, and I swing my arms at his, wildly trying to knock him loose.

But he only squeezes tighter, presses down harder.

A sandy-blond strand of hair—one that shook loose from the knot tied at the back of his head—falls over his eyes…

And they're dark—dark, cold, and callous.

I think of Violet Clare. I think of how hard she must have fought Ian while she was in his captivity. I think of her voice and the last words she spoke before the final video record ended—before *I* ended it because I couldn't bear to hear another word.

And though it's her voice I hear in my mind, I speak the words out loud, letting them whisper from my lips as Killian tries to steal my breath for good.

"*Circulus vitiosus in aeternum.*"

His rage-filled expression twists in confusion. "What did you just say to me?" He lets go with one hand to swing his arm as he turns his head. "Get *off*, Cambria!"

His shove sends her flying, and she drops harshly to the ground. Then, he returns the hand he pushed her with back to my throat. With both hands wrapped around my delicate neck, he squeezes.

He lifts my head, then slams it back to the ground again, so hard that my vision momentarily blackens at the edges.

I kick my foot, trying uselessly to get it out from beneath him…and the absurdity of this situation nearly makes me want to laugh.

Is this it?

After everything, is this the way I die?

I look past Killian, gazing up at the sky, noting the clouds above me have cleared.

I see the stars.

I see the full moon.

And in my mind, I see Violet Clare.

Somehow, the vision of her weakens me. All at once, I let my arms fall back…I stop kicking, I stop swinging, I stop fighting. My body is still beneath the crushing force of Killian's hands.

I'm lying on the ground, looking up at Violet Clare as she crawls over me, as though I'm the camera laid on the ground capturing her first night of horror as Ian Cole's captive. Her face appears above me, dirt-smudged and bloodied. She looks down at me when Ian demands it while she fights back her tears.

"*Circulus vitiosus in aeternum.*"

I don't know whether I said the words out loud or heard Violet's imaginary voice say them in my mind, but it doesn't matter. Her face above me begins to fade, but I'm not fading with her…I'm not dying. The haunting vision of her has breathed air into my lungs.

Her voice cuts through the fog in my mind, and it brings me clarity… it brings me back to reality. "Hey, hey! Vicious Circle!" Violet's voice is amplified, playing from the video she recorded at the concert.

Killian's grip loosens.

The servants' screaming ends.

The men's desperate demands fade.
And all of Ember Glen is quiet as the truth is finally revealed.

chapter thirty-two

Mercy

KILLIAN SLOWLY RISES, his gaze fixed on the screens in front of the Homestead—screens they'd intended to use to display Delle on trial.

But Delle is no longer on display as the video records play.

Everything around me has stopped…

The men and the servants all stare at the screens in silence.

Killian is on his feet, slowly taking a step away from me toward the Homestead. He seems bewildered, transfixed, as if he's drawn in by some unseen force.

This is my chance to free Delle.

His attention is focused on the screen, but I still need to move quietly. He won't give up on killing me so easily once he snaps out of it.

Drawing my knees and elbows beneath me, I sneak sideways, creeping like a crab as my eyes stay fixed on Killian, watching for any subtle indication that he's going to lunge for me. Cambria is on her hands and knees nearby, slowly rising to her feet, though she remains bent over to keep herself small and unseen.

She reaches out for me, her eyes darting up to watch Killian. I twist to grab her hand, let her help me to my feet, and we slowly, quietly back away.

Then, we turn toward the forest and run.

My lungs burn before we even reach the tree line that separates the square from the forest, but I keep pace with her all the same as we sprint into the darkness. We move as fast as we can, heading in the direction of the clearing with the bonfire, the twigs and leaves crunching beneath our boots.

Too soon, we hear footsteps behind us.

"Mercy Madness!" Killian roars.

"Go," I pant. "The clearing. Get Delle."

"Where are you—"

"Get Delle. He's after *me*. Let him chase me."

"Mercy—"

"Do it!"

I see her silhouette shift in the black forest, heading in the direction of the clearing.

I turn to circle around it, and just as I expected, I hear his footsteps behind me, keeping pace. It's not long before I see the tree line ahead of me and the meadow beyond it. The moon's spotlight glows above the wildflowers, guiding my path through the darkness among the trees.

The threshold is right in front of me, and I force myself to move faster toward it. But just as I reach it, my foot catches on a fallen branch, and I tumble into the tall grass.

Coming out of a roll, I scramble forward, fighting to get my feet beneath me. I try to run too soon and stumble over my own feet. My arms shoot out to catch my forward fall at the same moment Killian barrels into me from behind, slamming me face-down among the grass and wildflowers.

I clench my hand into a fist and swing my elbow back hard, twisting my body with the thrust to nail him in the ribs. He groans, his weight shifting sideways from the hit, and it gives me enough relief where I can push up to my hands and knees.

I manage to crawl out from under him and stumble ahead a few steps more, but then breathlessness catches up with me. My reserves are depleted after the run, my muscles are weak from the oxygen-deprivation, and my body gives out.

I fall to my hands and knees as he catches up to me, crawls over me, and climbs onto my back. The weight of him forces me down, flattening me beneath him.

I throw my arms out in front of me, claw my fingers into the ground, grasping at the stems of wildflowers that only snap in half.

"Well, this is a surprise." Killian reaches over me to grab my wrists, painfully yanking my arms behind me. He holds them in one hand, pressing them down against my lower back as I buck my hips, trying to throw him off me. He groans. "You made me hard with this little chase, sinner. I think God wants me to fuck you before I choke the life out of you."

"No!" I cry out, thrashing uselessly beneath his weight.

Still pinning my hands against my back with one hand, he lifts my skirt above my hips with the other. I fling madly, wildly, thrashing with every last ounce of energy I can muster. His rough fingers slip beneath my underwear and graze me dry as he tugs them to the side.

"Killian, don't! Don't do this!"

"Quiet, you little sinner. You deserve this for all the stress you've caused me."

"Stop!"

I hear his buckle.

"No, *please*!"

His zipper.

"Killian, st—"

He steals my voice.

He stuns me.

He forces himself inside me with a dry, grating thrust.

I can't think; I can't move. The world has gone quiet.

All I hear are his groans, the crude sounds of him moving inside me as unwanted wetness floods to protect me from the pain he inflicts.

I'm motionless.

I'm still for so long that he gradually loosens his grip, slowly releasing my hands. I let them slip from my back and drop to the ground at my sides. Arms restrained or freed, I'm still trapped beneath him, pinned to the ground in this nightmare.

A light breeze rustles the grass, and the wildflowers whisper as they dance around me…

Wildflowers and starlight.

The blooms are shades of amethyst and ruby, though they're shadowed in the night. And with each of Killian's painful movements, they grow darker. He's blackening my meadow, taking the color from this place with every vile thrust.

This place isn't for him.

This place is for love…

For wildflowers and starlight.

And he ruined it!

His palms grip my thighs so he can spread my legs, and he fucks me harder.

I bend my knee, sliding it up beside my hip.

"That's a good little sinner. Spread wider for me."

I twist my body toward my knee, reaching down with my hand. He's so consumed that he doesn't get what I'm doing. He doesn't know that I'm reaching for something. He's not aware that my fingers are grazing the handle of a knife that's sheathed inside my boot.

I grip it.

I start to pull.

Killian groans…

And then he's gone.

In a single motion, I unsheathe my knife and roll to my hands and knees. I look up to find Arlo tangled with Killian, tumbling through the grass. Arlo lands on top of him, slams his fist down into Killian's face, punching him over and over again.

I climb unsteadily to my feet, stumbling and shivering as I twist the knife in my hand while I move beside them...

Arlo continues to pummel Killian, his nose cracks and blood splatters. It splashes across my arm, dotting speckles of red across the wildflowers in my tattoo—the blood of a Cole spilled on the image meant to silence the Vicious Circle.

I want more of it...

I raise my arm.

I fall to my knees.

And finally, I drive my knife into Killian Cole's chest.

chapter thirty-three
ARLO

WHEN I SEE him on top of Mercy and realize what he's doing, violence mingles with adrenaline as it shoots through my veins. I charge after Killian, tumble with him through the meadow, and pin him to the ground.

My hand forms a fist that I pound against his face.

I keep hitting him, even when I hear a crack and blood sprays from his broken nose. I'm determined to hammer him with my fist until he stops moving, stops breathing, until he *stops fucking living.*

But I blink, startled back from the darkest part of my mind as blood erupts from Killian's chest. Then, more blood splashes up, so much that it makes me flinch as it covers my face.

Mercy...

She's on her knees beside us, pulling her knife out of his chest, driving it down again, causing another eruption of blood.

Her face is blood-soaked, twisted in rage, and the sight of her in action stuns me. I'm amazed by the look of her, confused by my reaction because all I see is beauty drenched in red...

My Mercy.

I slip off Killian as Mercy stabs, as she lifts, then lowers, and lifts her knife again. I stay there beside her as she unleashes her rage, watching her massacre this man who deserves every slice of her unbridled fury.

Gradually, her pace slows, and then she stops with her knife raised above him. She looks down at him as she fights for each breath. And then she drives her blade into his flesh—one final time—and her fingers remain settled there, gripping the handle.

I see the whites of her eyes as they slowly lift to look at me, peering through the red that soaks her face. "Arlo?" she mutters.

I reach forward, gently wrapping my fingers around her wrists, and as I rise to my feet, I pull her to stand with me. I step over Killian and drag her into my arms, reaching up into her tangled, starlight tresses, which are threaded with streaks of blood.

She hugs me around the waist, lifts her chin to look up at me, and for moments, we simply stand this way and stare. My hands move to her cheeks, unfazed by the blood that coats my palms as my thumbs brush with a comforting stroke.

In this quiet moment, it's only us.

I press my forehead to hers, tell her with my gaze that I'm so sorry I was late, that our delay caused this to happen to her. Her gentle eyes tell me that she's already forgiven me, yet we both know she'll never forget.

Just like all the pain I've caused her, she'll remember this. But this scar is not worth remembering how she got it. This pain is a burden that will haunt her. And though I did everything I could to be on time, though there was no avoiding being late from the malfunction with the technology, I will *always* blame myself for this.

I will always blame myself for *all* of this.

She should not have been alone. She should not have been Killian's target. But there's no doubt in my mind that this end was always coming. Mercy had to take back her power, and the only way was with violence—the men who built this place made sure of that.

And if violence is the only end, then I'll be violent with her. I'll fight to give her the life she deserves, because this brutal, beautiful, bloodied mess of a woman in front of me deserves peace, happiness, and freedom.

Mercy silently begs me for comfort, so I tilt my chin to kiss her lips softly. Though they're slick and red, I'm unbothered. His blood was meant to be spilled, and she earned the right to spill it.

I was just coming out of the Homestead when I saw Killian disappear into the woods, sprinting like he was chasing someone. I knew right away who he was chasing, but I scanned the crowd of servants and men, nonetheless. They were all just standing, staring, transfixed by the videos playing on the screens.

When I didn't quickly spot her in the throng, I ran into the forest after Killian. I went to the bonfire, assuming Mercy ran off to help Delle, and that's where Killian chased her.

Neither Mercy nor Killian were in the clearing. Instead, I found Cambria fighting tight knots in the ropes that held Delle, struggling to free her. I asked her where Mercy was, and she screamed at me to find her, that Killian had been chasing her, intent on killing her.

That's when I realized she'd lead him to the meadow.

Maybe she did it on purpose, or maybe she just felt the pull, but this meadow became ours the night we chose sin, when we declared our intentions to sin *together*.

That night—as we stood in the pouring rain, beneath the storming sky, with the wildflowers whipping around us in the wind—we'd declared a commitment to stop fighting the passion between us and give into it instead.

Maybe she knew I would find her here.

And when I did find her here, it took me moments too long to understand what I was seeing. I knew right away he was hurting her, but it took a few seconds trapped in shock to see *how* he was hurting her.

That monster was *fucking* my Mercy.

And when it hit me, I snapped.

I glance at Killian on the ground, Mercy turning her head to do the same. His chest doesn't rise and fall; he's as still as a statue. His blood still flows out of him in seemingly endless streams.

Killian is dead.

And my Mercy is the one who ended him.

Pride swells within me, and I feel no shame for it.

Still cradling her cheeks in my palms, I turn her head to face me. I dip to level my eyes with hers and let my wide grin tell her of my pride. Her smile shines through the crimson that coats her face, and though her eyes are filled with tears, I feel relief flow through her. I'm not sure whether the relief comes from the fact that he's dead or from my acceptance of her brutality against him. But it doesn't matter to me as long as she feels a burden lifted.

I take her hand, lock my fingers with hers, and lead her back to the bonfire.

"I'M SO SORRY," Theo's voice is frantic as he quickly works the buttons on his shirt.

The knots that held Delle have been undone, and I'm surprised to find her held in Luna's arms as she shivers. I don't spot Stefanie, but Cambria is nearby, hugging herself with her arms across her chest. Delle's arms are tucked up in front of her, pinned between her body and Luna's.

Mercy and I approach them, coming around from the opposite side of the fire. She tugs her hand from my grip, and I stop with her, both of us watching as Theo removes his button-down shirt. Then, he and Luna work together to put it on Delle, helping her slip her arms through before Luna quickly fastens the buttons in front of her.

"I knew y-you would c-come." Delle's voice tremors as she shivers through her words. Her head is turned toward us, and she's looking directly at Mercy. Delle smiles at her, then turns her gaze to look over at Theo. "I t-told you she'd come back and f-fight."

I look at Mercy, expecting to see her crying or grinning madly, maybe taking off at a run to drag Delle into a hug, so I'm shocked to find her expression impassive. Her face turns away as she casts her gaze toward the fire, then slowly, she walks toward the flames.

"Mercy?"

She crouches to her haunches beside the bonfire, watching the blaze expectantly—it looks as though the fire is speaking and she's listening intently.

Her hand moves forward, and my heart leaps.

Thinking that she's lost her mind—that she's going to thrust her hand into the flame—I cry out, "Mercy!"

She doesn't seem to hear me as she lowers her hand…but then it falls in *front* of the fire, not *through* it, and I let out a sigh of relief.

Her fingers wrap around the end of a small branch that sticks out from the burning pile of brush. She drags it out, bringing fire along with it, and she slowly rises. One end of the branch burns like a torch as she holds it out in front of her.

What is she doing?

She turns and slips away into the forest, heading back in the direction of the meadow. We all call after her, but she's either ignoring us or she's so focused on what's going on in her mind that she can't hear us. Either way, I'm frightened by her lack of response.

We all follow her.

We follow, though none of us makes a move to stop her.

Even when she's broken, even when she's hurting, even when her mind is lost to the darkness and pain, I have faith in her. I will follow her into flames and *burn* with her if that's where she leads me.

She enters the meadow, holding her makeshift torch in front of her, and though she continues forward, the rest of us stop. I can't speak for the others, but I feel *compelled* to stop. There's an internal sense of knowing that I should bear witness to whatever this is, though I'm not meant to participate.

So, we all wait, silently watching from the tree line.

She moves deeper into the meadow, to the spot where Killian lies nestled among the tall grass and wildflowers swaying ever so gently in the light breeze.

She stops beside him.

She stares down at him.

She takes in the vision of her brutality…

And I take in the vision of her reclaimed power.

Holding the flame, she's the light in the center of our meadow. Though darkness wraps around her—though shadows blacken the colors of our meadow—her glow remains bright, her internal flame still burning.

And when she speaks, we're compelled to listen.

Her voice is filled with malice, reflecting the contempt in her heart, and she directs her final words downward at Killian. "*Malo mori quam foedari.*"

Death before dishonor.

Chills ripple across my skin, a tremor running up my spine as goosebumps rise on my flesh.

She drops the burning branch over his body, then steps back.

The flames catch on his clothes.

The orange blaze spreads, then rises.

And we all watch as Killian Cole burns.

For moments, we're all transfixed, lost in a trance with Mercy as the fire dances. Sparking embers leap from his burning body, land on the blooms of wildflowers, and singe their petals.

Though her body faces the fire, Mercy's head turns to catch my stare. She draws in a breath so deep that her shoulders rise as her lungs fill. And when she lets it out again, I see the satisfaction in her subtle grin.

I will never forget her perfection in this moment.

She walks toward me, and I move to meet her halfway. I grab her cheeks and kiss her hard, stealing the last moment we'll ever see in this burning meadow.

Her hands touch my wrists as the kiss breaks, and with her sparkling silver-blue eyes on mine, she whispers, "Wildflowers and starlight."

My smile is wide and proud, and I'm immensely grateful that I get to call her *mine.* I drag her against me, embrace her close, and tangle my bare, bloodied fingers into her hair.

This burning meadow will forever hold the memory of the night we kissed in the rain, the moment when we declared our intent to sin together until the day death finds us.

But death hasn't found us yet.

And death won't find us today.

And now that he burns, Killian's violence won't sully our memory of this place. The fire is cleansing, and Mercy made it.

This meadow is ours again—hers and mine.

I whisper three words, "Wildflowers and starlight."

And they're the only three words she needs to hear to know that my love for her is eternal.

chapter thirty-four
ARLO

WE REACH THE square to find the entire village gathered in front of the Homestead—the servants and men were already there, but even the domestics have come out from their homes to join the population. A swarm of voices—loud in their confusion, fear, and outrage—all swirl together, creating hectic noise.

Wesley and Park stand halfway up the stone staircase, shouting down at the crowd, trying to give answers they don't have. Mercy and I walk hand-in-hand toward the back of the gathering with Theo, Delle, Cambria, and Luna all behind us.

Heads turn at our approach, and I'm certain the sight of us is jarring. Mercy looks like she's come straight from battle, as though she's killed a hundred men—and I suppose, in a way, she has.

Ending the life of Killian Cole—the ancestor of the man who's mad obsession resulted in the founding of Ember Glen—feels like poetic justice. She stabbed him countless times, and a part of me wonders if she stabbed once for each generation of Coles that survived and thrived in the brutality of this place.

Probably not, but the thought of it feels so *right*, that I decide it's what I'm going to believe.

One person from the throng spots us over their shoulder, and they draw the attention of others around them. More and more heads turn in our direction, looking back at us as we approach, and the crowd begins to part. A path opens for us through the gathering, and we follow it as voices gradually fade to silence.

Stefanie forces her way through the crowd ahead of us, and I follow her with my gaze. She runs for Luna and throws her arms around her in relief. I breathe a sigh of relief, too. It would hurt me if my sister's heart was broken—and it would have been broken if something had happened to Stefanie. She joins us as we approach the stone staircase.

Wesley and Park move in front of us about halfway up the steps. "What's going on?" Wesley asks. "Do you know anything about this?"

I ignore his question. "Where are Owen and Ryker?"

"They're inside, trying to get in touch with the Elders to find out if it's…Is it true? Is it all true?"

Mercy releases my hand and turns outward, facing the crowd. When she speaks, her voice is loud and clear. "What you've seen is the real story of Ember Glen from footage that was found hidden in the caves beneath our feet. And now that you know the truth, Ember Glen no longer exists.

"Men, in case you were wondering, there will be no purge tonight. The servants will no longer be happy to serve your violent and sexual needs. As you now understand, it is not God's will for them to serve you. It was the will of a madman named Ian Cole, and I'm certain no servant here would like to serve you in his honor.

"In two hours, we're leaving Ember Glen. Arlo Rainn will lead us through the caves to the world beyond the mountains. You may choose to come with us, or you can remain here in Ember Glen…" She turns her head toward the forest, looking out toward the smoke rising in the distance. "But if you choose to stay, then I suggest you hurry to put out the fire I set over Killian Cole's dead body before it spreads to the trees."

Everyone looks out toward the forest, but it's only about a dozen men who run from the crowd, shouting about hurrying to put it out.

Mercy turns on her heel. "Move," she tells Wesley and Park. They looked stunned, horrified, but they step aside to let us pass.

As we ascend, my gaze sweeps over the images of wildflowers etched into the massive wooden doors.

Did Ian Cole carve those images himself?

If he did, I'd like to watch them burn.

Stopping just in front of the doors, we move aside to let Theo reach out with his banded arm to unlock it. We enter the Homestead together, then turn left, heading directly for the courtroom.

Down the hallway, the courtroom door is open—which is unusual— and we can hear Owen's voice carry down the hall as we approach.

"And you *knew* this? You *knew* from the moment you became Elders?" Owen asks with a tone of incredulity.

"Yes." I hear Clyde's voice.

The Elders must be on screen.

Mercy and I glance at each other, then hurry to the door, rushing into the room.

"What are you—" Owen gapes at us with wide-eyes. He's leaning forward on his palms, standing behind the black, semi-circular table. I can see his face in the spotlight as he leans forward out of the shadows behind him. "I don't even care." He shakes his head, writes us off, and turns back to speak to the Elders. "How could you lie to us? How could you…Why would you…" he sputters, seemingly at a loss for words.

Ryker seems unfazed, sitting just a few seats away from Owen. "They still have to maintain control of this community. The so-called *truth* doesn't matter."

Owen swings his head to look over at Ryker. "The truth doesn't *matter?*"

"He's right," Lawrence says from the screen. "It didn't matter to you until you knew it."

"Well, now that I know, it *matters.*" Owen stands, putting his hands on his head as he spins away, pacing into the dark shadows behind the table.

Edgar appears somber on the screen. "Now that everyone knows the truth, it's over. It all ends at sunrise."

I step forward, moving to stand in the spotlight that shines over the center of the space in front of the table. "What do you mean? What ends at sunrise?"

"Arlo Rainn," Edgar snarls, "I suppose you're the culprit behind this little…*unveiling.*"

"Tell me what you mean." I put a hard edge to my voice. "It all ends at sunrise…?"

"You ask for truth so insistently," Edgar says. "So let me tell you the truth of the world outside of Ember Glen. Out here, you don't *exist*. You were never born, you never lived, you have no records…You are *nothing.* Because you don't exist, there is no life you can have beyond the mountains. You can't work, you can't earn, you can't purchase food or acquire housing. You would all *die*, starved and homeless if it weren't for us keeping this secret for you; if it weren't for us providing everything you need in Ember Glen—"

"We don't want you to provide for us!" Mercy shouts, stepping forward into the light. There's a chorus of gasps as they take in her rough appearance, but it doesn't give her a moment's pause. "We want to be free. We want to choose how we live our lives, and not be held to arbitrary rules made up by a madman."

"You *cannot* be free," Lawrence insists. "You don't exist beyond Ember Glen, and there is no way for you to survive. All that you have done, Mercy Madness, is provide hope to these people…hope where there is *none.*"

"There *is* hope," Mercy insists. "We're leaving this place tonight. You no longer control us."

The Elders laugh.

"How exactly do you think you're leaving?" Clyde asks. He tilts his head, regarding her. "Ah. I know. You're going to try to find your way through the caves, aren't you? Well, go right on ahead and try. We wish you luck."

Mercy's brow wrinkles—the response surprised her.

It surprises me, too.

"The caves lead to escape," I tell them. "I know they do."

"Sure," Lawrence says with a shrug. "I'm sure they do. But those tunnels and passages are vast and winding. One wrong turn will get you lost for days. How much food and water can you carry with you traveling through? How many mouths do you have to feed if they all follow you?"

"We'll make it through." Determination is unwavering in Mercy's voice.

"Go on and try," Edgar says. "No one here is going to stop you. But let's say you do escape. Let's say you do find your way out to the world beyond. What then? As I told you, *you do not exist*."

Mercy tilts her head. "You keep saying that, but it doesn't make sense. If *we* don't exist, then *you* don't exist. So, how are *you* surviving?"

The Elders seem to hesitate, each waiting for the other to speak. But they don't have to speak…because I think I know the answer.

"You've had to take on new identities on the outside, haven't you?" I ask.

"You were always bright, Arlo," Clyde says. "And if you'd only been patient, you would've known the truth when we made you an Elder at the next Shift."

"That wouldn't have been for…what? Another twenty-three years? Do you really believe that twenty-three years of our women suffering would have been worth the time it took for me to learn the truth at the Shift?" I chuckle without humor. "And I'm right, aren't I? What are your last names on the outside? I bet I can guess. You had to change them, didn't you?"

Slowly, quietly, Mercy says each name. "Cole. Bright. Creed."

"You've been given identities as though you were their descendants, haven't you? You gained their wealth and power on the outside, and you had to keep this secret or you'd lose it all. And in that case, as you've said, you wouldn't exist."

Edgar's expression indicates he's grown weary of the conversation. "Of course. There would be no other way to live outside of Ember Glen."

"So, that's why only three of the Control are selected to become Elders. And what of the Land of Kings? That's a lie, too, isn't it?"

"You seem to be answering your own questions," Lawrence says.

"Well, here's one I don't know the answer to. What happened to the three Elders before you? When the three of you became their replacements, what happened to them?"

"They were old," Edgar says with an air of annoyance. "They died."

"How?" Mercy takes a step forward. "How did they die?"

We're met with silence, and it's telling.

The conclusion we've all come to is spoken aloud by Luna. "You killed them."

"None of you are capable of understanding," Lawrence says. "It's an *honor* for the retiring Elders to give their lives, to make way for the next generation. They were seventy-five years old by then—they'd lived their lives on the outside and were ready to die."

"It's an *honor* to have kept these secrets from you," Edgar says. "We have kept you *alive* in Ember Glen. We've kept you housed; we've kept you fed. For God's sake, all your men would be *imprisoned* on the outside. They would be called *criminals* for the things they've done on nights of service."

"Then why didn't you simply *stop* them?" Mercy raises her voice. "Why did you continue this *game*? You could've put an end to it all—you *should* have!"

"It's too late to stop anything by the time one becomes an Elder. By then, we've spent twenty-five years with the Control and participated in countless nights of purging. By the time we reach fifty and learn the truth as new Elders at the Shift, it's already too late. If we put an end to it, then *we* would be the criminals. We'd be imprisoned for the things we've done in Ember Glen, and that hardly seems fair."

Mercy throws her head back and laughs. "Fair! Don't you dare speak to me about what's fair…"

"This conversation is pointless," Edgar says. "Come morning, Ember Glen will be gone. All of you will be dead, and it's all your fault."

"Let me make sure I understand," Mercy says. "You're going to wipe out an entire community of people, and all because you don't want the outside world to find out the truth about you? All because you're scared to admit that you're heinous, disgusting old men who get off on playing God? Because that's all this is; that's all that this has ever been. Ember Glen only exists because privileged men like you wanted to play God." She shakes her head. "But no more. We *will* find our way out."

"You'll never find the way out. You'll die in those caves."

"And so what if we do?" Mercy snaps. "If you're going to destroy this place anyway, at least we will have tried." Mercy takes a step closer to the screen. "Mark my words, gentlemen…we will find our way out. And when we do, I *will* find you. I will hunt you down, and I swear, it will be *my* face you see when you take your last breath."

Mercy turns, stomps from the room, and we follow her. She stops in the foyer, standing at the center of the starburst pattern on the tiled floor.

"Luna, Stefanie, start gathering everyone who wants to leave. Get the others to help you and lead them to the caves through my house. Tell them what the Elders said; tell them whatever you need to make them hurry. We have enough food and water to last four, maybe five days for the women and children who were with us, but we'll need more for the others. Have everyone gather as much as they can carry and tell them all to *hurry*."

She turns to look at Delle. "Go upstairs and get dressed. Then see what you and Theo can gather from the kitchen."

The front door suddenly opens, and Wesley enters.

Mercy charges toward him, boots stomping over the tile floor. "Are you with me or against me?" she asks Wesley, coming to a stop directly in front of him.

Wesley looks bewildered. "I…I don't know what I am."

"Well, make up your mind," she snaps. "We don't have time to wait for you to decide. If you're with me, then gather kindling for a fire, bring it here, and pile it in front of the staircase. We're leaving Ember Glen forever, but not before I watch it burn."

I SPENT FIFTEEN minutes in the shower with Mercy. It took that much time to help her scrub every last trace of Killian's blood from her skin and hair. She's dressed in red again—no black clothes in the Homestead for her to choose from.

We have everything we need packed and waiting for us to grab from the main cavern, so the only thing we cared to collect was her mother's journal which has the poems I'd written for Mercy tucked inside.

Some of the people have decided to stay. There's a group who don't believe the truth we revealed to them, and they most certainly don't believe the conversation we had with the Elders.

They think this is a test of faith.

They believe they'll meet God come sunrise.

The rest are ready to go, and they're all coming with us. I have to lead our people through the caves, and the idea of it is daunting. But the time to do it is now—whether I'm ready or not—and somehow, I'll find a way through for them.

Everyone who wants to leave has already been led through Mercy's home to the main cavern. They're waiting for us to meet them there…They're waiting for us to lead them.

Yet there's something that must be done before we go.

I tuck her mother's journal beneath my arm, pinning it to my side as I stand with Mercy in the foyer. The front doors of the Homestead are propped open wide, and there's a pile of brush and branches in the center of the sunburst tile.

"Ready?" I ask.

Mercy nods.

I strike the match, but this fire is hers to ignite.

I pass her the lit match and she takes it delicately between her fingertips. She steps closer to the kindling and crouches to her haunches. With one hand, she sweeps aside her crimson skirt, making the flower appliques dance with the motion. She lowers the small flame that's held between her fingers and keeps her hand in place until the brush catches fire.

She drops the match onto the pile as she rises, then returns to stand beside me. Together, we watch the flames grow, standing still as the entire pile catches fire, mesmerized for moments as the blaze reaches for the ceiling.

I tug on her hand. "Come on."

She turns with me, lets me lead her through the double doors, but then she stops. She lets go of my hand and turns around to face the flames. She stands centered within the frame of the open doors, just outside the threshold to the Homestead in an elegant red dress.

I need to see the entire picture…

I need to see her watching the fire she sparked.

I descend the stone steps, realizing this is the last time I'll ever walk them, that this is the last time I'll see the Homestead. I hesitate to turn, feeling the finality in my chest. Yet when I finally turn and look up, there is nothing in my heart but hope.

Beyond Mercy, there's nothing but fire.

It catches on the curtains, and it burns up the banister.

Flames fill the foyer entirely.

All I see is a backdrop of fire, and my Mercy standing at the center. Her starlight hair bounces as she turns her head over her shoulder. She sees me and smiles, and the world shifts into slow motion as she spins to face me.

Everything has slowed, my mind allowing me to catch every detail as she bends, as she lifts her skirt to reveal her black boots beneath, and she jogs down the steps to meet me.

She stops on the second to last step and reaches out to touch my cheek. The sound of the roaring fire crescendos—crackling, scorching heat behind us.

"Take my hand, Warden Rainn." She leans forward as her thumb brushes my cheek, pressing her lips to my ear. "Take us all away from here and lead me home."

My hands work secretly between us as she pulls back to look at me, her smile shining with a brightness that rivals all the stars in the sky.

I step back and hold out my hand for her.

She glances down at the fresh pair of black leather gloves I've put on, then looks at me quizzically.

"For old time's sake." I give her a smirk. "Come with me, sinner. I'll take you home."

Mercy lets out a cleansing breath as her grin rises.

She places her palm on mine, steps down beside me, and that's the moment all the stars in the sky align.

I have no fear of the journey ahead, no worry for life beyond Ember Glen. I only want to lead her home.

Yet our home isn't here.

Our home is beyond the mountains, waiting for us to find it.

So, I'll find it for her.

We run, hand-in-hand, crossing the empty village square beneath the star-speckled sky. Under the glow of the bright full moon, we leave the Homestead burning in our wake.

Our lives ended the night she ran from service, but a new one begins tonight, born from the ashes of Ember Glen.

We all rise from the sparking embers of Mercy.

circulus vitiosus in aeternum

epilogue

Mercy

July 21, 2188
Three Years Later

"EVEN MOM SAYS it's weird," Stefanie's oldest daughter, Heidi, informs me. "People out here don't wash their dishes by hand. They use a dishwasher machine. I know you have one."

Heidi and I are speaking through a small rectangular screen that's built into the wall beside my kitchen window. It's much like the screen in Ember Glen where the Control would speak to the Elders, but the screens in the outside world are much brighter and clearer, the technology far more advanced. I can speak to so many more people during the day than I could before—just a tap on the screen, and there they are.

I rinse a plate beneath the faucet. "Well, your mom also knows that I'm not the kind of person to do something just because everyone else is doing it. So, tell her I'll continue to be *weird*, and she should mind her own business."

Heidi turns and yells off screen, "Hey, Mom! Mercy says that you should—"

"Heidi!" I snatch her attention back, but it's too late.

Stefanie moves her face into the frame. "I heard every word. Happy birthday, by the way."

I grin. "Thank you."

I'm twenty-three years old today, which I've learned is considered rather young out here in the outer world. I've come to find that an Ember Glen twenty-three is about the same as an outer world forty.

Life moves slower out here…life is *kinder* out here.

When we fled Ember Glen, it took us four and a half days to navigate our way through the tunnels to escape. We came out onto a dirt path, which led us to a road. The road led us to people, and the people found us help.

We were granted government-issued housing for a while as things were sorted out. We all lived in the same apartment building in the city. It was a strange experience because it was nothing like Ember Glen, but at least we were able to be together so we could look after one another.

The Elders had been right about one thing—we didn't exist outside of Ember Glen. And because we didn't exist, we weren't able to secure jobs until about a year ago. That's when we were finally granted official documents and records.

That process was long, difficult, and exhausting.

But it wasn't impossible as we were made to believe.

We had to jump through a million hoops, tell and retell our individual stories to authorities, government officials, and social workers.

The men of the Control who fled—all but Ryker—were called to appear individually before a judge for rulings against any of their potential wrong-doings in Ember Glen. I can't speak for the others, but Arlo and Theo both had to jump hurdles to clear their names. But it was thanks to the testimonies from the other members of our community that they were cleared. Instead of imprisonment, they were appointed rehabilitative services instead.

And now we live happily, just outside the city. Our small house is within walking distance of everyone I love in our own little neighborhood that we call home.

"Is Arlo around?" Stefanie asks. "Luna and I were actually hoping we could talk to you both today…"

I freeze for a moment, my hands going still around the dish I'm holding beneath the faucet. I force myself to blink as I swallow hard. "Is it about… um…"

"Scoot," Stefanie tells Heidi, shooing her away. She moves closer to the screen. "It is about that, actually. Luna was going to drop all the kids off with Archer and Diane later today. Let them all run around at the new house."

"Oh, the new house *and* the new wife." I make a face. "How is Luna getting along with her?"

"Diane and Luna are basically the same person, so naturally, they don't get along at all." Stefanie grins.

I laugh. "Well, I'm glad Archer found Luna's double. He had the hardest time getting over her."

"Believe me, I know. It's better for all of us this way. Anyway, since we won't have the kids, we were hoping we could walk over and chat for a bit."

I try to mask my stuttering, anxious breath with a smile. "Of course, you're always welcome. You can come over anytime. You really don't have to ask first."

"Oh, yes, we do. We do have to ask."

"You're family, you don't—"

"We love you both, Mercy, very much, but not enough that I want to see you strung up naked in your living room because you and Arlo forgot we'd be coming by and you told us to 'let ourselves in' when we got there. We're not *that* close."

"And again, I am *so* sorry about that," I laugh.

"Speak of the devil…"

"Hi, Stefanie." I feel Arlo's heat at my back just before I hear his voice.

He comes in so close behind me that he pins me against the countertop. He brings his left arm around me, plants his hand on the counter, and leans forward. Except it's not just his hand that he's placed on the counter—he has a length of rope coiled in his grip.

My eyes widen a bit when I spot it, then I quickly draw my attention back to drying the dish I'm holding. I'm thankful our camera doesn't pan wide enough to show his hand on the counter.

"How's my sister?" Arlo asks casually.

His hips shift forward, and I feel him rock-hard against my ass. His right hand palms my cheek, and when he squeezes, I let out a small yelp. I quickly drop the dish as a cover, pretending that's what startled me.

"She's good. Everything okay over there?"

"Yes. I just dropped a dish. Soapy hands. Slippery."

"Maybe that's another good reason to use your dishwasher?"

"We'll see." I chuckle nervously. "I like to do it myself."

"You should at least make Arlo do it on your birthday."

His hand dips between my legs. "I couldn't agree more. That's exactly why I'm here, Stefanie. To give her a helping hand. She shouldn't have to do it herself on her birthday."

I glance at the upper corner of the screen to see whether my cheeks look flushed.

"Right. I get it." Stefanie rolls her eyes. "We'll come over at two. Do you think you can finish by then?"

"Two or three times, easy," Arlo says. He twists his head to look at me, but I don't dare look back. "Maybe four if we do it well? It *is* your birthday…"

"Oh, wow. Okay, see you at two," Stefanie says quickly, and the screen goes black.

He presses his lips to the curve of my neck. "I thought she'd never hang up…"

"We hardly spoke before you interrupted us."

"I'm sorry." He dips his hand further between my legs. "Would you like me to stop so you can call her back?"

"No need. She's coming over at two. I'll talk to her then."

"Good. Because I'm *desperate* to fuck you." He pushes harder against me, crushing my waist into the edge of the counter.

His hand slips down my throat, fingers tugging at the collar of my shirt. With a quick pull, he jerks down my top and my bra to expose my breasts. I'd sink to the floor with the way his fingers play with my nipple, except he's pushing so hard against me that I couldn't slip away if I wanted to.

And I definitely don't want to.

His lips sweep my neck. "Put your hands behind your back, starlight."

Instantly, I comply, folding onto the counter as he takes my arms behind me. He binds my wrists together with ease, and I'm already panting by the time he's done. He reaches around me to unfasten the button of my jeans, huffing a breath of frustration as he works the zipper.

"I fucking hate these." He chuckles, yanking my jeans down with a sharp motion. "I miss the accessibility…"

"I'll wear a skirt for you the next time I do the dishes if you'll quit complaining and get to work." I wiggle my hips.

One hand grips the rope as the other tangles in my long hair. He lifts me off the counter, my back arching as he curves me back against him.

"Lucky it's your birthday, Mercy Madness. Normally, that kind of snark earns you edging for hours."

My belly clenches. "No one asked you to make any exceptions for my birthday."

"Well, in that case…"

The screen on the wall interrupts us with a trill, showing that there's a call coming in from Theo.

"My phone's still connected to the screen…I think?" The technology is still a struggle sometimes. "Just grab it and turn it off. It's there by the sink."

With one hand still tangled in my hair, he reaches around me with the other to grab my phone. He fumbles with it in one hand, but then, the noise stops.

"Whatever I did worked," he says, just as confused about these things as I am.

"It didn't work the way you thought it did," Theo says, and our eyes pitch to the screen on the wall. There he is, looking directly at us, and we're frozen in awkward silence. "Call me right back. It's urgent." The screen goes black.

We're quiet for a beat.

"He didn't tell me to finish first…" Arlo says. "I think we should probably call him back."

We burst into laughter.

That's my favorite thing about the new world—I have things to smile and laugh about.

We put a pause on our activities, put ourselves back together, and return Theo's call.

As soon as he comes on screen, he says, "I found him."

And just like that, the day changes completely.

I couldn't have hoped for a better birthday present.

"THEO FOUND HIM." The words shoot from my lips the moment I open the door for Stefanie and Luna.

"He did?" Luna's eyes are wide with surprise. "When?"

"A few hours ago. Come in." I wave them inside.

Luna crosses to give Arlo a hug, and we all sit around the small table in the kitchen.

Stefanie glances over at Luna sitting beside her. "Do you think we should…"

Luna eagerly nods. "Definitely. We should definitely tell her because it's her birthday, and she's been waiting forever for an answer."

Stefanie's hesitancy makes my chest tight with anxiety. I *have* been waiting forever for an answer about this, but she doesn't owe me anything. She doesn't owe me an answer. She doesn't even owe me time spent considering it.

Arlo and I started talking about it a year ago when we found out I couldn't carry a pregnancy through to term—that was also when we found out that many of the former servants were getting similar results from their doctors.

Arlo reaches for my hand beneath the table, squeezing tight.

He wants a family. He wants it with me so much, and I want it, too. I'm just so afraid she'll say no.

"Stefanie," Luna says. "Would you just tell her?"

I close my eyes, certain from that statement alone that her answer is no.

"Luna and I have talked it over. We've been talking about it for a while now," Stefanie says. "And I'd be thrilled to carry your baby, Mercy. It's the least I could do for you."

I gape at her in shock.

I look at Arlo, and he's in tears.

He drags me into his arms and holds me.

This is the best birthday I've ever had.

"WELL, HAVE YOU told her yet?" I whisper to Theo.

We're standing beside my parked car, just across the street from the small house that Delle and her friend Juniper share. Cambria actually lives just a few houses down, so we've already stopped to pick her up, and she's waiting in the back seat of my car.

"She's not ready," Theo says.

"What do you mean?"

"You and I both know that out here, everything's different. Delle was still a kid when we left Ember Glen. The time she's spent out here has been different for her than it has been for you and me. She's only nineteen."

"And she was only sixteen in Ember Glen, but you thought having 'a connection' with her was okay then. So, what's different now?"

"The *world* is different, Mercy; that's what changed. *She* changed. And it's a good thing, I'm not saying it isn't. I'm glad she's free out here. I'm glad she can be like other people her age out here. But I'm thirty years old now, and I think differently than she does. It doesn't mean that it'll never happen, it just means..." The front door to Delle's house opens, and she appears, her head turning back over her shoulder as she laughs and waves goodbye to Juniper. "It just means not right now."

It's true that Delle has changed, and like Theo, I'm glad for it. It's been a good change for her. She's freer, happier, enjoying her life. She was so young when we left, and I think that was beneficial for her in transitioning. Where the rest of us felt a little more weathered than others our age, Delle seemed to blend in seamlessly with her peers.

She practically bounces down the sidewalk heading toward us, flipping her long, smooth hair over her shoulder. Her beautiful face is caked in experimental shades of make-up, and her clothes fit in easily with the other nineteen-year-olds in this world.

I'm happy for her.

And maybe one day Theo will tell her that he loves her…but for now, I think he might be right.

It's not time.

She's not ready for that with him yet.

All the same, she does have love for him in a certain context. It's evident in the way she leaps into his arms to give him a hug. "I haven't seen you in like, two weeks! Where have you been?"

"I've been around…" He grants her a small smile.

She comes to me next, and I drag her in for a tight squeeze.

"Ready?" Theo asks us both.

I nod. "We'll follow you."

I slip into the passenger seat of my car, though Delle goes immediately to Theo's parked behind us.

"Is everything okay there?" Arlo asks from the driver's seat.

"It will be. Some things just take time."

His brow wrinkles in confusion, because I don't think he knows what I'm talking about.

I just smile at him and shake my head. "Just drive, love."

"YOU DON'T HAVE to do this!" Edgar begs.

Theo found him.

Theo *finally* found the last of the three Elders.

He tracked down Lawrence within a year and found Clyde around the time our official citizenship documents were approved.

But Edgar has been a challenge.

I know Theo struggled with finding him, but I knew he could do it. I had faith that someday we could end this, once and for all.

Arlo and Theo have tied Edgar to a plush chair pulled from his luxury dining room. The others have all gathered around to witness, because they need to see it, too. We've all been struggling to find peace since we fled. We knew the Elders were still out there and knowing that made us angry and resentful.

Why should they get to live freely after what they put us through?

They had access to the same wealth and resources that funded Ian Cole's madness, and we couldn't risk them getting the bright idea to start it all over again somewhere else.

We had to find them, and we had to end them.

And once Edgar is dead, we'll all finally be able to rest.

Luna and Stefanie are on my right, Delle is on my left, and Cambria stands a few feet behind us. A glance over my shoulder reveals her arms tight across her chest—she struggles more than she lets on. I know ending Edgar's life alone won't help her, but maybe once this is done, she'll feel safe again.

Maybe once this is done, I can help her heal.

Theo moves to stand on the opposite side of Delle as Arlo circles behind me. His right arm swings forward with the gun in his hand, and I reach down my side to take it from him with care.

"I made you a promise." I take a step closer to Edgar. "I told you that my face would be the last one you see as you take your dying breath. And I'm here to make good on that promise."

"No, you don't have to do this. I'll give you money, more money than you can *dream* of..."

I shake my head. "I don't want money—none of us do. All we want is peace. It's all we *ever* wanted."

I raise my arm, gun in hand, and aim it at his head.

Edgar shouts.

I draw back the hammer and cock it.

Edgar begs.

I slip my finger over the trigger.

Arlo steps in close at my back. And just as he did with Lawrence and Clyde, he places his feet behind my heels to ease me from the kick-back.

"Any objections?" I ask the room.

I asked them the same when we ended Lawrence and Clyde. I may hold the gun, but they're all helping me pull the trigger. If even one of them decides they don't want this—even now—then I won't do it.

I'm only met with silence.

I squeeze, and the silence erupts.

Blood sprays.

Edgar dies.

And peace finally finds me.

I lower my arm as Arlo hugs my waist, and the energy around us changes. Ember Glen is destroyed. The final legacy of the Elders is gone. And all of us are *free*.

I finally feel safe.

I finally feel unburdened.

Cleansing tears fill my eyes and rinse down my cheeks.

And Arlo whispers a promise that sets my soul on fire...

"WILDFLOWERS AND STARLIGHT."

THE END

from the author

I have no idea how we made it here.

Writing this series has been a journey. There were times I thought it would never be finished. There were times I almost gave up on it, worried I could never give Mercy and Arlo the happily-ever-after they deserved. This world is deep, these characters are complex, and this story pushed me past my limits.

I have never cried so hard after finishing a story, and though that's partly because writing it kicked my ass, it's also because saying goodbye to Mercy and Arlo is heartbreaking for me. They've been with me for two years, existing with me daily inside my mind, telling me bits and pieces of this insane story and challenging me to actually write it. That's what this entire series has been for me—a challenge.

It's exhausted me, it's uplifted me, it's made me question my own sanity. But here, at the end of it all, I can say without a doubt that I'm in love with Mercy and Arlo and their strange, wicked, sexy, dark journey to love.

And with confidence, I'm happy to tell you…

They lived happily ever after.

With love,

Brynn

acknowledgments

This book would not exist without the support of my family, my friends, and my amazing team. There are many people who were involved in this process, but three in particular who deserve the most *major* of shoutouts.

Chris, love, there's no way I could have finished this book without you. Not only did you pick up my slack with the kids and the house while I spent hours upon hours sequestered behind my laptop, you encouraged me, you pushed me, you told me I could do it when I was ready to give up and tell the world I failed. You really are amazing, the best husband ever! *Wildflowers and starlight.*

Danielle. Real talk. This book would not exist if it weren't for you, and that's a hard fact. You have been my number one supporter from the very beginning of my writing journey. You encourage me, you uplift me, but more than anything else you *believe* in me—even on the days when I don't believe in myself. I need you to understand how amazing you are, and that I'm so lucky to have you in my corner. You've become one of my closest friends over the past few years, and I appreciate you more than you know. Love you!

Silvia, my AMAZING editor…you have gone above and beyond for me with this book! I could never say thank you enough! You know firsthand how much I struggled with this book, and I am beyond grateful for your flexibility, your time, and your endless support. Your feedback is always spot on, and I can always count on you to polish up my words so spectacularly. I don't know what I'd do without you, so I hope you plan on editing my books forever!

To my dearest beta readers, Danielle, Echo, Brandy, Mary, and Amanda. How do you continue to put up with me? With all of my last minute chapters and the cliffhangers, I would've abandoned me long ago if I were you! But seriously, I have to give you the biggest THANK YOU for your countless hours spent reading and giving me feedback. You are the most amazing people, and I appreciate you so much! (Also, I'm sorry I made you domestics who got left behind in the scuffle at the Homestead…that's my bad…I'm sure everything turned out okay for you in the end…)

To my Street and ARC team and everyone who has taken the time to read, review, or post about this series…THANK YOU! Your support means the world to me, and I'm so incredibly grateful for you.

Najla, Nada, and the team at Qamber Designs, thank you so much for making my book look beautiful! I adore your team and the work you do is always spectacular. I can always count on you to create gorgeous covers and stunning interior design for my stories. You all are amazing!

My final thank you goes directly to you, reader. You picked up this book, you read the words I wrote, and for that alone, I am grateful. If you connected with the characters or the story and enjoyed this read, just know that you and I have met through these words, and I'm forever thankful you took the journey with me.

brynn's books

The Four Families Trilogy
Counts of Eight
Dance with Death
Pas de Trois

The Four Families Spin-Off
King of Masters

Ember Glen
Spark of Madness
Blaze of Misery
Embers of Mercy

Senseless
Unheard
Unseen

Lawless
(Coming Soon!)
The Darkness We Hide

Standalones
Jagged Line Paradise
Sugar Wood
The Alter

connect with brynn

Author Newsletter
brynnford.com/connect

Goodreads
goodreads.com/brynnfordauthor

BookBub
bookbub.com/profile/brynn-ford

Instagram
@brynnfordauthor
instagram.com/brynnfordauthor

TikTok
@brynnfordauthor
tiktok.com/@brynnfordauthor

Facebook Page
facebook.com/brynnfordauthor

Facebook Reader's Group
Brynn's Daring Darlings
bit.ly/brynnsdarlings

about the author

Brynn Ford is a USA Today Bestselling Author of dark romance for daring readers. She writes emotionally heavy love stories that will twist your soul and shatter your heart before pulling you back together with a hopeful happily-ever-after.

Brynn's books are dark, sometimes disturbing, and often overwhelming. But they're always brightened by an insistent, spicy romance that will live rent-free in your head long after you've turned the final page.

When Brynn isn't obsessively writing, you may find her binge-watching favorite shows while eating far too much junk food or fanatically reading, always seeking to lose herself in the emotional roller coaster of a damn good story. She's a firm believer that her characters continue to live outside the pages in the minds of her readers. Stories don't end just because there aren't any more pages to turn.